The Editor

FRED KAPLAN is Distinguished Professor Emeritus of English at Queens College and The Graduate Center, City University of New York. A biographer and literary scholar, he is the author of *John Quincy Adams: American Visionary, The Singular Mark Twain: A Biography, Lincoln: The Biography of a Writer, Henry James: The Imagination of Genius: A Biography,* and *Dickens: A Biography,* among others. His *Thomas Carlyle: A Biography* was nominated for the National Book Critics' Circle Award and for the Pulitzer Prize. His *Sacred Tears: Sentimentality in Victorian Fiction, Dickens and Mesmerism: The Hidden Springs of Fiction,* and *Miracles of Rare Device: The Poet's Sense of Self in Nineteenth-Century Poetry* are important contributions to the study of Romantic and Victorian British literature and culture. He is currently at work on a study of Lincoln, John Quincy Adams, and slavery and a biography of Thomas Jefferson.

NORTON CRITICAL EDITIONS
VICTORIAN ERA

For a complete list of Norton Critical Editions, visit
wwnorton.com/nortoncriticals

A NORTON CRITICAL EDITION

Charles Dickens
HARD TIMES

AN AUTHORITATIVE TEXT
CONTEXTS
CRITICISM

FOURTH EDITION

Edited by

FRED KAPLAN
QUEENS COLLEGE AND THE GRADUATE CENTER,
CITY UNIVERSITY OF NEW YORK

W · W · NORTON & COMPANY · *New York* · *London*

W. W. Norton & Company has been independent since its founding in 1923, when William Warder Norton and Mary D. Herter Norton first published lectures delivered at the People's Institute, the adult education division of New York City's Cooper Union. The firm soon expanded its program beyond the Institute, publishing books by celebrated academics from America and abroad. By midcentury, the two major pillars of Norton's publishing program—trade books and college texts—were firmly established. In the 1950s, the Norton family transferred control of the company to its employees, and today—with a staff of four hundred and a comparable number of trade, college, and professional titles published each year—W. W. Norton & Company stands as the largest and oldest publishing house owned wholly by its employees.

Library of Congress Cataloging-in-Publication Data

Names: Dickens, Charles, 1812–1870, author. | Kaplan, Fred, 1937– editor.
Title: Hard times : an authoritative text, contexts, criticism / Charles
    Dickens ; edited by Fred Kaplan, Queens College and the Graduate
    Center, City University of New York.
Description: Fourth edition. | New York : W.W. Norton & Company, 2016. |
    Series: Norton critical edition | Includes bibliographical references.
Identifiers: LCCN 2016015310 | ISBN 9780393284386 (pbk.)
Subjects: LCSH: Social problems—Fiction. | England—Fiction. | Dickens,
    Charles, 1812–1870. Hard times.
Classification: LCC PR4561.A2 K36 2016 | DDC 823/.8—dc23
    LC record available at https://lccn.loc.gov/2016015310

W. W. Norton & Company, Inc., 500 Fifth Avenue, New York, NY 10110-0017
    wwnorton.com

W. W. Norton & Company Ltd., Castle House, 15 Carlisle Street, London
W1D 3BS

1 2 3 4 5 6 7 8 9 0

Contents

Criticism   379

Preface

Hard Times sustains its lasting and its ever-changing relevance to our modern world. In the almost 165 years since its publication in 1854, it has been a gift that keeps giving, from its relevance to the first and second waves of industrialization in the nineteenth and twentieth centuries to its pertinence to the twenty-first-century age of computers, machine intelligence, robotics, and the Internet.

This fourth edition of the Norton Critical Edition of *Hard Times* does not undervalue the traditional discussion that has emphasized the novel as a primer on the factory system, the exploitation of the working class, the role of unions in a capitalistic system, and the conflict between imagination (which Dickens calls "fancy") and the utilitarian frame of mind. To its first readers, it seemed the most un-Dickensian of Dickens' novels. Where was the humor, the comedy, the playfulness of language, the fullness of multiple plots, and the variety of social scenes that had made the author of *Pickwick Papers*, *David Copperfield*, and *Bleak House* the most famous writer of the Victorian world? Critics complained that *Hard Times* was exclusively and entirely somber, grim, and harshly critical. It focused on class, economic, and ideological conflict between employers and workers, between capitalists and human capital, and on the unforgiving, un-Christian nexus of cash and mechanistic rationality. The Dickens of *Hard Times* was not the optimistic cheerleader of Christmas benevolence in which the Scrooges of the world were made to see the error of their ways and exemplify in their personal redemption the potential redemption of the society as a whole. This disappointed many of the novelist's contemporaries. It was not the Dickens they knew and loved.

As the nineteenth century wore on, unregulated industrialization and capitalism made the exploited workers of Coketown a commonplace. Social critics and theorists began to find *Hard Times* a text for their times. Marx and Engels were in print and in the air. Writers like John Ruskin, George Gissing, and George Bernard Shaw found the novel rivetingly topical. It remains so today. In most of the developing countries, especially in the factories of Asia, we see many of the same conditions that Dickens dramatized. It does not take much imagination to read *Hard Times* with the sweatshops of the world and the powerlessness of the working class in mind. For Dickens, it would be a familiar scenario, and one wonders how he would view the complicated relationships between modern capitalism, the global economy, international trade agreements, the union movement, the minimum wage, and the condition of the working class. *Hard Times*, though it dramatizes an early stage in industrialization and capitalism, raises themes inseparable from later manifestations and its modern language: the substitution of machine technology for human workers; the increasing gap between rich and poor, widely referred to now as income inequality; and a society in which social and economic power are so unequally distributed that the political system favors those already in power. In Dickens' Victorian world, wage inequality is more grossly visible; the conditions of the working class are more unrelievedly dismal. Its representation in twenty-first-century British and American life is considerably softened by improvements in sanitation, disease control, the spread of inexpensive material goods, and by modern technology. But it still exists.

One level of Dickens' concern with factory labor and machine technology has its modern extension in the dynamics of the digital age. It is a short, though technologically complicated, road from Dickens' depiction of factory workers as dehumanized cogs in an industrial machine to the replacement of human workers by advanced machines and machine intelligence. What would Dickens think about computer intelligence and robots run by computers? In the "melancholy" mad elephants of Coketown factories do we have an anticipation of Hal, the paranoid computer that turns murderous in Stanley Kubrick's famous film, *2001: A Space Odyssey?* What would be Dickens' reaction to the dominant digital culture of the twenty-first century in which entertainment and education, unlike the circus of *Hard Times*, have become imagistic and personalized or to the interaction among individuals, entertainment machines (such as the computer and television), and mass culture? One feature new to the fourth edition of this Norton Critical Edition, a section of images associated with Victorian factory and working-class life, makes use of an aspect of the machine technology that originates in the early Industrial Revolution and to which the Victorians made a major contribution: the mass production of images, especially etchings, lithographs, and photographs, that is now facilitated by digital technology and the Internet.

This fourth edition of *Hard Times* carries forward most of the essays in the "Contexts" section of the third edition. They provide the tone and message of Dickens' contemporaries. The two exceptions are R. D. Butterworth's modern article about Dickens' use of the

Preston strike as a reference point for his depiction of labor relations and Sven Beckert's description of "one of the saddest sights to this day" in his *Empire of Cotton: A Global History*. The "Criticism" section has been substantially changed to accommodate a number of provocative and imaginative essays published in the last fifteen years. Four of the seminal critical articles that remain—Taine, Ruskin, Gissing, and Shaw—represent widely read, sharply intelligent views of the novel by writers of distinction in the late-nineteenth- and early-twentieth-century literary world.

F. R. Leavis's influential "*Hard Times*: An Analytic Note" (1960) also remains. It is essential to modern discussions of *Hard Times*, widely referred to for its success in arguing that *Hard Times* is a great work of literary art, equal in aesthetic merit, though different in its structure, to Dickens' canonically acknowledged masterpieces. It has inspired many critics to focus on the dynamic balance (or imbalance, as some have claimed) between *Hard Times* as social criticism and as literary art. Leavis attempts to tip the balance toward the latter. Five of the critical essays included in this volume represent this dynamic. Christopher Barnes, Christina Lupton, Efraim Sicher, and Nils Clausson provide provocative variations on ways of reading and categorizing *Hard Times* as a work of literary art.

Other new essays provide twenty-first-century variations on the widely discussed social, economic, and political themes of the novel. Kent Greenfield and John E. Nilsson, both lawyers, apply the lessons of Gradgrind's education to how the legal system deals with corporate responsibility as embodied in "The Business Judgment Rule." David M. Levy, an economist, argues that there is a moral equivalence between disempowered factory workers and American slavery in the nineteenth century. Like Paulette Kidder, whose main interest is the novel's Christian sensibility and themes, Levy's essay is in dialogue with Martha Nussbaum's "The Literary Imagination in Public Life," which is important enough to be carried over from the third edition. Nussbaum's essay (1991), the most influential attempt to reorient approaches to *Hard Times* since Leavis, makes the argument that *Hard Times* is a novel for modern times in its dramatization of income inequality and the perverse application of scientific rationalism to human beings and the human situation. Theodore Dalrymple makes the same argument in journalistic terms, a warning to twenty-first-century America that modern variants of the same socioeconomic conditions that Dickens condemned in *Hard Times* threaten the well-being, even the viability, of the world we live in now.

The improved text of the third edition of *Hard Times*, superbly edited by Sylvère Monod, remains the copy text for the fourth edition. It is based on the 1854 edition, which, to quote its modern editor, "possesses a kind of freshness and authenticity not to be found elsewhere." The "Preface" to the third edition contains its textual editor's rationale for his decisions, especially in regard to punctuation and other textual matters and can be consulted by those interested. The explanatory notes of the third edition are carried forward to the fourth, and they, like so much of this new edition, are the cumulative contributions of the three editors who, since the first edition, have collaborated on this enterprise. Two of them are no longer alive, George H. Ford (1914–1994) and Sylvère Monod (1921–2006). This august duo conceived of the edition and were the sole editors of its first two appearances, in 1966 and 1990. When George Ford died, I became Sylvère's co-editor for the third edition. In a world in which the newest generation too readily forgets its predecessors, it is important to remember those on whose shoulders we stand. George Ford and Sylvère Monod were men of character and principal; they had the inestimable blessing of loving their work; they were dedicated and exemplary scholars; and they played key roles in the post–World War II elevation of Dickens from one of the most highly regarded novelists of the Victorian world to his now supreme position, next to Shakespeare, in the pantheon of the great writers of the English literary canon. They were men who helped shape our literary history and culture. This fourth edition is dedicated to them.

FRED KAPLAN
BOOTHBAY, MAINE

Illustrations

The Text of
HARD TIMES

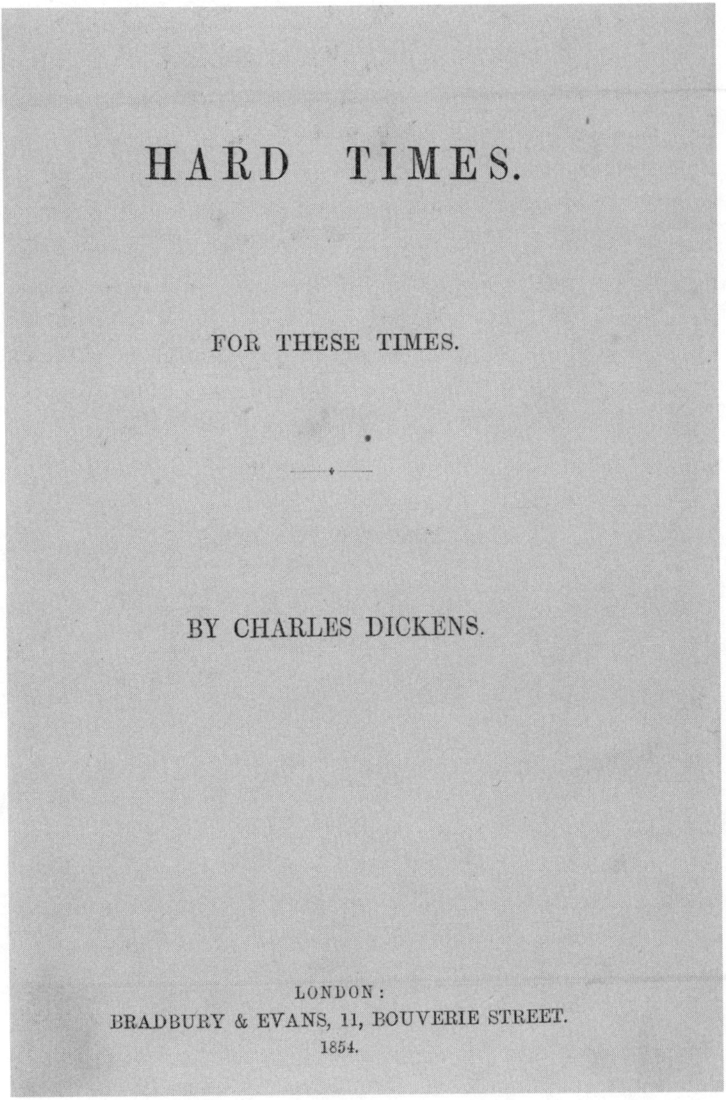

HARD TIMES.

FOR THESE TIMES.

BY CHARLES DICKENS.

LONDON:
BRADBURY & EVANS, 11, BOUVERIE STREET.
1854.

Fig. 1. 1854 title page (London: Bradbury & Evans). Courtesy of the Bodleian Library.

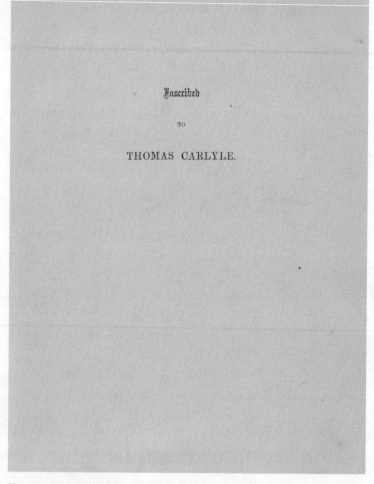

Inscribed

TO

THOMAS CARLYLE.

Fig. 2. 1854 dedication (London: Bradbury & Evans). Courtesy of the Bodleian Library.

CONTENTS

BOOK THE FIRST.
SOWING.

BOOK THE SECOND.
REAPING.

BOOK THE THIRD.
GARNERING.

Hard Times

Book the First—Sowing

Chapter I

THE ONE THING NEEDFUL.[1]

"Now, what I want is, Facts. Teach these boys and girls nothing but Facts. Facts alone are wanted in life. Plant nothing else, and root out everything else. You can only form the minds of reasoning animals upon Facts: nothing else will ever be of any service to them. This is the principle on which I bring up my own children, and this is the principle on which I bring up these children. Stick to Facts, sir!"

The scene was a plain, bare, monotonous vault of a schoolroom, and the speaker's square forefinger emphasised his observations by underscoring every sentence with a line on the schoolmaster's sleeve. The emphasis was helped by the speaker's square wall of a forehead, which had his eyebrows for its base, while his eyes found commodious cellarage[2] in two dark caves, overshadowed by the wall. The emphasis was helped by the speaker's mouth, which was wide, thin, and hard set. The emphasis was helped by the speaker's voice, which was inflexible, dry, and dictatorial. The emphasis was helped by the speaker's hair, which bristled on the skirts of his bald head, a plantation of firs to keep the wind from its shining surface, all covered with knobs, like the crust of a plum pie, as if the head had scarcely warehouse-room for the hard facts stored inside. The speaker's obstinate carriage, square coat, square legs, square shoulders,—nay, his very neckcloth, trained to take him by the throat with an unaccommodating grasp, like a stubborn fact, as it was,—all helped the emphasis.

"In this life, we want nothing but Facts, sir; nothing but Facts!"

The speaker, and the schoolmaster, and the third grown person present, all backed a little, and swept with their eyes the inclined

1. See Luke 10.40–42.
2. A cellar used as a large storage place, usually for provisions and wine.

plane of little vessels then and there arranged in order, ready to
have imperial gallons[3] of facts poured into them until they were full
to the brim.

Chapter II.

MURDERING THE INNOCENTS.[1]

Thomas Gradgrind, sir. A man of realities. A man of facts and calculations. A man who proceeds upon the principle that two and
two are four, and nothing over, and who is not to be talked into
allowing for anything over. Thomas Gradgrind, sir—peremptorily
Thomas—Thomas Gradgrind. With a rule and a pair of scales, and
the multiplication table always in his pocket, sir, ready to weigh and
measure any parcel of human nature, and tell you exactly what it
comes to. It is a mere question of figures, a case of simple arithmetic.
You might hope to get some other nonsensical belief into the head
of George Gradgrind, or Augustus Gradgrind, or John Gradgrind, or
Joseph Gradgrind (all supposititious, non-existent persons), but into
the head of Thomas Gradgrind—no, sir!

In such terms Mr. Gradgrind always mentally introduced himself, whether to his private circle of acquaintance, or to the public
in general. In such terms, no doubt, substituting the words "boys
and girls," for "sir," Thomas Gradgrind now presented Thomas
Gradgrind to the little pitchers before him, who were to be filled so
full of facts.

Indeed, as he eagerly sparkled at them from the cellarage before
mentioned, he seemed a kind of cannon loaded to the muzzle with
facts, and prepared to blow them clean out of the regions of childhood at one discharge. He seemed a galvanising apparatus, too,
charged with a grim mechanical substitute for the tender young
imaginations that were to be stormed away.

"Girl number twenty," said Mr. Gradgrind, squarely pointing
with his square forefinger, "I don't know that girl. Who is that girl?"

"Sissy Jupe, sir," explained number twenty, blushing, standing up,
and curtseying.

"Sissy is not a name," said Mr. Gradgrind. "Don't call yourself
Sissy. Call yourself Cecilia."

"It's father as calls me Sissy, sir," returned the young girl in a
trembling voice, and with another curtsey.

---

3. A unit of volume in the British Imperial system equal to 4.54 liters; a gallon in the
   United States Customary system is equal to 3.78 liters.
1. See Matthew 2.16–18. Believing his role threatened by the birth of Jesus, King Herod
   ordered the massacre in Bethlehem of all children younger than two years of age. This
   event is commemorated in The Book of Common Prayer by a ceremony held on December 28 called "Innocents' Day."

"Then he has no business to do it," said Mr. Gradgrind. "Tell him he mustn't. Cecilia Jupe. Let me see. What is your father?"

"He belongs to the horse-riding, if you please, sir."

Mr. Gradgrind frowned, and waved off the objectionable calling with his hand.

"We don't want to know anything about that, here. You mustn't tell us about that, here. Your father breaks horses, don't he?"

"If you please, sir, when they can get any to break, they do break horses in the ring, sir."

"You mustn't tell us about the ring, here. Very well, then. Describe your father as a horsebreaker. He doctors sick horses, I dare say?"

"Oh yes, sir."

"Very well, then. He is a veterinary surgeon, a farrier[2] and horse-breaker. Give me your definition of a horse."

(Sissy Jupe thrown into the greatest alarm by this demand.)

"Girl number twenty unable to define a horse!" said Mr. Gradgrind, for the general behoof of all the little pitchers. "Girl number twenty possessed of no facts, in reference to one of the commonest of animals! Some boy's definition of a horse. Bitzer, yours."

The square finger, moving here and there, lighted suddenly on Bitzer, perhaps because he chanced to sit in the same ray of sunlight which, darting in at one of the bare windows of the intensely white-washed room, irradiated Sissy. For, the boys and girls sat on the face of the inclined plane in two compact bodies, divided up the centre by a narrow interval; and Sissy, being at the corner of a row on the sunny side, came in for the beginning of a sunbeam, of which Bitzer, being at the corner of a row on the other side, a few rows in advance, caught the end. But, whereas the girl was so dark-eyed and dark-haired, that she seemed to receive a deeper and more lustrous color from the sun when it shone upon her, the boy was so light-eyed and light-haired that the self-same rays appeared to draw out of him what little color he ever possessed. His cold eyes would hardly have been eyes, but for the short ends of lashes which, by bringing them into immediate contrast with something paler than themselves, expressed their form. His short-cropped hair might have been a mere continuation of the sandy freckles on his forehead and face. His skin was so unwholesomely deficient in the natural tinge, that he looked as though, if he were cut, he would bleed white.

"Bitzer," said Thomas Gradgrind. "Your definition of a horse."

"Quadruped. Graminivorous.[3] Forty teeth, namely twenty-four grinders, four eye-teeth, and twelve incisive.[4] Sheds coat in the

---

2. Someone who shoes horses and/or treats them medically.
3. An animal that feeds on grain, grasses, or seeds.
4. Incisors.

spring; in marshy countries, sheds hoofs, too. Hoofs hard, but requiring to be shod with iron. Age known by marks in mouth." Thus (and much more) Bitzer.

"Now girl number twenty," said Mr. Gradgrind. "You know what a horse is."

She curtseyed again, and would have blushed deeper, if she could have blushed deeper than she had blushed all this time. Bitzer, after rapidly blinking at Thomas Gradgrind with both eyes at once, and so catching the light upon his quivering ends of lashes that they looked like the antennæ of busy insects, put his knuckles to his freckled forehead, and sat down again.

The third gentleman now stepped forth. A mighty man at cutting and drying, he was; a government officer; in his way (and in most other people's too), a professed pugilist; always in training, always with a system to force down the general throat like a bolus,[5] always to be heard of at the bar of his little Public-office, ready to fight all England. To continue in fistic phraseology, he had a genius for coming up to the scratch,[6] wherever and whatever it was, and proving himself an ugly customer. He would go in and damage any subject whatever with his right, follow up with his left, stop, exchange, counter, bore his opponent (he always fought All England)[7] to the ropes, and fall upon him neatly. He was certain to knock the wind out of common-sense, and render that unlucky adversary deaf to the call of time. And he had it in charge from high authority to bring about the great public-office Millennium, when Commissioners[8] should reign upon earth.

"Very well," said this gentleman, briskly smiling, and folding his arms. "That's a horse. Now, let me ask you girls and boys, Would you paper a room with representations of horses?"

After a pause, one half of the children cried in chorus, "Yes, sir!" Upon which the other half, seeing in the gentleman's face that Yes was wrong, cried out in chorus, "No, sir!"—as the custom is, in these examinations.

"Of course, No. Why wouldn't you?"

A pause. One corpulent slow boy, with a wheezy manner of breathing, ventured the answer, Because he wouldn't paper a room at all, but would paint it.

---

5. A large pill.
6. A line drawn across the center of the ring in the early days of prizefighting. Contestants would commence a match by stepping up to opposite sides of this line, and the match would end when one of the two could no longer come up to the scratch line at the beginning of a new round.
7. Fighting according to a national code of rules for the prize ring—one of the codes superseded by the adoption of the marquis of Queensbury's rules in 1866.
8. Administrative officials in various departments of government such as customs and income taxes. "Millennium": period of utopian perfection.

"You *must* paper it," said the gentleman, rather warmly.

"You must paper it," said Thomas Gradgrind, "whether you like it or not. Don't tell *us* you wouldn't paper it. What do you mean, boy?"

"I'll explain to you, then," said the gentleman, after another and a dismal pause, "why you wouldn't paper a room with representations of horses. Do you ever see horses walking up and down the sides of rooms in reality—in fact? Do you?"

"Yes, sir!" from one half. "No, sir!" from the other.

"Of course no," said the gentleman, with an indignant look at the wrong half. "Why, then, you are not to see anywhere, what you don't see in fact; you are not to have anywhere, what you don't have in fact. What is called Taste, is only another name for Fact."

Thomas Gradgrind nodded his approbation.

"This is a new principle, a discovery, a great discovery," said the gentleman. "Now, I'll try you again. Suppose you were going to carpet a room. Would you use a carpet having a representation of flowers upon it?"

There being a general conviction by this time that "No, sir!" was always the right answer to this gentleman, the chorus of No was very strong. Only a few feeble stragglers said Yes; among them Sissy Jupe.

"Girl number twenty," said the gentleman, smiling in the calm strength of knowledge.

Sissy blushed, and stood up.

"So you would carpet your room—or your husband's room, if you were a grown woman, and had a husband—with representations of flowers, would you," said the gentleman. "Why would you?"

"If you please, sir, I am very fond of flowers," returned the girl.

"And is that why you would put tables and chairs upon them, and have people walking over them with heavy boots?"

"It wouldn't hurt them, sir. They wouldn't crush and wither if you please, sir. They would be the pictures of what was very pretty and pleasant, and I would fancy[9]—"

"Ay, ay, ay! But you mustn't fancy," cried the gentleman, quite elated by coming so happily to his point. "That's it! You are never to fancy."

"You are not, Cecilia Jupe," Thomas Gradgrind solemnly repeated, "to do anything of that kind."

"Fact, fact, fact!" said the gentleman. And "Fact, fact, fact!" repeated Thomas Gradgrind.

"You are to be in all things regulated and governed," said the gentleman, "by fact. We hope to have, before long, a board of fact,

---

9. Dickens uses the word *fancy* in one of its important 19th-century usages; as a verb, *to fancy* means "to imagine," and as a noun *fancy* means "imagination."

composed of commissioners of fact, who will force the people to be
a people of fact, and of nothing but fact. You must discard the word
Fancy altogether. You have nothing to do with it. You are not to
have, in any object of use or ornament, what would be a contradiction in fact. You don't walk upon flowers in fact; you cannot be
allowed to walk upon flowers in carpets. You don't find that foreign
birds and butterflies come and perch upon your crockery; you cannot be permitted to paint foreign birds and butterflies upon your
crockery. You never meet with quadrupeds going up and down
walls; you must not have quadrupeds represented upon walls. You
must use," said the gentleman, "for all these purposes, combina-
tions and modifications (in primary colours) of mathematical figures which are susceptible of proof and demonstration. This is the
new discovery. This is fact. This is taste."

The girl curtseyed, and sat down. She was very young, and she
looked as if she were frightened by the matter of fact prospect
the world afforded.

"Now, if Mr. M'Choakumchild," said the gentleman, "will proceed to give his first lesson here, Mr. Gradgrind, I shall be happy, at
your request, to observe his mode of procedure."

Mr. Gradgrind was much obliged. "Mr. M'Choakumchild, we only
wait for you."

So, Mr. M'Choakumchild began in his best manner. He and some
one hundred and forty other schoolmasters, had been lately turned
at the same time, in the same factory, on the same principles, like so
many pianoforte legs. He had been put through an immense variety
of paces, and had answered volumes of head-breaking questions.
Orthography,[1] etymology, syntax, and prosody, biography, astronomy, geography, and general cosmography, the sciences of compound
proportion, algebra, land-surveying and levelling, vocal music, and
drawing from models, were all at the ends of his ten chilled fingers.
He had worked his stoney way into Her Majesty's most Honorable
Privy Council's Schedule B,[2] and had taken the bloom off the
higher branches of mathematics and physical science, French, Ger-
man, Latin, and Greek. He knew all about all the Water Sheds of
all the world (whatever they are), and all the histories of all the
peoples, and all the names of all the rivers and mountains, and all
the productions, manners, and customs of all the countries, and all
their boundaries and bearings on the two and thirty points of the
compass. Ah, rather overdone, M'Choakumchild. If he had only

---

1. The study of the principles and conventions of spelling.
2. A syllabus established in 1846 specifying what subjects were to be mastered by candi-
   dates training to become teachers. Schedule B was drawn up by a subcommittee of the
   Privy Council.

learnt a little less, how infinitely better he might have taught much more!

He went to work in this preparatory lesson, not unlike Morgiana[3] in the Forty Thieves: looking into all the vessels ranged before him, one after another, to see what they contained. Say, good M'Choakumchild. When from thy boiling store, thou shalt fill each jar brim full by and by, dost thou think that thou wilt always kill outright the robber Fancy lurking within—or sometimes only maim him and distort him!

Chapter III.

A LOOPHOLE.

Mr. Gradgrind walked homeward from the school, in a state of considerable satisfaction. It was his school, and he intended it to be a model. He intended every child in it to be a model—just as the young Gradgrinds were all models.

There were five young Gradgrinds, and they were models every one. They had been lectured at, from their tenderest years; coursed,[1] like little hares. Almost as soon as they could run alone, they had been made to run to the lecture-room. The first object with which they had an association, or of which they had a remembrance, was a large black board with a dry Ogre chalking ghastly white figures on it.

Not that they knew, by name or nature, anything about an Ogre. Fact forbid! I only use the word to express a monster in a lecturing castle, with Heaven knows how many heads manipulated into one, taking childhood captive, and dragging it into gloomy statistical dens by the hair.

No little Gradgrind had ever seen a face in the moon; it was up in the moon before it could speak distinctly. No little Gradgrind had ever learnt the silly jingle, Twinkle, twinkle, little star; how I wonder what you are![2] No little Gradgrind had ever known wonder on the subject, each little Gradgrind having at five years old dissected the Great Bear like a Professor Owen, and driven Charles's Wain[3] like a locomotive engine-driver. No little Gradgrind had ever asso-

3. Ali Baba's slave in the *Arabian Nights' Entertainments* who killed forty thieves by pouring boiling oil into the jars in which they were hiding.
1. Chased, usually in 19th-century England as a rabbit is chased by a greyhound in the popular sport of hunting hare with hounds.
2. The popular nursery rhyme by Jane Taylor was first published in 1806 under the title "The Star."
3. One of the names for the constellation called the Great Dipper or the Great Wain, so named for its resemblance to a wagon (wain) associated with King Charlemagne (Charles the Great). "Professor Owen": Sir Richard Owen (1804–1892), zoologist and author of *Comparative Anatomy and Physiology of Vertebrates*. Dickens had visited his home and discussed telescopes with him, an incident that may have prompted the reference to astronomy.

ciated a cow in a field with that famous cow[4] with the crumpled horn who tossed the dog who worried the cat who killed the rat who ate the malt, or with that yet more famous cow who swallowed Tom Thumb:[5] it had never heard of those celebrities, and had only been introduced to a cow as a graminivorous ruminating quadruped with several stomachs.

To his matter of fact home, which was called Stone Lodge, Mr. Gradgrind directed his steps. He had virtually retired from the wholesale hardware trade before he built Stone Lodge, and was now looking about for a suitable opportunity of making an arithmetical figure in Parliament. Stone Lodge was situated on a moor within a mile or two of a great town—called Coketown in the present faithful guide-book.

A very regular feature on the face of the country, Stone Lodge was. Not the least disguise toned down or shaded off that uncompromising fact in the landscape. A great square house, with a heavy portico darkening the principal windows, as its master's heavy brows overshadowed his eyes. A calculated, cast up, balanced, and proved house. Six windows on this side of the door, six on that side; a total of twelve in this wing, a total of twelve in the other wing; four and twenty carried over to the back wings. A lawn and garden and an infant avenue, all ruled straight like a botanical account-book. Gas and ventilation, drainage and water-service, all of the primest quality. Iron clamps and girders, fireproof from top to bottom; mechanical lifts[6] for the housemaids, with all their brushes and brooms; everything that heart could desire.

Everything? Well, I suppose so. The little Gradgrinds had cabinets in various departments of science too. They had a little conchological cabinet, and a little metallurgical cabinet, and a little mineralogical cabinet; and the specimens were all arranged and labelled, and the bits of stone and ore looked as though they might have been broken from the parent substances by those tremendously hard instruments their own names; and, to paraphrase the idle legend of Peter Piper,[7] who had never found his way into *their* nursery, If the greedy little Gradgrinds grasped at more than this, what was it for good gracious goodness sake, that the greedy little Gradgrinds grasped at!

Their father walked on in a hopeful and satisfied frame of mind. He was an affectionate father, after his manner; but he would prob-

4. A reference to one of the characters in a well-known accumulative rhyme titled "The House That Jack Built," first published in 1755.
5. The hero of Henry Fielding's play *The Life of Tom Thumb the Great* (1730).
6. Elevators.
7. Alluding to a line from a nursery rhyme: "Where's the peck of pickled peppers Peter Piper picked?"

ably have described himself (if he had been put, like Sissy Jupe, upon a definition) as "an eminently practical" father. He had a particular pride in the phrase eminently practical, which was considered to have a special application to him. Whatsoever the public meeting held in Coketown, and whatsoever the subject of such meeting, some Coketowner was sure to seize the occasion of alluding to his eminently practical friend Gradgrind. This always pleased the eminently practical friend. He knew it to be his due, but his due was acceptable.

He had reached the neutral ground upon the outskirts of the town, which was neither town nor country, and yet was either spoiled, when his ears were invaded by the sound of music. The clashing and banging band attached to the horse-riding establishment which had there set up its rest in a wooden pavilion, was in full bray. A flag, floating from the summit of the temple, proclaimed to mankind that it was "Sleary's Horse-riding" which claimed their suffrages.[8] Sleary himself, a stout modern statue with a money-box at its elbow, in an ecclesiastical niche of early Gothic architecture, took the money. Miss Josephine Sleary, as some very long and very narrow strips of printed bill announced, was then inaugurating the entertainments with her graceful equestrian Tyrolean flower-act.[9] Among the other pleasing but always strictly moral wonders which must be seen to be believed, Signor Jupe was that afternoon to "elucidate the diverting accomplishments of his highly trained performing dog Merrylegs." He was also to exhibit "his astounding feat of throwing seventy-five hundredweight in rapid succession backhanded over his head thus forming a fountain of solid iron in mid-air, a feat never before attempted in this or any other country and which having elicited such rapturous plaudits from enthusiastic throngs it cannot be withdrawn." The same Signor Jupe was to "enliven the varied performances at frequent intervals with his chaste Shaksperean quips and retorts." Lastly, he was to wind them up by appearing in his favorite character of Mr. William Button, of Tooley Street, in "the highly novel and laughable hippo-comedietta of The Tailor's Journey to Brentford."[1]

8. Votes, in the sense of their patronage to buy tickets.
9. The Tyrol is a picturesque region of northern Italy and of Austria that features colorful costumes and houses decorated with flowers. According to *The Dickens Index* (1988), "a noted equestrienne" of the 1830s, Laura Woolford, starred in solo performances at Astley's theater. One of her acts was called "The Italian Flower-Girl."
1. A pantomime staged on horseback. Performances of this kind, as described by Mr. Sleary in *Hard Times* (book 3, chapter 7), were popular in circuses and amusement halls such as Astley's in London. In February 1854, when Dickens and his friend Mark Lemon were visiting circuses to gather information to be used in *Hard Times*, Astley's was advertising a double bill featuring an elephant show ("Wise Elephants of the East") to be followed by "*Billy Button's Journey to Brentford; or Harlequin and the Ladies' Favourite.*" This production, described as a "grand Equestrian Comic Pantomime" recently written by Nelson Lee, was based on a popular pantomime of a tailor who rode his horse facing backward. The name Billy Button was applied to small boys. See *The Illustrated London News*, December 24, 1853, and February 4, 1854.

Thomas Gradgrind took no heed of these trivialities of course, but passed on as a practical man ought to pass on, after brushing the noisy insects from his thoughts, or consigning them to the House of Correction. But, the turning of the road took him by the back of the booth, and at the back of the booth a number of children were congregated in a number of stealthy attitudes, striving to peep in at the hidden glories of the place.

This brought him to a stop. "Now, to think of these vagabonds," said he, "attracting the young rabble from a model school."

A space of stunted grass and dry rubbish being between him and the young rabble, he took his eyeglass out of his waistcoat to look for any child he knew by name, and might order off. Phenomenon almost incredible though distinctly seen, what did he then behold but his own metallurgical Louisa peeping with all her might through a hole in a deal board,[2] and his own mathematical Thomas abasing himself on the ground to catch but a hoof of the graceful equestrian Tyrolean flower-act!

his kids having fun

Dumb with amazement, Mr. Gradgrind crossed to the spot where his family was thus disgraced, laid his hand upon each erring child, and said:

"Louisa!! Thomas!!"

Both rose, red and disconcerted. But, Louisa looked at her father with more boldness than Thomas did. Indeed, Thomas did not look at him, but gave himself up to be taken home like a machine.

"In the name of wonder, idleness, and folly!" said Mr. Gradgrind, leading each away by a hand; "what do you do here?"

"Wanted to see what it was like," returned Louisa shortly.

"What it was like?"

"Yes, father."

There was an air of jaded sullenness in them both, and particularly in the girl: yet, struggling through the dissatisfaction of her face, there was a light with nothing to rest upon, a fire with nothing to burn, a starved imagination keeping life in itself somehow, which brightened its expression. Not with the brightness natural to cheerful youth, but with uncertain, eager, doubtful flashes, which had something painful in them, analogous to the changes on a blind face groping its way.

She was a child now, of fifteen or sixteen; but at no distant day would seem to become a woman all at once. Her father thought so as he looked at her. She was pretty. Would have been self-willed (he thought in his eminently practical way), but for her bringing-up.

---

2. A board or plank made of fir or pine cut to a standard dimension, usually for fencing.

"Thomas, though I have the fact before me, I find it difficult to believe that you, with your education and resources, should have brought your sister to a scene like this."

"I brought *him*, father," said Louisa, quickly. "I asked him to come."

"I am sorry to hear it. I am very sorry indeed to hear it. It makes Thomas no better, and it makes you worse, Louisa."

She looked at her father again, but no tear fell down her cheek.

"You! Thomas and you, to whom the circle of the sciences is open; Thomas and you, who may be said to be replete with facts; Thomas and you, who have been trained to mathematical exactness; Thomas and you, here!" cried Mr. Gradgrind. "In this degraded position! I am amazed."

"I was tired, father. I have been tired a long time," said Louisa.

"Tired? Of what?" asked the astonished father.

"I don't know of what—of everything I think."

"Say not another word," returned Mr. Gradgrind. "You are childish. I will hear no more." He did not speak again until they had walked some half-a-mile in silence, when he gravely broke out with: "What would your best friends say, Louisa? Do you attach no value to their good opinion? What would Mr. Bounderby say?"

At the mention of this name, his daughter stole a look at him, remarkable for its intense and searching character. He saw nothing of it, for before he looked at her she had again cast down her eyes!

"What," he repeated presently, "would Mr. Bounderby say!" All the way to Stone Lodge, as with grave indignation he led the two delinquents home, he repeated at intervals "What would Mr. Bounderby say!"—as if Mr. Bounderby had been Mrs. Grundy.[3]

Chapter IV.

MR. BOUNDERBY.

Not being Mrs. Grundy, who *was* Mr. Bounderby?

Why, Mr. Bounderby was as near being Mr. Gradgrind's bosom friend, as a man perfectly devoid of sentiment can approach that spiritual relationship towards another man perfectly devoid of sentiment. So near was Mr. Bounderby—or, if the reader should prefer it, so far off.

He was a rich man: banker, merchant, manufacturer, and what not. A big, loud man, with a stare and a metallic laugh. A man made out of a coarse material, which seemed to have been stretched to make so much of him. A man with a great puffed head and forehead,

3. An embodiment of prudishness whose censorious comments are feared by her neighbors, in Thomas Morton's play *Speed the Plough* (1798).

swelled veins in his temples, and such a strained skin to his face that it seemed to hold his eyes open and lift his eyebrows up. A man with a pervading appearance on him of being inflated like a balloon, and ready to start. A man who could never sufficiently vaunt himself a self-made man. A man who was always proclaiming, through that brassy speaking-trumpet of a voice of his, his old ignorance and his old poverty. A man who was the Bully of humility.

A year or two younger than his eminently practical friend, Mr. Bounderby looked older; his seven or eight and forty might have had the seven or eight added to it again, without surprising anybody. He had not much hair. One might have fancied he had talked it off; and that what was left, all standing up in disorder, was in that condition from being constantly blown about by his windy boastfulness.

In the formal drawing-room of Stone Lodge, standing on the heartrug, warming himself before the fire, Mr. Bounderby delivered some observations to Mrs. Gradgrind on the circumstance of its being his birthday. He stood before the fire, partly because it was a cool spring afternoon, though the sun shone; partly because the shade of Stone Lodge was always haunted by the ghost of damp mortar; partly because he thus took up a commanding position, from which to subdue Mrs. Gradgrind.

"I hadn't a shoe to my foot. As to a stocking, I didn't know such a thing by name. I passed the day in a ditch, and the night in a pigsty. That's the way I spent my tenth birthday. Not that a ditch was new to me, for I was born in a ditch."

Mrs. Gradgrind, a little, thin, white, pink-eyed bundle of shawls, of surpassing feebleness, mental and bodily; who was always taking physic without any effect, and who, whenever she showed a symptom of coming to life, was invariably stunned by some weighty piece of fact tumbling on her; Mrs. Gradgrind hoped it was a dry ditch?

"No! As wet as a sop. A foot of water in it," said Mr. Bounderby.

"Enough to give a baby cold," Mrs. Gradgrind considered.

"Cold? I was born with inflammation of the lungs, and of everything else, I believe, that was capable of inflammation," returned Mr. Bounderby. "For years, ma'am, I was one of the most miserable little wretches ever seen. I was so sickly, that I was always moaning and groaning. I was so ragged and dirty, that you wouldn't have touched me with a pair of tongs."

Mrs. Gradgrind faintly looked at the tongs, as the most appropriate thing her imbecility could think of doing.

"How I fought through it, I don't know," said Bounderby. "I was determined, I suppose. I have been a determined character in later life, and I suppose I was then. Here I am, Mrs. Gradgrind, anyhow, and nobody to thank for my being here but myself."

Mrs. Gradgrind meekly and weakly hoped that his mother—

"*My* mother? Bolted, ma'am!" said Bounderby.

Mrs. Gradgrind, stunned as usual, collapsed and gave it up.

"My mother left me to my grandmother," said Bounderby; "and, according to the best of my remembrance, my grandmother was the wickedest and the worst old woman that ever lived. If I got a little pair of shoes by any chance, she would take 'em off and sell 'em for drink. Why, I have known that grandmother of mine lie in her bed and drink her fourteen glasses of liquor before breakfast!"

Mrs. Gradgrind, weakly smiling, and giving no other sign of vitality, looked (as she always did) like an indifferently executed transparency of a small female figure, without enough light behind it.

"She kept a chandler's shop,"[1] pursued Bounderby, "and kept me in an egg-box. That was the cot of *my* infancy; an old egg-box. As soon as I was big enough to run away, of course I ran away. Then I became a young vagabond; and instead of one old woman knocking me about and starving me, everybody of all ages knocked me about and starved me. They were right; they had no business to do anything else. I was a nuisance, an incumbrance, and a pest. I know that, very well."

His pride in having at any time of his life achieved such a great social distinction as to be a nuisance, an incumbrance, and a pest, was only to be satisfied by three sonorous repetitions of the boast.

"I was to pull through it I suppose, Mrs. Gradgrind. Whether I was to do it or not, ma'am, I did it. I pulled through it, though nobody threw me out a rope. Vagabond, errand-boy, vagabond, laborer, porter, clerk, chief manager, small partner, Josiah Bounderby of Coketown. Those are the antecedents, and the culmination. Josiah Bounderby of Coketown learnt his letters from the outsides of the shops, Mrs. Gradgrind, and was first able to tell the time upon a dial-plate,[2] from studying the steeple clock of St. Giles's Church, London, under the direction of a drunken cripple, who was a convicted thief and an incorrigible vagrant. Tell Josiah Bounderby of Coketown, of your district schools and your model schools, and your training schools, and your whole kettle-of-fish of schools; and Josiah Bounderby of Coketown, tells you plainly, all right, all correct—he hadn't such advantages—but let us have hard-headed, solid-fisted people—the education that made him won't do for everybody, he knows well—such and such his education was, however, and you may force him to swallow boiling fat, but you shall never force him to suppress the facts of his life."

Being heated when he arrived at this climax, Josiah Bounderby of Coketown stopped. He stopped just as his eminently practical

1. A grocery store.
2. The face-plate of a clock, usually of glass, on which the numbers are marked.

friend, still accompanied by the two young culprits, entered the room. His eminently practical friend, on seeing him, stopped also, and gave Louisa a reproachful look that plainly said, "Behold your Bounderby!"

"Well!" blustered Mr. Bounderby, "what's the matter? What is young Thomas in the dumps about?"

He spoke of young Thomas, but he looked at Louisa.

"We were peeping at the circus," muttered Louisa haughtily, without lifting up her eyes, "and father caught us."

"And Mrs. Gradgrind," said her husband in a lofty manner," I should as soon have expected to find my children reading poetry."

"Dear me," whimpered Mrs. Gradgrind. "How can you, Louisa and Thomas! I wonder at you. I declare you're enough to make one regret ever having had a family at all. I have a great mind to say I wish I hadn't. *Then* what would you have done, I should like to know."

Mr. Gradgrind did not seem favorably impressed by those cogent remarks. He frowned impatiently.

"As if, with my head in its present throbbing state, you couldn't go and look at the shells and minerals and things provided for you, instead of circuses!" said Mrs. Gradgrind. "You know, as well as I do, no young people have circus masters, or keep circuses in cabinets, or attend lectures about circuses. What can you possibly want to know of circuses then? I am sure you have enough to do, if that's what you want. With my head in its present state, I couldn't remember the mere names of half the facts you have got to attend to."

"That's the reason!" pouted Louisa.

"Don't tell me that's the reason, because it can be nothing of the sort," said Mrs. Gradgrind. "Go and be somethingological directly." Mrs. Gradgrind was not a scientific character, and usually dismissed her children to their studies with this general injunction to choose their pursuit.

In truth, Mrs. Gradgrind's stock of facts in general was woefully defective; but Mr. Gradgrind in raising her to her high matrimonial position, had been influenced by two reasons. Firstly, she was most satisfactory as a question of figures,[3] and, secondly, she had "no nonsense" about her. By nonsense he meant fancy; and truly it is probable she was as free from any alloy of that nature, as any human being not arrived at the perfection of an absolute idiot, ever was.

The simple circumstance of being left alone with her husband and Mr. Bounderby, was sufficient to stun this admirable lady again, without collision between herself and any other fact. So, she once more died away, and nobody minded her.

---

3. Her net worth, perhaps including a dowry, which would legally on marriage become Mr. Gradgrind's property.

"Bounderby," said Mr. Gradgrind, drawing a chair to the fireside, "you are always so interested in my young people—particularly in Louisa—that I make no apology for saying to you, I am very much vexed by this discovery. I have systematically devoted myself (as you know) to the education of the reason of my family. The reason is (as you know) the only faculty to which education should be addressed. And yet, Bounderby, it would appear from this unexpected circumstance of to-day; though in itself a trifling one, as if something had crept into Thomas's and Louisa's minds which is—or rather, which is not—I don't know that I can express myself better than by saying—which has never been intended to be developed, and in which their reason has no part."

"There certainly is no reason in looking with interest at a parcel of vagabonds," returned Bounderby. "When I was a vagabond myself, nobody looked with any interest at *me*; I know that."

"Then comes the question," said the eminently practical father, with his eyes on the fire, "in what has this vulgar curiosity its rise?"

"I'll tell you in what. In idle imagination."

"I hope not," said the eminently practical; "I confess, however, that the misgiving *has* crossed me on my way home."

"In idle imagination, Gradgrind," repeated Bounderby. "A very bad thing for anybody, but a cursed bad thing for a girl like Louisa. I should ask Mrs. Gradgrind's pardon for strong expressions, but that she knows very well I am not a refined character. Whoever expects refinement in *me* will be disappointed. I hadn't a refined bringing up."

"Whether," said Mr. Gradgrind, pondering with his hands in his pockets, and his cavernous eyes on the fire, "whether any instructor or servant can have suggested anything? Whether Louisa or Thomas can have been reading anything? Whether, in spite of all precautions, any idle storybook can have got into the house? Because, in minds that have been practically formed by rule and line, from the cradle upwards, this is so curious, so incomprehensible."

"Stop a bit!" cried Bounderby, who all this time had been standing, as before, on the hearth, bursting at the very furniture of the room with explosive humility. "You have one of those strollers'[4] children in the school."

"Cecilia Jupe, by name," said Mr. Gradgrind, with something of a stricken look at his friend.

"Now, stop a bit!" cried Bounderby again. "How did she come there?"

"Why, the fact is, I saw the girl myself, for the first time, only just now. She specially applied here at the house to be admitted, as not

4. Traveling performers.

regularly belonging to our town, and—yes, you are right, Bounderby, you are right."

"Now, stop a bit!" cried Bounderby, once more. "Louisa saw her when she came?"

"Louisa certainly did see her, for she mentioned the application to me. But Louisa saw her, I have no doubt, in Mrs. Gradgrind's presence."

"Pray, Mrs. Gradgrind," said Bounderby, "what passed?"

"Oh, my poor health!" returned Mrs. Gradgrind. "The girl wanted to come to the school, and Mr. Gradgrind wanted girls to come to the school, and Louisa and Thomas both said that the girl wanted to come, and that Mr. Gradgrind wanted girls to come, and how was it possible to contradict them when such was the fact!"

"Now I tell you what, Gradgrind!" said Mr. Bounderby. "Turn this girl to the rightabout,[5] and there's an end of it."

"I am much of your opinion."

"Do it at once," said Bounderby, "has always been my motto from a child. When I thought I would run away from my egg-box and my grandmother, I did it at once. Do you the same. Do this at once!"

"Are you walking?" asked his friend. "I have the father's address. Perhaps you would not mind walking to town with me?"

"Not the least in the world," said Mr. Bounderby, "as long as you do it at once!"

So, Mr. Bounderby threw on his hat—he always threw it on, as expressing a man who had been far too busily employed in making himself, to acquire any fashion of wearing his hat—and with his hands in his pockets, sauntered out into the hall. "I never wear gloves," it was his custom to say. "I didn't climb up the ladder in *them*. Shouldn't be so high up, if I had."

Being left to saunter in the hall a minute or two while Mr. Gradgrind went upstairs for the address, he opened the door of the children's study and looked into that serene floor-clothed apartment, which, notwithstanding its bookcases and its cabinets and its variety of learned and philosophical appliances, had much of the genial aspect of a room devoted to hair-cutting. Louisa languidly leaned upon the window looking out, without looking at anything, while young Thomas stood sniffing revengefully at the fire. Adam Smith and Malthus,[6] two younger Gradgrinds, were out at lecture

---

5. A command for soldiers on parade to turn around and march in the opposite direction.
6. The author of the widely read *Essay on the Principles of Population* (1798), Thomas Malthus (1766–1834) claimed that population increases at a far greater rate than food supply; consequently, overpopulation and starvation are inevitable. "Adam Smith": The most influential 18th-century economist (1723–1790) who advocated, in *An Inquiry into the Nature and Causes of the Wealth of Nations* (1776), a capitalistic economy free of government interference.

in custody; and little Jane, after manufacturing a good deal of moist pipe-clay on her face with slate-pencil and tears, had fallen asleep over vulgar fractions.

"It's all right now, Louisa; it's all right, young Thomas," said Mr. Bounderby; "you won't do so any more. I'll answer for its being all over with father. Well, Louisa, that's worth a kiss, isn't it?"

"You can take one, Mr. Bounderby," returned Louisa, when she had coldly paused, and slowly walked across the room, and ungraciously raised her cheek towards him, with her face turned away.

"Always my pet; an't you, Louisa?" said Mr. Bounderby. "Good-bye, Louisa!"

He went his way, but she stood on the same spot, rubbing the cheek he had kissed; with her handkerchief, until it was burning red. She was still doing this, five minutes afterwards.

"What are you about, Loo?" her brother sulkily remonstrated. "You'll rub a hole in your face."

"You may cut the piece out with your penknife if you like, Tom. I wouldn't cry!"

Chapter V.

THE KEY-NOTE.

Coketown, to which Messrs. Bounderby and Gradgrind now walked, was a triumph of fact; it had no greater taint of fancy in it than Mrs. Gradgrind herself. Let us strike the key-note, Coketown, before pursuing our tune.

It was a town of red brick, or of brick that would have been red if the smoke and ashes had allowed it; but, as matters stood it was a town of unnatural red and black like the painted face of a savage. It was a town of machinery and tall chimneys, out of which interminable serpents of smoke trailed themselves for ever and ever, and never got uncoiled. It had a black canal in it, and a river that ran purple with ill-smelling dye, and vast piles of building full of windows where there was a rattling and a trembling all day long, and where the piston of the steam-engine worked monotonously up and down, like the head of an elephant in a state of melancholy madness. It contained several large streets all very like one another, and many small streets still more like one another, inhabited by people equally like one another, who all went in and out at the same hours, with the same sound upon the same pavements, to do the same work, and to whom every day was the same as yesterday and to-morrow, and every year the counterpart of the last and the next.

These attributes of Coketown were in the main inseparable from the work by which it was sustained; against them were to be set off, comforts of life which found their way all over the world, and

elegancies of life which made, we will not ask how much of the fine
lady, who could scarcely bear to hear the place mentioned. The rest
of its features were voluntary, and they were these.

You saw nothing in Coketown but what was severely workful. If
the members of a religious persuasion built a chapel there—as the
members of eighteen religious persuasions had done—they made it
a pious warehouse of red brick, with sometimes (but this only in
highly ornamented examples) a bell in a bird-cage on the top of it.
The solitary exception was the New Church; a stuccoed edifice with
a square steeple over the door, terminating in four short pinnacles
like florid wooden legs. All the public inscriptions in the town were
painted alike, in severe characters of black and white. The jail
might have been the infirmary, the infirmary might have been the
jail, the town-hall might have been either, or both, or anything else,
for anything that appeared to the contrary in the graces of their
construction. Fact, fact, fact, everywhere in the material aspect of
the town; fact, fact, fact, everywhere in the immaterial. The
M'Choakumchild school was all fact, and the school of design was
all fact, and the relations between master and man were all fact,
and everything was fact between the lying-in hospital and the cem-
etery, and what you couldn't state in figures, or show to be purchaseable in the cheapest market and saleable in the dearest, was
not, and never should be, world without end,[1] Amen.

A town so sacred to fact, and so triumphant in its assertion, of
course got on well? Why no, not quite well. No? Dear me!

No. Coketown did not come out of its own furnaces, in all respects
like gold that had stood the fire. First, the perplexing mystery of the
place was, Who belonged to the eighteen denominations? Because,
whoever did, the laboring people did not. It was very strange to
walk through the streets on a Sunday morning, and note how few of
them the barbarous jangling of bells that was driving the sick and
nervous mad, called away from their own quarter, from their own
close rooms, from the corners of their own streets, where they
lounged listlessly, gazing at all the church and chapel[2] going, as at a
thing with which they had no manner of concern. Nor was it merely
the stranger who noticed this, because there was a native organisation in Coketown itself, whose members were to be heard of in
the House of Commons every session, indignantly petitioning for
acts of parliament that should make these people religious by
main force. Then, came the Teetotal Society, who complained that

1. From the "Gloria" (praise to God) in The Book of Common Prayer of the Church of
   England.
2. In Victorian Britain, *church* refers to Established Church (Anglican Church or Church
   of England) places of worship; *chapel* refers to places of worship created by the dissent-
   ing or nonconformist sects, such as the Baptists and Presbyterians.

these same people *would* get drunk, and showed in tabular statements that they did get drunk, and proved at tea parties that no
inducement, human or Divine (except a medal), would induce them
to forego their custom of getting drunk. Then, came the chemist and
druggist, with other tabular statements, showing that when they
didn't get drunk, they took opium. Then, came the experienced chaplain of the jail,[3] with more tabular statements, outdoing all the previous tabular statements, and showing that the same people *would*
resort to low haunts, hidden from the public eye, where they heard
low singing and saw low dancing, and mayhap joined in it; and
where A.B., aged twenty-four next birthday, and committed for
eighteen months' solitary, had himself said (not that he had ever
shown himself particularly worthy of belief) his ruin began, as he
was perfectly sure and confident that otherwise he would have been
a tip-top moral specimen. Then, came Mr. Gradgrind and Mr. Bounderby, the two gentlemen at this present moment walking through
Coketown, and both eminently practical, who could, on occasion,
furnish more tabular statements derived from their own personal
experience, and illustrated by cases they had known and seen,
from which it clearly appeared—in short it was the only clear thing
in the case—that these same people were a bad lot altogether,
gentlemen; that do what you would for them they were never
thankful for it, gentlemen; that they were restless, gentlemen;
that they never knew what they wanted; that they lived upon the
best, and bought fresh butter, and insisted on Mocha coffee, and
rejected all but prime parts of meat, and yet were eternally dissatisfied and unmanageable. In short it was the moral of the old
nursery fable:

> There was an old woman, and what do you think?
> She lived upon nothing but victuals and drink;
> Victuals and drink were the whole of her diet,
> And yet this old woman would NEVER be quiet.

Is it possible, I wonder, that there was any analogy between
the case of the Coketown population and the case of the little
Gradgrinds? Surely, none of us in our sober senses and acquainted
with figures, are to be told at this time of day, that one of the foremost elements in the existence of the Coketown working people
had been for scores of years, deliberately set at nought? That there
was any Fancy in them demanding to be brought into healthy

---

3. Probably a reference to the Reverend John Clay (1796–1858), an "experienced" prison
chaplain. In a letter of 1854, Clay wrote: "I see that Mr. Dickens, in *Hard Times,* has a
laugh at my 'tabular statements,' and at my credulity. He is not the only man I have met
who prefers to rely on his own theories and fancies rather than on well-ascertained
facts."

existence instead of struggling on in convulsions? That exactly in the ratio as they worked long and monotonously, the craving grew within them for some physical relief—some relaxation, encouraging good humour and good spirits, and giving them a vent—some recognised holiday, though it were but for an honest dance to a stirring band of music—some occasional light pie in which even M'Choakumchild had no finger—which craving must and would be satisfied aright, or must and would inevitably go wrong, until the laws of the Creation were repealed?

"This man lives at Pod's End, and I don't quite know Pod's End," said Mr. Gradgrind. "Which is it, Bounderby?"

Mr. Bounderby knew it was somewhere down town, but knew no more respecting it. So they stopped for a moment, looking about.

Almost as they did so, there came running round the corner of the street at a quick pace and with a frightened look, a girl whom Mr. Gradgrind recognised. "Halloa!" said he. "Stop! Where are you going? Stop!" Girl number twenty stopped then, palpitating, and made him a curtsey.

"Why are you tearing about the streets," said Mr. Gradgrind, "in this improper manner?"

"I was—I was run after, sir," the girl panted, "and I wanted to get away."

"Run after?" repeated Mr. Gradgrind. "Who would run after *you*?"

The question was unexpectedly and suddenly answered for her, by the colourless boy, Bitzer, who came round the corner with such blind speed and so little anticipating a stoppage on the pavement, that he brought himself up against Mr. Gradgrind's waistcoat, and rebounded into the road.

"What do you mean, boy?" said Mr. Gradgrind. "What are you doing? How dare you dash against—everybody—in this manner?"

Bitzer picked up his cap, which the concussion had knocked off; and backing, and knuckling his forehead, pleaded that it was an accident.

"Was this boy running after you, Jupe?" asked Mr. Gradgrind.

"Yes, sir," said the girl reluctantly.

"No, I wasn't, sir!" cried Bitzer. "Not till she run away from me. But the horse-riders never mind what they say, sir; they're famous for it. You know the horse-riders are famous for never minding what they say," addressing Sissy. "It's as well known in the town as—please, sir, as the multiplication table isn't known to the horseriders." Bitzer tried Mr. Bounderby with this.

"He frightened me so," said the girl, "with his cruel faces!"

"Oh!" cried Bitzer. "Oh! An't you one of the rest! An't you a horse-rider! I never looked at her, sir. I asked her if she would know how to define a horse tomorrow, and offered to tell her again, and she ran away, and I ran after her, sir, that she might know how to answer when she was asked. You wouldn't have thought of saying such mischief if you hadn't been a horse-rider!"

"Her calling seems to be pretty well known among 'em," observed Mr. Bounderby. "You'd have had the whole school peeping in a row, in a week."

"Truly, I think so," returned his friend. "Bitzer, turn you about and take yourself home. Jupe, stay here a moment. Let me hear of your running in this manner any more, boy, and you will hear of me through the master of the school. You understand what I mean. Go along."

The boy stopped in his rapid blinking, knuckled his forehead again, glanced at Sissy, turned about, and retreated.

"Now, girl," said Mr. Gradgrind, "take this gentleman and me to your father's; we are going there. What have you got in that bottle you are carrying?"

"Gin," said Mr. Bounderby.

"Dear, no sir! It's the nine oils."

"The what?" cried Mr. Bounderby.

"The nine oils, sir. To rub father with." Then, said Mr. Bounderby, with a loud, short laugh, "what the devil do you rub your father with nine oils for?"

"It's what our people always use, sir, when they get any hurts in the ring," replied the girl, looking over her shoulder, to assure herself that her pursuer was gone. "They bruise themselves very bad sometimes."

"Serve 'em right," said Mr. Bounderby, "for being idle." She glanced up at his face, with mingled astonishment and dread.

"By George!" said Mr. Bounderby, "when I was four or five years younger than you, I had worse bruises upon me than ten oils, twenty oils, forty oils, would have rubbed off. I didn't get 'em by posture-making, but by being banged about. There was no rope-dancing for me; I danced on the bare ground and was larruped[4] with the rope."

Mr. Gradgrind, though hard enough, was by no means so rough a man as Mr. Bounderby. His character was not unkind, all things considered; it might have been a very kind one indeed, if he had only made some round mistake in the arithmetic that balanced it, years ago. He said, in what he meant for a re-assuring tone, as they turned down a narrow road, "And this is Pod's End; is it, Jupe?"

"This is it, sir, and—if you wouldn't mind, sir—this is the house."

4. Thrashed.

She stopped, at twilight, at the door of a mean little public house,[5] with dim red lights in it. As haggard and as shabby, as if, for want of custom, it had itself taken to drinking, and had gone the way all drunkards go, and was very near the end of it.

"It's only crossing the bar, sir, and up the stairs, if you wouldn't mind, and waiting there for a moment till I get a candle. If you should hear a dog, sir, it's only Merrylegs, and he only barks."

"Merrylegs and nine oils, eh!" said Mr. Bounderby, entering last with his metallic laugh. "Pretty well this, for a self-made man!"

Chapter VI.

SLEARY'S HORSEMANSHIP.

The name of the public house was the Pegasus's Arms. The Pegasus's legs might have been more to the purpose; but, underneath the winged horse upon the sign-board, the Pegasus's Arms was inscribed in Roman letters. Beneath that inscription again, in a flowing scroll, the painter had touched off the lines:

> Good malt makes good beer,
> Walk in, and they'll draw it here;
> Good wine makes good brandy,
> Give us a call, and you'll find it handy.

Framed and glazed upon the wall behind the dingy little bar, was another Pegasus—a theatrical one—with real gauze let in for his wings, golden stars stuck on all over him, and his ethereal harness made of red silk.

As it had grown too dusky without, to see the sign, and as it had not grown light enough within to see the picture, Mr. Gradgrind and Mr. Bounderby received no offence from these idealities.[1] They followed the girl up some steep corner-stairs without meeting any one, and stopped in the dark while she went on for a candle. They expected every moment to hear Merrylegs give tongue, but the highly-trained performing dog had not barked when the girl and the candle appeared together.

"Father is not in our room, sir," she said, with a face of great surprise. "If you wouldn't mind walking in, I'll find him directly."

They walked in; and Sissy, having set two chairs for them, sped away with a quick light step. It was a mean, shabbily-furnished room, with a bed in it. The white night-cap[2] embellished with two

5. A tavern, "pub."
1. Things that exist only as creations of the imagination.
2. A cloth cap commonly worn in bed by Victorian men; here made a part of a clown's costume.

peacock's feathers and a pigtail bolt upright, in which Signor Jupe
had that very afternoon enlivened the varied performances with his
chaste Shakesperian quips and retorts, hung upon a nail; but no
other portion of his wardrobe, or other token of himself or his pursuits, was to be seen anywhere. As to Merrylegs, that respectable
ancestor of the highly-trained animal who went aboard the ark,
might have been accidentally shut out of it, for any sign of a dog
that was manifest to eye or ear in the Pegasus's Arms.

They heard the doors of rooms above, opening and shutting as
Sissy went from one to another in quest of her father; and presently
they heard voices expressing surprise. She came bounding down
again in a great hurry, opened a battered and mangey old hair trunk,[3]
found it empty, and looked round with her hands clasped and her
face full of terror.

"Father must have gone down to the Booth, Sir. I don't know why
he should go there, but he must be there; I'll bring him in a minute!"
She was gone directly, without her bonnet; with her long, dark,
childish hair streaming behind her.

"What does she mean!" said Mr. Gradgrind. "Back in a minute?
It's more than a mile off."

Before Mr. Bounderby could reply, a young man appeared at the
door, and introducing himself with the words, "By your leaves, gentlemen!" walked in with his hands in his pockets. His face, close-
shaven, thin, and sallow, was shaded by a great quantity of dark
hair brushed into a roll all round his head, and parted up the centre. His legs were very robust, but shorter than legs of good proportions should have been. His chest and back were as much too broad,
as his legs were too short. He was dressed in a Newmarket coat and
tight-fitting trousers; wore a shawl round his neck; smelt of lamp-
oil, straw, orange-peel, horses' provender, and sawdust; and looked
a most remarkable sort of Centaur,[4] compounded of the stable and
the play-house. Where the one began, and the other ended, nobody
could have told with any precision. This gentleman was mentioned
in the bills of the day as Mr. E. W. B. Childers, so justly celebrated
for his daring vaulting act as the Wild Huntsman of the North
American Prairies; in which popular performance, a diminutive boy
with an old face, who now accompanied him, assisted as his infant
son: being carried upside down over his father's shoulder, by one
foot, and held by the crown of his head, heels upwards, in the palm
of his father's hand, according to the violent paternal manner in

---

3. A trunk covered with an animal skin retaining its hair.
4. One of a race of Greek mythological monsters with the head, arms, and torso of a man
   and the body and legs of a horse. "Newmarket coat": a flashy style of overcoat favored
   by patrons of Newmarket, a center for racing and horse trading.

which wild huntsmen may be observed to fondle their offspring. Made up with curls, wreaths, wings, white bismuth, and carmine,[5] this hopeful young person soared into so pleasing a Cupid as to constitute the chief delight of the maternal part of the spectators; but, in private, where his characteristics were a precocious cutaway coat and an extremely gruff voice, he became of the Turf, turfy.

"By your leaves, gentlemen," said Mr. E. W. B. Childers, glancing round the room. "It was you, I believe, that were wishing to see Jupe?"

"It was," said Mr. Gradgrind. "His daughter has gone to fetch him, but I can't wait; therefore, if you please, I will leave a message for him with you."

"You see, my friend," Mr. Bounderby put in, "we are the kind of people who know the value of time, and you are the kind of people who don't know the value of time."

"I have not," retorted Mr. Childers, after surveying him from head to foot, "the honor of knowing you;—but if you mean that you can make more money of your time than I can of mine, I should judge from your appearance, that you are about right."

"And when you have made it, you can keep it too, I should think," said Cupid.

"Kidderminster, stow that!"[6] said Mr. Childers. (Master Kidderminster was Cupid's mortal name.)

"What does he come here cheeking us for, then?" cried Master Kidderminster, showing a very irascible temperament. "If you want to cheek us, pay your ochre[7] at the doors and take it out."

"Kidderminster," said Mr. Childers, raising his voice, "stow that!—Sir," to Mr. Gradgrind, "I was addressing myself to you. You may or you may not be aware (for perhaps you have not been much in the audience), that Jupe has missed his tip very often, lately."

"Has—what has he missed?" asked Mr. Gradgrind, glancing at the potent Bounderby for assistance.

"Missed his tip."

"Offered at the Garters four times last night, and never done 'em once," said Master Kidderminster. "Missed his tip at the banners, too, and was loose in his ponging."[8]

"Didn't do what he ought to do. Was short in his leaps and bad in his tumbling," Mr. Childers interpreted.

---

5. Used as cosmetics. "Bismuth": a white crystalline metallic element. "Carmine": a purple-red pigment from chochineal.
6. Put that away! *or*, Stop that!
7. A yellow pigment signifying, here, money, in the form of gold coins.
8. Kidderminster's speech was translated by Angus Easson as follows: "Garters": "refused to jump through a hoop though he had four opportunities." "Banners": "failed in his jump over streamers stretched in the ring." "Ponging": "faulty in his somersaulting" (*Hard Times: Critical Commentary and Notes* [1973]).

"Oh!" said Mr. Gradgrind, "that is tip, is it?"

"In a general way that's missing his tip," Mr. E. W. B. Childers answered.

"Nine-oils, Merrylegs, missing tips, garters, banners, and Ponging, eh!" ejaculated Bounderby, with his laugh of laughs. "Queer sort of company, too, for a man who has raised himself."

"Lower yourself, then," retorted Cupid, "Oh Lord! if you've raised yourself so high as all that comes to, let yourself down a bit."

"This is a very obtrusive lad!" said Mr. Gradgrind, turning, and knitting his brows on him.

"We'd have had a young gentleman to meet you, if we had known you were coming," retorted Master Kidderminster, nothing abashed. "It's a pity you don't have a bespeak,[9] being so particular. You're on the Tight-Jeff, ain't you?"

"What does this unmannerly boy mean," asked Mr. Gradgrind, eyeing him in a sort of desperation, "by Tight-Jeff?"

"There! Get out, get out!" said Mr. Childers, thrusting his young friend from the room, rather in the prairie manner. "Tight-Jeff or Slack-Jeff, it don't much signify: it's only tight-rope and slack-rope. You were going to give me a message for Jupe?"

"Yes, I was."

"Then," continued Mr. Childers, quickly, "my opinion is, he will never receive it. Do you know much of him?"

"I never saw the man in my life."

"I doubt if you ever *will* see him now. It's pretty plain to me, he's off."

"Do you mean that he has deserted his daughter?"

"Ay! I mean," said Mr. Childers, with a nod, "that he has cut. He was goosed[1] last night, he was goosed the night before last, he was goosed to-day. He has lately got in the way of being always goosed, and he can't stand it."

"Why has he been—so very much—Goosed?" asked Mr. Gradgrind, forcing the word out of himself, with great solemnity and reluctance.

"His joints are turning stiff, and he is getting used up," said Childers. "He has his points as a Cackler still, but he can't get a living out of *them*."

"A Cackler!" Bounderby repeated. "Here we go again!"

"A speaker, if the gentleman likes it better," said Mr. E. W. B. Childers, superciliously throwing the interpretation over his shoulder, and accompanying it with a shake of his long hair—which all shook at once. "Now, it's a remarkable fact, sir, that it cut that man

9. A special show; here, for the benefit of the circus performers.
1. Hissed by the audience.

deeper, to know that his daughter knew of his being goosed, than to go through with it."

"Good!" interrupted Mr. Bounderby. "This is good, Gradgrind! A man so fond of his daughter, that he runs away from her! This is devilish good! Ha! ha! Now, I'll tell you what, young man. I haven't always occupied my present station of life. I know what these things are. You may be astonished to hear it, but my mother ran away from *me*."

E. W. B. Childers replied pointedly, that he was not at all astonished to hear it.

"Very well," said Bounderby. "I was born in a ditch, and my mother ran away from me. Do I excuse her for it? No. Have I ever excused her for it? Not I. What do I call her for it? I call her probably the very worst woman that ever lived in the world, except my drunken grandmother. There's no family pride about me, there's no imaginative sentimental humbug about me. I call a spade a spade; and I call the mother of Josiah Bounderby of Coketown, without any fear or any favor, what I should call her if she had been the mother of Dick Jones of Wapping.[2] So, with this man. He is a runaway rogue and a vagabond, that's what he is, in English."

"It's all the same to me what he is or what he is not, whether in English or whether in French," retorted Mr. E. W. B. Childers, facing about. "I am telling your friend what's the fact; if you don't like to hear it, you can avail yourself of the open air. You give it mouth enough,[3] you do; but give it mouth in your own building at least," remonstrated E. W. B. with stern irony. "Don't give it mouth in this building, till you're called upon. You have got some building of your own, I dare say, now?"

"Perhaps so," replied Mr. Bounderby, rattling his money and laughing.

"Then give it mouth in your own building, will you, if you please?" said Childers. "Because this isn't a strong building, and too much of you might bring it down!"

Eyeing Mr. Bounderby from head to foot again, he turned from him, as from a man finally disposed of, to Mr. Gradgrind.

"Jupe sent his daughter out on an errand not an hour ago, and then was seen to slip out himself, with his hat over his eyes and a bundle tied up in a handkerchief under his arm. She will never believe it of him, but he has cut away and left her."

"Pray," said Mr. Gradgrind, "why will she never believe it of him?"

"Because those two were one. Because they were never asunder. Because, up to this time, he seemed to dote upon her," said Childers,

2. A phrase used to denote "anyone," an ordinary person, similar to "Mr. Smith" or "Mr. Jones" today. Wapping is a dockside area in East London.
3. Talk too much about it.

taking a step or two to look into the empty trunk. Both Mr. Childers and Master Kidderminster walked in a curious manner; with their legs wider apart than the general run of men, and with a very knowing assumption of being stiff in the knees. This walk was common to all the male members of Sleary's company, and was understood to express, that they were always on horseback.

"Poor Sissy! He had better have apprenticed her," said Childers, giving his hair another shake, as he looked up from the empty box. "Now, he leaves her without anything to take to."

"It is creditable to you who have never been apprenticed, to express that opinion," returned Mr. Gradgrind, approvingly.

"*I* never apprenticed? I was apprenticed when I was seven year old."

"Oh! Indeed?" said Mr. Gradgrind, rather resentfully, as having been defrauded of his good opinion. "I was not aware of its being the custom to apprentice young persons to—"

"Idleness," Mr. Bounderby put in with a loud laugh. "No, by the Lord Harry![4] Nor I!"

"Her father always had it in his head," resumed Childers, feigning unconsciousness of Mr. Bounderby's existence, "that she was to be taught the deuce-and-all[5] of education. How it got into his head, I can't say; I can only say that it never got out. He has been picking up a bit of reading for her, here—and a bit of writing for her, there—and a bit of cyphering for her, somewhere else—these seven years."

Mr. E. W. B. Childers took one of his hands out of his pockets, stroked his face and chin, and looked, with a good deal of doubt and a little hope, at Mr. Gradgrind. From the first he had sought to conciliate that gentleman, for the sake of the deserted girl.

"When Sissy got into the school here," he pursued, "her father was as pleased as Punch.[6] I couldn't altogether make out why, myself, as we were not stationary here, being but comers and goers anywhere. I suppose, however, he had this move in his mind—he was always half-cracked—and then considered her provided for. If you should happen to have looked in to-night, for the purpose of telling him that you were going to do her any little service," said Mr. Childers, stroking his face again, and repeating his look, "it would be very fortunate and well timed; *very* fortunate and well-timed."

"On the contrary," returned Mr. Gradgrind. "I came to tell him that her connexions made her not an object for the school, and that

4. The devil.
5. Everything there is to know.
6. In the puppet show "Punch and Judy," the smiling male character is portrayed as persistently pleased with himself.

she must not attend any more. Still, if her father really has left her, without any connivance on her part—Bounderby, let me have a word with you."

Upon this, Mr. Childers politely betook himself, with his equestrian walk, to the landing outside the door, and there stood stroking his face and softly whistling. While thus engaged, he overheard such phrases in Mr. Bounderby's voice as "No. *I* say no. I advise you not. I say by no means." While, from Mr. Gradgrind, he heard in his much lower tone the words, "But even as an example to Louisa, of what this pursuit which has been the subject of a vulgar curiosity, leads to and ends in. Think of it, Bounderby, in that point of view."

Meanwhile, the various members of Sleary's company gradually gathered together from the upper regions, where they were quartered, and, from standing about, talking in low voices to one another and to Mr. Childers, gradually insinuated themselves and him into the room. There were two or three handsome young women among them, with their two or three husbands, and their two or three mothers, and their eight or nine little children, who did the fairy business when required. The father of one of the families was in the habit of balancing the father of another of the families on the top of a great pole; the father of a third family often made a pyramid of both those fathers, with Master Kidderminster for the apex, and himself for the base; all the fathers could dance upon rolling casks, stand upon bottles, catch knives and balls, twirl hand-basins, ride upon anything, jump over everything, and stick at nothing. All the mothers could (and did) dance, upon the slack wire and the tight rope, and perform rapid acts on bare-backed steeds; none of them were at all particular in respect of showing their legs; and one of them, alone in a Greek chariot, drove six in hand[7] into every town they came to. They all assumed to be mighty rakish and knowing, they were not very tidy in their private dresses, they were not at all orderly in their domestic arrangements, and the combined literature of the whole company would have produced but a poor letter on any subject. Yet there was a remarkable gentleness and childishness about these people, a special inaptitude for any kind of sharp practice, and an untiring readiness to help and pity one another, deserving, often of as much respect, and always of as much generous construction, as the every-day virtues of any class of people in the world.

Last of all appeared Mr. Sleary: a stout man as already mentioned, with one fixed eye and one loose eye, a voice (if it can be called so) like the efforts of a broken old pair of bellows, a flabby surface, and a muddled head which was never sober and never drunk.

7. Controlling six horses.

"Thquire!" said Mr. Sleary, who was troubled with asthma, and whose breath came far too thick and heavy for the letters, "Your thervant! Thith ith a bad piethe of bithnith, thith ith. You've heard of my Clown and hith dog being thuppothed to have morrithed?"[8]

He addressed Mr. Gradgrind, who answered "Yes."

"Well Thquire," he returned, taking off his hat, and rubbing the lining with his pocket-handkerchief, which he kept inside it for the purpose. "Ith it your intenthion to do anything for the poor girl, Thquire?"

"I shall have something to propose to her when she comes back," said Mr. Gradgrind.

"Glad to hear it, Thquire. Not that I want to get rid of the child, any more than I want to thtand in her way. I'm willing to take her prentith, though at her age ith late. My voithe ith a little huthky, Thquire, and not eathy heard by them ath don't know me; but if you'd been chilled and heated, heated and chilled, chilled and heated in the ring when you wath young, ath often ath I have been, *your* voithe wouldn't have lathted out, Thquire, no more than mine."

"I dare say not," said Mr. Gradgrind.

"What thall it be, Thquire, while you wait? Thall it be Therry? Give it a name, Thquire!" said Mr. Sleary, with hospitable ease.

"Nothing for me, I thank you," said Mr. Gradgrind.

"Don't thay nothing, Thquire. What doth your friend thay? If you haven't took your feed yet, have a glath of bitterth."[9]

Here his daughter Josephine—a pretty fair-haired girl of eighteen, who had been tied on a horse at two years old, and had made a will at twelve, which she always carried about with her, expressive of her dying desire to be drawn to the grave by the two piebald[1] ponies—cried "Father, hush! she has come back!" Then came Sissy Jupe, running into the room as she had run out of it. And when she saw them all assembled, and saw their looks, and saw no father there, she broke into a most deplorable cry, and took refuge on the bosom of the most accomplished tight-rope lady (herself in the family way), who knelt down on the floor to nurse her, and to weep over her.

"Ith an infernal thame, upon my thoul it ith," said Sleary.

"O my dear father, my good kind father, where are you gone? You are gone to try to do me some good, I know! You are gone away for my sake, I am sure. And how miserable and helpless you will be without me, poor, poor father, until you come back!" It was so pathetic to hear her saying many things of this kind, with her face turned

8. Morrised; i.e., run away or decamped.
9. Bitters; a kind of beer.
1. Spotted, usually black and white.

upward, and her arms stretched out as if she were trying to stop his departing shadow and embrace it, that no one spoke a word until Mr. Bounderby (growing impatient) took the case in hand.

"Now, good people all," said he, "this is wanton waste of time. Let the girl understand the fact. Let her take it from me, if you like, who have been run away from, myself. Here, what's your name! Your father has absconded—deserted you—and you mustn't expect to see him again as long as you live."

They cared so little for plain Fact, these people, and were in that advanced state of degeneracy on the subject, that instead of being impressed by the speaker's strong common sense, they took it in extraordinary dudgeon. The men muttered "Shame!" and the women "Brute!" and Sleary, in some haste, communicated the following hint, apart to Mr. Bounderby.

"I tell you what, Thquire. To thpeak plain to you, my opinion ith that you had better cut it thort, and drop it. They're a very good natur'd people, my people, but they're accuthtomed to be quick in their movementh; and if you don't act upon my advithe, I'm damned if I don't believe they'll pith you out o' winder."

Mr. Bounderby being restrained by this mild suggestion, Mr. Gradgrind found an opening for his eminently practical exposition of the subject.

"It is of no moment," said he, "whether this person is to be expected back at any time, or the contrary. He is gone away, and there is no present expectation of his return. That, I believe, is agreed on all hands."

"Thath agreed, Thquire. Thtick to that!" From Sleary.

"Well then. I, who came here to inform the father of the poor girl, Jupe, that she could not be received at the school any more, in consequence of there being practical objections, into which I need not enter, to the reception there of the children of persons so employed, am prepared in these altered circumstances to make a proposal. I am willing to take charge of you, Jupe, and to educate you, and provide for you. The only condition (over and above your good behaviour) I make is, that you decide now, at once, whether to accompany me or remain here. Also, that if you accompany me now, it is understood that you communicate no more with any of your friends who are here present. These observations comprise the whole of the case."

"At the thame time," said Sleary, "I mutht put in my word, Thquire, tho that both thides of the banner may be equally theen. If you like, Thethilia, to be prentitht, you know the nature of the work and you know your companionth. Emma Gordon, in whothe lap you're a lyin' at prethent, would be a mother to you, and Joth'phine would be a thithter to you. I don't pretend to be of the angel breed mythelf, and I don't thay but what, when you mith'd your tip, you'd find me cut up rough, and thwear a oath or two at you. But what I thay, Thquire, ith, that good tempered or bad tempered, I never did a horthe a injury yet, no more than thwearing at him went, and that I don't expect I thall begin otherwithe at my time of life, with a rider. I never wath much of a Cackler, Thquire, and I have thed my thay."

The latter part of this speech was addressed to Mr. Gradgrind, who received it with a grave inclination of his head, and then remarked.

"The only observation I will make to you, Jupe, in the way of influencing your decision, is, that it is highly desirable to have a sound practical education, and that even your father himself (from what I understand) appears, on your behalf, to have known and felt that much."

The last words had a visible effect upon her. She stopped in her wild crying, a little detached herself from Emma Gordon, and turned her face full upon her patron. The whole company perceived the force of the change, and drew a long breath together, that plainly said, "she will go!"

"Be sure you know your own mind, Jupe," Mr. Gradgrind cautioned her; "I say no more. Be sure you know your own mind!"

"When father comes back," cried the girl, bursting into tears again after a minute's silence, "how will he ever find me if I go away!"

"You may be quite at ease," said Mr. Gradgrind, calmly; he worked out the whole matter like a sum: "you may be quite at ease, Jupe, on that score. In such a case, your father, I apprehend, must find out Mr.—."

"Thleary. Thath my name, Thquire. Not athamed of it. Known all over England, and alwayth paythe ith way."

"Must find out Mr. Sleary, who would then let him know where you went. I should have no power of keeping you against his wish, and he would have no difficulty, at any time, in finding Mr. Thomas Gradgrind of Coketown. I am well known."

"Well known," assented Mr. Sleary, rolling his loose eye. "You're one of the thort, Thquire, that keepth a prethious thight of money out of the houthe.[2] But never mind that at prethent."

There was another silence; and then she exclaimed, sobbing with her hands before her face, "Oh give me my clothes, give me my clothes, and let me go away before I break my heart!"

Tho women sadly bestirred themselves to get the clothes together—it was soon done, for they were not many—and to pack them in a basket which had often travelled with them. Sissy sat all the time,

---

2. Dissuades people from spending money on the circus.

upon the ground, still sobbing and covering her eyes: Mr. Gradgrind and his friend Bounderby stood near the door, ready to take her away. Mr. Sleary stood in the middle of the room, with the male members of the company about him, exactly as he would have stood in the centre of the ring during his daughter Josephine's performance. He wanted nothing but his whip.

The basket packed in silence, they brought her bonnet to her, and smoothed her disordered hair, and put it on. Then they pressed about her, and bent over her in very natural attitudes, kissing and embracing her; and brought the children to take leave of her; and were a tender-hearted, simple, foolish set of women altogether.

"Now, Jupe," said Mr. Gradgrind. "If you are quite determined, come!"

But she had to take her farewell of the male part of the company yet, and every one of them had to unfold his arms (for they all assumed the professional attitude when they found themselves near Sleary), and give her a parting kiss—Master Kidderminster excepted, in whose young nature there was an original flavor of the misanthrope, who was also known to have harbored matrimonial. views, and who moodily withdrew. Mr. Sleary was reserved until the last. Opening his arms wide he took her by both her hands, and would have sprung her up and down, after the riding-master manner of congratulating young ladies on their dismounting from a rapid act; but there was no rebound in Sissy, and she only stood before him crying.

"Good-bye, my dear!" said Sleary. "You'll make your fortun, I hope, and none of our poor folkth will ever trouble you, I'll pound it.[3] I with your father hadn't taken hith dog with him; ith a ill-conwenienth to have the dog out of the billth. But on thecond thoughth, he wouldn't have performed without hith mathter, tho ith ath broad ath ith long!"[4]

With that he regarded her attentively with his fixed eye, surveyed his company with his loose one, kissed her, shook his head, and handed her to Mr. Gradgrind as to a horse.

"There the ith, Thquire," he said, sweeping her with a professional glance as if she were being adjusted in her seat, "and the'll do you juthtithe. Good-bye, Thethilia!"

"Good-bye, Cecilia!" "Good-bye, Sissy!" "God bless you, dear!" In a variety of voices from all the room.

But the riding-master eye had observed the bottle of the nine oils in her bosom, and he now interposed with "Leave the bottle,

---

3. Bet a pound on it or guarantee it.
4. Either way is the same.

my dear; ith large to carry; it will be of no uthe to you now. Give it to me!"

"No, no!" she said, in another burst of tears. "Oh no! Pray let me keep it for father till he comes back! He will want it when he comes back. He had never thought of going away, when he sent me for it. I must keep it for him, if you please!"

"Tho be it, my dear. (You thee how it ith, Thquire!) Farewell, Thethilia! My latht wordth to you ith thith, Thtick to the termth of your engagement, be obedient to the Thquire, and forget uth. But if, when you're grown up and married and well off, you come upon any horthe-riding ever, don't be hard upon it, don't be croth with it, give it a Bethpeak if you can, and think you might do wurth. People mutht be amuthed, Thquire, thomehow," continued Sleary, rendered more pursy[5] than ever, by so much talking; "they can't be alwayth a work-ing, nor yet they can't be alwayth a learning. Make the betht of uth; not the wurtht. I've got my living out of the horthe-riding all my life, I know; but I conthider that I lay down the philothophy of the thubject when I thay to you, Thquire, make the betht of uth: not the wurtht!"

The Sleary philosophy was propounded as they went down-stairs; and the fixed eye of Philosophy—and its rolling eye, too—soon lost the three figures and the basket in the darkness of the street.

Chapter VII.

MRS. SPARSIT.

Mr. Bounderby being a bachelor, an elderly lady presided over his establishment, in consideration of a certain annual stipend. Mrs. Sparsit was this lady's name; and she was a prominent figure in attendance on Mr. Bounderby's car,[1] as it rolled along in triumph with the Bully of humility inside.

For, Mrs. Sparsit had not only seen different days, but was highly connected. She had a great aunt living in these very times called Lady Scadgers. Mr. Sparsit, deceased, of whom she was the relict,[2] had been by the mother's side what Mrs. Sparsit still called "a Pow-ler." Strangers of limited information and dull apprehension were sometimes observed not to know what a Powler was, and even to appear uncertain whether it might be a business, or a political party, or a profession of faith. The better class of minds, however, did not need to be informed that the Powlers were an ancient stock, who could trace themselves so exceedingly far back that it was not

5. Puckered.
1. Chariot.
2. Widow.

surprising if they sometimes lost themselves—which they had rather frequently done, as respected horse-flesh, blind-hookey, Hebrew monetary transactions, and the Insolvent Debtors' Court.[3]

The late Mr. Sparsit, being by the mother's side a Powler, married this lady, being by the father's side a Scadgers. Lady Scadgers (an immensely fat old woman, with an inordinate appetite for butcher's meat, and a mysterious leg which had now refused to get out of bed for fourteen years) contrived the marriage, at a period when Sparsit was just of age, and chiefly noticeable for a slender body, weakly supported on two long slim props, and surmounted by no head worth mentioning. He inherited a fair fortune from his uncle, but owed it all before he came into it, and spent it twice over immediately afterwards. Thus, when he died, at twenty-four (the scene of his decease, Calais,[4] and the cause brandy), he did not leave his widow, from whom he had been separated soon after the honeymoon, in affluent circumstances. That bereaved lady, fifteen years older than he, fell presently at deadly feud with her only relative, Lady Scadgers; and, partly to spite her ladyship, and partly to maintain herself, went out at a salary. And here she was now, in her elderly days, with the Coriolanian style of nose[5] and the dense black eyebrows which had captivated Sparsit, making Mr. Bounderby's tea as he took his breakfast.

If Bounderby had been a Conqueror, and Mrs. Sparsit a captive Princess whom he took about as a feature in his state-processions, he could not have made a greater flourish with her than he habitually did. Just as it belonged to his boastfulness to depreciate his own extraction, so it belonged to it to exalt Mrs. Sparsit's. In the measure that he would not allow his own youth to have been attended by a single favorable circumstance, he brightened Mrs. Sparsit's juvenile career with every possible advantage, and showered wagon-loads of early roses all over that lady's path. "And yet, sir," he would say, "how does it turn out after all? Why here she is at a hundred a year (I give her a hundred, which she is pleased to term handsome), keeping the house of Josiah Bounderby of Coketown!"

3. The bankruptcy court designated exclusively for individuals as opposed to businesses. Individuals could be imprisoned by a litigious creditor until the debt had been cleared; the practice was abolished by the Debtor's Act of 1869. "Blind hookey": a card game in which the player places bets before seeing the cards in his or her own hand (hence *blind*). "Hebrew monetary transactions": borrowing from Jewish money-lenders, usually at high interest rates; in Victorian Britain, as in Europe as a whole, Jews were associated, often anti-Semitically, with money-lending, over which they had had a monopoly in the Middle Ages since Christians had been forbidden to lend money at interest.
4. A city in France just across the English Channel and outside the reach of English law whose proximity made it a popular place of refuge for those fleeing from legal obligations or criminal charges.
5. A "Roman nose," associated with Coriolanus, a haughty Roman general who is the title character in Shakespeare's tragedy *Coriolanus*.

Nay, he made this foil of his so very widely known, that third parties took it up, and handled it on some occasions with considerable briskness. It was one of the most exasperating attributes of Bounderby, that he not only sang his own praises but stimulated other men to sing them. There was a moral infection of clap-trap in him. Strangers, modest enough elsewhere, started up at dinners in Coketown, and boasted, in quite a rampant way, of Bounderby. They made him out to be the Royal arms, the Union-Jack, Magna Charta, John Bull, Habeas Corpus, the Bill of Rights,[6] An Englishman's house is his castle, Church and State, and God save the Queen, all put together. And as often (and it was very often) as an orator of this kind brought into his peroration,

> "Princes and Lords may flourish or may fade,
> A breath can make them, as a breath has made,[7]

—it was, for certain, more or less understood among the company that he had heard of Mrs. Sparsit.

"Mr. Bounderby," said Mrs. Sparsit, "you are unusually slow, sir, with your breakfast this morning."

"Why, ma'am," he returned, "I am thinking about Tom Gradgrind's whim;" Tom Gradgrind, for a bluff independent manner of speaking—as if somebody were always endeavouring to bribe him with immense sums to say Thomas, and he wouldn't; "Tom Gradgrind's whim, ma'am, of bringing up the tumbling-girl."[8]

"The girl is now waiting to know," said Mrs. Sparsit, "whether she is to go straight to the school, or up to the Lodge."

"She must wait, ma'am," answered Bounderby, "till I know myself. We shall have Tom Gradgrind down here presently, I suppose. If he should wish her to remain here a day or two longer, of course she can, ma'am."

"Of course she can if you wish it, Mr. Bounderby."

"I told him I would give her a shake-down[9] here, last night, in order that he might sleep on it before he decided to let her have any association with Louisa."

"Indeed, Mr. Bounderby? Very thoughtful of you!"

---

6. All references to evoke British patriotism and national pride. "Royal arms": the coat of arms of the British sovereign. "Union-Jack": the British national flag. Magna Charta": the declaration issued by King John in 1215 in which he agreed to extend certain freedoms and privileges to his nobles. "Habeas Corpus": dating back to 1215 and reaffirmed in the Habeas Corpus Act of 1679, prohibits the government both from imprisoning a person without sufficient evidence to support a criminal charge and from keeping a person imprisoned for an indefinite time without a trial. "Bill of Rights": enacted in 1689, after the peaceful Revolution of 1688, reestablished constitutional rule in Britain and asserted the rights of citizens and of the Parliament.
7. From *The Deserted Village* (1770) by Oliver Goldsmith.
8. Circus girl, from the use of tumbling to mean performing acrobatic feats.
9. A temporary place to sleep.

Mrs. Sparsit's Coriolanian nose underwent a slight expansion of the nostrils, and her black eyebrows contracted as she took a sip of tea.

"It's tolerably clear to *me*," said Bounderby, "that the little puss can get small good out of such companionship."

"Are you speaking of young Miss Gradgrind, Mr. Bounderby?"

"Yes, ma'am, I am speaking of Louisa."

"Your observation being limited to 'little puss,'" said Mrs. Sparsit, "and there being two little girls in question, I did not know which might be indicated by that expression."

"Louisa," repeated Mr. Bounderby. "Louisa, Louisa."

"You are quite another father to Louisa, sir." Mrs. Sparsit took a little more tea; and, as she bent her again contracted eyebrows over her steaming cup, rather looked as if her classical countenance were invoking the infernal gods.

"If you had said I was another father to Tom—young Tom, I mean, not my friend Tom Gradgrind—you might have been nearer the mark. I am going to take young Tom into my office. Going to have him under my wing, ma'am."

"Indeed? Rather young for that, is he not, sir?" Mrs. Sparsit's "sir," in addressing Mr. Bounderby, was a word of ceremony, rather exacting consideration for herself in the use, than honoring him.

"I'm not going to take him at once; he is to finish his educational cramming before then," said Bounderby. "By the Lord Harry, he'll have enough of it, first and last! He'd open his eyes, that boy would, if he knew how empty of learning *my* young maw[1] was, at his time of life." Which, by the by,.he probably did know, for he had heard of it often enough. "But it's extraordinary the difficulty I have on scores of such subjects, in speaking to any one on equal terms. Here, for example, I have been speaking to you this morning about tumblers. Why, what do *you* know about tumblers? At the time when, to have been a tumbler in the mud of the streets, would have been a godsend to me, a prize in the lottery to me, you were at the Italian Opera.[2] You were coming out of the Italian Opera, ma'am, in white satin and jewels, a blaze of splendor, when I hadn't a penny to buy a link[3] to light you."

"I certainly, sir," returned Mrs. Sparsit, with a dignity serenely mournful, "was familiar with the Italian Opera at a very early age."

"Egad, ma'am, so was I," said Bounderby, "—with the wrong side of it. A hard bed the pavement of its Arcade used to make, I assure you. People like you, ma'am, accustomed from infancy to lie on

---

1. The mouth or stomach of an animal with a voracious appetite.
2. A theatre in Pall Mall in London.
3. A flaming torch used to light up the street for pedestrians.

Down feathers, have no idea *how* hard a paving-stone is, without trying it. No no, it's of no use my talking to *you* about tumblers. I should speak of foreign dancers, and the West End of London, and May Fair,[4] and lords and ladies and honorables."

"I trust, sir," rejoined Mrs. Sparsit, with decent resignation, "it is not necessary that you should do anything of that kind. I hope I have learnt how to accommodate myself to the changes of life. If I have acquired an interest in hearing of your instructive experiences, and can scarcely hear enough of them, I claim no merit for that, since I believe it is a general sentiment."

"Well, ma'am," said her patron, "perhaps some people may be pleased to say that they do like to hear, in his own unpolished way, what Josiah Bounderby of Coketown, has gone through. But you must confess that you were born in the lap of luxury, yourself. Come, ma'am, you know you were born in the lap of luxury."

"I do not, sir," returned Mrs. Sparsit with a shake of her head, "deny it."

Mr. Bounderby was obliged to get up from table, and stand with his back to the fire, looking at her; she was such an enhancement of his position.

"And you were in crack society. Devilish high society," he said, warming his legs.

"It is true, sir," returned Mrs. Sparsit, with an affectation of humility the very opposite of his, and therefore in no danger of jostling it.

"You were in the tiptop fashion, and all the rest of it," said Mr. Bounderby.

"Yes, sir," returned Mrs. Sparsit, with a kind of social widowhood upon her. "It is unquestionably true."

Mr. Bounderby, bending himself at the knees, literally embraced his legs in his great satisfaction and laughed aloud. Mr. and Miss Gradgrind being then announced, he received the former with a shake of the hand, and the latter with a kiss.

"Can Jupe be sent here, Bounderby?" asked Mr. Gradgrind.

Certainly. So Jupe was sent there. On coming in, she curtseyed to Mr. Bounderby, and to his friend Tom Gradgrind, and also to Louisa; but in her confusion unluckily omitted Mrs. Sparsit. Observing this, the blustrous Bounderby had the following remarks to make:

"Now, I tell you what, my girl. The name of that lady by the teapot, is Mrs. Sparsit. That lady acts as mistress of this house, and she is a highly connected lady. Consequently, if ever you come again into any

4. A fashionable section of the West End of London, originally the site of an annual fair held in May.

room in this house, you will make a short stay in it if you don't behave towards that lady in your most respectful manner. Now, I don't care a button what you do to *me*, because I don't affect to be anybody. So far from having high connections I have no connections at all, and I come of the scum of the earth. But towards that lady, I do care what you do; and you shall do what is deferential and respectful, or you shall not come here."

"I hope, Bounderby," said Mr. Gradgrind, in a conciliatory voice, "that this was merely an oversight."

"My friend Tom Gradgrind suggests, Mrs. Sparsit," said Bounderby, "that this was merely an oversight. Very likely. However, as you are aware, ma'am, I don't allow of even oversights towards you."

"You are very good indeed, sir," returned Mrs. Sparsit, shaking her head with her State humility. "It is not worth speaking of."

Sissy, who all this time had been faintly excusing herself with tears in her eyes, was now waved over by the master of the house to Mr. Gradgrind. She stood, looking intently at him, and Louisa stood coldly by, with her eyes upon the ground, while he proceeded thus:

"Jupe, I have made up my mind to take you into my house; and, when you are not in attendance at the school, to employ you about Mrs. Gradgrind, who is rather an invalid. I have explained to Miss Louisa—this is Miss Louisa—the miserable but natural end of your late career; and you are to expressly understand that the whole of that subject is past, and is not to be referred to any more. From this time you begin your history. You are, at present, ignorant, I know."

"Yes, sir, very," she answered, curtseying.

"I shall have the satisfaction of causing you to be strictly educated; and you will be a living proof to all who come into communication with you, of the advantages of the training you will receive. You will be reclaimed and formed. You have been in the habit, now, of reading to your father, and those people I found you among, I dare say?" said Mr. Gradgrind, beckoning her nearer to him before he said so, and dropping his voice.

"Only to father and Merrylegs, sir. At least I mean to father, when Merrylegs was always there."

"Never mind Merrylegs, Jupe," said Mr. Gradgrind, with a passing frown. "I don't ask about him. I understand you to have been in the habit of reading to your father?"

"O yes, sir, thousands of times. They were the happiest—O, of all the happy times we had together, sir!"

It was only now, when her sorrow broke out, that Louisa looked at her.

"And what," asked Mr. Gradgrind, in a still lower voice, "did you read to your father, Jupe?"

"About the Fairies, sir, and the Dwarf, and the Hunchback, and the Genies,"[5] she sobbed out; "and about—"

"Hush!" said Mr. Gradgrind, "that is enough. Never breathe a word of such destructive nonsense any more. Bounderby, this is a case for rigid training, and I shall observe it with interest."

"Well," returned Mr. Bounderby, "I have given you my opinion already, and I shouldn't do as you do. But, very well, very well. Since you are bent upon it, *very* well!"

So, Mr. Gradgrind and his daughter took Cecilia Jupe off with them to Stone Lodge, and on the way Louisa never spoke one word, good or bad. And Mr. Bounderby went about his daily pursuits. And Mrs. Sparsit got behind her eyebrows and meditated in the gloom of that retreat, all the morning.

Chapter VIII.

NEVER WONDER.

Let us strike the key-note again, before pursuing the tune.

When she was half a dozen years younger, Louisa had been over-heard to begin a conversation with her brother one day, by saying "Tom, I wonder"—upon which Mr. Gradgrind, who was the person overhearing, stepped forth into the light, and said, "Louisa, never wonder!"

Herein lay the spring of the mechanical art and mystery of educating the reason without stooping to the cultivation of the sentiments and affections. Never wonder. By means of addition, subtraction, multiplication, and division, settle everything somehow, and never wonder. Bring to me, says M'Choakumchild, yonder baby just able to walk, and I will engage that it shall never wonder.

Now, besides very many babies just able to walk, there happened to be in Coketown a considerable population of babies who had been walking against time towards the infinite world, twenty, thirty, forty, fifty years and more. These portentous infants being alarming creatures to stalk about in any human society, the eighteen denominations incessantly scratched one another's faces and pulled one another's hair, by way of agreeing on the steps to be taken for their improvement—which they never did; a surprising circumstance, when the happy adaptation of the means to the end is considered. Still, although they differed in every other particular, conceivable and inconceivable (especially inconceivable), they were

5. From the *Arabian Nights' Entertainments.*

pretty well united on the point that these unlucky infants were never to wonder. Body number one, said they must take everything on trust. Body number two, said they must take everything on political economy. Body number three, wrote leaden little books for them, showing how the good grown-up baby invariably got to the Savings-bank, and the bad grown-up baby invariably got transported. Body number four, under dreary pretences of being droll (when it was very melancholy indeed), made the shallowest pretences of concealing pitfalls of knowledge, into which it was the duty of these babies to be smuggled and inveigled. But, all the bodies agreed that they were never to wonder.

There was a library in Coketown, to which general access was easy. Mr. Gradgrind greatly tormented his mind about what the people read in this library: a point whereon little rivers of tabular statements periodically flowed into the howling ocean of tabular statements, which no diver ever got to any depth in and came up sane. It was a dis-heartening circumstance, but a melancholy fact, that even these readers persisted in wondering. They wondered about human nature, human passions, human hopes and fears, the struggles, triumphs and defeats, the cares and joys and sorrows, the lives and deaths, of com-mon men and women! They sometimes, after fifteen hours' work, sat down to read mere fables about men and women, more or less like themselves, and about children, more or less like their own. They took De Foe to their bosoms, instead of Euclid, and seemed to be on the whole more comforted by Goldsmith than by Cocker.[1] Mr. Gradgrind was for ever working, in print and out of print, at this eccentric sum, and he never could make out how it yielded this un-accountable product.

"I am sick of my life, Loo. I hate it altogether, and I hate every-body except you," said the unnatural young Thomas Gradgrind in the haircutting chamber at twilight.

"You don't hate Sissy, Tom?"

"I hate to be obliged to call her Jupe. And she hates me," said Tom moodily.

"No she does not, Tom, I am sure."

"She must," said Tom. "She must just hate and detest the whole set-out of us. They'll bother her head off, I think, before they have done with her. Already she's getting as pale as wax, and as heavy as—I am."

1. Edward Cocker (1631–1675), author of a treatise on arithmetic. "De Foe": Daniel De Foe (1660?–1731), author of *Robinson Crusoe* (1719) and *Moll Flanders* (1722) and one of the initiators of the novel as a literary genre. "Euclid": Greek mathematician, ca. 4th century b.c.e., who systematized geometry as a mathematical science and initiated the deductive system in mathematics. "Goldsmith": Oliver Goldsmith (1730?–1774), Anglo-Irish poet and novelist, author of *The Vicar of Wakefield* (1766), who, like De Foe, was one of Dickens' favorite writers.

Young Thomas expressed these sentiments, sitting astride of a chair before the fire, with his arms on the back, and his sulky face on his arms. His sister sat in the darker corner by the fireside, now looking at him, now looking at the bright sparks as they dropped upon the hearth.

"As to me," said Tom, tumbling his hair all manner of ways with his sulky hands, "I am a Donkey, that's what *I* am. I am as obstinate as one, I am more stupid than one, I get as much pleasure as one, and I should like to kick like one."

"Not me, I hope, Tom?"

"No, Loo; I wouldn't hurt *you*. I made an exception of you at first. I don't know what this—jolly old—Jaundiced Jail," Tom had paused to find a sufficiently complimentary and expressive name for the parental roof, and seemed to relieve his mind for a moment by the strong alliteration of this one, "would be without you."

"Indeed, Tom? Do you really and truly say so?"

"Why, of course I do. What's the use of talking about it!" returned Tom, chafing his face on his coat-sleeve, as if to mortify his flesh, and have it in unison with his spirit.

"Because Tom," said his sister, after silently watching the sparks awhile, "as I get older, and nearer growing up, I often sit wondering here, and think how unfortunate it is for me that I can't reconcile you to home better than I am able to do. I don't know what other girls know. I can't play to you, or sing to you. I can't talk to you so as to lighten your mind, for I never see any amusing sights or read any amusing books that it would be a pleasure or a relief to you to talk about, when you are tired."

"Well, no more do I. I am as bad as you in that respect; and I am a Mule too, which you're not. If father was determined to make me either a Prig or a Mule, and I am not a Prig, why, it stands to reason, I must be a Mule. And so I am," said Tom, desperately.

"It's a great pity," said Louisa, after another pause, and speaking thoughtfully out of her dark corner; "it's a great pity, Tom. It's very unfortunate for both of us."

"Oh! You," said Tom; "you are a girl, Loo, and a girl comes out of it better than a boy does. I don't miss anything in you. You are the only pleasure I have—you can brighten even this place—and you can always lead me as you like."

"You are a dear brother, Tom; and while you think I can do such things, I don't so much mind knowing better. Though I do know better, Tom, and am very sorry for it." She came and kissed him, and went back into her corner again.

"I wish I could collect all the Facts we hear so much about," said. Tom, spitefully setting his teeth, "and all the Figures, and all the people who found them out; and I wish I could put a thousand barrels of gunpowder under them, and blow them all up together! However, when I go to live with old Bounderby, I'll have my revenge."

"Your revenge, Tom?"

"I mean, I'll enjoy myself a little, and go about and see something, and hear something. I'll recompense myself for the way in which I have been brought up."

"But don't disappoint yourself beforehand, Tom. Mr. Bounderby thinks as father thinks, and is a great deal rougher, and not half so kind."

"Oh!" said Tom, laughing; "I don't mind that. I shall very well know how to manage and smoothe old Bounderby!"

Their shadows were defined upon the wall, but those of the high presses[2] in the room were all blended together on the wall and on the ceiling, as if the brother and sister were overhung by a dark cavern. Or, a fanciful imagination—if such treason could have been there—might have made it out to be the shadow of their subject, and of its lowering[3] association with their future.

"What is your great mode of smoothing and managing, Tom? Is it a secret?"

"Oh!" said Tom, "if it is a secret, it's not far off. It's you. You are his little pet, you are his favourite; he'll do anything for you. When he says to me what I don't like, I shall say to him, 'My sister Loo will be hurt and disappointed, Mr. Bounderby. She always used to tell me she was sure you would be easier with me than this.' That'll bring him about, or nothing will."

After waiting for some answering remark, and getting none, Tom wearily relapsed into the present time, and twined himself yawning round and about the rails of his chair, and rumpled his head more and more, until he suddenly looked up, and asked:

"Have you gone to sleep, Loo?"

"No, Tom. I am looking at the fire."

"You seem to find more to look at in it than ever I could find," said Tom. "Another of the advantages, I suppose, of being a girl."

"Tom," enquired his sister, slowly, and in a curious tone, as if she were reading what she asked, in the fire, and it were not quite plainly written there, "do you look forward with any satisfaction to this change to Mr. Bounderby's?"

"Why, there's one thing to be said of it," returned Tom, pushing his chair from him, and standing up; "it will be getting away from home."

"There is one thing to be said of it," Louisa repeated in her former curious tone; "it will be getting away from home. Yes."

2. Large cupboards, usually recessed in a wall, for storage.
3. Threatening.

"Not but what I shall be very unwilling, both to leave you, Loo, and to leave you here. But I must go, you know, whether I like it or not; and I had better go where I can take with me some advantage of your influence, than where I should lose it altogether. Don't you see?"

"Yes, Tom."

The answer was so long in coming, though there was no indecision in it, that Tom went and leaned on the back of her chair, to contemplate the fire which so engrossed her, from her point of view, and see what he could make of it.

"Except that it is a fire," said Tom, "it looks to me as stupid and blank as everything else looks. What do you see in it? Not a circus?"

"I don't see anything in it, Tom, particularly. But since I have been looking at it, I have been wondering about you and me, grown up."

"Wondering again!" said Tom.

"I have such unmanageable thoughts," returned his sister, "that they *will* wonder."

"Then I beg of you, Louisa," said Mrs. Gradgrind, who had opened the door without being heard, "to do nothing of that description, for goodness' sake you inconsiderate girl, or I shall never hear the last of it from your father. And Thomas, it is really shameful, with my poor head continually wearing me out, that a boy brought up as you have been, and whose education has cost what yours has, should be found encouraging his sister to wonder, when he knows his father has expressly said that she is not to do it."

Louisa denied Tom's participation in the offence; but her mother stopped her with the conclusive answer, "Louisa, don't tell me, in my state of health; for unless you had been encouraged, it is morally and physically impossible that you could have done it."

"I was encouraged by nothing, mother, but by looking at the red sparks dropping out of the fire, and whitening and dying. It made me think, after all, how short my life would be, and how little I could hope to do in it."

"Nonsense!" said Mrs. Gradgrind, rendered almost energetic. "Nonsense! Don't stand there and tell me such stuff, Louisa, to my face, when you know very well that if it was ever to reach your father's ears I should never hear the last of it. After all the trouble that has been taken with you! After the lectures you have attended, and the experiments you have seen! After I have heard you myself, when the whole of my right side has been benumbed, going on with your master about combustion, and calcination, and calorification, and I may say every kind of ation that could drive a poor invalid distracted, to hear you talking in this absurd way about sparks and ashes! I wish," whimpered Mrs. Gradgrind, taking a chair, and discharging her strongest point before succumbing under these mere shadows of facts, "yes, I really *do* wish that I had never had a family, and then you would have known what it was to do without me!"

Chapter IX.

SISSY'S PROGRESS.

Sissy Jupe had not an easy time of it, between Mr. M'Choakumchild and Mrs. Gradgrind, and was not without strong impulses, in the first months of her probation, to run away. It hailed facts all day long so very hard, and life in general was opened to her as such a closely-ruled cyphering-book, that assuredly she would have run away, but for only one restraint.

It is lamentable to think of; but this restraint was the result of no arithmetical process, was self-imposed in defiance of all calculation, and went dead against any table of probabilities that any Actuary would have drawn up from the premises. The girl believed that her father had not deserted her; she lived in the hope that he would come back, and in the faith that he would be made the happier by her remaining where she was.

The wretched ignorance with which Jupe clung to this consolation, rejecting the superior comfort of knowing, on a sound arithmetical basis, that her father was an unnatural vagabond, filled Mr. Gradgrind with pity. Yet, what was to be done? M'Choakumchild reported that she had a very dense head for figures; that, once possessed with a general idea of the globe, she took the smallest conceivable interest in its exact measurements; that she was extremely slow in the acquisition of dates, unless some pitiful incident happened to be connected therewith; that she would burst into tears on being required (by the mental process) immediately to name the cost of two hundred and forty-seven muslin caps at fourteenpence halfpenny; that she was as low down, in the school, as low could be; that after eight weeks of induction into the elements of Political Economy, she had only yesterday been set right by a prattler three feet high, for returning to the question, "What is the first principle of this science?" the absurd answer, "To do unto others as I would that they should do unto me."[1]

Mr. Gradgrind observed, shaking his head, that all this was very bad; that it showed the necessity of infinite grinding at the mill of knowledge, as per system, schedule, blue book,[2] report, and tabular

1. Cf. the Catechism of the Church of England: "My duty towards my neighbor is . . . to do to all men as I would they should do unto me."
2. Blue-bound statistical reports issued by the government.

statements A to Z; and that Jupe "must be kept to it." So Jupe was kept to it, and became low-spirited, but no wiser.

"It would be a fine thing to be you, Miss Louisa!" she said, one night, when Louisa had endeavoured to make her perplexities for next day something clearer to her.

"Do you think so?"

"I should know so much, Miss Louisa. All that is difficult to me now, would be so easy then."

"You might not be the better for it, Sissy."

Sissy submitted, after a little hesitation, "I should not be the worse, Miss Louisa." To which Miss Louisa answered, "I don't know that."

There had been so little communication between these two— both because life at Stone Lodge went monotonously round like a piece of machinery which discouraged human interference, and because of the prohibition relative to Sissy's past career—that they were still almost strangers. Sissy, with her dark eyes wonderingly directed to Louisa's face, was uncertain whether to say more or to remain silent.

"You are more useful to my mother, and more pleasant with her than I can ever be," Louisa resumed. "You are pleasanter to yourself, than *I* am to *my* self."

"But, if you please Miss Louisa," Sissy pleaded, "I am—O so stupid!"

Louisa, with a brighter laugh than usual, told her she would be wiser by and by.

"You don't know," said Sissy, half crying, "what a stupid girl I am. All through school hours I make mistakes. Mr. and Mrs. M'Choakumchild call me up, over and over again, regularly to make mistakes. I can't help them. They seem to come natural to me."

"Mr. and Mrs. M'Choakumchild never make any mistakes themselves, I suppose, Sissy?"

"O no!" she eagerly returned. "They know everything."

"Tell me some of your mistakes."

"I am almost ashamed," said Sissy, with reluctance. "But to-day, for instance, Mr. M'Choakumchild was explaining to us about Natural Prosperity."

"National, I think it must have been," observed Louisa.

"Yes, it was.—But isn't it the same?" she timidly asked.

"You had better say, National, as he said so," returned Louisa, with her dry reserve.

"National Prosperity. And he said, Now, this schoolroom is a Nation. And in this nation, there are fifty millions of money. Isn't this a prosperous nation? Girl number twenty, isn't this a prosperous nation, and a'n't you in a thriving state?"

"What did you say?" asked Louisa.

"Miss Louisa, I said I didn't know. I thought I couldn't know whether it was a prosperous nation or not, and whether I was in a thriving state or not, unless I knew who had got the money, and whether any of it was mine. But that had nothing to do with it. It was not in the figures at all," said Sissy, wiping her eyes.

"That was a great mistake of yours," observed Louisa.

"Yes, Miss Louisa, I know it was, now. Then Mr. M'Choakumchild said he would try me again. And he said, This schoolroom is an immense town, and in it there are a million of inhabitants, and only five-and-twenty are starved to death in the streets, in the course of a year. What is your remark on that proportion? And my remark was—for I couldn't think of a better one—that I thought it must be just as hard upon those who were starved, whether the others were a million, or a million million. And that was wrong, too."

"Of course it was."

"Then Mr. M'Choakumchild said he would try me once more. And he said, Here are the stutterings—"

"Statistics," said Louisa.

"Yes, Miss Louisa—they always remind me of stutterings, and that's another of my mistakes—of accidents upon the sea. And I find (Mr. M'Choakumchild said) that in a given time a hundred thousand persons went to sea on long voyages, and only five hundred of them were drowned or burnt to death. What is the percentage? And I said, Miss;" here Sissy fairly sobbed as confessing with extreme contrition to her greatest error; "I said it was nothing."

"Nothing, Sissy?"

"Nothing, Miss—to the relations and friends of the people who were killed. I shall never learn," said Sissy. "And the worst of all is, that although my poor father wished me so much to learn, and although I am so anxious to learn because he wished me to, I am afraid I don't like it."

Louisa stood looking at the pretty modest head, as it drooped abashed before her, until it was raised again to glance at her face. Then she asked:

"Did your father know so much himself, that he wished you to be well taught too, Sissy?"

Sissy hesitated before replying, and so plainly showed her sense that they were entering on forbidden ground, that Louisa added, "No one hears us; and if any one did, I am sure no harm could be found in such an innocent question."

"No, Miss Louisa," answered Sissy, upon this encouragement, shaking her head; "father knows very little indeed. It's as much as he can do to write; and it's more than people in general can do to read his writing. Though it's plain to *me*."

"Your mother?"

"Father says she was quite a scholar. She died when I was born. She was;" Sissy made the terrible communication nervously; "she was a dancer."

"Did your father love her?" Louisa asked these questions with a strong, wild, wandering interest peculiar to her; an interest gone astray like a banished creature, and hiding in solitary places.

"O yes! As dearly as he loves me. Father loved me, first, for her sake. He carried me about with him when I was quite a baby. We have never been asunder from that time."

"Yet he leaves you now, Sissy?"

"Only for my good. Nobody understands him as I do; nobody knows him as I do. When he left me for my good—he never would have left me for his own—I know he was almost broken-hearted with the trial. He will not be happy for a single minute, till he comes back."

"Tell me more about him," said Louisa, "I will never ask you again. Where did you live?"

"We travelled about the country, and had no fixed place to live in. Father's a;" Sissy whispered the awful word; "a clown."

"To make the people laugh?" said Louisa, with a nod of intelligence.

"Yes. But they wouldn't laugh sometimes, and then father cried. Lately, they very often wouldn't laugh, and he used to come home despairing. Father's not like most. Those who didn't know him as well as I do, and didn't love him as dearly as I do, might believe he was not quite right. Sometimes they played tricks upon him; but they never knew how he felt them, and shrunk up, when he was alone with me. He was far, far timider than they thought!"

"And you were his comfort through everything?"

She nodded, with the tears rolling down her face. "I hope so, and father said I was. It was because he grew so scared and trembling, and because he felt himself to be a poor, weak, ignorant, helpless man (those used to be his words), that he wanted me so much to know a great deal and be different from him. I used to read to him to cheer his courage, and he was very fond of that. They were wrong books—I am never to speak of them here—but we didn't know there was any harm in them."

"And he liked them?" said Louisa, with her searching gaze on Sissy all this time.

"O very much! They kept him, many times, from what did him real harm. And often and often of a night, he used to forget all his troubles in wondering whether the Sultan would let the lady[3] go on with the story, or would have her head cut off before it was finished."

---

3. Scheherazade, the sultan's wife in the *Arabian Nights*, whose skill as a storyteller saved her from having her head cut off, the customary fate of the sultan's wives.

"And your father was always kind? To the last?" asked Louisa;
contravening the great principle, and wondering very much.

"Always, always!" returned Sissy, clasping her hands. "Kinder and
kinder than I can tell. He was angry only one night, and that was
not to me, but Merrylegs. Merrylegs;" she whispered the awful fact;
"is his performing dog."

"Why was he angry with the dog?" Louisa demanded.

"Father, soon after they came home from performing, told Merrylegs to jump up on the backs of the two chairs and stand across
them—which is one of his tricks. He looked at father, and didn't do
it at once. Everything of father's had gone wrong that night, and he
hadn't pleased the public at all. He cried out that the very dog knew
he was failing, and had no compassion on him. Then he beat the
dog, and I was frightened, and said, 'Father; father! Pray don't hurt
the creature who is so fond of you! O Heaven forgive you, father,
stop!' And he stopped, and the dog was bloody, and father lay down
crying on the floor with the dog in his arms, and the dog licked his
face."

Louisa saw that she was sobbing; and going to her, kissed her,
took her hand, and sat down beside her.

"Finish by telling me how your father left you, Sissy. Now that I
have asked you so much, tell me the end. The blame, if there is any
blame, is mine, not yours."

"Dear Miss Louisa," said Sissy, covering her eyes, and sobbing
yet; "I came home from the school that afternoon, and found poor
father just come home too, from the booth. And he sat rocking himself over the fire, as if he was in pain. And I said, 'Have you hurt
yourself, father?' (as he did sometimes, like they all did), and he said,
'A little, my darling.' And when I came to stoop down and look up at
his face, I saw that he was crying. The more I spoke to him, the
more he hid his face; and at first he shook all over, and said nothing
but 'My darling!' and 'My love!'"

Here Tom came lounging in, and stared at the two with a coolness not particularly savouring of interest in anything but himself,
and not much of that at present.

"I am asking Sissy a few questions, Tom," observed his sister. "You
have no occasion to go away; but don't interrupt us for a moment,
Tom dear."

"Oh! very well!" returned Tom. "Only father has brought old
Bounderby home, and I want you to come into the drawing-room.
Because if you come, there's a good chance of old Bounderby's ask-
ing me to dinner; and if you don't, there's none."

"I'll come directly."

"I'll wait for you," said Tom, "to make sure."

Sissy resumed in a lower voice. "At last poor father said that he had given no satisfaction again, and never did give any satisfaction now, and that he was a shame and disgrace, and I should have done better without him all along. I said all the affectionate things to him that came into my heart, and presently he was quiet and I sat down by him, and told him all about the school and everything that had been said and done there. When I had no more left to tell, he put his arms round my neck, and kissed me a great many times. Then he asked me to fetch some of the stuff he used, for the little hurt he had had, and to get it at the best place, which was at the other end of town from there; and then, after kissing me again, he let me go. When I had gone down stairs, I turned back that I might be a little bit more company to him yet, and looked in at the door, and said, 'Father dear, shall I take Merrylegs?' Father shook his head and said, 'No, Sissy, no; take nothing that's known to be mine, my darling;' and I left him sitting by the fire. Then the thought must have come upon him, poor poor father! of going away to try something for my sake; for, when I came back, he was gone."

"I say! Look sharp for old Bounderby, Loo!" Tom remonstrated.

"There's no more to tell, Miss Louisa. I keep the nine oils ready for him, and I know he will come back. Every letter that I see in Mr. Gradgrind's hand takes my breath away and blinds my eyes, for I think it comes from father, or from Mr. Sleary about father. Mr. Sleary promised to write as soon as ever father should be heard of, and I trust to him to keep his word."

"Do look sharp for old Bounderby, Loo!" said Tom, with an impatient whistle. "He'll be off, if you don't look sharp!"

After this, whenever Sissy dropped a curtsey to Mr. Gradgrind in the presence of his family, and said in a faltering way, "I beg your pardon, sir, for being troublesome—but—have you had any letter yet about me?" Louisa would suspend the occupation of the moment, whatever it was, and look for the reply as earnestly as Sissy did. And when Mr. Gradgrind regularly answered, "No, Jupe, nothing of the sort," the trembling of Sissy's lip would be repeated in Louisa's face, and her eyes would follow Sissy with compassion to the door. Mr. Gradgrind usually improved these occasions by remarking, when she was gone, that if Jupe had been properly trained from an early age she would have demonstrated to herself on sound principles the baselessness of these fantastic hopes. Yet it did seem (though not to him, for he saw nothing of it) as if fantastic hope could take as strong a hold as Fact.

This observation must be limited exclusively to his daughter. As to Tom, he was becoming that not unprecedented triumph of calculation which is usually at work on number one. As to Mrs. Gradgrind, if she said anything on the subject, she would come a little way out of her wrappers, like a feminine dormouse,[4] and say:

"Good gracious bless me how my poor head is vexed and worried by that girl Jupe's so perseveringly asking, over and over again, about her tiresome letters! Upon my word and honour I seem to be fated, and destined, and ordained, to live in the midst of things that I am never to hear the last of. It really is a most extraordinary circumstance that it appears as if I never was to hear the last of anything!"

At about this point, Mr. Gradgrind's eye would fall upon her; and under the influence of that wintry piece of fact, she would become torpid again.

Chapter X.

STEPHEN BLACKPOOL.

I entertain a weak idea that the English people are as hard-worked as any people upon whom the sun shines. I acknowledge to this ridiculous idiosyncrasy, as a reason why I would give them a little more play.

In the hardest working part of Coketown; in the innermost fortifications of that ugly citadel, where Nature was as strongly bricked out as killing airs and gases were bricked in; at the heart of the labyrinth of narrow courts[1] upon courts, and close streets upon streets, which had come into existence piecemeal, every piece in a violent hurry for some one man's purpose, and the whole an unnatural family, shouldering, and trampling, and pressing one another to death; in the last close nook of this great exhausted receiver, where the chimneys, for want of air to make a draught, were built in an immense variety of stunted and crooked shapes, as though every house put out a sign of the kind of people who might be expected to be born in it; among the multitude of Coketown, generically called "the Hands,"—a race who would have found more favour with some people, if Providence had seen fit to make them only hands, or, like the lower creatures of the sea-shore, only hands and stomachs—lived a certain Stephen Blackpool, forty years of age.

Stephen looked older, but he had had a hard life. It is said that every life has its roses and thorns; there seemed, however, to have been a misadventure or mistake in Stephen's case, whereby somebody else had become possessed of his roses, and he had become

---

4. A small rodent, noted for long hibernation, of a family intermediate between the mouse and the squirrel.
1. Short alleys, usually closed off at one end.

possessed of the same somebody else's thorns in addition to his own. He had known, to use his words, a peck[2] of trouble. He was usually called Old Stephen, in a kind of rough homage to the fact.

A rather stooping man, with a knitted brow, a pondering expression of face, and a hard-looking head sufficiently capacious, on which his iron-grey hair lay long and thin, Old Stephen might have passed for a particularly intelligent man in his condition. Yet he was not. He took no place among those remarkable "Hands," who, piecing together their broken intervals of leisure through many years, had mastered difficult sciences, and acquired a knowledge of most unlikely things. He held no station among the Hands who could make speeches and carry on debates. Thousands of his compeers could talk much better than he, at any time. He was a good power-loom weaver, and a man of perfect integrity. What more he was, or what else he had in him, if anything, let him show for himself.

The lights in the great factories, which looked, when they were illuminated, like Fairy palaces—or the travellers by express-train said so—were all extinguished; and the bells had rung for knocking off for the night, and had ceased again; and the Hands, men and women, boy and girl, were clattering home. Old Stephen was standing in the street, with the odd sensation upon him which the stoppage of the machinery always produced—the sensation of its having worked and stopped in his own head.

"Yet I don't see Rachael, still!" said he.

It was a wet night, and many groups of young women passed him, with their shawls drawn over their bare heads and held close under their chins to keep the rain out. He knew Rachael well, for a glance at any one of these groups was sufficient to show him that she was not there. At last, there were no more to come; and then he turned away, saying in a tone of disappointment, "Why, then, I ha' missed her!"

But, he had not gone the length of three streets, when he saw another of the shawled figures in advance of him, at which he looked so keenly that perhaps its mere shadow indistinctly reflected on the wet pavement—if he could have seen it without the figure itself moving along from lamp to lamp, brightening and fading as it went—would have been enough to tell him who was there. Making his pace at once much quicker and much softer, he darted on until he was very near this figure, then fell into his former walk, and called "Rachael!"

She turned, being then in the brightness of a lamp; and raising her hood a little, showed a quiet oval face, dark and rather delicate, irradiated by a pair of very gentle eyes, and further set off by the

2. A great deal; from a unit of volume used in a dry measure equal in the British Imperial system to almost 555 cubic inches.

perfect order of her shining black hair. It was not a face in its first bloom; she was a woman five and thirty years of age.

"Ah, lad! 'Tis thou?" When she had said this, with a smile which would have been quite expressed, though nothing of her had been seen but her pleasant eyes, she replaced her hood again, and they went on together.

"I thought thou wast ahind me, Rachael?"

"No."

"Early t'night, lass?"

" 'Times I'm a little early, Stephen; 'times a little late. I'm never to be counted on, going home."

"Nor going t'other way, neither, t'seems to me, Rachael?"

"No, Stephen."

He looked at her with some disappointment in his face, but with a respectful and patient conviction that she must be right in whatever she did. The expression was not lost upon her; she laid her hand lightly on his arm a moment, as if to thank him for it.

"We are such true friends, lad, and such old friends, and getting to be such old folk, now."

"No, Rachael, thou'rt as young as ever thou wast."

"One of us would be puzzled how to get old, Stephen, without t'other getting so too, both being alive," she answered, laughing; "but, any ways, we're such old friends, that t'hide a word of honest truth fro' one another would be a sin and a pity. 'Tis better not to walk too much together; 'Times, yes! 'Twould be hard, indeed, if 'twas not to be at all," she said, with a cheerfulness she sought to communicate to him.

" 'Tis hard, anyways, Rachael."

"Try to think not; and 'twill seem better."

"I've tried a long time, and 'ta'nt got better. But thou'rt right; 'tmight mak fok talk, even of thee. Thou hast been that to me, Rachael, through so many year: thou hast done me so much good, and heartened of me in that cheering way, that thy word is a law to me. Ah lass, and a bright good law! Better than some real ones."

"Never fret about them, Stephen," she answered quickly, and not without an anxious glance at his face. "Let the laws be."

"Yes," he said, with a slow nod or two. "Let 'em be. Let everything be. Let all sorts alone. 'Tis a muddle, and that's aw."

"Always a muddle?" said Rachael, with another gentle touch upon his arm, as if to recall him out of the thoughtfulness, in which he was biting the long ends of his loose neckerchief as he walked along. The touch had its instantaneous effect. He let them fall, turned a smiling face upon her, and said, as he broke into a good-humoured laugh, "Ay, Rachael, lass, alwus a muddle. That's where

I stick. I come to the muddle many times and agen, and I never get beyond it."

They had walked some distance, and were near their own homes. The woman's was the first reached. It was in one of the many small streets for which the favourite undertaker (who turned a handsome sum out of the one poor ghastly pomp of the neighbourhood) kept a black ladder, in order that those who had done their daily groping up and down the narrow stairs might slide out of this working world by the windows. She stopped at the corner, and putting her hand in his, wished him good night.

"Good night, dear lass; good night!"

She went, with her neat figure and her sober womanly step, down the dark street, and he stood looking after her until she turned into one of the small houses. There was not a flutter of her coarse shawl, perhaps, but had its interest in this man's eyes; not a tone of her voice but had its echo in his innermost heart.

When she was lost to his view, he pursued his homeward way, glancing up sometimes at the sky, where the clouds were sailing fast and wildly. But, they were broken now, and the rain had ceased, and the moon shone—looking down the high chimneys of Coketown on the deep furnaces below, and casting Titanic shadows of the steam engines at rest, upon the walls where they were lodged. The man seemed to have brightened with the night, as he went on.

His home, in such another street as the first, saving that it was narrower, was over a little shop. How it came to pass that any people found it worth their while to sell or buy the wretched little toys, mixed up in its window with cheap newspapers and pork (there was a leg to be raffled for to-morrow night), matters not here. He took his end of candle from a shelf, lighted it at another end of candle on the counter, without disturbing the mistress of the shop who was asleep in her little room, and went up stairs into his lodging.

It was a room, not unacquainted with the black ladder under various tenants; but as neat, at present, as such a room could be. A few books and writings were on an old bureau in a corner, the furniture was decent and sufficient, and, though the atmosphere was tainted, the room was clean.

Going to the hearth to set the candle down upon a round three-legged table standing there, he stumbled against something. As he recoiled, looking down at it, it raised itself up into the form of a woman in a sitting attitude.

"Heaven's mercy, woman!" he cried, falling farther off from the figure. "Hast thou come back again!"

Such a woman! A disabled, drunken creature, barely able to preserve her sitting posture by steadying herself with one begrimed hand on the floor, while the other was so purposeless in trying to push away her tangled hair from her face, that it only blinded her the more with the dirt upon it. A creature so foul to look at, in her tatters, stains, and splashes, but so much fouler than that in her moral infamy, that it was a shameful thing even to see her.

After an impatient oath or two, and some stupid clawing of herself with the hand not necessary to her support, she got her hair away from her eyes sufficiently to obtain a sight of him. Then she sat swaying her body to and fro, and making gestures with her unnerved arm, which seemed intended as the accompaniment to a fit of laughter, though her face was stolid and drowsy.

"Eigh lad? What, yo'r there?" Some hoarse sounds meant for this, came mockingly out of her at last; and her head dropped forward on her breast.

"Back agen?" she screeched, after some minutes, as if he had that moment said it. "Yes! And back agen. Back agen ever and ever so often. Back? Yes, back. Why not?"

Roused by the unmeaning violence with which she cried it out, she scrambled up, and stood supporting herself with her shoulders against the wall; dangling in one hand by the string, a dunghill-fragment[3] of a bonnet, and trying to look scornfully at him.

"I'll sell thee off again, and I'll sell thee off again, and I'll sell thee off a score of times!" she cried, with something between a furious menace and an effort at a defiant dance. "Come awa' from th' bed!" He was sitting on the side of it, with his face hidden in his hands. "Come awa' from 't. 'Tis mine, and I've a right to 't!"

As she staggered to it, he avoided her with a shudder, and passed— his face still hidden—to the opposite end of the room. She threw herself upon the bed heavily, and soon was snoring hard. He sunk into a chair, and moved but once all that night. It was to throw a covering over her; as if his hands were not enough to hide her, even in the darkness.

Chapter XI.

NO WAY OUT.

The Fairy palaces burst into illumination, before pale morning showed the monstrous serpents of smoke trailing themselves over Coketown. A clattering of clogs upon the pavement; a rapid ringing of bells; and all the melancholy-mad elephants, polished and oiled up for the day's monotony, were at their heavy exercise again.

---

3. Befouled, as if it had been pulled out of a pile of excrement.

Stephen bent over his loom, quiet, watchful, and steady. A special contrast, as every man was in the forest of looms where Stephen worked, to the crashing, smashing, tearing piece of mechanism at which he laboured. Never fear, good people of an anxious turn of mind, that Art will consign Nature to oblivion. Set anywhere, side by side, the work of GOD and the work of man; and the former, even though it be a troop of Hands of very small account, will gain in dignity from the comparison.

So many hundred Hands in this Mill; so many hundred horse Steam Power. It is known, to the force of a single pound weight, what the engine will do; but, not all the calculators of the National Debt can tell me the capacity for good or evil, for love or hatred, for patriotism or discontent, for the decomposition of virtue into vice, or the reverse, at any single moment in the soul of one of these its quiet servants, with the composed faces and the regulated actions. There is no mystery in it; there is an unfathomable mystery in the meanest of them, for ever.—Supposing we were to reserve our arithmetic for material objects, and to govern these awful unknown quantities by other means!

The day grew strong, and showed itself outside, even against the flaming lights within. The lights were turned out, and the work went on. The rain fell, and the Smoke-serpents, submissive to the curse of all that tribe, trailed themselves upon the earth. In the waste-yard outside, the steam from the escape-pipe, the litter of barrels and old iron, the shining heaps of coals, the ashes everywhere, were shrouded in a veil of mist and rain.

The work went on, until the noon-bell rang. More clattering upon the pavements. The looms, and wheels, and Hands, all out of gear for an hour.

Stephen came out of the hot mill into the damp wind and cold wet streets, haggard and worn. He turned from his own class and his own quarter, taking nothing but a little bread as he walked along, towards the hill on which his principal employer lived, in a red house with black outside shutters, green inside blinds, a black street door, up two white steps, BOUNDERBY (in letters very like himself) upon a brazen plate, and a round brazen door-handle underneath it like a brazen full-stop.

Mr. Bounderby was at his lunch. So Stephen had expected. Would his servant say that one of the Hands begged leave to speak to him? Message in return, requiring name of such Hand. Stephen Blackpool. There was nothing troublesome against Stephen Blackpool; yes, he might come in.

Stephen Blackpool in the parlour. Mr. Bounderby (whom he just knew by sight), at lunch on chop and sherry. Mrs. Sparsit netting¹ at the fire-side, in a side-saddle attitude, with one foot in a cotton stirrup. It was a part, at once of Mrs. Sparsit's dignity and service, not to lunch. She supervised the meal officially, but implied that in her own stately person she considered lunch a weakness.

"Now, Stephen," said Mr. Bounderby, "what's the matter with *you?*"

Stephen made a bow. Not a servile one—these Hands will never do that! Lord bless you, sir, you'll never catch them at that, if they have been with you twenty years!—and, as a complimentary toilet for Mrs. Sparsit, tucked his neckerchief ends into his waistcoat.

"Now, you know," said Mr. Bounderby, taking some sherry, "we have never had any difficulty with you, and you have never been one of the unreasonable ones. You don't expect to be set up in a coach and six, and to be fed on turtle soup and venison, with a gold spoon, as a good many of 'em do!" Mr. Bounderby always represented this to be the sole, immediate, and direct object of any Hand who was not entirely satisfied; "and therefore I know already that you have not come here to make a complaint. Now, you know, I am certain of that, beforehand."

"No, sir, sure I ha' not coom for nowt o' th' kind."

Mr. Bounderby seemed agreeably surprised, notwithstanding his previous strong conviction. "Very well," he returned. "You're a steady Hand, and I was not mistaken. Now, let me hear what it's all about. As it's not that, let me hear what it is. What have you got to say? Out with it, lad!"

Stephen happened to glance towards Mrs. Sparsit. "I can go, Mr. Bounderby, if you wish it," said that self-sacrificing lady, making a feint of taking her foot out of the stirrup.

Mr. Bounderby stayed her, by holding a mouthful of chop in suspension before swallowing it, and putting out his left hand. Then, withdrawing his hand and swallowing his mouthful of chop, he said to Stephen:

"Now, you know, this good lady is a born lady, a high lady. You are not to suppose because she keeps my house for me, that she hasn't been very high up the tree—ah, up at the top of the tree! Now, if you have got anything to say that can't be said before a born lady, this lady will leave the room. If what you have got to say *can* be said before a born lady, this lady will stay where she is."

"Sir, I hope I never had nowt to say, not fitten for a born lady to year, sin' I were born mysen'," was the reply, accompanied with a slight flush.

---

1. Engaged in a form of needlework, formerly used for making fancy purses and other objects, in which the stitching was similar to that used for making fishnets. Netting involved looping some of the threads round the lady's shoe so as to form a frame in which other threads could be worked; hence Dickens' reference to the "cotton stirrup."

"Very well," said Mr. Bounderby, pushing away his plate, and leaning back. "Fire away!"

"I ha' coom," Stephen began, raising his eyes from the floor, after a moment's consideration, "to ask yo yor advice. I need't overmuch. I were married on Eas'r Monday nineteen year sin, long and dree.[2] She were a young lass—pretty enow—wi' good accounts of herseln. Well! She went bad—soon. Not along of me. Gonnows[3] I were not a unkind husband to her."

"I have heard all this before," said Mr. Bounderby. "She took to drinking, left off working, sold the furniture, pawned the clothes, and played old Gooseberry."[4]

"I were patient wi' her."

("The more fool you, I think," said Mr. Bounderby, in confidence to his wine-glass.)

"I were very patient wi' her. I tried to wean her fra't, ower and ower agen. I tried this, I tried that, I tried t'other. I ha' gone home, many's the time, and found all vanished as I had in the world, and her without a sense left to bless herseln lying on bare ground. I ha' dun't not once, not twice—twenty time!"

Every line in his face deepened as he said it, and put in its affecting evidence of the suffering he had undergone.

"From bad to worse, from worse to worsen. She left me. She disgraced herseln everyways, bitter and bad. She coom back, she coom back, she coom back. What could I do t' hinder her? I ha' walked the streets nights long, ere ever I'd go home. I ha' gone t' th' brigg[5] minded to fling myseln ower, and ha' no more on't. I ha' bore that much, that I were owd when I were young."

Mrs. Sparsit, easily ambling along with her netting-needles, raised the Coriolanian eyebrows and shook her head, as much as to say, "The great know trouble as well as the small. Please to turn your humble eye in My direction."

"I ha' paid her to keep awa' fra' me. These five year I ha' paid her. I ha' gotten decent fewtrils[6] about me agen. I ha' lived hard and sad, but not ashamed and fearfo' a' the minnits o' my life. Last night, I went home. There she lay upon my har-stone! There she is!"

In the strength of his misfortune, and the energy of his distress, he fired for the moment like a proud man. In another moment, he stood as he had stood all the time—his usual stoop upon him; his pondering face addressed to Mr. Bounderby, with a curious expres-

2. Tedious.
3. "God knows." For such north of England expressions, Dickens seems to have used a book that he owned: John Colliet, *A View of the Lancashire Dialect* (1770). See Angus Easson, *Hard Times: A Critical Commentary.*
4. Played the deuce (or devil) with everything.
5. Bridge.
6. Trifles, inexpensive household objects.

sion on it, half shrewd, half perplexed, as if his mind were set upon unravelling something very difficult; his hat held tight in his left hand, which rested on his hip; his right arm, with a rugged propriety and force of action, very earnestly emphasising what he said: not least so when it always paused, a little bent, but not withdrawn, as he paused.

"I was acquainted with all this, you know," said Mr. Bounderby, "except the last clause, long ago. It's a bad job; that's what it is. You had better have been satisfied as you were, and not have got married. However, it's too late to say that."

"Was it an unequal marriage, sir, in point of years?" asked Mrs. Sparsit.

"You hear what this lady asks. Was it an unequal marriage in point of years, this unlucky job of yours?" said Mr. Bounderby.

"Not e'en so. I were one-and-twenty myseln; she were twenty nigh-but."[7]

"Indeed, sir?" said Mrs. Sparsit to her Chief, with great placidity. "I inferred, from its being so miserable a marriage, that it was probably an unequal one in point of years."

Mr. Bounderby looked very hard at the good lady in a sidelong way that had an odd sheepishness about it. He fortified himself with a little more sherry.

"Well? Why don't you go on?" he then asked, turning rather irritably on Stephen Blackpool.

"I ha' coom to ask yo, sir, how I am to be ridded o' this woman." Stephen infused a yet deeper gravity into the mixed expression of his attentive face. Mrs. Sparsit uttered a gentle ejaculation, as having received a moral shock.

"What do you mean?" said Bounderby, getting up to lean his back against the chimney-piece. "What are you talking about? You took her for better for worse."

"I mun' be ridden o' her. I cannot bear't nommore. I ha' lived under't so long, for that I ha' had'n the pity and comforting words o' th' best lass living or dead. Haply, but for her, I should ha' gone hottering[8] mad."

"He wishes to be free, to marry the female of whom he speaks, I fear, sir," observed Mrs. Sparsit in an undertone, and much dejected by the immorality of the people.

"I do. The lady says what's right. I do. I were a coming to't. I ha' read i' th' papers that great fok (fair faw 'em a'l[9] I wishes 'em no hurt!) are not bonded together for better for worse so fast, but that they can be set free fro' *their* misfortnet marriages, an marry ower

7. About.
8. Boiling or raging (Lancashire dialect).
9. Fair fall them all! I.e., may good luck fall to all of them!

agen. When they dunnot agree, for that their tempers is ill-sorted, they has rooms o' one kind an another in their houses, above a bit, and they can live asunders. We fok ha' only one room, an we can't. When that won't do, they ha' gowd an other cash, an they can say 'This for yo, an that for me,' an they can go their separate ways. We can't. Spite o' all that, they can be set free for smaller wrongs than mine. So, I mun be ridden o' this woman, an I want t'know how?"

"No how," returned Mr. Bounderby.

"If I do her any hurt, sir, there's a law to punish me?"

"Of course there is."

"If I flee from her, there's a law to punish me?"

"Of course there is."

"If I marry t'oother dear lass, there's a law to punish me?"

"Of course there is."

"If I was to live wi' her an not marry her—saying such a thing could be, which it never could or would, an her so good—there's a law to punish me, in every innocent child belonging to me?"

"Of course there is."

"Now, a' God's name," said Stephen Blackpool, "show me the law to help me!"

"Hem! There's a sanctity in this relation of life," said Mr. Bounderby, "and—and—it must be kept up."

"No no, dunnot say that, sir. 'Tan't kep' up that way. Not that way. 'Tis kep' down that way. I'm a weaver, I were in a fact'ry when a chilt, but I ha' gotten een to see wi' and eern to year wi'. I read in th' papers every 'Sizes, every Sessions—and you read too—I know it!—with dismay—how th' supposed unpossibility o' ever getting unchained from one another, at any price, on any terms, brings blood upon this land, and brings many common married fok to battle, murder, and sudden death.[1] Let us ha' this, right understood. Mine's a grievous case, an I want—if yo will be so good—t'know the law that helps me."

"Now, I tell you what!" said Mr. Bounderby, putting his hands in his pockets. "There *is* such a law."

Stephen, subsiding into his quiet manner, and never wandering in his attention, gave a nod.

"But it's not for you at all. It costs money. It costs a mint of money."

How much might that be? Stephen calmly asked.

"Why, you'd have to go to Doctors' Commons[2] with a suit, and you'd have to go to a court of Common Law with a suit, and you'd have to go to the House of Lords with a suit, and you'd have to get

---

1. See the Litany in The Book of Common Prayer: "From plague, pestilence, and famine; from battle, and murder, and from sudden death, Good Lord, deliver us." "'Sizes": Assizes; the periodical sittings of the superior courts in English counties.
2. Law courts with jurisdiction over divorce cases. See *David Copperfield*, chapter 23.

an Act of Parliament to enable you to marry again, and it would cost you (if it was a case of very plain-sailing), I suppose from a thousand to fifteen hundred pound," said Mr. Bounderby. "Perhaps twice the money."

"There's no other law?"

"Certainly not."

"Why then, sir," said Stephen, turning white, and motioning with that right hand of his, as if he gave everything to the four winds, " 'tis a muddle. 'Tis just a muddle a'toogether, an the sooner I am dead, the better."

(Mrs. Sparsit again dejected by the impiety of the people.)

"Pooh, pooh! Don't you talk nonsense, my good fellow," said Mr. Bounderby, "about things you don't understand; and don't you call the Institutions of your country a muddle, or you'll get yourself into a real muddle one of these fine mornings. The institutions of your country are not your piece-work, and the only thing you have got to do, is, to mind your piece-work. You didn't take your wife for fast and for loose; but for better for worse. If she has turned out worse—why, all we have got to say is; she might have turned out better."

" 'Tis a muddle," said Stephen, shaking his head as he moved to the door. " 'Tis a' a muddle!"

"Now, I'll tell you what!" Mr. Bounderby resumed, as a valedictory address. "With what I shall call your unhallowed opinions, you have been quite shocking this lady: who, as I have already told you, is a born lady, and who, as I have not already told you, has had her own marriage misfortunes to the tune of tens of thousands of pounds—tens of Thousands of Pounds!" (he repeated it with great relish). "Now, you have always been a steady Hand hitherto; but my opinion is, and so I tell you plainly, that you are turning into the wrong road. You have been listening to some mischievous stranger or other—they're always about—and the best thing you can do is, to come out of that. Now you know;" here his countenance expressed marvellous acuteness; "I can see as far into a grindstone as another man; farther than a good many, perhaps, because I had my nose well kept to it when I was young. I see traces of the turtle soup, and venison, and gold spoon in this. Yes, I do!" cried Mr. Bounderby, shaking his head with obstinate cunning. "By the Lord Harry, I do!"

With a very different shake of the head and a deep sigh, Stephen said, "Thank you, sir, I wish you good day." So he left Mr. Bounderby swelling at his own portrait on the wall, as if he were going to explode himself into it; and Mrs. Sparsit still ambling on with her foot in her stirrup, looking quite cast down by the popular vices.

Chapter XII.

THE OLD WOMAN.

Old Stephen descended the two white steps, shutting the black door with the brazen door-plate, by the aid of the brazen full-stop, to which he gave a parting polish with the sleeve of his coat, observing that his hot hand clouded it. He crossed the street with his eyes bent upon the ground, and thus was walking sorrowfully away, when he felt a touch upon his arm.

It was not the touch he needed most at such a moment—the touch that could calm the wild waters of his soul, as the uplifted hand of the sublimest love and patience could abate the raging of the sea[1]—yet it was a woman's hand too. It was an old woman, tall and shapely still, though withered by Time, on whom his eyes fell when he stopped and turned. She was very cleanly and plainly dressed, had country mud upon her shoes, and was newly come from a journey. The flutter of her manner, in the unwonted noise of the streets; the spare shawl, carried unfolded on her arm; the heavy umbrella, and little basket; the loose long-fingered gloves, to which her hands were unused; all bespoke an old woman from the country, in her plain holiday clothes, come into Coketown on an expedition of rare occurrence. Remarking this at a glance, with the quick observation of his class, Stephen Blackpool bent his attentive face— his face, which, like the faces of many of his order, by dint of long working with eyes and hands in the midst of a prodigious noise, had acquired the concentrated look with which we are familiar in the countenances of the deaf—the better to hear what she asked him.

"Pray, sir," said the old woman, "didn't I see you come out of that gentleman's house?" pointing back to Mr. Bounderby's. "I believe it was you, unless I have had the bad luck to mistake the person in following?"

"Yes, missus," returned Stephen, "it were me."

"Have you—you'll excuse an old woman's curiosity—have you seen the gentleman?"

"Yes, missus."

"And how did he look, sir? Was he portly, bold, outspoken, and hearty?" As she straightened her own figure, and held up her head in adapting her action to her words, the idea crossed Stephen that he had seen this old woman before, and had not quite liked her.

"O yes," he returned, observing her more attentively, "he were all that."

---

1. See Matthew 8.23–27, referring to the miracle performed by Jesus during a stormy voyage when he "rebuked the winds and the sea; and there was a great calm."

"And healthy," said the old woman, "as the fresh wind?"

"Yes," returned Stephen. "He were ett'n and drinking—as large and as loud as a Hummobee."[2]

"Thank you!" said the old woman with infinite content. "Thank you!"

He certainly never had seen this old woman before. Yet there was a vague remembrance in his mind, as if he had more than once dreamed of some old woman like her.

She walked along at his side, and, gently accommodating himself to her humour, he said Coketown was a busy place, was it not? To which she answered "Eigh sure! Dreadful busy!" Then he said, she came from the country, he saw? To which she answered in the affirmative.

"By Parliamentary,[3] this morning. I came forty mile by Parliamentary this morning, and I'm going back the same forty mile this afternoon. I walked nine mile to the station this morning, and if I find nobody on the road to give me a lift, I shall walk the nine mile back to-night. That's pretty well, sir, at my age!" said the chatty old woman, her eye brightening with exultation.

" 'Deed 'tis. Don't do't too often, missus."

"No, no. Once a year," she answered, shaking her head. "I spend my savings so, once every year. I come regular, to tramp about the streets, and see the gentlemen."

"Only to see 'em?" returned Stephen.

"That's enough for me," she replied, with great earnestness and interest of manner. "I ask no more! I have been standing about, on this side of the way, to see that gentleman," turning her head back towards Mr. Bounderby's again, "come out. But, he's late this year, and I have not seen him. You came out, instead. Now, if I am obliged to go back without a glimpse of him—I only want a glimpse—well! I have seen you, and you have seen him, and I must make that do." Saying this, she looked at Stephen as if to fix his features in her mind, and her eye was not so bright as it had been.

With a large allowance for difference of tastes, and with all submission to the patricians of Coketown, this seemed so extraordinary a source of interest to take so much trouble about, that it perplexed him. But they were passing the church now, and as his eye caught the clock, he quickened his pace.

He was going to his work? the old woman said, quickening hers, too, quite easily. Yes, time was nearly out. On his telling her where he worked, the old woman became a more singular old woman than before.

2. A humblebee (or bumblebee), a large wild bee which makes a loud humming sound.
3. Designating the cheapest form of railway travel, one penny a mile. Railway companies were required, by act of Parliament, to run one such "Parliamentary" train, every day, on all their principal lines.

"An't you happy?" she asked him.

"Why—there's awmost nobbody but has their troubles, missus."
He answered evasively, because the old woman appeared to take it
for granted that he would be very happy indeed, and he had not the
heart to disappoint her. He knew that there was trouble enough in
the world; and if the old woman had lived so long, and could count
upon his having so little, why so much the better for her, and none
the worse for him.

"Ay, ay! You have your troubles at home, you mean?" she said.

"Times. Just now and then," he answered slightly.

"But, working under such a gentleman, they don't follow you to
the Factory?"

No, no; they didn't follow him there, said Stephen. All correct
there. Everything accordant there. (He did not go so far as to say,
for her pleasure, that there was a sort of Divine Right there; but, I
have heard claims almost as magnificent of late years.)

They were now in the black by-road near the place, and the
Hands were crowding in. The bell was ringing, and the Serpent was
a Serpent of many coils, and the Elephant was getting ready. The
strange old woman was delighted with the very bell. It was the beau-
tifullest bell she had ever heard, she said, and sounded grand!

She asked him, when he stopped goodnaturedly to shake hands
with her before going in, how long he had worked there?

"A dozen year," he told her.

"I must kiss the hand," said she, "that has worked in this fine factory for a dozen year!" And she lifted it, though he would have prevented her, and put it to her lips. What harmony, besides her age
and her simplicity, surrounded her, he did not know, but even in this
fantastic action there was a something neither out of time nor place:
a something which it seemed as if nobody else could have made as
serious, or done with such a natural and touching air.

He had been at his loom full half an hour, thinking about this old
woman, when, having occasion to move round the loom for its
adjustment, he glanced through a window which was in his corner,
and saw her still looking up at the pile of building, lost in admiration. Heedless of the smoke and mud and wet, and of her two long
journeys, she was gazing at it, as if the heavy thrum that issued from
its many stories were proud music to her.

She was gone by and by, and the day went after her, and the lights
sprung up again, and the Express whirled in full sight of the Fairy
Palace over the arches near: little felt amid the jarring of the machinery, and scarcely heard above its crash and rattle. Long before then,
his thoughts had gone back to the dreary room above the little
shop, and to the shameful figure heavy on the bed, but heavier on
his heart.

Machinery slackened; throbbing feebly like a fainting pulse; stopped. The bell again; the glare of light and heat dispelled; the factories, looming heavy in the black wet night—their tall chimneys rising up into the air like competing Towers of Babel.

He had spoken to Rachael only last night, it was true, and had walked with her a little way; but he had his new misfortune on him in which no one else could give him a moment's relief, and, for the sake of it, and because he knew himself to want that softening of his anger which no voice but hers could effect, he felt he might so far disregard what she had said as to wait for her again. He waited, but she had eluded him. She was gone. On no other night in the year could he so ill have spared her patient face.

O! Better to have no home in which to lay his head, than to have a home and dread to go to it, through such a cause. He ate and drank, for he was exhausted—but, he little knew or cared what; and he wandered about in the chill rain, thinking and thinking, and brooding and brooding.

No word of a new marriage had ever passed between them; but Rachael had taken great pity on him years ago, and to her alone he had opened his closed heart all this time, on the subject of his miseries; and he knew very well that if he were free to ask her, she would take him. He thought of the home he might at that moment have been seeking with pleasure and pride; of the different man he might have been that night; of the lightness then in his now heavy-laden breast; of the then restored honor, self-respect, and tranquility, now all torn to pieces. He thought of the waste of the best part of his life, of the change it made in his character for the worse every day, of the dreadful nature of his existence, bound hand and foot to a dead woman, and tormented by a demon in her shape. He thought of Rachael, how young when they were first brought together in these circumstances, how mature now, how soon to grow old. He thought of the number of girls and women she had seen marry, how many homes with children in them she had seen grow up around her, how she had contentedly pursued her own lone quiet path—for him—and how he had sometimes seen a shade of melancholy on her blessed face, that smote him with remorse and despair. He set the picture of her up, beside the infamous image of last night; and thought, Could it be, that the whole earthly course of one so gentle, good, and self-denying, was subjugate to such a wretch as that!

Filled with these thoughts—so filled that he had an unwholesome sense of growing larger, of being placed in some new and diseased relation towards the objects among which he passed, of seeing the iris round every misty light turn red—he went home for shelter.

Chapter XIII.

RACHAEL.

A candle faintly burned in the window, to which the black ladder had often been raised for the sliding away of all that was most precious in this world to a striving wife and a brood of hungry babies; and Stephen added to his other thoughts the stern reflection, that of all the casualties of this existence upon earth, not one was dealt out with so unequal a hand as Death. The inequality of Birth was nothing to it. For, say that the child of a King and the child of a Weaver were born to-night in the same moment, what was that disparity, to the death of any human creature who was serviceable to, or beloved by, another, while this abandoned woman lived on!

From the outside of his home he gloomily passed to the inside, with suspended breath and with a slow footstep. He went up to his door, opened it, and so into the room.

Quiet and peace were there. Rachael was there, sitting by the bed.

She turned her head, and the light of her face shone in upon the midnight of his mind. She sat by the bed, watching and tending his wife. That is to say, he saw that some one lay there, and he knew too well it must be she; but Rachael's hands had put a curtain up, so that she was screened from his eyes. Her disgraceful garments were removed, and some of Rachael's were in the room. Everything was in its place and order as he had always kept it, the little fire was newly trimmed, and the hearth was freshly swept. It appeared to him that he saw all this in Rachael's face, and looked at nothing besides. While looking at it, it was shut out from his view by the softened tears that filled his eyes; but, not before he had seen how earnestly she looked at him, and how her own eyes were filled too.

She turned again towards the bed, and satisfying herself that all was quiet there, spoke in a low, calm, cheerful voice.

"I am glad you have come at last, Stephen. You are very late."

"I ha' been walking up an down."

"I thought so. But 'tis too bad a night for that. The rain falls very heavy, and the wind has risen."

The wind? True. It was blowing hard. Hark to the thundering in the chimney, and the surging noise! To have been out in such a wind, and not to have known it was blowing!

"I have been here once before, to-day, Stephen. Landlady came round for me at dinner-time. There was some one here that needed looking to, she said. And 'deed she was right. All wandering and lost, Stephen. Wounded too, and bruised."

He slowly moved to a chair and sat down, drooping his head before her.

"I came to do what little I could, Stephen; first, for that she worked with me when we were girls both, and for that you courted her and married her when I was her friend—"

He laid his furrowed forehead on his hand, with a low groan.

"And next, for that I know your heart, and am right sure and certain that 'tis far too merciful to let her die, or even so much as suffer, for want of aid. Thou knowest who said, 'Let him who is without sin among you, cast the first stone at her!'[1] There have been plenty to do that. Thou art not the man to cast the last stone, Stephen, when she is brought so low."

"O Rachael, Rachael!"

"Thou hast been a cruel sufferer, Heaven reward thee!" she said, in compassionate accents. "I am thy poor friend, with all my heart and mind."

The wounds of which she had spoken, seemed to be about the neck of the self-made outcast. She dressed them now, still without showing her. She steeped a piece of linen in a basin, into which she poured some liquid from a bottle, and laid it with a gentle hand upon the sore. The three-legged table had been drawn close to the bedside, and on it there were two bottles. This was one.

It was not so far off, but that Stephen, following her hands with his eyes, could read what was printed on it, in large letters. He turned of a deadly hue, and a sudden horror seemed to fall upon him.

"I will stay here, Stephen," said Rachael, quietly resuming her seat, "till the bells go Three. 'Tis to be done again at three, and then she may be left till morning."

"But thy rest agen to-morrow's work, my dear."

"I slept sound last night. I can wake many nights, when I am put to it. 'Tis thou who art in need of rest—so white and tired. Try to sleep in the chair there, while I watch. Thou hadst no sleep last night, I can well believe. Tomorrow's work is far harder for thee than for me."

He heard the thundering and surging out of doors, and it seemed to him as if his late angry mood were going about trying to get at him. She had cast it out; she would keep it out; he trusted to her to defend him from himself.

"She don't know me, Stephen; she just drowsily mutters and stares. I have spoken to her times and again, but she don't notice! 'Tis as well so. When she comes to her right mind once more, I shall have done what I can, and she never the wiser."

"How long, Rachael, is't looked for, that she'll be so?"

"Doctor said she would haply come to her mind to-morrow."

1. John 8.7.

His eyes again fell on the bottle, and a tremble passed over him, causing him to shiver in every limb. She thought he was chilled with the wet. "No," he said; "it was not that. He had had a fright."

"A fright?"

"Ay, ay! coming in. When I were walking. When I were thinking. When I—" It seized him again; and he stood up, holding by the mantel-shelf, as he pressed his dank cold hair down with a hand that shook as if it were palsied.

"Stephen!"

She was coming to him, but he stretched out his arm to stop her.

"No! Don't please; don't! Let me see thee setten by the bed. Let me see thee, a' so good, and so forgiving. Let me see thee as I see thee when I coom in. I can never see thee better than so. Never, never, never!"

He had a violent fit of trembling, and then sunk into his chair. After a time he controlled himself, and, resting with an elbow on one knee, and his head upon that hand, could look towards Rachael. Seen across the dim candle with his moistened eyes, she looked as if she had a glory shining round her head. He could have believed she had. He did believe it, as the noise without shook the window, rattled at the door below, and went about the house clamoring and lamenting.

"When she gets better, Stephen, 'tis to be hoped she'll leave thee to thyself again, and do thee no more hurt. Anyways we will hope so now. And now I shall keep silence, for I want thee to sleep."

He closed his eyes, more to please her than to rest his weary head; but, by slow degrees as he listened to the great noise of the wind, he ceased to hear it, or it changed into the working of his loom, or even into the voices of the day (his own included) saying what had been really said. Even this imperfect consciousness faded away at last, and he dreamed a long, troubled dream.

He thought that he, and some one on whom his heart had long been set—but she was not Rachael, and that surprised him, even in the midst of his imaginary happiness—stood in the church being married. While the ceremony was performing, and while he recognised among the witnesses some whom he knew to be living, and many whom he knew to be dead, darkness came on, succeeded by the shining of a tremendous light. It broke from one line in the table of commandments at the altar, and illuminated the building with the words. They were sounded through the church too, as if there were voices in the fiery letters. Upon this, the whole appearance before him and around him changed, and nothing was left as it had been, but himself and the clergyman. They stood in the daylight before a crowd so vast, that if all the people in the world could have been brought together into one space, they could not have looked, he thought, more numerous; and they all abhorred him, and there was not one pitying or friendly eye among the millions that were fastened on his face. He stood on a raised stage, under his own loom; and, looking up at the shape the loom took, and hearing the burial service distinctly read, he knew that he was there to suffer death. In an instant what he stood on fell below him, and he was gone.

Out of what mystery he came back to his usual life, and to places that he knew, he was unable to consider; but, he was back in those places by some means, and with this condemnation upon him, that he was never, in this world or the next, through all the unimaginable ages of eternity, to look on Rachael's face or hear her voice. Wandering to and fro, unceasingly, without hope, and in search of he knew not what (he only knew that he was doomed to seek it), he was the subject of a nameless, horrible dread, a mortal fear of one particular shape which everything took. Whatsoever he looked at, grew into that form sooner or later. The object of his miserable existence was to prevent its recognition by any one among the various people he encountered. Hopeless labor! If he led them out of rooms where it was, if he shut up drawers and closets where it stood, if he drew the curious from places where he knew it to be secreted, and got them out into the streets, the very chimneys of the mills assumed that shape, and round them was the printed word.

The wind was blowing again, the rain was beating on the housetops, and the larger spaces through which he had strayed contracted to the four walls of his room. Saving that the fire had died out, it was as his eyes had closed upon it. Rachael seemed to have fallen into a doze, in the chair by the bed. She sat wrapped in her shawl, perfectly still. The table stood in the same place, close by the bedside, and on it, in its real proportions and appearance, was the shape so often repeated.

He thought he saw the curtain move. He looked again, and he was sure it moved. He saw a hand come forth, and grope about a little. Then the curtain moved more perceptibly, and the woman in the bed put it back, and sat up.

With her woful eyes, so haggard and wild, so heavy and large, she looked all round the room, and passed the corner where he slept in his chair. Her eyes returned to that corner, and she put her hand over them as a shade, while she looked into it. Again they went all round the room, scarcely heeding Rachael if at all, and returned to that corner. He thought, as she once more shaded them—not so much looking at him, as looking for him with a brutish instinct that he was there—that no single trace was left in those debauched features, or in the mind that went along with them, of the woman he had married eighteen years before. But that he had seen her come to this by inches, he never could have believed her to be the same.

All this time, as if a spell were on him, he was motionless and powerless, except to watch her.

Stupidly dozing, or communing with her incapable self about nothing, she sat for a little while with her hands at her ears, and her head resting on them. Presently, she resumed her staring round the room. And now, for the first time, her eyes stopped at the table with the bottles on it.

Straightway she turned her eyes back to his corner, with the defiance of last night, and, moving very cautiously and softly, stretched out her greedy hand. She drew a mug into the bed, and sat for a while considering which of the two bottles she should choose. Finally, she laid her insensate grasp upon the bottle that had swift and certain death in it, and, before his eyes, pulled out the cork with her teeth.

Dream or reality, he had no voice, nor had he power to stir. If this be real, and her allotted time be not yet come, wake, Rachael, wake!

She thought of that, too. She looked at Rachael, and very slowly, very cautiously, poured out the contents. The draught was at her lips. A moment and she would be past all help, let the whole world wake and come about her with its utmost power. But, in that moment Rachael started up with a suppressed cry. The creature struggled, struck her, seized her by the hair; but Rachael had the cup.

Stephen broke out of his chair. "Rachael, am I wakin' or dreamin' this dreadfo' night!"

" 'Tis all well, Stephen. I have been asleep myself. 'Tis near three. Hush! I hear the bells."

The wind brought the sounds of the church clock to the window. They listened, and it struck three. Stephen looked at her, saw how pale she was, noted the disorder of her hair, and the red marks of fingers on her forehead, and felt assured that his senses of sight and hearing had been awake. She held the cup in her hand even now.

"I thought it must be near three," she said, calmly pouring from the cup into the basin, and steeping the linen as before. "I am thankful I stayed! 'Tis done now, when I have put this on. There! And now she's quiet again. The few drops in the basin I'll pour away, for 'tis bad stuff to leave about, though ever so little of it." As she spoke, she drained the basin into the ashes of the fire, and broke the bottle on the hearth.

She had nothing to do, then, but to cover herself with her shawl before going out into the wind and rain.

"Thou'lt let me walk wi' thee at this hour, Rachael?"

"No, Stephen, 'Tis but a minute and I'm home."

"Thou'rt not fearfo';" he said it in a low voice, as they went out at the door; "to leave me alone wi' her!"

As she looked at him, saying "Stephen?" he went down on his knee before her, on the poor mean stairs, and put an end of her shawl to his lips.

"Thou art an Angel. Bless thee, bless thee!"

"I am, as I have told thee, Stephen, thy poor friend. Angels are not like me. Between them, and a working woman fu' of faults, there is a deep gulf[2] set. My little sister is among them, but she is changed."

She raised her eyes for a moment as she said the words; and then they fell again, in all their gentleness and mildness, on his face.

"Thou changest me from bad to good. Thou mak'st me humbly wishfo' to be more like thee, and fearfo' to lose thee when this life is ower, an a' the muddle cleared awa'. Thou'rt an Angel; it may be, thou hast saved my soul alive!"

She looked at him, on his knee at her feet, with her shawl still in his hand, and the reproof on her lips died away when she saw the working of his face.

"I coom home desp'rate. I coom home wi'out a hope, and mad wi' thinking that when I said a word o' complaint, I was reckoned a onreasonable Hand. I told thee I had had a fright. It were the Poison-bottle on table. I never hurt a livin' creetur; but happenin' so suddenly upon't, I thowt, 'How can I say what I might ha' done to myseln, or her, or both!'"

She put her two hands on his mouth, with a face of terror, to stop him from saying more. He caught them in his unoccupied hand, and holding them, and still clasping the border of her shawl, said, hurriedly:

"But I see thee, Rachael, setten by the bed. I ha' seen thee, aw this night. In my troublous sleep I ha' known thee still to be there. Evermore I will see thee there. I nevermore will see her or think o' her, but thou shalt be beside her. I nevermore will see or think o' anything that angers me, but thou, so much better than me, shalt be by th' side on't. And so I will try t' look t' th' time, and so I will try t' trust t' th' time, when thou and me at last shall walk together far awa', beyond the deep gulf, in th' country where thy little sister is."

He kissed the border of her shawl again, and let her go. She bade him good night in a broken voice, and went out into the street.

The wind blew from the quarter where the day would soon appear, and still blew strongly. It had cleared the sky before it, and the rain had spent itself or travelled elsewhere, and the stars were bright. He stood bare-headed in the road, watching her quick disappear-

---

2. A reference to the "gulf" between the rich man in Hell and Lazarus in Heaven (Luke 16.26).

ance. As the shining stars were to the heavy candle in the window, so was Rachael, in the rugged fancy of this man, to the common experiences of his life.

Chapter XIV.

THE GREAT MANUFACTURER.

Time went on in Coketown like its own machinery; so much material wrought up, so much fuel consumed, so many powers worn out, so much money made. But, less inexorable than iron, steel, and brass, it brought its varying seasons even into that wilderness of smoke and brick, and made the only stand that ever *was* made in the place against its direful uniformity.

"Louisa is becoming," said Mr. Gradgrind, "almost a young woman."

Time, with his innumerable horse-power, worked away, not minding what anybody said, and presently turned out young Thomas a foot taller than when his father had last taken particular notice of him.

"Thomas is becoming," said Mr. Gradgrind, "almost a young man."

Time passed Thomas on in the mill, while his father was thinking about it, and there he stood in a long-tailed coat and a stiff shirt-collar.

"Really," said Mr. Gradgrind, "the period has arrived when Thomas ought to go to Bounderby."

Time, sticking to him, passed him on into Bounderby's Bank, made him an inmate of Bounderby's house, necessitated the purchase of his first razor, and exercised him diligently in his calculations relative to number one.

The same great manufacturer, always with an immense variety of work on hand, in every stage of development, passed Sissy onward in his mill, and worked her up into a very pretty article indeed.

"I fear, Jupe," said Mr. Gradgrind, "that your continuance at the school any longer, would be useless."

"I am afraid it would, sir," Sissy answered with a curtsey.

"I cannot disguise from you, Jupe," said Mr. Gradgrind, knitting his brow, "that the result of your probation there has disappointed me; has greatly disappointed me. You have not acquired, under Mr. and Mrs. M'Choakumchild, anything like that amount of exact knowledge which I looked for. You are extremely deficient in your facts. Your acquaintance with figures is very limited. You are altogether backward, and below the mark."

"I am sorry, sir," she returned; "but I know it is quite true. Yet I have tried hard, sir."

"Yes," said Mr. Gradgrind, "yes, I believe you have tried hard; I have observed you, and I can find no fault in that respect."

"Thank you, sir. I have thought sometimes;" Sissy very timid here; "that perhaps I tried to learn too much, and that if I had asked to be allowed to try a little less, I might have—"

"No, Jupe, no," said Mr. Gradgrind, shaking his head in his profoundest and most eminently practical way. "No. The course you pursued, you pursued according to the system—the system—and there is no more to be said about it. I can only suppose that the circumstances of your early life were too unfavorable to the development of your reasoning powers, and that we began too late. Still, as I have said already, I am disappointed."

"I wish I could have made a better acknowledgment, sir, of your kindness to a poor forlorn girl who had no claim upon you, and of your protection of her."

"Don't shed tears," said Mr. Gradgrind. "Don't shed tears. I don't complain of you. You are an affectionate, earnest, good young woman, and—and we must make that do."

"Thank you, sir, very much," said Sissy, with a grateful curtsey.

"You are useful to Mrs. Gradgrind, and (in a generally pervading way) you are serviceable in the family also; so I understand from Miss Louisa, and, indeed, so I have observed myself. I therefore hope," said Mr. Gradgrind, "that you can make yourself happy in those relations."

"I should have nothing to wish, sir, if—"

"I understand you," said Mr. Gradgrind; "you still refer to your father. I have heard from Miss Louisa that you still preserve that bottle. Well! If your training in the science of arriving at exact results had been more successful, you would have been wiser on these points. I will say no more."

He really liked Sissy too well to have a contempt for her; otherwise he held her calculating powers in such very slight estimation that he must have fallen upon that conclusion. Somehow or other, he had become possessed by an idea that there was something in this girl which could hardly be set forth in a tabular form. Her capacity of definition might be easily stated at a very low figure, her mathematical knowledge at nothing; yet he was not sure that if he had been required, for example, to tick her off into columns in a parliamentary return, he would have quite known how to divide her.

In some stages of his manufacture of the human fabric, the processes of Time are very rapid. Young Thomas and Sissy being both at such a stage of their working up, these changes were effected in a year or two; while Mr. Gradgrind himself seemed stationary in his course, and underwent no alteration.

Except one, which was apart from his necessary progress through the mill. Time hustled him into a little noisy and rather dirty machinery, in a by-corner, and made him Member of Parliament for Coketown: one of the respected members for ounce weights and measures, one of the representatives of the multiplication table, one of the deaf honorable gentlemen, dumb honorable gentlemen, blind honorable gentlemen, lame honorable gentlemen, dead honorable gentlemen, to every other consideration. Else wherefore live we in a Christian land, eighteen hundred and odd years after our Master?[1]

All this while, Louisa had been passing on, so quiet and reserved, and so much given to watching the bright ashes at twilight as they fell into the grate and became extinct, that from the period when her father had said she was almost a young woman—which seemed but yesterday—she had scarcely attracted his notice again, when he found her quite a young woman.

"Quite a young woman," said Mr. Gradgrind, musing. "Dear me!"

Soon after this discovery, he became more thoughtful than usual for several days, and seemed much engrossed by one subject. On a certain night, when he was going out, and Louisa came to bid him good-bye before his departure—as he was not to be home until late and she would not see him again until the morning—he held her in his arms, looking at her in his kindest manner, and said:

"My dear Louisa, you are a woman!"

She answered with the old, quick, searching look of the night when she was found at the Circus; then cast down her eyes. "Yes, father."

"My dear," said Mr. Gradgrind, "I must speak with you alone and seriously. Come to me in my room after breakfast to-morrow, will you?"

"Yes, father."

"Your hands are rather cold, Louisa. Are you not well?"

"Quite well, father."

"And cheerful?"

She looked at him again, and smiled in her peculiar manner. "I am as cheerful, father, as I usually am, or usually have been."

"That's well," said Mr. Gradgrind. So, he kissed her and went away; and Louisa returned to the serene apartment of the hair-cutting character, and leaning her elbow on her hand, looked again at the short-lived sparks that so soon subsided into ashes.

"Are you there, Loo?" said her brother, looking in at the door. He was quite a young gentleman of pleasure now, and not quite a prepossessing one.

1. Jesus.

"Dear Tom," she answered, rising and embracing him, "how long it is since you have been to see me!"

"Why, I have been otherwise engaged, Loo, in the evenings; and in the daytime old Bounderby has been keeping me at it rather. But I touch him up with you, when he comes it too strong, and so we preserve an understanding. I say! Has father said anything particular to you, to-day or yesterday, Loo?"

"No, Tom. But he told me to-night that he wished to do so in the morning."

"Ah! That's what I mean," said Tom. "Do you know where he is tonight?"—with a very deep expression.

"No."

"Then I'll tell you. He's with old Bounderby. They are having a regular confab together, up at the Bank. Why at the Bank, do you think? Well, I'll tell you again. To keep Mrs. Sparsit's ears as far off as possible, I expect."

With her hand upon her brother's shoulder, Louisa still stood looking at the fire. Her brother glanced at her face with greater interest than usual, and, encircling her waist with his arm, drew her coaxingly to him.

"You are very fond of me, an't you, Loo?"

"Indeed I am, Tom, though you do let such long intervals go by without coming to see me."

"Well, sister of mine," said Tom, "when you say that, you are near my thoughts. We might be so much oftener together—mightn't we? Always together, almost—mightn't we? It would do me a great deal of good if you were to make up your mind to I know what, Loo. It would be a splendid thing for me. It would be uncommonly jolly!"

Her thoughtfulness baffled his cunning scrutiny. He could make nothing of her face. He pressed her in his arm, and kissed her cheek. She returned the kiss, but still looked at the fire.

"I say, Loo! I thought I'd come, and just hint to you what was going on: though I supposed you'd most likely guess, even if you didn't know. I can't stay, because I'm engaged to some fellows to-night. You won't forget how fond you are of me?"

"No, dear Tom, I won't forget."

"That's a capital girl," said Tom. "Good-bye, Loo."

She gave him an affectionate good-night, and went out with him to the door, whence the fires of Coketown could be seen, making the distance lurid. She stood there, looking stedfastly towards them, and listening to his departing steps. They retreated quickly, as glad to get away from Stone Lodge; and she stood there yet, when he was gone and all was quiet. It seemed as if, first in her own fire within the house, and then in the fiery haze without, she tried to discover what kind of woof Old Time, that greatest and longest-established

Spinner of all, would weave from the threads he had already spun into a woman. But, his factory is a secret place, his work is noiseless, and his Hands are mutes.

Chapter XV.

FATHER AND DAUGHTER.

Although Mr. Gradgrind did not take after Blue Beard,[1] his room was quite a blue chamber in its abundance of blue books. Whatever they could prove (which is usually anything you like), they proved there, in an army constantly strengthening by the arrival of new recruits. In that charmed apartment, the most complicated social questions were cast up, got into exact totals, and finally settled—if those concerned could only have been brought to know it. As if an astronomical observatory should be made without any windows, and the astronomer within should arrange the starry universe solely by pen, ink and paper, so Mr. Gradgrind, in *his* Observatory (and there are many like it), had no need to cast an eye upon the teeming myriads of human beings around him, but could settle all their destinies on a slate, and wipe out all their tears with one dirty little bit of sponge.

To this Observatory, then: a stern room, with a deadly-statistical clock in it, which measured every second with a beat like a rap upon a coffin-lid: Louisa repaired on the appointed morning. A window looked towards Coketown; and when she sat down near her father's table, she saw the high chimneys and the long tracts of smoke looming in the heavy distance gloomily.

"My dear Louisa," said her father, "I prepared you last night to give me your serious attention in the conversation we are now going to have together. You have been so well trained, and you do, I am happy to say, so much justice to the education you have received, that I have perfect confidence in your good sense. You are not impulsive, you are not romantic, you are accustomed to view everything from the strong dispassionate ground of reason and calculation. From that ground alone, I know you will view and consider what I am going to communicate."

He waited, as if he would have been glad that she said something. But she said never a word.

"Louisa my dear, you are the subject of a proposal of marriage that has been made to me."

1. In the tale of Blue Beard, first translated into English in 1729 from a French story by Charles Perrault, a wealthy, evil man, disfigured by a blue beard, whose first seven wives have mysteriously disappeared, is discovered by his final wife, Fatima, to have murdered the previous seven. When Blue Beard attempts to kill her, she is rescued, and Blue Beard is killed by her brothers.

Again he waited, and again she answered not one word. This so far surprised him, as to induce him gently to repeat, "a proposal of marriage, my dear." To which she returned, without any visible emotion whatever:

"I hear you, father. I am attending, I assure you."

"Well!" said Mr. Gradgrind, breaking into a smile, after being for the moment at a loss, "you are even more dispassionate than I expected, Louisa. Or, perhaps, you are not unprepared for the announcement I have it in charge to make?"

"I cannot say that, father, until I hear it. Prepared or unprepared, I wish to hear it all from you. I wish to hear you state it to me, father."

Strange to relate, Mr. Gradgrind was not so collected at this moment as his daughter was. He took a paper-knife in his hand, turned it over, laid it down, took it up again, and even then had to look along the blade of it, considering how to go on.

"What you say, my dear Louisa, is perfectly reasonable. I have undertaken then to let you know that—in short, that Mr. Bounderby has informed me that he has long watched your progress with particular interest and pleasure, and has long hoped that the time might ultimately arrive when he should offer you his hand in marriage. That time, to which he has so long, and certainly with great constancy, looked forward, is now come. Mr. Bounderby has made his proposal of marriage to me, and has entreated me to make it known to you, and to express his hope that you will take it into your favorable consideration."

Silence between them. The deadly-statistical clock very hollow. The distant smoke very black and heavy.

"Father," said Louisa, "do you think I love Mr. Bounderby?"

Mr. Gradgrind was extremely discomfited by this unexpected question. "Well, my child," he returned, "I—really—cannot take upon myself to say."

"Father," pursued Louisa in exactly the same voice as before, "do you ask me to love Mr. Bounderby?"

"My dear Louisa, no. No. I ask nothing."

"Father," she still pursued, "does Mr. Bounderby ask me to love him?"

"Really, my dear," said Mr. Gradgrind, "it is difficult to answer your question—"

"Difficult to answer it, Yes or No, father?"

"Certainly, my dear. Because;" here was something to demonstrate, and it set him up again; "because the reply depends so materially, Louisa, on the sense in which we use the expression. Now, Mr. Bounderby does not do you the injustice, and does not do himself the injustice, of pretending to anything fanciful, fantastic, or (I am using synonymous terms) sentimental. Mr. Bounderby would have seen you grow up under his eyes, to very little purpose, if he could so far forget what is due to your good sense, not to say to his, as to address you from any such ground. Therefore, perhaps the expression itself—I merely suggest this to you, my dear—may be a little misplaced."

"What would you advise me to use in its stead, father?"

"Why, my dear Louisa," said Mr. Gradgrind, completely recovered by this time, "I would advise you (since you ask me) to consider this question, as you have been accustomed to consider every other question, simply as one of tangible Fact. The ignorant and the giddy may embarrass such subjects with irrelevant fancies, and other absurdities that have no existence, properly viewed—really no existence—but it is no compliment to you to say, that you know better. Now, what are the Facts of this case? You are, we will say in round numbers, twenty years of age; Mr. Bounderby is, we will say in round numbers, fifty. There is some disparity in your respective years, but in your means and positions there is none; on the contrary, there is a great suitability. Then the question arises, Is this one disparity sufficient to operate as a bar to such a marriage? In considering this question, it is not unimportant to take into account the statistics of marriage, so far as they have yet been obtained, in England and Wales. I find, on reference to the figures, that a large proportion of these marriages are contracted between parties of very unequal ages, and that the elder of these contracting parties is, in rather more than three-fourths of these instances, the bridegroom. It is remarkable as showing the wide prevalence of this law, that among the natives of the British possessions in India, also in a considerable part of China, and among the Calmucks of Tartary,[2] the best means of computation yet furnished us by travellers, yield similar results. The disparity I have mentioned, therefore, almost ceases to be disparity, and (virtually) all but disappears."

"What do you recommend, father," asked Louisa, her reserved composure not in the least affected by these gratifying results, "that I should substitute for the term I used just now? For the misplaced expression?"

"Louisa," returned her father, "it appears to me that nothing can be plainer. Confining yourself rigidly to Fact, the question of Fact you state to yourself is: Does Mr. Bounderby ask me to marry him? Yes, he does. The sole remaining question then is: Shall I marry him? I think nothing can be plainer than that."

"Shall I marry him?" repeated Louisa, with great deliberation.

"Precisely. And it is satisfactory to me, as your father, my dear Louisa, to know that you do not come to the consideration of that

2. Or Kalmucks; a semi-nomadic branch of the Oirat Mongols, who inhabit an area of southeastern Russia on the Caspian Sea.

question with the previous habits of mind, and habits of life, that belong to many young women."

"No, father," she returned, "I do not."

"I now leave you to judge for yourself," said Mr. Gradgrind. "I have stated the case, as such cases are usually stated among practical minds; I have stated it, as the case of your mother and myself was stated in its time. The rest, my dear Louisa, is for you to decide."

From the beginning, she had sat looking at him fixedly. As he now leaned back in his chair, and bent his deep-set eyes upon her in his turn, perhaps he might have seen one wavering moment in her, when she was impelled to throw herself upon his breast, and give him the pent-up confidences of her heart. But, to see it, he must have over-leaped at a bound the artificial barriers he had for many years been erecting, between himself and all those subtle essences of humanity which will elude the utmost cunning of algebra until the last trumpet ever to be sounded[3] shall blow even algebra to wreck. The barriers were too many and too high for such a leap. With his unbending, utilitarian, matter-of-fact face, he hardened her again; and the moment shot away into the plumbless depths of the past, to mingle with all the lost opportunities that are drowned there.

Removing her eyes from him, she sat so long looking silently towards the town, that he said, at length: "Are you consulting the chimneys of the Coketown works, Louisa?"

"There seems to be nothing there, but languid and monotonous smoke. Yet when the night comes, Fire bursts out, father!" she answered, turning quickly.

"Of course I know that, Louisa. I do not see the application of the remark." To do him justice he did not, at all.

She passed it away with a slight motion of her hand, and concentrating her attention upon him again, said, "Father, I have often thought that life is very short."—This was so distinctly one of his subjects that he interposed:

"It is short, no doubt, my dear. Still, the average duration of human life is proved to have increased of late years. The calculations of various life assurance[4] and annuity offices, among other figures which cannot go wrong, have established the fact."

"I speak of my own life, father."

"O indeed? Still," said Mr. Gradgrind, "I need not point out to you, Louisa, that it is governed by the laws which govern lives in the aggregate."

"While it lasts, I would wish to do the little I can, and the little I am fit for. What does it matter!"

3. 1 Corinthians 15.52.
4. Insurance.

Mr. Gradgrind seemed rather at a loss to understand the last four words; replying, "How, matter? What, matter, my dear?"

"Mr. Bounderby," she went on in a steady, straight way, without regarding this, "asks me to marry him. The question I have to ask myself is, shall I marry him? That is so, father, is it not? You have told me so, father. Have you not?"

"Certainly, my dear."

"Let it be so. Since Mr. Bounderby likes to take me thus, I am satisfied to accept his proposal. Tell him, father, as soon as you please, that this was my answer. Repeat it, word for word, if you can, because I should wish him to know what I said."

"It is quite right, my dear," retorted her father, approvingly, "to be exact. I will observe your very proper request. Have you any wish, in reference to the period of your marriage, my child?"

"None, father. What does it matter!"

Mr. Gradgrind had drawn his chair a little nearer to her, and taken her hand. But, her repetition of these words seemed to strike with some little discord on his ear. He paused to look at her, and, still holding her hand, said:

"Louisa, I have not considered it essential to ask you one question, because the possibility implied in it appeared to me to be too remote. But, perhaps, I ought to do so. You have never entertained in secret any other proposal?"

"Father," she returned, almost scornfully, "what other proposal can have been made to *me*? Whom have I seen? Where have I been? What are my heart's experiences?"

"My dear Louisa," returned Mr. Gradgrind, reassured and satisfied, "you correct me justly. I merely wished to discharge my duty."

"What do *I* know, father," said Louisa in her quiet manner, "of tastes and fancies; of aspirations and affections; of all that part of my nature in which such light things might have been nourished? What escape have I had from problems that could be demonstrated, and realities that could be grasped?" As she said it, she unconsciously closed her hand, as if upon a solid object, and slowly opened it as though she were releasing dust or ash.

"My dear," assented her eminently practical parent, "quite true, quite true."

"Why, father," she pursued, "what a strange question to ask *me*! The baby-preference that even I have heard of as common among children, has never had its innocent resting-place in my breast. You have been so careful of me, that I never had a child's heart. You have trained me so well, that I never dreamed a child's dream. You have dealt so wisely with me, father, from my cradle to this hour, that I never had a child's belief or a child's fear."

Mr. Gradgrind was quite moved by his success, and by this testimony to it. "My dear Louisa," said he, "you abundantly repay my
care. Kiss me, my dear girl."

So, his daughter kissed him. Detaining her in his embrace, he
said, "I may assure you now, my favourite child, that I am made
happy by the sound decision at which you have arrived. Mr. Bounderby is a very remarkable man; and what little disparity can be
said to exist between you—if any—is more than counterbalanced
by the tone your mind has acquired. It has always been my object
so to educate you, as that you might, while still in your early youth,
be (if I may so express myself) almost any age. Kiss me once more,
Louisa. Now, let us go and find your mother."

Accordingly, they went down to the drawing-room, where the
esteemed lady with no nonsense about her, was recumbent as usual,
while Sissy worked beside her. She gave some feeble signs of
returning animation when they entered, and presently the faint
transparency was presented in a sitting attitude.

"Mrs. Gradgrind," said her husband, who had waited for the
achievement of this feat with some impatience, "allow me to present
to you Mrs. Bounderby."

"Oh!" said Mrs. Gradgrind, "so you have settled it! Well, I'm sure I
hope your health may be good, Louisa; for if your head begins to split
as soon as you are married, which was the case with mine, I cannot
consider that you are to be envied, though I have no doubt you think
you are, as all girls do. However, I give you joy, my dear—and I hope
you may now turn all your ological studies to good account, I am sure
I do! I must give you a kiss of congratulation, Louisa; but don't touch
my right shoulder, for there's something running down it all day long.
And now you see," whimpered Mrs. Gradgrind, adjusting her shawls
after the affectionate ceremony, "I shall be worrying myself, morning, noon, and night, to know what I am to call him!"

"Mrs. Gradgrind," said her husband, solemnly, "what do you mean?"

"Whatever I am to call him, Mr. Gradgrind, when he is married
to Louisa! I must call him something. It's impossible," said Mrs.
Gradgrind, with a mingled sense of politeness and injury, "to be constantly addressing him, and never giving him a name. I cannot call
him Josiah, for the name is insupportable to me. You yourself
wouldn't hear of Joe, you very well know. Am I to call my own son-
in-law, Mister? Not, I believe, unless the time has arrived when, as
an invalid, I am to be trampled upon by my relations. Then, what
am I to call him!"

Nobody present having any suggestion to offer in the remarkable emergency, Mrs. Gradgrind departed this life for the time
being, after delivering the following codicil to her remarks already
executed:

"As to the wedding, all I ask, Louisa, is,—and I ask it with a flut-tering in my chest, which actually extends to the soles of my feet,—that it may take place soon. Otherwise, I know it is one of those subjects I shall never hear the last of."

When Mr. Gradgrind had presented Mrs. Bounderby, Sissy had suddenly turned her head, and looked, in wonder, in pity, in sorrow, in doubt, in a multitude of emotions, towards Louisa. Louisa had known it, and seen it, without looking at her. From that moment she was impassive, proud, and cold—held Sissy at a distance—changed to her altogether.

Chapter XVI.

HUSBAND AND WIFE.

Mr. Bounderby's first disquietude, on hearing of his happiness, was occasioned by the necessity of imparting it to Mrs. Sparsit. He could not make up his mind how to do that, or what the consequences of the step might be. Whether she would instantly depart, bag and baggage, to Lady Scadgers, or would positively refuse to budge from the premises; whether she would be plaintive or abusive, tearful or tearing; whether she would break her heart, or break the looking-glass; Mr. Bounderby could not at all foresee. However, as it must be done, he had no choice but to do it; so, after attempting several let-ters, and failing in them all, he resolved to do it by word of mouth.

On his way home, on the evening he set aside for this momen-tous purpose, he took the precaution of stepping into a chemist's shop and buying a bottle of the very strongest smelling-salts. "By George!" said Mr. Bounderby, "if she takes it in the fainting way, I'll have the skin off her nose, at all events!" But, in spite of being thus forearmed, he entered his own house with anything but a coura-geous air; and appeared before the object of his misgivings, like a dog who was conscious of coming direct from the pantry.

"Good evening, Mr. Bounderby!"

"Good evening, ma'am, good evening." He drew up his chair, and Mrs. Sparsit drew back hers, as who should say, "Your fireside, sir. I freely admit it. It is for you to occupy it all, if you think proper."

"Don't go to the North Pole, ma'am!" said Mr. Bounderby.

"Thank you, sir," said Mrs. Sparsit, and returned, though short of her former position.

Mr. Bounderby sat looking at her, as, with the points of a stiff, sharp pair of scissors, she picked out holes for some inscrutable ornamental purpose, in a piece of cambric. An operation which, taken in connexion with the bushy eye-brows and the Roman nose, suggested with some liveliness the idea of a hawk engaged upon the eyes of a tough little bird. She was so stedfastly occupied, that many minutes elapsed before she looked up from her work; when she did so, Mr. Bounderby bespoke her attention with a hitch of his head.

"Mrs. Sparsit ma'am," said Mr. Bounderby, putting his hands in his pockets, and assuring himself with his right hand that the cork of the little bottle was ready for use, "I have no occasion to say to you, that you are not only a lady born and bred, but a devilish sensible woman."

"Sir," returned the lady, "this is indeed not the first time that you have honored me with similar expressions of your good opinion."

"Mrs. Sparsit ma'am," said Mr. Bounderby, "I am going to astonish you."

"Yes, sir?" returned Mrs. Sparsit, interrogatively, and in the most tranquil manner possible. She generally wore mittens,[1] and she now laid down her work, and smoothed those mittens.

"I am going, ma'am," said Bounderby, "to marry Tom Gradgrind's daughter."

"Yes, sir?" returned Mrs. Sparsit. "I hope you may be happy, Mr. Bounderby. Oh, indeed I hope you may be happy, sir!" And she said it with such great condescension, as well as with such great compassion for him, that Bounderby,—far more disconcerted than if she had thrown her work-box at the mirror, or swooned on the hearth-rug,—corked up the smelling-salts tight in his pocket, and thought, "Now confound this woman, who could have ever guessed that she would take it in this way!"

"I wish with all my heart, sir," said Mrs. Sparsit, in a highly superior manner; somehow she seemed, in a moment, to have established a right to pity him ever afterwards; "that you may be in all respects very happy."

"Well, ma'am," returned Bounderby, with some resentment in his tone: which was clearly lowered, though in spite of himself, "I am obliged to you. I hope I shall be."

"*Do* you, sir!" said Mrs. Sparsit, with great affability. "But naturally you do; of course you do."

A very awkward pause on Mr. Bounderby's part, succeeded. Mrs. Sparsit sedately resumed her work, and occasionally gave a small cough, which sounded like the cough of conscious strength and forbearance.

"Well, ma'am," resumed Bounderby, "under these circumstances, I imagine it would not be agreeable to a character like yours to remain here, though you would be very welcome here?"

"Oh dear no, sir, I could on no account think of that!" Mrs. Sparsit shook her head, still in her highly superior manner, and a little

1. Gloves of lace or knitted work that cover the forearms and part of the hands but not the fingers.

changed the small cough—coughing now, as if the spirit of prophecy rose within her, but had better be coughed down.

"However, ma'am," said Bounderby, "there are apartments at the Bank, where a born and bred lady, as keeper of the place, would be rather a catch than otherwise; and if the same terms—"

"I beg your pardon, sir. You were so good as to promise that you would always substitute the phrase, annual compliment."

"Well, ma'am, annual compliment. If the same annual compliment would be acceptable there, why, I see nothing to part us unless you do."

"Sir," returned Mrs. Sparsit. "The proposal is like yourself, and if the position I should assume at the Bank is one that I could occupy without descending lower in the social scale—"

"Why, of course it is," said Bounderby. "If it was not, ma'am, you don't suppose that I should offer it to a lady who has moved in the society you have moved in. Not that I care for such society, you know! But *you* do."

"Mr. Bounderby, you are very considerate."

"You'll have your own private apartments, and you'll have your coals and your candles and all the rest of it, and you'll have your maid to attend upon you, and you'll have your light porter[2] to protect you, and you'll be what I take the liberty of considering precious comfortable," said Bounderby.

"Sir," rejoined Mrs. Sparsit, "say no more. In yielding up my trust here, I shall not be freed from the necessity of eating the bread of dependence:" she might have said the sweetbread,[3] for that delicate article in a savoury brown sauce was her favourite supper: "and I would rather receive it from your hand, than from any other. Therefore, sir, I accept your offer gratefully, and with many sincere acknowledgments for past favors. And I hope sir," said Mrs. Sparsit, concluding in an impressively compassionate manner, "I fondly hope that Miss Gradgrind may be all you desire, and deserve!"

Nothing moved Mrs. Sparsit from that position any more. It was in vain for Bounderby to bluster, or to assert himself in any of his explosive ways; Mrs. Sparsit was resolved to have compassion on him, as a Victim. She was polite, obliging, cheerful, hopeful; but, the more polite, the more obliging, the more cheerful, the more hopeful, the more exemplary altogether, she; the forlorner Sacrifice and Victim, he. She had that tenderness for his melancholy fate, that his great red countenance used to break out into cold perspirations when she looked at him.

2. One who carries light packages (here a bank messenger).
3. The thymus gland of a veal, when cooked, was considered a great delicacy. Its popularity is indicated by the many pages devoted to its preparation in Mrs. Beeton's classic Victorian cookbook, *Book of Household Management* (1861).

Meanwhile the marriage was appointed to be solemnised in eight weeks' time, and Mr. Bounderby went every evening to Stone Lodge as an accepted wooer. Love was made on these occasions in the form of bracelets; and, on all occasions during the period of betrothal, took a manufacturing aspect. Dresses were made, jewellery was made, cakes and gloves were made, settlements were made, and an extensive assortment of Facts did appropriate honour to the contract. The business was all Fact, from first to last. The Hours did not go through any of those rosy performances,[4] which foolish poets have ascribed to them at such times; neither did the clocks go any faster, or any slower, than at other seasons. The deadly-statistical recorder in the Gradgrind observatory knocked every second on the head as it was born, and buried it with his accustomed regularity.

So the day came, as all other days come to people who will only stick to reason; and when it came, there were married in the church of the florid wooden legs—that popular order of architecture—Josiah Bounderby Esquire of Coketown, to Louisa eldest daughter of Thomas Gradgrind Esquire of Stone Lodge, M.P. for that borough. And when they were united in holy matrimony, they went home to breakfast at Stone Lodge aforesaid.

There was an improving party assembled on the auspicious occasion, who knew what everything they had to eat and drink was made of, and how it was imported or exported, and in what quantities, and in what bottoms, whether native or foreign, and all about it. The bridesmaids, down to little Jane Gradgrind, were, in an intellectual point of view, fit helpmates for the calculating boy;[5] and there was no nonsense about any of the company.

After breakfast, the bridegroom addressed them in the following terms.

"Ladies and gentlemen, I am Josiah Bounderby of Coketown. Since you have done my wife and myself the honor of drinking our healths and happiness, I suppose I must acknowledge the same; though, as you all know me, and know what I am, and what my extraction was, you won't expect a speech from a man who, when he sees a Post, says 'that's a Post,' and when he sees a Pump, says 'that's a Pump,' and is not to be got to call a Post a Pump, or a Pump a Post, or either of them a Toothpick. If you want a speech this morning, my friend and father-in-law, Tom Gradgrind, is a Member of Parliament, and you know where to get it. I am not your man. However, if I feel a little independent when I look around this table to-day, and reflect how little I thought of marrying Tom Gradgrind's daughter when I was a

4. Romantic activities.
5. George Bidder (1806–1878), a boyhood prodigy whose remarkable feats of mental arithmetic were featured at public exhibitions. He was billed as "The Calculating Phenomenon" (noted by Guiliano and Collins in *The Annotated Dickens* [1987]).

ragged street-boy, who never washed his face unless it was at a pump, and that not oftener than once a fortnight, I hope I may be excused. So, I hope you like my feeling independent; if you don't, I can't help it. I *do* feel independent. Now, I have mentioned, and you have mentioned, that I am this day married to Tom Gradgrind's daughter. I am very glad to be so. It has long been my wish to be so. I have watched her bringing-up, and I believe she is worthy of me. At the same time—not to deceive you—I believe I am worthy of her. So, I thank you, on both our parts, for the good-will you have shown towards us; and the best wish I can give the unmarried part of the present company, is this: I hope every bachelor may find as good a wife as I have found. And I hope every spinster may find as good a husband as my wife has found."

Shortly after which oration, as they were going on a nuptial trip to Lyons,[6] in order that Mr. Bounderby might take the opportunity of seeing how the Hands got on in those parts, and whether they, too, required to be fed with gold spoons; the happy pair departed for the railroad. The bride, in passing down stairs, dressed for her journey, found Tom waiting for her—flushed, either with his feelings or the vinous part of the breakfast.

"What a game girl you are, to be such a first-rate sister, Loo!" whispered Tom.

She clung to him, as she should have clung to some far better nature that day, and was a little shaken in her reserved composure for the first time.

"Old Bounderby's quite ready," said Tom. "Time's up. Good-bye! I shall be on the look-out for you, when you come back. I say, my dear Loo! An't it uncommonly jolly now!"

END OF THE FIRST BOOK

Book the Second—Reaping[1]

Chapter I.

EFFECTS IN THE BANK.

A sunny midsummer day. There was such a thing sometimes, even in Coketown.

Seen from a distance in such weather, Coketown lay shrouded in a haze of its own, which appeared impervious to the sun's rays. You

6. Manufacturing city in east-central France, a center of the silk industry, whose industrial pollution Dickens had found ugly; consequently, it was an appropriate destination
for Bounderby's honeymoon.
1. See Galatians 6.7: "for whatsoever a man soweth, that shall he also reap."

only knew the town was there, because you knew there could have have been no such sulky blotch upon the prospect without a town. A blur of soot and smoke, now confusedly tending this way, now that way, now aspiring to the vault of Heaven, now murkily creeping along the earth, as the wind rose and fell, or changed its quarter: a dense formless jumble, with sheets of cross light in it, that showed nothing but masses of darkness:—Coketown in the distance was suggestive of itself, though not a brick of it could be seen.

The wonder was, it was there at all. It had been ruined so often, that it was amazing how it had borne so many shocks. Surely there never was such fragile china-ware as that of which the millers of Coketown were made. Handle them never so lightly, and they fell to pieces with such ease that you might suspect them of having been flawed before. They were ruined, when they were required to send labouring children to school; they were ruined, when inspectors were appointed to look into their works; they were ruined, when such inspectors considered it doubtful whether they were quite justified in chopping people up with their machinery; they were utterly undone, when it was hinted that perhaps they need not always make quite so much smoke. Besides Mr. Bounderby's gold spoon which was generally received in Coketown, another prevalent fiction was very popular there. It took the form of a threat. Whenever a Coketowner felt he was ill-used—that is to say, whenever he was not left entirely alone, and it was proposed to hold him accountable for the consequences of any of his acts—he was sure to come out with the awful menace, that he would "sooner pitch his property into the Atlantic." This had terrified the Home Secretary within an inch of his life, on several occasions.

However, the Coketowners were so patriotic after all, that they never had pitched their property into the Atlantic yet, but on the contrary, had been kind enough to take mighty good care of it. So there it was, in the haze yonder; and it increased and multiplied.[2]

The streets were hot and dusty on the summer day, and the sun was so bright that it even shone through the heavy vapour drooping over Coketown, and could not be looked at steadily. Stokers emerged from low underground doorways into factory yards, and sat on steps, and posts, and palings, wiping their swarthy visages, and contemplating coals. The whole town seemed to be frying in oil. There was a stifling smell of hot oil everywhere. The steamengines shone with it, the dresses of the Hands were soiled with it, the mills throughout their many stories oozed and trickled it. The atmosphere of those Fairy palaces was like the breath of the

---

2. Evocative of Genesis 9.1: "And God blessed Noah and his sons, and said unto them, Be fruitful and multiply, and replenish the earth."

simoom,[3] and their inhabitants, wasting with heat, toiled languidly in the desert. But no temperature made the melancholy mad elephants more mad or more sane. Their wearisome heads went up and down at the same rate, in hot weather and cold, wet weather and dry, fair weather and foul. The measured motion of their shadows on the walls, was the substitute Coketown had to show for the shadows of rustling woods; while, for the summer hum of insects, it could offer, all the year round, from the dawn of Monday to the night of Saturday, the whirr of shafts and wheels.

Drowsily they whirred all through this sunny day, making the passenger more sleepy and more hot as he passed the humming walls of the mills. Sun-blinds, and sprinklings of water, a little cooled the main streets and the shops; but the mills, and the courts and alleys, baked at a fierce heat. Down upon the river that was black and thick with dye, some Coketown boys who were at large—a rare sight there—rowed a crazy boat; which made a spumous[4] track upon the water as it jogged along, while every dip of an oar stirred up vile smells. But the sun itself, however beneficent generally, was less kind to Coketown than hard frost, and rarely looked intently into any of its closer regions without engendering more death than life. So does the eye of Heaven itself become an evil eye, when incapable or sordid hands are interposed between it and the things it looks upon to bless.

Mrs. Sparsit sat in her afternoon apartment at the Bank, on the shadier side of the frying street. Office-hours were over: and at that period of the day, in warm weather, she usually embellished with her genteel presence, a managerial board-room over the public office. Her own private sitting-room was a story higher, at the window of which post of observation she was ready, every morning, to greet Mr. Bounderby as he came across the road, with the sympathising recognition appropriate to a Victim. He had been married now, a year; and Mrs. Sparsit had never released him from her determined pity a moment.

The Bank offered no violence to the wholesome monotony of the town. It was another red brick house, with black outside shutters, green inside blinds, a black street-door up two white steps, a brazen door-plate, and a brazen door-handle full stop. It was a size larger than Mr. Bounderby's house, as other houses were from a size to half-a-dozen sizes smaller; in all other particulars, it was strictly according to pattern.

Mrs. Sparsit was conscious that by coming in the evening-tide among the desks and writing implements, she shed a feminine, not

3. A hot, powerful, sand-laden wind of the Sahara and Arabian deserts.
4. Foamy or frothy.

to say also aristocratic, grace upon the office. Seated, with her needlework or netting apparatus, at the window, she had a self-laudatory
sense of correcting, by her ladylike deportment, the rude business
aspect of the place. With this impression of her interesting character upon her, Mrs. Sparsit considered herself, in some sort, the
Bank Fairy. The townspeople who, in their passing and repassing,
saw her there, regarded her as the Bank Dragon, keeping watch over
the treasures of the mine.

What those treasures were, Mrs. Sparsit knew as little as they
did. Gold and silver coin, precious paper, secrets that if divulged
would bring vague destruction upon vague persons (generally, however, people whom she disliked), were the chief items in her ideal
catalogue thereof. For the rest, she knew that after office-hours, she
reigned supreme over all the office furniture, and over a locked-up
iron room with three locks, against the door of which strong chamber the light porter laid his head every night, on a truckle bed,[5] that
disappeared at cockcrow. Further, she was lady paramount over
certain vaults in the basement, sharply spiked off from communication with the predatory world; and over the relics of the current
day's work, consisting of blots of ink, worn-out pens, fragments of
wafers, and scraps of paper torn so small, that nothing interesting
could ever be deciphered on them when Mrs. Sparsit tried. Lastly,
she was guardian over a little armoury of cutlasses and carbines,
arrayed in vengeful order above one of the official chimney-pieces;
and over that respectable tradition never to be separated from a
place of business claiming to be wealthy—a row of fire-buckets—
vessels calculated to be of no physical utility on any occasion, but
observed to exercise a fine moral influence, almost equal to bullion,
on most beholders.

A deaf serving-woman and the light porter completed Mrs. Sparsit's
empire. The deaf serving-woman was rumoured to be wealthy; and
a saying had for years gone about among the lower orders of Coketown, that she would be murdered some night when the Bank was
shut, for the sake of her money. It was generally considered, indeed,
that she had been due some time, and ought to have fallen long ago;
but she had kept her life, and her situation, with an ill-conditioned
tenacity that occasioned much offence and disappointment.

Mrs. Sparsit's tea was just set for her on a pert little table, with
its tripod of legs in an attitude, which she insinuated after office-
hours, into the company of the stern, leathern-topped, long board-
table that bestrode the middle of the room. The light porter placed
the tea-tray on it, knuckling his forehead as a form of homage.

5. Also known as a trundle bed; A low bed on casters or corded grooved wheels usually
   stored when not in use under a bed of regular height.

"Thank you, Bitzer," said Mrs. Sparsit.

"Thank *you*, ma'am," returned the light porter. He was a very light porter indeed; as light as in the days when he blinkingly defined a horse, for girl number twenty.

"All is shut up, Bitzer?" said Mrs. Sparsit.

"All is shut up, ma'am."

"And what," said Mrs. Sparsit, pouring out her tea, "is the news of the day? Anything?"

"Well, ma'am, I can't say that I have heard anything particular. Our people are a bad lot, ma'am; but that is no news, unfortunately."

"What are the restless wretches doing now?" asked Mrs. Sparsit.

"Merely going on in the old way, ma'am. Uniting, and leaguing, and engaging to stand by one another."

"It is much to be regretted," said Mrs. Sparsit, making her nose more Roman and her eyebrows more Coriolanian in the strength of her severity, "that the united masters allow of any such class-combinations."[6]

"Yes, ma'am," said Bitzer.

"Being united themselves, they ought one and all to set their faces against employing any man who is united with any other man," said Mrs. Sparsit.

"They have done that, ma'am," returned Bitzer; "but it rather fell through, ma'am."

"I do not pretend to understand these things," said Mrs. Sparsit, with dignity, "my lot having been originally cast in a widely different sphere; and Mr. Sparsit, as a Powler, being also quite out of the pale of any such dissensions. I only know that these people must be conquered, and that it's high time it was done, once for all."

"Yes, ma'am," returned Bitzer, with a demonstration of great respect for Mrs. Sparsit's oracular authority. "You couldn't put it clearer, I am sure, ma'am."

As this was his usual hour for having a little confidential chat with Mrs. Sparsit, and as he had already caught her eye and seen that she was going to ask him something, he made a pretence of arranging the rulers, inkstands, and so forth, while that lady went on with her tea, glancing through the open window down into the street.

"Has it been a busy day, Bitzer?" asked Mrs. Sparsit.

"Not a very busy day, my lady. About an average day." He now and then slided into my lady, instead of ma'am, as an involuntary acknowledgment of Mrs. Sparsit's personal dignity and claims to reverence.

6. An organization or union of workers was referred to as a "combination." Unions were permissible but legally constrained in what representations they could make to employers by the Combination of Workmen Act of 1825.

"The clerks," said Mrs. Sparsit, carefully brushing an imperceptible crumb of bread and butter from her left-hand mitten, "are trustworthy, punctual, and industrious, of course?"

"Yes, ma'am, pretty fair, ma'am. With the usual exception."

He held the respectable office of general spy and informer in the establishment, for which volunteer service he received a present at Christmas, over and above his weekly wage. He had grown into an extremely clear-headed, cautious, prudent young man, who was safe to rise in the world. His mind was so exactly regulated, that he had no affections or passions. All his proceedings were the result of the nicest and coldest calculation; and it was not without cause that Mrs. Sparsit habitually observed of him, that he was a young man of the steadiest principle she had ever known. Having satisfied himself, on his father's death, that his mother had a right of settlement in Coketown, this excellent young economist had asserted that right for her with such a steadfast adherence to the principle of the case, that she had been shut up in the workhouse[7] ever since. It must be admitted that he allowed her half a pound of tea a year, which was weak in him: first, because all gifts have an inevitable tendency to pauperise the recipient, and secondly, because his only reasonable transaction in that commodity would have been to buy it for as little as he could possibly give, and sell it for as much as he could possibly get; it having been clearly ascertained by philosophers that in this is comprised the whole duty of man[8]—not a part of man's duty, but the whole.

"Pretty fair, ma'am. With the usual exception, ma'am," repeated Bitzer.

"Ah—h!" said Mrs. Sparsit, shaking her head over her tea-cup, and taking a long gulp.

"Mr. Thomas, ma'am, I doubt Mr. Thomas very much, ma'am, I don't like his ways at all."

"Bitzer," said Mrs. Sparsit, in a very impressive manner, "do you recollect my having said anything to you respecting names?"

"I beg your pardon, ma'am. It's quite true that you did object to names being used, and they're always best avoided."

"Please to remember that I have a charge here," said Mrs. Sparsit, with her air of state. "I hold a trust here, Bitzer, under Mr. Bound-

---

7. The Poor Law Amendment Act of 1834 divided England and Wales into twenty-four districts, each responsible for creating large institutional homes called "workhouses" (which were not places of work) for the indigent poor of all ages and states of health. The intent was to discourage the poor from living in the workhouses by providing a standard of living lower than what the poorest worker outside the workhouse might achieve.

8. *The Whole Duty of Man,* by the Royalist clergyman Richard Allestree, was at one time an exceptionally popular religious treatise. During the forty years after its first publication in 1638, it went through thirty-six editions.

erby. However improbable both Mr. Bounderby and myself might have deemed it years ago, that he would ever become my patron, making me an annual compliment, I cannot but regard him in that light. From Mr. Bounderby I have received every acknowledgment of my social station, and every recognition of my family descent, that I could possibly expect. More, far more. Therefore, to my patron I will be scrupulously true. And I do not consider, I will not consider, I cannot consider," said Mrs. Sparsit, with a most extensive stock on hand of honor and morality, "that I *should* be scrupulously true, if I allowed names to be mentioned under this roof, that are unfortunately—most unfortunately—no doubt of that—connected with his."

Bitzer knuckled his forehead again, and again begged pardon.

"No, Bitzer," continued Mrs. Sparsit, "say an individual, and I will hear you; say Mr. Thomas, and you must excuse me."

"With the usual exception, ma'am," said Bitzer, trying back, "of an individual."

"Ah—h!" Mrs. Sparsit repeated the ejaculation, the shake of the head over her tea-cup, and the long gulp, as taking up the conversation again at the point where it had been interrupted.

"An individual, ma'am," said Bitzer, "has never been what he ought to have been, since he first came into the place. He is a dissipated, extravagant idler. He is not worth his salt, ma'am. He wouldn't get it either, if he hadn't a friend and relation at court, ma'am!"

"Ah—h!" said Mrs. Sparsit, with another melancholy shake of her head.

"I only hope, ma'am," pursued Bitzer, "that his friend and relation may not supply him with the means of carrying on. Otherwise, ma'am, we know out of whose pocket *that* money comes."

"Ah—h!" sighed Mrs. Sparsit again, with another melancholy shake of her head.

"He is to be pitied, ma'am. The last party I have alluded to, is to be pitied, ma'am," said Bitzer.

"Yes, Bitzer," said Mrs. Sparsit. "I have always pitied the delusion, always."

"As to an individual, ma'am," said Bitzer, dropping his voice and drawing nearer, "he is as improvident as any of the people in this town. And you know what *their* improvidence is, ma'am. No one could wish to know it better than a lady of your eminence does."

"They would do well," returned Mrs. Sparsit, "to take example by you, Bitzer."

"Thank you, ma'am. But, since you do refer to me, now look at me, ma'am. I have put by a little, ma'am, already. That gratuity which I receive at Christmas, ma'am: I never touch it. I don't even go the length of my wages, though they're not high, ma'am. Why can't they do as I have done, ma'am? What one person can do, another can do."

This, again, was among the fictions of Coketown. Any capitalist there, who had made sixty thousand pounds out of sixpence, always professed to wonder why the sixty thousand nearest Hands didn't each make sixty thousand pounds out of sixpence, and more or less reproached them every one for not accomplishing the little feat. What I did you can do. Why don't you go and do it?

"As to their wanting recreations, ma'am," said Bitzer, "it's stuff and nonsense. *I* don't want recreations. I never did, and I never shall; I don't like 'em. As to their combining together; there are many of them, I have no doubt, that by watching and informing upon one another could earn a trifle now and then, whether in money or good will, and improve their livelihood. Then, why don't they improve it, ma'am? It's the first consideration of a rational creature, and it's what they pretend to want."

"Pretend indeed!" said Mrs. Sparsit.

"I am sure we are constantly hearing ma'am, till it becomes quite nauseous, concerning their wives and families," said Bitzer. "Why look at me, ma'am! *I* don't want a wife and family. Why should they?"

"Because they are improvident," said Mrs. Sparsit.

"Yes, ma'am," returned Bitzer, "that's where it is. If they were more provident, and less perverse, ma'am, what would they do? They would say, 'While my hat covers my family,' or, 'while my bonnet covers my family'—as the case might be, ma'am—'I have only one to feed, and that's the person I most like to feed.'"

"To be sure," assented Mrs. Sparsit, eating muffin.

"Thank you, ma'am," said Bitzer, knuckling his forehead again, in return for the favor of Mrs. Sparsit's improving conversation. "Would you wish a little more hot water, ma'am, or is there anything else that I could fetch you?"

"Nothing just now, Bitzer."

"Thank you, ma'am. I shouldn't wish to disturb you at your meals, ma'am, particularly tea, knowing your partiality for it," said Bitzer, craning a little to look over into the street from where he stood; "but there's a gentleman been looking up here for a minute or so, ma'am, and he has come across as if he was going to knock. That *is* his knock, ma'am, no doubt."

He stepped to the window; and looking out, and drawing in his head again, confirmed himself with, "Yes, ma'am. Would you wish the gentleman to be shown in, ma'am?"

"I don't know who it can be," said Mrs. Sparsit, wiping her mouth and arranging her mittens.

"A stranger, ma'am, evidently."

"What a stranger can want at the Bank at this time of the evening, unless he comes upon some business for which he is too late, I don't know," said Mrs. Sparsit; "but I hold a charge in this establishment from Mr. Bounderby, and I will never shrink from it. If to see him is any part of the duty I have accepted, I will see him. Use your own discretion, Bitzer."

Here the visitor, all unconscious of Mrs. Sparsit's magnanimous words, repeated his knock so loudly that the light porter hastened down to open the door; while Mrs. Sparsit took the precaution of concealing her little table, with all its appliances upon it, in a cupboard, and then decamped up stairs that she might appear, if needful, with the greater dignity.

"If you please, ma'am, the gentleman would wish to see you," said Bitzer, with his light eye at Mrs. Sparsit's key-hole. So, Mrs. Sparsit, who had improved the interval by touching up her cap, took her classical features down stairs again, and entered the board-room in the manner of a Roman matron[9] going outside the city walls to treat with an invading general.

The visitor having strolled to the window, and being then engaged in looking carelessly out, was as unmoved by this impressive entry as man could possibly be. He stood whistling to himself with all imaginable coolness, with his hat still on, and a certain air of exhaustion upon him, in part arising from excessive summer, and in part from excessive gentility. For, it was to be seen with half an eye that he was a thorough gentleman, made to the model of the time; weary of everything, and putting no more faith in anything than Lucifer.

"I believe, sir," quoth Mrs. Sparsit, "you wished to see me."

"I beg your pardon," he said, turning and removing his hat; "pray excuse me."

"Humph!" thought Mrs. Sparsit, as she made a stately bend. "Five and thirty, good-looking, good figure, good teeth, good voice, good breeding, well-dressed, dark hair, bold eyes." All which Mrs. Sparsit observed in her womanly way—like the Sultan who put his head in the pail of water[1]—merely in dipping down and coming up again.

"Please to be seated, sir," said Mrs. Sparsit.

"Thank you. Allow me." He placed a chair for her, but remained himself carelessly lounging against the table. "I left my servant at the railway looking after the luggage—very heavy train and vast quantity of it in the van—and strolled on, looking about me. Exceedingly odd place. Will you allow me to ask you if it's *always* as black as this?"

"In general much blacker," returned Mrs. Sparsit, in her uncompromising way.

"Is it possible! Excuse me: you are not a native, I think?"

"No, sir," returned Mrs. Sparsit. "It was once my good or ill fortune, as it may be—before I became a widow—to move in a very different sphere. My husband was a Powler."

"Beg your pardon, really!" said the stranger. "Was—?"

Mrs. Sparsit repeated, "A Powler."

"Powler Family," said the stranger, after reflecting a few moments. Mrs. Sparsit signified assent. The stranger seemed a little more fatigued than before.

"You must be very much bored here?" was the inference he drew from the communication.

"I am the servant of circumstances, sir," said Mrs. Sparsit, "and I have long adapted myself to the governing power of my life."

"Very philosophical," returned the stranger, "and very exemplary and laudable, and—" It seemed to be scarcely worth his while to finish the sentence, so he played with his watch-chain wearily.

"May I be permitted to ask, sir," said Mrs. Sparsit, "to what I am indebted for the favor of—"

"Assuredly," said the stranger. "Much obliged to you for reminding me. I am the bearer of a letter of introduction to Mr. Bounderby the banker. Walking through this extraordinarily black town, while they were getting dinner ready at the hotel, I asked a fellow whom I met; one of the working people; who appeared to have been taking a shower-bath of something fluffy,[2] which I assume to be the raw material;—"

Mrs. Sparsit inclined her head.

"—Raw material—where Mr. Bounderby the banker, might reside. Upon which, misled no doubt by the word Banker, he directed me to the Bank. Fact being, I presume, that Mr. Bounderby the Banker, does *not* reside in the edifice in which I have the honour of offering this explanation?"

"No, sir," returned Mrs. Sparsit, "he does not."

"Thank you. I had no intention of delivering my letter at the present moment, nor have I. But, strolling on to the Bank to kill time, and having the good fortune to observe at the window," towards which he languidly waved his hand, then slightly bowed, "a lady of a very superior and agreeable appearance, I considered that I could not do better than take the liberty of asking that lady where

---

2. Fluff produced in the process of manufacturing cotton cloth from raw cotton.

Mr. Bounderby the Banker, *does* live. Which I accordingly venture, with all suitable apologies, to do."

The inattention and indolence of his manner were sufficiently relieved, to Mrs. Sparsit's thinking, by a certain gallantry at ease, which offered her homage too. Here he was, for instance, at this moment, all but sitting on the table, and yet lazily bending over her, as if he acknowledged an attraction in her that made her charming— in her way.

"Banks, I know, are always suspicious, and officially must be," said the stranger, whose lightness and smoothness of speech were pleasant likewise; suggesting matter far more sensible and humorous than it ever contained—which was perhaps a shrewd device of the founder of this numerous sect, whosoever may have been that great man; "therefore I may observe that my letter—here it is—is from the member for this place—Gradgrind—whom I have had the pleasure of knowing in London."

Mrs. Sparsit recognised the hand, intimated that such confirmation was quite unneccessary, and gave Mr. Bounderby's address, with all needful clues and directions in aid.

"Thousand thanks," said the stranger. "Of course you know the Banker well?"

"Yes, sir," rejoined Mrs. Sparsit. "In my dependent relation towards him, I have known him ten years."

"Quite an eternity! I think he married Gradgrind's daughter?"

"Yes," said Mrs. Sparsit, suddenly compressing her mouth. "He had that—honor."

"The lady is quite a philosopher, I am told?"

"Indeed, sir," said Mrs. Sparsit. "*Is* she?"

"Excuse my impertinent curiosity," pursued the stranger, fluttering over Mrs. Sparsit's eyebrows, with a propitiatory air, "but you know the family, and know the world. I am about to know the family, and may have much to do with them. Is the lady so very alarming? Her father gives her such a portentously hard-headed reputation, that I have a burning desire to know. Is she absolutely unapproachable? Repellently and stunningly clever? I see, by your meaning smile, you think not. You have poured balm into my anxious soul. As to age, now. Forty! Five and thirty?"

Mrs. Sparsit laughed outright. "A chit," said she. "Not twenty when she was married."

"I give you my honor, Mrs. Powler," returned the stranger, detaching himself from the table, "that I never was so astonished in my life!"

It really did seem to impress him, to the utmost extent of his capacity of being impressed. He looked at his informant for full a quarter of a minute, and appeared to have the surprise in his mind all the time. "I assure you, Mrs. Powler," he then said, much exhausted, "that the father's manner prepared me for a grim and stony maturity.

I am obliged to you, of all things, for correcting so absurd a mistake. Pray excuse my intrusion. Many thanks. Good day!"

He bowed himself out; and Mrs. Sparsit, hiding in the window-curtain, saw him languishing down the street on the shady side of the way, observed of all the town.

"What do you think of the gentleman, Bitzer?" she asked the light porter, when he came to take away.

"Spends a deal of money on his dress, ma'am."

"It must be admitted," said Mrs. Sparsit, "that it's very tasteful."

"Yes, ma'am," returned Bitzer, "if that's worth the money."

"Besides which, ma'am," resumed Bitzer, while he was polishing the table, "he looks to me as if he gamed."

"It's immoral to game," said Mrs. Sparsit.

"It's ridiculous, ma'am," said Bitzer, "because the chances are against the players."

Whether it was that the heat prevented Mrs. Sparsit from work-ing, or whether it was that her hand was out, she did no work that night. She sat at the window, when the sun began to sink behind the smoke; she sat there when the smoke was burning red, when the color faded from it, when darkness seemed to rise slowly out of the ground, and creep upward, upward, up to the house-tops, up the church steeple, up to the summits of the factory chimneys, up to the sky. Without a candle in the room, Mrs. Sparsit sat at the window, with her hands before her, not thinking much of the sounds of eve-ning: the whooping of boys, the barking of dogs, the rumbling of wheels, the steps and voices of passengers, the shrill street cries, the clogs upon the pavement when it was their hour for going by, the shutting-up of shop-shutters. Not until the light porter announced that her nocturnal sweetbread was ready, did Mrs. Sparsit arouse herself from her reverie, and convey her dense black eye-brows—by that time creased with meditation, as if they needed ironing out—up stairs.

"O, you Fool!" said Mrs. Sparsit, when she was alone at her sup-per. Whom she meant, she did not say; but she could scarcely have meant the sweetbread.

Chapter II.

MR. JAMES HARTHOUSE.

The Gradgrind party wanted assistance in cutting the throats of the Graces.[1] They went about recruiting; and where could they enlist recruits more hopefully, than among the fine gentlemen who, having

---

1. Three Greek goddesses associated with the pleasures of art and the general enjoyment of life.

found out everything to be worth nothing, were equally ready for anything?

Moreover, the healthy spirits who had mounted to this sublime height were attractive to many of the Gradgrind school. They liked fine gentlemen; they pretended that they did not, but they did. They became exhausted in imitation of them; and they yaw-yawed in their speech like them; and they served out, with an enervated air, the little mouldy rations of political economy, on which they regaled their disciples. There never before was seen on earth such a wonderful hybrid race as was thus produced.

Among the fine gentlemen not regularly belonging to the Gradgrind school, there was one of a good family and a better appearance, with a happy turn of humour which had told immensely with the House of Commons on the occasion of his entertaining it with his (and the Board of Directors') view of a railway accident, in which the most careful officers ever known, employed by the most liberal managers ever heard of, assisted by the finest mechanical contrivances ever devised, the whole in action on the best line ever constructed, had killed five people and wounded thirty-two, by a casualty without which the excellence of the whole system would have been positively incomplete. Among the slain was a cow, and among the scattered articles unowned, a widow's cap. And the honourable member had so tickled the House (which has a delicate sense of humour) by putting the cap on the cow, that it became impatient of any serious reference to the Coroner's Inquest, and brought the railway off with Cheers and Laughter.

Now, this gentleman had a younger brother of still better appearance than himself, who had tried life as a Cornet of Dragoons,[2] and found it a bore; and had afterwards tried it in the train of an English minister abroad, and found it a bore; and had then strolled to Jerusalem, and got bored there; and had then gone yachting about the world, and got bored everywhere. To whom this honorable and jocular member fraternally said one day, "Jem, there's a good opening among the hard Fact fellows, and they want men: I wonder you don't go in for statistics." Jem, rather taken by the novelty of the idea, and very hard up for a change, was as ready to "go in" for statistics as for anything else. So, he went in. He coached himself up with a blue book or two;[3] and his brother put it about among the hard Fact fellows, and said, "If you want to bring in, for any place, a handsome dog who can make you a devilish good speech, look after my brother Jem, for he's your man." After a few dashes in the public meeting way, Mr. Gradgrind and a council of political sages approved of

2. A cavalry officer.
3. He studied blue-bound books of statistics.

Jem, and it was resolved to send him down to Coketown, to become known there and in the neighbourhood. Hence the letter Jem had last night shown to Mrs. Sparsit, which Mr. Bounderby now held in his hand; superscribed, "Josiah Bounderby, Esquire, Banker, Coketown. Specially to introduce James Harthouse, Esquire. Thomas Gradgrind."

Within an hour of the receipt of this dispatch and Mr. James Harthouse's card, Mr. Bounderby put on his hat and went down to the Hotel. There he found Mr. James Harthouse looking out of window, in a state of mind so disconsolate, that he was already half disposed to "go in" for something else.

"My name, sir," said his visitor, "is Josiah Bounderby of Coketown."

Mr. James Harthouse was very happy indeed (though he scarcely looked so), to have a pleasure he had long expected.

"Coketown, sir," said Bounderby, obstinately taking a chair, "is not the kind of place you have been accustomed to. Therefore, if you'll allow me—or whether you will or not, for I am a plain man—I'll tell you something about it before we go any further."

Mr. Harthouse would be charmed.

"Don't be too sure of that," said Bounderby. "I don't promise it. First of all, you see our smoke. That's meat and drink to us. It's the healthiest thing in the world in all respects, and particularly for the lungs. If you are one of those who want us to consume it, I differ from you. We are not going to wear the bottoms of our boilers out any faster than we wear 'em out now, for all the humbugging sentiment in Great Britain and Ireland."

By way of "going in" to the fullest extent, Mr. Harthouse rejoined, "Mr. Bounderby, I assure you I am entirely and completely of your way of thinking. On conviction."

"I am glad to hear it," said Bounderby. "Now, you have heard a lot of talk about the work in our mills, no doubt. You have? Very good. I'll state the fact of it to you. It's the pleasantest work there is, and it's the lightest work there is, and it's the best paid work there is. More than that, we couldn't improve the mills themselves, unless we laid down Turkey carpets on the floors. Which we're not a-going to do."

"Mr. Bounderby, perfectly right."

"Lastly," said Bounderby, "as to our Hands. There's not a Hand in this town, sir, man, woman, or child, but has one ultimate object in life. That object is, to be fed on turtle soup and venison with a gold spoon. Now, they're not a-going—none of 'em—ever to be fed on turtle soup and venison with a gold spoon. And now you know the place."

Mr. Harthouse professed himself in the highest degree instructed and refreshed, by this condensed epitome of the whole Coketown question.

"Why, you see," replied Mr. Bounderby, "it suits my disposition to have a full understanding with a man, particularly with a public man, when I make his acquaintance. I have only one thing more to say to you, Mr. Harthouse, before assuring you of the pleasure with which I shall respond, to the utmost of my poor ability, to my friend Tom Gradgrind's letter of introduction. You are a man of family. Don't you deceive yourself by supposing for a moment that *I* am a man of family. I am a bit of dirty riff-raff, and a genuine scrap of tag, rag, and bobtail."

If anything could have exalted Jem's interest in Mr. Bounderby, it would have been this very circumstance. Or, so he told him.

"So now," said Bounderby, "we may shake hands on equal terms. I say, equal terms, because although I know what I am, and the exact depth of the gutter I have lifted myself out of, better than any man does, I am as proud as you are. I am just as proud as you are. Having now asserted my independence in a proper manner, I may come to how do you find yourself, and I hope you're pretty well."

The better, Mr. Harthouse gave him to understand as they shook hands, for the salubrious air of Coketown. Mr. Bounderby received the answer with favor.

"Perhaps you know," said he, "or perhaps you don't know, I married Tom Gradgrind's daughter. If you have nothing better to do than to walk up town with me, I shall be glad to introduce you to Tom Gradgrind's daughter."

"Mr. Bounderby," said Jem, "you anticipate my dearest wishes."

They went out without further discourse; and Mr. Bounderby piloted the new acquaintance who so strongly contrasted with him, to the private red brick dwelling, with the black outside shutters, the green inside blinds, and the black street door up the two white steps. In the drawing-room of which mansion, there presently entered to them the most remarkable girl Mr. James Harthouse had ever seen. She was so constrained, and yet so careless; so reserved, and yet so watchful; so cold and proud, and yet so sensitively ashamed of her husband's braggart humility—from which she shrunk as if every example of it were a cut or a blow; that it was quite a new sensation to observe her. In face she was no less remarkable than in manner. Her features were handsome; but their natural play was so locked up, that it seemed impossible to guess at their genuine expression. Utterly indifferent, perfectly self-reliant, never at a loss, and yet never at her ease, with her figure in company with them there, and her mind apparently quite alone—it was of no use "going in" yet awhile to comprehend this girl, for she baffled all penetration.

From the mistress of the house, the visitor glanced to the house itself. There was no mute sign of a woman in the room. No graceful

little adornment, no fanciful little device, however trivial, anywhere
expressed her influence. Cheerless and comfortless, boastfully and
doggedly rich, there the room stared at its present occupants, unsoft-
ened and unrelieved by the least trace of any womanly occupation. As Mr. Bounderby stood in the midst of his household gods,
so those unrelenting divinities occupied their places around
Mr. Bounderby, and they were worthy of one another, and well
matched.

"This, sir," said Bounderby, "is my wife, Mrs. Bounderby: Tom
Gradgrind's eldest daughter. Loo, Mr. James Harthouse. Mr. Harthouse has joined your father's muster-roll. If he is not Tom
Gradgrind's colleague before long, I believe we shall at least hear of
him in connexion with one of our neighbouring towns. You observe,
Mr. Harthouse, that my wife is my junior. I don't know what she
saw in me to marry me, but she saw something in me, I suppose, or
she wouldn't have married me. She has lots of expensive knowledge, sir, political and otherwise. If you want to cram for anything,
I should be troubled to recommend you to a better adviser than Loo
Bounderby."

To a more agreeable adviser, or one from whom he would be
more likely to learn, Mr. Harthouse could never be recommended.

"Come!" said his host. "If you're in the complimentary line, you'll
get on here, for you'll meet with no competition. I have never been
in the way of learning compliments myself, and I don't profess to
understand the art of paying 'em. In fact, despise 'em. But, your
bringing-up was different from mine; mine was a real thing, by
George! You're a gentleman, and I don't pretend to be one. I am
Josiah Bounderby of Coketown, and that's enough for me. However,
though *I* am not influenced by manners and station, Loo Bounderby
may be. She hadn't my advantages—disadvantages you would call
'em, but I call 'em advantages—so you'll not waste your power, I
dare say."

"Mr. Bounderby," said Jem, turning with a smile to Louisa, "is a
noble animal in a comparatively natural state, quite free from the
harness in which a conventional hack like myself works."

"You respect Mr. Bounderby very much," she quietly returned. "It
is natural that you should."

He was disgracefully thrown out, for a gentleman who had seen
so much of the world, and thought, "Now, how am I to take this?"

"You are going to devote yourself, as I gather from what Mr. Bounderby has said, to the service of your country. You have made up your
mind," said Louisa, still standing before him where she had first
stopped—in all the singular contrariety of her self-possession, and
her being obviously very ill at ease—"to show the nation the way
out of all its difficulties."

"Mrs. Bounderby," he returned, laughing, "upon my honor, no. I will make no such pretence to you. I have seen a little, here and there, up and down; I have found it all to be very worthless, as everybody has, and as some confess they have, and some do not; and I am going in for your respected father's opinions—really because I have no choice of opinions, and may as well back them as anything else."

"Have you none of your own?" asked Louisa.

"I have not so much as the slightest predilection left. I assure you I attach not the least importance to any opinions. The result of the varieties of boredom I have undergone, is a conviction (unless conviction is too industrious a word for the lazy sentiment I entertain on the subject), that any set of ideas will do just as much good as any other set, and just as much harm as any other set. There's an English family with a charming Italian motto. What will be, will be.[4] It's the only truth going!"

This vicious assumption of honesty in dishonesty—a vice so dangerous, so deadly, and so common—seemed, he observed, a little to impress her in his favor. He followed up the advantage, by saying in his pleasantest manner: a manner to which she might attach as much or as little meaning as she pleased: "The side that can prove anything in a line of units, tens, hundreds, and thousands, Mrs. Bounderby, seems to me to afford the most fun, and to give a man the best chance. I am quite as much attached to it as if I believed it. I am quite ready to go in for it, to the same extent as if I believed it. And what more could I possibly do, if I did believe it!"

"You are a singular politician," said Louisa.

"Pardon me; I have not even that merit. We are the largest party in the state, I assure you, Mrs. Bounderby, if we all fell out of our adopted ranks and were reviewed together."

Mr. Bounderby, who had been in danger of bursting in silence, interposed here with a project for postponing the family dinner till half-past six, and taking Mr. James Harthouse in the meantime on a round of visits to the voting and interesting notabilities of Coketown and its vicinity. The round of visits was made; and Mr. James Harthouse, with a discreet use of his blue coaching, came off triumphantly, though with a considerable accession of boredom.

In the evening, he found the dinner-table laid for four, but they sat down only three. It was an appropriate occasion for Mr. Bounderby to discuss the flavour of the hap'orth of stewed eels he had purchased in the streets at eight years old; and also of the inferior water, specially used for laying the dust, with which he had washed down that repast. He likewise entertained his guest, over the soup

---

4. *Che sarà, sarà* was the "charming Italian motto" of the family of Lord John Russell, who was prime minister of England (1846–52 and 1865–66).

and fish, with the calculation that he (Bounderby) had eaten in his youth at least three horses under the guise of polonies and saveloys.[5] These recitals, Jem, in a languid manner, received with "charming!" every now and then; and they probably would have decided him to "go in" for Jerusalem again tomorrow morning, had he been less curious respecting Louisa.

"Is there nothing," he thought, glancing at her as she sat at the head of the table, where her youthful figure, small and slight, but very graceful, looked as pretty as it looked misplaced; "is there nothing that will move that face?"

Yes! By Jupiter, there was something, and here it was, in an unexpected shape! Tom appeared. She changed as the door opened, and broke into a beaming smile.

A beautiful smile. Mr. James Harthouse might not have thought so much of it, but that he had wondered so long at her impassive face. She put out her hand—a pretty little soft hand; and her fingers closed upon her brother's, as if she would have carried them to her lips.

"Ay, ay?" thought the visitor. "This whelp[6] is the only creature she cares for. So, so!"

The whelp was presented, and took his chair. The appellation was not flattering, but not unmerited.

"When I was your age, young Tom," said Bounderby, "I was punctual, or I got no dinner!"

"When you were my age," returned Tom, "you hadn't a wrong balance to get right, and hadn't to dress afterwards."

"Never mind that now," said Bounderby.

"Well, then," grumbled Tom. "Don't begin with me."

"Mrs. Bounderby," said Harthouse, perfectly hearing this understrain as it went on; "your brother's face is quite familiar to me. Can I have seen him abroad? Or at some public school,[7] perhaps?"

"No," she returned, quite interested, "he has never been abroad yet, and was educated here, at home. Tom, love, I am telling Mr. Harthouse that he never saw you abroad."

"No such luck, sir," said Tom.

There was little enough in him to brighten her face, for he was a sullen young fellow, and ungracious in his manner even to her. So much the greater must have been the solitude of her heart, and her need of some one on whom to bestow it. "So much the more is this whelp the only creature she has ever cared for," thought Mr. James Harthouse, turning it over and over. "So much the more. So much the more."

5. Kinds of highly flavored sausages.
6. As defined by *OED*, a whelp is "a saucy, or impertinent young fellow, a puppy."
7. In Great Britain, an endowed boarding school traditionally for the upper class.

Both in his sister's presence, and after she had left the room, the whelp took no pains to hide his contempt for Mr. Bounderby, whenever he could indulge it without the observation of that independent man, by making wry faces, or shutting one eye. Without responding to these telegraphic communications, Mr. Harthouse encouraged him much in the course of the evening, and showed an unusual liking for him. At last, when he rose to return to his hotel, and was a little doubtful whether he knew the way by night, the whelp immediately proffered his services as guide, and turned out with him to escort him thither.

Chapter III.

THE WHELP.

It was very remarkable that a young gentleman who had been brought up under one continuous system of unnatural restraint, should be a hypocrite; but it was certainly the case with Tom. It was very strange that a young gentleman who had never been left to his own guidance for five consecutive minutes, should be incapable at last of governing himself; but so it was with Tom. It was altogether unaccountable that a young gentleman whose imagination had been strangled in his cradle, should be still inconvenienced by its ghost in the form of grovelling sensualities; but such a monster, beyond all doubt, was Tom.

"Do you smoke?" asked Mr. James Harthouse, when they came to the hotel.

"I believe you!" said Tom.

He could do no less than ask Tom up; and Tom could do no less than go up. What with a cooling drink adapted to the weather, but not so weak as cool; and what with a rarer tobacco than was to be bought in those parts; Tom was soon in a highly free and easy state at his end of the sofa, and more than ever disposed to admire his new friend at the other end.

Tom blew his smoke aside, after he had been smoking a little while, and took an observation of his friend. "He don't seem to care about his dress," thought Tom, "and yet how capitally he does it. What an easy swell he is!"

Mr. James Harthouse, happening to catch Tom's eye, remarked that he drank nothing, and filled his glass with his own negligent hand.

"Thank'ee," said Tom. "Thank'ee. Well, Mr. Harthouse, I hope you have had about a dose of old Bounderby to-night." Tom said this with one eye shut up again, and looking over his glass knowingly, at his entertainer.

"A very good fellow indeed!" returned Mr. James Harthouse.

"You think so, don't you?" said Tom. And shut up his eye again.

Mr. James Harthouse smiled; and rising from his end of the sofa, and lounging with his back against the chimney-piece, so that he stood before the empty fire-grate as he smoked, in front of Tom and looking down at him, observed:

"What a comical brother-in-law you are!"

"What a comical brother-in-law old Bounderby is, I think you mean," said Tom.

"You are a piece of caustic,[1] Tom," retorted Mr. James Harthouse.

There was something so very agreeable in being so intimate with such a waistcoat; in being called Tom, in such an intimate way, by such a voice; in being on such off-hand terms so soon, with such a pair of whiskers; that Tom was uncommonly pleased with himself.

"Oh! I don't care for old Bounderby," said he, "if you mean that. I have always called old Bounderby by the same name when I have talked about him, and I have always thought of him in the same way. I am not going to begin to be polite now, about old Bounderby. It would be rather late in the day."

"Don't mind me," returned James; "but take care when his wife is by, you know."

"His wife?" said Tom. "My sister Loo? O yes!" And he laughed, and took a little more of the cooling drink.

James Harthouse continued to lounge in the same place and attitude, smoking his cigar in his own easy way, and looking pleasantly at the whelp, as if he knew himself to be a kind of agreeable demon who had only to hover over him, and he must give up his whole soul if required. It certainly did seem that the whelp yielded to this influence. He looked at his companion sneakingly, he looked at him admiringly, he looked at him boldly, and put up one leg on the sofa.

"My sister Loo?" said Tom. "*She* never cared for old Bounderby."

"That's the past tense, Tom," returned Mr. James Harthouse, striking the ash from his cigar with his little finger. "We are in the present tense, now."

"Verb neuter, not to care. Indicative mood, present tense. First person singular, I do not care; second person singular, thou dost not care; third person singular, she does not care," returned Tom.

"Good! Very quaint!" said his friend. "Though you don't mean it."

"But I *do* mean it," cried Tom. "Upon my honor! Why, you won't tell me, Mr. Harthouse, that you really suppose my sister Loo does care for old Bounderby."

"My dear fellow," returned the other, "what am I bound to suppose, when I find two married people living in harmony and happiness?"

1. A person with a cutting wit.

Tom had by this time got both his legs on the sofa. If his second leg had not been already there when he was called a dear fellow, he would have put it up at that great stage of the conversation. Feeling it necessary to do something then, he stretched himself out at greater length, and, reclining with the back of his head on the end of the sofa, and smoking with an infinite assumption of negligence, turned his common face, and not too sober eyes, towards the face looking down upon him so carelessly yet so potently.

"You know our governor, Mr. Harthouse," said Tom, "and therefore you needn't be surprised that Loo married old Bounderby. She never had a lover, and the governor proposed old Bounderby, and she took him."

"Very dutiful in your interesting sister," said Mr. James Harthouse.

"Yes, but she wouldn't have been as dutiful, and it would not have come off as easily," returned the whelp, "if it hadn't been for me."

The tempter merely lifted his eyebrows; but the whelp was obliged to go on.

"*I* persuaded her," he said, with an edifying air of superiority. "I was stuck into old Bounderby's bank (where I never wanted to be), and I knew I should get into scrapes there, if she put old Bounderby's pipe out; so I told her my wishes, and she came into them. She would do anything for me. It was very game of her, wasn't it?"

"It was charming, Tom!"

"Not that it was altogether so important to her as it was to me," continued Tom coolly, "because my liberty and comfort, and perhaps my getting on, depended on it; and she had no other lover, and staying at home was like staying in jail—especially when I was gone. It wasn't as if she gave up another lover for old Bounderby; but still it was a good thing in her."

"Perfectly delightful. And she gets on so placidly."

"Oh," returned Tom, with contemptuous patronage, "she's a regular girl. A girl can get on anywhere. She has settled down to the life, and *she* don't mind. It does just as well as another. Besides, though Loo is a girl, she's not a common sort of girl. She can shut herself up within herself, and think—as I have often known her sit and watch the fire—for an hour at a stretch."

"Ay, ay? Has resources of her own," said Harthouse, smoking quietly.

"Not so much of that as you may suppose," returned Tom; "for our governor had her crammed with all sorts of dry bones and sawdust. It's his system."

"Formed his daughter on his own model?" suggested Harthouse.

"His daughter? Ah! and everybody else. Why, he formed Me that way," said Tom.

"Impossible!"

"He did though," said Tom, shaking his head. "I mean to say,
Mr. Harthouse, that when I first left home and went to old Bounderby's, I was as flat as a warming-pan,[2] and knew no more about
life, than any oyster does."

"Come, Tom! I can hardly believe that. A joke's a joke."

"Upon my soul!" said the whelp. "I am serious; I am indeed!" He
smoked with great gravity and dignity for a little while, and then
added, in a highly complacent tone, "Oh! I have picked up a little,
since. I don't deny that. But I have done it myself; no thanks to the
governor."

"And your intelligent sister?"

"My intelligent sister is about where she was. She used to complain to me that she had nothing to fall back upon, that girls usually fall back upon; and I don't see how she is to have got over that
since. But *she* don't mind," he sagaciously added, puffing at his cigar,
again. "Girls can always get on, somehow."

"Calling at the Bank yesterday evening, for Mr. Bounderby's
address, I found an ancient lady there, who seems to entertain great
admiration for your sister," observed Mr. James Harthouse, throwing away the last small remnant of the cigar he had now smoked out.

"Mother Sparsit?" said Tom. "What! you have seen her already,
have you?"

His friend nodded. Tom took his cigar out of his mouth, to shut
up his eye (which had grown rather unmanageable) with the greater
expression, and to tap his nose several times with his finger.

"Mother Sparsit's feeling for Loo is more than admiration, I
should think," said Tom. "Say affection and devotion. Mother Sparsit never set her cap at Bounderby when he was a bachelor. Oh no!"

These were the last words spoken by the whelp, before a giddy
drowsiness came upon him, followed by complete oblivion. He was
roused from the latter state by an uneasy dream of being stirred up
with a boot, and also of a voice saying: "Come, it's late. Be off!"

"Well!" he said, scrambling from the sofa. "I must take my leave
of you though. I say. Yours is very good tobacco. But it's too mild."

"Yes, it's too mild," returned his entertainer.

"It's—it's ridiculously mild," said Tom. "Where's the door? Good
night!"

He had another odd dream of being taken by a waiter through a
mist, which, after giving him some trouble and difficulty, resolved
itself into the main street, in which he stood alone. He then walked
home pretty easily, though not yet free from an impression of the
presence and influence of his new friend—as if he were lounging

2. A temporary employee, one who holds down a job (i.e., keeps it warm) until he or she is
replaced by someone more competent (slang). "Flat": here, stupid or inexperienced.

somewhere in the air, in the same negligent attitude, regarding him with the same look.

The whelp went home, and went to bed. If he had had any sense of what he had done that night, and had been less of a whelp and more of a brother, he might have turned short on the road, might have gone down to the ill-smelling river that was dyed black, might have gone to bed in it for good and all, and have curtained his head for ever with its filthy waters.

Chapter IV.

MEN AND BROTHERS.

"Oh my friends, the down-trodden operatives of Coketown! Oh my friends and fellow countrymen, the slaves of an iron-handed and a grinding despotism! Oh my friends and fellow-sufferers, and fellow-workmen, and fellow-men! I tell you that the hour is come, when we must rally round one another as One united power, and crumble into dust the oppressors that too long have battened upon the plunder of our families, upon the sweat of our brows, upon the labor of our hands, upon the strength of our sinews, upon the God-created glorious rights of Humanity, and upon the holy and eternal privileges of Brotherhood!"

"Good!" "Hear, hear, hear!" "Hurrah!" and other cries, arose in many voices from various parts of the densely crowded and suffocatingly close Hall, in which the orator, perched on a stage, delivered himself of this and what other froth and fume he had in him. He had declaimed himself into a violent heat, and was as hoarse as he was hot. By dint of roaring at the top of his voice under a flaring gaslight, clenching his fists, knitting his brows, setting his teeth, and pounding with his arms, he had taken so much out of himself by this time, that he was brought to a stop and called for a glass of water.

As he stood there, trying to quench his fiery face with his drink of water, the comparison between the orator and the crowd of attentive faces turned towards him, was extremely to his disadvantage. Judging him by Nature's evidence, he was above the mass in very little but the stage on which he stood. In many great respects, he was essentially below them. He was not so honest, he was not so manly, he was not so good-humoured; he substituted cunning for their simplicity, and passion for their safe solid sense. An ill-made high-shouldered man, with lowering brows, and his features crushed into an habitually sour expression, he contrasted most unfavourably, even in his mongrel dress, with the great body of his hearers in their plain working clothes. Strange as it always is to consider any assembly in the act of submissively resigning itself to the dreariness

of some complacent person, lord or commoner, whom three-fourths
of it could, by no human means, raise out of the slough of inanity
to their own intellectual level, it was particularly strange, and it
was even particularly affecting, to see this crowd of earnest faces,
whose honesty in the main no competent observer free from bias
could doubt, so agitated by such a leader.

Good! Hear, hear! Hurrah! The eagerness, both of attention and
intention, exhibited in all the countenances, made them a most
impressive sight. There was no carelessness, no languor, no idle curiosity; none of the many shades of indifference to be seen in all other
assemblies, visible for one moment there. That every man felt his
condition to be, somehow or other, worse than it might be; that
every man considered it incumbent on him to join the rest, towards
the making of it better; that every man felt his only hope to be in
his allying himself to the comrades by whom he was surrounded;
and that in this belief, right or wrong (unhappily wrong then), the
whole of that crowd were gravely, deeply, faithfully in earnest; must
have been as plain to any one who chose to see what was there, as
the bare beams of the roof, and the whitened brick walls. Nor could
any such spectator fail to know in his own breast, that these men,
through their very delusions, showed great qualities, susceptible of
being turned to the happiest and best account; and that to pretend
(on the strength of sweeping axioms, howsoever cut and dried) that
they went astray wholly without cause, and of their own irrational
wills, was to pretend that there could be smoke without fire, death
without birth, harvest without seed, anything or everything produced from nothing.

The orator having refreshed himself, wiped his corrugated forehead from left to right several times with his handkerchief folded
into a pad, and concentrated all his revived forces in a sneer of
great disdain and bitterness.

"But, oh my friends and brothers! Oh men and Englishmen, the
down-trodden operatives of Coketown! What shall we say of that
man—that working-man, that I should find it necessary so to libel
the glorious name—who, being practically and well acquainted
with the grievances and wrongs of you, the injured pith and mar-
row of this land, and having heard you, with a noble and majestic
unanimity that will make Tyrants tremble, resolve for to subscribe
to the funds of the United Aggregate Tribunal, and to abide by the
injunctions issued by that body for your benefit, whatever they may
be—what, I ask you, will you say of that working-man, since such I
must acknowledge him to be, who, at such a time, deserts his post,
and sells his flag; who, at such a time, turns a traitor and a craven
and a recreant; who, at such a time, is not ashamed to make to you
the dastardly and humiliating avowal that he will hold himself aloof,

and will *not* be one of those associated in the gallant stand for Freedom and for Right?"

The assembly was divided at this point. There were some groans and hisses, but the general sense of honor was much too strong for the condemnation of a man unheard. "Be sure you're right, Slackbridge!" "Put him up!" "Let's hear him!" Such things were said on many sides. Finally, one strong voice called out, "Is the man heer? If the man's heer, Slackbridge, let's hear the man himseln, 'stead o' yo." Which was received with a round of applause.

Slackbridge, the orator, looked about him with a withering smile; and, holding out his right hand at arm's length (as the manner of all Slackbridges is), to still the thundering sea, waited until there was a profound silence.

"Oh my friends and fellow-men!" said Slackbridge then, shaking his head with violent scorn, "I do not wonder that you, the prostrate sons of labor, are incredulous of the existence of such a man. But he who sold his birthright for a mess of pottage existed, and Judas Iscariot existed, and Castlereagh[1] existed, and this man exists!"

Here, a brief press and confusion near the stage, ended in the man himself standing at the orator's side before the concourse. He was pale and a little moved in the face—his lips especially showed it; but he stood quiet, with his left hand at his chin, waiting to be heard. There was a chairman to regulate the proceedings, and this functionary now took the case into his own hands.

"My friends," said he, "by virtue o' my office as your president, I ashes o' our friend Slackbridge, who may be a little over hetter[2] in this business, to take his seat, whiles this man Stephen Blackpool is heern. You all know this man Stephen Blackpool. You know him awlung o' his misfort'ns, and his good name."

With that, the chairman shook him frankly by the hand, and sat down again. Slackbridge likewise sat down, wiping his hot forehead—always from left to right, and never the reverse way.

"My friends," Stephen began, in the midst of a dead calm; "I ha' hed what's been spok'n o' me, and 'tis lickly that I shan't mend it. But I'd liefer you'd hearn the truth concernin myseln, fro my lips than fro onny other man's, though I never cud'n speak afore so monny, wi'out bein moydert[3] and muddled."

Slackbridge shook his head as if he would shake it off, in his bitterness.

---

1. An important statesman during the Napoleonic period, Lord Castlereagh (1769–1822) was regarded as a tyrannical reactionary by the working classes, in particular for his part in the suppression of a meeting in 1819, an event afterward known as the Peterloo Massacre. See Genesis 25.30–34, for the story of Esau's giving up his birthright in return for food offered to him by his brother, Jacob.
2. Embittered.
3. Bewildered.

"I'm th' one single Hand in Bounderby's mill, o' a' the men theer, as don't coom in wi' th' proposed reg'lations. I canna' coom in wi' 'em. My friends, I doubt their doin' yo onny good. Licker they'll do yo hurt."

Slackbridge laughed, folded his arms, and frowned sarcastically.

"But't ant sommuch for that as I stands out. If that were aw, I'd coom in wi' th' rest. But I ha' my reasons—mine, yo see—for being hindered; not on'y now, but awlus—awlus—life long!"

Slackbridge jumped up and stood beside him, gnashing and tearing. "Oh my friends, what but this did I tell you? Oh my fellow-countrymen, what warning but this did I give you? And how shows this recreant conduct in a man on whom unequal laws are known to have fallen heavy? Oh you Englishmen, I ask you how does this subornation show in one of yourselves, who is thus consenting to his own undoing and to yours, and to your children's and your children's children's?"

There was some applause, and some crying of Shame upon the man; but the greater part of the audience were quiet. They looked at Stephen's worn face, rendered more pathetic by the homely emotions it evinced; and, in the kindness of their nature, they were more sorry than indignant.

"'Tis this Delegate's trade for t' speak," said Stephen, "an he's paid for't, an he knows his work. Let him keep to't. Let him give no heed to what I ha had'n to bear. That's not for him. That's not for nobbody but me."

There was a propriety, not to say a dignity in these words, that made the hearers yet more quiet and attentive. The same strong voice called out, "Slackbridge, let the man be heern, and howd thee tongue!" Then the place was wonderfully still.

"My brothers," said Stephen, whose low voice was distinctly heard, "and my fellow-workmen—for that you are to me, though not, as I knows on, to this delegate heer—I ha but a word to sen, and I could sen nommore if I was to speak till Strike o' day. I know weel, aw what's afore me. I know weel that yo are aw resolved to ha nommore ado wi' a man who is not wi' yo in this matther. I know weel that if I was a lyin parisht i' th' road, yo'd feel it right to pass me by, as a forrenner and stranger. What I ha getn, I mun mak th' best on."

"Stephen Blackpool," said the chairman, rising, "think on't agen. Think on't once agen, lad, afore thou'rt shunned by aw owd friends."

There was an universal murmur to the same effect, though no man articulated a word. Every eye was fixed on Stephen's face. To repent of his determination, would be to take a load from all their minds. He looked around him, and knew that it was so. Not a grain of anger with them was in his heart; he knew them, far below their surface weaknesses and misconceptions, as no one but their fellow-laborer could.

"I ha thowt on't, above a bit, sir. I simply canna coom in. I mun go th' way as lays afore me. I mun tak my leave o' aw heer."

He made a sort of reverence to them by holding up his arms, and stood for the moment in that attitude: not speaking until they slowly dropped at his sides.

"Monny's the pleasant word as soom heer has spok'n wi' me: monny's the face I see heer, as I first seen when I were yoong and lighter heart'n than now. I ha never had no fratch[4] afore, sin ever I were born, wi' any o' my like; Gonnows I ha' none now that's o' my makin'. Yo'll ca' me traitor and that—yo I mean t' say," addressing Slackbridge, "but 'tis easier to ca' than mak' out. So let be."

He had moved away a pace or two to come down from the platform, when he remembered something he had not said, and returned again.

"Haply," he said, turning his furrowed face slowly about that he might as it were individually address the whole audience, those both near and distant; "haply, when this question has been tak'n up and discoosed, there'll be a threat, to turn out if I'm let to work among yo. I hope I shall die ere ever such a time cooms, and I shall work solitary among yo unless it cooms—truly, I mun do 't, my friends; not to brave[5] yo, but to live. I ha nobbut work to live by; and wheerever can I go, I who ha worked sin I were no heighth at aw, in Coketown heer? I mak' no complaints o' bein turned to the wa', o' being outcasten and overlooken fro this time forrard, but I hope I shall be let to work. If there is any right for me at aw, my friends, I think 'tis that."

Not a word was spoken. Not a sound was audible in the building, but the slight rustle of men moving a little apart, all along the centre of the room, to open a means of passing out, to the man with whom they had all bound themselves to renounce companionship. Looking at no one, and going his way with a lowly steadiness upon him that asserted nothing and sought nothing, Old Stephen, with all his troubles on his head, left the scene.

Then Slackbridge, who had kept his oratorical arm extended during the going out, as if he were repressing with infinite solicitude and by a wonderful moral power the vehement passions of the multitude, applied himself to raising their spirits. Had not the Roman Brutus, oh my British countrymen, condemned his son to death; and had not the Spartan mothers, oh my soon to be victorious friends, driven their flying children on the points of their enemies'

4. Quarrel.
5. Defy.

swords?[6] Then was it not the sacred duty of the men of Coketown, with forefathers before them, an admiring world in company with them, and a posterity to come after them, to hurl out traitors from the tents they had pitched in a sacred and a Godlike cause? The winds of Heaven answered Yes; and bore Yes, east, west, north, and south. And consequently three cheers for the United Aggregate Tribunal!

Slackbridge acted as fugleman,[7] and gave the time. The multitude of doubtful faces (a little conscience-stricken) brightened at the sound, and took it up. Private feeling must yield to the common cause. Hurrah! The roof yet vibrated with the cheering, when the assembly dispersed.

Thus easily did Stephen Blackpool fall into the loneliest of lives, the life of solitude among a familiar crowd. The stranger in the land who looks into ten thousand faces for some answering look and never finds it, is in cheering society as compared with him who passes ten averted faces daily, that were once the countenances of friends. Such experience was to be Stephen's now, in every waking moment of his life; at his work, on his way to it and from it, at his door, at his window, everywhere. By general consent, they even avoided that side of the street on which he habitually walked; and left it, of all the working men, to him only.

He had been for many years, a quiet silent man, associating but little with other men, and used to companionship with his own thoughts. He had never known before, the strength of the want in his heart for the frequent recognition of a nod, a look, a word; or the immense amount of relief that had been poured into it by drops, through such small means. It was even harder than he could have believed possible, to separate in his own conscience his abandonment by all his fellows, from a baseless sense of shame and disgrace.

The first four days of his endurance were days so long and heavy, that he began to be appalled by the prospect before him. Not only did he see no Rachael all the time, but he avoided every chance of seeing her; for, although he knew that the prohibition did not yet formally extend to the women working in the factories, he found that some of them with whom he was acquainted were changed to him, and he feared to try others, and dreaded that Rachael might be even singled out from the rest if she were seen in his company. So, he had been quite alone during the four days, and had spoken

---

6. The fearless bravery of Spartan soldiers was legendary; they were expected never to retreat. If they ever tried to flee from battle, their own mothers were ready to sacrifice them by driving them back to confront the swords of the enemy. Lucius Junius Brutus sentenced his two sons to death when they were convicted of conspiring against Rome.
7. A soldier, expert in parade drill, who marched in front of his company as a model for his less-experienced companions.

to no one, when, as he was leaving his work at night, a young man of a very light complexion accosted him in the street.

"Your name's Blackpool, an't it?" said the young man.

Stephen colored to find himself with his hat in his hand, in his gratitude for being spoken to, or in the suddenness of it, or both. He made a feint of adjusting the lining, and said, "Yes."

"You are the Hand they have sent to Coventry,[8] I mean?" said Bitzer, the very light young man in question.

Stephen answered "Yes," again.

"I supposed so, from their all appearing to keep away from you. Mr. Bounderby wants to speak to you. You know his house, don't you?"

Stephen said "Yes," again.

"Then go straight up there, will you?" said Bitzer. "You're expected, and have only to tell the servant it's you. I belong to the Bank; so, if you go straight up without me (I was sent to fetch you), you'll save me a walk."

Stephen, whose way had been in the contrary direction, turned about, and betook himself as in duty bound, to the red brick castle of the giant Bounderby.

Chapter V.

MEN AND MASTERS.

"Well Stephen," said Bounderby, in his windy manner, "what's this I hear? What have these pests of the earth been doing to *you*? Come in, and speak up."

It was into the drawing-room that he was thus bidden. A tea-table was set out; and Mr. Bounderby's young wife, and her brother, and a great gentleman from London, were present. To whom Stephen made his obeisance, closing the door and standing near it, with his hat in his hand.

"This is the man I was telling you about, Harthouse," said Mr. Bounderby. The gentleman he addressed, who was talking to Mrs. Bounderby on the sofa, got up, saying in an indolent way, "Oh really?" and dawdled to the hearthrug where Mr. Bounderby stood.

"Now," said Bounderby, "speak up!"

After the four days he had passed, this address fell rudely and discordantly on Stephen's ear. Besides being a rough handling of his wounded mind, it seemed to assume that he really was the self-interested deserter he had been called.

"What were it, sir," said Stephen, "as yo were pleased to want wi' me?"

8. Ostracized.

"Why, I have told you," returned Bounderby. "Speak up like a man, since you are a man, and tell us about yourself and this Combination."

"Wi' yor pardon, sir," said Stephen Blackpool, "I ha' nowt to sen about it."

Mr. Bounderby, who was always more or less like a Wind, finding something in his way here, began to blow at it directly.

"Now, look here, Harthouse," said he, "here's a specimen of 'em. When this man was here once before, I warned this man against the mischievous strangers who are always about—and who ought to be hanged wherever they are found—and I told this man that he was going in the wrong direction. Now, would you believe it, that although they have put this mark upon him, he is such a slave to them still, that he's afraid to open his lips about them?"

"I sed as I had nowt to sen, sir; not as I was fearfo' o' openin' my lips."

"You said. Ah! I know what you said; more than that, I know what you mean, you see. Not always the same thing, by the Lord Harry! Quite different things. You had better tell us at once, that that fellow Slackbridge is not in the town, stirring up the people to mutiny; and that he is not a regular qualified leader of the people: that is, a most confounded scoundrel. You had better tell us so at once; you can't deceive me. You want to tell us so. Why don't you?"

"I'm as sooary as yo, sir, when the people's leaders is bad," said Stephen, shaking his head. "They taks such as offers. Haply 'tis na' the sma'est o' their misfortuns when they can get no better."

The wind began to be boisterous.

"Now, you'll think this pretty well, Harthouse," said Mr. Bounderby. "You'll think this tolerably strong. You'll say, upon my soul this is a tidy specimen of what my friends have to deal with; but this is nothing, sir! You shall hear me ask this man a question. Pray, Mr. Blackpool"—wind springing up very fast—"may I take the liberty of asking you how it happens that you refused to be in this Combination?"

"How 't happens?"

"Ah!" said Mr. Bounderby, with his thumbs in the arms of his coat, and jerking his head and shutting his eyes in confidence with the opposite wall: "how it happens."

"I'd leefer not coom to't, sir; but sin you put th' question—an not want'n t' be ill-manner'n—I'll answer. I ha passed a promess."

"Not to me, you know," said Bounderby. (Gusty weather with deceitful calms. One now prevailing.)

"O no, sir. Not to yo."

"As for me, any consideration for me has had just nothing at all to do with it," said Bounderby, still in confidence with the wall. "If only Josiah Bounderby of Coketown had been in question, you would have joined and made no bones about it?"

"Why yes, sir. 'Tis true."

"Though he knows," said Mr. Bounderby, now blowing a gale, "that these are a set of rascals and rebels whom transportation[1] is too good for! Now, Mr. Harthouse, you have been knocking about in the world some time. Did you ever meet with anything like that man out of this blessed country?" And Mr. Bounderby pointed him out for inspection, with an angry finger.

"Nay, ma'am," said Stephen Blackpool, staunchly protesting against the words that had been used, and instinctively addressing himself to Louisa, after glancing at her face. "Not rebels, nor yet rascals. Nowt o' th' kind, ma'am, nowt o' th' kind. They've not doon me a kindness, ma'am, as I know and feel. But there's not a dozen men amoong 'em, ma'am—a dozen? Not six—but what believes as he has doon his duty by the rest and by himseln. God forbid as I, that ha known an had'n experience o' these men aw my life—I, that ha' ett'n an droonken wi' em, an seet'n wi' em, and toil'n wi' em, and lov'n 'em, should fail fur to stan by 'em wi' the truth, let 'em ha doon to me what they may!"

He spoke with the rugged earnestness of his place and character—deepened perhaps by a proud consciousness that he was faithful to his class under all their mistrust; but he fully remembered where he was, and did not even raise his voice.

"No, ma'am, no. They're true to one another, faithfo' to one another, fectionate to one another, e'en to death. Be poor amoong 'em, be sick amoong 'em, grieve amoong 'em for onny o' th' monny causes that carries grief to the poor man's door, an they'll be tender wi' yo, gentle wi' yo, comfortable wi' yo, Chrisen wi' yo. Be sure o' that, ma'am. They'd be riven to bits, ere ever they'd be different."

"In short," said Mr. Bounderby, "it's because they are so full of virtues that they have turned you adrift. Go through with it while you are about it. Out with it."

"How 'tis, ma'am," resumed Stephen, appearing still to find his natural refuge in Louisa's face, "that what is best in us fok, seems to turn us most to trouble an misfort'n an mistake, I dunno. But 'tis so. I know 'tis, as I know the heavens is over me ahint the smoke. We're patient too, an wants in general to do right. An' I canna think the fawt is aw wi' us."

"Now, my friend," said Mr. Bounderby, whom he could not have exasperated more, quite unconscious of it though he was, than by seeming to appeal to any one else, "if you will favour me with your

---

1. The widely practiced deportation of convicts to British penal colonies in Australia and New Zealand.

attention for half a minute, I should like to have a word or two with you. You said just now, that you had nothing to tell us about this business. You are quite sure of that, before we go any further?"

"Sir, I am sure on't."

"Here's a gentleman from London present," Mr. Bounderby made a back-handed point at Mr. James Harthouse with his thumb, "a Parliament gentleman. I should like him to hear a short bit of dialogue between you and me, instead of taking the substance of it—for I know precious well, beforehand, what it will be; nobody knows better than I do, take notice!—instead of receiving it on trust, from my mouth."

Stephen bent his head to the gentleman from London, and showed a rather more troubled mind than usual. He turned his eyes involuntarily to his former refuge, but at a look from that quarter (expressive though instantaneous) he settled them on Mr. Bounderby's face.

"Now, what do you complain of?" asked Mr. Bounderby.

"I ha' not coom here, sir," Stephen reminded him, "to complain. I coom for that I were sent for."

"What," repeated Mr. Bounderby, folding his arms, "do you people, in a general way, complain of?"

Stephen looked at him with some little irresolution for a moment, and then seemed to make up his mind.

"Sir, I were never good at showin o't, though I ha had'n my share in feeling o't. 'Deed we are in a muddle, sir. Look round town—so rich as 'tis—and see the numbers o' people as has been broughten into bein heer, fur to weave, an to card,[2] an to piece out a livin', aw the same one way, somehows, twixt their cradles and their graves. Look how we live, an wheer we live, an in what numbers, an by what chances, and wi' what sameness; and look how the mills is awlus a goin, and how they never works us no nigher to ony dis'ant object—ceptin awlus, Death. Look how you considers of us, an writes of us, an talks of us, and goes up wi' yor deputations to Secretaries o' State 'bout us, and how yo are awlus right, and how we are awlus wrong, and never had'n no reason in us sin ever we were born. Look how this ha growen an growen, sir, bigger an bigger, broader an broader, harder an harder, fro year to year, fro generation unto generation. Who can look on't, sir, and fairly tell a man 'tis not a muddle?"

"Of course," said Mr. Bounderby. "Now perhaps you'll let the gentleman know, how you would set this muddle (as you're so fond of calling it) to rights."

2. To operate a carding machine in a cotton mill, extracting impurities such as seeds or stalks from partially processed cotton.

"I donno, sir. I canna be expecten to't. 'Tis not me as should be looken to for that, sir. 'Tis them as is put ower me, and ower aw the rest of us. What do they tak upon themseln, sir, if not to do't?"

"I'll tell you something towards it, at any rate," returned Mr. Bounderby. "We will make an example of half a dozen Slackbridges. We'll indict the blackguards for felony, and get 'em shipped off to penal settlements."

Stephen gravely shook his head.

"Don't tell me we won't, man," said Mr. Bounderby, by this time blowing a hurricane, "because we will, I tell you!"

"Sir," returned Stephen, with the quiet confidence of absolute certainty, "if yo was t' tak a hundred Slackbridges—aw as there is, and aw the number ten times towd—an was t' sew 'em up in seperate sacks, an sink 'em in the deepest ocean as were made ere ever dry land coom to be, yo'd leave the muddle just wheer 'tis. Mischeevous strangers!" said Stephen, with an anxious smile; "when ha we not heern, I am sure, sin ever we can call to mind, o' th' mischeevous strangers! 'Tis not by *them* the trouble's made, sir. 'Tis not wi' *them* 't commences. I ha no favor for 'em—I ha no reason to favor 'em—but 'tis hopeless an useless to dream o' takin them fro their trade, 'stead o' takin their trade fro them! Aw that's now about me in this room were heer afore I coom, an will be heer when I am gone. Put that clock aboard a ship an pack it off to Norfolk Island,[3] an the time will go on just the same. So 'tis wi' Slackbridge every bit."

Reverting for a moment to his former refuge, he observed a cautionary movement of her eyes towards the door. Stepping back, he put his hand upon the lock. But, he had not spoken out of his own will and desire; and he felt it in his heart a noble return for his late injurious treatment, to be faithful to the last to those who had repudiated him. He stayed to finish what was in his mind.

"Sir, I canna, wi' my little learning an my common way, tell the genelman what will better aw this—though some working men o' this town could, above my powers—but I can tell him what I know will never do't. The strong hand will never do't. Vict'ry and triumph will never do't. Agreeing fur to mak one side unnat'rally awlus and for ever right, and toother side unnat'rally awlus and for ever wrong, will never, never do't. Nor yet lettin alone will never do't. Let thousands upon thousands alone, aw leadin the like lives and aw faw'en into the like muddle, and they will be as one, and yo will be as anoother, wi' a black unpassable world betwixt yo, just as long or short a time as sitch-like misery can last. Not drawin nigh

---

3. A remote island in the Pacific Ocean to which convicts were transported—thus one of the "penal settlements" referred to by Mr. Bounderby as a suitable place to have Slackbridge "shipped."

to fok, wi' kindness and patience an cheery ways, that so draws nigh to one another in their monny troubles, and so cherishes one another in their distresses wi' what they need themseln—like, I humbly believe, as no people the genelman ha seen in aw his travels can beat—will never do't till th' Sun turns t' ice. Most o' aw, ratin 'em as so much Power, and reg'latin 'em as if they was figures in a soom, or machines: wi'out loves and likeins, wi'out memories and inclinations, wi'out souls to weary and souls to hope—when aw goes quiet, draggin on wi' 'em as if they'd nowt o' th' kind, an when aw goes onquiet, reproachin 'em for their want o' sitch humanly feelins in their dealins wi' yo—this will never do't, sir, till God's work is onmade."

Stephen stood with the open door in his hand, waiting to know if anything more were expected of him.

"Just stop a moment," said Mr. Bounderby, excessively red in the face. "I told you, the last time you were here with a grievance, that you had better turn about and come out of that. And I also told you, if you remember, that I was up to the gold spoon look-out."

"I were not up to't myseln, sir; I do assure yo."

"Now, it's clear to me," said Mr. Bounderby, "that you are one of those chaps who have always got a grievance. And you go about, sowing it and raising crops. That's the business of *your* life, my friend."

Stephen shook his head, mutely protesting that indeed he had other business to do for his life.

"You are such a waspish, raspish, ill-conditioned chap, you see," said Mr. Bounderby, "that even your own Union, the men who know you best, will have nothing to do with you. I never thought those fellows could be right in anything; but I tell you what! I so far go along with them for a novelty, that *I'*ll have nothing to do with you either."

Stephen raised his eyes quickly to his face.

"You can finish off what you're at," said Mr. Bounderby, with a meaning nod, "and then go elsewhere."

"Sir, yo know weel," said Stephen expressively, "that if I canna get work wi' yo, I canna get it elsewheer."

The reply was, "What I know, I know; and what you know, you know. I have no more to say about it."

Stephen glanced at Louisa again, but her eyes were raised to his no more; therefore, with a sigh, and saying, barely above his breath, "Heaven help us aw in this world!" he departed.

Chapter VI.

FADING AWAY.

It was falling dark when Stephen came out of Mr. Bounderby's house. The shadows of night had gathered so fast, that he did not look about him when he closed the door, but plodded straight along the street. Nothing was further from his thoughts than the curious old woman he had encountered on his previous visit to the same house, when he heard a step behind him that he knew, and, turning, saw her in Rachael's company.

He saw Rachael first, as he had heard her only.

"Ah Rachael, my dear! Missus, thou wi' her!"

"Well, and now you are surprised to be sure, and with reason I must say," the old woman returned. "Here I am again, you see."

"But how wi' Rachael?" said Stephen, falling into their step, walking between them, and looking from the one to the other.

"Why, I come to be with this good lass pretty much as I came to be with you," said the old woman cheerfully, taking the reply upon herself. "My visiting time is later this year than usual, for I have been rather troubled with shortness of breath, and so put it off till the weather was fine and warm. For the same reason I don't make all my journey in one day, but divide it into two days, and get a bed to-night at the Travellers' Coffee House down by the railroad (a nice clean house), and go back Parliamentary, at six in the morning. Well, but what has this to do with this good lass, says you? I'm going to tell you. I have heard of Mr. Bounderby being married. I read it in the paper, where it looked grand—oh, it looked fine!" the old woman dwelt on it with strange enthusiasm; "and I want to see his wife. I have never seen her yet. Now, if you'll believe me, she hasn't come out of that house since noon to-day. So, not to give her up too easily, I was waiting about, a little last bit more, when I passed close to this good lass two or three times; and her face being so friendly I spoke to her, and she spoke to me. There!" said the old woman to Stephen, "you can make all the rest out for yourself now, a deal shorter than I can, I dare say!"

Once again, Stephen had to conquer an instinctive propensity to dislike this old woman, though her manner was as honest and simple as a manner possibly could be. With a gentleness that was as natural to him as he knew it to be to Rachael, he pursued the subject that interested her in her old age.

"Well, missus," said he, "I ha seen the lady, and she were yoong and hansom. Wi' fine dark thinkin eyes, and a still way, Rachael, as I ha never seen the like on."

"Young and handsome. Yes!" cried the old woman, quite delighted. "As bonny as a rose! And what a happy wife!"

"Aye, missus, I suppose she be," said Stephen. But with a doubtful glance at Rachael.

"Suppose she be? She must be. She's your master's wife," returned the old woman.

Stephen nodded assent. "Though as to master," said he, glancing again at Rachael, "not master onny more. That's aw enden twixt him and me."

"Have you left his work, Stephen?" asked Rachael, anxiously and quickly.

"Why Rachael," he replied, "whether I ha lef'n his work, or whether his work ha left'n me, cooms t' th' same. His work and me are parted. 'Tis as weel so—better, I were thinkin when yo coom up wi' me. It would ha brought'n trouble upon trouble if I had stayed theer. Haply 'tis a kindness to monny that I go; haply 'tis a kindness to myseln; anyways it mun be done. I mun turn my face fro Coketown fur th' time, and seek a fort'n, dear, by beginnin fresh."

"Where will you go, Stephen?"

"I donno t'night," said he, lifting off his hat, and smoothing his thin hair with the flat of his hand. "But I'm not goin t'night, Rachael; nor yet t'morrow. Tan't easy overmuch, t'know wheer t' turn, but a good heart will coom to me."

Herein, too, the sense of even thinking unselfishly aided him. Before he had so much as closed Mr. Bounderby's door, he had reflected that at least his being obliged to go away was good for her, as it would save her from the chance of being brought into question for not withdrawing from him. Though it would cost him a hard pang to leave her, and though he could think of no similar place in which his condemnation would not pursue him, perhaps it was almost a relief to be forced away from the endurance of the last four days, even to unknown difficulties and distresses.

So he said, with truth, "I'm more leetsome,[1] Rachael, under 't, than I couldn ha believed." It was not her part to make his burden heavier. She answered with her comforting smile, and the three walked on together.

Age, especially when it strives to be self-reliant and cheerful, finds much consideration among the poor. The old woman was so decent and contented, and made so light of her infirmities, though they had increased upon her since her former interview with Stephen, that they both took an interest in her. She was too sprightly to allow of their walking at a slow pace on her account, but she was very grateful to be talked to, and very willing to talk to any extent:

1. Lighthearted or cheerful.

so, when they came to their part of the town, she was more brisk and vivacious than ever.

"Coom to my poor place, missus," said Stephen, "and tak a coop o' tea. Rachael will coom then; and arterwards I'll see thee safe t' thy Travellers' lodgin. 'T may be long, Rachael, ere ever I ha th' chance o' thy coompany agen."

They complied, and the three went on to the house where he lodged. When they turned into a narrow street, Stephen glanced at his window with a dread that always haunted his desolate home; but it was open, as he had left it, and no one was there. The evil spirit of his life had flitted away again, months ago, and he had heard no more of her since. The only evidences of her last return now, were the scantier moveables in his room, and the grayer hair upon his head.

He lighted a candle, set out his little tea-board, got hot water from below, and brought in small portions of tea and sugar, a loaf, and some butter, from the nearest shop. The bread was new and crusty, the butter fresh, and the sugar lump,[2] of course—in fulfilment of the standard testimony of the Coketown magnates, that these people lived like princes, sir. Rachael made the tea (so large a party necessitated the borrowing of a cup), and the visitor enjoyed it mightily. It was the first glimpse of sociality the host had had for many days. He too, with the world a wide heath before him, enjoyed the meal—again in corroboration of the magnates, as exemplifying the utter want of calculation on the part of these people, sir.

"I ha never thowt yet, missus," said Stephen, "o' askin thy name."

The old lady announced herself as "Mrs. Pegler."

"A widder, I think?" said Stephen.

"Oh, many long years!" Mrs. Pegler's husband (one of the best on record) was already dead, by Mrs. Pegler's calculation, when Stephen was born.

" 'Twere a bad job too, to lose so good a one," said Stephen. "Onny children?"

Mrs. Pegler's cup, rattling against her saucer as she held it, denoted some nervousness on her part. "No," she said. "Not now, not now."

"Dead, Stephen," Rachael softly hinted.

"I'm sooary I ha spok'n on't," said Stephen, "I ought t' hadn in my mind as I might touch a sore place. I—I blame myseln."

While he excused himself, the old lady's cup rattled more and more. "I had a son," she said, curiously distressed, and not by any of the usual appearances of sorrow; "and he did well, wonderfully

2. The per capita consumption of sugar (in former centuries a luxury enjoyed only by the wealthy classes) rose rapidly in 19th-century England. Lump sugar, the most expensive form of the commodity, would impress the "magnates" as evidence of a pampered life.

well. But he is not to be spoken of if you please. He is—" Putting down her cup, she moved her hands as if she would have added, by her action, "dead!" Then she said, aloud, "I have lost him."

Stephen had not yet got the better of his having given the old lady pain, when his landlady came stumbling up the narrow stairs, and calling him to the door, whispered in his ear. Mrs. Pegler was by no means deaf, for she caught a word as it was uttered.

"Bounderby!" she cried, in a suppressed voice, starting up from the table. "Oh hide me! Don't let me be seen for the world. Don't let him come up till I've got away. Pray, pray!" She trembled, and was excessively agitated; getting behind Rachael, when Rachael tried to reassure her; and not seeming to know what she was about.

"But hearken, missus, hearken," said Stephen, astonished. " 'Tisn't Mr. Bounderby; 'tis his wife. Yor not fearfo' o' her. Yo was hey-go-mad[3] about her, but an hour sin."

"But are you sure it's the lady, and not the gentleman?" she asked, still trembling.

"Certain sure!"

"Well then, pray don't speak to me, nor yet take any notice of me," said the old woman. "Let me be quite to myself in this corner."

Stephen nodded; looking to Rachael for an explanation, which she was quite unable to give him; took the candle, went down-stairs, and in a few moments returned, lighting Louisa into the room. She was followed by the whelp.

Rachael had risen, and stood apart with her shawl and bonnet in her hand, when Stephen, himself profoundly astonished by this visit, put the candle on the table. Then he too stood, with his doubled hand upon the table near it, waiting to be addressed.

For the first time in her life, Louisa had come into one of the dwellings of the Coketown Hands; for the first time in her life, she was face to face with anything like individuality in connexion with them. She knew of their existence by hundreds and by thousands. She knew what results in work a given number of them would produce, in a given space of time. She knew them in crowds passing to and from their nests, like ants or beetles. But she knew from her reading infinitely more of the ways of toiling insects than of these toiling men and women.

Something to be worked so much and paid so much, and there ended; something to be infallibly settled by laws of supply and demand; something that blundered against those laws, and floundered into difficulty; something that was a little pinched when wheat was dear, and over-ate itself when wheat was cheap; something that increased at such a rate of percentage, and yielded such

3. Wildly excited.

another percentage of crime, and such another percentage of pauperism; something wholesale, of which vast fortunes were made; something that occasionally rose like a sea, and did some harm and waste (chiefly to itself), and fell again; this she knew the Coketown Hands to be. But, she had scarcely thought more of separating them into units, than of separating the sea itself into its component drops.

She stood for some moments looking round the room. From the few chairs, the few books, the common prints, and the bed, she glanced to the two women, and to Stephen.

"I have come to speak to you, in consequence of what passed just now. I should like to be serviceable to you, if you will let me. Is this your wife?"

Rachael raised her eyes, and they sufficiently answered no, and dropped again.

"I remember," said Louisa, reddening at her mistake; "I recollect, now, to have heard your domestic misfortunes spoken of, though I was not attending to the particulars at the time. It was not my meaning to ask a question that would give pain to any one here. If I should ask any other question that may happen to have that result, give me credit, if you please, for being in ignorance how to speak to you as I ought."

As Stephen had but a little while ago instinctively addressed himself to her, so she now instinctively addressed herself to Rachael. Her manner was short and abrupt, yet faltering and timid.

"He has told you what has passed between himself and my husband? You would be his first resource, I think."

"I have heard the end of it, young lady," said Rachael.

"Did I understand, that, being rejected by one employer, he would probably be rejected by all? I thought he said as much?"

"The chances are very small, young lady—next to nothing—for a man who gets a bad name among them."

"What shall I understand that you mean by a bad name?"

"The name of being troublesome."

"Then, by the prejudices of his own class, and by the prejudices of the other, he is sacrificed alike? Are the two so deeply separated in this town, that there is no place whatever, for an honest workman between them?"

Rachael shook her head in silence.

"He fell into suspicion," said Louisa, "with his fellow-weavers, because he had made a promise not to be one of them. I think it must have been to you that he made that promise. Might I ask you why he made it?"

Rachael burst into tears. "I didn't seek it of him, poor lad. I prayed him to avoid trouble for his own good, little thinking he'd come to it through me. But I know he'd die a hundred deaths, ere ever he'd break his word. I know that of him well."

Stephen had remained quietly attentive, in his usual thoughtful attitude, with his hand at his chin. He now spoke in a voice rather less steady than usual.

"No one, excepting myseln, can ever know what honor, an what love, an respect, I bear to Rachael, or wi' what cause. When I passed that promess, I towd her true, she were th' Angel o' my life. 'Twere a solemn promess. 'Tis gone fro me, for ever."

Louisa turned her head to him, and bent it with a deference that was new in her. She looked from him to Rachael, and her features softened. "What will you do?" she asked him. And her voice had softened too.

"Weel, ma'am," said Stephen, making the best of it, with a smile; "when I ha finished off, I mun quit this part, an try another. Fortnet or misfortnet, a man can but try; there's nowt to be done wi'out tryin'—cept laying down an dying."

"How will you travel?"

"Afoot, my kind ledy, afoot."

Louisa colored, and a purse appeared in her hand. The rustling of a bank-note was audible, as she unfolded one and laid it on the table.

"Rachael, will you tell him—for you know how, without offence—that this is freely his, to help him on his way? Will you entreat him to take it?"

"I canna do that, young lady," she answered, turning her head aside; "Bless you for thinking o' the poor lad wi' such tenderness. But 'tis for him to know his heart, and what is right according to it."

Louisa looked, in part incredulous, in part frightened, in part overcome with quick sympathy, when this man of so much self-command, who had been so plain and steady through the late interview, lost his composure in a moment, and now stood with his hand before his face. She stretched out hers, as if she would have touched him; then checked herself, and remained still.

"Not e'en Rachael," said Stephen, when he stood again with his face uncovered, "could mak sitch a kind offerin, by onny words, kinder. T' show that I'm not a man wi'out reason and gratitude, I'll tak two pound. I'll borrow't for t' pay't back. 'Twill be the sweetest work as ever I ha done, that puts it in my power t'acknowledge once more my lastin thankfulness for this present action."

She was fain to take up the note again, and to substitute the much smaller sum he had named. He was neither courtly, nor handsome, nor picturesque, in any respect; and yet his manner of accepting it, and of expressing his thanks without more words, had a grace in it that Lord Chesterfield[4] could not have taught his son in a century.

Tom had sat upon the bed, swinging one leg and sucking his walking-stick with sufficient unconcern, until the visit had attained this stage. Seeing his sister ready to depart, he got up, rather hurriedly, and put in a word.

"Just wait a moment, Loo! Before we go, I should like to speak to him a moment. Something comes into my head. If you'll step out on the stairs, Blackpool, I'll mention it. Never mind a light, man!" Tom was remarkably impatient of his moving towards the cupboard, to get one. "It don't want a light."

Stephen followed him out, and Tom closed the room door, and held the lock in his hand.

"I say!" he whispered. "I think I can do you a good turn. Don't ask me what it is, because it may not come to anything. But there's no harm in my trying."

His breath fell like a flame of fire on Stephen's ear, it was so hot.

"That was our light porter at the Bank," said Tom, "who brought you the message to-night. I call him our light porter, because I belong to the Bank too."

Stephen thought "What a hurry he is in!" He spoke so confusedly.

"Well!" said Tom. Now look here! When are you off?"

"T'day's Monday," replied Stephen, considering. "Why, sir, Friday or Saturday, nigh 'bout."

"Friday or Saturday," said Tom. "Now, look here! I am not sure that I can do you the good turn I want to do you—that's my sister, you know, in your room—but I may be able to, and if I should not be able to, there's no harm done. So I tell you what. You'll know our light porter again?"

"Yes sure," said Stephen.

"Very well," returned Tom. "When you leave work of a night, between this and your going away, just hang about the Bank an hour or so, will you? Don't take on, as if you meant anything, if he should see you hanging about there; because I shan't put him up to speak to you, unless I find I can do you the service I want to do you. In that case he'll have a note or a message for you, but not else. Now look here! You are sure you understand."

He had wormed a finger, in the darkness, through a button-hole of Stephen's coat, and was screwing that corner of the garment tight up, round and round, in an extraordinary manner.

"I understand, sir," said Stephen.

4. Philip Dormer Stanhope, fourth Earl of Chesterfield (1694–1773), in a series of letters to his illegitimate son published as *Letters to His Son* (1774), advocated the importance of flattery, deceit, and the social graces in getting ahead in the world.

"Now look here!" repeated Tom. "Be sure you don't make any mistake then, and don't forget. I shall tell my sister as we go home, what I have in view, and she'll approve, I know. Now look here! You're all right, are you? You understand all about it? Very well then. Come along, Loo!"

He pushed the door open as he called to her, but did not return into the room, or wait to be lighted down the narrow stairs. He was at the bottom when she began to descend, and was in the street before she could take his arm.

Mrs. Pegler remained in her corner until the brother and sister were gone, and until Stephen came back with the candle in his hand. She was in a state of inexpressible admiration of Mrs. Bounderby, and, like an unaccountable old woman, wept, "because she was such a pretty dear." Yet Mrs. Pegler was so flurried lest the object of her admiration should return by chance, or anybody else should come, that her cheerfulness was ended for that night. It was late too, to people who rose early and worked hard; therefore the party broke up; and Stephen and Rachael escorted their mysterious acquaintance to the door of the Travellers' Coffee House, where they parted from her.

They walked back together to the corner of the street where Rachael lived, and as they drew nearer and nearer to it, silence crept upon them. When they came to the dark corner where their unfrequent meetings always ended, they stopped, still silent, as if both were afraid to speak.

"I shall strive t' see thee agen, Rachael, afore I go, but if not—"

"Thou wilt not, Stephen, I know. 'Tis better that we make up our minds to be open wi' one another."

"Thou'rt awlus right. 'Tis bolder and better. I ha been thinkin then, Rachael, that as 'tis but a day or two that remains, 'twere better for thee, my dear, not t' be seen wi' me. 'T might bring thee into trouble, fur no good."

" 'Tis not for that, Stephen, that I mind. But thou know'st our old agreement. 'Tis for that."

"Well, well," said he. " 'Tis better, onnyways."

"Thou'lt write to me, and tell me all that happens, Stephen?"

"Yes. What can I say now, but Heaven be wi' thee, Heaven bless thee, Heaven thank thee and reward thee?"

"May it bless thee, Stephen, too, in all thy wanderings, and send thee peace and rest at last!"

"I towd thee, my dear," said Stephen Blackpool—"that night— that I would never see or think o' onnything that angered me, but thou, so much better than me, should'st be beside it. Thou'rt beside it now. Thou mak'st me see it wi' a better eye. Bless thee. Good night. Good-bye!"

It was but a hurried parting in the common street, yet it was a sacred remembrance to these two common people. Utilitarian economists, skeletons of schoolmasters, Commissioners of Fact, genteel and used-up infidels, gabblers of many little dog's-eared creeds, the poor you will have always with you.[5] Cultivate in them, while there is yet time, the utmost graces of the fancies and affections, to adorn their lives so much in need of ornament; or, in the day of your triumph, when romance is utterly driven out of their souls, and they and a bare existence stand face to face, Reality will take a wolfish turn, and make an end of you!

Stephen worked the next day, and the next, uncheered by a word from any one, and shunned in all his comings and goings as before. At the end of the second day, he saw land; at the end of the third, his loom stood empty.

He had overstayed his hour in the street outside the Bank, on each of the two first evenings; and nothing had happened there, good or bad. That he might not be remiss in his part of the engagement, he resolved to wait full two hours, on this third and last night.

There was the lady who had once kept Mr. Bounderby's house, sitting at the first floor window as he had seen her before; and there was the light porter, sometimes talking with her there, and sometimes looking over the blind below which had BANK upon it, and sometimes coming to the door and standing on the steps for a breath of air. When he first came out, Stephen thought he might be looking for him, and passed near; but the light porter only cast his winking eyes upon him slightly, and said nothing.

Two hours were a long stretch of lounging about, after a long day's labor. Stephen sat upon the step of a door, leaned against a wall under an archway, strolled up and down, listened for the church clock, stopped and watched children playing in the street. Some purpose or other is so natural to every one, that a mere loiterer always looks and feels remarkable. When the first hour was out, Stephen even began to have an uncomfortable sensation upon him of being for the time a disreputable character.

Then came the lamplighter, and two lengthening lines of light all down the long perspective of the street, until they were blended and lost in the distance. Mrs. Sparsit closed the first floor window, drew down the blind, and went up stairs. Presently, a light went up stairs after her, passing first the fanlight of the door, and

---

5. Matthew 26.11. "Utilitarian economists": influential Victorian economists and political theorists, such as Jeremy Bentham, who believed that the greatest good for the greatest number should be the operative principle of all public policy and private ethics; Dickens uses the word "utilitarian" pejoratively to indicate an ultrarational, dehumanized approach to the human condition.

afterwards the two staircase windows, on its way up. By and by, one corner of the second floor blind was disturbed, as if Mrs. Sparsit's eye were there; also the other corner, as if the light porter's eye were on that side. Still, no communication was made to Stephen. Much relieved when the two hours were at last accomplished, he went away at a quick pace, as a recompense for so much loitering.

He had only to take leave of his landlady, and lie down on his temporary bed upon the floor; for his bundle was made up for tomorrow, and all was arranged for his departure. He meant to be clear of the town very early; before the Hands were in the streets.

It was barely daybreak, when, with a parting look round his room, mournfully wondering whether he should ever see it again, he went out. The town was as entirely deserted as if the inhabitants had abandoned it, rather than hold communication with him. Everything looked wan at that hour. Even the coming sun made but a pale waste in the sky, like a sad sea.

By the place where Rachael lived, though it was not in his way; by the red brick streets; by the great silent factories, not trembling yet; by the railway, where the danger-lights were waning in the strengthening day; by the railway's crazy neighbourhood, half pulled down and half built up; by scattered red brick villas, where the besmoked evergreens were sprinkled with a dirty powder, like untidy snuff-takers; by coal-dust paths and many varieties of ugliness; Stephen got to the top of the hill, and looked back.

Day was shining radiantly upon the town then, and the bells were going for the morning work. Domestic fires were not yet lighted, and the high chimneys had the sky to themselves. Puffing out their poisonous volumes, they would not be long in hiding it; but, for half an hour, some of the many windows were golden, which showed the Coketown people a sun eternally in eclipse, through a medium of smoked glass.

So strange to turn from the chimneys to the birds. So strange to have the road-dust on his feet instead of the coal-grit. So strange to have lived to his time of life, and yet to be beginning like a boy this summer morning! With these musings in his mind, and his bundle under his arm, Stephen took his attentive face along the high road. And the trees arched over him, whispering that he left a true and loving heart behind.

Chapter VII.

GUNPOWDER.

Mr. James Harthouse, "going in"[1] for his adopted party, soon began to score. With the aid of a little more coaching for the political sages, a little more genteel listlessness for the general society, and a tolerable management of the assumed honesty in dishonesty, most effective and most patronised of the polite deadly sins, he speedily came to be considered of much promise. The not being troubled with earnestness was a grand point in his favour, enabling him to take to the hard Fact fellows with as good a grace as if he had been born one of the tribe, and to throw all other tribes overboard, as conscious hypocrites.

"Whom none of us believe, my dear Mrs. Bounderby, and who do not believe themselves. The only difference between us and the professors of virtue or benevolence, or philanthropy—never mind the name—is, that we know it is all meaningless, and say so; while they know it equally and will never say so."

Why should she be shocked or warned by this reiteration? It was not so unlike her father's principles, and her early training, that it need startle her. Where was the great difference between the two schools, when each chained her down to material realities, and inspired her with no faith in anything else? What was there in her soul for James Harthouse to destroy, which Thomas Gradgrind had nurtured there in its state of innocence!

It was even the worse for her at this pass, that in her mind— implanted there before her eminently practical father began to form it—a struggling disposition to believe in a wider and nobler humanity than she had ever heard of, constantly strove with doubts and resentments. With doubts, because the aspiration had been so laid waste in her youth. With resentments, because of the wrong that had been done her, if it were indeed a whisper of the truth. Upon a nature long accustomed to self-suppression, thus torn and divided, the Harthouse philosophy came as a relief and justification. Everything being hollow and worthless, she had missed nothing and sacrificed nothing. What did it matter, she had said to her father, when he proposed her husband. What did it matter, she said still. With a scornful self-reliance, she asked herself, What did anything matter—and went on.

---

1. Usual meaning is "taking up something," as when Harthouse goes in for statistics (book II, chapter II). Here the phrase has a special meaning from the game of cricket. A player "goes in" when he is taking over as batsman and begins to "score" runs (noted by Guiliano and Collins in *The Annotated Dickens* [1987]).

Towards what? Step by step, onward and downward, towards some
end, yet so gradually, that she believed herself to remain motionless.
As to Mr. Harthouse, whither *he* tended, he neither considered nor
cared. He had no particular design or plan before him: no energetic
wickedness ruffled his lassitude. He was as much amused and
interested, at present, as it became so fine a gentleman to be; perhaps even more than it would have been consistent with his reputation to confess. Soon after his arrival he languidly wrote to his
brother, the honorable and jocular member, that the Bounderbys
were "great fun;" and further, that the female Bounderby, instead
of being the Gorgon[2] he had expected, was young, and remarkably
pretty. After that, he wrote no more about them, and devoted his
leisure chiefly to their house. He was very often in their house, in his
flittings and visitings about the Coketown district; and was much
encouraged by Mr. Bounderby. It was quite in Mr. Bounderby's gusty
way to boast to all his world that *he* didn't care about your highly
connected people, but that if his wife Tom Gradgrind's daughter did,
she was welcome to their company.

Mr. James Harthouse began to think it would be a new sensation,
if the face which changed so beautifully for the whelp, would change
for him.

He was quick enough to observe; he had a good memory, and did
not forget a word of the brother's revelations. He interwove them with
everything he saw of the sister, and he began to understand her. To be
sure, the better and profounder part of her character was not within
his scope of perception; for in natures, as in seas, depth answers unto
depth;[3] but he soon began to read the rest with a student's eye.

Mr. Bounderby had taken possession of a house and grounds,
about fifteen miles from the town, and accessible within a mile
or two, by a railway striding on many arches over a wild country,
undermined by deserted coal-shafts, and spotted at night by fires
and black shapes of stationary engines at pits' mouths. This country, gradually softening towards the neighbourhood of Mr. Bounderby's retreat, there mellowed into a rustic landscape, golden with
heath, and snowy with hawthorn in the spring of the year, and
tremulous with leaves and their shadows all the summer time. The
bank had foreclosed a mortgage effected on the property thus
pleasantly situated, by one of the Coketown magnates, who, in his
determination to make a shorter cut than usual to an enormous fortune, overspeculated himself by about two hundred thousand pounds.
Those accidents did sometimes happen in the best-regulated fami-

2. Referring to Medusa, the best known of the three Gorgons, characters in Greek
   mythology. All those who look at Medusa, a female monster whose hair is composed of
   live serpents, are turned to stone.
3. Cf. Psalms 42.7, "Deep calleth unto deep."

lies of Coketown, but the bankrupts had no connexion whatever with the improvident classes.

It afforded Mr. Bounderby supreme satisfaction to instal himself in this snug little estate, and with demonstrative humility to grow cabbages in the flower-garden. He delighted to live, barrack-fashion, among the elegant furniture, and he bullied the very pictures with his origin. "Why, sir," he would say to a visitor, "I am told that Nickits," the late owner, "gave seven hundred pound for that Sea-beach.[4] Now, to be plain with you, if I ever, in the whole course of my life, take seven looks at it, at a hundred pound a look, it will be as much as I shall do. No, by George! I don't forget that I am Josiah Bounderby of Coketown. For years upon years, the only pictures in my possession, or that I could have got into my possession by any means, unless I stole 'em, were the engravings of a man shaving himself in a boot,[5] on the blacking bottles that I was overjoyed to use in cleaning boots with, and that I sold when they were empty for a farthing a-piece, and glad to get it!"

Then he would address Mr. Harthouse in the same style.

"Harthouse, you have a couple of horses down here. Bring half a dozen more if you like, and we'll find room for 'em. There's stabling in this place for a dozen horses; and unless Nickits is belied, he kept the full number. A round dozen of 'em, sir. When that man was a boy, he went to Westminster School. Went to Westminster School as a King's Scholar,[6] when I was principally living on garbage, and sleeping in market baskets. Why, if I wanted to keep a dozen horses— which I don't, for one's enough for me—I couldn't bear to see 'em in their stalls here, and think what my own lodging used to be. I couldn't look at 'em, sir, and not order 'em out. Yet so things come round. You see this place; you know what sort of a place it is; you are aware that there's not a completer place of its size in this kingdom or elsewhere—I don't care where—and here, got into the middle of it, like a maggot into a nut, is Josiah Bounderby. While Nickits (as a man came into my office, and told me yesterday), Nickits, who used to act in Latin, in the Westminster School plays, with the chief-justices and nobility of this country applauding him till they were

4. It is difficult to determine whether this is a reference to the subject of the painting or to its painter; if the latter, Bounderby has probably mangled the name of Charles Henry Seaforth or of Dickens' friend, Clarkson Stanfield, both well known for their seascapes.
5. An engraved advertisement pasted on a bottle of black shoe polish. To indicate how shiny a surface could be obtained with this polish, the picture featured a man using a boot as a mirror while shaving. Cf. *David Copperfield,* chapters 11–12.
6. A pupil awarded free tuition, board, and lodging for his performance in a special entrance examination, a privilege first established by the Crown during the reign of Elizabeth I. Westminster, one of the leading public schools in England, has many traditional observances, including the annual staging of a Latin play such as the one in which Nickits acted.

black in the face, is drivelling at this minute—drivelling, sir!—in a fifth floor, up a narrow dark back street in Antwerp."[7]

It was among the leafy shadows of this retirement, in the long sultry summer days, that Mr. Harthouse began to prove[8] the face which had set him wondering when he first saw it, and to try if it would change for him.

"Mrs. Bounderby, I esteem it a most fortunate accident that I find you alone here. I have for some time had a particular wish to speak to you."

It was not by any wonderful accident that he found her, the time of day being that at which she was always alone, and the place being her favorite resort. It was an opening in a dark wood, where some felled trees lay, and where she would sit watching the fallen leaves of last year, as she had watched the falling ashes at home.

He sat down beside her, with a glance at her face.

"Your brother. My young friend Tom—"

Her color brightened, and she turned to him with a look of interest. "I never in my life," he thought, "saw anything so remarkable and so captivating as the lighting of those features!" His face betrayed his thoughts—perhaps without betraying him, for it might have been according to its instructions so to do.

"Pardon me. The expression of your sisterly interest is so beautiful—Tom should be so proud of it—I know this is inexcusable, but I am so compelled to admire."

"Being so impulsive," she said composedly.

"Mrs. Bounderby, no: you know I make no pretence with you. You know I am a sordid piece of human nature, ready to sell myself at any time for any reasonable sum, and altogether incapable of any Arcadian[9] proceeding whatever."

"I am waiting," she returned, "for your further reference to my brother."

"You are rigid with me, and I deserve it. I am as worthless a dog as you will find, except that I am not false—not false. But you surprised and started me from my subject, which was your brother. I have an interest in him."

"Have you an interest in anything, Mr. Harthouse?" she asked, half incredulously and half gratefully.

"If you had asked me when I first came here, I should have said no. I must say now—even at the hazard of appearing to make a pretence, and of justly awakening your incredulity—yes."

7. A major port in Belgium.
8. To test.
9. Simple or unaffected, like a shepherd in the countryside of Arcadia in Greece, as represented in pastoral poetry.

She made a slight movement, as if she were trying to speak, but could not find voice; at length she said, "Mr. Harthouse, I give you credit for being interested in my brother."

"Thank you. I claim to deserve it. You know how little I do claim, but I will go that length. You have done so much for him, you are so fond of him; your whole life, Mrs. Bounderby, expresses such charming self-forgetfulness on his account—pardon me again—I am running wide of the subject. I am interested in him for his own sake."

She had made the slightest action possible, as if she would have risen in a hurry and gone away. He had turned the course of what he said at that instant, and she remained.

"Mrs. Bounderby," he resumed, in a lighter manner, and yet with a show of effort in assuming it, which was even more expressive than the manner he dismissed; "it is no irrevocable offence in a young fellow of your brother's years, if he is heedless, inconsiderate, and expensive—a little dissipated, in the common phrase. Is he?"

"Yes."

"Allow me to be frank. Do you think he games at all?"

"I think he makes bets." Mr. Harthouse waiting, as if that were not her whole answer, she added, "I know he does."

"Of course he loses?"

"Yes."

"Everybody does lose who bets. May I hint at the probability of your sometimes supplying him with money for these purposes?"

She sat, looking down; but, at this question, raised her eyes searchingly and a little resentfully.

"Acquit me of impertinent curiosity, my dear Mrs. Bounderby. I think Tom may be gradually falling into trouble, and I wish to stretch out a helping hand to him from the depths of my wicked experience.—Shall I say again, for his sake? Is that necessary?"

She seemed to try to answer, but nothing came of it.

"Candidly to confess everything that has occurred to me," said James Harthouse, again gliding with the same appearance of effort into his more airy manner; "I will confide to you my doubt whether he has had many advantages. Whether—forgive my plainness—whether any great amount of confidence is likely to have been established between himself and his most worthy father."

"I do not," said Louisa, flushing with her own great remembrance in that wise, "think it likely."

"Or, between himself, and—I may trust to your perfect understanding of my meaning, I am sure—and his highly esteemed brother-in-law."

She flushed deeper and deeper, and was burning red when she replied in a fainter voice, "I do not think that likely, either."

"Mrs. Bounderby," said Harthouse, after a short silence, "may there be a better confidence between yourself and me? Tom has borrowed a considerable sum of you?"

"You will understand, Mr. Harthouse," she returned, after some indecision: she had been more or less uncertain, and troubled throughout the conversation, and yet had in the main preserved her self-contained manner; "you will understand that if I tell you what you press to know, it is not by way of complaint or regret. I would never complain of anything, and what I have done I do not in the least regret."

"So spirited, too!" thought James Harthouse.

"When I married, I found that my brother was even at that time heavily in debt. Heavily for him, I mean. Heavily enough to oblige me to sell some trinkets. They were no sacrifice. I sold them very willingly. I attached no value to them. They were quite worthless to me."

Either she saw in his face that he knew, or she only feared in her conscience that he knew, that she spoke of some of her husband's gifts. She stopped, and reddened again. If he had not known it before, he would have known it then, though he had been a much duller man than he was.

"Since then, I have given my brother, at various times, what money I could spare: in short, what money I have had. Confiding in you at all, on the faith of the interest you profess for him, I will not do so by halves. Since you have been in the habit of visiting here, he has wanted in one sum as much as a hundred pounds. I have not been able to give it to him. I have felt uneasy for the consequences of his being so involved, but I have kept these secrets until now, when I trust them to your honor. I have held no confidence with any one, because—you anticipated my reason just now." She abruptly broke off.

He was a ready man, and he saw, and seized, an opportunity here of presenting her own image to her, slightly disguised as her brother.

"Mrs. Bounderby, though a graceless person, of the world worldly, I feel the utmost interest, I assure you, in what you tell me. I cannot possibly be hard upon your brother. I understand and share the wise consideration with which you regard his errors. With all possible respect both for Mr. Gradgrind and for Mr. Bounderby, I think I perceive that he has not been fortunate in his training. Bred at a disadvantage towards the society in which he has his part to play, he rushes into these extremes for himself, from opposite extremes that have long been forced—with the very best intentions we have no doubt—upon him. Mr. Bounderby's fine bluff English independence, though a most charming characteristic, does not—as we have agreed—invite confidence. If I might venture to remark that it is the least in the world deficient in that delicacy to which a youth mistaken, a character misconceived, and abilities misdirected, would turn for relief and guidance, I should express what it presents to my own view."

As she sat looking straight before her, across the changing lights upon the grass into the darkness of the wood beyond, he saw in her face her application of his very distinctly uttered words.

"All allowance," he continued, "must be made. I have one great fault to find with Tom, however, which I cannot forgive, and for which I take him heavily to account."

Louisa turned her eyes to his face, and asked him what fault was that?

"Perhaps," he returned, "I have said enough. Perhaps it would have been better, on the whole, if no allusion to it had escaped me."

"You alarm me, Mr. Harthouse. Pray let me know it."

"To relieve you from needless apprehension—and as this confidence regarding your brother, which I prize I am sure above all possible things, has been established between us—I obey. I cannot forgive him for not being more sensible, in every word, look, and act of his life, of the affection of his best friend; of the devotion of his best friend; of her unselfishness; of her sacrifice. The return he makes her, within my observation, is a very poor one. What she has done for him demands his constant love and gratitude, not his ill-humour and caprice. Careless fellow as I am, I am not so indifferent, Mrs. Bounderby, as to be regardless of this vice in your brother, or inclined to consider it a venial offence."

The wood floated before her, for her eyes were suffused with tears. They rose from a deep well, long concealed, and her heart was filled with acute pain that found no relief in them.

"In a word, it is to correct your brother in this, Mrs. Bounderby, that I must aspire. My better knowledge of his circumstances, and my direction and advice in extricating him—rather valuable, I hope, as coming from a scapegrace on a much larger scale—will give me some influence over him, and all I gain I shall certainly use towards this end. I have said enough, and more than enough. I seem to be protesting that I am a sort of good fellow, when, upon my honor, I have not the least intention to make any protestation to that effect, and openly announce that I am nothing of the sort. Yonder, among the trees," he added, having lifted up his eyes and looked about; for he had watched her closely until now; "is your brother himself; no doubt, just come down. As he seems to be loitering in this direction, it may be as well, perhaps, to walk towards him, and throw ourselves in his way. He has been very silent and doleful of late. Perhaps, his brotherly conscience is touched—if there are such things as consciences. Though, upon my honor, I hear of them much too often to believe in them."

He assisted her to rise, and she took his arm, and they advanced to meet the whelp. He was idly beating the branches as he lounged along: or he stooped viciously to rip the moss from the trees with his stick. He was startled when they came upon him while he was engaged in this latter pastime, and his color changed.

"Holloa!" he stammered; "I didn't know you were here."

"Whose name, Tom," said Mr. Harthouse, putting his hand upon his shoulder and turning him, so that they all three walked towards the house together, "have you been carving on the trees?"

"Whose name?" returned Tom. "Oh! You mean what girl's name?"

"You have a suspicious appearance of inscribing some fair creature's on the bark, Tom."

"Not much of that, Mr. Harthouse, unless some fair creature with a slashing fortune at her own disposal would take a fancy to me. Or she might be as ugly as she was rich, without any fear of losing me. I'd carve her name as often as she liked."

"I am afraid you are mercenary, Tom."

"Mercenary," repeated Tom. "Who is not mercenary? Ask my sister."

"Have you so proved it to be a failing of mine, Tom?" said Louisa, showing no other sense of his discontent and ill-nature.

"You know whether the cap fits you, Loo," returned her brother sulkily. "If it does, you can wear it."

"Tom is misanthropical to-day, as all bored people are now and then," said Mr. Harthouse. "Don't believe him, Mrs. Bounderby. He knows much better. I shall disclose some of his opinions of you, privately expressed to me, unless he relents a little."

"At all events, Mr. Harthouse," said Tom, softening in his admiration of his patron, but shaking his head sullenly too, "you can't tell her that I ever praised her for being mercenary. I may have praised her for being the contrary, and I should do it again if I had as good reason. However, never mind this now; it's not very interesting to you, and I am sick of the subject."

They walked on to the house, where Louisa quitted her visitor's arm and went in. He stood looking after her, as she ascended the steps, and passed into the shadow of the door; then put his hand upon her brother's shoulder again, and invited him with a confidential nod to a walk in the garden.

"Tom, my fine fellow, I want to have a word with you."

They had stopped among a disorder of roses—it was part of Mr. Bounderby's humility to keep Nickits's roses on a reduced scale—and Tom sat down on a terrace-parapet, plucking buds and picking them to pieces; while his powerful Familiar[1] stood over him, with a foot upon the parapet, and his figure easily resting on the arm supported by that knee. They were just visible from her window. Perhaps she saw them.

"Tom, what's the matter?"

"Oh! Mr. Harthouse," said Tom, with a groan, "I am hard up, and bothered out of my life."

"My good fellow, so am I."

"You!" returned Tom. "You are the picture of independence. Mr. Harthouse, I am in a horrible mess. You have no idea what a state I have got myself into—what a state my sister might have got me out of, if she would only have done it."

He took to biting the rose-buds now, and tearing them away from his teeth with a hand that trembled like an infirm old man's. After one exceedingly observant look at him, his companion relapsed into his lightest air.

"Tom, you are inconsiderate: you expect too much of your sister. You have had money of her, you dog, you know you have."

"Well, Mr. Harthouse, I know I have. How else was I to get it? Here's old Bounderby always boasting that at my age he lived upon two-pence a month, or something of that sort. Here's my father drawing what he calls a line, and tying me down to it from a baby, neck and heels. Here's my mother who never has anything of her own, except her complaints. What *is* a fellow to do for money, and where *am* I to look for it, if not to my sister?"

He was almost crying, and scattered the buds about by dozens. Mr. Harthouse took him persuasively by the coat.

"But, my dear Tom, if your sister has not got it—"

"Not got it, Mr. Harthouse? I don't say she has got it. I may have wanted more than she was likely to have got. But then she ought to get it. She could get it. It's of no use pretending to make a secret of matters now, after what I have told you already; you know she didn't marry old Bounderby for her own sake, or for his sake, but for my sake. Then why doesn't she get what I want, out of him, for my sake? She is not obliged to say what she is going to do with it; she is sharp enough; she could manage to coax it out of him, if she chose. Then why doesn't she choose, when I tell her of what consequence it is? But no. There she sits in his company like a stone, instead of making herself agreeable and getting it easily. I don't know what you may call this, but *I* call it unnatural conduct."

There was a piece of ornamental water immediately below the parapet, on the other side, into which Mr. James Harthouse had a very strong inclination to pitch Mr. Thomas Gradgrind Junior, as

1. An attendant evil spirit or devil who seeks control over his companion.

the injured men of Coketown threatened to pitch their property into the Atlantic. But he preserved his easy attitude; and nothing more solid went over the stone balustrades than the accumulated rosebuds now floating about, a little surface-island.

"My dear Tom," said Harthouse, "let me try to be your banker."

"For God's sake," replied Tom, suddenly, "don't talk about bankers!" And very white he looked, in contrast with the roses. Very white.

Mr. Harthouse, as a thoroughly well bred man, accustomed to the best society, was not to be surprised—he could as soon have been affected—but he raised his eyelids a little more, as if they were lifted by a feeble touch of wonder. Albeit it was as much against the precepts of his school to wonder, as it was against the doctrines of the Gradgrind College.

"What is the present need, Tom? Three figures? Out with them. Say what they are."

"Mr. Harthouse," returned Tom, now actually crying; and his tears were better than his injuries, however pitiful a figure he made; "it's too late; the money is of no use to me at present. I should have had it before, to be of use to me. But I am very much obliged to you; you're a true friend."

A true friend! "Whelp, whelp!" thought Mr. Harthouse, lazily; "what an Ass you are!"

"And I take your offer as a great kindness," said Tom grasping his hand. "As a great kindness, Mr. Harthouse."

"Well," returned the other, "it may be of more use by and by. And, my good fellow, if you will open your bedevilments to me when they come thick upon you, I may show you better ways out of them than you can find for yourself."

"Thank you," said Tom, shaking his head dismally, and chewing rosebuds. "I wish I had known you sooner, Mr. Harthouse."

"Now, you see, Tom," said Mr. Harthouse in conclusion, himself tossing over a rose or two, as a contribution to the island, which was always drifting to the wall as if it wanted to become a part of the mainland; "every man is selfish in everything he does, and I am exactly like the rest of my fellow creatures. I am desperately intent;" the languor of his desperation being quite tropical; "on your softening towards your sister—which you ought to do; and on your being a more loving and agreeable sort of brother—which you ought to be."

"I will be, Mr. Harthouse."

"No time like the present, Tom. Begin at once."

"Certainly I will. And my sister Loo shall say so."

"Having made which bargain, Tom," said Harthouse, clapping him on the shoulder again, with an air which left him at liberty to infer—as he did, poor fool—that this condition was imposed upon him in mere careless good nature, to lessen his sense of obligation, "we will tear ourselves asunder until dinner-time."

When Tom appeared before dinner, though his mind seemed heavy enough, his body was on the alert; and he appeared before Mr. Bounderby came in. "I didn't mean to be cross, Loo," he said, giving her his hand, and kissing her. "I know you are fond of me, and you know I am fond of you."

After this, there was a smile upon Louisa's face that day, for some one else. Alas, for some one else!

"So much the less is the whelp the only creature that she cares for," thought James Harthouse, reversing the reflection of his first day's knowledge of her pretty face. "So much the less, so much the less."

Chapter VIII.

EXPLOSION.

The next morning was too bright a morning for sleep, and James Harthouse rose early, and sat in the pleasant bay window of his dressing-room, smoking the rare tobacco that had had so wholesome an influence on his young friend. Reposing in the sunlight, with the fragrance of his eastern pipe about him, and the dreamy smoke vanishing into the air, so rich and soft with summer odors, he reckoned up his advantages as an idle winner might count his gains. He was not at all bored for the time, and could give his mind to it.

He had established a confidence with her, from which her husband was excluded. He had established a confidence with her, that absolutely turned upon her indifference towards her husband, and the absence, now and at all times, of any congeniality between them. He had artfully, but plainly assured her, that he knew her heart in its last most delicate recesses; he had come so near to her through its tenderest sentiment; he had associated himself with that feeling; and the barrier behind which she lived, had melted away. All very odd, and very satisfactory!

And yet he had not, even now, any earnest wickedness of purpose in him. Publicly and privately, it were much better for the age in which he lived, that he and the legion of whom he was one were designedly bad, than indifferent and purposeless. It is the drifting icebergs setting with any current anywhere, that wreck the ships.

When the Devil goeth about like a roaring lion, he goeth about in a shape by which few but savages and hunters are attracted. But, when he is trimmed, smoothed, and varnished, according to the mode: when he is aweary of vice, and aweary of virtue, used up as to brimstone, and used up as to bliss; then, whether he take to the serving out of red tape, or to the kindling of red fire, he is the very Devil.[1]

So, James Harthouse reclined in the window, indolently smoking, and reckoning up the steps he had taken on the road by which he happened to be travelling. The end to which it led was before him, pretty plainly; but he troubled himself with no calculations about it. What will be, will be.[2]

As he had rather a long ride to take that day—for there was a public occasion "to do" at some distance, which afforded a tolerable opportunity of going in for the Gradgrind men—he dressed early, and went down to breakfast. He was anxious to see if she had relapsed since the previous evening. No. He resumed where he had left off. There was a look of interest for him again.

He got through the day as much (or as little) to his own satisfaction, as was to be expected under the fatiguing circumstances; and came riding back at six o'clock. There was a sweep of some half mile between the lodge and the house, and he was riding along at a foot pace over the smooth gravel, once Nickits's, when Mr. Bounderby burst out of the shrubbery, with such violence as to make his horse shy across the road.

"Harthouse!" cried Mr. Bounderby. "Have you heard?"

"Heard what?" said Harthouse, soothing his horse, and inwardly favoring Mr. Bounderby with no good wishes.

"Then you *haven't* heard!"

"I have heard you, and so has this brute. I have heard nothing else."

Mr. Bounderby, red and hot, planted himself in the centre of the path before the horse's head, to explode his bombshell with more effect.

"The Bank's robbed!"

"You don't mean it!"

"Robbed last night, sir. Robbed in an extraordinary manner. Robbed with a false key."

"Of much?"

Mr. Bounderby, in his desire to make the most of it, really seemed mortified by being obliged to reply, "Why, no; not of very much. But it might have been."

"Of how much?"

---

1. Various biblical references are incorporated into this passage: "My name is Legion" (Mark 5.9); "as a roaring lion" (1 Peter 5.8); "But the . . . idolaters, and all liars, shall have their part in the lake which burneth with fire and brimstone" (Revelation 21.8). And according to Michael Wheeler, the expression "he is the very Devil" can be read in two ways: "as the clubman's cliché for a dashed roguish fellow or as the actual Devil incarnate" (*Allusion in Victorian Poetry* [1979]).
2. See p. 107, n. 4.

"Oh! as a sum—if you stick to a sum—of not more than a hundred and fifty pound," said Bounderby, with impatience. "But it's not the sum; it's the fact. It's the fact of the Bank being robbed, that's the important circumstance. I am surprised you don't see it."

"My dear Bounderby," said James, dismounting, and giving his bridle to his servant, "I *do* see it; and am as overcome as you can possibly desire me to be, by the spectacle afforded to my mental view. Nevertheless, I may be allowed, I hope, to congratulate you— which I do with all my soul, I assure you—on your not having sustained a greater loss."

"Thank'ee," replied Bounderby, in a short, ungracious manner. "But I tell you what. It might have been twenty thousand pound."

"I suppose it might."

"Suppose it might! By the Lord, you *may* suppose so. By George!" said Mr. Bounderby, with sundry menacing nods and shakes of his head, "It might have been twice twenty. There's no knowing what it would have been, or wouldn't have been, as it was, but for the fellows' being disturbed."

Louisa had come up now, and Mrs. Sparsit, and Bitzer.

"Here's Tom Gradgrind's daughter knows pretty well what it might have been, if you don't," blustered Bounderby. "Dropped, sir, as if she was shot when I told her! Never knew her do such a thing before. Does her credit, under the circumstances, in my opinion!"

She still looked faint and pale. James Harthouse begged her to take his arm; and as they moved on very slowly, asked her how the robbery had been committed.

"Why, I am going to tell you," said Bounderby, irritably giving his arm to Mrs. Sparsit. "If you hadn't been so mighty particular about the sum, I should have begun to tell you before. You know this lady (for she *is* a lady), Mrs. Sparsit?"

"I have already had the honor"—

"Very well. And this young man, Bitzer, you saw him too on the same occasion?" Mr. Harthouse inclined his head in assent, and Bitzer knuckled his forehead.

"Very well. They live at the Bank. You know they live at the Bank, perhaps? Very well. Yesterday afternoon, at the close of business hours, everything was put away as usual. In the iron room that this young fellow sleeps outside of, there was never mind how much. In the little safe in young Tom's closet, the safe used for petty purposes, there was a hundred and fifty odd pound."

"A hundred and fifty-four, seven, one," said Bitzer.

"Come!" retorted Bounderby, stopping to wheel round upon him, "let's have none of *your* interruptions. It's enough to be robbed while you're snoring because you're too comfortable, without being put right with *your* four seven ones. I didn't snore, myself, when I was your age, let me tell you. I hadn't victuals enough to snore. And I didn't four seven one. Not if I knew it."

Bitzer knuckled his forehead again, in a sneaking manner, and seemed at once particularly impressed and depressed by the instance last given of Mr. Bounderby's moral abstinence.

"A hundred and fifty odd pound," resumed Mr. Bounderby. "That sum of money, young Tom locked in his safe; not a very strong safe, but that's no matter now. Everything was left, all right. Some time in the night, while this young fellow snored—Mrs. Sparsit, ma'am, you say you have heard him snore?"

"Sir," returned Mrs. Sparsit, "I cannot say that I have heard him precisely snore, and therefore must not make that statement. But on winter evenings, when he has fallen asleep at his table, I have heard him, what I should prefer to describe as partially choke. I have heard him on such occasions produce sounds of a nature similar to what may be sometimes heard in Dutch clocks.[3] Not," said Mrs. Sparsit, with a lofty sense of giving strict evidence, "that I would convey any imputation on his moral character. Far from it, I have always considered Bitzer a young man of the most upright principle; and to that I beg to bear my testimony."

"Well!" said the exasperated Bounderby, "while he was snoring, *or* choking, *or* Dutch-clocking, *or* something or other—being asleep—some fellows, somehow, whether previously concealed in the house or not remains to be seen, got to young Tom's safe, forced it, and abstracted the contents. Being then disturbed, they made off; letting themselves out at the main door, and double-locking it again (it was double-locked, and the key under Mrs. Sparsit's pillow) with a false key, which was picked up in the street near the Bank, about twelve o'clock to-day. No alarm takes place, till this chap, Bitzer, turns out this morning and begins to open and prepare the offices for business. Then, looking at Tom's safe, he sees the door ajar, and finds the lock forced, and the money gone."

"Where is Tom, by the by?" asked Harthouse, glancing round.

"He has been helping the police," said Bounderby, "and stays behind at the Bank. I wish these fellows had tried to rob me when I was at his time of life. They would have been out of pocket, if they had invested eighteenpence in the job; I can tell 'em that."

"Is anybody suspected?"

"Suspected? I should think there was somebody suspected. Egod!" said Bounderby, relinquishing Mrs. Sparsit's arm to wipe his heated

---

3. Wheezy noises made by the mechanisms of a Dutch clock when the hours are sounded. These popular wooden clocks were made in the Black Forest of Germany (*Deutsch* became *Dutch*—as in Pennsylvania).

head. "Josiah Bounderby of Coketown, is not to be plundered and nobody suspected. No, thank you!"

Might Mr. Harthouse inquire Who was suspected?

"Well," said Bounderby, stopping and facing about to confront them all, "I'll tell you. It's not to be mentioned everywhere; it's not to be mentioned anywhere: in order that the scoundrels concerned (there's a gang of 'em) may be thrown off their guard. So take this in confidence. Now wait a bit." Mr. Bounderby wiped his head again. "What should you say to;" here he violently exploded: "to a Hand being in it?"

"I hope," said Harthouse, lazily, "not our friend Blackpot?"

"Say Pool instead of Pot, sir," returned Bounderby, "and that's the man."

Louisa faintly uttered some word of incredulity and surprise.

"O yes! I know!" said Bounderby, immediately catching at the sound. "I know! I am used to that. I know all about it. They are the finest people in the world, these fellows are. They have got the gift of the gab, they have. They only want to have their rights explained to them, they do. But I tell you what. Show me a dissatisfied Hand, and I'll show you a man that's fit for anything bad, I don't care what it is."

Another of the popular fictions of Coketown, which some pains had been taken to disseminate—and which some people really believed.

"But I am acquainted with these chaps," said Bounderby. "I can read 'em off, like books. Mrs. Sparsit, ma'am, I appeal to you. What warning did I give that fellow, the first time he set foot in the house, when the express object of his visit was to know how he could knock Religion over, and floor the Established Church? Mrs. Sparsit, in point of high connexions, you are on a level with the aristocracy,—did I say, or did I not say, to that fellow, 'you can't hide the truth from me: you are not the kind of fellow I like; you'll come to no good.'?"

"Assuredly, sir," returned Mrs. Sparsit, "you did, in a highly impressive manner, give him such an admonition."

"When he shocked you, ma'am," said Bounderby; "when he shocked your feelings?"

"Yes, sir," returned Mrs. Sparsit, with a meek shake of her head, "he certainly did so. Though I do not mean to say but that my feelings may be weaker on such points—more foolish, if the term is preferred—than they might have been, if I had always occupied my present position."

Mr. Bounderby stared with a bursting pride at Mr. Harthouse, as much as to say, "I am the proprietor of this female, and she's worth your attention, I think." Then, resumed his discourse.

"You can recall for yourself, Harthouse, what I said to him when you saw him. I didn't mince the matter with him. I am never mealy with 'em. I know 'em. Very well, sir. Three days after that, he bolted. Went off, nobody knows where: as my mother did in my infancy—only with this difference, that he is a worse subject than my mother, if possible What did he do before he went? What do you say;" Mr. Bounderby, with his hat in his hand, gave a beat upon the crown at every little division of his sentences, as if it were a tambourine; "to his being seen—night after night—watching the Bank?—to his lurking about there—after dark?—To its striking Mrs. Sparsit— that he could be lurking for no good—To her calling Bitzer's attention to him, and their both taking notice of him—And to its appearing on inquiry to-day—that he was also noticed by the neighbours?" Having come to the climax, Mr. Bounderby, like an oriental dancer, put his tambourine on his head.[4]

"Suspicious," said James Harthouse, "certainly."

"I think so, sir," said Bounderby, with a defiant nod. "I think so. But there are more of 'em in it. There's an old woman. One never hears of these things till the mischief's done; all sorts of defects are found out in the stable door after the horse is stolen; there's an old woman turns up now. An old woman who seems to have been flying into town on a broomstick, every now and then. *She* watches the place a whole day before this fellow begins, and, on the night when you saw him, she steals away with him and holds a council with him—I suppose, to make her report on going off duty, and be damned to her."

There was such a person in the room that night, and she shrunk from observation, thought Louisa.

"This is not all of 'em, even as we already know 'em," said Bounderby, with many nods of hidden meaning. "But I have said enough for the present. You'll have the goodness to keep it quiet, and mention it to no one. It may take time, but we shall have 'em. It's policy to give 'em line enough, and there's no objection to that."

"Of course, they will be punished with the utmost rigor of the law, as notice-boards observe," replied James Harthouse, "and serve them right. Fellows who go in for Banks must take the consequences. If there were no consequences, we should all go in for Banks." He had gently taken Louisa's parasol from her hand, and had put it up for her; and she walked under its shade, though the sun did not shine there.

"For the present, Loo Bounderby," said her husband, "here's Mrs. Sparsit to look after. Mrs. Sparsit's nerves have been acted upon by

4. Oriental street-dancers in London would signal the "climax" of a performance by banging their heads with tambourines (afterward, they would seek to collect money from onlookers). See Angus Easson, *Hard Times: A Critical Commentary*.

this business, and she'll stay here a day or two. So, make her comfortable."

"Thank you very much, sir," that discreet lady observed, "but pray do not let My comfort be a consideration. Anything will do for Me."

It soon appeared that if Mrs. Sparsit had a failing in her association with that domestic establishment, it was that she was so excessively regardless of herself and regardful of others, as to be a nuisance. On being shown her chamber, she was so dreadfully sensible of its comforts as to suggest the inference that she would have preferred to pass the night on the mangle[5] in the laundry. True, the Powlers and the Scadgerses were accustomed to splendor, "but it is my duty to remember," Mrs. Sparsit was fond of observing with a lofty grace: particularly when any of the domestics were present, "that what I was, I am no longer. Indeed," said she, "if I could altogether cancel the remembrance that Mr. Sparsit was a Powler, or that I myself am related to the Scadgers family; or if I could even revoke the fact, and make myself a person of common descent and ordinary connexions; I would gladly do so. I should think it, under existing circumstances, right to do so." The same Hermitical[6] State of mind led to her renunciation of made dishes and wines at dinner, until fairly commanded by Mr. Bounderby to take them; when she said, "Indeed you are very good, sir;" and departed from a resolution of which she had made rather formal and public announcement, to "wait for the simple mutton." She was likewise deeply apologetic for wanting the salt; and, feeling amiably bound to bear out Mr. Bounderby to the fullest extent in the testimony he had borne to her nerves, occasionally sat back in her chair and silently wept; at which periods a tear of large dimensions, like a crystal earring, might be observed (or rather, must be, for it insisted on public notice) sliding down her Roman nose.

But Mrs. Sparsit's greatest point, first and last, was her determination to pity Mr. Bounderby. There were occasions when in looking at him she was involuntarily moved to shake her head, as who would say, "Alas poor Yorick![7] After allowing herself to be betrayed into these evidences of emotion, she would force a lambent brightness, and would be fitfully cheerful, and would say, "You have still good spirits, sir, I am thankful to find;" and would appear to hail it as a blessed dispensation that Mr. Bounderby bore up as he did. One idiosyncrasy for which she often apologised, she found it excessively difficult to conquer. She had a curious propensity to call

5. A rolling press with two cylinders used to dry and press laundry.
6. Ascetic, as in the act of forgoing anything comfortable or pleasurable.
7. *Hamlet* 5.1.202.

Mrs. Bounderby "Miss Gradgrind," and yielded to it some three or four score times in the course of the evening. Her repetition of this mistake covered Mrs. Sparsit with modest confusion; but indeed, she said, it seemed so natural to say Miss Gradgrind: whereas, to persuade herself that the young lady whom she had had the happiness of knowing from a child could be really and truly Mrs. Bounderby, she found almost impossible. It was a further singularity of this remarkable case, that the more she thought about it, the more impossible it appeared; "the differences," she observed, "being such."

In the drawing-room after dinner, Mr. Bounderby tried the case of the robbery, examined the witnesses, made notes of the evidence, found the suspected persons guilty, and sentenced them to the extreme punishment of the law. That done, Bitzer was dismissed to town with instructions to recommend Tom to come home by the mail-train.

When candles were brought, Mrs. Sparsit murmured, "Don't be low, sir. Pray let me see you cheerful, sir, as I used to do." Mr. Bounderby, upon whom these consolations had begun to produce the effect of making him, in a bull-headed blundering way, sentimental, sighed like some large sea-animal. "I cannot bear to see you so, sir," said Mrs. Sparsit. "Try a hand at backgammon, sir, as you used to do when I had the honour of living under your roof." "I haven't played backgammon, ma'am," said Mr. Bounderby, "since that time." "No, sir," said Mrs. Sparsit, soothingly, "I am aware that you have not. I remember that Miss Gradgrind takes no interest in the game. But I shall be happy, sir, if you will condescend."[8]

They played near a window, opening on the garden. It was a fine night: not moonlight, but sultry and fragrant. Louisa and Mr. Harthouse strolled out into the garden, where their voices could be heard in the stillness, though not what they said. Mrs. Sparsit, from her place at the backgammon board, was constantly straining her eyes to pierce the shadows without. "What's the matter, ma'am?" said Mr. Bounderby; "you don't see a Fire, do you?" "Oh dear no, sir," returned Mrs. Sparsit, "I was thinking of the dew." "What have you got to do with the dew, ma'am?" said Mr. Bounderby. "It's not myself, sir," returned Mrs. Sparsit, "I am fearful of Miss Gradgrind's taking cold." "She never takes cold," said Mr. Bounderby. "Really, sir?" said Mrs. Sparsit. And was affected with a cough in her throat.

When the time drew near for retiring, Mr. Bounderby took a glass of water. "Oh, sir?" said Mrs. Sparsit. "Not your sherry warm, with lemon-peel and nutmeg?" "Why I have got out of the habit of taking it now, ma'am," said Mr. Bounderby. "The more's the pity, sir,"

8. Graciously lower yourself.

returned Mrs. Sparsit; "you are losing all your good old habits. Cheer up, sir! If Miss Gradgrind will permit me, I will offer to make it for you, as I have often done."

Miss Gradgrind readily permitting Mrs. Sparsit to do anything she pleased, that considerate lady made the beverage, and handed it to Mr. Bounderby. "It will do you good, sir. It will warm your heart. It is the sort of thing you want, and ought to take, sir." And when Mr. Bounderby said, "Your health, ma'am!" she answered with great feeling. "Thank you, sir. The same to you, and happiness also." Finally, she wished him good night, with great pathos; and Mr. Bounderby went to bed, with a maudlin persuasion that he had been crossed in something tender, though he could not, for his life, have mentioned what it was.

Long after Louisa had undressed and lain down, she watched and waited for her brother's coming home. That could hardly be, she knew, until an hour past midnight; but in the country silence, which did anything but calm the trouble of her thoughts, time lagged wearily. At last, when the darkness and stillness had seemed for hours to thicken one another, she heard the bell at the gate. She felt as though she would have been glad that it rang on until daylight; but it ceased, and the circles of its last sound spread out fainter and wider in the air, and all was dead again.

She waited yet some quarter of an hour, as she judged. Then she arose, put on a loose robe, and went out of her room in the dark, and up the staircase to her brother's room. His door being shut, she softly opened it and spoke to him, approaching his bed with a noiseless step.

She kneeled down beside it, passed her arm over his neck, and drew his face to hers. She knew that he only feigned to be asleep, but she said nothing to him.

He started by and by as if he were just then awakened, and asked who that was, and what was the matter?

"Tom, have you anything to tell me? If ever you loved me in your life, and have anything concealed from every one besides, tell it to me."

"I don't know what you mean, Loo. You have been dreaming."

"My dear brother:" she laid her head down on his pillow, and her hair flowed over him as if she would hide him from every one but herself: "is there nothing that you have to tell me? Is there nothing you can tell me, if you will? You can tell me nothing that will change me. O Tom, tell me the truth!"

"I don't know what you mean, Loo!"

"As you lie here alone, my dear, in the melancholy night, so you must lie somewhere one night, when even I, if I am living then, shall have left you. As I am here beside you, barefoot, unclothed, undistinguishable in darkness, so must I lie through all the night of my decay, until I am dust. In the name of that time, Tom, tell me the truth now!"

"What is it you want to know?"

"You may be certain;" in the energy of her love she took him to her bosom as if he were a child; "that I will not reproach you. You may be certain that I will be compassionate and true to you. You may be certain that I will save you at whatever cost. O Tom, have you nothing to tell me? Whisper very softly. Say only 'yes,' and I shall understand you!"

She turned her ear to his lips, but he remained doggedly silent.

"Not a word, Tom?"

"How can I say Yes, or how can I say No, when I don't know what you mean? Loo, you are a brave, kind girl, worthy I begin to think of a better brother than I am. But I have nothing more to say. Go to bed, go to bed."

"You are tired," she whispered presently, more in her usual way.

"Yes, I am quite tired out."

"You have been so hurried and disturbed to-day. Have any fresh discoveries been made?"

"Only those you have heard of, from—him."

"Tom, have you said to any one that we made a visit to those people, and that we saw those three together?"

"No. Didn't you yourself particularly ask me to keep it quiet, when you asked me to go there with you?"

"Yes. But I did not know then what was going to happen."

"Nor I neither. How could I?"

He was very quick upon her with this retort.

"Ought I to say, after what has happened," said his sister, standing by the bed—she had gradually withdrawn herself and risen, "that I made that visit? Should I say so? Must I say so?"

"Good Heavens, Loo," returned her brother, "you are not in the habit of asking my advice. Say what you like. If you keep it to yourself, I shall keep it to *myself*. If you disclose it, there's an end of it."

It was too dark for either to see the other's face; but each seemed very attentive, and to consider before speaking.

"Tom, do you believe the man I gave the money to, is really implicated in this crime?"

"I don't know. I don't see why he shouldn't be."

"He seemed to me an honest man."

"Another person may seem to you dishonest, and yet not be so."

There was a pause, for he had hesitated and stopped.

"In short," resumed Tom, as if he had made up his mind, "if you come to that, perhaps I was so far from being altogether in his favor, that I took him outside the door to tell him quietly, that I thought he might consider himself very well off to get such a windfall as he had got from my sister, and that I hoped he would make good use of it. You remember whether I took him out or not. I say nothing against the man; he may be a very good fellow, for anything I know; I hope he is."

"Was he offended by what you said?"

"No, he took it pretty well; he was civil enough. Where are you, Loo?" He sat up in bed and kissed her. "Good night, my dear, good night!"

"You have nothing more to tell me?"

"No. What should I have? You wouldn't have me tell you a lie?"

"I wouldn't have you do that to-night, Tom, of all the nights in your life; many and much happier as I hope they will be."

"Thank you, my dear Loo. I am so tired, that I am sure I wonder I don't say anything, to get to sleep. Go to bed, go to bed."

Kissing her again, he turned round, drew the coverlet over his head, and lay as still as if that time had come by which she had adjured him. She stood for some time at the bedside before she slowly moved away. She stopped at the door, looked back when she had opened it, and asked him if he had called her? But he lay still, and she softly closed the door and returned to her room.

Then the wretched boy looked cautiously up and found her gone, crept out of bed, fastened his door, and threw himself upon his pillow again: tearing his hair, morosely crying, grudgingly loving her, hatefully but impenitently spurning himself, and no less hatefully and unprofitably spurning all the good in the world.

Chapter IX.

HEARING THE LAST OF IT.

Mrs. Sparsit, lying by to recover the tone of her nerves in Mr. Bounderby's retreat, kept such a sharp look-out, night and day, under her Coriolanian eyebrows, that her eyes, like a couple of lighthouses on an iron-bound coast, might have warned all prudent mariners from that bold rock her Roman nose and the dark and craggy region in its neighbourhood, but for the placidity of her manner. Although it was hard to believe that her retiring for the night could be anything but a form, so severely wide awake were those classical eyes of hers, and so impossible did it seem that her rigid nose could yield to any relaxing influence, yet her manner of sitting, smoothing her uncomfortable, not to say, gritty, mittens (they were constructed of a cool fabric like a meat-safe),[1] or of ambling to unknown places of destination with her foot in her cotton

---

1. "A cupboard for storing meat, usually made of wire gauze or perforated zinc" (*OED*). The device provided for ventilation and also for protection from flies.

stirrup, was so perfectly serene, that most observers would have been constrained to suppose her a dove, embodied, by some freak of nature, in the earthly tabernacle of a bird of the hook-beaked order.

She was a most wonderful woman for prowling about the house. How she got from story to story, was a mystery beyond solution. A lady so decorous in herself, and so highly connected, was not to be suspected of dropping over the banisters or sliding down them, yet her extraordinary facility of locomotion suggested the wild idea. Another noticeable circumstance in Mrs. Sparsit was, that she was never hurried. She would shoot with consummate velocity from the roof to the hall, yet would be in full possession of her breath and dignity on the moment of her arrival there. Neither was she ever seen by human vision to go at a great pace.

She took very kindly to Mr. Harthouse, and had some pleasant conversation with him soon after her arrival. She made him her stately curtsey in the garden, one morning before breakfast.

"It appears but yesterday, sir," said Mrs. Sparsit, "that I had the honor of receiving you at the Bank, when you were so good as to wish to be made acquainted with Mr. Bounderby's address."

"An occasion, I am sure, not to be forgotten by myself in the course of Ages," said Mr. Harthouse, inclining his head to Mrs. Sparsit with the most indolent of all possible airs.

"We live in a singular world, sir," said Mrs. Sparsit.

"I have had the honor, by a coincidence of which I am proud, to have made a remark, similar in effect, though not so epigrammatically expressed."

"A singular world, I would say, sir," pursued Mrs. Sparsit; after acknowledging the compliment with a drooping of her dark eyebrows, not altogether so mild in its expression as her voice was in its dulcet tones; "as regards the intimacies we form at one time, with individuals we were quite ignorant of, at another. I recall, sir, that on that occasion you went so far as to say you were actually apprehensive of Miss Gradgrind."

"Your memory does me more honor than my insignificance deserves. I availed myself of your obliging hints to correct my timidity, and it is unnecessary to add that they were perfectly accurate. Mrs. Sparsit's talent for—in fact for anything requiring accuracy—with a combination of strength of mind—and Family—is too habitually developed to admit of any question." He was almost falling asleep over this compliment; it took him so long to get through, and his mind wandered so much in the course of its execution.

"You found Miss Gradgrind—I really cannot call her Mrs. Bounderby; it's very absurd of me—as youthful as I described her?" asked Mrs. Sparsit, sweetly.

"You drew her portrait perfectly," said Mr. Harthouse. "Presented her dead image."

"Very engaging, sir," said Mrs. Sparsit, causing her mittens slowly to revolve over one another.

"Highly so."

"It used to be considered," said Mrs. Sparsit, "that Miss Gradgrind was wanting in animation, but I confess she appears to me considerably and strikingly improved in that respect. Ay, and indeed here *is* Mr. Bounderby!" cried Mrs. Sparsit, nodding her head a great many times, as if she had been talking and thinking of no one else. "How do you find yourself this morning, sir? Pray let us see you cheerful, sir."

Now, these persistent assuagements of his misery, and lightenings of his load, had by this time begun to have the effect of making Mr. Bounderby softer than usual towards Mrs. Sparsit, and harder than usual to most other people from his wife downward. So, when Mrs. Sparsit said with forced lightness of heart, "You want your breakfast, sir, but I daresay Miss Gradgrind will soon be here to preside at the table," Mr. Bounderby replied, "If I waited to be taken care of by my wife, ma'am, I believe you know pretty well I should wait till Doomsday, so I'll trouble *you* to take charge of the teapot." Mrs. Sparsit complied, and assumed her old position at table.

This again made the excellent woman vastly sentimental. She was so humble withal, that when Louisa appeared, she rose, protesting she never could think of sitting in that place under existing circumstances, often as she had had the honor of making Mr. Bounderby's breakfast, before Mrs. Gradgrind—she begged pardon, she meant to say, Miss Bounderby—she hoped to be excused, but she really could not get it right yet, though she trusted to become familiar with it by and by—had assumed her present position. It was only (she observed) because Miss Gradgrind happened to be a little late, and Mr. Bounderby's time was so very precious, and she knew it of old to be so essential that he should breakfast to the moment, that she had taken the liberty of complying with his request: long as his will had been a law to her.

"There! Stop where you are, ma'am," said Mr. Bounderby, "stop where you are! Mrs. Bounderby will be very glad to be relieved of the trouble, I believe."

"Don't say that, sir," returned Mrs. Sparsit, almost with severity, "because that is very unkind to Mrs. Bounderby. And to be unkind is not to be you, sir."

"You may set your mind at rest, ma'am.—You can take it very quietly, can't you, Loo?" said Mr. Bounderby, in a blustering way to his wife.

"Of course. It is of no moment. Why should it be of any impor-tance to me?"

"Why should it be of any importance to any one, Mrs. Sparsit, ma'am?" said Mr. Bounderby, swelling with a sense of slight. "You attach too much importance to these things, ma'am. By George, you'll be corrupted in some of your notions here. You are old fash-ioned, ma'am. You are behind Tom Gradgrind's children's time."

"What is the matter with you?" asked Louisa, coldly surprised. "What has given you offence?"

"Offence!" repeated Bounderby. "Do you suppose if there was any offence given me, I shouldn't name it, and request to have it cor-rected? I am a straightforward man, I believe. I don't go beating about for side-winds."

"I suppose no one ever had occasion to think you too diffident, or too delicate," Louisa answered him composedly: "I have never made that objection to you, either as a child or as a woman. I don't under-stand what you would have."

"Have?" returned Mr. Bounderby. "Nothing. Otherwise, don't you, Loo Bounderby, know thoroughly well that I, Josiah Bound-erby of Coketown, would have it?"

She looked at him, as he struck the table and made the teaoups ring, with a proud colour in her face that was a new change, Mr. Harthouse thought. "You are incomprehensible this morning," said Louisa. "Pray take no further trouble to explain yourself. I am not curious to know your meaning. What does it matter!"

Nothing more was said on this theme, and Mr. Harthouse was soon idly gay on indifferent subjects. But from this day, the Sparsit action upon Mr. Bounderby threw Louisa and James Harthouse more together, and strengthened the dangerous alienation from her husband and confidence against him with another, into which she had fallen by degrees so fine that she could not retrace them if she tried. But, whether she ever tried or no, lay hidden in her own closed heart.

Mrs. Sparsit was so much affected on this particular occasion, that, assisting Mr. Bounderby to his hat after breakfast, and being then alone with him in the hall, she imprinted a chaste kiss upon his hand, murmured "My benefactor!" and retired, overwhelmed with grief. Yet it is an indubitable fact, within the cognizance of this history, that five minutes after he had left the house in the self same hat, the same descendant of the Scadgerses and connexion by matrimony of the Powlers, shook her right-hand mitten at his por-trait, made a contemptuous grimace at that work of art, and said "Serve you right, you Noodle, and I am glad of it!"

Mr. Bounderby had not been long gone, when Bitzer appeared. Bitzer had come down by train, shrieking and rattling over the long line of arches that bestrode the wild country of past and present coal pits, with an express from Stone Lodge. It was a hasty note to inform Louisa, that Mrs. Gradgrind lay very ill. She had never been well, within her daughter's knowledge; but, she had declined within the last few days, had continued sinking all through the night, and was now as nearly dead, as her limited capacity of being in any state that implied the ghost of an intention to get out of it, allowed.

Accompanied by the lightest of porters, fit colourless servitor at Death's door when Mrs. Gradgrind knocked, Louisa rumbled to Coketown, over the coalpits past and present, and was whirled into its smoky jaws. She dismissed the messenger to his own devices, and rode away to her old home.

She had seldom been there, since her marriage. Her father was usually sifting and sifting at his parliamentary cinder-heap in London (without being observed to turn up many precious articles among the rubbish), and was still hard at it in the national dust-yard.[2] Her mother had taken it rather as a disturbance than otherwise, to be visited, as she reclined upon her sofa; young people, Louisa felt herself all unfit for; Sissy she had never softened to again, since the night when the stroller's child had raised her eyes to look at Mr. Bounderby's intended wife. She had no inducements to go back, and had rarely gone.

Neither, as she approached her old home now, did any of the best influences of old home descend upon her. The dreams of childhood—its airy fables; its graceful, beautiful, humane, impossible adornments of the world beyond: so good to be believed in once, so good to be remembered when outgrown, for then the least among them rises to the stature of a great Charity in the heart, suffering little children[3] to come into the midst of it, and to keep with their pure hands a garden in the stony ways of this world, wherein it were better for all the children of Adam that they should oftener sun themselves, simple and trustful, and not worldly-wise—what had she to do with these? Remembrances of how she had journeyed to the little that she knew, by the enchanted roads of what she and millions of innocent creatures had hoped and imagined; of how, first coming upon Reason through the tender light of Fancy, she had seen it a beneficent god, deferring to gods as great as itself: not a grim Idol, cruel and cold, with its victims bound hand to foot, and its big dumb shape set up with a sightless stare, never to be moved by anything but so many calculated tons of leverage—what had she to do with these? Her remembrances of home and childhood, were

2. Garbage dump.
3. See Mark 10.14–15. After telling his disciples to "suffer" (allow) some little children to come to him to be blessed, Jesus affirmed: "Whosoever shall not receive the kingdom of God as a little child, he shall not enter therein."

remembrances of the drying up of every spring and fountain in her young heart as it gushed out. The golden waters were not there. They were flowing for the fertilisation of the land where grapes are gathered from thorns, and figs from thistles.[4]

She went, with a heavy, hardened kind of sorrow upon her, into the house and into her mother's room. Since the time of her leaving home, Sissy had lived with the rest of the family on equal terms. Sissy was at her mother's side; and Jane, her sister, now ten or twelve years old, was in the room.

There was great trouble before it could be made known to Mrs. Gradgrind that her eldest child was there. She reclined, propped up, from mere habit, on a couch: as nearly in her old usual attitude, as anything so helpless could be kept in. She had positively refused to take to her bed; on the ground that if she did, she would never hear the last of it.

Her feeble voice sounded so far away in her bundle of shawls, and the sound of another voice addressing her seemed to take such a long time in getting down to her ears, that she might have been lying at the bottom of a well. The poor lady was nearer Truth[5] than she ever had been: which had much to do with it.

On being told that Mrs. Bounderby was there, she replied, at cross-purposes, that she had never called him by that name since he married Louisa; that pending her choice of an unobjectionable name, she had called him J; and that she could not at present depart from that regulation, not being yet provided with a permanent substitute. Louisa had sat by her for some minutes, and had spoken to her often, before she arrived at a clear understanding who it was. She then seemed to come to it all at once.

"Well, my dear," said Mrs. Gradgrind, "and I hope you are going on satisfactorily to yourself. It was all your father's doing. He set his heart upon it. And he ought to know."

"I want to hear of you, mother; not of myself."

"You want to hear of me, my dear? That's something new, I am sure, when anybody wants to hear of me. Not at all well, Louisa. Very faint and giddy."

"Are you in pain, dear mother?"

"I think there's a pain somewhere in the room," said Mrs. Gradgrind, "but I couldn't positively say that I have got it."

After this strange speech, she lay silent for some time. Louisa, holding her hand, could feel no pulse; but kissing it, could see a slight thin thread of life in fluttering motion.

---

4. Matthew 7.16.
5. The idea that truth is difficult to find is figuratively expressed by the old saying that "Truth is lying at the bottom of a well." This saying, originated by the Greek philosopher Democritus, has been extensively repeated by later authors.

"You very seldom see your sister," said Mrs. Gradgrind. "She grows like you. I wish you would look at her. Sissy, bring her here."

She was brought, and stood with her hand in her sister's. Louisa had observed her with her arm round Sissy's neck, and she felt the difference of this approach.

"Do you see the likeness, Louisa?"

"Yes, mother. I should think her like me. But—"

"Eh? Yes, I always say so," Mrs. Gradgrind cried, with unexpected quickness. "And that reminds me. I—I want to speak to you, my dear. Sissy, my good girl, leave us alone a minute."

Louisa had relinquished the hand: had thought that her sister's was a better and brighter face than hers had ever been: had seen in it, not without a rising feeling of resentment, even in that place and at that time, something of the gentleness of the other face in the room: the sweet face with the trusting eyes, made paler than watching and sympathy made it, by the rich dark hair.

Left alone with her mother, Louisa saw her lying with an awful lull upon her face, like one who was floating away upon some great water, all resistance over, content to be carried down the stream. She put the shadow of a hand to her lips again, and recalled her.

"You were going to speak to me, mother."

"Eh? Yes, to be sure, my dear. You know your father is almost always away now, and therefore I must write to him about it."

"About what, mother? Don't be troubled. About what?"

"You must remember, my dear; that whenever I have said anything, on any subject, I have never heard the last of it; and consequently, that I have long left off saying anything."

"I can hear you, mother." But, it was only by dint of bending down to her ear, and at the same time attentively watching the lips as they moved, that she could link such faint and broken sounds into any chain of connexion.

"You learnt a great deal, Louisa, and so did your brother. Ologies of all kinds, from morning to night. If there is any Ology left, of any description, that has not been worn to rags in this house, all I can say is, I hope I shall never hear its name."

"I can hear you, mother, when you have strength to go on." This, to keep her from floating away.

"But there is something—not an Ology at all—that your father has missed, or forgotten, Louisa. I don't know what it is. I have often sat with Sissy near me, and thought about it. I shall never get its name now. But your father may. It makes me restless. I want to write to him, to find out for God's sake, what it is. Give me a pen, give me a pen."

Even the power of restlessness was gone, except from the poor head, which could just turn from side to side.

She fancied, however, that her request had been complied with, and that the pen she could not have held was in her hand. It matters little what figures of wonderful no-meaning she began to trace upon her wrappers. The hand soon stopped in the midst of them; the light that had always been feeble and dim behind the weak transparency, went out; and even Mrs. Gradgrind, emerged from the shadow in which man walketh and disquieteth himself in vain,[6] took upon her the dread solemnity of the sages and patriarchs.

Chapter X.

MRS. SPARSIT'S STAIRCASE.

Mrs. Sparsit's nerves being slow to recover their tone, the worthy woman made a stay of some weeks in duration at Mr. Bounderby's retreat, where, notwithstanding her anchorite turn of mind based upon her becoming consciousness of her altered station, she resigned herself with noble fortitude, to lodging, as one may say, in clover, and feeding on the fat of the land.[1] During the whole term of this recess from the guardianship of the Bank, Mrs. Sparsit was a pattern of consistency; continuing to take such pity on Mr. Bounderby to his face, as is rarely taken on man, and to call his portrait a Noodle to *its* face, with the greatest acrimony and contempt.

Mr. Bounderby, having got it into his explosive composition that Mrs. Sparsit was a highly superior woman to perceive that he had that general cross upon him in his deserts (for he had not yet settled what it was), and further that Louisa would have objected to her as a frequent visitor if it had comported with his greatness that she should object to anything he chose to do, resolved not to lose sight of Mrs. Sparsit easily. So, when her nerves were strung up to the pitch of again consuming sweet-breads in solitude, he said to her at the dinner-table, on the day before her departure, "I tell you what, ma'am; you shall come down here of a Saturday while the fine weather lasts, and stay till Monday." To which Mrs. Sparsit returned, in effect, though not of the Mahommedan[2] persuasion: "To hear is to obey."

Now, Mrs. Sparsit was not a poetical woman; but she took an idea, in the nature of an allegorical fancy, into her head. Much watching of Louisa, and much consequent observation of her impenetrable demeanor, which keenly whetted and sharpened

---

6. Cf. the Church of England Order for the Burial of the Dead in The Book of Common Prayer: "For man walketh in a vain shadow, and disquieteth himself in vain" (Psalms 39.5).
1. Genesis 45.18. "Anchorite": a person who has retired into seclusion, usually for religious reasons.
2. A Muslim, or follower of Mohammed.

Mrs. Sparsit's edge, must have given her as it were a lift, in the way of inspiration. She erected in her mind a mighty Staircase, with a dark pit of shame and ruin at the bottom; and down those stairs, from day to day and hour to hour, she saw Louisa coming.

It became the business of Mrs. Sparsit's life, to look up at her staircase, and to watch Louisa coming down. Sometimes slowly, sometimes quickly, sometimes several steps at one bout, sometimes stopping, never turning back. If she had once turned back, it might have been the death of Mrs. Sparsit in spleen and grief.

She had been descending steadily, to the day, and on the day, when Mr. Bounderby issued the weekly invitation recorded above. Mrs. Sparsit was in good spirits, and inclined to be conversational.

"And pray, sir," said she, "if I may venture to ask a question appertaining to any subject on which you show reserve—which is indeed hardy in me, for I well know you have a reason for everything you do—have you received intelligence respecting the robbery?"

"Why, ma'am, no; not yet. Under the circumstances, I didn't expect it yet. Rome wasn't built in a day, ma'am."

"Very true, sir," said Mrs. Sparsit, shaking her head.

"Nor yet in a week, ma'am."

"No, indeed, sir," returned Mrs. Sparsit, with a gentle melancholy upon her.

"In a similar manner, ma'am," said Bounderby, "I can wait, you know. If Romulus and Remus[3] could wait, Josiah Bounderby can wait. They were better off in their youth than I was, however. They had a she-wolf for a nurse; I had only a she-wolf for a grandmother. She didn't give any milk, ma'am; she gave bruises. She was a regular Alderney[4] at that."

"Ah!" Mrs. Sparsit sighed and shuddered.

"No, ma'am," continued Bounderby, "I have not heard anything more about it. It's in hand, though; and young Tom, who rather sticks to business at present—something new for him; he hadn't the schooling I had—is helping. My injunction is, Keep it quiet, and let it seem to blow over. Do what you like under the rose,[5] but don't give a sign of what you're about; or half a hundred of 'em will combine together and get this fellow who has bolted, out of reach for good. Keep it quiet, and the thieves will grow in confidence by little and little, and we shall have 'em."

---

3. Legendary leaders of early Rome. In childhood they were orphaned and abandoned but were sustained by being suckled by a she-wolf. They thus had a long wait before assuming power.
4. A breed of dairy cattle from the Channel Islands.
5. English translation of the Latin expression *sub rosa*. According to legend, a rose was associated with the god of silence, and hence to hang a rose above a meeting place would indicate that proceedings were to be secret.

"Very sagacious indeed, sir," said Mrs. Sparsit. "Very interesting. The old woman you mentioned, sir—"

"The old woman I mentioned, ma'am," said Bounderby, cutting the matter short, as it was nothing to boast about, "is not laid hold of; but, she may take her oath she will be, if that is any satisfaction to her villainous old mind. In the mean time, ma'am, I am of opinion, if you ask me my opinion, that the less she is talked about, the better."

That same evening, Mrs. Sparsit, in her chamber window, resting from her packing operations, looked towards her great staircase and saw Louisa still descending.

She sat by Mr. Harthouse, in an alcove in the garden, talking very low, he stood leaning over her, as they whispered together, and his face almost touched her hair. "If not quite!" said Mrs. Sparsit, straining her hawk's eyes to the utmost. Mrs. Sparsit was too distant to hear a word of their discourse, or even to know that they were speaking softly, otherwise than from the expression of their figures; but what they said was this:

"You recollect the man, Mr. Harthouse?"

"Oh, perfectly!"

"His face, and his manner, and what he said?"

"Perfectly. And an infinitely dreary person he appeared to me to be. Lengthy and prosy in the extreme. It was knowing to hold forth, in the humble-virtue school of eloquence; but, I assure you I thought at the time, 'My good fellow, you are over-doing this!'"

"It has been very difficult to me to think ill of that man."

"My dear Louisa—as Tom says." Which he never did say. "You know no good of the fellow?"

"No, certainly."

"Nor of any other such person?"

"How can I," she returned, with more of her first manner on her than he had lately seen, "when I know nothing of them, men or women?"

"My dear Louisa, then consent to receive the submissive representation of your devoted friend, who knows something of several varieties of his excellent fellow-creatures—for excellent they are, I am quite ready to believe, in spite of such little foibles as always helping themselves to what they can get hold of. This fellow talks. Well; every fellow talks. He professes morality. Well; all sorts of humbugs profess morality. From the House of Commons to the House of Correction, there is a general profession of morality, except among our people; it really is that exception which makes our people quite reviving. You saw and heard the case. Here was one of the fluffy classes pulled up extremely short by my esteemed friend Mr. Bounderby—who, as we know, is not possessed of that delicacy which would soften so tight a hand. The member of the fluffy classes was injured, exasperated, left the house grumbling, met somebody who proposed to him to go in for some share in this Bank business, went in, put something in his pocket which had nothing in it before, and relieved his mind extremely. Really he would have been an uncommon, instead of a common, fellow, if he had not availed himself of such an opportunity. Or he may have originated it altogether, if he had the cleverness."

"I almost feel as though it must be bad in me," returned Louisa, after sitting thoughtful awhile, "to be so ready to agree with you, and to be so lightened in my heart by what you say."

"I only say what is reasonable; nothing worse. I have talked it over with my friend Tom more than once—of course I remain on terms of perfect confidence with Tom—and he is quite of my opinion, and I am quite of his. Will you walk?"

They strolled away, among the lanes beginning to be indistinct in the twilight—she leaning on his arm—and she little thought how she was going down, down, down, Mrs. Sparsit's staircase.

Night and day, Mrs. Sparsit kept it standing. When Louisa had arrived at the bottom and disappeared in the gulf, it might fall in upon her if it would; but, until then, there it was to be, a Building, before Mrs. Sparsit's eyes. And there Louisa always was, upon it. And always gliding down, down, down!

Mrs. Sparsit saw James Harthouse come and go; she heard of him here and there; she saw the changes of the face he had studied; she, too, remarked to a nicety how and when it clouded, how and when it cleared; she kept her black eyes wide open, with no touch of pity, with no touch of compunction, all absorbed in interest. In the interest of seeing her, ever drawing, with no hand to stay her, nearer and nearer to the bottom of this new Giants' Staircase.[6]

With all her deference for Mr. Bounderby as contra-distinguished from his portrait, Mrs. Sparsit had not the smallest intention of interrupting the descent. Eager to see it accomplished, and yet patient, she waited for the last fall, as for the ripeness and fulness of the harvest of her hopes. Hushed in expectancy, she kept her wary gaze upon the stairs; and seldom so much as darkly shook her right mitten (with her fist in it), at the figure coming down.

6. Referring to a grand staircase in the courtyard of the ducal palace in Venice, which Dickens had visited in 1844 and 1853 (the name derives from two colossal statues of Mars and Neptune that flank the top of the steps). On this staircase the historic hero of Byron's play *Marino Faliero, Doge of Venice* was crowned and later assassinated, and the staircase was also associated, by Dickens, with another Doge whose life ended unhappily, Francesco Foscari, who died after his abdication of office in 1457. In his *Pictures from Italy* (1846), Dickens reports his own impression of the palace courtyard: "Descending from the palace by a staircase, called . . . the Giant's—I had . . . recollections of an old man abdicating, coming, more slowly and more feebly, down it, when he heard the bell, proclaiming his successor."

Chapter XI.

LOWER AND LOWER.

The figure descended the great stairs, steadily, steadily; always verging, like a weight in deep water, to the black gulf at the bottom.

Mr. Gradgrind, apprised of his wife's decease, made an expedition from London, and buried her in a business-like manner. He then returned with promptitude to the national cinder-heap, and resumed his sifting for the odds and ends he wanted, and his throwing of the dust about into the eyes of other people who wanted other odds and ends—in fact, resumed his parliamentary duties.

In the meantime, Mrs. Sparsit kept unwinking watch and ward. Separated from her staircase, all the week, by the length of iron road dividing Coketown from the country-house, she yet maintained her cat-like observation of Louisa, through her husband, through her brother, through James Harthouse, through the outsides of letters and packets, through everything animate and inanimate that at any time went near the stairs. "Your foot on the last step, my lady," said Mrs. Sparsit, apostrophising the descending figure, with the aid of her threatening mitten, "and all your art shall never blind me."

Art or nature though, the original stock of Louisa's character or the graft of circumstances upon it,—her curious reserve did baffle, while it stimulated, one as sagacious as Mrs. Sparsit. There were times when Mr. James Harthouse was not sure of her. There were times when he could not read the face he had studied so long; and when this lonely girl was a greater mystery to him, than any woman of the world with a ring of satellites to help her.

So the time went on; until it happened that Mr. Bounderby was called away from home by business which required his presence elsewhere, for three or four days. It was on a Friday that he intimated this to Mrs. Sparsit at the Bank, adding: "But you'll go down to-morrow, ma'am, all the same. You'll go down just as if I was there. It will make no difference to you."

"Pray, sir," returned Mrs. Sparsit, reproachfully, "let me beg you not to say that. Your absence will make a vast difference to me, sir, as I think you very well know."

"Well, ma'am, then you must get on in my absence as well as you can," said Bounderby, not displeased.

"Mr. Bounderby," retorted Mrs. Sparsit, "your will is to me a law, sir; otherwise, it might be my inclination to dispute your kind commands, not feeling sure that it will be quite so agreeable to Miss Gradgrind to receive me, as it ever is to your own munificent hospitality. But you shall say no more, sir. I will go, upon your invitation."

"Why, when I invite you to my house, ma'am," said Bounderby, opening his eyes, "I should hope you want no other invitation."

"No indeed, sir," returned Mrs. Sparsit, "I should hope not. Say no more, sir. I would, sir, I could see you gay again."

"What do you mean, ma'am?" blustered Bounderby.

"Sir," rejoined Mrs. Sparsit, "there was wont to be an elasticity in you which I sadly miss. Be buoyant, sir!"

Mr. Bounderby, under the influence of this difficult adjuration, backed up by her compassionate eye, could only scratch his head in a feeble and ridiculous manner, and afterwards assert himself at a distance, by being heard to bully the small fry of business all the morning.

"Bitzer," said Mrs. Sparsit that afternoon, when her patron was gone on his journey, and the Bank was closing, "present my compliments to young Mr. Thomas, and ask him if he would step up and partake of a lamb chop and walnut ketchup, with a glass of India ale?"[1] Young Mr. Thomas being usually ready for anything in that way, returned a gracious answer, and followed on its heels. "Mr. Thomas," said Mrs. Sparsit, "these plain viands being on table, I thought you might be tempted." "Thank'ee, Mrs. Sparsit," said the whelp. And gloomily fell to.

"How is Mr. Harthouse, Mr. Tom?" asked Mrs. Sparsit.

"Oh, he's all right," said Tom.

"Where may he be at present?" Mrs. Sparsit asked in a light conversational manner, after mentally devoting the whelp to the Furies for being so uncommunicative.

"He is shooting in Yorkshire," said Tom. "Sent Loo a basket half as big as a church, yesterday."

"The kind of gentleman, now," said Mrs. Sparsit, sweetly, "whom one might wager to be a good shot!"

"Crack," said Tom.

He had long been a down-looking young fellow, but this characteristic had so increased of late, that he never raised his eyes to any face for three seconds together. Mrs. Sparsit consequently had ample means of watching his looks, if she were so inclined.

"Mr. Harthouse is a great favourite of mine," said Mrs. Sparsit, "as indeed he is of most people. May we expect to see him again shortly, Mr. Tom?"

"Why, *I* expect to see him to-morrow," returned the whelp.

"Good news!" cried Mrs. Sparsit, blandly.

"I have got an appointment with him to meet him in the evening at the station here," said Tom, "and I am going to dine with him

---

1. A type of pale ale developed for British residents in India. This brew was supposed not to deteriorate in a tropical climate.

afterwards, I believe. He is not coming down to the country-house for a week or so, being due somewhere else. At least, he says so; but I shouldn't wonder if he was to stop here over Sunday, and stray that way."

"Which reminds me!" said Mrs. Sparsit. "Would you remember a message to your sister, Mr. Tom, if I was to charge you with one?"

"Well? I'll try," returned the reluctant whelp, "if it isn't a long un."

"It is merely my respectful compliments," said Mrs. Sparsit, "and I fear I may not trouble her with my society this week; being still a little nervous, and better perhaps by my poor self."

"Oh! If that's all," observed Tom, "it wouldn't much matter, even if I was to forget it, for Loo's not likely to think of you unless she sees you."

Having paid for his entertainment with this agreeable compliment, he relapsed into a hangdog silence until there was no more India ale left, when he said, "Well, Mrs. Sparsit, I must be off!" and went off.

Next day, Saturday, Mrs. Sparsit sat at her window all day long: looking at the customers coming in and out, watching the postmen, keeping an eye on the general traffic of the street, revolving many things in her mind, but, above all, keeping her attention on her staircase. The evening come, she put on her bonnet and shawl, and went quietly out: having her reasons for hovering in a furtive way about the station by which a passenger would arrive from Yorkshire, and for preferring to peep into it round pillars and corners, and out of ladies' waiting-room windows, to appearing in its precincts openly.

Tom was in attendance, and loitered about until the expected train came in. It brought no Mr. Harthouse. Tom waited until the crowd had dispersed, and the bustle was over; and then referred to a posted list of trains, and took counsel with porters. That done, he strolled away idly, stopping in the street and looking up it and down it, and lifting his hat off and putting it on again, and yawning and stretching himself, and exhibiting all the symptoms of mortal weariness to be expected in one who had still to wait until the next train should come in, an hour and forty minutes hence.

"This is a device to keep him out of the way," said Mrs. Sparsit, starting from the dull office window whence she had watched him last. "Harthouse is with his sister now!"

It was the conception of an inspired moment, and she shot off with her utmost swiftness to work it out. The station for the country-house was at the opposite end of the town, the time was short, the road not easy; but she was so quick in pouncing on a disengaged coach, so quick in darting out of it, producing her money, seizing her ticket, and diving into the train, that she was borne along the arches spanning the land of coal-pits past and present, as if she had been caught up in a cloud and whirled away.

All the journey, immovable in the air though never left behind; plain to the dark eyes of her mind, as the electric wires[2] which ruled a colossal strip of music-paper out of the evening sky, were plain to the dark eyes of her body; Mrs. Sparsit saw her staircase, with the figure coming down. Very near the bottom now. Upon the brink of the abyss.

An overcast September evening, just at nightfall, saw beneath its drooping eyelid Mrs. Sparsit glide out of her carriage, pass down the wooden steps of the little station into a stony road, cross it into a green lane, and become hidden in a summer-growth of leaves and branches. One or two late birds sleepily chirping in their nests, and a bat heavily crossing and recrossing her, and the reek[3] of her own tread in the thick dust that felt like velvet, were all Mrs. Sparsit heard or saw until she very softly closed a gate.

She went up to the house, keeping within the shrubbery, and went round it, peeping between the leaves at the lower windows. Most of them were open, as they usually were in such warm weather, but there were no lights yet, and all was silent. She tried the garden with no better effect. She thought of the wood, and stole towards it, heedless of long grass and briers: of worms, snails, and slugs, and all the creeping things[4] that be. With her dark eyes and her hook nose warily in advance of her, Mrs. Sparsit softly crushed her way through the thick undergrowth, so intent upon her object that she probably would have done no less, if the wood had been a wood of adders.

Hark!

The smaller birds might have tumbled out of their nests, fascinated by the glittering of Mrs. Sparsit's eyes in the gloom, as she stopped and listened.

Low voices close at hand. His voice and hers. The appointment *was* a device to keep the brother away! There they were yonder, by the felled tree.

Bending low among the dewy grass, Mrs. Sparsit advanced closer to them. She drew herself up, and stood behind a tree, like Robinson Crusoe in his ambuscade[5] against the savages; so near to them that at a spring, and that no great one, she could have touched them both. He was there secretly, and had not shown himself at the

2. Telegraph wires strung on poles alongside the railway.
3. Fine dust kicked up, with the appearance of smoke.
4. Acts 10.12.
5. In hiding in preparation for an ambush. *Robinson Crusoe* was De Foe's novel (see p. 46, n. 1) about the adventures of a shipwrecked Englishman.

house. He had come on horseback, and must have passed through the neighbouring fields; for his horse was tied to the meadow side of the fence, within a few paces.

"My dearest love," said he, "what could I do? Knowing you were alone, was it possible that I could stay away?"

"You may hang your head, to make yourself the more attractive; *I* don't know what they see in you when you hold it up," thought Mrs. Sparsit; "but you little think, my dearest love, whose eyes are on you!"

That she hung her head, was certain. She urged him to go away, she commanded him to go away; but she neither turned her face to him, nor raised it. Yet it was remarkable that she sat as still, as ever the amiable woman in ambuscade had seen her sit, at any period in her life. Her hands rested in one another, like the hands of a statue; and even her manner of speaking was not hurried.

"My dear child," said Harthouse; Mrs. Sparsit saw with delight that his arm embraced her; "will you not bear with my society for a little while?"

"Not here."

"Where, Louisa?"

"Not here."

"But we have so little time to make so much of, and I have come so far, and am altogether so devoted, and distracted. There never was a slave at once so devoted and ill-used by his mistress. To look for your sunny welcome that has warmed me into life, and to be received in your frozen manner, is heart-rending."

"Am I to say again, that I must be left to myself here?"

"But we must meet, my dear Louisa. Where shall we meet?"

They both started. The listener started guiltily, too; for she thought there was another listener among the trees. It was only rain, beginning to fall fast, in heavy drops.

"Shall I ride up to the house a few minutes hence, innocently supposing that its master is at home and will be charmed to receive me?"

"No!"

"Your cruel commands are implicitly to be obeyed; though I am the most unfortunate fellow in the world, I believe, to have been insensible to all other women, and to have fallen prostrate at last under the foot of the most beautiful, and the most engaging, and the most imperious. My dearest Louisa, I cannot go myself, or let you go, in this hard abuse of your power."

Mrs. Sparsit saw him detain her with his encircling arm, and heard him then and there, within her (Mrs. Sparsit's) greedy hearing, tell her how he loved her, and how she was the stake for which he ardently desired to play away all that he had in life. The objects he had lately pursued, turned worthless beside her; such success as was almost in his grasp, he flung away from him like the dirt it was, compared with her. Its pursuit, nevertheless, if it kept him near her, or its renunciation if it took him from her, or flight if she shared it, or secrecy if she commanded it, or any fate, or every fate, all was alike to him, so that she was true to him,—the man who had seen how cast away she was, whom she had inspired at their first meeting with an admiration, an interest, of which he had thought himself incapable, whom she had received into her confidence, who was devoted to her and adored her. All this, and more, in his hurry, and in hers, in the whirl of her own gratified malice, in the dread of being discovered, in the rapidly increasing noise of heavy rain among the leaves, and a thunder-storm rolling up—Mrs. Sparsit received into her mind, set off with such an unavoidable halo of confusion and indistinctness, that when at length he climbed the fence and led his horse away, she was not sure where they were to meet, or when, except that they had said it was to be that night.

But one of them yet remained in the darkness before her; and while she tracked that one she must be right. "Oh, my dearest love," thought Mrs. Sparsit, "you little think how well attended you are."

Mrs. Sparsit saw her out of the wood, and saw her enter the house. What to do next? It rained now, in a sheet of water. Mrs. Sparsit's white stockings were of many colors, green predominating; prickly things were in her shoes; caterpillars slung themselves, in hammocks of their own making, from various parts of her dress; rills ran from her bonnet, and her Roman nose. In such condition, Mrs. Sparsit stood hidden in the density of the shrubbery, considering what next?

Lo, Louisa coming out of the house! Hastily cloaked and muffled, and stealing away. She elopes! She falls from the lowermost stair, and is swallowed up in the gulf!

Indifferent to the rain, and moving with a quick determined step, she struck into a side-path parallel with the ride.[6] Mrs. Sparsit followed in the shadow of the trees, at but a short distance; for it was not easy to keep a figure in view going quickly through the umbrageous darkness.

When she stopped to close the side-gate without noise, Mrs. Sparsit stopped. When she went on, Mrs. Sparsit went on. She went by the way Mrs. Sparsit had come, emerged from the green lane, crossed the stony road, and ascended the wooden steps to the railroad. A train for Coketown would come through presently, Mrs. Sparsit knew; so she understood Coketown to be her first place of destination.

6. A path for horseback riders, usually through a wood.

In Mrs. Sparsit's limp and streaming state, no extensive precautions were necessary to change her usual appearance; but, she stopped under the lee of the station wall, tumbled her shawl into a new shape, and put it on over her bonnet. So disguised, she had no fear of being recognised when she followed up the railroad steps, and paid her money in the small office. Louisa sat waiting in a corner. Mrs. Sparsit sat waiting in another corner. Both listened to the thunder, which was loud, and to the rain, as it washed off the roof, and pattered on the parapets of the arches. Two or three lamps were rained out and blown out; so, both saw the lightning to advantage as it quivered and zig-zagged on the iron tracks.

The seizure of the station with a fit of trembling, gradually deepening to a complaint of the heart, announced the train. Fire and steam, and smoke, and red light; a hiss, a crash, a bell, and a shriek; Louisa put into one carriage, Mrs. Sparsit put into another: the little station a desert speck in the thunder-storm.

Though her teeth chattered in her head from wet and cold, Mrs. Sparsit exulted hugely. The figure had plunged down the precipice, and she felt herself, as it were, attending on the body. Could she, who had been so active in the getting up of the funeral triumph, do less than exult? "She will be at Coketown long before him," thought Mrs. Sparsit, "though his horse is never so good. Where will she wait for him? And where will they go together? Patience. We shall see."

The tremendous rain occasioned infinite confusion, when the train stopped at its destination. Gutters and pipes had burst, drains had overflowed, and streets were under water. In the first instant of alighting, Mrs. Sparsit turned her distracted eyes towards the waiting coaches, which were in great request. "She will get into one," she considered, "and will be away before I can follow in another. At all risks of being run over, I must see the number, and hear the order given to the coachman."

But, Mrs. Sparsit was wrong in her calculation. Louisa got into no coach, and was already gone. The black eyes kept upon the railroad-carriage in which she had travelled, settled upon it a moment too late. The door not being opened after several minutes, Mrs. Sparsit passed it and repassed it, saw nothing, looked in, and found it empty. Wet through and through: with her feet squelching and squashing in her shoes whenever she moved; with a rash of rain upon her classical visage; with a bonnet like an overripe fig; with all her clothes spoiled; with damp impressions of every button, string, and hook-and-eye she wore, printed off upon her highly-connected back; with a stagnant verdure on her general exterior, such as accumulates on an old park fence in a mouldy lane; Mrs. Sparsit had no resource but to burst into tears of bitterness and say, "I have lost her!"

Chapter XII.

DOWN.

The national dustmen,[1] after entertaining one another with a great many noisy little fights among themselves, had dispersed for the present, and Mr. Gradgrind was at home for the vacation.

He sat writing in the room with the deadly-statistical clock, proving something no doubt—probably, in the main, that the Good Samaritan was a Bad Economist.[2] The noise of the rain did not disturb him much; but it attracted his attention sufficiently to make him raise his head sometimes, as if he were rather remonstrating with the elements. When it thundered very loudly, he glanced towards Coketown, having it in his mind that some of the tall chimneys might be struck by lightning.

The thunder was rolling into distance, and the rain was pouring down like a deluge, when the door of his room opened. He looked round the lamp upon his table, and saw, with amazement, his eldest daughter.

"Louisa!"

"Father, I want to speak to you."

"What is the matter? How strange you look! And good Heaven," said Mr. Gradgrind, wondering more and more, "have you come here exposed to this storm?"

She put her hands to her dress, as if she hardly knew. "Yes." Then she uncovered her head, and letting her cloak and hood fall where they might, stood looking at him: so colorless, so dishevelled, so defiant and despairing, that he was afraid of her.

"What is it? I conjure you, Louisa, tell me what is the matter."

She dropped into a chair before him, and put her cold hand on his arm.

"Father, you have trained me from my cradle."

"Yes, Louisa."

"I curse the hour in which I was born to such a destiny."

He looked at her in doubt and dread, vacantly repeating, "Curse the hour? Curse the hour?"

"How could you give me life, and take from me all the inappreciable things that raise it from the state of conscious death? Where are the graces of my soul? Where are the sentiments of my heart? What have you done, O father, what have you done, with the garden that should have bloomed once, in this great wilderness here!"

---

1. Members of Parliament in London are likened here to dustmen; i.e., persons employed to collect garbage and trash.
2. See Luke 10.29–37, for the parable of the Samaritan who gave help and money to a stranger who had been robbed.

She struck herself with both her hands upon her bosom.

"If it had ever been here, its ashes alone would save me from the void in which my whole life sinks. I did not mean to say this; but, father, you remember the last time we conversed in this room?"

He had been so wholly unprepared for what he heard now, that it was with difficulty he answered, "Yes, Louisa."

"What has risen to my lips now, would have risen to my lips then, if you had given me a moment's help. I don't reproach you, father. What you have never nurtured in me, you have never nurtured in yourself; but O! if you had only done so long ago, or if you had only neglected me, what a much better and much happier creature I should have been this day!"

On hearing this, after all his care, he bowed his head upon his hand and groaned aloud.

"Father, if you had known, when we were last together here, what even I feared while I strove against it—as it has been my task from infancy to strive against every natural prompting that has arisen in my heart; if you had known that there lingered in my breast, sensibilities, affections, weaknesses capable of being cherished into strength, defying all the calculations ever made by man, and no more known to his arithmetic than his Creator is,—would you have given me to the husband whom I am now sure that I hate?"

He said, "No. No, my poor child."

"Would you have doomed me, at any time, to the frost and blight that have hardened and spoiled me? Would you have robbed me— for no one's enrichment—only for the greater desolation of this world—of the immaterial part of my life, the spring and summer of my belief, my refuge from what is sordid and bad in the real things around me, my school in which I should have learned to be more humble and more trusting with them, and to hope in my little sphere to make them better?"

"O no, no. No, Louisa."

"Yet, father, if I had been stone blind; if I had groped my way by my sense of touch, and had been free, while I knew the shapes and surfaces of things, to exercise my fancy somewhat, in regard to them; I should have been a million times wiser, happier, more loving, more contented, more innocent and human in all good respects, than I am with the eyes I have. Now, hear what I have come to say."

He moved, to support her with his arm. She rising as he did so, they stood close together: she, with a hand upon his shoulder, looking fixedly in his face.

"With a hunger and thirst upon me, father, which have never been for a moment appeased; with an ardent impulse towards some region where rules, and figures, and definitions were not quite absolute; I have grown up, battling every inch of my way."

"I never knew you were unhappy, my child."

"Father, I always knew it. In this strife I have almost repulsed and crushed my better angel into a demon. What I have learned has left me doubting, misbelieving, despising, regretting, what I have not learned, and my dismal resource has been to think that life would soon go by, and that nothing in it could be worth the pain and trouble of a contest."

"And you so young, Louisa!" he said with pity.

"And I so young. In this condition, father—for I show you now, without fear or favor, the ordinary deadened state of my mind as I know it—you proposed my husband to me. I took him. I never made a pretence to him or you that I loved him. I knew, and, father, you knew, and he knew, that I never did. I was not wholly indifferent, for I had a hope of being pleasant and useful to Tom. I made that wild escape into something visionary, and have slowly found out how wild it was. But Tom had been the subject of all the little tenderness of my life; perhaps he became so because I knew so well how to pity him. It matters little now, except as it may dispose you to think more leniently of his errors."

As her father held her in his arms, she put her other hand upon his other shoulder, and still looking fixedly in his face, went on.

"When I was irrevocably married, there rose up into rebellion against the tie, the old strife, made fiercer by all those causes of disparity which arise out of our two individual natures, and which no general laws shall ever rule or state for me, father, until they shall be able to direct the anatomist where to strike his knife into the secrets of my soul."

"Louisa!" he said, and said imploringly; for he well remembered what had passed between them in their former interview.

"I do not reproach you, father, I make no complaint. I am here with another object."

"What can I do, child? Ask me what you will."

"I am coming to it. Father, chance then threw into my way a new acquaintance; a man such as I had had no experience of; used to the world; light, polished, easy; making no pretences; avowing the low estimate of everything, that I was half afraid to form in secret; conveying to me almost immediately, though I don't know how or by what degrees, that he understood me, and read my thoughts. I could not find that he was worse than I. There seemed to be a near affinity between us. I only wondered it should be worth his while, who cared for nothing else, to care so much for me."

"For you, Louisa!"

Her father might instinctively have loosened his hold, but that he felt her strength departing from her, and saw a wild dilating fire in the eyes steadfastly regarding him.

"I say nothing of his plea for claiming my confidence. It matters very little how he gained it. Father, he did gain it. What you know of the story of my marriage, he soon knew, just as well."

Her father's face was ashy white, and he held her in both his arms.

"I have done no worse, I have not disgraced you. But if you ask me whether I have loved him, or do love him, I tell you plainly, father, that it may be so. I don't know!"

She took her hands suddenly from his shoulders and pressed them both upon her side; while in her face, not like itself—and in her figure, drawn up, resolute to finish by a last effort what she had to say—the feelings long suppressed broke loose.

"This night, my husband being away, he has been with me, declaring himself my lover. This minute he expects me, for I could release myself of his presence by no other means. I do not know that I am sorry, I do not know that I am ashamed, I do not know that I am degraded in my own esteem. All that I know is, your philosophy and your teaching will not save me. Now, father, you have brought me to this. Save me by some other means!"

He tightened his hold in time to prevent her sinking on the floor, but she cried out in a terrible voice, "I shall die if you hold me! Let me fall upon the ground!" And he laid her down there, and saw the pride of his heart and the triumph of his system, lying, an insensible heap, at his feet.

END OF THE SECOND BOOK

Book the Third—Garnering

Chapter I.

ANOTHER THING NEEDFUL.

Louisa awoke from a torpor, and her eyes languidly opened on her old bed at home, and her old room. It seemed, at first, as if all that had happened since the days when these objects were familiar to her were the shadows of a dream; but gradually, as the objects became more real to her sight, the events became more real to her mind.

She could scarcely move her head for pain and heaviness, her eyes were strained and sore, and she was very weak. A curious passive inattention had such possession of her, that the presence of her little sister in the room did not attract her notice for some time. Even when their eyes had met, and her sister had approached the bed, Louisa lay for minutes looking at her in silence, and suffering her timidly to hold her passive hand, before she asked:

"When was I brought to this room?"

"Last night, Louisa."

"Who brought me here?"

"Sissy, I believe."

"Why do you believe so?"

"Because I found her here this morning. She didn't come to my bedside to wake me, as she always does; and I went to look for her. She was not in her own room either; and I went looking for her all over the house, until I found her here, taking care of you and cooling your head. Will you see father? Sissy said I was to tell him when you woke."

"What a beaming face you have, Jane!" said Louisa, as her young sister—timidly still—bent down to kiss her.

"Have I? I am very glad you think so. I am sure it must be Sissy's doing."

The arm Louisa had begun to twine about her neck, unbent itself. "You can tell father, if you will." Then, staying her a moment, she said, "It was you who made my room so cheerful, and gave it this look of welcome?"

"Oh no, Louisa, it was done before I came. It was—"

Louisa turned upon her pillow, and heard no more. When her sister had withdrawn, she turned her head back again, and lay with her face towards the door, until it opened and her father entered.

He had a jaded anxious look upon him, and his hand, usually steady, trembled in hers. He sat down at the side of the bed, tenderly asking how she was, and dwelling on the necessity of her keeping very quiet after her agitation and exposure to the weather last night. He spoke in a subdued and troubled voice, very different from his usual dictatorial manner; and was often at a loss for words.

"My dear Louisa. My poor daughter." He was so much at a loss at that place, that he stopped altogether. He tried again.

"My unfortunate child." The place was so difficult to get over, that he tried again.

"It would be hopeless for me, Louisa, to endeavour to tell you how overwhelmed I have been, and still am, by what broke upon me last night. The ground on which I stand has ceased to be solid under my feet. The only support on which I leaned, and the strength of which it seemed and still does seem, impossible to question, has given way in an instant. I am stunned by these discoveries. I have no selfish meaning in what I say; but I find the shock of what broke upon me last night, to be very heavy indeed."

She could give him no comfort herein. She had suffered the wreck of her whole life upon the rock.

"I will not say, Louisa, that if you had by any happy chance undeceived me some time ago, it would have been better for us both;

better for your peace, and better for mine. For I am sensible that it may not have been a part of my system to invite any confidence of that kind. I have proved my—my system to myself, and I have rigidly administered it; and I must bear the responsibility of its failures. I only entreat you to believe, my favorite child, that I have meant to do right."

He said it earnestly, and to do him justice he had. In gauging fathomless deeps with his little mean excise-rod,[1] and in staggering over the universe with his rusty stiff-legged compasses, he had meant to do great things. Within the limits of his short tether he had tumbled about, annihilating the flowers of existence with greater singleness of purpose than many of the blatant personages whose company he kept.

"I am well assured of what you say, father. I know I have been your favorite child. I know you have intended to make me happy. I have never blamed you, and I never shall."

He took her outstretched hand, and retained it in his.

"My dear, I have remained all night at my table, pondering again and again on what has so painfully passed between us. When I consider your character; when I consider that what has been known to me for hours, has been concealed by you for years; when I consider under what immediate pressure it has been forced from you at last; I come to the conclusion that I cannot but mistrust myself."

He might have added more than all, when he saw the face now looking at him. He did add it in effect, perhaps, as he softly moved her scattered hair from her forehead with his hand. Such little actions, slight in another man, were very noticeable in him; and his daughter received them as if they had been words of contrition.

"But," said Mr. Gradgrind, slowly, and with hesitation, as well as with a wretched sense of helplessness, "if I see reason to mistrust myself for the past, Louisa, I should also mistrust myself for the present and the future. To speak unreservedly to you, I do. I am far from feeling convinced now, however differently I might have felt only this time yesterday, that I am fit for the trust you repose in me; that I know how to respond to the appeal you have come home to make to me; that I have the right instinct—supposing it for the moment to be some quality of that nature—how to help you, and to set you right, my child."

She had turned upon her pillow, and lay with her face upon her arm, so that he could not see it. All her wildness and passion had subsided; but, though softened, she was not in tears. Her father was

---

1. A measuring stick used by an official for taking samples of various commodities and in gauging how much excise tax would have to be paid on them.

changed in nothing so much as in the respect that he would have
been glad to see her in tears.

"Some persons hold," he pursued, still hesitating, "that there is a
wisdom of the Head, and that there is a wisdom of the Heart. I have
not supposed so; but, as I have said, I mistrust myself now. I have
supposed the Head to be all-sufficient. It may not be all-sufficient;
how can I venture this morning to say it is! If that other kind of wisdom should be what I have neglected, and should be the instinct that
is wanted, Louisa—"

He suggested it very doubtfully, as if he were half unwilling to
admit it even now. She made him no answer; lying before him on
her bed, still half-dressed, much as he had seen her lying on the
floor of his room last night.

"Louisa," and his hand rested on her hair again, "I have been absent
from here, my dear, a good deal of late; and though your sister's
training has been pursued according to—the system," he appeared
to come to that word with great reluctance always, "it has necessarily been modified by daily associations begun, in her case, at an
early age. I ask you—ignorantly and humbly, my daughter—for the
better, do you think?"

"Father," she replied, without stirring, "if any harmony has been
awakened in her young breast that was mute in mine until it turned
to discord, let her thank Heaven for it, and go upon her happier
way, taking it as her greatest blessing that she has avoided my way."

"O my child, my child!" he said, in a forlorn manner, "I am an
unhappy man to see you thus! What avails it to me that you do not
reproach me, if I so bitterly reproach myself!" He bent his head,
and spoke low to her. "Louisa, I have a misgiving that some change
may have been slowly working about me in this house, by mere love
and gratitude; that what the Head had left undone and could not
do, the Heart may have been doing silently. Can it be so?"

She made him no reply.

"I am not too proud to believe it, Louisa. How could I be arro-
gant, and you before me! Can it be so? Is it so my dear?"

He looked upon her, once more, lying cast away there; and without another word went out of the room. He had not been long gone,
when she heard a light tread near the door, and knew that some one
stood beside her.

She did not raise her head. A dull anger that she should be seen
in her distress, and that the involuntary look she had so resented
should come to this fulfilment, smouldered within her like an
unwholesome fire. All closely imprisoned forces rend and destroy.
The air that would be healthful to the earth, the water that would
enrich it, the heat that would ripen it, tear it when caged up. So in
her bosom even now; the strongest qualities she possessed, long

turned upon themselves, became a heap of obduracy, that rose against a friend.

It was well that soft touch came upon her neck, and that she understood herself to be supposed to have fallen asleep. The sympathetic hand did not claim her resentment. Let it lie there, let it lie.

It lay there, warming into life a crowd of gentler thoughts; and she rested. As she softened with the quiet, and the consciousness of being so watched, some tears made their way into her eyes. The face touched hers, and she knew that there were tears upon it too, and she the cause of them.

As Louisa feigned to rouse herself, and sat up, Sissy retired, so that she stood placidly near the bed-side.

"I hope I have not disturbed you. I have come to ask if you would let me stay with you."

"Why should you stay with me? My sister will miss you. You are everything to her."

"Am I?" returned Sissy, shaking her head. "I would be something to you, if I might."

"What?" said Louisa, almost sternly.

"Whatever you want most, if I could be that. At all events, I would like to try to be as near it as I can. And however far off that may be, I will never tire of trying. Will you let me?"

"My father sent you to ask me."

"No indeed," replied Sissy. "He told me that I might come in now, but he sent me away from the room this morning—or at least—" She hesitated and stopped.

"At least, what?" said Louisa, with her searching eyes upon her.

"I thought it best myself that I should be sent away, for I felt very uncertain whether you would like to find me here."

"Have I always hated you so much?"

"I hope not, for I have always loved you, and have always wished that you should know it. But you changed to me a little, shortly before you left home. Not that I wondered at it. You knew so much, and I knew so little, and it was so natural in many ways, going as you were among other friends, that I had nothing to complain of, and was not at all hurt."

Her color rose as she said it modestly and hurriedly. Louisa understood the loving pretence, and her heart smote her.

"May I try?" said Sissy, emboldened to raise her hand to the neck that was insensibly drooping towards her.

Louisa, taking down the hand that would have embraced her in another moment, held it in one of hers, and answered:

"First, Sissy, do you know what I am? I am so proud and so hardened, so confused and troubled, so resentful and unjust to every one and to myself, that everything is stormy, dark, and wicked to me. Does not that repel you?"

"No!"

"I am so unhappy, and all that should have made me otherwise is so laid waste, that if I had been bereft of sense to this hour, and instead of being as learned as you think me, had to begin to acquire the simplest truths, I could not want a guide to peace, content-ment, honor, all the good of which I am quite devoid, more abjectly than I do. Does not that repel you?"

"No!"

In the innocence of her brave affection, and the brimming up of her old devoted spirit, the once deserted girl shone like a beautiful light upon the darkness of the other.

Louisa raised the hand that it might clasp her neck, and join its fellow there. She fell upon her knees, and clinging to this stroller's child looked up at her almost with veneration.

"Forgive me, pity me, help me! Have compassion on my great need, and let me lay this head of mine upon a loving heart!"

"O lay it here!" cried Sissy. "Lay it here, my dear."

Chapter II.

VERY RIDICULOUS.

Mr. James Harthouse passed a whole night and a day in a state of so much hurry, that the World, with its best glass[1] in its eye, would scarcely have recognised him during that insane interval, as the brother Jem of the honorable and jocular member. He was positively agitated. He several times spoke with an emphasis, similar to the vulgar manner. He went in and went out in an unaccountable way, like a man without an object. He rode like a highwayman. In a word, he was so horribly bored by existing circumstances, that he forgot to go in for boredom in the manner prescribed by the authorities.

After putting his horse at Coketown through the storm, as if it were a leap, he waited up all night: from time to time ringing his bell with the greatest fury, charging the porter who kept watch with delinquency in withholding letters or messages that could not fail to have been entrusted to him, and demanding restitution on the spot. The dawn coming, the morning coming, and the day coming, and neither message nor letter coming with either, he went down to the country-house. There, the report was, Mr. Bounderby away, and Mrs. Bounderby in town. Left for town suddenly last evening. Not even known to be gone until receipt of message, importing that her return was not to be expected for the present.

1. A monocle.

In these circumstances he had nothing for it but to follow her to town. He went to the house in town. Mrs. Bounderby not there. He looked in at the Bank. Mr. Bounderby away, and Mrs. Sparsit away. Mrs. Sparsit away? Who could have been reduced to sudden extremity for the company of that griffin!

"Well! I don't know," said Tom, who had his own reasons for being uneasy about it. "She was off somewhere at daybreak this morning. She's always full of mystery; I hate her. So I do that white chap; he's always got his blinking eyes upon a fellow."

"Where were you last night, Tom?"

"Where was I last night!" said Tom. "Come! I like that. I was waiting for you, Mr. Harthouse, till it came down as I never saw it come down before. Where was I too! Where were you, you mean."

"I was prevented from coming—detained."

"Detained!" murmured Tom. "Two of us were detained. I was detained looking for you, till I lost every train but the mail. It would have been a pleasant job to go down by that on such a night, and have to walk home through a pond. I was obliged to sleep in town after all."

"Where?"

"Where? Why, in my own bed at Bounderby's."

"Did you see your sister?"

"How the deuce," returned Tom, staring, "could I see my sister when she was fifteen miles off?"

Cursing these quick retorts of the young gentleman to whom he was so true a friend, Mr. Harthouse disembarrassed himself of that interview with the smallest conceivable amount of ceremony, and debated for the hundredth time what all this could mean? He made only one thing clear. It was, that whether she was in town or out of town, whether he had been premature with her who was so hard to comprehend, or she had lost courage, or they were discovered, or some mischance or mistake, at present incomprehensible had occurred, he must remain to confront his fortune, whatever it was. The hotel where he was known to live when condemned to that region of blackness, was the stake to which he was tied. As to all the rest—What will be, will be.

"So, whether I am waiting for a hostile message, or an assignation, or a penitent remonstrance, or an impromptu wrestle with my friend Bounderby in the Lancashire manner[2]—which would seem as likely as anything else in the present state of affairs—I'll dine," said Mr. James Harthouse. "Bounderby has the advantage in point of weight; and if anything of a British nature is to come off between us, it may be as well to be in training."

2. A kind of wrestling in which many varieties of holds were allowed.

Therefore he rang the bell, and tossing himself negligently on a sofa, ordered "Some dinner at six—with a beefsteak in it," and got through the intervening time as well as he could. That was not particularly well; for he remained in the greatest perplexity, and, as the hours went on, and no kind of explanation offered itself, his perplexity augmented at compound interest.

However, he took affairs as coolly as it was in human nature to do, and entertained himself with the facetious idea of the training more than once. "It wouldn't be bad," he yawned at one time, "to give the waiter five shillings, and throw him." At another time it occurred to him, "Or a fellow of about thirteen or fourteen stone[3] might be hired by the hour." But these jests did not tell materially on the afternoon, or his suspense; and, sooth to say, they both lagged fearfully.

It was impossible, even before dinner, to avoid often walking about in the pattern of the carpet, looking out of the window, listening at the door for footsteps, and occasionally becoming rather hot when any steps approached that room. But, after dinner, when the day turned to twilight, and the twilight turned to night, and still no communication was made to him, it began to be as he expressed it, "like the Holy Office and slow torture."[4] However, still true to his conviction that indifference was the genuine high-breeding (the only conviction he had), he seized this crisis as the opportunity for ordering candles and a newspaper.

He had been trying in vain, for half an hour, to read this newspaper, when the waiter appeared and said, at once mysteriously and apologetically:

"Beg your pardon, sir. You're wanted, sir, if you please."

A general recollection that this was the kind of thing the Police said to the swell mob,[5] caused Mr. Harthouse to ask the waiter in return, with bristling indignation, what the Devil he meant by "wanted?"

"Beg your pardon, sir. Young lady outside, sir, wishes to see you."

"Outside? Where?"

"Outside this door, sir."

Giving the waiter to the personage before-mentioned, as a blockhead duly qualified for that consignment, Mr. Harthouse hurried into the gallery. A young woman whom he had never seen stood there. Plainly dressed, very quiet, very pretty. As he conducted her into the room and placed a chair for her, he observed, by the light of the candles, that she was even prettier than he had at first believed.

---

3. In English measurement, a stone is equivalent to 14 pounds. The hired wrestling partner would therefore weigh between 180 and 200 pounds.

4. The tortures inflicted by the Roman Catholic Inquisition, especially in Spain.

5. According to Eric Partridge's *Dictionary of Slang*, a gang of pickpockets "who, to escape detection, dress and behave like respectable people."

Her face was innocent and youthful, and its expression remarkably pleasant. She was not afraid of him, or in any way disconcerted; she seemed to have her mind entirely pre-occupied with the occasion of her visit, and to have substituted that consideration for herself.

"I speak to Mr. Harthouse?" she said, when they were alone.

"To Mr. Harthouse." He added in his mind, "And you speak to him with the most confiding eyes I ever saw, and the most earnest voice (though so quiet) I ever heard."

"If I do not understand—and I do not, sir"—said Sissy, "what your honor as a gentleman binds you to, in other matters:" the blood really rose in his face as she began in these words: "I am sure I may rely upon it to keep my visit secret, and to keep secret what I am going to say. I will rely upon it, if you will tell me I may so far trust—"

"You may, I assure you."

"I am young, as you see; I am alone, as you see. In coming to you, sir, I have no advice or encouragement beyond my own hope."

He thought, "But that is very strong," as he followed the momentary upward glance of her eyes. He thought besides, "This is a very odd beginning. I don't see where we are going."

"I think," said Sissy, "you have already guessed whom I left just now?"

"I have been in the greatest concern and uneasiness during the last four-and-twenty hours (which have appeared as many years)," he returned, "on a lady's account. The hopes I have been encouraged to form that you come from that lady, do not deceive me, I trust."

"I left her within an hour."

"At—?"

"At her father's."

Mr. Harthouse's face lengthened in spite of his coolness, and his perplexity increased. "Then I certainly," he thought, "do *not* see where we are going."

"She hurried there last night. She arrived there in great agitation, and was insensible all through the night. I live at her father's, and was with her. You may be sure, sir, you will never see her again as long as you live."

Mr. Harthouse drew a long breath; and, if ever man found himself in the position of not knowing what to say, made the discovery beyond all question that he was so circumstanced. The child-like ingenuousness with which his visitor spoke, her modest fearlessness, her truthfulness which put all artifice aside, her entire forgetfulness of herself in her earnest quiet holding to the object with which she had come; all this, together with her reliance on his easily-given promise—which in itself shamed him—presented something in which he was so inexperienced, and against which he knew any of his usual weapons would fall so powerless; that not a word could he rally to his relief.

At last he said:

"So startling an announcement, so confidently made, and by such lips, is really disconcerting in the last degree. May I be permitted to inquire, if you are charged to convey that information to me in those hopeless words, by the lady of whom we speak?"

"I have no charge from her."

"The drowning man catches at the straw. With no disrespect for your judgment, and with no doubt of your sincerity, excuse my saying that I cling to the belief that there is yet hope that I am not condemned to perpetual exile from that lady's presence."

"There is not the least hope. The first object of my coming here, sir, is to assure you that you must believe that there is no more hope of your ever speaking with her again, than there would be if she had died when she came home last night."

"Must believe? But if I can't—or if I should, by infirmity of nature, be obstinate—and won't—"

"It is still true. There is no hope."

James Harthouse looked at her with an incredulous smile upon his lips; but her mind looked over and beyond him, and the smile was quite thrown away.

He bit his lip, and took a little time for consideration.

"Well! If it should unhappily appear," he said, "after due pains and duty on my part, that I am brought to a position so desolate as this banishment, I shall not become the lady's persecutor. But you said you had no commission from her?"

"I have only the commission of my love for her, and her love for me. I have no other trust, than that I have been with her since she came home, and that she has given me her confidence. I have no further trust, than that I know something of her character and her marriage. O Mr. Harthouse, I think you had that trust too!"

He was touched in the cavity where his heart should have been—in that nest of addled eggs, where the birds of heaven would have lived if they had not been whistled away—by the fervor of this reproach.

"I am not a moral sort of fellow," he said, "and I never make any pretensions to the character of a moral sort of fellow. I am as immoral as need be. At the same time, in bringing any distress upon the lady who is the subject of the present conversation, or in unfortunately compromising her in any way, or in committing myself by any expression of sentiments towards her, not perfectly reconcilable with—in fact with—the domestic hearth; or in taking any advantage of her father's being a machine, or of her brother's being a whelp, or of her husband's being a bear; I beg to be allowed to assure you that I have had no particularly evil intentions, but have glided on from one step to another with a smoothness so perfectly diabolical, that I had not the slightest idea the catalogue was half so long until I began to turn it over. Whereas I find," said Mr. James Harthouse, in conclusion, "that it is really in several volumes."

Though he said all this in his frivolous way, the way seemed, for that once, a conscious polishing of but an ugly surface. He was silent for a moment; and then proceeded with a more self-possessed air, though with traces of vexation and disappointment that would not be polished out.

"After what has been just now represented to me, in a manner I find it impossible to doubt—I know of hardly any other source from which I could have accepted it so readily—I feel bound to say to you, in whom the confidence you have mentioned has been reposed, that I cannot refuse to contemplate the possibility (however unexpected) of my seeing the lady no more. I am solely to blame for the thing having come to this—and—and, I cannot say," he added, rather hard up for a general peroration, "that I have any sanguine expectation of ever becoming a moral sort of fellow, or that I have any belief in any moral sort of fellow whatever."

Sissy's face sufficiently showed that her appeal to him was not finished.

"You spoke," he resumed, as she raised her eyes to him again, "of your first object. I may assume that there is a second to be mentioned?"

"Yes."

"Will you oblige me by confiding it?"

"Mr. Harthouse," returned Sissy, with a blending of gentleness and steadiness that quite defeated him, and with a simple confidence in his being bound to do what she required, that held him at a singular disadvantage, "the only reparation that remains with you, is to leave here immediately and finally. I am quite sure that you can mitigate in no other way the wrong and harm you have done. I am quite sure that it is the only compensation you have left it in your power to make. I do not say that it is much, or that it is enough; but it is something, and it is necessary. Therefore, though without any other authority than I have given you, and even without the knowledge of any other person than yourself and myself, I ask you to depart from this place to-night, under an obligation never to return to it."

If she had asserted any influence over him beyond her plain faith in the truth and right of what she said; if she had concealed the least doubt or irresolution, or had harboured for the best purpose any reserve or pretence; if she had shown, or felt, the lightest trace of any sensitiveness to his ridicule or his astonishment, or any remonstrance he might offer; he would have carried it against her at this point. But he could as easily have changed a clear sky by looking at it in surprise, as affect her.

"But do you know," he asked, quite at a loss, "the extent of what you ask? You probably are not aware that I am here on a public kind of business, preposterous enough in itself, but which I have gone in for, and sworn by, and am supposed to be devoted to in quite a desperate manner? You probably are not aware of that, but I assure you it's the fact."

It had no effect on Sissy, fact or no fact.

"Besides which," said Mr. Harthouse, taking a turn or two across the room, dubiously, "it's so alarmingly absurd. It would make a man so ridiculous, after going in for these fellows, to back out in such an incomprehensible way."

"I am quite sure," repeated Sissy, "that it is the only reparation in your power, sir. I am quite sure, or I would not have come here."

He glanced at her face, and walked about again. "Upon my soul, I don't know what to say. So immensely absurd!"

It fell to his lot, now, to stipulate for secresy.

"If I were to do such a very ridiculous thing," he said, stopping again presently, and leaning against the chimney-piece, "it could only be in the most inviolable confidence."

"I will trust to you, sir," returned Sissy, "and you will trust to me."

His leaning against the chimney-piece reminded him of the night with the whelp. It was the self-same chimney-piece, and somehow he felt as if *he* were the whelp to-night. He could make no way at all.

"I suppose a man never was placed in a more ridiculous position," he said, after looking down, and looking up, and laughing, and frowning, and walking off, and walking back again. "But I see no way out of it. What will be, will be. *This* will be, I suppose. I must take off myself, I imagine—in short, I engage to do it."

Sissy rose. She was not surprised by the result, but she was happy in it, and her face beamed brightly.

"You will permit me to say," continued Mr. James Harthouse, "that I doubt if any other ambassador, or ambassadress, could have addressed me with the same success. I must not only regard myself as being in a very ridiculous position, but as being vanquished at all points. Will you allow me the privilege of remembering my enemy's name?"

"*My* name?" said the ambassadress.

"The only name I could possibly care to know, to-night."

"Sissy Jupe."

"Pardon my curiosity at parting. Related to the family?"

"I am only a poor girl," returned Sissy. "I was separated from my father—he was only a stroller—and taken pity on by Mr. Gradgrind. I have lived in the house ever since."

She was gone.

"It wanted this to complete the defeat," said Mr. James Harthouse, sinking, with a resigned air, on the sofa, after standing transfixed a little while. "The defeat may now be considered perfectly accomplished. Only a poor girl—only a stroller—only James Harthouse made nothing of—only James Harthouse a Great Pyramid of failure."

The Great Pyramid put it into his head to go up the Nile. He took a pen upon the instant, and wrote the following note (in appropriate hieroglyphics) to his brother:

> Dear Jack. All up at Coketown. Bored out of the place, and going in for camels. Affectionately, JEM.

He rang the bell.

"Send my fellow here."

"Gone to bed, sir."

"Tell him to get up, and pack up."

He wrote two more notes. One, to Mr. Bounderby, announcing his retirement from that part of the country, and showing where he would be found for the next fortnight. The other, similar in effect, to Mr. Gradgrind. Almost as soon as the ink was dry upon their superscriptions, he had left the tall chimneys of Coketown behind, and was in a railway carriage, tearing and glaring over the dark landscape.

The moral sort of fellows might suppose that Mr. James Harthouse derived some comfortable reflections afterwards, from this prompt retreat, as one of his few actions that made any amends for anything, and as a token to himself that he had escaped the climax of a very bad business. But it was not so, at all. A secret sense of having failed and been ridiculous—a dread of what other fellows who went in for similar sorts of things, would say at his expense if they knew it—so oppressed him, that what was about the very best passage in his life was the one of all others he would not have owned to on any account, and the only one that made him ashamed of himself.

Chapter III.

VERY DECIDED.

The indefatigable Mrs. Sparsit, with a violent cold upon her, her voice reduced to a whisper, and her stately frame so racked by continual sneezes that it seemed in danger of dismemberment, gave chase to her patron until she found him in the metropolis; and there, majestically sweeping in upon him at his hotel in St. James's Street, exploded the combustibles with which she was charged, and blew up. Having executed her mission with infinite relish, this high-minded woman then fainted away on Mr. Bounderby's coat-collar.

Mr. Bounderby's first procedure was to shake Mrs. Sparsit off, and leave her to progress as she might through various stages of suffering on the floor. He next had recourse to the administration of potent restoratives, such as screwing the patient's thumbs, smiting her hands, abundantly watering her face, and inserting salt in her mouth. When these attentions had recovered her (which they speedily did), he hustled her into a fast train[1] without offering any other refreshment, and carried her back to Coketown more dead than alive.

Regarded as a classical ruin, Mrs. Sparsit was an interesting spectacle on her arrival at her journey's end; but considered in any other light, the amount of damage she had by that time sustained was excessive, and impaired her claims to admiration. Utterly heedless of the wear and tear of her clothes and constitution, and adamant to her pathetic sneezes, Mr. Bounderby immediately crammed her into a coach, and bore her off to Stone Lodge.

"Now, Tom Gradgrind," said Bounderby, bursting into his father-in-law's room late at night; "here's a lady here—Mrs. Sparsit—you know Mrs. Sparsit—who has something to say to you that will strike you dumb."

"You have missed my letter!" exclaimed Mr. Gradgrind, surprised by the apparition.

"Missed your letter, sir!" bawled Bounderby. "The present time is no time for letters. No man shall talk to Josiah Bounderby of Coketown about letters, with his mind in the state it's in now."

"Bounderby," said Mr. Gradgrind, in a tone of temperate remonstrance, "I speak of a very special letter I have written to you, in reference to Louisa."

"Tom Gradgrind," replied Bounderby, knocking the flat of his hand several times with great vehemence on the table, "I speak of a

1. Express train.

very special messenger that has come to me, in reference to Louisa. Mrs. Sparsit ma'am, stand forward!"

That unfortunate lady hereupon essaying to offer testimony, without any voice and with painful gestures expressive of an inflamed throat, became so aggravating and underwent so many facial contortions, that Mr. Bounderby, unable to bear it, seized her by the arm and shook her.

"If you can't get it out ma'am," said Bounderby, "leave *me* to get it out. This is not a time for a lady, however highly connected, to be totally inaudible, and seemingly swallowing marbles. Tom Gradgrind, Mrs. Sparsit latterly found herself, by accident, in a situation to overhear a conversation out of doors between your daughter and your precious gentleman-friend, Mr. James Harthouse."

"Indeed?" said Mr. Gradgrind.

"Ah! Indeed!" cried Bounderby. "And in that conversation—"

"It is not necessary to repeat its tenor, Bounderby. I know what passed."

"You do? Perhaps," said Bounderby, staring with all his might at his so quiet and assuasive father-in-law, "you know where your daughter is at the present time?"

"Undoubtedly. She is here."

"Here?"

"My dear Bounderby, let me beg you to restrain these loud outbreaks, on all accounts. Louisa is here. The moment she could detach herself from that interview with the person of whom you speak, and whom I deeply regret to have been the means of introducing to you, Louisa hurried here, for protection. I myself had not been at home many hours, when I received her—here, in this room. She hurried by the train to town, she ran from town to this house through a raging storm, and presented herself before me in a state of distraction. Of course, she has remained here ever since. Let me entreat you, for your own sake and for hers, to be more quiet."

Mr. Bounderby silently gazed about him for some moments, in every direction except Mrs. Sparsit's direction; and then, abruptly turning upon the niece of Lady Scadgers, said to that wretched woman:

"Now, ma'am! We shall be happy to hear any little apology you may think proper to offer, for going about the country at express pace, with no other luggage than a Cock-and-a-Bull,[2] ma'am!"

"Sir," whispered Mrs. Sparsit, "my nerves are at present too much shaken, and my health is at present too much impaired, in your service, to admit of my doing more than taking refuge in tears."

(Which she did.)

2. A misleading story.

"Well, ma'am," said Bounderby, "without making any observation to you that may not be made with propriety to a woman of good family, what I have got to add to that, is, that there's something else in which it appears to me you may take refuge, namely, a coach. And the coach in which we came here, being at the door, you'll allow me to hand you down to it, and pack you home to the Bank: where the best course for you to pursue, will be to put your feet into the hottest water you can bear, and take a glass of scalding rum and butter after you get into bed." With these words, Mr. Bounderby extended his right hand to the weeping lady and escorted her to the conveyance in question, shedding many plaintive sneezes by the way. He soon returned alone.

"Now, as you showed me in your face, Tom Gradgrind, that you wanted to speak to me," he resumed, "here I am. But, I am not in a very agreeable state, I tell you plainly; not relishing this business even as it is, and not considering that I am at any time as dutifully and submissively treated by your daughter, as Josiah Bounderby of Coketown ought to be treated by his wife. You have your opinion, I dare say; and I have mine, I know. If you mean to say anything to me to-night, that goes against this candid remark, you had better let it alone."

Mr. Gradgrind, it will be observed, being much softened, Mr. Bounderby took particular pains to harden himself at all points. It was his amiable nature.

"My dear Bounderby," Mr. Gradgrind began in reply.

"Now, you'll excuse me," said Bounderby, "but I don't want to be too dear. That, to start with. When I begin to be dear to a man, I generally find that his intention is to come over me. I am not speaking to you politely; but, as you are aware, I am *not* polite. If you like politeness, you know where to get it. You have your gentleman-friends you know, and they'll serve you with as much of the article as you want. I don't keep it myself."

"Bounderby," urged Mr. Gradgrind, "we are all liable to mistakes—"

"I thought you couldn't make 'em," interrupted Bounderby.

"Perhaps I thought so. But, I say we are all liable to mistakes; and I should feel sensible of your delicacy, and grateful for it, if you would spare me these references to Harthouse. I shall not associate him in our conversation with your intimacy and encouragement; pray do not persist in connecting him with mine."

"I never mentioned his name!" said Bounderby.

"Well, well!" returned Mr. Gradgrind, with a patient, even a submissive, air. And he sat for a little while pondering. "Bounderby, I see reason to doubt whether we have ever quite understood Louisa."

"Who do you mean by We?"

"Let me say I, then," he returned, in answer to the coarsely blurted question; "I doubt whether I have understood Louisa. I doubt whether I have been quite right in the manner of her education."

"There you hit it," returned Bounderby. "There I agree with you. You have found it out at last, have you? Education! I'll tell you what education is—To be tumbled out of doors, neck and crop, and put upon the shortest allowance of everything except blows. That's what *I* call education."

"I think your good sense will perceive," Mr. Gradgrind remonstrated in all humility, "that whatever the merits of such a system may be, it would be difficult of general application to girls."

"I don't see it at all, sir," returned the obstinate Bounderby.

"Well," sighed Mr. Gradgrind, "We will not enter into the question. I assure you I have no desire to be controversial. I seek to repair what is amiss, if I possibly can; and I hope you will assist me in a good spirit, Bounderby, for I have been very much distressed."

"I don't understand you, yet," said Bounderby, with determined obstinacy, "and therefore I won't make any promises."

"In the course of a few hours, my dear Bounderby," Mr. Gradgrind proceeded, in the same depressed and propitiatory manner, "I appear to myself to have become better informed as to Louisa's character, than in previous years. The enlightenment has been painfully forced upon me, and the discovery is not mine. I think there are—Bounderby, you will be surprised to hear me say this—I think there are qualities in Louisa, which—which have been harshly neglected, and—and a little perverted. And—and I would suggest to you, that—that if you would kindly meet me in a timely endeavour to leave her to her better nature for a while—and to encourage it to develope itself by tenderness and consideration—it— it would be the better for the happiness of all of us. Louisa," said Mr. Gradgrind, shading his face with his hand, "has always been my favorite child."

The blustrous Bounderby crimsoned and swelled to such an extent on hearing these words, that he seemed to be, and probably was, on the brink of a fit. With his very ears a bright purple shot with crimson, he pent up his indignation, however, and said:

"You'd like to keep her here for a time?"

"I—I had intended to recommend, my dear Bounderby, that you should allow Louisa to remain here on a visit, and be attended by Sissy (I mean of course Cecilia Jupe), who understands her, and in whom she trusts."

"I gather from all this, Tom Gradgrind," said Bounderby, standing up with his hands in his pockets, "that you are of opinion that there's what people call some incompatibility between Loo Bounderby and myself."

"I fear there is at present a general incompatibility between Louisa, and—and—and almost all the relations in which I have placed her," was her father's sorrowful reply.

"Now, look you here, Tom Gradgrind," said Bounderby the flushed, confronting him with his legs wide apart, his hands deeper in his pockets, and his hair like a hayfield wherein his windy anger was boisterous. "You have said your say; I am going to say mine. I am a Coketown man. I am Josiah Bounderby of Coketown. I know the bricks of this town, and I know the works of this town, and I know the chimneys of this town, and I know the smoke of this town, and I know the Hands of this town. I know 'em all pretty well. They're real. When a man tells me anything about imaginative qualities, I always tell that man, whoever he is, that I know what he means. He means turtle-soup and venison, with a gold spoon, and that he wants to be set up with a coach and six. That's what your daughter wants. Since you are of opinion that she ought to have what she wants, I recommend you to provide it for her. Because, Tom Gradgrind, she will never have it from me."

"Bounderby," said Mr. Gradgrind, "I hoped, after my entreaty, you would have taken a different tone."

"Just wait a bit," retorted Bounderby, "you have said your say, I believe. I heard you out; hear me out, if you please. Don't make yourself a spectacle of unfairness as well as inconsistency, because, although I am sorry to see Tom Gradgrind reduced to his present position, I should be doubly sorry to see him brought so low as that. Now, there's an incompatibility of some sort or another, I am given to understand by you, between your daughter and me. I'll give *you* to understand, in reply to that, that there unquestionably is an incompatibility of the first magnitude—to be summed up in this—that your daughter don't properly know her husband's merits, and is not impressed with such a sense as would become her, by George! of the honor of his alliance. That's plain speaking, I hope."

"Bounderby," urged Mr. Gradgrind, "this is unreasonable."

"Is it?" said Bounderby. "I am glad to hear you say so. Because when Tom Gradgrind with his new lights, tells me that what I say is unreasonable, I am convinced at once it must be devilish sensible. With your permission I am going on. You know my origin; and you know that for a good many years of my life I didn't want a shoeing-horn, in consequence of not having a shoe. Yet you may believe or not, as you think proper, that there are ladies—born ladies—belonging to families—Families!—who next to worship the ground I walk on."

He discharged this, like a Rocket, at his father-in-law's head.

"Whereas your daughter," proceeded Bounderby, "is far from being a born lady. That you know, yourself. Not that I care a pinch of candle-snuff about such things, for you are very well aware I don't, but that such is the fact, and you, Tom Gradgrind, can't change it. Why do I say this?"

"Not, I fear," observed Mr. Gradgrind, in a low voice, "to spare me."

"Hear me out," said Bounderby, "and refrain from cutting in till your turn comes round. I say this, because highly connected females have been astonished to see the way in which your daughter has conducted herself, and to witness her insensibility. They have wondered how I have suffered it. And I wonder myself now, and I won't suffer it."

"Bounderby," returned Mr. Gradgrind, rising, "the less we say to-night the better, I think."

"On the contrary, Tom Gradgrind, the more we say to-night, the better, I think. That is," the consideration checked him, "till I have said all I mean to say, and then I don't care how soon we stop. I come to a question that may shorten the business: What do you mean by the proposal you made just now?"

"What do I mean, Bounderby?"

"By your visiting proposition," said Bounderby, with an inflexible jerk of the hayfield.

"I mean that I hope you may be induced to arrange, in a friendly manner, for allowing Louisa a period of repose and reflection here, which may tend to a gradual alteration for the better in many respects."

"To a softening down of your ideas of the incompatibility?" said Bounderby.

"If you put it in those terms."

"What made you think of this?" said Bounderby.

"I have already said, I fear Louisa has not been understood. Is it asking too much, Bounderby, that you, so far her elder, should aid in trying to set her right? You have accepted a great charge of her; for better for worse, for—"

Mr. Bounderby may have been annoyed by the repetition of his own words to Stephen Blackpool, but he cut the quotation short with an angry start.

"Come!" said he, "I don't want to be told about that. I know what I took her for, as well as you do. Never you mind what I took her for; that's my look-out."

"I was merely going on to remark, Bounderby, that we may all be more or less in the wrong, not even excepting you; and that some yielding on your part, remembering the trust you have accepted, may not only be an act of true kindness, but perhaps a debt incurred towards Louisa."

"I think differently," blustered Bounderby. "I am going to finish this business according to my own opinions. Now, I don't want to make a quarrel of it with you, Tom Gradgrind. To tell you the truth, I don't think it would be worthy of my reputation to quarrel on such a subject. As to your gentleman-friend, he may take himself off, wherever he likes best. If he falls in my way, I shall tell him my mind; if he don't fall in my way, I shan't, for it won't be worth my while to do it. As to your daughter, whom I made Loo Bounderby, and might have done better by leaving Loo Gradgrind, if she don't come home tomorrow, by twelve o'clock at noon, I shall understand that she prefers to stay away, and I shall send her wearing apparel and so forth over here, and you'll take charge of her for the future. What I shall say to people in general, of the incompatibility that led to my so laying down the law, will be this. I am Josiah Bounderby, and I had my bringing-up; she's the daughter of Tom Gradgrind, and she had her bringing-up; and the two horses wouldn't pull together. I am pretty well known to be rather an uncommon man, I believe; and most people will understand fast enough that it must be a woman rather out of the common, also, who, in the long run, would come up to my mark."

"Let me seriously entreat you to re-consider this, Bounderby," urged Mr. Gradgrind, "before you commit yourself to such a decision."

"I always come to a decision," said Bounderby, tossing his hat on: "and whatever I do, I do at once. I should be surprised at Tom Gradgrind's addressing such a remark to Josiah Bounderby of Coke-town, knowing what he knows of him, if I could be surprised by anything Tom Gradgrind did, after his making himself a party to sentimental humbug. I have given you my decision, and I have got no more to say. Goodnight!"

So Mr. Bounderby went home to his town house to bed. At five minutes past twelve o'clock next day, he directed Mrs. Bounderby's property to be carefully packed up and sent to Tom Gradgrind's; advertised his country retreat for sale by private contract; and resumed a bachelor life.

Chapter IV.

LOST.

The robbery at the Bank had not languished before, and did not cease to occupy a front place in the attention of the principal of that establishment now. In boastful proof of his promptitude and activity, as a remarkable man, and a self-made man, and a commercial wonder more admirable than Venus,[1] who had risen out of the mud instead of the sea, he liked to show how little his domestic affairs abated his business ardor. Consequently, in the first few

---

1. According to Hesiod, Venus (or Aphrodite) sprang to life out of the foam of the sea.

weeks of his resumed bachelorhood, he even advanced upon his usual display of bustle, and every day made such a rout in renewing his investigations into the robbery, that the officers who had it in hand almost wished it had never been committed.

They were at fault too, and off the scent. Although they had been so quiet since the first outbreak of the matter, that most people really did suppose it to have been abandoned as hopeless, nothing new occurred. No implicated man or woman took untimely courage, or made a self-betraying step. More remarkable yet, Stephen Blackpool could not be heard of, and the mysterious old woman remained a mystery.

Things having come to this pass, and showing no latent signs of stirring beyond it, the upshot of Mr. Bounderby's investigations was, that he resolved to hazard a bold burst. He drew up a placard, offering Twenty Pounds reward for the apprehension of Stephen Blackpool, suspected of complicity in the robbery of the Coketown Bank on such a night; he described the said Stephen Blackpool by dress, complexion, estimated height, and manner, as minutely as he could; he recited how he had left the town, and in what direction he had been last seen going; he had the whole printed in great black letters on a staring broadsheet; and he caused the walls to be posted with it in the dead of night, so that it should strike upon the sight of the whole population at one blow.

The factory-bells had need to ring their loudest that morning to disperse the groups of workers who stood in the tardy daybreak, collected round the placards, devouring them with eager eyes. Not the least eager of the eyes assembled, were the eyes of those who could not read. These people, as they listened to the friendly voice that read aloud—there was always some such ready to help them— stared at the characters which meant so much with a vague awe and respect that would have been half ludicrous, if any aspect of public ignorance could ever be otherwise than threatening and full of evil. Many ears and eyes were busy with a vision of the matter of these placards, among turning spindles, rattling looms, and whir-ring wheels, for hours afterwards; and when the Hands cleared out again into the streets, there were still as many readers as before.

Slackbridge, the delegate, had to address his audience too that night; and Slackbridge had obtained a clean bill from the printer, and had brought it in his pocket. Oh my friends and fellow country-men, the down-trodden operatives of Coketown, oh my fellow brothers and fellow workmen and fellow citizens and fellow men, what a to-do was there, when Slackbridge unfolded what he called "that damning document," and held it up to the gaze, and for the execration, of the working-man community! "Oh my fellow men, behold of what a traitor in the camp of those great spirits who are

enrolled upon the holy scroll of Justice and of Union, is appropriately capable! Oh my prostrate friends, with the galling yoke of
tyrants on your necks and the iron foot of despotism treading down
your fallen forms into the dust of the earth, upon which right glad
would your oppressors be to see you creeping on your bellies all the
days of your lives, like the serpent in the garden[2]—oh my brothers,
and shall I as a man not add, my sisters too, what do you say, *now*,
of Stephen Blackpool, with a slight stoop in his shoulders and about
five foot seven in height, as set forth in this degrading and disgusting document, this blighting bill, this pernicious placard, this abom-
inable advertisement; and with what majesty of denouncement will
you crush the viper, who would bring this stain and shame upon the
Godlike race that happily has cast him out for ever! Yes my compa-
triots, happily cast him out and sent him forth! For you remember
how he stood here before you on this platform; you remember how,
face to face and foot to foot, I pursued him through all his intricate
windings; you remember how, he sneaked, and slunk, and sidled,
and splitted of straws, until, with not an inch of ground to which to
cling, I hurled him out from amongst us: an object for the undying
finger of scorn to point at, and for the avenging fire of every free
and thinking mind, to scorch and sear! And now my friends—my
laboring friends, for I rejoice and triumph in that stigma—my friends
whose hard but honest beds are made in toil, and whose scanty but
independent pots are boiled in hardship; and, now I say, my friends,
what appellation has that dastard craven taken to himself, when,
with the mask torn from his features, he stands before us in all his
native deformity, a What? A thief! A plunderer! A proscribed fugitive, with a price upon his head; a fester and a wound upon the noble
character of the Coketown operative! Therefore, my band of brothers[3]
in a sacred bond, to which your children and your children's children
yet unborn have set their infant hands and seals, I propose to you on
the part of the United Aggregate Tribunal, ever watchful for your
welfare, ever zealous for your benefit, that this meeting does Resolve:
That Stephen Blackpool, weaver, referred to in this placard, having
been already solemnly disowned by the community of Coketown
Hands, the same are free from the shame of his misdeeds, and cannot as a class be reproached with his dishonest actions!"

Thus Slackbridge; gnashing and perspiring after a prodigious
sort. A few stern voices called out "No!" and a score or two hailed,
with assenting cries of "Hear hear!" the caution from one man,
"Slackbridge, y'or over hetter int; y'or a goen too fast!" But these
were pigmies against an army; the general assemblage subscribed

2. See Genesis 3.14.
3. See *Henry V* 4.3.60.

to the gospel according to Slackbridge, and gave three cheers for him, as he sat demonstratively panting at them.

These men and women were yet in the streets, passing quietly to their homes, when Sissy, who had been called away from Louisa some minutes before, returned.

"Who is it?" asked Louisa.

"It is Mr. Bounderby," said Sissy, timid of the name, "and your brother Mr. Tom, and a young woman who says her name is Rachael, and that you know her."

"What do they want, Sissy dear?"

"They want to see you. Rachael has been crying, and seems angry."

"Father," said Louisa, for he was present, "I cannot refuse to see them, for a reason that will explain itself. Shall they come in here?"

As he answered in the affirmative, Sissy went away to bring them. She reappeared with them directly. Tom was last; and remained standing in the obscurest part of the room, near the door.

"Mrs. Bounderby," said her husband, entering with a cool nod, "I don't disturb you, I hope. This is an unseasonable hour, but here is a young woman who has been making statements which render my visit necessary. Tom Gradgrind, as your son, young Tom, refuses for some obstinate reason or other to say anything at all about those statements, good or bad, I am obliged to confront her with your daughter."

"You have seen me once before, young lady," said Rachael, standing in front of Louisa.

Tom coughed.

"You have seen me, young lady," repeated Rachael, as she did not answer, "once before."

Tom coughed again.

"I have."

Rachael cast her eyes proudly towards Mr. Bounderby, and said, "Will you make it known, young lady, where, and who was there?"

"I went to the house where Stephen Blackpool lodged, on the night of his discharge from his work, and I saw you there. He was there too: and an old woman who did not speak, and whom I could scarcely see, stood in a dark corner. My brother was with me."

"Why couldn't you say so, young Tom?" demanded Bounderby.

"I promised my sister I wouldn't." Which Louisa hastily confirmed. "And besides," said the whelp bitterly, "she tells her own story so precious well—and so full—that what business had I to take it out of her mouth!"

"Say, young lady, if you please," pursued Rachael, "why in an evil hour, you ever came to Stephen's that night."

"I felt compassion for him," said Louisa, her color deepening, "and I wished to know what he was going to do and wished to offer him assistance."

"Thank you, ma'am," said Bounderby. "Much flattered and obliged."

"Did you offer him," asked Rachael, "a bank note?"

"Yes; but he refused it, and would only take two pounds in gold."

Rachael cast her eyes towards Mr. Bounderby again.

"Oh certainly!" said Bounderby. "If you put the question whether your ridiculous and improbable account was true or not, I am bound to say it's confirmed."

"Young lady," said Rachael, "Stephen Blackpool is now named as a thief in public print all over this town, and where else! There have been a meeting to-night where he have been spoken of in the same shameful way. Stephen! The honestest lad, the truest lad, the best!" Her indignation failed her, and she broke off, sobbing.

"I am very, very sorry," said Louisa.

"O young lady, young lady," returned Rachael, "I hope you may be, but I don't know! I can't say what you may ha' done! The like of you don't know us, don't care for us, don't belong to us. I am not sure why you may ha' come that night. I can't tell but what you may ha' come wi' some aim of your own, not mindin to what trouble you brought such as the poor lad. I said then, Bless you for coming; and I said it of my heart, you seemed to take so pitifully to him; but I don't know now, I don't know!"

Louisa could not reproach her for her unjust suspicions; she was so faithful to her idea of the man, and so afflicted.

"And when I think," said Rachael through her sobs, "that the poor lad was so grateful, thinkin you so good to him—when I mind that he put his hand over his hard-worken face to hide the tears that you brought up there—O, I hope you may be sorry, and ha' no bad cause to be it; but I don't know, I don't know!"

"You're a pretty article," growled the whelp, moving uneasily in his dark corner, "to come here with these precious imputations! You ought to be bundled out for not knowing how to behave yourself, and you would be by rights."

She said nothing in reply; and her low weeping was the only sound that was heard, until Mr. Bounderby spoke.

"Come!" said he, "you know what you have engaged to do. You had better give your mind to that; not this."

" 'Deed, I am loath," returned Rachael, drying her eyes, "that any here should see me like this; but I won't be seen so again. Young lady, when I had read what's put in print of Stephen—and what has just as much truth in it as if it had been put in print of you—I went straight to the Bank to say I knew where Stephen was, and to give a sure and certain promise that he should be here in two days. I couldn't meet wi' Mr. Bounderby then, and your brother sent me away, and I tried to find you, but you was not to be found, and I went back to work. Soon as I come out of the Mill to-night, I hastened to hear what was said of Stephen—for I know wi' pride he will come back to shame it!—and then I went again to seek Mr. Bounderby, and I found him, and I told him every word I knew; and he believed no word I said, and brought me here."

"So far, that's true enough," assented Mr. Bounderby, with his hands in his pockets and his hat on. "But I have known you people before today, you'll observe, and I know you never die for want of talking. Now, I recommend you not so much to mind talking just now, as doing. You have undertaken to do something; all I remark upon that at present is, do it!"

"I have written to Stephen by the post that went out this afternoon, as I have written to him once before sin' he went away," said Rachael; "and he will be here, at furthest, in two days."

"Then, I'll tell you something. You are not aware, perhaps," retorted Mr. Bounderby, "that you yourself have been looked after now and then, not being considered quite free from suspicion in this business, on account of most people being judged according to the company they keep. The post-office hasn't been forgotten either. What I'll tell you is, that no letter to Stephen Blackpool has ever got into it. Therefore, what has become of yours, I leave you to guess. Perhaps you're mistaken, and never wrote any."

"He hadn't been gone from here, young lady," said Rachael, turning appealingly to Louisa, "as much as a week, when he sent me the only letter I have had from him, saying that he was forced to seek work in another name."

"Oh, by George!" cried Bounderby, shaking his head, with a whistle, "he changes his name, does he! That's rather unlucky, too, for such an immaculate chap. It's considered a little suspicious in Courts of Justice, I believe, when an Innocent happens to have many names."

"What," said Rachael, with the tears in her eyes again, "what, young lady, in the name of Mercy, was left the poor lad to do! The masters against him on one hand, the men against him on the other, he only wantin to work hard in peace, and do what he felt right. Can a man have no soul of his own, no mind of his own? Must he go wrong all through wi' this side, or must he go wrong all through wi' that, or else be hunted like a hare?"

"Indeed, indeed, I pity him from my heart," returned Louisa; "and I hope that he will clear himself."

"You need have no fear of that, young lady. He is sure!"

"All the surer, I suppose," said Mr. Bounderby, "for your refusing to tell where he is? Eh?"

"He shall not, through any act of mine, come back wi' the unmerited reproach of being brought back. He shall come back of his own accord to clear himself, and put all those that have injured his good character, and he not here for its defence, to shame. I have told him what has been done against him," said Rachael, throwing off all distrust as a rock throws off the sea, "and he will be here, at furthest, in two days."

"Notwithstanding which," added Mr. Bounderby, "if he can be laid hold of any sooner, he shall have an earlier opportunity of clearing himself. As to you, I have nothing against you; what you came and told me turns out to be true, and I have given you the means of proving it to be true, and there's an end of it. I wish you good night all! I must be off to look a little further into this."

Tom came out of his corner when Mr. Bounderby moved, moved with him, kept close to him, and went away with him. The only parting salutation of which he delivered himself was a sulky "Good night, father!" With that brief speech, and a scowl at his sister, he left the house.

Since his sheet-anchor[4] had come home, Mr. Gradgrind had been sparing of speech. He still sat silent, when Louisa mildly said:

"Rachael, you will not distrust me one day, when you know me better."

"It goes against me," Rachael answered, in a gentler manner, "to mistrust any one; but when I am so mistrusted—when we all are—I cannot keep such things quite out of my mind. I ask your pardon for having done you an injury. I don't think what I said now. Yet I might come to think it again, wi' the poor lad so wronged."

"Did you tell him in your letter," inquired Sissy, "that suspicion seemed to have fallen upon him, because he had been seen about the bank at night? He would then know what he would have to explain on coming back, and would be ready."

"Yes, dear," she returned; "but I can't guess what can have ever taken him there. He never used to go there. It was never in his way. His way was the same as mine, and not near it."

Sissy had already been at her side asking her where she lived, and whether she might come tomorrow-night, to inquire if there were news of him.

"I doubt," said Rachael, "if he can be here till next day."

"Then I will come next night too," said Sissy.

When Rachael, assenting to this, was gone, Mr. Gradgrind lifted up his head, and said to his daughter:

---

4. "A large anchor used only in an emergency. Hence, figuratively, that on which one places one's reliance when everything else has failed" (*OED*).

"Louisa, my dear, I have never, that I know of, seen this man. Do you believe him to be implicated?"

"I think I have believed it, father, though with great difficulty. I do not believe it now."

"That is to say, you once persuaded yourself to believe it, from knowing him to be suspected. His appearance and manner; are they so honest?"

"Very honest."

"And her confidence not to be shaken! I ask myself," said Mr. Gradgrind, musing, "does the real culprit know of these accusations? Where is he? Who is he?"

His hair had latterly began to change its color. As he leaned upon his hand again, looking gray and old, Louisa, with a face of fear and pity, hurriedly went over to him, and sat close at his side. Her eyes by accident met Sissy's at the moment. Sissy flushed and started, and Louisa put her finger on her lip.

Next night, when Sissy returned home and told Louisa that Stephen was not come, she told it in a whisper. Next night again, when she came home with the same account, and added that he had not been heard of, she spoke in the same low frightened tone. From the moment of that interchange of looks, they never uttered his name, or any reference to him, aloud; nor ever pursued the subject of the robbery, when Mr. Gradgrind spoke of it.

The two appointed days ran out, three days and nights ran out, and Stephen Blackpool was not come, and remained unheard of. On the fourth day, Rachael, with unabated confidence, but considering her despatch to have miscarried, went up to the Bank, and showed her letter from him with his address, at a working colony, one of many, not upon the main road, sixty miles away. Messengers were sent to that place, and the whole town looked for Stephen to be brought in next day.

During this whole time the whelp moved about with Mr. Bounderby like his shadow, assisting in all the proceedings. He was greatly excited, horribly fevered, bit his nails down to the quick, spoke in a hard rattling voice, and with lips that were black and burnt up. At the hour when the suspected man was looked for, the whelp was at the station; offering to wager that he had made off before the arrival of those who were sent in quest of him, and that he would not appear.

The whelp was right. The messengers returned alone. Rachael's letter had gone, Rachael's letter had been delivered, Stephen Blackpool had decamped in that same hour; and no soul knew more of him. The only doubt in Coketown was, whether Rachael had written in good faith, believing that he really would come back, or warning him to fly. On this point opinion was divided.

Six days, seven days, far on into another week. The wretched whelp plucked up a ghastly courage, and began to grow defiant. "*Was* the suspected fellow the thief? A pretty question! If not, where was the man, and why did he not come back?"

Where was the man, and why did he not come back? In the dead of night the echoes of his own words, which had rolled Heaven knows how far away in the daytime, came back instead, and abided by him until morning.

Chapter V.

FOUND.

Day and night again, day and night again. No Stephen Blackpool. Where was the man, and why did he not come back?

Every night, Sissy went to Rachael's lodging, and sat with her in her small neat room. All day, Rachael toiled as such people must toil, whatever their anxieties. The smoke-serpents were indifferent who was lost or found, who turned out bad or good; the melancholy mad elephants, like the Hard Fact men, abated nothing of their set routine, whatever happened. Day and night again, day and night again. The monotony was unbroken. Even Stephen Blackpool's disappearance was falling into the general way, and becoming as monotonous a wonder as any piece of machinery in Coketown.

"I misdoubt," said Rachael, "if there is as many as twenty left in all this place, who have any trust in the poor dear lad now."

She said it to Sissy, as they sat in her lodging, lighted only by the lamp at the street corner. Sissy had come there when it was already dark, to await her return from work; and they had since sat at the window where Rachael had found her, wanting no brighter light to shine on their sorrowful talk.

"If it hadn't been mercifully brought about, that I was to have you to speak to," pursued Rachael, "times are, when I think my mind would not have kept right. But I get hope and strength through you; and you believe that though appearances may rise against him, he will be proved clear?"

"I do believe so," returned Sissy, "with my whole heart. I feel so certain, Rachael, that the confidence you hold in yours against all discouragement, is not like to be wrong, that I have no more doubt of him than if I had known him through as many years of trial as you have."

"And I, my dear," said Rachael, with a tremble in her voice, "have known him through them all, to be, according to his quiet ways, so faithful to everything honest and good, that if he was never to be heard of more, and I was to live to be a hundred years old, I could say with my last breath, God knows my heart. I have never once left trusting Stephen Blackpool!"

"We all believe, up at the Lodge, Rachael, that he will be freed from suspicion, sooner or later."

"The better I know it to be so believed there, my dear," said Rachael, "and the kinder I feel it that you come away from there, purposely to comfort me, and keep me company, and be seen wi' me when I am not yet free from all suspicion myself, the more grieved I am that I should ever have spoken those mistrusting words to the young lady. And yet—"

"You don't mistrust her now, Rachael?"

"Now that you have brought us more together, no. But I can't at all times keep out of my mind—"

Her voice so sunk into a low and slow communing with herself, that Sissy, sitting by her side, was obliged to listen with attention.

"I can't at all times keep out of my mind, mistrustings of some one. I can't think who 'tis, I can't think how or why it may be done, but I mistrust that some one has put Stephen out of the way. I mistrust that by his coming back of his own accord, and showing himself innocent before them all, some one would be confounded, who—to prevent that—has stopped him, and put him out of the way."

"That is a dreadful thought," said Sissy, turning pale.

"It is a dreadful thought to think he may be murdered."

Sissy shuddered, and turned paler yet.

"When it makes its way into my mind, dear," said Rachael, "and it will come sometimes, though I do all I can to keep it out, wi' counting on to high numbers as I work, and saying over and over again pieces that I knew when I were a child—I fall into such a wild, hot hurry, that, however tired I am, I want to walk fast, miles and miles. I must get the better of this before bed-time. I'll walk home wi' you."

"He might fall ill upon the journey back," said Sissy, faintly offering a worn-out scrap of hope; "and in such a case, there are many places on the road where he might stop."

"But he is in none of them. He has been sought for in all, and he's not there."

"True," was Sissy's reluctant admission.

"He'd walk the journey in two days. If he was footsore and couldn't walk, I sent him, in the letter he got, the money to ride, lest he should have none of his own to spare."

"Let us hope that to-morrow will bring something better, Rachael. Come into the air!"

Her gentle hand adjusted Rachael's shawl upon her shining black hair in the usual manner of her wearing it, and they went out. The night being fine, little knots of Hands were here and there lingering at street-corners; but it was supper-time with the greater part of them, and there were but few people in the streets.

"You're not so hurried now, Rachael, and your hand is cooler."

"I get better dear, if I can only walk, and breathe a little fresh. 'Times when I can't, I turn weak and confused."

"But you must not begin to fail, Rachael, for you may be wanted at any time to stand by Stephen. To-morrow is Saturday. If no news comes to-morrow, let us walk in the country on Sunday morning, and strengthen you for another week. Will you go?"

"Yes, dear."

They were by this time in the street where Mr. Bounderby's house stood. The way to Sissy's destination led them past the door, and they were going straight towards it. Some train had newly arrived in Coketown, which had put a number of vehicles in motion, and scattered a considerable bustle about the town. Several coaches were rattling before them and behind them as they approached Mr. Bounderby's, and one of the latter drew up with such briskness as they were in the act of passing the house, that they looked round involuntarily. The bright gaslight over Mr. Bounderby's steps showed them Mrs. Sparsit in the coach, in an ecstacy of excitement, struggling to open the door; Mrs. Sparsit seeing them at the same moment, called to them to stop.

"It's a coincidence," exclaimed Mrs. Sparsit, as she was released by the coachman. "It's a Providence! Come out, ma'am!" then said Mrs. Sparsit, to some one inside, "come out, or we'll have you dragged out!"

Hereupon, no other than the mysterious old woman descended. Whom Mrs. Sparsit incontinently collared.

"Leave her alone, everybody!" cried Mrs. Sparsit, with great energy. "Let nobody touch her. She belongs to me. Come in, ma'am!" then said Mrs. Sparsit, reversing her former word of command. "Come in, ma'am, or we'll have you dragged in!"

The spectacle of a matron of classical deportment, seizing an ancient woman by the throat, and haling her into a dwelling-house, would have been, under any circumstances, sufficient temptation to all true English stragglers so blest as to witness it, to force a way into that dwelling-house and see the matter out. But when the phenomenon was enhanced by the notoriety and mystery by this time associated all over the town, with the Bank robbery, it would have lured the stragglers in, with an irresistible attraction, though the roof had been expected to fall upon their heads. Accordingly, the chance witnesses on the ground, consisting of the busiest of the neighbours to the number of some five-and-twenty, closed in after Sissy and Rachael, as they closed in after Mrs. Sparsit and her prize; and the whole body made a disorderly irruption into Mr. Bounderby's dining-room, where the people behind lost not a moment's time in mounting on the chairs, to get the better of the people in front.

"Fetch Mr. Bounderby down!" cried Mrs. Sparsit. "Rachael, young woman; you know who this is?"

"It's Mrs. Pegler," said Rachael.

"I should think it is!" cried Mrs. Sparsit, exulting. "Fetch Mr. Bounderby. Stand away, everybody!" Here old Mrs. Pegler, muffling herself up, and shrinking from observation, whispered a word of entreaty. "Don't tell me," said Mrs. Sparsit, aloud, "I have told you twenty times, coming along, that I will *not* leave you till I have handed you over to him myself."

Mr. Bounderby now appeared, accompanied by Mr. Gradgrind and the whelp, with whom he had been holding conference upstairs. Mr. Bounderby looked more astonished than hospitable, at sight of this uninvited party in his dining-room.

"Why, what's the matter now!" said he. "Mrs. Sparsit, ma'am?"

"Sir," explained that worthy woman, "I trust it is my good fortune to produce a person you have much desired to find. Stimulated by my wish to relieve your mind, sir, and connecting together such imperfect clues to the part of the country in which that person might be supposed to reside, as have been afforded by the young woman Rachael, fortunately now present to identify, I have had the happiness to succeed, and to bring that person with me—I need not say most unwillingly on her part. It has not been, sir, without some trouble that I have effected this; but trouble in your service is to me a pleasure, and hunger, thirst, and cold a real gratification."

Here Mrs. Sparsit ceased; for Mr. Bounderby's visage exhibited an extraordinary combination of all possible colors and expressions of discomfiture, as old Mrs. Pegler was disclosed to his view.

"Why, what do you mean by this?" was his highly unexpected demand, in great warmth. "I ask you, what do you mean by this, Mrs. Sparsit, ma'am?"

"Sir!" exclaimed Mrs. Sparsit, faintly.

"Why don't you mind your own business, ma'am?" roared Bounderby. "How dare you go and poke your officious nose into my family affairs?"

This allusion to her favorite feature overpowered Mrs. Sparsit. She sat down stiffly in a chair, as if she were frozen; and, with a fixed stare at Mr. Bounderby, slowly grated her mittens against one another, as if they were frozen too.

"My dear Josiah!" cried Mrs. Pegler, trembling. "My darling boy! I am not to blame. It's not my fault, Josiah. I told this lady over and over again, that I knew she was doing what would not be agreeable to you, but she would do it."

"What did you let her bring you for? Couldn't you knock her cap off, or her tooth out, or scratch her, or do something or other to her?" asked Bounderby.

"My own boy! She threatened me that if I resisted her, I should be brought by constables, and it was better to come quietly than make that stir in such a—" Mrs. Pegler glanced timidly but proudly round the walls—"such a fine house as this. Indeed, indeed, it is not my fault! My dear, noble, stately boy! I have always lived quiet and secret, Josiah, my dear. I have never broken the condition once. I have never said I was your mother. I have admired you at a distance; and if I have come to town sometimes, with long times between, to take a proud peep at you, I have done it unbeknown, my love, and gone away again."

Mr. Bounderby, with his hands in his pockets, walked in impatient mortification up and down at the side of the long dining-table, while the spectators greedily took in every syllable of Mrs. Pegler's appeal, and at each succeeding syllable became more and more round-eyed. Mr. Bounderby still walking up and down when Mrs. Pegler had done, Mr. Gradgrind addressed that maligned old lady:

"I am surprised, madam," he observed with severity, "that in your old age you have the face to claim Mr. Bounderby for your son, after your unnatural and inhuman treatment of him."

"*Me* unnatural!" cried poor old Mrs. Pegler. "*Me* inhuman! To my dear boy?"

"Dear!" repeated Mr. Gradgrind. "Yes; dear in his self-made prosperity, madam, I dare say. Not very dear, however, when you deserted him in his infancy, and left him to the brutality of a drunken grandmother."

"*I* deserted my Josiah!" cried Mrs. Pegler, clasping her hands. "Now, Lord forgive you, sir, for your wicked imaginations, and for your scandal against the memory of my poor mother, who died in my arms before Josiah was born. May you repent of it, sir, and live to know better!"

She was so very earnest and injured, that Mr. Gradgrind, shocked by the possibility which dawned upon him, said in a gentler tone:

"Do you deny, then, madam, that you left your son to—to be brought up in the gutter?"

"Josiah in the gutter!" exclaimed Mrs. Pegler. "No such a thing, sir. Never! For shame on you! My dear boy knows, and will give *you* to know, that though he come of humble parents, he come of parents that loved him as dear as the best could, and never thought it hardship on themselves to pinch a bit that he might write and cypher beautiful, and I've his books at home to show it! Aye, have I!" said Mrs. Pegler, with indignant pride. "And my dear boy knows, and will give *you* to know, sir, that after his beloved father died when he was eight year old, his mother, too, could pinch a bit, as it was her duty and her pleasure and her pride to do it, to help him out in life, and put him 'prentice. And a steady lad he was, and a kind master he had to lend him a hand, and well he worked his own way forward to be rich and thriving. And I'll give you to know, sir—for this my dear boy won't—that though his mother kept but a little village shop, he never forgot her, but pensioned me on thirty pound a-year— more than I want, for I put by out of it—only making the condition that I was to keep down in my own part, and make no boasts about him, and not trouble him. And I never have, except with looking at him once a year, when he has never knowed it. And it's right," said poor old Mrs. Pegler, in affectionate championship, "that I *should* keep down in my own part, and I have no doubts that if I was here I should do a many unbefitting things, and I am well contented, and I can keep my pride in my Josiah to myself, and I can love for love's own sake! And I am ashamed of you, sir," said Mrs. Pegler, lastly, "for your slanders and suspicions. And I never stood here before, nor never wanted to stand here when my dear son said no. And I shouldn't be here now, if it hadn't been for being brought here. And for shame upon you, O for shame, to accuse me of being a bad mother to my son, with my son standing here to tell you so different!"

The bystanders, on and off the dining-room chairs, raised a murmur of sympathy with Mrs. Pegler, and Mr. Gradgrind felt himself innocently placed in a very distressing predicament, when Mr. Bounderby, who had never ceased walking up and down, and had every moment swelled larger and larger, and grown redder and redder, stopped short.

"I don't exactly know," said Mr. Bounderby, "how I come to be favoured with the attendance of the present company, but I don't inquire. When they're quite satisfied, perhaps they'll be so good as to disperse; whether they're satisfied or not, perhaps they'll be so good as to disperse. I'm not bound to deliver a lecture on my family affairs, I have not undertaken to do it, and I'm not a going to do it. Therefore those who expect any explanation whatever upon that branch of the subject, will be disappointed—particularly Tom Gradgrind, and he can't know it too soon. In reference to the Bank robbery, there has been a mistake made, concerning my mother. If there hadn't been over-officiousness it wouldn't have been made, and I hate over-officiousness at all times, whether or no. Good evening!"

Although Mr. Bounderby carried it off in these terms, holding the door open for the company to depart, there was a blustering sheepishness upon him, at once extremely crest-fallen and superlatively absurd. Detected as the Bully of humility, who had built his windy reputation upon lies, and in his boastfulness had put the honest truth as far away from him as if he had advanced the mean claim (there is no meaner) to tack himself on to a pedigree, he cut a most ridiculous figure. With the people filing off at the door he held, who he knew would carry what had passed to the whole town, to be given to the four winds, he could not have looked a Bully more shorn and forlorn, if he had had his ears cropped. Even that unlucky female, Mrs. Sparsit, fallen from her pinnacle of exultation into the Slough of Despond,[1] was not in so bad a plight as that remarkable man and self-made Humbug, Josiah Bounderby of Coketown.

Rachael and Sissy, leaving Mrs. Pegler to occupy a bed at her son's for that night, walked together to the gate of Stone Lodge and there parted. Mr. Gradgrind joined them before they had gone very far, and spoke with much interest of Stephen Blackpool; for whom he thought this signal failure of the suspicions against Mrs. Pegler was likely to work well.

As to the whelp; throughout this scene as on all other late occasions, he had stuck close to Bounderby. He seemed to feel that as long as Bounderby could make no discovery without his knowledge, he was so far safe. He never visited his sister, and had only seen her once since she went home: that is to say, on the night when he still stuck close to Bounderby, as already related.

There was one dim unformed fear lingering about his sister's mind, to which she never gave utterance, which surrounded the graceless and ungrateful boy with a dreadful mystery. The same dark possibility had presented itself in the same shapeless guise, this very day, to Sissy, when Rachael spoke of some one who would be confounded by Stephen's return, having put him out of the way. Louisa had never spoken of harboring any suspicion of her brother, in connexion with the robbery, she and Sissy had held no confidence on the subject, save in that one interchange of looks when the unconscious father rested his gray head on his hand; but it was understood between them, and they both knew it. This other fear was so awful, that it hovered about each of them like a ghostly shadow; neither daring to think of its being near herself, far less of its being near the other.

And still the forced spirit which the whelp had plucked up, throve with him. If Stephen Blackpool was not the thief, let him show himself. Why didn't he?

Another night. Another day and night. No Stephen Blackpool. Where was the man, and why did he not come back?

---

1. In John Bunyan's *Pilgrim's Progress* (1678), an allegorical representation of the state of despair into which people may sink.

Chapter VI.

THE STARLIGHT.

The Sunday was a bright Sunday in autumn, clear and cool, when early in the morning Sissy and Rachael met, to walk in the country.

As Coketown cast ashes not only on its own head but on the neighbourhood's too—after the manner of those pious persons who do penance for their own sins by putting other people into sackcloth—it was customary for those who now and then thirsted for a draught of pure air, which is not absolutely the most wicked among the vanities of life, to get a few miles away by the railroad, and then begin their walk, or their lounge in the fields. Sissy and Rachael helped themselves out of the smoke by the usual means, and were put down at a station about midway between the town and Mr. Bounderby's retreat.

Though the green landscape was blotted here and there with heaps of coal, it was green elsewhere, and there were trees to see, and there were larks singing (though it was Sunday),[1] and there were pleasant scents in the air, and all was overarched by a bright blue sky. In the distance one way, Coketown showed as a black mist; in another distance, hills began to rise; in a third, there was a faint change in the light of the horizon, where it shone upon the far-off sea. Under their feet, the grass was fresh; beautiful shadows of branches flickered upon it, and speckled it; hedgerows were luxuriant; everything was at peace. Engines at pits' mouths, and lean old horses that had worn the circle of their daily labor into the ground, were alike quiet; wheels had ceased for a short space to turn; and the great wheel of earth seemed to revolve without the shocks and noises of another time.

They walked on across the fields and down the shady lanes, sometimes getting over a fragment of a fence so rotten that it dropped at a touch of the foot, sometimes passing near a wreck of bricks and beams overgrown with grass, marking the site of deserted works. They followed paths and tracks, however slight. Mounds where the grass was rank and high, and where brambles, dock-weed, and suchlike vegetation, were confusedly heaped together, they always avoided; for dismal stories were told in that country of the old pits hidden beneath such indications.

The sun was high when they sat down to rest. They had seen no one, near or distant, for a long time; and the solitude remained unbroken. "It is so still here, Rachael, and the way is so untrodden,

---

1. An ironic reference to Victorian laws forbidding public entertainments and recreational activities on Sunday, which Dickens believed particularly penalized the working class and had opposed in his pamphlet *Sunday under Three Heads* (1836).

that I think we must be the first who have been here all the summer."

As Sissy said it, her eyes were attracted by another of those rotten fragments of fence upon the ground. She got up to look at it. "And yet I don't know. This has not been broken very long. The wood is quite fresh where it gave way. Here are footsteps too.—O Rachael!"

She ran back, and caught her round the neck. Rachael had already started up.

"What is the matter?"

"I don't know. There is a hat lying in the grass."

They went forward together. Rachael took it up, shaking from head to foot. She broke into a passion of tears and lamentations: Stephen Blackpool was written in his own hand on the inside.

"O the poor lad, the poor lad! He has been made away with. He is lying murdered here!"

"Is there—has the hat any blood upon it?" Sissy faltered.

They were afraid to look; but they did examine it, and found no mark of violence, inside or out. It had been lying there some days, for rain and dew had stained it, and the mark of its shape was on the grass where it had fallen. They looked fearfully about them, without moving, but could see nothing more. "Rachael," Sissy whispered, "I will go on a little by myself."

She had unclasped her hand, and was in the act of stepping forward, of a black ragged chasm, hidden by the thick grass. They sprang back, and fell upon their knees, each hiding her face upon the other's neck.

"O, my good Lord! He's down there! Down there!" At first this, and her terrific screams, were all that could be got from Rachael, by any tears, by any prayers, by any representations, by any means. It was impossible to hush her; and it was deadly necessary to hold her, or she would have flung herself down the shaft.

"Rachael, dear Rachael, good Rachael, for the love of Heaven not these dreadful cries! Think of Stephen, think of Stephen, think of Stephen!"

By an earnest repetition of this entreaty, poured out in all the agony of such a moment, Sissy at last brought her to be silent, and to look at her with a tearless face of stone.

"Rachael, Stephen may be living. You wouldn't leave him lying maimed at the bottom of this dreadful place, a moment, if you could bring help to him!"

"No, no, no!"

"Don't stir from here, for his sake! Let me go and listen."

She shuddered to approach the pit; but she crept towards it on her hands and knees, and called to him as loud as she could call. She listened, but no sound replied. She called again and listened;

still no answering sound. She did this, twenty, thirty, times. She took a little clod of earth from the broken ground where he had stumbled, and threw it in. She could not hear it fall.

The wide prospect, so beautiful in its stillness but a few minutes ago, almost carried despair to her brave heart, as she rose and looked all round her, seeing no help. "Rachael, we must lose not a moment. We must go in different directions, seeking aid. You shall go by the way we have come, and I will go forward by the path. Tell any one you see, and every one what has happened. Think of Stephen, think of Stephen!"

She knew by Rachael's face that she might trust her now. And after standing for a moment to see her running, wringing her hands as she ran, she turned and went upon her own search; she stopped at the hedge to tie her shawl there as a guide to the place, then threw her bonnet aside, and ran as she had never run before.

Run, Sissy, run, in Heaven's name! Don't stop for breath. Run, run! Quickening herself by carrying such entreaties in her thoughts, she ran from field to field, and lane to lane, and place to place, as she had never run before; until she came to a shed by an engine-house, where two men lay in the shade, asleep on straw.

First to wake them, and next to tell them, all so wild and breathless as she was, what had brought her there, were difficulties; but they no sooner understood her than their spirits were on fire like hers. One of the men was in a drunken slumber, but on his comrade's shouting to him that a man had fallen down the Old Hell Shaft, he started out to a pool of dirty water, put his head in it, and came back sober.

With these two men she ran to another half-a-mile further, and with that one to another, while they ran elsewhere. Then a horse was found; and she got another man to ride for life or death to the railroad, and send a message to Louisa, which she wrote and gave him. By this time a whole village was up; and windlasses,[2] ropes, poles, candles, lanterns, all things necessary, were fast collecting and being brought into one place, to be carried to the Old Hell Shaft.

It seemed now hours and hours since she had left the lost man lying in the grave where he had been buried alive. She could not bear to remain away from it any longer—it was like deserting him—and she hurried swiftly back, accompanied by half-a-dozen laborers, including the drunken man whom the news had sobered, and who was the best man of all. When they came to the Old Hell Shaft, they found it as lonely as she had left it. The men called and listened as she had done, and examined the edge of the chasm, and settled

2. Lifting machines with a rope wound around a cylinder and turned by a crank.

how it had happened, and then sat down to wait until the implements they wanted should come up.

Every sound of insects in the air, every stirring of the leaves, every whisper among these men, made Sissy tremble, for she thought it was a cry at the bottom of the pit. But the wind blew idly over it, and no sound arose to the surface, and they sat upon the grass, waiting and waiting. After they had waited some time, straggling people who had heard of the accident began to come up; then the real help of implements began to arrive. In the midst of this, Rachael returned; and with her party there was a surgeon, who brought some wine and medicines. But, the expectation among the people that the man would be found alive, was very slight indeed.

There being now people enough present, to impede the work, the sobered man put himself at the head of the rest, or was put there by the general consent, and made a large ring round the Old Hell Shaft, and appointed men to keep it. Besides such volunteers as were accepted to work, only Sissy and Rachael were at first permitted within this ring; but, later in the day, when the message brought an express from Coketown, Mr. Gradgrind and Louisa, and Mr. Bounderby, and the whelp, were also there.

The sun was four hours lower than when Sissy and Rachael had first sat down upon the grass, before a means of enabling two men to descend securely was rigged with poles and ropes. Difficulties had arisen in the construction of this machine, simple as it was; requisites had been found wanting, and messages had had to go and return. It was five o'clock in the afternoon of the bright autumnal Sunday, before a candle was sent down to try the air, while three or four rough faces stood crowded close together, attentively watching it: the men at the windlass lowering as they were told. The candle was brought up again, feebly burning, and then some water was cast in. Then the bucket was hooked on; and the sobered man and another got in with lights, giving the word. "Lower away!"

As the rope went out, tight and strained, and the windlass creaked, there was not a breath among the one or two hundred men and women looking on, that came as it was wont to come. The signal was given and the windlass stopped, with abundant rope to spare. Apparently so long an interval ensued with the men at the windlass standing idle, that some women shrieked that another accident had happened! But the surgeon who held the watch, declared five minutes not to have elapsed yet, and sternly admonished them to keep silence. He had not well done speaking, when the windlass was reversed and worked again. Practised eyes knew that it did not go as heavily as it would if both workmen had been coming up, and that only one was returning.

The rope came in tight and strained; and ring after ring was coiled upon the barrel of the windlass, and all eyes were fastened on the pit. The sobered man was brought up, and leaped out briskly on the grass. There was an universal cry of "Alive or dead?" and then a deep, profound hush.

When he said. "Alive!" a great shout arose, and many eyes had tears in them.

"But he's hurt very bad," he added, as soon as he could make himself heard again. "Where's doctor? He's hurt so very bad, sir, that we donno how to get him up."

They all consulted together, and looked anxiously at the surgeon, as he asked some questions, and shook his head on receiving the replies. The sun was setting now; and the red light in the evening sky touched every face there, and caused it to be distinctly seen in all its wrapt suspense.

The consultation ended in the men returning to the windlass, and the pitman going down again, carrying the wine and some other small matters with him. Then the other man came up. In the meantime, under the surgeon's directions, some men brought a hurdle,[3] on which others made a thick bed of spare clothes covered with loose straw, while he himself contrived some bandages and slings from shawls and handkerchiefs. As these were made, they were hung upon an arm of the pitman who had last come up, with instructions how to use them; and as he stood, shown by the light he carried, leaning his powerful loose hand upon one of the poles, and sometimes glancing down the pit, and sometimes glancing round upon the people, he was not the least conspicuous figure in the scene. It was dark now, and torches were kindled.

It appeared from the little this man said to those about him, which was quickly repeated all over the circle, that the lost man had fallen upon a mass of crumbled rubbish with which the pit was half choked up, and that his fall had been further broken by some jagged earth at the side. He lay upon his back with one arm doubled under him, and according to his own belief had hardly stirred since he fell, except that he had moved his free hand to a side pocket, in which he remembered to have some bread and meat (of which he had swallowed crumbs), and had likewise scooped up a little water in it now and then. He had come straight away from his work, on being written to, and had walked the whole journey; and was on his way to Mr. Bounderby's country-house after dark, when he fell. He was crossing that dangerous country at such a dangerous time, because he was innocent of what was laid to his charge, and couldn't

---

3. In Britain, a portable section of fencing used for containing sheep; also a frame used to carry condemned persons to their executions.

rest from coming the nearest way to deliver himself up. The Old Hell Shaft, the pitman said, with a curse upon it, was worthy of its bad name to the last; for, though Stephen could speak now, he believed it would soon be found to have mangled the life out of him.

When all was ready, this man, still taking his last hurried charges from his comrades and the surgeon after the windlass had begun to lower him, disappeared into the pit. The rope went out as before, the signal was made as before, and the windlass stopped. No man removed his hand from it now. Every one waited with his grasp set, and his body bent down to the work, ready to reverse and wind in. At length the signal was given, and all the ring leaned forward.

For, now, the rope came in, tightened and strained to its utmost as it appeared, and the men turned heavily, and the windlass complained. It was scarcely endurable to look at the rope, and think of its giving way. But, ring after ring was coiled upon the barrel of the windlass safely, and the connecting chains appeared, and finally the bucket with the two men holding on at the sides—a sight to make the head swim, and oppress the heart—and tenderly supporting between them, slung and tied within, the figure of a poor, crushed, human creature.

A low murmur of pity went round the throng, and the women wept aloud, as this form, almost without form, was moved very slowly from its iron deliverance, and laid upon the bed of straw. At first, none but the surgeon went close to it. He did what he could in its adjustment on the couch, but the best that he could do was to cover it. That gently done, he called to him Rachael and Sissy. And at that time the pale, worn, patient face was seen looking up at the sky, with the broken right hand lying bare on the outside of the covering garments, as if waiting to be taken by another hand.

They gave him drink, moistened his face with water, and administered some drops of cordial and wine. Though he lay quite motionless looking up at the sky, he smiled and said, "Rachael."

She stooped down on the grass at his side, and bent over him until her eyes were between his and the sky, for he could not so much as turn them to look at her.

"Rachael, my dear."

She took his hand. He smiled again and said, "Don't let't go."

"Thou'rt in great pain, my own dear Stephen?"

"I ha' been, but not now. I ha' been—dreadful, and dree, and long, my dear—but 'tis ower now. Ah, Rachael, aw a muddle! Fro' first to last, a muddle!"

The spectre of his old look seemed to pass as he said the word.

"I ha' fell into th' pit, my dear, as have cost wi'in the knowledge o' old fok now livin, hundreds and hundreds o' men's lives—fathers,

sons, brothers, dear to thousands an thousands, an keepin 'em fro'
want and hunger. I ha' fell into a pit that ha' been wi' th' Fire-damp[4]
crueller than battle. I ha' read on't in the public petition, as onny
one may read, fro' the men that works in pits, in which they ha'
pray'n an pray'n the lawmakers for Christ's sake not to let their
work be murder to 'em, but to spare 'em for th' wives and children
that they loves as well as gentlefok loves theirs. When it were in
work, it killed wi'out need; when 'tis let alone, it kills wi'out need.
See how we die an no need, one way an another—in a muddle—
every day!"

He faintly said it, without any anger against any one. Merely as
the truth.

"Thy little sister, Rachael, thou has not forgot her. Thou'rt not like
to forget her now, and me so nigh her. Thou know'st—poor, patient,
suff'rin, dear—how thou didst work for her, seet'n all day long in her
little chair at thy winder, and how she died, young and misshapen,
awlung o' sickly air as had'n no need to be, an awlung o' working
people's miserable homes. A muddle! Aw a muddle!"

Louisa approached him; but he could not see her, lying with his
face turned up to the night sky.

"If aw th' things that tooches us, my dear, was not so muddled, I
should'n ha' had'n need to coom heer. If we was not in a muddle
among ourseln, I should'n ha' been, by my own fellow weavers and
workin' brothers, so mistook. If Mr. Bounderby had ever know'd me
right—if he'd ever know'd me at aw—he would'n ha' took'n offence
wi' me. He would'n ha' suspect'n me. But look up yonder, Rachael!
Look aboove!"

Following his eyes, she saw that he was gazing at a star.

"It ha' shined upon me," he said reverently, "in my pain and
trouble down below. It ha' shined into my mind. I ha' lookn at 't an
thowt o' thee, Rachael, till the muddle in my mind have cleared
awa, above a bit, I hope. If soom ha' been wantin' in unnerstan'in
me better, I, too, ha' been wantin' in unnerstan'in them better.
When I got thy letter, I easily believe that what the yoong ledy sen
an done to me, an what her brother sen an done to me, was one, an
that there were a wicked plot betwixt 'em. When I fell, I were in
anger wi' her, an hurryin on t' be as onjust t' her as oothers was
t' me. But in our judgments, like as in our doins, we mun bear
and forbear. In my pain an trouble, lookin up yonder,—wi' it
shinin' on me—I ha' seen more clear, and ha' made it my dyin
prayer that aw th' world may on'y coom toogether more, an get a

---

4. A combustible gas generated by coal. Its propensity to explode led to frequent disasters
   in the coal mines until 1816, when a safety lamp for miners was invented by Sir Hum-
   phrey Davy, a chemist. The invention dramatically reduced the dangers of this much-
   dreaded gas.

better unnerstan'in o'one another, than when I were in't my own weak seln."

Louisa hearing what he said, bent over him on the opposite side to Rachael, so that he could see her.

"You ha' heard?" he said after a few moments' silence. "I ha' not forgot yo, ledy."

"Yes, Stephen, I have heard you. And your prayer is mine."

"You ha' a father. Will yo tak' a message to him?"

"He is here," said Louisa, with dread. "Shall I bring him to you?"

"If yo please."

Louisa returned with her father. Standing hand-in-hand, they both looked down upon the solemn countenance.

"Sir, yo will clear me an mak my name good wi' aw men. This I leave to yo."

Mr. Gradgrind was troubled and asked how?

"Sir," was the reply; "yor son will tell yo how. Ask him. I mak no charges: I leave none ahint me: not a single word. I ha' seen an spok'n wi' yor son, one night. I ask no more o' yo than that yo clear me—an I trust to you to do't."

The bearers being now ready to carry him away, and the surgeon being anxious for his removal, those who had torches or lanterns, prepared to go in front of the litter. Before it was raised, and while they were arranging how to go, he said to Rachael, looking upward at the star:

"Often as I coom to myseln, and found it shinin on me down there in my trouble, I thowt it were the star as guided to Our Saviour's home. I awmust think it be the very star!"

They lifted him up, and he was overjoyed to find that they were about to take him in the direction whither the star seemed to him to lead.

"Rachael, beloved lass! Don't let go my hand. We may walk together t'night, my dear!"

"I will hold thy hand, and keep beside thee, Stephen, all the way."

"Bless thee! Will soombody be pleased to coover my face!"

They carried him very gently along the fields, and down the lanes, and over the wide landscape; Rachael always holding the hand in hers. Very few whispers broke the mournful silence. It was soon a funeral procession. The star had shown him where to find the God of the poor; and through humility, and sorrow, and forgiveness, he had gone to his Redeemer's rest.

Chapter VII.

WHELP-HUNTING.

Before the ring formed round the Old Hell Shaft was broken, one figure had disappeared from within it. Mr. Bounderby and his shadow had not stood near Louisa, who held her father's arm, but in a retired place by themselves. When Mr. Gradgrind was summoned to the couch, Sissy, attentive to all that happened, slipped behind that wicked shadow—a sight in the horror of his face, if there had been eyes there for any sight but one—and whispered in his ear. Without turning his head, he conferred with her a few moments, and vanished. Thus the whelp had gone out of the circle before the people moved.

When the father reached home, he sent a message to Mr. Bounderby's, desiring his son to come to him directly. The reply was, that Mr. Bounderby having missed him in the crowd, and seeing nothing of him since, had supposed him to be at Stone Lodge.

"I believe, father," said Louisa, "he will not come back to town tonight." Mr. Gradgrind turned away, and said no more.

In the morning, he went down to the Bank himself as soon as it was opened, and seeing his son's place empty (he had not the courage to look in at first), went back along the street to meet Mr. Bounderby on his way there. To whom he said that, for reasons he would soon explain, but entreated not then to be asked for, he had found it necessary to employ his son at a distance for a little while. Also, that he was charged with the duty of vindicating Stephen Blackpool's memory, and declaring the thief. Mr. Bounderby, quite confounded, stood stock-still in the street after his father-in-law had left him, swelling like an immense soap-bubble, without its beauty.

Mr. Gradgrind went home, locked himself in his room, and kept it all that day. When Sissy and Louisa tapped at his door, he said, without opening it, "Not now, my dears; in the evening." On their return in the evening, he said, "I am not able yet—to-morrow." He ate nothing all day, and had no candle after dark; and they heard him walking to and fro late at night.

But, in the morning he appeared at breakfast at the usual hour, and took his usual place at the table. Aged and bent he looked, and quite bowed down; and yet he looked a wiser man, and a better man, than in the days when in this life he wanted nothing but Facts. Before he left the room, he appointed a time for them to come to him; and so, with his gray head drooping, went away.

"Dear father," said Louisa, when they kept their appointment, "you have three young children left. They will be different, *I* will be different yet, with Heaven's help."

She gave her hand to Sissy, as if she meant with her help too.

"Your wretched brother," said Mr. Gradgrind. "Do you think he had planned this robbery, when he went with you to the lodging?"

"I fear so, father. I know he had wanted money very much, and had spent a great deal."

"The poor man being about to leave the town, it came into his evil brain to cast suspicion on him?"

"I think it must have flashed upon him while he sat there, father. For, I asked him to go there with me. The visit did not originate with him."

"He had some conversation with the poor man. Did he take him aside?"

"He took him out of the room. I asked him afterwards, why he had done so, and he made a plausible excuse; but since last night, father, and when I remember the circumstances by its light, I am afraid I can imagine too truly what passed between them."

"Let me know," said her father, "if your thoughts present your guilty brother in the same dark view as mine."

"I fear, father," hesitated Louisa, "that he must have made some representation to Stephen Blackpool—perhaps in my name, perhaps in his own—which induced him to do in good faith and honesty, what he had never done before, and to wait about the Bank those two or three nights before he left the town."

"Too plain!" returned the father. "Too plain!"

He shaded his face, and remained silent for some moments. Recovering himself, he said:

"And now, how is he to be found? How is he to be saved from justice? In the few hours that I can possibly allow to elapse before I publish the truth, how is he to be found by us, and only by us? Ten thousand pounds could not effect it."

"Sissy has effected it, father."

He raised his eyes to where she stood, like a good fairy in his house, and said in a tone of softened gratitude and grateful kindness, "It is always you, my child!"

"We had our fears," Sissy explained, glancing at Louisa, "before yesterday; and when I saw you brought to the side of the litter last night, and heard what passed (being close to Rachael all the time), I went to him when no one saw, and said to him. 'Don't look at me. See where your father is. Escape at once, for his sake and your own!' He was in a tremble before I whispered to him, and he started and trembled more then, and said, 'Where can I go? I have very little money, and I don't know who will hide me!' I thought of father's old circus. I have not forgotten where Mr. Sleary goes at this time of year, and I read of him in a paper only the other day. I told him to hurry there, and tell his name, and ask Mr. Sleary to hide him till I came. 'I'll get to him before the morning,' he said. And I saw him shrink away among the people."

"Thank Heaven!" exclaimed his father. "He may be got abroad yet."

It was the more hopeful as the town to which Sissy had directed him was within three hours' journey of Liverpool, whence he could be swiftly dispatched to any part of the world. But, caution being necessary in communicating with him—for there was a greater danger every moment of his being suspected now, and nobody could be sure at heart but that Mr. Bounderby himself, in a bullying vein of concerted public zeal, might play a Roman part—it was concerted that Sissy and Louisa should repair to the place in question, by a circuitous course, alone; and that the unhappy father, setting forth at another time and leaving the town by an opposite direction, should get round to the same bourne[1] by another and wider route. It was further agreed that he should not present himself to Mr. Sleary, lest his intentions should be mistrusted, or the intelligence of his arrival should cause his son to take flight anew; but, that the communication should be left to Sissy and Louisa to open; and that they should inform the cause of so much misery and disgrace, of his father's being at hand and of the purpose for which they had come. When these arrangements had been well considered and were fully understood by all three, it was time to begin to carry them into execution. Early in the afternoon, Mr. Gradgrind walked direct from his own house into the country, to be taken up on the line by which he was to travel; and at night the remaining two set forth upon their different course, encouraged by not seeing any face they knew.

The two travelled all night, except when they were left, for odd numbers of minutes, at branch-places[2] up illimitable flights of steps, or down wells—which was the only variety of those branches—and, early in the morning, were turned out on a swamp, a mile or two from the town they sought. From this dismal spot they were rescued by a savage old postilion, who happened to be up early, kicking a horse in a fly; and so were smuggled into the town by all the back lanes where the pigs lived: which, although not a magnificent or even savoury approach, was, as is usual in such cases, the legitimate highway.

The first thing they saw on entering the town was the skeleton of Sleary's Circus. The company had departed for another town more than twenty miles off, and had opened there last night. The con-

1. Destination. "To play a Roman part": to repudiate family ties by turning Tom over to the police—as the Roman Brutus had sentenced his own two sons to death after they were discovered to be conspirators.
2. Railroad stops where tracks diverge and passengers change trains.

nection between the two places was by a hilly turnpike-road, and the travelling on that road was very slow. Though they took but a hasty breakfast, and no rest (which it would have been in vain to seek under such anxious circumstances), it was noon before they began to find the bills of Sleary's Horseriding on barns and walls, and one o'clock when they stopped in the market-place.

A Grand Morning Performance[3] by the Riders, commencing at that very hour, was in course of announcement by the bellman as they set their feet upon the stones of the street. Sissy recommended that, to avoid making inquiries and attracting attention in the town, they should present themselves to pay at the door. If Mr. Sleary were taking the money, he would be sure to know her, and would proceed with discretion. If he were not, he would be sure to see them inside; and, knowing what he had done with the fugitive, would proceed with discretion still.

Therefore they repaired, with fluttering hearts, to the well-remembered booth. The flag with the inscription SLEARY'S HORSE-RIDING, was there; and the Gothic niche was there; but Mr. Sleary was not there. Master Kidderminster, grown too maturely turfy to be received by the wildest credulity as Cupid any more, had yielded to the invincible force of circumstances (and his beard), and, in the capacity of a man who made himself generally useful, presided on this occasion over the exchequer[4]—having also a drum in reserve, on which to expend his leisure moments and superfluous forces. In the extreme sharpness of his look out for base coin, Mr. Kidderminster, as at present situated, never saw anything but money; so Sissy passed him unrecognised, and they went in.

The Emperor of Japan, on a steady old white horse stencilled with black spots, was twirling five wash-hand basins at once, as it is the favourite recreation of that monarch to do. Sissy, though well acquainted with his Royal line, had no personal knowledge of the present Emperor, and his reign was peaceful. Miss Josephine Sleary, in her celebrated graceful Equestrian Tyrolean Flower-Act, was then announced by a new clown (who humorously said Cauliflower Act), and Mr. Sleary appeared, leading her in.

Mr. Sleary had only made one cut at the Clown with his long whiplash, and the Clown had only said, "If you do it again, I'll throw the horse at you!" when Sissy was recognised both by father and daughter. But they got through the Act with great self-possession; and Mr. Sleary, saving for the first instant, conveyed no more expression into his locomotive eye than into his fixed one. The performance

---

3. In early theatrical usage, an afternoon performance. Similarly today, the word "matinée" (from the French *matin* meaning "morning") means an afternoon showing.
4. Box office.

seemed a little long to Sissy and Louisa, particularly when it stopped
to afford the Clown an opportunity of telling Mr. Sleary (who said
"Indeed, sir!" to all his observations in the calmest way, and with
his eye on the house), about two legs sitting on three legs looking at
one leg, when in came four legs, and laid hold of one leg, and up got
two legs, caught hold of three legs, and threw 'em at four legs, who
ran away with one leg. For, although an ingenious Allegory relating
to a butcher, a three-legged stool, a dog, and a leg of mutton, this
narrative consumed time; and they were in great suspense. At last,
however, little fair-haired Josephine made her curtsey amid great
applause; and the Clown, left alone in the ring, had just warmed
himself, and said, "Now I'll have a turn!" when Sissy was touched
on the shoulder, and beckoned out.

    She took Louisa with her; and they were received by Mr. Sleary
in a very little private apartment, with canvas sides, a grass floor,
and a wooden ceiling all aslant, on which the box company stamped
their approbation as if they were coming through. "Thethilia," said
Mr. Sleary, who had brandy and water at hand, "it doth me good to
thee you. You wath alwayth a favourite with uth, and you've done uth
credit thinth the old timeth I'm thure. You mutht thee our people,
my dear, afore we thpeak of bithnith, or they'll break their hearth—
ethpethially the women. Here'th Jothphine hath been and got married to E. W. B. Childerth, and thee hath got a boy, and though
he'th only three yearth old, he thtickth on to any pony you can
bring againtht him. He'th named The Little Wonder Of Thcolathic
Equitation; and if you don't hear of that boy at Athley'th,[5] you'll
hear of him at Parith. And you recollect Kidderminthter, that wath
thought to be rather thweet upon yourthelf? Well. He'th married
too. Married a widder. Old enough to be hith mother. Thee wath
Tightrope, thee wath, and now thee'th nothing—on accounth of
fat. They've got two children, tho we're thtrong in the Fairy bithnith and the Nurthery dodge. If you wath to thee our Children in
the Wood, with their father and mother both a dyin' on a horthe—
their uncle a rethieving of 'em ath hith wardth, upon a horthe—
themthelvth a goin' a blackberryin' on a horthe—and the Robinth a
coming in to cover 'em with leavth, upon a horthe—you'd thay it
wath the completetht thing ath ever you thet your eyeth on! And
you remember Emma Gordon, my dear, ath wath a'motht a mother
to you? Of courthe you do; I needn't athk. Well! Emma; thee lotht
her huthband. He wath throw'd a heavy back-fall off a Elephant
in a thort of a Pagoda thing ath the Thultan of the Indieth, and
he never got the better of it; and thee married a thecond time—

5. Astley's, a famous circus in London. See Dickens' *Sketches by Boz* and also *The Old
   Curiosity Shop*, chapter 39.

married a Cheethemonger ath fell in love with her from the front—
and he'th a Overtheer and makin' a fortun."

These various changes, Mr. Sleary, very short of breath now,
related with great heartiness, and with a wonderful kind of innocence, considering what a bleary and brandy-and-watery old veteran
he was. Afterwards he brought in Josephine, and E. W. B. Childers
(rather deeply-lined in the jaws by daylight), and The Little Wonder
of Scholastic Equitation, and, in a word, all the company. Amazing
creatures they were in Louisa's eyes, so white and pink of complexion, so scant of dress, and so demonstrative of leg; but it was very
agreeable to see them crowding about Sissy, and very natural in
Sissy to be unable to refrain from tears.

"There! Now Thethilia hath kithd all the children, and hugged
all the women, and thaken handth all round with all the men, clear,
every one of you, and ring in the band for the thecond part!"

As soon as they were gone, he continued in a low tone. "Now,
Thethilia, I don't athk to know any thecreth, but I thuppothe I may
conthider thith to be Mith Thquire."

"This is his sister. Yes."

"And t'other one'th daughter. That'h what I mean. Hope I thee
you well, mith. And I hope the Thquire'th well?"

"My father will be here soon," said Louisa, anxious to bring him
to the point. "Is my brother safe?"

"Thafe and thound!" he replied. I want you jutht to take a peep at
the Ring, mith, through here. Thethilia, you know the dodgeth;
find a thpyhole for yourthelf."

They each looked through a chink in the boards.

"That'h Jack the Giant Killer—piethe of comic infant bithnith,"
said Sleary. "There'th a property-houthe, you thee, for Jack to
hide in; there'th my Clown with a thauthepan-lid and a thpit, for
Jack'th thervant; there'th little Jack himthelf in a thplendid thoot
of armour; there'th two comic black thervanth twithe ath big ath
the houthe, to thtand by it and to bring it in and clear it; and the
Giant (a very ecthpenthive bathket one), he an't on yet. Now, do you
thee 'em all?"

"Yes," they both said.

"Look at 'em again," said Sleary, "look at 'em well. You thee 'em
all? Very good. Now, mith;" he put a form for them to sit on; "I
have my opinionth, and the Thquire your father hath hith. I don't
want to know what your brother'th been up to; ith better for me
not to know. All I thay ith, the Thquire hath thtood by Thethilia,
and I'll thtand by the Thquire. Your brother ith one o' them black
thervanth."

Louisa uttered an exclamation, partly of distress, partly of
satisfaction.

"Ith a fact," said Sleary, "and even knowin' it, you couldn't put your finger on him. Let the Thquire come. I thall keep your brother here after the performanth. I thant undreth him, nor yet wath hith paint off. Let the Thquire come here after the performanth, or come here yourthelf after the performanth, and you thall find your brother, and have the whole plathe to talk to him in. Never mind the lookth of him, ath long ath he'th well hid."

Louisa, with many thanks and with a lightened load, detained Mr. Sleary no longer then. She left her love for her brother, with her eyes full of tears; and she and Sissy went away until later in the afternoon.

Mr. Gradgrind arrived within an hour afterwards. He too had encountered no one whom he knew; and was now sanguine, with Sleary's assistance, of getting his disgraced son to Liverpool in the night. As neither of the three could be his companion without almost identifying him under any disguise, he prepared a letter to a correspondent whom he could trust, beseeching him to ship the bearer off, at any cost, to North or South America, or any distant part of the world to which he could be the most speedily and privately dispatched. This done, they walked about, waiting for the Circus to be quite vacated; not only by the audience, but by the company and by the horses. After watching it a long time, they saw Mr. Sleary bring out a chair and sit down by the side-door, smoking; as if that were his signal that they might approach.

"Your thervant, Thquire," was his cautious salutation as they passed in. "If you want me you'll find me here. You muthn't mind your thon having a comic livery on."

They all three went in; and Mr. Gradgrind sat down, forlorn, on the Clown's performing chair in the middle of the ring. On one of the back benches, remote in the subdued light and the strangeness of the place, sat the villainous whelp, sulky to the last, whom he had the misery to call his son.

In a preposterous coat, like a beadle's,[6] with cuffs and flaps exaggerated to an unspeakable extent; in an immense waistcoat, knee-breeches, buckled shoes, and a mad cocked hat; with nothing fitting him, and everything of coarse material, moth-eaten, and full of holes; with seams in his black face, where fear and heat had started through the greasy composition daubed all over it; anything so grimly, detestably, ridiculously shameful as the whelp in his comic livery, Mr. Gradgrind never could by any other means have believed in, weighable and measurable fact though it was. And one of his model children had come to this!

---

6. A low-ranking officer whose duty it was to implement and enforce the rules of the parish board in regard to local law and social services.

At first the whelp would not draw any nearer, but persisted in remaining up there by himself. Yielding at length, if any concession so sullenly made can be called yielding, to the entreaties of Sissy—for Louisa he disowned altogether—he came down, bench by bench, until he stood in the sawdust, on the verge of the circle, as far as possible, within its limits from where his father sat.

"How was this done?" asked the father.

"How was what done?" moodily answered the son.

"This robbery," said the father, raising his voice upon the word.

"I forced the safe myself over night, and shut it up ajar before I went away. I had had the key that was found, made long before. I dropped it that morning, that it might be supposed to have been used. I didn't take the money all at once. I pretended to put my balance away every night, but I didn't. Now you know all about it."

"If a thunderbolt had fallen on me," said the father, "it would have shocked me less than this!"

"I don't see why," grumbled the son. "So many people are employed in situations of trust; so many people, out of so many, will be dishonest. I have heard you talk, a hundred times, of its being a law. How can I help laws? You have comforted others with such things, father. Comfort yourself!"

The father buried his face in his hands, and the son stood in his disgraceful grotesqueness, biting straw; his hands, with the black partly worn away inside, looking like the hands of a monkey. The evening was fast closing in; and, from time to time, he turned the whites of his eyes restlessly and impatiently towards his father. They were the only parts of his face that showed any life or expression, the pigment upon it was so thick.

"You must be got to Liverpool, and sent abroad."

"I suppose I must. I can't be more miserable anywhere," whimpered the whelp, "than I have been here, ever since I can remember. That's one thing."

Mr. Gradgrind went to the door, and returned with Sleary, to whom he submitted the question, How to get this deplorable object away?

"Why, I've been thinking of it, Thquire. There'th not muth time to lothe, tho you muth thay yeth or no. Ith over twenty mileth to the rail. Thereth a coath in half an hour, that goeth *to* the rail, 'purpothe to cath the mail train. That train will take him right to Liverpool."

"But look at him," groaned Mr. Gradgrind. "Will any coach—"

"I don't mean that he thould go in the comic livery," said. Sleary. "Thay the word, and I'll make a Jothkin[7] of him, out of the wardrobe, in five minutes."

7. A bumpkin, an uncouth farmhand.

"I don't understand," said Mr. Gradgrind.

"A Jothkin—a Carter. Make up your mind quick, Thquire. There'll be beer to feth. I've never met with nothing but beer ath'll ever clean a comic blackamoor."

Mr. Gradgrind rapidly assented; Mr. Sleary rapidly turned out from a box, a smock frock, a felt hat, and other essentials; the whelp rapidly changed clothes behind a screen of baize; Mr. Sleary rapidly brought beer, and washed him white again.

"Now," said Sleary, "come along to the coath, and jump up behind; I'll go with you there, and they'll thuppothe you one of my people. Thay farewell to your family, and tharp'th the word!" With which he delicately retired.

"Here is your letter," said Mr. Gradgrind. "All necessary means will be provided for you. Atone, by repentance and better conduct, for the shocking action you have committed, and the dreadful consequences to which it has led. Give me your hand, my poor boy, and may God forgive you as I do!"

The culprit was moved to a few abject tears by these words and their pathetic tone. But, when Louisa opened her arms, he repulsed her afresh.

"Not you. I don't want to have anything to say to you!"

"O Tom, Tom, do we end so, after all my love!"

"After all your love!" he returned, obdurately. "Pretty love! Leaving old Bounderby to himself, and packing my best friend Mr. Harthouse off, and going home, just when I was in the greatest danger. Pretty love that! Coming out with every word about our having gone to that place, when you saw the net was gathering round me. Pretty love that! You have regularly given me up. You never cared for me."

"Tharp'th the word!" said Sleary at the door.

They all confusedly went out: Louisa crying to him that she forgave him, and loved him still, and that he would one day be sorry to have left her so, and glad to think of these her last words, far away: when some one ran against them. Mr. Gradgrind and Sissy, who were both before him while his sister yet clung to his shoulder, stopped and recoiled.

For, there was Bitzer, out of breath, his thin lips parted, his thin nostrils distended, his white eyelashes quivering, his colorless face more colorless than ever, as if he ran himself into a white heat, when other people ran themselves into a glow. There he stood, panting and heaving, as if he had never stopped since the night, now long ago, when he had run them down before.

"I'm sorry to interfere with your plans," said Bitzer, shaking his head, "but I can't allow myself to be done by horseriders. I must have young Mr. Tom; he mustn't be got away by horseriders; here he is in a smock frock, and I must have him!"

By the collar, too, it seemed. For, so he took possession of him.

Chapter VIII.

PHILOSOPHICAL.

They went back into the booth, Sleary shutting the door to keep intruders out. Bitzer, still holding the paralysed culprit by the collar, stood in the Ring, blinking at his old patron through the darkness of the twilight.

"Bitzer," said Mr. Gradgrind, broken down, and miserably submissive to him, "have you a heart?"

"The circulation, sir," returned Bitzer, smiling at the oddity of the question, "couldn't be carried on without one. No man, sir, acquainted with the facts established by Harvey[1] relating to the circulation of the blood, can doubt that I have a heart."

"Is it accessible," cried Mr. Gradgrind, "to any compassionate influence?"

"It is accessible to Reason, sir," returned the excellent young man. "And to nothing else."

They stood looking at each other; Mr. Gradgrind's face as white as the pursuer's.

"What motive—even what motive in reason—can you have for preventing the escape of this wretched youth," said Mr. Gradgrind, "and crushing his miserable father? See his sister here. Pity us!"

"Sir," returned Bitzer, in a very business-like and logical manner, "since you ask me what motive I have in reason, for taking young Mr. Tom back to Coketown, it is only reasonable to let you know. I have suspected young Mr. Tom of this bank-robbery from the first. I had had my eye upon him before that time, for I knew his ways. I have kept my observations to myself, but I have made them; and I have got ample proofs against him now, besides his running away, and besides his own confession, which I was just in time to overhear. I had the pleasure of watching your house yesterday morning, and following you here. I am going to take young Mr. Tom back to Coketown, in order to deliver him over to Mr. Bounderby. Sir, I have no doubt whatever that Mr. Bounderby will then promote me to young Mr. Tom's situation. And I wish to have his situation, sir, for it will be a rise to me, and will do me good."

---

1. The English scientist William Harvey (1578–1657), author of *On the Motion of the Heart and Blood in Animals* (1628), discovered the circulation of the blood and the activity of the heart.

"If this is solely a question of self-interest with you—" Mr. Gradgrind began.

"I beg your pardon for interrupting you, sir," returned Bitzer; "but I am sure you know that the whole social system is a question of self-interest. What you must always appeal to, is a person's self-interest. It's your only hold. We are so constituted. I was brought up in that catechism when I was very young, sir, as you are aware."

"What sum of money," said Mr. Gradgrind, "will you set against your expected promotion?"

"Thank you, sir," returned Bitzer, "for hinting at the proposal; but I will not set any sum against it. Knowing that your clear head would propose that alternative, I have gone over the calculations in my mind; and I find that to compound a felony, even on very high terms indeed, would not be as safe and good for me as my improved prospects in the Bank."

"Bitzer," said Mr. Gradgrind, stretching out his hands as though he would have said, See how miserable I am! "Bitzer, I have but one chance left to soften you. You were many years at my school. If, in remembrance of the pains bestowed upon you there, you can persuade yourself in any degree to disregard your present interest and release my son, I entreat and pray you to give him the benefit of that remembrance."

"I really wonder, sir," rejoined the old pupil in an argumentative manner, "to find you taking a position so untenable. My schooling was paid for; it was a bargain; and when I came away, the bargain ended."

It was a fundamental principle of the Gradgrind philosophy, that everything was to be paid for. Nobody was ever on any account to give anybody anything, or render anybody help without purchase. Gratitude was to be abolished, and the virtues springing from it were not to be Every inch of the existence of mankind, from birth to death, was to be a bargain across a counter. And if we didn't get to Heaven that way, it was not a politico-economical place, and we had no business there.

"I don't deny," added Bitzer, "that my schooling was cheap. But that comes right, sir. I was made in the cheapest market, and have to dispose of myself in the dearest."

He was a little troubled here, by Louisa and Sissy crying.

"Pray don't do that," said he, "it's of no use doing that: it only worries. You seem to think that I have some animosity against young Mr. Tom; whereas I have none at all. I am only going, on the reasonable grounds I have mentioned, to take him back to Coketown. If he was to resist, I should set up the cry of Stop Thief! But, he won't resist, you may depend upon it."

Mr. Sleary, who, with his mouth open and his rolling eye as immoveably jammed in his head as his fixed one, had listened to these doctrines with profound attention; here stepped forward.

"Thquire, you know perfectly well, and your daughter knowth perfectly well (better than you, becauthe I thed it to her), that I didn't know what your thon had done, and that I didn't want to know—I thed it wath better not, though I only thought, then, it wath thome thkylarking. However, thith young man having made it known to be a robbery of a bank, why, that'h a theriouth thing; muth too theriouth a thing for me to compound, ath thith young man hath very properly called it. Conthequently, Thquire, you muthn't quarrel with me if I take thith young man'th thide, and thay he'th right and there'th no help for it. But I tell you what I'll do, Thquire; I'll drive your thon and thith young man over to the rail, and prevent expothure here. I can't conthent to do more, but I'll do that."

Fresh lamentations from Louisa, and deeper affliction on Mr. Gradgrind's part, followed this desertion of them by their last friend. But, Sissy glanced at him with great attention; nor did she in her own breast misunderstand him. As they were all going out again, he favored her with one slight roll of his moveable eye, desiring her to linger behind. As he locked the door, he said excitedly:

"The Thquire thtood by you, Thethilia, and I'll thtand by the Thquire. More than that: thith ith a prethiouth rathcal, and belongth to that bluthtering Cove that my people nearly pitht out o' winder. It'll be a dark night; I've got a horthe that'll do anything but thpeak; I've got a pony that'll go fifteen mile an hour with Childerth driving of him; I've got a dog that'll keep a man to one plathe four-and-twenty hourth. Get a word with the young Thquire. Tell him, when he theeth our horthe begin to danthe, not to be afraid of being thpilt, but to look out for a pony-gig coming up. Tell him, when he theeth that gig clothe by, to jump down, and it'll take him off at a rattling pathe. If my dog leth thith young man thtir a peg on foot, I give him leave to go. And if my horthe ever thtirth from that thpot where he beginth a danthing, till the morning—I don't know him!—Tharp'th the word!"

The word was so sharp, that in ten minutes Mr. Childers, sauntering about the market-place in a pair of slippers, had his cue, and Mr. Sleary's equipage was ready. It was a fine sight, to behold the learned dog barking round it, and Mr. Sleary instructing him, with his one practicable eye, that Bitzer was the object of his particular attentions. Soon after dark they all three got in and started; the learned dog (a formidable creature) already pinning Bitzer with his eye, and sticking close to the wheel on his side, that he might

be ready for him in the event of his showing the slightest disposition to alight.

The other three sat up at the inn all night in great suspense. At
eight o'clock in the morning Mr. Sleary and the dog re-appeared:
both in high spirits.

"All right, Thquire!" said Mr. Sleary, "your thon may be aboard-a-
thip by thith time. Childerth took him off, an hour and a half after
we left here latht night. The horthe danthed the Polka till he wath
dead beat (he would have walthed, if he hadn't been in harneth),
and then I gave him the word and he went to thleep comfortable.
When that prethiouth young Rathcal thed he'd go for'ard afoot, the
dog hung on to hith neck-hankercher with all four legth in the air
and pulled him down and rolled him over. Tho he come back into
the drag,[2] and there he that, 'till I turned the horthe'th head, at
halfpatht thixth thith morning."

Mr. Gradgrind overwhelmed him with thanks, of course; and
hinted as delicately as he could, at a handsome remuneration in
money.

"I don't want money mythelf, Thquire; but Childerth ith a family
man, and if you wath to like to offer him a five-pound note, it mightn't
be unaccheptable. Likewithe if you wath to thtand a collar for the
dog, or a thet of bellth for the horthe, I thould be very glad to take
'em. Brandy and water I alwayth take." He had already called for a
glass, and now called for another. "If you wouldn't think it going too
far, Thquire, to make a little thpread for the company at about three
and thixth ahead, not reckoning Luth,[3] it would make 'em happy."

All these little tokens of his gratitude, Mr. Gradgrind very willingly undertook to render. Though he thought them far too slight,
he said, for such a service.

"Very well, Thquire; then, if you'll only give a Horthe-riding, a
bethpeak, whenever you can, you'll more than balanthe the account.
Now, Thquire, if your daughter will ethcuthe me, I thould like one
parting word with you."

Louisa and Sissy withdrew into an adjoining room; Mr. Sleary,
stirring, and drinking his brandy and water as he stood, went on:

"Thquire, you don't need to be told that dogth ith wonderful
animalth."

"Their instinct," said Mr. Gradgrind, "is surprising."

"Whatever you call it—and I'm bletht if *I* know what to call it"—
said Sleary, "it ith athtonithing. The way in with a dog'll find you—
the dithtanthe he'll come!"

2. A heavy cart.
3. Lush, a slang term for alcoholic drinks. "Three and thixth": three shillings and six-
    pence in predecimal English currency; equal to thirty pence, which in modern value is
    about £3 British and about $5 in the United States.

"His scent," said Mr. Gradgrind, "being so fine."

"I'm bletht if I know what to call it," repeated Sleary, shaking his head, "but I have had dogth find me, Thquire, in a way that made me think whether that dog hadn't gone to another dog, and thed, 'You don't happen to know a perthon of the name of Thleary, do you? Perthon of the name of Thleary, in the Horthe-Riding way—thtout man—game eye?' And whether that dog mightn't have thed, 'Well, I can't thay I know him mythelf, but I know a dog that I think would be likely to be acquainted with him.' And whether that dog mightn't have thought it over, and thed, 'Thleary, Thleary! O yeth, to be thure! A friend of mine menthioned him to me at one time. I can get you hith addreth directly.' In conthequenth of my being afore the public, and going about tho muth, you thee, there mutht be a number of dogth acquainted with me, Thquire, that I don't know!"

Mr. Gradgrind seemed to be quite confounded by this speculation.

"Any way," said Sleary, after putting his lips to his brandy and water, "ith fourteen month ago, Thquire, thinthe we wath at Chethter. We wath getting up our Children in the Wood one morning, when there cometh into our Ring, by the thtage door, a dog. He had travelled a long way, he wath in very bad condithon, he wath lame, and pretty well blind. He went round to our children, one after another, as if he wath a theeking for a child he know'd; and then he come to me, and throwd hithelf up behind, and thtood on hith two fore-legth, weak ath he wath, and then he wagged hith tail and died. Thquire, that dog wath Merrylegth."

"Sissy's father's dog!"

"Thethilia'th father'th old dog. Now, Thquire, I can take my oath, from my knowledge of that dog, that that man wath dead—and buried—afore that dog come back to me. Joth'phine and Childerth and me talked it over a long time, whether I thould write or not. But we agreed, 'No. There'th nothing comfortable to tell; why unthettle her mind, and make her unhappy?' Tho, whether her father bathely detherted her; or whether he broke hith own heart alone, rather than pull her down along with him; never will be known, now, Thquire, till—no, not till we know how the dogth findth uth out!"

"She keeps the bottle that he sent her for, to this hour; and she will believe in his affection to the last moment of her life," said Mr. Gradgrind.

"It theemth to prethent two thingth to a perthon, don't it, Thquire?" said Mr. Sleary, musing as he looked down into the depths of his brandy and water: "one, that there ith a love in the world, not all Thelf-interetht after all, but thomething very different; t'other, that it hath a way of ith own of calculating or not calculating, whith thomehow or another ith at leatht ath hard to give a name to, ath the wayth of the dogth ith!"

Mr. Gradgrind looked out of window, and made no reply. Mr. Sleary emptied his glass and recalled the ladies.

"Thethilia my dear, kith me and good-bye! Mith Thquire, to thee you treating of her like a thithter, and a thithter that you trutht and honor with all your heart and more, ith a very pretty thight to me. I hope your brother may live to be better detherving of you, and a greater comfort to you. Thquire, thake handth, firtht and latht! Don't be croth with uth poor vagabondth. People mutht be amuthed. They can't be alwayth a learning, nor yet they can't be alwayth a working, they an't made for it. You *mutht* have uth, Thquire. Do the withe thing and the kind thing too, and make the betht of uth; not the wurtht!

"And I never thought before," said Mr. Sleary, putting his head in at the door again to say it, "that I wath tho muth of a Cackler!"

Chapter IX.

FINAL.

It is a dangerous thing to see anything in the sphere of a vain blusterer, before the vain blusterer sees it himself. Mr. Bounderby felt that Mrs. Sparsit had audaciously anticipated him, and presumed to be wiser than he. Inappeasably indignant with her for her triumphant discovery of Mrs. Pegler, he turned this presumption, on the part of a woman in her dependent position, over and over in his mind, until it accumulated with turning like a great snowball. At last he made the discovery that to discharge this highly-connected female—to have it in his power to say, "She was a woman of family, and wanted to stick to me, but I wouldn't have it, and got rid of her"—would be to get the utmost possible amount of crowning glory out of the connection, and at the same time to punish Mrs. Sparsit according to her deserts.

Filled fuller than ever, with this great idea, Mr. Bounderby came in to lunch, and sat himself down in the dining-room of former days, where his portrait was. Mrs. Sparsit sat by the fire, with her foot in her cotton stirrup, little thinking whither she was posting.

Since the Pegler affair, this gentlewoman had covered her pity for Mr. Bounderby with a veil of quiet melancholy and contrition. In virtue thereof, it had become her habit to assume a woful look; which woful look she now bestowed upon her patron.

"What's the matter now, ma'am?" said Mr. Bounderby, in a very short, rough way.

"Pray, sir," returned Mrs. Sparsit, "do not bite my nose off."

"Bite your nose off, ma'am!" repeated Mr. Bounderby. "Your nose!" meaning, as Mrs. Sparsit conceived, that it was too developed a nose for the purpose. After which offensive implication, he cut himself a crust of bread, and threw the knife down with a noise.

Mrs. Sparsit took her foot out of her stirrup, and said, "Mr. Bounderby, sir!"

"Well, ma'am?" retorted Mr. Bounderby. "What are you staring at?"

"May I ask, sir," said Mrs. Sparsit, "have you been ruffled this morning?"

"Yes, ma'am."

"May I inquire, sir," pursued the injured woman, "whether I am the unfortunate cause of your having lost your temper?"

"Now, I'll tell you what, ma'am," said Bounderby, "I am not come here to be bullied. A female may be highly connected, but she can't be permitted to bother and badger a man in my position, and I am not going to put up with it." (Mr. Bounderby felt it necessary to get on; foreseeing that if he allowed of details, he would be beaten.)

Mrs. Sparsit first elevated, then knitted, her Coriolanian eyebrows; gathered up her work into its proper basket; and rose.

"Sir," said she, majestically. "It is apparent to me that I am in your way at present. I will retire to my own apartment."

"Allow me to open the door, ma'am."

"Thank you, sir; I can do it for myself."

"You had better allow me, ma'am," said Bounderby, passing her, and getting his hand upon the lock; "because I can take the opportunity of saying a word to you, before you go. Mrs. Sparsit, ma'am, I rather think you are cramped here, do you know? It appears to me, that, under my humble roof, there's hardly opening enough for a lady of your genius in other people's affairs."

Mrs. Sparsit gave him a look of the darkest scorn, and said with great politeness, "Really, sir?"

"I have been thinking it over, you see, since the late affairs have happened, ma'am," said Bounderby; "and it appears to my poor judgment—"

"Oh! Pray, sir," Mrs. Sparsit interposed, with sprightly cheerfulness, "don't disparage your judgment. Everybody knows how unerring Mr. Bounderby's judgment is. Everybody has had proofs of it. It must be the theme of general conversation. Disparage anything in yourself but your judgment, sir," said Mrs. Sparsit, laughing.

Mr. Bounderby, very red and uncomfortable, resumed:

"It appears to me, ma'am, I say, that a different sort of establishment altogether, would bring out a lady of your powers. Such an establishment as your relation, Lady Scadgers's, now. Don't you think you might find some affairs there, ma'am, to interfere with?"

"It never occurred to me before, sir," returned Mrs. Sparsit; "but now you mention it, I should think it highly probable."

"Then suppose you try, ma'am," said Bounderby, laying an enve-
lope with a cheque in it, in her little basket. "You can take your own
time for going, ma'am; but perhaps in the meanwhile, it will be
more agreeable to a lady of your powers of mind, to eat her meals by
herself, and not to be intruded upon. I really ought to apologise to
you—being only Josiah Bounderby of Coketown—for having stood
in your light so long."

"Pray don't name it, sir," returned Mrs. Sparsit. "If that portrait
could speak, sir,—but it has the advantage over the original of not
possessing the power of committing itself and disgusting others,—
it would testify, that a long period has elapsed since I first habitually
addressed it as the picture of a Noodle. Nothing that a Noodle does,
can awaken surprise or indignation; the proceedings of a Noodle
can only inspire contempt."

Thus saying, Mrs. Sparsit, with her Roman features like a medal
struck to commemorate her scorn of Mr. Bounderby, surveyed him
fixedly from head to foot, swept disdainfully past him, and ascended
the staircase. Mr. Bounderby closed the door, and stood before
the fire; projecting himself after his old explosive manner into his
portrait—and into futurity.

Into how much of futurity? He saw Mrs. Sparsit fighting out a daily
fight, at the points of all the weapons in the female armory, with
the grudging, smarting, peevish, tormenting Lady Scadgers, still
laid up in bed with her mysterious leg, and gobbling her insufficient
income down by about the middle of every quarter, in a mean little
airless lodging, a mere closet for one, a mere crib for two; but did he
see more? Did he catch any glimpse of himself making a show of
Bitzer to strangers, as the rising young man, so devoted to his master's great merits, who had won young Tom's place, and had almost
captured young Tom himself, in the times when by various rascals
he was spirited away? Did he see any faint reflection of his own
image making a vain-glorious will, whereby five-and-twenty Humbugs, past five and fifty years of age, each taking upon himself the
name, Josiah Bounderby of Coketown, should for ever dine in
Bounderby Hall,[1] for ever lodge in Bounderby Buildings, for ever
attend a Bounderby chapel, for ever go to sleep under a Bounderby
chaplain, for ever be supported out of a Bounderby estate, and for
ever nauseate all healthy stomachs with a vast amount of Bounderby
balderdash and bluster? Had he any prescience of the day, five years
to come, when Josiah Bounderby of Coketown was to die of a fit in
the Coketown street, and this same precious will was to begin its

---

1. Victorian old age homes, privately endowed, often had their benefactors' names and
   even required their residents to identify themselves by the names of the founders.

long career of quibble, plunder, false pretences, vile example, little service and much law? Probably not. Yet the portrait was to see it all out.

Here was Mr. Gradgrind on the same day, and in the same hour, sitting thoughtful in his own room. How much of futurity did *he* see? Did he see himself, a white-haired decrepit man, bending his hitherto inflexible theories to appointed circumstances; making his facts and figures subservient to Faith, Hope, and Charity;[2] and no longer trying to grind that Heavenly trio in his dusty little mills? Did he catch sight of himself, therefore much despised by his late political associates? Did he see them, in the era of its being quite settled that the national dustmen have only to do with one another, and owe no duty to an abstraction called a People, "taunting the honorable gentleman" with this and with that and with what not, five nights a-week, until the small hours of the morning?[3] Probably he had that much fore-knowledge, knowing his men.

Here was Louisa on the night of the same day, watching the fire as in days of yore, though with a gentler and a humbler face. How much of the future might arise before *her* vision? Broadsides in the streets, signed with her father's name, exonerating the late Stephen Blackpool, weaver, from misplaced suspicion, and publishing the guilt of his own son, with such extenuation as his years and temptation (he could not bring himself to add, his education) might beseech; were of the Present. So, Stephen Blackpool's tombstone, with her father's record of his death, was almost of the Present, for she knew it was to be. These things she could plainly see. But, how much of the Future?

A working woman, christened Rachael, after a long illness once again appearing at the ringing of the Factory bell, and passing to and fro at the set hours, among the Coketown Hands; a woman of a pensive beauty, always dressed in black, but sweet-tempered and serene, and even cheerful; who, of all the people in the place, alone appeared to have compassion on a degraded, drunken wretch of her own sex, who was sometimes seen in the town secretly begging of her, and crying to her; a woman working, ever working, but content to do it, and preferring to do it as her natural lot, until she should be too old to labor any more? Did Louisa see this? Such a thing was to be.

A lonely brother, many thousands of miles away, writing, on paper blotted with tears, that her words had too soon come true, and that all the treasures in the world would be cheaply bartered

2. See 1 Corinthians 13.1–13.
3. Parliamentary debates frequently last all night.

for a sight of her dear face? At length this brother coming nearer home, with hope of seeing her, and being delayed by illness; and then a letter in a strange hand, saying "he died in hospital, of fever, such a day, and died in penitence and love of you: his last word being your name"? Did Louisa see these things? Such things were to be.

Herself again a wife—a mother—lovingly watchful of her children, ever careful that they should have a childhood of the mind no less than a childhood of the body, as knowing it to be even a more beautiful thing, and a possession, any hoarded scrap of which, is a blessing and happiness to the wisest? Did Louisa see this? Such a thing was never to be.

But, happy Sissy's happy children loving her; all children loving her; she, grown learned in childish lore; thinking no innocent and pretty fancy ever to be despised; trying hard to know her humbler fellow-creatures, and to beautify their lives of machinery and reality with those imaginative graces and delights, without which the heart of infancy will wither up, the sturdiest physical manhood will be morally stark death, and the plainest national prosperity figures can show, will be the Writing on the Wall,[4]—she holding this course as part of no fantastic vow, or bond, or brotherhood, or sisterhood, or pledge, or covenant, or fancy dress, or fancy fair; but simply as a duty to be done,—did Louisa see these things of herself? These things were to be.

Dear reader! It rests with you and me, whether, in our two fields of action, similar things shall be or not. Let them be! We shall sit with lighter bosoms on the hearth, to see the ashes of our fires turn gray and cold.

THE END

4. Daniel 5.5–31.

A Note on the Text

The Genesis of *Hard Times*: A History of the Text[†]

Hard Times was first published as a serial in Dickens' own weekly magazine, *Household Words*, over a five-month period from April 1, 1854, through August 12, and shortly afterward as a single volume of 352 pages. As Dickens stated, in a letter to Thomas Carlyle, his novel had been "constructed * * * patiently, with a view to its publication altogether in a compact cheap form." His patience had, in fact, been severely stretched by the challenging difficulties of telling his story in short weekly installments, a mode he had not used since writing *Barnaby Rudge* thirteen years earlier. After he had remastered this art of weekly serialization in the process of writing *Hard Times*, he did return to it again in two of his later novels, *A Tale of Two Cities* and *Great Expectations*, but in 1854, he had lost the habit of the strict limits imposed; he found them, as he said, "crushing."

One result of this mode of publication is the relative shortness of *Hard Times* (approximately 117,000 words as compared with the 350,000 words of *Bleak House* or *David Copperfield*, the two novels preceding *Hard Times*). There are some seventy-nine characters in *Bleak House*, as against only twenty-five in *Hard Times*.

The proposal to publish *Hard Times* as a weekly serial was not initiated by Dickens himself but by the printers of *Household Words*, who were concerned about the magazine's sagging sales. It was they who argued that the inclusion of a novel by Dickens in its pages would provide the transfusion necessary to restore the magazine's circulation. Their prediction was sound. As Dickens' friend and biographer John Forster reports, the serialization of *Hard Times* "more than doubled the circulation of his journal."

When his publishers made their proposal to him, late in 1853, Dickens was somewhat reluctant to accept, partly because of the restrictions imposed by weekly serialization, partly because, at that time, he had hoped to enjoy a year's rest. In August 1853, after completing *Bleak House*, he had felt unusually tired and therefore resolved

---

[†] This and the textual notes were created by George Ford and Sylvère Monod and revised by Monod for the third edition.

to write no more full-length fiction until the following summer at the earliest. *Rest* never meant for him what it means for most people: he went on editing his magazine, writing articles, taking part in amateur theatricals, reading his works in public, lending his energy to philanthropic enterprises, and looking after the education and welfare of his nine children. His idea of *rest* was simply an interruption of novel writing. And the temptation to shorten the period allotted to rest was often vivid. His printers' suggestion provided the necessary incentive, and by January 23, 1854, he had written the first page of *Hard Times*.

The student of Dickens' fiction is in a privileged position to follow the history of the text, for valuable documents about no fewer than six stages of the novelist's work have been preserved:

1. The number plans or Memoranda, i.e., notes Dickens made while writing *Hard Times* that concern the arrangement of his story in serial form.

2. The original manuscript in its entirety.

3. Corrected proofs. For parts of chapters XI and XII (book I) two sets of proofs have been preserved. Most of the proofs are galley proofs, in long slips, but for chapters XI and XII of book II, and chapters I and II of book III they are page proofs, already set in the *Household Words* format.

4. The text as it was published in *Household Words* (April 1 through August 12, 1854). Unlike *A Tale of Two Cities* later, *Hard Times* was *not* reprinted in monthly parts, illustrated, in a green cover, immediately after the appearance of each batch of four consecutive weekly numbers.

5. The text as it was published in the first edition in book form (one volume, 352 pages, 1854). Unlike the first edition of *Bleak House* and Dickens' other full-length novels, the 1854 *Hard Times* had to be reset, since it had not appeared in monthly parts that could be simply stitched and bound together.

6. The text as reprinted in several popular editions brought out in the author's lifetime: the Library Edition of 1858, the Cheap Edition of 1860, the People's Edition of 1865—which used the text of the Cheap Edition—and, finally and more significantly, the Charles Dickens Edition of 1867–68, proudly reproducing, on both title page and hard cover, the author's signature with its well-known sensational flourish.

The general history of the text is interesting and sufficiently clear. The *Working Plans* or *Mems.* (see p. 239) show how the book gradually took shape. The second and third stages (manuscript and proofs) can best be traced by reading the textual notes. Meanwhile, the reader can examine the organization of the story through its fourth and fifth stages by looking at the calendar on p. 298, which shows the correspondence between the two printed forms of 1854, the weekly serial and the one-volume version.

As regards the text proper, there is evidence of considerable work on the manuscript itself, extensive revision at proof stage, further revision (still of some significance) before publication in book form, and only minor, perhaps perfunctory, revision in 1867–68 for the Charles Dickens Edition.

Detailed comparison has shown, and even a cursory examination of the textual notes makes abundantly clear, that one and in some cases two sets of proofs, besides those we possess, must have existed, but have not been preserved. In many cases, there are substantial differences between manuscript and proof (other than excusable misreadings by an overworked compositor of an excruciatingly difficult manuscript); and in many other cases, changes not made at proof stage are incorporated into the *Household Words* text; chapters III, IV, and V of book I contain evidence that there must have been an earlier proof; chapter VI, that there must have been both earlier and later proofs than those we have.

The text as first written and published in *Household Words* had no chapter titles; the division into three books, although conceived while Dickens was working on the early section (as is shown by the Working Plans), and also the chapter titles were first introduced in the one-volume edition of 1854.

Dickens' Working Plans

From the time of his writing *Dombey and Son* (1846–48), it became Dickens' practice to jot down on loose sheets of paper a series of briefly worded suggestions for his own guidance about his work in progress; the suggestions were about plot and theme, names of characters, significant phrases to be used in narrative or dialogue, and more particularly about how his story might best be divided into installments for periodical publication. These sheets of working memoranda (or *Mems.* as he called them) provide us with exceptionally interesting glimpses of a novelist at work.

The *Mems.* for *Hard Times* occupy six handwritten pages,[1] but because each of these pages was folded down the center to provide for two columns of entries, we have, in effect, twelve pages. At the top of the opening page (which contains speculations about length and suitable titles for the novel) the entries are written from one side across to the other, but later the division into separate columns is consistently maintained. As a rule, Dickens seems to have used the left-hand side of each page for one kind of note and the right-hand

---

1. They are available in facsimile, thanks to Harry Stone's splendid edition of *Dickens' Working Notes for His Novels* (Chicago: U of Chicago P, 1987), pp. 246–61.

side for another. On the left-hand side are lists of incidents, key phrases, and queries (not always in chronological order), which would seem to constitute the raw material of the "number" in the making. On the right-hand side the same material is more methodically divided into chapters, which suggests that it represents a later stage of Dickens' planning. Some points, however, remain unclear, and one among the many queries that the *Mems.* can raise is whether their function was entirely prospective; was it not also, and at the same time, retrospective? Did not the novelist occasionally record in the *Mems.* work that he had already done? And is it not likely that he sometimes added to both sides of his sheet while already at work on the current number?

A specially intriguing aspect of the memoranda for *Hard Times* is that they are written in the same form as those of the long "monthly" novels, although *Hard Times* was never published or conceived as a monthly serial. This form seems to have been adopted by Dickens for half-technical, half-sentimental reasons. In any case, the division of *Hard Times* into five "numbers," corresponding neither to the twenty[2] weekly intallments of *Household Words* nor to the three-book division of the first edition in volume form, is a purely artificial one.

[*Page 1—Left-hand side*]

Friday January 20th 1854

Mems: Quantity

One sheet (16 pages) of Bleak House, will make 10
pages and a quarter of Household Words. Fifteen pages of
my writing, will make a sheet of Bleak House.
~~A line or two more than a~~ A page and a half
of my writing, will make a page of Household Words.
—

The quantity of the story to be published weekly, being
about five pages of Household Words, will require about
seven pages and a half of my writing.

[*Page 1—Right-hand side*]

Friday January 20th 1854

Mr Gradgrind	Stubborn Things
Mrs Gradgrind	Fact
	Thomas Gradgrind's facts
	~~George~~ John Gradgrind's facts

---

2. The chapters described in the *Mems.* as *Weekly No. 20* and *Weekly No. 21* were in fact
   published in the same number (no. 229) of *Household Words*.

Hard-headed Gradgrind
The Grindstone
Hard heads and soft hearts
<u>The Time Grinders</u>
Mr. Gradgrind's grindstone
~~The Family grindstone~~
~~Hard Times~~
The ~~universal~~ general
grindstone
Hard Times
Heads and Tales
Two and two are four
Prove it!
<u>Black and white</u>
/According to Cocker
/Prove it!
/Stubborn things
/~~Facts are stubborn things~~

~~The real times~~
~~days~~
~~There's no~~
~~No such thing Sir.~~
/~~Extremes meet.~~
/~~Unknown quantities~~
/Simple arithmetic
/A ~~mere~~ matter of
calculation
/A mere question of figures
/

Mr. Gradgrind's ~~grindstone~~
facts
/The ~~John Thomas Thomas~~
~~Thomas Mr. Gradgrind's~~
grindstone
Hard Times
/Two and two are four
/~~Calculations~~
~~According to Cocker~~
~~Damaging Facts~~
/Something tangible
/Our hard-headed friend
/Rust and dust

[Page 2—Left-hand side]

Mem: write and calculate the story in the old monthly N^os

—

Mr Gradgrind. Facts and figures. "Teach these children nothing but facts. Nothing but facts."/

—

M'Choakumchild. If he only knew less, how much better he might have taught much more!

—

Dolly Jupe
Sissy
Bitzer—Pale winking boy.

—

Louisa Gradgrind
Young Thomas
Mrs. Gradgrind—or Miss? Wife or sister? <u>Wife</u>

Any little Gradgrinds? Say 3

Adam Smith	
Malthus	No parts to play
Jane	

Circus
"Horse-riding"/
Sleary

The man who by being utterly sensual and careless comes
to very much the same thing in the end as the Gradgrind
school?

<u>Not yet</u>

[*Page 2—Right-hand side*]

<u>Hard Times</u>   Nº 1

Chapter I

"Teach these children nothing but facts"

Chapter II

Mr Gradgrind.   <u>Cole</u>
        /   Marlborough House Doctrine   <u>Sissy</u>
                        /   <u>Bitzer</u>
                                                        /

<u>Nº 1 weekly</u>   Chapter III

Mrs. Gradgrind badly done transparency, without enough
light behind. <u>No not yet.</u> Mr. Gradgrind take
Tom and Louisa home.
<u>"What will Mr. Bound say?"</u> Bounder—
                        Bounderby

Chapter IV

Mr. Bounderby. The Bully of humility
——
<u>Now, Mrs. Gradgrind</u>   The Children's study
                        Dawn of Bounderby
                        and Louisa

N° 2 weekly   Chapter V

"Let us strike the keynote Coketown"
Take them to Sleary's headquarters—

N° 3 weekly   Chapter VI

The Pegasus's Arms. The circus company. Sissy's father
has deserted her. Over-"goosed".

Chapter VII

Mrs. Sparsit. Without whom Bounderby's glory
incomplete.

N° 4 weekly   Chapter VIII

Indication of Louisa's marrying Bounderby
bye & bye.

[*Page 3—Left-hand side*]

Man of N° 1?—Not yet

    Law of Divorce
John Prodge?
Stephen?
George?   Mill Pictures
old Stephen?

                                Stephen Blackpool   Rachael

Turtle and Venison & a gold spoon
"That's what the Hands want Sir!"—
____

Bounderby's mother? Yes

____   /
Bitzer's father and mother? No
                        /
children grow up and Louisa married
Carry on Tom—selfish-calculations all go to N° 1.
Carry on Louisa—Never had a ~~childh~~   child's belief
    or a child's fear.
Carry on Sissy—Power of affection

Republish in 3 books?   1. Sowing
                                         2. Reaping
                                         3. Garnering

[Page 3—Right-hand side]

Hard Times   N° II
_____

Weekly N° 5   Chapter IX

  Present Sissy in her simple & affectionate position—
  low down in the school—no arithmetic—Interests
  Louisa—tells her story.

                             Chapter X

  Open Law of Divorce. Stephen Blackpool and Rachael.
     (Wolverhampton black ladder)
          Finds his bad wife at home "Come awa' from
             th'bed!
          'Tis mine! Drunk agen? Ah! why not?"
_____

Weekly N° 6   Chapter XI

  Mill Picture. Interview with Bounderby and Mrs
  Sparsit. "I mun' be ridded o' her. How? Law to punish
  me. What law to help me!"
Goldspoon

                             Chapter XII

  Bounderby's mother / Mill Picture, Stephen goes home,
                                              wrathful.
_____

Weekly N° 7   Chapter XIII

  "Quiet and peace were there. Rachael was there, sitting
  by the bed." Poison bottle. "Thou hast saved my
  soul alive."

                             Chapter XIV

Children grow up. Time, a manufacturer. Passes them through his
mill.
                     /Time for Mr Gradgrind "to talk to" Louisa. /
                                              Tom
_____

Weekly N° 8   Chapter XV

  Scene between Mr Gradgrind and Louisa, in which he
  communicates Bounderby's proposal. Force of figures.
  Bounderby accepted.

Chapter XVI

Mrs Sparsit   Great intelligence conveyed to her/
To keep the bank/Happy pair married/
and Bounderby's speech

[*Page 4—Left-hand side*]

Mrs. Sparsit's life at the Bank? Yes

Bitzer light porter Yes

Tom's progress Yes

Louisa's married life—Dawn of knowledge of her immaterial
self. Too late.   Scarcely yet

Man dropped in N° 1? Yes.   Percy Harthouse
                                   Jem
                                   James

A sunny day in Coketown? Picture? Yes

Popular leader? Yes

Lover for Sissy? No. Decide on no love at all.
Sissy and Rachael to become acquainted? No

[*Page 4—Right-hand side*]

Hard Times   N° III

Weekly N° 9   Chapter XVII

   Mrs. Sparsit & Bitzer—Bank description—Fire buckets

   Introduce Mr. James Harthouse
            /"Ugh—You—Fool!" said Mrs. Sparsit.

Weekly N° 10   Chapter XVIII

   James Harthouse's antecedents.

   Bounderby explains Coketown "And now you know the place."

   sees Louisa for the first time.—and Tom.

Chapter XIX

Tom goes home with James Harthouse to smoke—Genteel demon.

———

Tom shews him everything—and had better have drowned himself.

Weekly Nº 11   Chapter XX

Working men's meeting—Slackbridge the orator
Stephen won't join—and is sent to Coventry.

Chapter XXI

Scene at Bounderby's/Stephen's exposition of the Slackbridge question. "Ill-conditioned fellow—your own people get rid of you—well then—I'll get rid of you too."

Weekly Nº 12   Chapter XXII

Bounderby's old mother again—and Rachael.

———

Scene at Stephens. Louisa
         and Tom (with his Bank scheme)
      in the dark

———

Morning picture of Stephen going away from Coketown out of the coal ashes on to the country dust.

[Page 5—Left-hand side]

Tom to rob Bounderby? Yes
Louisa to be acted on by Harthouse through Tom? Yes

———

Louisa's danger slowly drawn about her. Yes

———

Sissy? No
Rachael?
—   ‖ No
Bring her with Louisa again? ‖
=
Stephen?
—   No

To shew Louisa, how alike in their creeds, her father and Harthouse are?—How the two heartless things come to the same in the end?

Yes. But almost imperceptibly

Louisa

"you have brought me to this, father. Now, save me!"

[*Page 5—Right-hand side*]

Hard Times   Nº IV

Weekly Nº 13   Chapter XXIII

Country house. Bounderby has foreclosed a mortgage on it.
James Harthouse undermines her through Tom
Scene with Tom.
                    Plucking rosebuds. Tom softens to his
sister. "So much the less is the whelp the only creature
she cares for."

Weekly Nº 14   Chapter XXIV

Take up from last chapter Account of the robbery
                    Bitzer and Mrs. Sparsit: Bounderby
made by that good lady to feel "as if he had been crossed
in something, though he has no idea in what."
        Scene with Tom and Louisa. Tom in bed. Dogged and hard.
                    Nø "What can I say? I don't know
                    what you mean."

Weekly Nº 15   Chapter XXV

Take up Mrs Sparsit again. Mrs Gradgrind dies.
"Mr Gradgrind must have forgotten some Ology. Can't have had
had them all taught. Something wanting in Louisa surely."

Chapter XXVI

Mrs Sparsit's Giant staircase. Louisa always coming
Down, Down, Down.

Weekly Nº 16   Chapter XXVII

Mrs Sparsit watching her staircase. Overhears them
together—Follows Louisa. Loses her.
                    Wet night picture
She seems to have eloped.

Chapter XXVIII

The National Dustman in his study—Another scene
between them. Companion to the former.
    "You have brought me to this father. Now save me!"

[Page 6—Left-hand side]

Weekly N⁰ˢ to be enlarged to 10 of my sides each—about.

<u>Sissy and Louisa</u>/

<u>Sissy with James Harthouse</u>/

Stephen Blackpool to disappear/

<u>Rachael</u>/

Stephen Blackpool to be found

His wife? <u>No</u>

Slackbridge/

Bounderby and Mrs Sparsit/

(Bitzer)
Mrs Pegler

Tom, and his
discovery

Sleary's Horsemanship and
Sissy's father—Merrylegs

[Page 6—Right-hand side]

Hard Times   N⁰ˢ V & VI

Weekly N⁰ 17   Chapter XXIX

Sissy and Louisa. Head and heart—"O lay your head here
    my dear, lay it here!"

Chapter XXX

—Sissy and James Harthouse   He goes away. One of the best
    Goes in for camels   actions of his life, quite a silent
                                   sorrow to him afterwards.

Weekly N⁰ 18   Chapter XXXI

Bounderby and Mrs Sparsit together—Separation scene
with Mr Gradgrind.

Chapter XXXII

Pursue the robbery—<u>disappearance of Stephen</u>

                                                   Rachael

Tom plucking up a spirit because
        <u>still no Stephen.</u>

Weekly Nº 19   Chapter XXXIII

                                           The great effect
Still no Stephen Mrs Sparsit fearfully energetic.
Mrs Pegler Bounderby's mother—Excellent
woman. Brought him up capitally
Still no Stephen

                    Chapter XXXIV

             coal pit & death
"I leave 't to yo to clear my good name. Ask
yor son Sir."   Stephen and Rachael
Stephen found and Tom vanishes.
                    Bear and forbear   The star that
                                            leads the way.

Weekly Nº 20 ˙   Chapter XXXV

Sissy and ~~Rachael~~   Louisa pursue Tom
                        "Comic Livery"
Find him with travelling riders/ and so work round Sissy's own
story.

                    Chapter XXXVI

Bitzer true to his bringing-up. Tom saved by Sleary. Finish Sissy
here.

Weekly Nº 21

Conclusion
Dispose of Mrs Sparsit
Wind up
The ashes of our fires grow grey and cold

The Running Headlines

Experts on Dickens' texts have reached agreement about the lack of specific textual authority possessed by the Charles Dickens Edition of the novels of Charles Dickens.

It does, however, supply one novelty: the running headlines were introduced into it as an attractive feature of that edition. They were very probably written by Dickens himself. It has been proved that this had been the case for *Bleak House*. Inevitably, to fit new paginations in later editions, the headlines have often been modified, subtracted from and/or added to. It is evident that these descriptive headlines contribute relatively little to an understanding of *Hard Times*, though they are a kind of running commentary on the story and the characters and express, as often as not ironically, the way in which the author looked at his work, after a dozen years. So, because, at least in their original form, they are part of the text of his novel as Dickens prepared it in its final version, they do deserve to be preserved in some manner. As it is impracticable to adopt the pagination of the cheap and cramped Charles Dickens Edition, the only efficient method for presenting the running headlines in a modern edition is to print them all together, with a brief allusion to the relevant episode whenever the headline is not self-explanatory.

HOUSEHOLD WORDS			ONE-VOLUME EDITION OF 1854	
No.	Date	Chapters		
210	April 1	I–II–III	Book I	I–II–III
211	April 8	IV–V		IV–V
212	April 15	VI		VI
213	April 22	VII–VIII		VII–VIII
214	April 29	IX–X		IX–X
215	May 6	XI–XII		XI–XII
216	May 13	XIII–XIV		XIII–XIV
217	May 20	XV–XVI		XV–XVI
218	May 27	XVII	Book II	I
219	June 3	XVIII–XIX		II–III
220	June 10	XX–XXI		IV–V
221	June 17	XXII		VI
222	June 24	XXIII		VII
223	July 1	XXIV		VIII
224	July 8	XXV–XXVI		IX–X
225	July 15	XXVII–XXVIII		XI–XII
226	July 22	XXIX–XXX	Book III	I–II
227	July 29	XXXI–XXXII		III–IV
228	August 5	XXXIII–XXXIV		V–VI
229	August 12	XXXV–XXXVI–XXVII		VII–VIII–IX

Book One—Chapter I: no headlines. Chapter II: ALWAYS IN TRAIN-
ING; MATTERS OF FACT. Chapter III: THE TOUCH OF NATURE (the
children peeping at the Circus). Chapter IV: AN AUTOBIOGRAPHY
(Bounderby holding forth to Mrs. Gradgrind); BOUNDERBY'S PENE-
TRATION AND ADVICE. Chapter V: THE COKETOWN INSTITUTIONS.
Chapter VI: THE PEGASUS'S ARMS; MR. BOUNDERBY IS INSTRUCTED IN
TERMS OF ART (by the circus people); SLEARY'S COMPANY; BOTH SIDES
OF THE BANNER (Sleary leaves Cecilia free to choose). Chapter VII:
A LADY HOUSEKEEPER; GENTILITY AND HUMILITY. Chapter VIII: COKE-
TOWN LITERATURE (the library); UNMANAGEABLE THOUGHTS (Loui-
sa's, they *will* wonder). Chapter XI: STATISTICS; SISSY'S STORY. Chapter
X: STEPHEN BLACKPOOL; "BACK AGAIN!". Chapter XI: STEPHEN'S
CROSS; THE ONLY WAY OUT. Chapter XII: THE OLD WOMAN ON HER
PILGRIMAGE; GOING HOME. Chapter XIII: STEPHEN'S DREAM; LOOK-
ING BEYOND THE GULF (Stephen's grateful speech to Rachael). Chap-
ter XIV: BROAD HINTS (from Tom to Louisa, about marriage with
Bounderby). Chapter XV: IMPORTANT FACTS (the statistics of mar-
riage); LOUISA CONVEYS HER DECISION. Chapter XVI: APPROACHING
THE FIRST DIFFICULTY; MR. BOUNDERBY'S MARRIAGE ORATION.

Book Two—Chapter I. MRS. SPARSIT ON THE PEOPLE (expressing her
views to Bitzer); BITZER TAKES A MORAL VIEW OF HIMSELF; A VISITOR
AT THE BANK. Chapter II: RECRUITING; "LOO, MR. JAMES HARTHOUSE";
THE WHELP. Chapter III: THE WHELP UNDER A SPELL (Harthouse's).
Chapter IV: A PROFESSIONAL LEADER (Slackbridge); STEPHEN CAST
OUT. Chapter V: THE WIND RISES (Bounderby's ill temper); ALL A
MUDDLE. Chapter VI: THE OLD WOMAN AGAIN; LOUISA AND RACHAEL;
TOM THINKS OF SOMETHING; STEPHEN'S DEPARTURE. Chapter VII:
MR. BOUNDERBY'S RETREAT (country-house); JAMES HARTHOUSE IN
CONFIDENCE (with Louisa, about Tom); UNNATURAL CONDUCT (Tom's
view of Louisa's to him). Chapter VIII: MR. BOUNDERBY'S BURST
(first announcement of the robbery); WHO DID IT?; SO NATURAL TO
SAY MISS GRADGRIND (Mrs. Sparsit's idiosyncrasy); TOM HAS NOTH-
ING TO TELL (Louisa, about the robbery). Chapter IX: MRS. SPARSIT
MORE SUPERIOR THAN EVER (in Bounderby's eyes); MRS. GRADGRIND'S
SICK CHAMBER. Chapter X: MR. BOUNDERBY CAN WAIT (for arrest of
culprits); COMING DOWN THE STAIRCASE. Chapter XI: MRS. SPARSIT'S
JOURNEY; MRS. SPARSIT'S TRIUMPH. Chapter XII: GREAT FAILURE OF
THE HOUSE OF GRADGRIND; SHIPWRECKED (Louisa insensible at her
father's feet).

Book Three—Chapter I: A LESSON IN HUMILITY (learned by Mr.
Gradgrind); MAY SISSY TRY? Chapter II: MR. HARTHOUSE IS WANTED;
SISSY'S APPEAL. Chapter III: A CLASSICAL RUIN (Mrs. Sparsit after
her journey); MR. GRADGRIND HITS IT (incriminates Louisa's educa-

The Text

As shown earlier, the textual history of *Hard Times*, in spite of a few
gaps, is richly documented. This has enabled the editors to establish a text that, on its first publication, was praised by experts, and
abundantly used by teachers and students. That text was improved
for the second edition, which took advantage of new findings, notes
privately sent by several colleagues, and the labors of the Japanese
scholar Mr. Takashi Terauchi. The text of *Hard Times* published in
the second edition met with criticism by Joel C. Brattin, who in particular pointed out that the 1854 one-volume edition was not used
consistently as the copy-text. This fourth edition, like the second
and third, reproduces the 1854 edition, not exactly warts and all,
but, with scrupulous fidelity. The warts, that is, the very few downright
mistakes in the 1854 edition, are corrected, and they are the basis of
the Emendations list on p. 287. One unexpected consequence of so
much textual work done on Dickens' novels is an increased awareness
of how few misprints and other errors were left in the various editions published in those days; and yet compositors worked, not from
typescripts or disks, but from pen-and-ink sheets covered with
often hardly legible handwriting, and did that work under high
pressure and in tremendous haste.

The two objectives in mind from the beginning remain unal-
tered. The first was to present a freshly edited text based on a comparative study of all the relevant versions of *Hard Times*. The second
was to provide the reader with all the materials necessary for a study
of the history of this text by means of textual notes showing its evolution from manuscript to book.

The original manuscript and even the corrected proofs appear to
treat the novel as still, as it were, in the workshop and thus could
not be considered as providing a suitable copy-text. Dickens left
much of the punctuation to be inserted later and gave himself every

opportunity of changing his mind about his way of expressing ideas, creating images, and sometimes conducting his story. Even after publication in his periodical, he altered his work significantly. On the other hand, the amount of revision done by Dickens in preparation for the Charles Dickens Edition of his novels seems to have been minimal, apart from introducing the running headlines (see p. 250), but cannot be used in a new edition that does not adhere to the Charles Dickens pagination. No revision was done for the other popular series that preceded the Charles Dickens Edition. Thus did, and does, the first edition of *Hard Times* in volume form as published in 1854, appear as the only possible copy-text to be followed.

That text has been emended at a limited number of points, sometimes significantly, though the policy has been extremely prudent. Emendations have been introduced only when the 1854 text contained an obvious mistake, or when its departures from the *Household Words* version seemed to result from accident or unusual carelessness rather than purpose. Likewise, it has not been judged desirable to restore to the text readings from the manuscript that had been overlooked or misinterpreted by the early printer. Dickens' very careful work on his text at every stage amounted to an acceptance of such deviations from his original purpose: what he did not reject, he made his own. What he did not exclude after reading several sets of proofs, he sanctioned. Yet the relevant materials are, of course, given in the notes.

The Textual Notes

The textual notes, of which there are nearly fifteen hundred, are placed together in a separate section. They are of uneven importance and interest. They would make dull reading, if perused consecutively. Such is not their purpose: they are here to be dipped into, in connection with a specific passage one happens to be studying or a specific problem of style or tone or theme one is interested in.

In compiling these textual notes, we have deliberately left aside a number of points about which Dickens' practice was erratic and inconsistent in his manuscript, so that he left himself to a large extent in the hands of his printers. In addition to punctuation, there are capitalization, hyphenation, italicizing, and the choice of certain spellings (*-ising/-izing* and *-or /-our*). Showing variations on such points from edition to edition would have at least doubled the number of the notes without proving anything.

But the notes do provide information about every other aspect of the history, growth, development, and evolution of the text of *Hard Times*. Thus by consulting the notes the reader will realize, for instance, what the printer had to put up with from Dickens, and what Dickens put up with from the printer. Dickens' z looked like *n*, and his final -*ly* was a mere vertical bar, often so thin that it was almost invisible; his *my* was hardly any better; on the other hand, a chapter like chapter VII (book III) could almost be described as a "bad" chapter, in the technical sense in which one speaks of a "bad" Shakespeare quarto: it was very inefficiently set in type and less efficiently corrected than most others.[3] One will also find from the notes that Dickens' spelling was sometimes peculiar, sometimes even erroneous. One will see what immense pains, worthy perhaps of a better cause, he took over the pronunciations of Sleary and Stephen Blackpool, without in either case achieving complete consistency.

But one will see most of all that Dickens put into the writing and polishing of this text a remarkable amount of energy and conscientious craftsmanship.

3. See S. Monod, "Dickens at Work on the Text of *Hard Times*," *The Dickensian* 355 (May 1968): 86–99.

Textual Notes

The abbreviations used in the textual notes are as follows:

MS = original manuscript

CP = corrected proofs (CP$_1$, CP$_2$, where there are two sets)

HW = text as published in *Household Words*

54 = first edition in volume form (1854)

CD = Charles Dickens Edition, slightly revised by author in 1867–68

p.t. = present text

(?) doubtful word

corr. = corrected

canc. = cancelled

D. = Charles Dickens

Whenever a textual note refers to MS only, the word or spelling concerned was disregarded by the compositor and does not appear in CP. When 54 occurs at the end of a textual note, it implies that the 54 reading was preserved in CD. 54-CD is used only when a textual note is not given in chronological order, or when CD perpetuates an error or oddity of 54.

7.17–18
MS: *speaker's bristled hair, which on the skirts of his bald head formed a plantation* corr. on CP to p.t.

8.01
there and then corr. on CP to *then and there*

8.17
MS only: *acquaintances,*

8.25
Canc. fragment of MS here reads: *He seemed a powder-magazine of facts whose explosion would disperse their tender young imaginations into dust, atoms never to be gathered together any more; a galvanizing apparatus into the bargain.*

8.27
that were added on CP

8.27
stowed corr. on CP to *stormed* as in MS

9.20
MS only: *hovering* CP to CD: *moving*

9.21
Here, and through book I, the boy's name was printed on CP as *Bitner* and corr. to *Bitzer* as in MS (but D.'s z is peculiar)

9.40
MS: *Gramnivorous.*

10.12
After *stepped forth*: *A bustling, pleasant little gentleman, he was.* canc. on CP

10.13
he was; added on CP

10.13–14
Before *most other*: *in* added on CP

10.17
CP: *in the fistic* corr. to *in fistic* thus in HW to CD

10.19
a glutton. corr. on CP to *an ugly customer.*

257

10.22
nearly. corr. on CP to *neatly.* as in MS
10.24
MS: *He was sure to make opponents when none were ready, by wire-drawing the simplest principle into a complicated absurdity,* canc. on CP after *call of time.*
11.10
" here he complacently smiled again, " canc. on CP after *then,*
11.27
cheerfully. canc. on CP after *gentleman*
11.37
MS to HW: *Mary Jupe* 54: *Cecilia Jupe*
11.39
with three brisk little claps of his hands. canc. on CP after *gentleman*
11.40
with three confirmatory frowns. canc. on CP after *Gradgrind*
12.11
with a blithe sentenciousness peculiar to him. canc. on CP after *gentleman*
12.16
rather canc. on CP before *matter of fact*
12.18
MS: *McChoakumchild,"* (?) through whole chapter; CP: *M'Choakumchild,"* not corr.
12.27
a volume corr. on CP to *volumes*
12.32
MS to 54: *stoney* CD: *stony*
12.37
and all the names . . . mountains, added in 54
13.01
known corr. on CP to *learnt*
13.06
CP: *the* corr. to *thy* as in MS
13.08
Fang corr. on CP to *Fancy* as in MS
13.10
MS: *homewards* CP to CD: *homeward*
13.28
MS to HW: *It had never known* 54: *No little Gradgrind had ever known*
13.29
each little Gradgrind added in 54
13.30
a not in MS (?) after first *like*
14.05
MS: *gramnivorous*
14.08
veritably corr. on CP to *virtually* as in MS
14.15
shadowed corr. on CP to *shaded*
14.21
came down corr. on CP to *carried over* as in MS
14.21
wings. added in 54
14.29
MS & CP: *botanical* HW: *metallurgical*
14.31
lists corr. on CP to *bits* as in MS

14.32
been added on CP
15.09
that corr. on CP to *the* as in MS after *reached*
15.16
MS: *stone* (after *modern*) not in CP or later
15.16
MS & CP: *a patch over its eye and* (before *a money-box*) not in HW
15.19
there corr. on CP to *then* as in MS
15.22–23
performing is in HW, but not in MS or on CP
15.30
Shakspearean Thus from MS to CD, though often emended in later editions: on Sept. 12, 1847, D. wrote to J. Forster: ". . . Shakspearian (put an e before the s; I like it much better) . . ."
15.30
witticisms." corr. on CP to *quips and retorts'*
16.02
after in MS; *either* in CP, HW, and all later editions (MS reading restored as making better sense)
16.08
those vagabonds corr. on CP to *these vagabonds*
16.14
MS & CP: *conchological* HW: *metallurgical*
16.15
mineralogical corr. on CP to *mathematical*
16.17
MS: *equestrial*
16.22
very canc. on CP before *red*
16.24
downcast canc. on CP before *machine*
16.38
MS & CP: *fourteen or fifteen;* HW: *fifteen or sixteen;*
17.20
(here and to end of chapter) *Bound* corr. on CP to *Bounderby*
17.24
And all corr. on CP to *All*
17.28
MS & CP: *And, not* HW: *Not*
17.35
lift added on CP
18.11
barked corr. on CP to *talked* as in MS
18.12
standing on end corr. on CP to *standing up*
18.13
constantly added on CP
18.33
body corr. on CP to *baby* as in MS
18.42
54: *do'nt* (an obvious mistake) corr. to *don't*
18.45
my added on CP, but was in MS
19.08
her added on CP

19.11
usually corr. on CP to *always*
19.24
ma'am, added on CP
19.35
plain, corr. on CP to *plainly,* as in MS
20.02
too, corr. on CP to *also,*
20.10
salt corr. on CP to *lofty* as in MS
20.14
her corr. on CP to *ever* as in MS after *regret*
20.14
had corr. on CP to *have* before *a great mind*
20.14
to-day to corr. on CP to *to say I* as in MS
20.27
it's corr, on CP to *it can be*
20.36
and added on CP, but was in MS
20.37
alloy so illegible on MS that printer left blank on CP; inserted on CP
20.38
position corr. on CP to *perfection* as in MS
21.01
up canc. on CP after *drawing*
21.09
or rather, is in HW, but not in MS or CP
21.17
girl, corr. on CP to *fire,* as in MS
21.19
father; canc. on CP (but was not in MS) after *practical*
21.20
MS: *the* CP to CD: *my*
21.22
MS & CP: *damned* HW: *cursed*
21.23
for a strong expression, added on CP; HW to CD: *for strong expressions,*
21.31
an corr. on CP to *any* before *idle*
21.32
MS & CP: *practically and mathematically formed, from* HW: p.t.
21.36
these corr. on CP to *those*
22.13
it corr. on CP to *such* after *when*
22.21
wouldn't corr. on CP to *would not*
22.35
general corr. on CP to *genial* as in MS
22.38
young corr. on CP to *younger* as in MS
23.05
MS to 54: *it's* CD: *its*
23.10
MS to 54: *an't* CD: *ain't*
23.15
sulkily is in HW, but not in MS or CP
23.25
an ugly savage. corr. on CP to *a savage.*

23.26
MS: *chimnies,* (spelling consistently used by D. through MS)
23.27
sluggishly canc. on CP after *themselves*
23.36
the pavement, corr. on CP to p.t.
24.03
there corr. on CP to *they*
24.04
MS & CP: *useful* HW to CD: *workful*
24.06
about canc. on CP before *eighteen*
24.10
principal canc. on CP before *door*
24.10
MS & CP: *four stunted* HW: *four short*
24.14
MS & CP: *and* before *the town-hall* not in HW
24.21–22
or show . . . dearest, not in MS or CP, is in HW (HW: *purchasable* 54-CD: *purchaseable*)
24.31
MS & CP: *chorus* HW: *jangling*
24.34
all added on CP
24.39–40
go to church. corr. on CP to *religious by force* HW: *religious by main force*
24.40
-the corr. on CP to *these*
25.07
MS & CP: *confirming* HW: *outdoing*
25.08
MS: *shewing* (D.'s consistent spelling of this word through MS)
25.11
-two corr. on CP to *-four*
25.13
a subject to be particularly believed) corr. on CP to *particularly worthy of belief)*
25.17
would, corr. on CP to *could,* as in MS
25.17
MS: *on any occasion* CP: *on an occasion* on CP *an* canc.
25.18
MS: *produce* CP: *furnish*
25.23
, gentlemen added on CP after *for it*
25.36
can believe, corr. on CP to *are to be told . . . of day,*
25.38
MS: *was set* corr. on CP to *was utterly set* but HW has: *had been . . . deliberately set*
25.38–26.01
That there was . . . in convulsions? added on CP
26.01–02
MS: *in the ratio of dreary fact, so the craving grew, as they worked long and monot-*

onously corr. on CP to p.t. (CP: *monotonous* corr. to *monotonously*)
26.03
and mental entertainment corr. on CP to *relief*
26.03–06
some relaxation . . . of music added on CP (but *recognised* appears only in HW)
26.06
even added on CP
26.08
inevitably in HW, but not in MS or CP
26.26
Name again printed as *Bitner*, and corr. on CP to *Bitzer*, as in MS
26.45
should corr. on CP to *would*
27.38
MS & CP: *a positively kind one*, HW: p.t.
27.38–39
MS: *if he had but made a round mistake in the arithmetic* CP: *if he had not made a round mistake in his arithmetic* corr. to *if he had only made a good round mistake in the arithmetic* HW: p.t.
27.40
some time corr. on CP to *years*
28.01
MS: *At twilight, she stopped at the door of a mean rickety public-house*, CP: *She stopped at the door of a mean hut, at twilight like a public-house*, corr. to p.t.
28.08
eh!' added on CP, but was in MS
28.19
a stand corr. on CP to *the wall* as in MS
28.27
there canc. on CP after *stopped*
28.31
an't corr. on CP to *is not*
28.33
So they corr. on CP to *They*
29.08
visible corr. on CP to *manifest*
29.11
or advising her where to seek him. canc. on CP after *surprise*
29.24
black corr. on CP to *dark*
29.29
-fitting added on CP
29.30
and added on CP before *looked*
29.31
Centaur compound corr. on CP to *Centaur, compounded*
29.33
tell corr. on CP to *have told*
29.33
MS: *approach to* not on CP before *precision*
29.35
after *vaulting act* MS: *to the ground and lofty* CP: *to the ground and off* corr. to *to the ground and lofty* not in HW
30.01
MS: *may be usually* CP: *may generally be* corr. to p.t.

30.08
looking round the room and shaking his head. corr. on CP to p.t.
30.16–17
after surveying . . . to foot, added on CP
30.19
about added on CP
30.29
and perhaps you have canc. on CP before *not been*
30.35
"Miss'd corr. on CP to *"Missed*
30.36
in his loose corr. on CP to *loose in his* as in MS
30.38
hustling," corr. on CP to *tumbling,"* as in MS
31.05
MS: *Mr.* not in CP before *Bounderby*
31.07
you'd corr. on CP to *you've*
31.08
little," corr. on CP to *bit."*
31.12
MS: *Kidder,* changed to *Kidderminster,*
31.12
nothing abashed. is in HW, but not in MS or CP
31.16
54: *eying* corr. to *eyeing*
31.25
MS: *he's* CP: *he is*
31.28
"All I mean," corr. on CP to *"Ay! I mean,"* as in MS.
31.34
"Because his corr. on CP to *"His*
31.35
after *Childers* MS & CP: *"That's about the size of it.* not in HW
31.38
gentlemen like corr. on CP to *gentleman likes*
32.09
at all added on CP
32.19
a added on CP, but is in MS before *vagabond*
32.20
now, canc. on CP after *is*
32.21
"I don't care corr. on CP to p.t.
32.22–23
facing about. added on CP
32.30
chuckling. corr. on CP to *laughing*
32.34
again, added on CP
32.35
again canc. on CP after *Gradgrind*
32.38
MS: *belcher* CP: *dark* (?) canc. before *handkerchief*
33.03
common corr. on CP to *general*
33.12

CP: *years* corr. to *year*
33.13–14
After *seven year old*. MS & CP (but not HW) have: *Did the canvass, more or less every day of the year* [CP: *of my life*] *till I was out of my time," said Childers. Seeing Mr. Gradgrind at a loss, he explained very clearly by a circular motion of his hand that doing the canvass was synonymous with riding round the ring. "Oh, you mean that.* Between *of his hand* and *that doing the canvass* CP has in addition: *and [by the* added on CP] *rapid interjections "Hi' hi! hi!" as stimulants to a supposititious* [corr. on CP to *supposititious*] *horse*
33.25
after *seven years*. MS & CP (but not HW) have: *If she had been apprenticed, she would have been doing the garlands in an independent way by this time.*
32.28
thought corr. on CP to *sought* as in MS
32.32
MS: *stationery*
32.34
was always added to fill blank left on CP (thus in MS, but difficult to read)
32.36
now," canc. on CP after *service*
33.38
Indeed it would be!" canc. on CP after *well-timed*
34.11
"No!" canc. on CP after *view*.
34.22
nex, corr. on CP to *apex,* as in MS
34.24
and corr. on CP to *twirl*
34.28
showing added on CP
34.32
strength corr. on CP to *literature*
35.01
who was . . . and added on CP
35.07
CD omits *it* after *inside*
35.08
MS to HW: *intenthionth* 54: *intenthion*
35.17
been, added on CP
35.17
MS: *voice* CP: *voithe*
35.20
Thery? corr. on CP to *Therry?* as in MS
35.22
I not in MS or CP, but is in HW before *thank*
36.04
I tell you what, canc. on CP after *"Now,*
36.04
Bounderby, corr. on CP to *he,*
36.12
MS & CP: *cried* HW: *muttered*
36.15
speak corr. on CP to *thpeak*
36.18
d—d corr. on CP to *damned* as in MS

36.27
MS: *"That'th* corr. on CP to *"Thatth* HW: *"Thath*
36.27
MS to 54: *Thtick* CD: *Thick* probably by mistake
36.31
MS & CP: *parties* HW: *persons*
36.42
MS: *prentithd,* CP: *prentithet,* corr. to *prentitht*
36.44
prethenth, corr. on CP to *prethent,*
36.45
thither corr. on CP to *thithter*
37.02
MS to 54: *a* CD: *an* before *oath*
37.04
no added on CP, but is in MS
37.06
much corr. on CP to *muth* HW: *muth* 54: *much*
37.06
MS: *I've* CP: *I have*
37.10
54: *remarked.* corr. to *remarked:* (as required by sense)
37.36
MS to 54: *prethious* CD: *prethiouth*
37.37
house. corr. on CP to *houthe.*
38.03
small corr. on CP to *male* as in MS
38.05
observing corr. on CP to *during* as in MS
38.21
MS & CP: *hands* HW: *arms* before *wide*
38.24
now, canc. on CP after *Sissy*
38.26
fortune, corr. on CP to *fortun,* as in MS
38.27
foakth corr. on CP to *folkth* as in MS
38.27
know corr. on CP to *trouble*
38.28
convenienth corr. on CP to *conwenienth* as in MS
38.33
MS to HW: *the* 54: *his* before *loose*
38.36
MS & CP: *she'll* HW: *the'll*
38.40
riding-master's corr. on CP to *riding-master*
38.40
after *eye* MS: *(supposed in the profession to be the fixed one)* CP: *(supposed to be the fixed one)* canc.
39.8–9
Be obedient . . . and forget uth. Thtick to . . . engagement. The two sentences transposed on CP and turned into clauses in one sentence
39.12
MS to HW: *mutht* 54-CD: *must* (*mutht* adopted here as more coherent)

39.14
54: *alwath* corr. to *alwayth*
39.16
wortht. corr. on CP to *wurtht.*
39.17
admit; corr. on CP to *know;*
39.21
MS for this chapter contains at the back of two of its pages canceled fragments. page 16 (1st sentence of chapter): *The name of the public house was The first and Last,* implying that Page 18: "This is a very obtrusive boy," said Mr. Gradgrind, turning and frowning on the offender [the offender deleted] "Oh, indeed! . . . Raly!" "We'd have had a young gentle man provided for you, if we'd known you were coming," retorted Mr. Kidder. "It's a pity you don't have a bespeak, since you're so particular. I never heard of our pulling you in myself. Perhaps you'd like an order for a saving?'
39.30
still added on CP
39.34
friends, corr. on CP to *minds,* as in MS
40.01
it must be confessed canc. on CP after *which*
40.08
out of bed added on CP to fill blank (MS difficult to read)
40.10
very canc. on CP after *two,* but is not in MS
40.17
surviving canc. on CP after *only*
40.19
MS & CP (not corr.): *as a companion.* HW: *at a salary.*
40.20
elder corr. on CP to *elderly* as in MS
41.08
National corr. on CP to *Royal*
41.13
MS & CP: *and* HW: *or* after *flourish*
41.21
trick corr. on CP to *bribe* as in MS
41.22
an immense sum corr. on CP to *immense sums*
41.22
it showers, corr. on CP to *Thomas,* as in MS
41.22
54: *would'nt* corr. to *wouldn't*
41.30
"*Oh!* corr. on CP to "*O!* before *Of course* but *O!* not in HW
41.30
if you wish it added on CP
42.07
MS to 54: *I am* CD: *I'm*
42.34
no doubt canc. on CP after *ma'am,*

42.37–38
with a dignity serenely mournful, added on CP
43.03
and—canc. on CP after *London,*
43.05
dignity, corr. on CP to *resignation,*
43.08
own canc. on CP before *instructive*
43.10
very canc. on CP before *general*
43.11
are corr. on CP to *may be*
43.13–14
you must confess that added on CP
43.15
know you added on CP
43.20
MS & CP: *virtues.* HW: *merits.* 54: *position.*
43.26
that," corr. on CP to *the rest of it,"*
43.28–29
stately resignation corr. on CP to *kind of social widowhood*
43.41
the canc. on CP before *mistress*
44.05
came corr. on CP to *come*
44.06
must corr. on CP to *shall* before *do*
44.06
what's corr. on CP to *what is*
44.07
you shall added on CP before *not*
44.08
should canc. on CP before *hope*
44.08
before *conciliatory* MS: *low* not in CP
44.28
ignorant," canc. on CP after *very*
44.28
after *curtseying* MS & CP: *with a trembling lip.* not in HW
44.29
After *educated* MS: *in a knowledge of Facts;* canc. on CP
44.32
You can read. canc. on CP after *formed.*
44.41
the— canc. on CP after *They were*
44.43
MS to HW: *grief* 54: *sorrow*
44.43
glanced corr. on CP to *looked*
45.01
said corr. on CP to *asked*
45.02
to your father, added on CP
45.04
MS to HW: *sobbed out.* 54-CD: *sobbed out; "and about—"*
45.05
MS to HW: "*There!*" 54: "*Hush!*"
45.05
that is enough. not in MS, but is in CP

45.14–15
remained there, corr. on CP to *meditated in the gloom of that retreat,*

45.15
MS to HW: *morning,* 54-CD: *evening.* (an obvious mistake, *so morning.,* adopted here)

45.18
morning, corr. on CP to *day,*

45.22–24
the M'Choakumchild mystery. corr. on CP to *the mechanical . . . and affections.*

45.25
for ever, corr. on CP to *somehow,*

45.30
against time towards the infinite world, added on CP

45.31
and more. added on CP

45.33–34
MS & CP: *incessantly tugged and scratched at one another by way of agreeing on what should be done* HW: p.t.

45.38
(especially inconceivable), added on CP

46.07
before droll MS & CP: *amusing or even* not in HW

46.08–09
concealed corr. on CP to *made the shallowest pretences of concealing*

46.09–10
tried to smuggle and inveigle them. corr. on CP to *was the duty of these babies to be smuggled and inveigled*

46.11
at end of ¶ MS: *and all the babies agreed in wondering on their own accounts. Therefore it is perhaps not absolutely wonderful if their wondering faculty sometimes went into dangerous directions and got itself imposed upon.* canc. on CP

46.12
Whole ¶ added on CP

46.21
MS addition on CP after *women* reads: *Facts and figures were not always all sufficient for them as they would have been for good machines.* not in HW

46.23
about before *children* not in MS addition to CP or in HW, but is in 54 & CD

47.08
and corr. on CP to *I am* before *more*

47.08
and corr. on CP to *I* before *get*

47.09
and added on CP after *as one,*

47.09
if it comes to that." canc. on CP at end of speech

47.11
after *at first. I should be a fool indeed, as well as a brute, to hurt the person I love.* canc. on CP

47.12–13
MS & CP: *said Tom, pausing to find* HW: *Tom had paused to find*

47.14
MS & CP: *seeming* HW: *seemed*

47.21–22
sit wondering here, and added on CP

47.25
have never corr. on CP to *never see any amusing sights or*

47.28
have I. corr. on CP to *do I.*

47.29
besides. corr. on CP to *too, which you're not.*

47.36
most disadvantages corr. on CP to *it before better*

47.36
At least I know you do. canc. on CP after *does.*

47.39
kind good corr. on CP to *dear*

47.44
MS: *spitefully,* on CP *clenching his fist* added, but HW has p.t.

48.06
was corr. on CP *to have been*

48.10
54: *"Oh;"* corr. to *"Oh!"*

48.25
down, corr. on CP to *about,*

48.27
turned corr. on CP to *twined* as in MS

48.33
"That must be another corr. on CP to *"Another*

48.33
should think, corr. on CP to *suppose,*

48.35
as if canc. on CP before *it were not*

48.38 & 41
this corr. on CP to *one thing*

48.42
Yes." added on CP, but is in MS

49.03–04
take your influence with me; corr. on CP to p.t.

49.04
altogether. added on CP

49.11
anything corr. on CP to *everything*

49.11
MS: *a* CP: *a* corr. to *the* HW: *a*

49.12
particular. corr. on CP to *particularly.* as in MS

49.15
tool" corr. on CP to *again!"*

49.16
returned his sister, added on CP

49.17
sometimes." canc. on CP after *wonder*

49.21
it's corr. on CP to *it is*

49.24
in wondering, corr. on CP to *to wonder,*
49.32
after all, added on CP
49.36
ever in HW, though not in MS or CP
49.41
and calcination, added on CP, but is in MS
49.42
would corr. on CP to *could* as in MS
49.42
an corr. on CP to *a poor*
49.44
said corr. on CP to *whimpered*
49.45
final corr. on CP to *strongest*
50.03
Mr. not in MS & CP, but is in HW
50.13
before *lived* MS to HW: *and she* 54: *she*
50.25
powers) corr. on CP to *process)* as in MS
50.28
instruction corr. on CP to *induction* as in MS
51.02
not corr. on CP to *no* as in MS before *wiser*
51.12
the corr. on CP to *these* before *two*
51.22
MS & CP: *Miss,"* HW: *Miss Louisa,"*
51.30
any added on CP
52.02
54: *could'nt* corr. to *couldn't*
52.10
there is corr. on CP to *there are* (MS has no verb here)
52.18
the added on CP, but is in MS
52.18
stuttering tables corr. on CP to *stutterings*
52.19
"Statistical tables," corr. on CP to *"Statistics,"*
52.21
tables canc. on CP before *of accidents*
52.21
MS: *seas.* CP: *sea.*
52.23
persons added on CP: MS has *people* (?)
52.25
faintly corr. on CP to *fairly* as in MS
52.26
MS: *errors;* CP: *error;*
52.28
relatives corr. on CP to *relations* as in MS
52.43
after *her head* MS & CP: *at the same time;* not in HW
53.01
?" in HW & 54 *!"* in CD
53.01
after *my good* MS & CP: *, Miss Louisa.* not in HW

53.22 & 23
MS & CP: *do it* HW: *laugh*
53.24
54: *did'nt* corr. to *didn't*
53.38
MS to 54: *her* CD: *a* (probably by mistake)
54.08
from performing, in HW, though not in MS or CP
54.13
for corr. on CP to *on* after *compassion*
54.15
MS & CP: *God* HW: *Heaven*
54.19
before *Louisa* MS & CP: *She turned away her head.* not in HW
54.37
needn't corr. on CP to *have no occasion to*
55.08
CP: *arm* corr. to *arms*
55.16
at corr. on CP to *by* after *sitting*
55.25
to added on CP after *trust*
55.29
54: *faltering way.* corr. to *faltering way,* (as required by sense)
55.38
MS to 54: *demonstrated* CD: *remonstrated* (an obvious mistake)
55.39
unaccountably canc. on CP after *seem*
55.41
MS & CP: *Facts and figures.* HW: *Fact.*
55.43
deducing corr. on CP to *becoming* as in MS
56.11
freezy corr. on CP to *wintry* as in MS (?)
56.14
to added on CP, but is in MS
56.19
MS seems to have *hitting* (?), not *killing* here.
56.28–29
generally corr. on CP to *generically* as in MS
57.21
MS to 54: *odd* CD: *old* (probably by mistake)
57.41
head corr. on CP to *hood* as in MS
58.12
before *going* MS & CP: *in* not in HW
58.17
MS & CP: *upon* HW: *on* after *lightly*
58.24
MS: *truth* to CP: *truth to* corr. to *truth fra'* thus in HW 54 & CD: *truth fro'*
58.29
after *not* MS & CP: *lad* not in HW
58.31
MS to HW: *make* 54: *mak*
58.32
MS: *years* corr. to *year* [?] CP: *years,* corr. to *year:*

58.38
MS to HW: *all.*" 54: *aw.*"

58.39
MS & CP: *muddle, lad? Eh?" Eh?* canc. on CP , *lad* not in HW

58.41
MS: *neck-kerchief*

58.44
MS & CP: *always* HW: *awlus*

59.06
pump corr. on CP to *pomp* as in MS

59.16
after *heart.* MS: *It may be one of the difficulties of casting up and ticking off human figures by the hundred thousand that they have their individual varieties of affection and passions which are of so perverse a nature that they will not come under any rule into the account.* whole sentence canc. on CP

59.17
MS & CP: *eyes,* HW: *view,*

59.18
looking corr. on CP to *glancing up*

59.21
MS: *Tytanic*

59.32
MS: *unaquainted*

59.38
MS & CP: *stumbled upon* HW: *stumbled against*

59.43–44
after *preserve* MS to HW: *the* 54: *her*

60.13
after *and* MS & CP: *then* not in HW

60.15
MS & CP: *again?"* HW: *agen?"*

60.16
MS & CP: *again,* HW: *agen.*

60.16
MS & CP: *again* HW: *agen* before *ever and*

60.20
her corr. on CP to *one* before *hand*

60.24 & 26
MS & CP: *away* HW: *awa*

60.30
MS: *over* CP: *in* HW: *into*

60.31
after *burst* MS to HW: *out* not in 54

61.03
pieces corr. on CP to *piece* as in MS

61.07
troop (as in MS) added on CP to fill blank left by printer

61.08
before *dignity* MS to HW: *solemn* not in 54

61.09
MS to HW: *Four hundred and more* before *Hands* 54: p.t.

61.09
MS to HW: *two hundred and fifty* before *horse* 54: p.t.

61.12
MS: *can* CP_1: *can* corr. to *shall* CP_2: *shall* HW: *can*

61.18
then, canc. on CP after *objects,*

61.18
to added on CP before *govern*

61.21
CP_1: *and work* corr. to *and the work*

61.28
bands corr. on CP to *Hands* as in MS

61.30
MS to HW: *the* before *cold* not in 54

61.32
MS: *Eating nothing . . . along, he turned . . . quarter* corr. on CP_1 to p.t. (CP_1 has *taking* instead of *eating*)

61.35
with corr. on CP to *up two* as in MS

61.36
MS: *brazen* CP_1: an illegible word corr. to *brazen*

61.43–44
whom he just knew by sight), added on CP_1

62.03
and corr. on CP to *but*

62.14
often corr. on CP to *of 'em* as in MS

62.19
MS-CP_1: *come* CP_2: *come* corr. to *coom*

62.19
MS: *nought* corr. on CP_2 to *nowt*

62.27
point corr. on CP to *feint* as in MS

62.28
MS: *mouth full*

62.38
nought corr. on CP_2 to *nowt*

62.39
HW: *hear,* all other texts: *year,*

63.03
come," corr. on CP_2 to *coom,"*

63.05
MS to HW: *a* before *Eas'r* not in 54

63.06
yoong corr. on CP to *young*

63.06
MS to HW: *hersen'* 54: *herseln*

63.09
MS: *of* before *this* not on CP_1

63.09
HW only: *found other companions,* before *took*

63.13–14
Whole parenthesis added on CP_1, as in MS

63.16
MS to CP_2: *t'other* HW: *t'oother.* 54 *t'other.*

63.18
CP_1: *without sense* corr. to *without a sense*

63.18
MS to HW: *hersen'* 54: *herseln*

63.18
MS: *lyin* CP_1: *lying*

63.19
MS: *time!"* CP_1: *times!"* corr. to *time!"*

63.22
MS to CP_2: *worsen.* HW: *worse.* 54: *worsen.*

63.23
MS to HW: *hersen'* 54: *herseln*
63.25
when it was raining Heavens hard. corr. on
    CP$_2$ to *ere ever I'd go home.*
63.26
MS to HW: *mysen'* 54: *myseln*
63.27
MS: *yoong."* corr. on CP$_1$ to *young."*
63.33
MS to CP$_2$: *gotten some decent* HW: *gotten
    decent*
63.35
on corr. on CP to *upon*
63.35
MS to HW: *harston!* 54: *har-stone!*
63.35
is!" corr. on CP to *IS!"*
64.15
MS to HW: *mysen';* 54: *myseln;*
64.16
MS: *nighb't."* CP$_1$: word omitted, *nighb't.'*
    added; corr. on CP$_2$ to *nighbut."* HW:
    nighbout." 54: *nightbut."*
64.25
MS & CP$_1$: *come* corr. on CP$_2$ to *coom*
64.32
MS to CP$_2$: *ridded* HW to CD: *ridden*
64.32
MS to HW: *connot* 54: *cannot*
64.33
this ten last year, corr. on CP to *so long,*
64.33
before *comforting* MS to HW: *the* not in 54
64.34
MS: *Happly,*
64.40
MS-CP$_1$-CP$_2$: *folks* HW: *fok*
64.40
fan corr. on CP to *faw* as in MS
64.41
MS: *jisted* CP$_1$: *fested* corr. on CP$_2$ to
    bonded
64.41
MS to 54: *worse* CD: *worst* (probably by
    mistake)
64.42
MS to HW: *fra'* 54: *fro'*
65.02
MS to HW: *have* 54: *has*
65.02
after *rooms* MS to HW: *of* 54: *o'*
65.02
above a bit is in MS CP & 54-CD, but not
    in HW
65.03
MS to CP$_2$: *folk* HW: *fok*
65.06
after *wrongs* HW only: *than is suffered by
    hundreds an' hundreds of us—by women
    fur more than men—they can be set free.*
65.07
MS & CP: *ridded* HW: *ridden*
65.08
HW: *wife o' mine,* all other texts: *woman,*

65.13
MS & CP: *t'other* HW: *t'oother*
65.17
MS: *chilt*
65.21
Hem! omitted in HW only
65.23–24
MS & CP: *kept* HW: *kep'*
65.25
MS to CP$_2$: *year* HW: *hear* 54: *year*
65.27
supposed omitted in HW only
65.27
MS & CP$_1$: *eever* corr. on CP$_2$ to *ever*
65.29
MS & CP: *folk* HW: *fok*
65.30
HW only: *(agen, I say, women fur of'ener
    than men)* before *to battle*
65.30–31
understood, added on CP
66.02
very added on CP
66.09
MS: *awtogether,* CP: *at together,* corr. to
    aw'together, HW: *a'toogether,*
66.22
MS & CP: *aw* HW: *a'*
66.23
MS: *I tell* CP$_1$ to CD: *I'll tell*
66.28
MS: *a* before *great*
66.33
MS-CP & 54-CD: *you know;"* HW only:
    you understand;"
66.40
a before *deep* omitted in CD (possibly by
    mistake), but is in all other texts
66.42
smiling corr. on CP to *swelling* as in MS
67.19
quiet corr. on CP to *quick* as in MS
67.29
missis," corr. on CP to *missus,"*
67.33–34
and omitted in HW only before *hearty?"*
67.34
MS: *straitened*
68.14
MS: *I am* CP: *I'm*
68.18
HW only: *eyes*
68.19
MS-CP$_1$-CP$_2$: *missis."* HW: *missus."*
68.32
HW: *eyes were* all other texts: *eye was*
68.32
HW: *they* all other texts: *it*
68.33
MS: *differences of taste,* CP$_1$: *difference of
    taste,* on CP$_2$ *taste,* corr. to *tastes,*
69.02
MS: *awmust*
69.02
MS: *nobboddy*

69.02
missis." corr. on CP_2 to *missus."*
69.09
MS: *Aye, aye!* CP: *Ay, ay!*
69.11–12
MS: *here?"* corr. on CP_1 to *to the factory?"*
CP_2: *to the Factory?"*
69.17
MS: *bye-road* CP_1: *by-road* corr. on CP_2 to
bye-road thus in HW; 54-CD: *by-road*
69.28
MS: *didn't* corr. on CP_1 to *did not*
69.30
it seemed as if added on CP_1
69.41
Palaces corr. on CP_1 to *Palace* as in MS
70.02
(after *dispelled*) MS: *the four high walls,
seen from the street, a black mass—
indistinctly blotting the black rainy night*
corr. on CP_1 to *the factories, black
masses, looming heavy . . . (*end like p.t.*);
black masses* canc. on CP_2
70.26
now in MS to 54; omitted in CD
70.28
MS to HW: *way,* 54: *day,*
70.41
MS: *And filled* CP_1: *And so filled* corr. to
And filled corr. on CP_2 to *Filled*
71.04
he corr. on CP to *Stephen*
71.10
—still corr. on CP to *while* as in MS
71.22
neatly corr. on CP to *newly* as in MS
71.35
to have not in MS or CP, but is in HW
71.40
bowing corr. on CP to *drooping*
72.07
MS: *know'st* (?) CP: *knowest*
72.13
passionate corr. on CP to *compassionate* as
in MS
72.31
MS & CP: *hads't* HW: *hadst*
72.35
word corr. on CP to *mood* as in MS
72.43
MS: *happly*
73.01
MS to 54: *again fell* CD: *fell again*
73.16
MS to HW: *controuled* 54: *controlled*
73.24
MS: *new* CP: *more*
73.36
company corr. on CP to *witnesses*
73.44–45
would corr. on CP to *could* as in MS (?)
74.14
bound corr. on CP to *doomed* as in MS
74.26
Seeing corr. on CP to *Saving* as in MS

74.31
at end of ¶—*the bottle with the cautionary
word Poison.* canc. on CP
74.32
he added on CP after *and*
74.33
that canc. on CP after *sure*
74.34–35
she corr. on CP to *the woman in the bed*
74.35
in bed. canc. on CP after *sat up*
74.45
might be or canc. on CP after *that he*
75.13
take corr. on CP to *choose.*
75.21
was corr. on CP to *would be*
75.26
burst corr. on CP to *broke*
75.26
wakkin' corr. on CP to *wakin'*
75.27
dreadful corr. on CP to *dreadfo'*
75.32
mark corr. on CP to *marks*
76.01
afeerd;' corr. on CP to *fearfo';'*
76.12
before *Thou* MS: *"Rachael!* not on CP
76.13
MS & CP: *wishfu'* HW: *wishfo'*
76.13
fearfu' corr. on CP to *fearfo'* as in MS (?)
76.14
after *cleared awa':* The following fragment
is in MS, and was not canc. on CP, yet
did not appear in HW. Text given here
as in MS, with CP corrections shown
where they occur: *"Thou'st spokken* [corr.
to *spokken*] *o' thy little sisther. There agen!
Wi' her child arm tore off afore thy face!"*
She turned her head aside, and put her
hand up [up canc.] *to her eyes. "Where
dost thou ever hear or read o' us—the
like o' us—as being otherwise than onreasonable and cause o' trouble? Yet think o'
that. Government gentlemen comes down
and mak's report. Fend* [CP: *Plad* (?) corr.
to *Fend*] *off the dangerous machinery, box
it off, save life and limb,* [CP:, corr. to,]
*don't rend and tear human creeturs to bits
in a Chris'en country! What follers?
Owners sets up their throats, cries out,
'Onreasonable! Inconvenient! Troublesome!' Gets to Secretaries o' States wi'
deputations, and nothing's done. When
do we get there wi'* our *deputations, God
help us! We are too much int'rested and
nat'rally too far wrong t' have a right judgment. Happly* [CP: Haply] *we are: but
what are they then? I' th' name o' th' muddle in which we are born and live and die,
what are they then?" "Let such things be,
Stephen. They only lead to hurt. Let them
be!" "I will, since thou tell'st me so. I will.*

I pass my promise." After *nothing's done.* D. inserted on CP a footnote: *See Household Words vol.* IX *page* 224, *article entitled* GROUND IN THE MILL. Note not published in HW, of course, the relevant passage having been canc.

76.19
cam' corr. on CP to *coom* after *"I* and before *home wi'out*

76.19
mad at corr. on CP to *mad wi'*

76.22
Poison—added on CP

76.23
thought, corr. on CP to *thowt,*

76.24
MS to HW: *mysen',* 54: *myseln,*

76.29
MS: *all* corr. on CP to *a'* HW: *a'* 54: *aw*

77.19
MS to HW: *long tail-coat* 54: *long-tailed coat*

77.24
in corr. on CP to *of* after *inmate*

77.27
before *the same* MS: *Meanwhiles* not on CP

77.30–31
the added on CP before *school,* but is in MS

78.09
Your natural capacity is not a bad one. canc. on CP before *I can*

78.28
sciences corr. on CP to *science*

79.02
through corr. on CP to *into*

79.28
"It is necessary that I should corr. on CP to *"I must*

79.35
a corr. on CP to *her*

80.24
You know," corr. on CP to *sister of mine,"*

80.41
if canc. on CP before *glad;* not in MS

80.44
that corr. on CP to *the* before *fiery*

81.01
one of the few I have heard of who is not at once a Croesus and a Victim canc. on CP after *of all,*

81.20
before *window* MS to HW: *The* 54: A

81.22
MS: *chimnies* CP: *chimney* corr. to *chimneys*

81.24–25
for giving corr. on CP to *to give*

81.33
very canc. on CP before *glad*

82.03
this corr. on CP to *which*

82.06
before *smile* MS & CP: *an embarrassed* HW: *a*

82.07
after *moment* MS & CP: *quite* not in HW

82.16
reasonable, canc. on CP before *perfectly*

82.17
inform you corr. on CP to *let you know*

82.17
MS: *that* on CP *in short, that* added; HW: *that—that* 54: p.t.

82.31
can't corr. on CP to *cannot*

83.03
false canc. on CP before *ground*

83.12
proved canc. on CP before *existence*

83.14
nineteen corr. on CP to *twenty*

83.25
those corr. on CP to *these*

84.03
after *returned,* MS & CP: *with much expression,* not in HW

84.10
a corr. on CP to *one*

84.12
pent-up added on CP

84.12
confidence corr. on CP to *confidences*

84.16
algebra itself corr. on CP to *even algebra*

84.17
after *leap.* MS to HW: *He did not see it;* not in 54

84.20
lie corr. on CP to *are drowned*

84.26
suddenly. corr. on CP to *quickly.*

84.27
," he returned, " canc. on CP after *Louisa*

84.29
head, corr. on CP to *hand,* as in MS

85.04
MS: *The one question* CP: *The question*

85.15
at all, canc. on CP after *"None*

85.21–22
MS: *appeared to me too remote to be recognised.* CP: *appeared to me to be too remote to be recognised. to be recognised* canc. on CP

85.22
MS & CP: *not* HW: *never*

85.30
but most emphatically too, after *manner,* is in MS & CP, but not in HW

85.31
before *aspirations* MS: *stray* CP: *easy* canc.

85.37
asserted corr. on CP to *assented* as in MS

85.39
after *pursued* MS & CP: *stedfastly* [CP: *stead-fastly* corr. to *stedfastly*] *regarding him with her peculiar smile* HW: p.t.

85.41
narrow corr. on CP to *innocent* as in MS

86.04
him, and, detaining corr. on CP to *him.
Detaining*
86.07
very added on CP
86.21
"Good gracious me!" corr. on CP to *"Oh!"*
86.26–27
sure! corr. on CP to *sure I do!*
86.28
whatever you do, canc. on CP after *shoulder,*
86.29
whispered corr. on CP to *whimpered* as in
MS
87.04
that canc. on CP after *subjects*
87.06
quickly corr. on CP to *suddenly*
87.15
MS: *Scadgers's,* (?)
87.23
very added on CP
87.24
that corr. on CP to *the fainting*
87.34
again, canc. on CP after *returned*
87.38
lawn, corr. on CP to *cambric.*
87.39
Cyclops (?) corr. on CP to *eyebrows* as in
MS
88.19
great added on CP
88.33
you do." added on CP
89.12
MS to 54: *should* CD: *shall*
90.18
MS: *Gradgrind*[!] after *Josiah*
91.03
it; corr. on CP to *my feeling independent;*
91.04
But, whether excused or not, canc. on CP
before *I do feel*
91.18
the corr. on CP to *her* before *journey,*
91.24
a little added on CP
92.02
smoky corr. on CP to *sulky* as in MS
92.06
cross sheets of corr. on CP to *sheets of cross*
(order not clear on MS)
92.22
gloomy canc. on CP before *threat.*
92.26
dismal corr. on CP to *awful*
92.39
suffocating corr. on CP to *stifling*
92.39
warm corr. on CP to *hot*
92.42
blast corr. on CP to *breath*
93.07
MS & CP: *trees;* HW: *woods;*

93.09
MS: *whir* corr. on CP to *whirr*
93.13
mill-walls, corr. on CP to *mills,*
93.14
with corr. on CP to *at*
93.17
slip (?) corr. on CP to *dip* as in MS
93.20
quickening destructive scents, and canc. on
CP after *without*
93.39
respects, corr. on CP to *particulars,*
93.39
strictly added on CP
94.05
after *upon her,* MS & CP: *it is possible that*
not in HW
94.05
as canc. on CP after *herself*
94.06
It is certain that the corr. on CP to *The*
before *townspeople*
94.16
lay corr. on CP to *laid*
94.22–23
She corr. on CP to *Lastly, she*
94.23
small corr. on CP to *little*
94.30
54: *deaf-serving woman* corr. to *deaf
serving-woman* (as required by sense)
95.07
town canc. on CP before *news*
95.25
MS to 54: originally CD: *signally*
95.27
discussions, corr. on CP to *dissensions.* as
in MS
95.27–28
MS & CP: *I only know that if the people
will not be conquered by smooth means,
they must be conquered by rough. Conquered they must be, and it's high time it
was done, once for all."* [the corr on CP to
these] HW: p.t.
95.29
Bitner corr. on CP to *Bitzer* as in MS (and
thus through present chapter)
96.06
services corr. on CP to *service*
96.09
MS: *fully certain* CP: *pretty certain* HW:
safe
96.18
confessed corr. on CP to *admitted*
96.21
must corr. on CP to *would*
96.23–24
MS & CP: *but to err is human, and this was
his solitary error.* HW: p.t. (*it having
been . . . but the whole.*)
96.37
solemn canc. on CP before *state.*
97.09
Italics added to *should* on CP

97.14
after *Sparsit* MS & CP: *firmly,* not in HW
97.24
couldn't corr. on CP to *wouldn't* as in MS
97.38
MS & CP: *Hands* HW: *people*
98.01
MS & CP: *the Hands* HW: *they* after *can't*
98.05
always added on CP
98.14
wrong corr. on CP to *money* as in MS
98.20
after *families,* MS & CP: *and concerning their wives being wanted in their homes, and schools being attended by their children,"* not in HW
98.21
Italics added to *I* on CP
98.25
obstinately ignorant, corr. on CP to *perverse,*
98.26
and shawl canc. on CP after *bonnet*
98.29
a canc. on CP before *muffin;* not in MS
99.22
possibly in HW; not in MS or CP
100.02
Exceeding corr. on CP to *Exceedingly* as in MS
100.04–05
in her uncompromising way. not in MS or CP, but is in HW
100.11–12
54 runs on *"Powler family,"* after *"A Powler."* instead of opening new line. This is unjustified, and there is only one other case in the novel. New line restored.
100.14
exhausted corr. on CP to *fatigued*
100.24
CP: *"True,"* (not corr.) HW: *"Assuredly,"*
100.24
for reminding me. not in MS or CP, but is in HW
100.26
extraordinary corr. on CP to *extraordinarily*
100.26
to escape being bored out of my life at the hotel, canc. on CP after *town*
100.27
at the hotel, added on CP
101.09
always added on CP
101.09
necessarily corr. on CP to *officially*
101.19
of the same. canc. on CP after *aid*
101.38
54: *chit"* corr. to *chit,"* and period added after *Mrs*
101.45
fatigued, corr. on CP to *exhausted,*
102.05
shopkeepers and passengers. corr. on CP to *town.*

102.09–10
54 runs on *"It's ridiculous* after *said Mrs. Sparsit.* New line restored, as in 92.25–26.
102.32
MS to HW: *murdering* 54: *cutting the throats of*
102.34
MS to HW: *readily,* 54: *hopefully.*
103.01
equally added on CP
103.04
of knowledge canc. on CP after *height*
103.11
not added on CP, but is in MS
103.23
always canc. on CP after *which has*
103.27
MS: *of a still better* CP-CD: *of still better*
103.29
MS: *line* (?) CP: *train*
103.38
him corr. on CP to *it* after *put*
104.10
desolate, corr. on CP to *disconsolate,*
104.15
severely corr. on CP to *obstinately*
104.15–16
MS to 54: *if you'll* CD: *if you will*
104.16
you will or no, corr. on CP to *you will or not,*
104.20
Well! added on CP, but is not in HW or MS after *smoke*
104.20
, sir. canc. on CP after *to us*
104.38
ultimate added on CP
105.01
"You may corr. on CP to *"Why, you*
105.08
MS: *dirty* CP: *duty* (?) corr. to *the dirty* HW: p.t.
105.14
raised corr. on CP to *lifted*
105.15
MS: *can tell of* (?) *me* CP: *can tell it me,* HW: *does,*
105.16
now added on CP
105.16
in a proper manner, added on CP
105.16
now canc. on CP after *I may*
105.32
so added on CP after *she was*
105.33
sensitive corr. on CP to *sensitively*
105.38
before *locked up,* MS to HW: *suppressed* *and* not in 54
106.02
Childless corr. on CP to *Cheerless* as in MS
106.02
wastefully corr. on CP to *boastfully* as in MS

106.04
even canc. on CP after *unrelieved*
106.11
is on the right side and canc. on CP before *has joined*
106.17
Would do no discredit to Parliament if she could get there. canc. on CP after *otherwise.*
106.17
in the way of Facts or Figures, canc. on CP after *anything*
106.24
, sir, canc. on CP after *myself,*
106.25
before *despise* MS to HW: *I* not in 54
106.25
altogether. canc. on CP after *despise 'em*
106.41
the corr. on CP to *your*
106.42
he corr. on CP to *she*
106.44
her added on CP, but is in MS before *being*
106.44
MS & HW: *obviously so very ill* CP & 54-CD: *obviously very ill*
107.02
to you. added on CP
107.03
been very much bored, corr. on CP to *found it all to be very worthless,*
107.04
been, canc. on CP after *they have*
107.09
after *result of* MS & CP: *all* not in HW
107.14
MS & CP: *a capital motto, Che sara, sara.* HW: *a capital Italian motto.* 54: *a charming Italian motto.*
107.20–21
MS: "*The side that states everything in units, tens, hundreds, and thousands, and can prove anything by that means,* corr. on CP to *in a line of figures* HW: p.t.
107.31
MS to HW: *to* 54: *till*
107.34
and its vicinity. added on CP
107.34
accordingly canc. on CP before *made;*
108.01
taken corr. on CP to *eaten* as in MS
108.05
again not in MS or CP, but is in HW
108.14
Mr. not in MS or CP, but is in HW
108.17
taken corr. on CP to *carried*
108.37
But so corr. on CP to *So*
108.40
whelp added on CP
108.40
Mr. not in MS or CP, but is in HW

109.12
from his birth, canc. on CP after *restraint*
109.15
consecutive added on CP
109.19
sensuality corr. on CP to *sensualities*
109.21
James in HW, but not in MS or CP
109.27
got corr. on CP to *bought*
109.34 & 41
James in HW, but not in MS or CP
110.02
Mr. in HW, but not in MS or CP
110.04
as he smoked, added on CP
110.11
in such an intimate way, not in HW, but is in MS, CP & 54-CD
110.12–13
MS & CP: *man;* HW: *pair of whiskers;*
110.25
felt corr. on CP to *knew*
110.25
to be added on CP
110.28
silent canc. on CP before *influence*
110.31
Mr. in HW, but not in MS or CP
111.02
MS & CP: *my* HW: *a*
111.04
there, corr. on CP to *then,* as in MS
111.13
Mr. in HW, but not in MS or CP
113.14
MS: *wouldn't* CP & HW: *would not*
111.16
up canc. on CP after *lifted*
111.16
and smiled; canc. on CP after *eyebrows*
111.18
after *superiority* MS & CP: *and power* not in HW
111.25
coolly, added on CP
111.29
to do." corr. on CP to *in her."*
111.31
with contemptuous patronage, added on CP
111.33
HW only: *The life does just as well for her,* as MS, CP, 54: p.t.
111.37
"Aye, aye? added on CP; HW: *"Ay, ay?*
111.37
MS & CP: *within herself,"* HW: *of her own,"*
112.04
an corr. on CP to *any*
112.19
Mr. in HW, but not in MS or CP
112.21
MS & CP: *"Oh!* HW: *"What!*
112.24
rather added on CP

112.25
"What do you say?" canc. on CP after *finger.*, but is not in MS
112.27
"What do you say to corr. on CP to *"Say*
112.27
For canc. on CP before *Mother*
112.33
off corr. on CP to *from*
112.34
CP & HW: *Your's* MS & 54: *Yours*
112.39
a good deal of corr. on CP to *some*
112.40
under a lamp-post, canc. on CP after *alone*
113.07
finally, corr. on CP to *for good and all,*
113.07
have added on CP before *curtained*
113.08
filthy added on CP
113.13
all canc. on CP after *must,* but is not in MS
113.14
MS: *into thin* CP: *into the* and *the* canc.
113.14
have too long corr. on CP to *too long have*
113.20
roaring corr. on CP to *many* as in MS
113.22
and fume added on CP
113.32
very added on CP
113.39
shabby-genteel canc. on CP before *dress*
114.04
then (?) corr. on CP to *even* as in MS
114.07
and canc. on CP after *hear!*
114.12
ought to corr. on CP to *might*
114.20
heart, corr. on CP to *breast,* as in MS
114.22
or corr. on CP to *and*
114.23
sweeping added on CP
114.25
monstrously canc. on CP before *to pretend*
114.27
MS: whole ¶ ending here, from *exhibited*
on, inserted on separate slip pasted on to
back of page
114.38
for added on CP, but is in MS
114.39
Delegate corr. on CP to *Aggregate*
115.01
for (?) corr. on CP to *in* as in MS
115.08
MS & CP: *himsen,* HW: *himseln,*
115.09
general canc. on CP before *round*
115.16
operatives of Coketown, corr. on CP to *sons
of labour,*

115.23
however canc. on CP after *chairman*
115.26
askes corr. on CP to *ashes* as in MS
115.30
MS: *frankly shook him* CP: *shook him
frankly*
115.34
MS & CP: *said* HW: *spok'n*
115.35
MS & CP: *mysen,* HW: *myseln,*
115.35–36
fra corr. on CP to *fro* before *my lips* and
before *onny*
116.01
of corr. on CP to *o'*
116.06
a', corr. on CP to *aw,*
116.22
"an No attempt is made here to list the variations from edition to edition of *and*
(*and, an', an*) and *have* (*have, ha', ha*) in
Stephen's dialect.
116.26
CP: *the words* corr. to *these words*
116.29
wonderful corr. on CP to *wonderfully* as in
MS
116.32
MS to 54: *heer* CD: *here*
116.32
MS: *hadn* CP: *had* corr. to *ha'*
116.33
a' corr. on CP to *aw*
116.34
HW & 54: *yo are aw resolved*   MS & CD:
p.t. (*a'* corr. on CP to *aw*)
116.40
a' corr. on CP to *aw*
116.44
hearts. corr. on CP to *minds.*
116.44
MS & CP: *Stephen* HW: *He*
116.45
MS: *breast;* CP: *heart;*
116.45
for he corr. on CP to *he*
117.02
Whole ¶ ending here inserted in MS on
separate slip pasted on to back of page
117.04
MS & CP: *of* HW: *o'*
117.04
a' corr. on CP to *aw*
117.12
yo added on CP before *I mean,* but is in MS
117.13
"that corr. on CP to *"but*
117.23
MS: *you*   CP: *yo*
117.23
leave corr. on CP to *brave* as in MS
117.24
a', corr. on CP to *aw,*
117.26
fra' corr. on CP to *fro*

118.01
after *swords* MS & CP: *for patriotic purposes* not in HW
118.06
CP: *Delegate* corr. to *Aggregate*
118.11
same canc. on CP before *roof*
118.29
MS: *this* (?) CP: *his* after *conscience*
118.33
this corr. on CP to *the* as in MS before *time*,
118.38
now corr. on CP to *even* as in MS
119.03
MS to 54: *an't* CD: *ain't*
119.35
very canc. on CP before *rough*
119.37
after *called* MS & CP: *and was punished like* not in HW
120.10
who added on CP after *and*
120.11
where corr. on CP to *wherever* as in MS
120.13
their corr. on CP to *this* as in MS
120.25
MS: *tak's* CP: *takes* corr. to *taks*
120.26
MS: *smaa'est* CP: *sma'est*
120.26
MS to 54: *be* CD: *get*
120.33
happened corr. on CP to *happens* as in MS
120.39
sin' corr. on CP to *sin*
121.05
MS to 54: *these* CD: *there*
121.13
Nou't corr. on CP to *Nowt* as in MS
121.13
the corr. on CP to *th'* before *kind*. the correction is made twice in this line
121.13
MS & CP: *vara weel* not in HW
121.16
MS: *th'* CP: *the*
121.16
hissen. corr. on CP to *himsen.* as in MS (?) thus in HW; 54: *himseln.*
121.17
a' corr. on CP to *aw*
121.25
awlus canc. on CP before *true*
121.26
'fectionate corr. on CP to *fectionate*
121.29
Chrise'n corr. on CP to *Chrisen*
121.35
folk, corr. on CP to *fok,* as in MS
121.36
us added on CP, but is in MS
121.37
after *ahint* MS: *th'* CP: *the*
121.38
We're patient too . . . to do right. added on CP

122.26
before *numbers* MS to HW: *th'* 54: *the*
122.28
bad canc. on CP before *way,* but is not in MS
122.30
sameness; added on CP to fill blank left by printer because word illegible on MS; then: *an' wi'out a thing to grace our lives;* canc. on CP
122.32
exceptin corr. on CP to *ceptin*
122.32–33
CP: *considers* added to fill blank left by printer because word difficult to read on MS *write* corr. to *writes* and *talk* to *talks*
122.37
fra corr. on CP to *fro* before *year to* and before *generation unto*
123.02
ower in HW before *aw the rest,* but not in MS or CP
123.03
MS to HW: *themsen,* 54: *themseln,*
123.12
MS: *take* CP: *tak*
123.20–21
fra corr. on CP to *fro*
123.21
MS: *ahint* CP: *about*
123.32
MS & CP: *gentleman* HW: *genelman*
123.32
though added on CP
123.33
fur canc. on CP before *above*
123.35
CP: *Agreein' to mak'* corr. to *Agreein to mak* HW: *Agreein fur to mak* 54: *Agreeing fur to mak*
123.39
they'll corr. on CP to *they will*
123.40
MS & CP: *another,* HW: *anoother,*
123.40
impassable corr. on CP to *unpassable* as in MS
123.41
-like added on CP
124.01
that canc. on CP after *fok,*
124.01
that so added on CP
124.02
cheers corr. on CP to *cherishes*
124.03
MS & CP: *themsen* HW: *themseln*
124.04
MS to HW: *gentleman* 54: *genelman*
124.05
MS to HW: *Last* 54: *Most*
124.07
MS to 54: *likeins,* CD: *likens,*
124.09
nout (?) corr. on CP to *nowt* as in MS

124.11
Sir, added on CP
124.17
about added on CP
124.19
MS to HW: *mysen,* 54: *myseln,*
124.19
do added on CP
125.21
by canc. on CP after *back,* but is not in MS
125.30
me, and—there!" corr. on CP to *me. There!"*
125.38
MS: *ledy,* CP: *lady,*
126.13
MS to 54: *left'n* CD: *lef'n*
126.15
MS: *T'would* CP: *I would* corr. to *It would*
126.17
MS & CP: *mysen;* HW: *myseln;*
126.21
MS to HW: *a goin* 54: *goin*
126.28
MS: *As to himself though* CP: *or whimpering though* corr. to *Though*
126.38
before *old* MS & CP: *This* HW: *The*
127.08
MS & CP: *the narrow place,* HW: *the narrow street,* 54: p.t.
127.12
MS to 54: *evidences* CD: *evidence*
127.17
some added on CP
127.26
thout corr. on CP to *thowt*
127.38
MS to HW: *t'ha hadn* 54: *t'hadn*
127.39
MS & CP: *mysen."* HW: *myseln."*
128.03
MS: *After a while* CP: *While* corr. to *Then*
128.06
after *whispered* MS & CP: *some words* not in HW
128.10
MS to HW: *I have* 54: *I've*
128.11
she corr. on CP to *Rachael* before *tried*
128.13
54: *hearken;" said Stephen, astonished, " 'Tisn't* corr. to *hearken," said Stephen, astonished. " 'Tisn't*
128.14
MS: *Yo'r* CP: *Yo're* HW: *Yor*
128.19
yet added on CP
128.32
by in HW before *thousands,* but not in MS or CP
128.35
holes, corr. on CP to *nests,*
129.03
and added on CP

129.14
she corr. on CP to *they* as in MS
129.25
His corr. on CP to *Her* as in MS
129.27
dare say.' corr. on CP to *think."*
129.06
MS & CP: *mysen;* HW: *myseln,*
129.07
MS: *t',* CP: *to* before *Rachael,*
129.09
fro' me, added on CP
129.09
MS to HW: *fur* 54: *for*
129.16
nout corr. on CP to *nowt* as in MS
129.17
MS to HW: *doon* 54: *down*
129.27
MS & CP: *"God bless* HW: *"Bless*
129.29
ridiculous, corr. on CP to *incredulous,* as in MS
129.30
quiet corr. on CP to *quick* as in MS
129.37
after *kinder* MS: *an gentler.* CP: *and gentler.* not in HW
129.37
aw canc. on CP before *reason*
129.38
MS: *fur* CP: *for*
131.41
MS: *unnerstan,* CP-HW: *understan,* 54: *understand,*
132.15
before *chance,* MS to HW: *any* not in 54-CD
132.32
for corr. on CP to *fur*
132.35
MS: *"Weel, weel,"* CP: *"Well, well,"*
132.38
after *thee* MS & CP: *for me!"* not in HW
132.41
CP & HW: *Blackfoot* MS, 54: *Blackpool*
133.01
MS: *It* corr. on CP to *This* HW: *It*
133.01
MS to 54: *the* CD: *a*
133.01
became corr. on CP to *was* after *yet it*
133.04
dirty corr. on CP to *dog's-eared*
133.05
MS & CP: *ye* HW: *you* correction made twice
133.06
while there is yet time, added on CP
133.08
MS to HW: *moment* 54: *day*
133.08
our corr. on CP to *your* as in MS
133.08
departed from corr. on CP to *driven out of*

133.09
their corr. on CP to *a* before *bare*
133.10
MS to 54: *you!* CD: *you.*
133.13
after *land;* MS & CP: *and*   not in HW
133.27
long added on CP
133.32
even added on CP
133.33
even canc. on CP before *being*
133.39
after her, added on CP
134.05
MS & CP: *him.*   HW: *Stephen.*
134.06
MS & CP: *Stephen*   HW: *he*
134.10
was added on CP, but is in MS
134.13
mournfully added on CP
134.14
MS & CP: *streets were*   HW: *town was*
134.15
MS & CP: *the town,*   HW: *it,*
134.16
MS: *hour, and even*   CP: *hour; and even*
   on CP *and* canc.   HW: *hour. Even*
134.18
the place where. . . . his way; by added
   on CP
134.21
its corr. on CP to *the railway's*
134.22
before *scattered* MS: *the first*   CP: *the fast*
   (?) canc.
134.23
dusty corr. on CP to *dirty*
134.28
MS: *chimnies*   CP: *chimneys* corr. to
   chimnies   HW: *chimneys*
134.36
MS & CP: *such*   HW: *these*
135.03
the added on CP, but is in MS
135.06
much added on CP
135.06
as a rising public man. canc. on CP after
   promise
135.07
CP: *with any earnestness* corr. to *with
   earnestness*
135.09
born added on CP
135.10
MS: *imposters.* CP-HW: *impostors.* 54:
   hypocrites.
135.11–12
don't corr. on CP to *do not*
135.12
myself, for example, corr. on CP to *us*
135.12–13
any professor corr. on CP to *the professors*

135.14
I corr. on CP to *we*
135.15
he knows corr. on CP to *they know*
135.25
MS: *nobler* corr. on CP to *higher* HW: *higher*
   54: *nobler*
135.31
new corr. on CP to *Harthouse*
135.32
of little worth, corr. on CP to *worthless,*
135.35
now. corr. on CP to *still.*
136.03
tended, added on CP to fill blank left by
   printer, because word difficult to read
   on MS
136.08
languidly added on CP
136.16
roar (?) corr. on CP to *boast* as in MS
136.31
MS to HW: *coalpits,*   54: *coal-shafts,*
136.32
MS to HW: *engines.*   54: *stationary engines
   at pits' mouths.*
136.34
CP: *mellowed down into* corr. to *mellowed
   into*
136.37
banker corr. on CP to *bank* as in MS
136.37
effected in 54; not in MS to HW
136.37–38
thus pleasantly situated, added on CP; then
   effected in MS to HW; not in 54
136.40
afterwards added on CP after *himself;* is in
   HW; not in 54
137.01
MS to HW: *though*   54: *but*
137.05
Samilarly he lived in a kind of corr. on CP
   to *He delighted to live,*
137.06
he added on CP
137.16
before *boots* MS: *my own*   CP: *your* canc.
137.16
with added on CP after *boots*
137.19
got canc. on CP before *a couple*
137.23
54: *Westmister* corr. to *Westminster*
137.29
well canc. on CP before *aware*
137.32
(through this chapter) MS: *Nikits*   CP:
   Nickits
138.01
, Sir! added on CP
138.37
54: *increduously* corr. to *incredulously*
139.02
before *voice;* MS: *a* (?) not on CP

139.02
will canc. on CP before *give*
139.16
if added on CP
139.17
good people's corr. on CP to *the common*
139.20
makes added on CP
139.24
MS to HW: *loses* 54: *does lose*
139.24
who bets: added on CP
139.30
in corr. on CP to *from the depths of*
139.36
bluntness corr. on CP to *plainness*
139.39
resemblance corr. on CP to *remembrance*
as in MS
140.05
trembled corr. on CP to *troubled* as in MS
140.09
this thing corr. on CP to *what I have done*
140.14
did so corr. on CP to *sold them*
140.23–24
ought not to corr. on CP to *will not*
140.26
sometimes been corr. on CP to *felt*
140.39
very canc. on CP before *fortunate*
140.39
Placed corr. on CP to *Bred*
141.01
*" He was very slow and distinct in what fol-
lowed. "* canc. on CP after *confidence.*
141.06
he corr. on CP to *she* as in MS
141.08
very distinctly uttered added on CP
141.24
respect corr. on CP to *love*
141.30
Yet she restrained her tears from falling.
canc. on CP at end of ¶
141.32
MS to HW: *most* 54: *must*
141.32
aspire, by corr. on CP to *aspire. My* as in
MS
141.33
MS to 54: *extricating him* CD: *extricating
them* (an obvious error)
141.44
MS: *lately.* CP: *of late.*
142.03
, knowing the world.' canc. on CP at end of
speech
142.06
MS to HW: *stopped* 54: *stooped*
142.11
as corr. on CP to *and turning him, so that*
142.20
MS: *"I am* CP & HW: *"I'm* 54: *"I am* (sic)
CD: *"I am*

142.26
if you like." canc. on CP at end of speech
142.27
54: *to day* corr. to *to-day*
142.30
this deponent, canc. on CP after *to me*
142.36
it." corr. on CP to *the subject."*
142.45
MS: *terace*
143.08
boy, corr. on CP to *fellow,*
143.11
and corr. on CP to —*what a state* before *my
sister*
143.22
from a baby, added on CP
143.28
my added on CP, but is in MS
144.06
to me canc. on CP after *talk*
144.11
Though corr. on CP to *Albeit*
144.16
on CP *now* added before *actually* and canc.
after *crying*
144.27
next canc. on CP before *come*
144.29
eating corr. on CP to *chewing*
144.31–32
MS: *tossing a rose or two over himself,* corr.
on CP to *himself tossing over a rose or
two,*
145.12
pretty not in MS, but is in CP
145.20
a corr. on CP to *an idle*
145.21
the subject, corr. on CP to *it.*
145.33–34
CP: *he was only one* corr. to *he was one* as
in MS
145.34
utterly canc. on CP before *indifferent*
145.34
and purposeless. added on CP
145.39
MS to HW: *varnished, and polished,* 54:
smoothed, and varnished,
145.41
takes corr. on CP to *take*
146.06
close canc. on CP before *calculations*
146.11
MS: *curious* CP: *anxious*
146.18
good corr. on CP to *foot*
147.02
importance. corr. on CP to *impatience.* as
in MS
147.03
at all, canc. on CP after *robbed*
147.25
her in 54-CD, but not in MS to HW

147.39
that's corr. on CP to *the safe*
147.41
"A in 54-CD before *hundred;* not in MS to HW
148.06
quoted corr. on CP to *given*
148.13
snore precisely, corr. on CP to *precisely snore,* as in MS
148.20
strictest corr. on CP to *most upright*
148.23
MS: *choaking,* CP: *choking,*
148.40
Ecod!" corr. on CP to *Egod!"*
149.11
lazily, added on CP
149.14
MS: *or* CP: *and*
149.17
men corr. on CP to *fellows*
149.20
fellow corr. on CP to *man*
149.28
express added on CP
150.01
MS: *recal*
150.34
the canc. on CP before *notice-boards*
150.34
say," corr. on CP to *observe,"*
150.34
observed corr. on CP to *replied*
151.01
shall corr. on CP to *she'll*
151.20
hermetical corr. on CP to *Hermitical* as in MS
151.24–25
proclamation, corr. on CP to *announcement,*
151.26
the added on CP before *salt;*
151.28
she canc. on CP before *occasionally*
151.28
silently added on CP
151.29
extremely canc. on CP before *large*
151.35
MS to HW: *should* 54: *would*
152.01–02
four score corr. on CP to *eighty or ninety* HW: *three or four score*
152.02
MS: *This repetition of the* CP: *Her repetition of this*
152.20
bull-headed added on CP. This part of the CP has a note (useless, merely repeating the altered text) not in D.'s hand; possibly in John Forster's.
153.01
good added on CP

153.05
worthy corr. on CP to *considerate*
153.14
she corr. on CP to *Louisa*
153.14
Louisa corr. on CP to *she*
153.15
It corr. on CP to *That*
153.24
room. added on CP
153.28
only added on CP
153.30
first corr. on CP to *just then*
153.41
Loo!' added on CP
154.06
CP: *be as compassionate* corr. to *be compassionate* (MS not clear)
154.08
it canc. on CP after *Whisper*
154.17
quite added on CP
154.18
more corr. on CP to *fresh*
154.21
to any one added on CP
154.33
Italics added on CP
154.38
I am not bound to believe anything about him, canc. on CP after *know.*
155.01
before *good use* MS to HW: *a* not in 54-CD
155.13
am sure I added on CP
155.16
the corr. on CP to *that* before *time*
156.07
MS to HW: *bannisters* 54: *banisters*
156.11
health corr. on CP to *breath* as in MS
156.28
54: *ackowledging* corr. to *acknowledging*
156.28
dropping corr. on CP to *drooping*
156.41
MS: *execution.* (?)
157.03
MS to HW: *Sir?"* 54: *Sir,"*
157.15
MS & CP: *harder and louder than* HW: *harder than*
157.22
before *Mrs. Sparsit* MS & CP: *Accordingly* not in HW
157.34
even canc. on CP after *liberty*
158.06
MS to HW: *corrected* 54: *corrupted*
158.43
"Served corr. on CP to *"Serve*
159.21
MS: *She had had* CP: *She had*

159.26
after *good* MS: *to have* CP: *where* corr. to *to be*

159.28
statue corr. on CP to *stature* as in MS

159.29
with added on CP to fill blank left by printer; *with* not clear in MS

159.37
greater gods than itself: corr. on CP to *gods as great as itself:*

160.23
MS to HW: *unobjectionable* 54-CD: *objectionable* (*unobjectionable* adopted here as making better sense)

160.38
Jane don't corr. on CP to *I couldn't* as in MS

160.38
had corr. on CP to *have*

161.07
54: *"But"*— (an obvious mistake) corr. to *"But—"*

161.09
I— in 54 before *I want,* but not in MS to HW

161.19
stream, (?) corr. on CP to *water,*

161.31
to in 54, but not in MS to HW

161.32
learnt (?) corr. on CP to *learnt* as in MS

161.35
that canc. on CP before *I hope*

162.06
then corr. on CP to *even* as in MS

162.07
and canc. on CP after *in vain,*

162.30
MS to 54: *Mahommedan* CD: *Mahomedan*

163.03
MS: *the* corr. on CP to *these* HW: *these* 54: *those*

163.05
MS to HW: *the* 54: *her*

163.06
her corr. on CP to *Louisa*

163.16
robber?" corr. on CP to *robbery?"* as in MS

163.21
MS to HW: *an air of* 54: *a gentle*

163.22
upon her. in 54, but not in MS to HW

163.23
ma'am," in 54, but not in MS to HW

163.32
MS: *new* CP: *more*

164.06
MS: *villianous* (?)

164.10
before *great* MS & CP: *the* HW: *her*

164.15
She corr. on CP to *Mrs. Sparsit*

164.23
very in MS to HW before *knowing;* not in 54

164.25
MS & CP: , *you really are!"* "at end of speech; not in HW

164.26
so corr. on CP to *very*

164.34
MS: *"My dear—Mrs. Bounderby! Then* dash canc. on CP; HW: *My dear Mrs. Bounderby! Then* 54: p.t.

164.35
MS to HW: *your most devoted* 54: *your devoted*

164.36
for added on CP

164.36
they are, added on CP

164.37
MS to HW: *I have no doubt,* 54: *I am quite ready to believe,*

164.38
MS: *hold of—and of this variety among the rest. He talks.* corr. on CP to *hold of. This fellow talks.*

164.39
; *I assure you* corr. on CP to . *Well;*

164.39
MS: *everybody talks. You really cannot regard his professing morality, beyond its deserving a moment's consideration, as a very suspicious circumstance.* CP: MS text, with *deserving* corr. to *requiring,* HW: *every fellow talks. His professing morality only deserves a moment's consideration, as being a very suspicious circumstance. All* 54: *every fellow talks. He professes morality. Well; all*

164.41
there is a general profession of morality, not in MS to HW

164.42
among not in MS to HW

164.43
There corr. on CP to *Here*

164.44
MS to HW: *a common man* 54: *one of the fluffy classes*

164.45
MS: *of exactly that delicacy* CP: *exactly of that delicacy exactly* not in HW

165.01
MS to HW: *common man* 54: *member of the fluffy classes*

165.03
Bank added on CP

165.06
MS to HW: *man* 54: *fellow*

165.07
MS to HW: *made* 54: *originated*

165.07
altogether added on CP

165.08
MS to HW: *Equally probable!'* at end of speech; not in 54

165.12
MS & CP: *It is only* HW: *I only say what is*

165.19–20
should arrive corr. on CP to *had arrived*
165.20
disappear corr. on CP to *disappeared*
165.22–23
MS: *upon it, and always* corr. on CP to *upon it. Always* thus in HW; 54: *upon it. And always*
165.28
MS to HW: *; but, in* 54: In
165.30
MS to 54: *Giants'* CD: *Giant's* see explanatory footnote to that word, p. 155.
166.18
not avail you." corr. on CP to *never blind me."*
166.20
drift corr. on CP to *graft* as in MS
166.20
that corr. on CP to *her* before *curious*
166.28
perhaps canc. on CP before *for three*
167.18
himself, canc. on CP after *heels*
167.23
MS to HW: *he is*   54: *he's*
167.40
blandly. added on CP
168.01
MS to HW: *Nickits's for*   54: *the country house for*
168.01
54: *country house* corr. to *country-house* (cf. 156, 171, 202)
168.12
MS to HW: *matter much,*   54: *much matter,*
168.42–43
54: *country house* corr. to *country-house*
169.16
that canc. on CP after *were all*
169.40
yet canc. on CP before *shown*
170.22
make much of corr. on CP to *make so much of*
170.23
and ill-used. canc. on CP after *distracted*
170.24
by his mistress. added on CP
170.32
(as you know I have often done before) canc. on CP after *house*
171.01
the success that corr. on CP to *such success as*
171.05
MS to 54: *secresy*   CD: *secrecy*
171.05
or not in MS before *any*
171.05
or added on CP before *every*
171.08
an in 54-CD; *and* in HW before *interest*
171.09
in corr. on CP to *into*

172.10
MS & CP: *rained and blown out* HW-CD: *rained out and blown out*
172.11
MS to HW: *zig-zaged*   54: *zig-zagged*
172.12–13
declining corr. on CP to *deepening* as in MS
172.29
in another, added on CP
172.38–39
with in CP, but not in MS
172.39–40
her damp clothes spoiled; with impressions corr. on CP to p.t., as in MS
173.05
perhaps, corr. on CP to *probably,*
174.06
some canc. on CP before *difficulty*
174.10
but corr. on CP to *only* before *done*
174.10
if you added on CP after *or*
174.10
but corr. on CP to *only* before *neglected*
174.16
to repress corr. on CP to *against*
174.29
learnt corr. on CP to *learned*
174.35
express corr. on CP to *exercise* as in MS
174.41
and earnestly canc. on CP after *fixedly*
175.11
a corr. on CP to *my* as in MS
175.13
and he knew, added on CP
175.15
MS to HW: *gradually*   54: *slowly*
175.16–17
before *tenderness* MS to HW: *imaginative* not in 54
175.21
into corr. on CP to *in*
175.42
Louisa!" added on CP
175.45
MS: *still* before *steadfastly*   not on CP
176.04
MS: *ashey*   CP: *ashy*
177.36
for the first time canc. on CP before *last night.*
178.02
has not corr. on CP to *may not have*
178.03
MS to 54: *have*   CD: *had* before *proved*
178.07
MS: *guaging*   CP: *gauging*
178.27
the palm of canc. of CP before *his hand*
179.07
before *it is!* MS to HW: *that*   not in 54
179.19
a very corr. on CP to *an* before *early*

179.23
God corr. on CP to Heaven
179.27
so added on CP
179.29
in this house, added on CP
180.03
before soft MS: a not in CP
180.07
MS to HW: So it   54: It
180.08
MS to HW: lay still.   54: rested.
180.10
stooped closer to her, corr. on CP to touched
hers,
180.13
at corr. on CP to near
180.14–15
MS to HW: if you will let 54: if you would let
180.18
smiling and canc. on CP before shaking
180.19
dear Miss Louisa, canc. on CP after you,
180.32
been truly attached to corr. on CP to loved
180.32
deeply wishful corr. on CP to have always
wished
180.43
tight canc. on CP after held it
180.44
you should corr. on CP to do you
181.11
trimming corr. on CP to brimming as in MS
181.19
at end of chapter: Brief ¶ here in MS, canc.
on CP: Louisa's tears fell like the blessed
rain after a long drought. The sullen glare
was over, and in every drop there was a
germ of hope and promise for the dried-
up ground.
181.22
have scarcely corr. on CP to scarcely have
181.25
a most corr. on CP to an after out in
181.26
MS to HW: with   54: without
181.27
real canc. on CP before existing
182.02
; not even been heard of. canc. on CP after
not there
182.09
eye corr. on CP to eyes
182.15
said corr. on CP to murmured
182.21
your corr. on CP to my own as in MS
183.17
they corr. on CP to any steps
183.20
uncommonly canc. on CP before like
183.20
54: However still   CD: However, still (omission of comma in 54 seems accidental)
183.21
coolness corr. on CP to indifference

183.28
sort corr. on CP to kind
183.32
wished corr. on CP to wishes
184.14
MS to HW: trust you."   54: trust—"
184.21
MS: "Perhaps, Sir,"   CP: "Perhaps," corr. to
"I think,"
184.29
"So lately! canc. on CP before At—?
184.40
, James Harthouse, canc. on CP after that
he
185.01
any of added on CP
185.08
54: of whom we speak CD: of whom we
speak? (question mark adopted as called
for by interrogative turn of sentence)
185.25
"Well! added on CP
185.31
fled corr. on CP to came
185.36
simple canc. on CP before fervor
185.40
, I daresay. canc. on CP after need be
185.44
—in fact with— added on CP
186.03–04
MS: entirely diabolical, corr. on CP to perfectly irresistible, thus in HW; 54: perfectly diabolical,
186.05
When corr. on CP to Whereas
186.07
really added on CP
186.09
courtly corr. on CP to self-possessed
186.13
really canc. on CP before know
186.20
expectations corr. on CP to expectation
186.21
anywhere." corr. on CP to whatever."
186.30
perfect corr. on CP to simple
186.42
simple corr. on CP to plain
187.14
and biting his nails, canc. on CP after room
187.16
unaccountable corr. on CP to incomprehensible
187.21
MS to 54: secresy.   CD: secrecy.
187.23
MS: chimnie-piece,
187.39
at the same advantage. corr. on CP to with
the same success.
187.43
, blushing, canc. on CP after ambassadress
188.09
And now it may corr. on CP to The defeat
may now

188.11
floored corr. on CP to *made nothing of*
188.16–17
This being set in ordinary type in CP, D.
  writes: *Printer. Print this letter in another
  type.*
188.30
thereafter corr. on CP to *afterwards*
188.33
MS: *sad* CP: *bad*
188.34
made himself corr. on CP to *been*
188.36
very added on CP
188.38
on any account, added on CP
188.38
that often corr. on CP to *the only one that*
188.38
quite canc. on CP before *ashamed*
189.05
majestically added on CP
189.10
MS: *proceedure*
189.28
make known corr. on CP to *say*
190.11
MS: *lately* CP: *latterly*
190.18
MS to HW: *staring*   54-CD *starting* (an
  obvious mistake)
190.32
too, canc. on CP after *for hers*
190.43
MS to HW: *Which she did.*   54: *(Which she
  did.)*
191.03
MS to 54: *there's*   CD: *there is*
191.21
leave corr. on CP to *let*
191.36
really canc. on CP before *grateful*
192.22
all canc. on CP before *previous*
192.25
imaginative canc. on CP before *qualities*
192.26
hardly dealt with, corr. on CP to *harshly
  neglected,*
192.36
put corr. on CP to *pent* as in MS
192.43
that added on CP before *there's*
193.04
54: *Gadgrind* corr. to *Gradgrind*
193.06
and added on CP before *his hair*
193.36
that canc. on CP after *at once*
193.37
54: *permision* corr. to *permission*
194.32
you took her canc. on CP before *for better.*
194.32
MS: *worse,—* on CP *for—"* added
194.36
he said, corr. on CP to *said he,*

194.41
consideration canc. on CP after *yielding*
194.45
Now, added on CP
195.03
poor canc. on CP before *subject*
195.03
Your corr. on CP to *As to your* as in MS
195.05
MS: *shan't,*   CP & HW: *sha'nt,*   54: *shan't,*
195.20
such added on CP
195.31
Nickits's corr. on CP to *his country*
195.35
trustful corr. on CP to *boastful* as in MS
196.02
lustre, corr. on CP to *bustle,* as in MS
196.03
professional persons corr. on CP to *officers*
196.10
was not found, corr. on CP to *could not be
  heard of,*
196.21
he in HW before *caused* but not in MS
  or CP
196.30
started corr. on CP to *stared* as in MS
196.31
After *half ludicrous, if* MS & CP have: *such a
  picture of a Country as a suicidal idiot with
  its sword of state [pointed* added on CP] *at
  its own heart could ever be otherwise than
  wholly shocking* but HW has p.t.
196.31
54: *ludicrous* corr. to *ludicrous,* (the comma
  having apparently been dropped by accident, at end of line and bottom of page)
196.36
still added on CP
196.42
stir corr. on CP to *to-do*
197.17
MS: *skunked,* (?) corr. on CP to *slunk,*
197.18
of added on CP before *straws,* but is in MS
197.21
slur! corr. on CP to *sear!* as in MS
197.41
MS: *in't;*   CP to CD: *int;*
198.14
you will soon understand. corr. on CP to
  that will explain itself.
198.44
young lady, added on CP
198.45
MS to HW: *come*   54: *came*
199.02
went corr. on CP to *was*
199.12
robber corr. on CP to *thief*
199.13
spoke corr. on CP to *spoken*
199.19
feel for us corr. on CP to *know us*
199.26
unhappy. corr. on CP to *afflicted.*

199.41
MS: *greet*;   CP: *great*; corr. to *like this*;
199.43
and no more canc. on CP before—*I went*
200.16
after *Rachael*   MS: *confidently*;   not in CP
200.27
from him, added on CP
200.29
shaking his head, added on CP
200.31
lad. corr. on CP to *chap.*
200.43
it, corr. on CP to *that*,
200.45
lass canc. on CP after *Eh*
201.09
any added on CP
201.17
MS to HW: *that*   54-CD: *a* here *that* adopted,
    as alone making sense
201.24
gentle corr. on CP to *gentler*
201.24–35
"*It goes against me. . . . and not near it.*"
    inserted in MS on separate slip pasted
    on to back of page
201.28
belied," corr. on CP to *wronged.*"
201.30
bad corr. on CP to *had* as in MS
201.31
MS only: *He would know then* (?)
201.38
of him added on CP
202.09
then," canc. on CP after *myself*
202.12
MS to HW: *begun*   54-CD: *began*
202.15
this corr. on CP to *the* before *moment*
202.28
MS: *its*   CP & HW: *his*
202.29
some canc. on CP before *sixty*
202.32
All this corr. on CP to *During this whole*
202.33
great corr. on CP to *greatly* as in MS
202.36
time corr. on CP to *hour*
203.01
days, added on CP after *seven*, but is in MS
203.14
was corr. on CP to *turned out*
203.17
unshaken. corr. on CP to *unbroken.* as in
    MS
203.25
wait for corr. on CP to *await*
203.32
living or dead canc. on CP after *clear*
203.35
MS: *likely* CP: *like*
203.41
would corr. on CP to *could* as in MS

204.09
MS: *mistrustin* CP: *mistrusting*
204.12
not her canc. on CP after *no*
204.31
my canc. on CP before *bed-time.*
204.31–32
now canc on CP after *wi' you*
204.33
back added on CP
204.36
MS: *he's*   CP: *he is*
204.36
He's corr. on CP to *He has*
204.39
54: *couldn't* corr. to *couldn't*
205.04
MS to HW: *You are*   54: *You're*
205.08
for corr. on CP to *by* as in MS
205.14
just corr. on CP to *newly*
205.34
Roman-nosed canc. on CP before *matron*
205.41
lined corr. on CP to *lured* as in MS
205.41
in, added on CP but is in MS
205.41
inevitable corr. on CP to *irresistible* as in
    MS
205.43
MS: *laziest* (?)   CP: *busiest*
206.02
54: *dining room* corr. to *dining-room* (as
    elsewhere)
206.34
MS to HW: *wrath*.   54: *warmth.*
206.44
said corr. on CP to *cried*
207.02
to you, added on CP
207.04
or other added on CP
207.09
MS: *it's*   CP: *it is*
207.33
"*Now*, added on CP
207.35
afore corr. on CP to *before*
207.39
to—added on CP after *son*
207.45
MS to 54: *cypher*   CD: *cipher*
208.04
MS to 54: *year*   CD: *years*
208.10
forget corr. on CP to *forgot* as in MS
208.20
for in CD only before *I never*
208.20
afore, corr. on CP to *before*,
208.20
or corr. on CP to *nor*
208.20
never added on CP

208.22
here added on CP after *brought*
208.23
O added on CP, but is in MS
208.34 & 35
to added on CP before *disperse*
209.03
preferred corr. on CP to *advanced*
209.30
her canc. on CP before *harboring*
209.32
saving corr. on CP to *save*
210.14
elsewhere, added on CP
210.18
MS: *begin* CP: *began*
210.30
some canc. on CP after *site of*
211.04
54: *to look it it* corr. to *to look at it*
211.19
it left canc. on CP before *the mark* and *was* added after *shape*
211.27
MS to HW: *God!* 54: *Lord!*
211.31
distractedly canc. on CP before *flung*
211.36
time, corr. on CP to *moment,*
212.02
little in 54-CD, but not in MS to HW
212.11–12
MS to HW: *After* 54: *And after*
212.13
went, corr. on CP to *ran,*
212.25–26
MS: *Old Hell Shaft,* CP: *OLD HELL SHAFT,* corr. to *Old Hell Shaft,*
212.33
after *poles,* MS to HW: *buckets,* not in 54
212.33
lanthorns, corr. on CP to *lanterns,*
213.12
working pitmen corr. on CP to *people*
213.26
a corr. on CP to *the* before *bright*
213.28–29
all actively corr. on CP to *attentively* as in MS
213.39
that added on CP before *another*
213.44
MS: *both men* CP: *workmen* on CP *both* added
214.15
MS: *suspence.*
214.21
loose added on CP
214.23
the corr. on CP to *an* before *arm*
214.24
shown in the light corr. on CP to *shown by the light* as in MS (?)
214.27
around corr. on CP to *round*

214.32
further been corr. on CP to *been further* as in MS
214.34
own added on CP
214.42
wholly canc. on CP before *innocent*
215.38
let it corr. on CP to *let't*
216.01
All apostrophes in words like *an', fro', sufferin',* were canc. on CP; they did not appear in HW or 54; but in CD, many have come back.
216.13–15
MS had: *not forgot her. Thou'rt not like to forget her now, poor patient suff'rin dear and me so nigh her. Thou knowst* (order probably misread by compositor)
216.15–16
thou didst work . . . winder, and added on CP
216.16
how in 54-CD, but not in CP & HW
216.21
touches corr. on CP to *tooches*
216.25
rather canc. on CP after *right*—(had already been canc. in MS, but not very clearly)
216.29
MS: *revrently,*
216.29
my added on CP
216.30
at't added on CP
216.31
thout corr. on CP to *thowt* as in MS
216.34
believed corr. on CP to *believen*
216.34
MS to HW: *lady* 54: *ledy*
216.35
were one corr. on CP to *was one*
216.36
all. (?) corr. on CP to *'em.* as in MS
216.37
MS to HW: *others* 54: *oothers*
216.38
judgment, corr. on CP to *judgments,*
216.39
You in corr. on CP to *In my* as in MS (?)
216.41
MS: *coom* CP & HW: *came* 54: *coom*
217.03
before *said* MS: *had* not in CP
217.06
HW & 54: *yo,* CD: *you,*
217.12
his corr. on CP to *the*
217.18
to corr. on CP to *yo* as in MS before *clear*
217.32
my added on CP
218.08
for she had begun by telling him not even to look round, canc. on CP after *head,*

218.13–14
MS to HW: *seen*　　54: *seeing*
219.01
the help of her loving heart. corr. on CP to *her help too.*
219.03
after *robbery,* MS: *Louisa,* not on CP
219.15
after *remember,* MS: *all* not on CP
219.18
do." canc. on CP after *mine*
219.19
am afraid, corr. on CP to *fear,*
219.19
reiterated corr. on CP to *hesitated*
219.27
MS: *is to*　　CP: *is he to*
219.33
grateful had been canc. in MS, but is in CP
219.41
then, added on CP
220.03
God!" corr. on CP to *Heaven!"*
220.10
view corr. on CP to *vein* as in MS
220.11
MS: *concerted*　　CP and all later texts: *consented* here *concerted* adopted, as making better sense
220.13–15
In CP *setting forth at* occurs at bottom of a column; *at* corr. to *in an* to fit in with next line at top of following column: *opposite direction,* But MS has p.t., restored here for the first time, in the belief that the words *another time and leaving the town by an* making up exactly one average line of HW print, had been either overlooked by compositor or dropped from set-up type.
222.01
after *Louisa,* MS: *in their suspence,*　　CP: *in their suspense,* canc.
222.06
MS: *'em* corr. on CP to *them*　　thus in HW 54: *'em*
222.09
painfully anxious. corr. on CP to *in great suspense.*
222.20
MS: *credit* CP to CD: *credith* (*credit* adopted as more consistent than perpetuated misreading of MS)
222.21
MS: *heartth*　　CP: *hearth*
222.22
MS: *thethpethially*　　CP: *ethpethially*
222.24
stickth corr. on CP to *thtickth*
222.28
MS: *on* (first written *upon* but *up* canc.): CP: *upon*
222.34
on corr. on CP to *upon*
222.35
MS: *themthelvth* CP: *then the both.* on CP *then the* corr. to *themthelvth* but *both* (an

obvious mistake) left to subsist to this day! *both* rejected here
223.11
pleasant for all that corr. on CP to *agreeable*
223.15
after *part!"* MS to HW: *said Sleary.* not in 54
223.17
MS: *thecretth,*　　CP: *thecreth,*
223.28
a canc. on CP before *piethe*
223.34
MS to HW: *expenthive*　　54: *ecthpenthive*
224.01
that, corr. on CP to *it,*
224.24
In MS to 54, the ¶ goes on to *might approach.* New ¶ at *This done* in CD only
225.17
returned corr. on CP to *grumbled*
225.29
on board." (?) corr. on CP to *abroad."* as in MS
225.38
MS & CP: *gothe* HW: *goeth*
226.15
this shocking act of dishonesty, corr. on CP to *the shocking action you have committed,*
226.21
No. canc. on CP before *I don't*
226.31–32
his ingratitude, canc. on CP after *forgave him*
226.33
those corr. on CP to *these* as in MS
227.05
CP: *out; and Bitzer,* corr to *out. Bitzer,*
227.13
must canc. on CP after *that I*
227.16
MS: *Reason*　　CP: *treason* (?) corr. to *reason*
227.26
before *bank-robbery* MS: *the*　　CP: *this*
227.27
and corr. on CP to *for* before *I knew*
228.07
very added on CP
228.19
there, added on CP (*there,* written, but canc., in MS)
228.29
MS & CP: *return.*　　HW: *purchase.*
228.31
MS: *The whole existence* HW: *Every inch of the whole existence* 54: p.t.
228.36
sir, added on CP
229.07
that canc. on CP before *I thed*
229.07
then, added on CP
229.09
MS: *thath*　　CP: *that'th* HW: *that'h*
229.11
called it; conthequently, corr. on CP to *called it. Conthequently,*

229.11
54: *muth'nt* corr. to *muthn't*

229.19
MS: *heart*   CP: *breast*

229.19
him; for as corr. on CP to *him. As*

229.20
MS to 54: *moveable*   CD: *movable*.

229.30
danth. corr. on CP to *danthe,* as in MS

229.33
or corr. on CP after *a peg* to *on* as in MS

229.35
54: *know him ?* corr. to *know him!*

230.03
other added on CP

230.08
here added on CP

230.11
Bitther corr. on CP to *When that pre-thiouth young Rathcal*

230.11
afoot added on CP; *and* canc. on CP before *the dog*

230.14
got the better of the acthident, and canc. on CP before *turned*

230.19
"Well! I don't corr. on CP to *"I don't*

230.26
sixth corr. on CP to *thixth*

230.32
MS & CP: *excuthe*   HW: *ethcuthe*

230.34
and canc. on CP after *room;*

230.40
no doubt canc. on CP after *it ith*

231.11
lived with him corr. on CP to *menthioned him to me*

231.17–18
and very good bithnith we wath a doing, canc. on CP after *Chethter*

231.22
looking corr. on CP to *theeking*

231.24
MS: *forelegth,*   HW to 54: *fore-legs.*

231.32
bathely canc. in MS, does not appear in CP, but is in HW to CD

231.35
MS & CP: *till—not*   HW-CD: *till—no, not*

231.39
54: *prethnt* corr. to *prethent*

232.36
with you, corr. on CP to *now,*

233.11
MS: *I tell* CP: *I'll tell*

233.44
in a light, social style of conversation; canc. on CP after *Mrs. Sparsit*

234.20
white line added on CP after *futurity.*

234.29
now corr. on CP to *won* as in MS

234.32–33
self-made men, corr. on CP to *Humbugs,*

234.33
fifty corr. on CP to *five-and-fifty*

234.39
that corr. on CP to *the* before *day,*

235.01
meanness, corr. on CP to *vile example,*

235.02–03
MS had white line after *see it all out.*

235.16
so corr. on CP to *that*

235.17
White line added after *his men.* on CP. In MS D. had written: *No white line here.*

235.22
unhappy canc. on CP after *his own*

235.30
a woman in MS: canc. on CP; but is in HW

235.32
before who, of all MS & CP: *a woman* not in HW to CD.

235.40
too added on CP

236.05
54: *name?"* corr. to *name"?*

236.10–11
MS: *and any hoarded scrap of the possession a blessing* CP: and [*a possession* added on CP] *any hoarded scrap of the former* [*the former* corr. to *which is*] *a blessing* HW: p.t.

236.22
simply added on CP

Emendations List

The text of *Hard Times* printed here is that of the first edition in book form, published in 1854 by Bradbury and Evans. The few changes made are listed below. They are mostly corrections of accidental mistakes in the 1854 text.

16.02
54: *either brushing* corr. to *after brushing* (MS reading restored as making better sense)

18.42
54: *do'nt* (an obvious mistake) corr. to *don't*

23.05
54: *it's* (almost certainly by mistake) corr. to *its*

31.16
54: *eying* corr. to *eyeing* (as the only accepted form—used by D. in 29.19)

37.10
54: has period after *remarked* colon substituted, as required by sense

39.12
54: *must* corr. to *mutht* for consistency's sake

39.14–15
54: *alwath* (an obvious mistake) corr. to *alwayth*

41.22
54: *would'nt* (an obvious error) corr. to *wouldn't*

45.15
54: *evening* (obviously erroneous) corr. to *morning*

48.10
54: *"Oh;"* (punctuation obviously wrong) corr. to *"Oh!"*

52.02
54: *could'nt* (an obvious mistake) corr. to *couldn't*

53.24
54: *did'nt* corr. to *didn't*

55.29
54: *faltering way.* corr. to *faltering way,* (as required by sense)

94.30
54: *deaf-serving woman* corr. to *deaf serving-woman* (as required by sense)

100.11–12
54 runs on *"Powler family,"* after *"A Powler."* instead of opening new line. This is unjustified and there is only one other case in the novel. New line restored.

101.38
54: comma added after *chit"*

101.40
period added after *Mrs*

102.13–14
54 again runs on *"It's ridiculous* after *said Mrs. Sparsit.* New line restored, as in 93.29–30

125.26
54: *has'nt* (an obvious mistake) corr. to *hasn't*

128.13
54: *hearken;" said Stephen, astonished, "'Tisn't* erroneous punctuation corr. to *hearken," said Stephen, astonished. "'Tisn't*

137.23
54: *Westmister* corr. to *Westminster*

138.37
54: *incredulously* corr. to *incredulously*

142.20
54: *I'am afraid* corr. to *I am afraid* as in MS to HW, and CD

142.27
54: *to day* corr. to *to-day*

156.28
54: *ackowledging* corr. to *acknowledging*

160.23
54: *objectionable* corr. to *unobjectionable* as required by sense

161.07
54: *"But"*—(an obvious error) corr. to *But—"*

168.01
54: *country house* corr. to *country-house* (cf. 156, 171, 202)

168.42–43
54: *country house* corr. to *country-house*

183.20
54: *However still* CD: *However, still* (CD comma adopted, as its omission in 54 seems accidental)

185.08
54: *of whom we speak.* CD: *of whom we speak?*
(CD question mark adopted as called for by
interrogative turn of sentence)
190.18
54: *starting* (an obvious error) corr. to *staring*
193.04
54: *Gadgrind* corr. to *Gradgrind*
193.37
54: *permision* (an obvious error) corr. to
permission
196.31
54: *ludicrous* corr. to *ludicrous,* (the comma
having apparently been dropped by accident, at end of line and bottom of page)
199.40
54: *that any* corr. to *"that any* (the inverted
commas having apparently been dropped
by accident)
201.17
54: *with a brief speech* HW reading (*with
that brief speech*) restored here, as alone
making sense
204.39
54: *could't* corr. to *couldn't*
206.02
54: *dining room* corr. to *dining-room* as
elsewhere

211.04
54: *to look it it* (an obvious mistake) corr.
to *to look at it*
220.11–12
54: *consented* MS reading (*concerted*)
restored here, as making better sense
220.14
54: *in an opposite* MS reading (*at another
time and leaving the town by an opposite*)
restored here (see textual note)
222.20
54: *credith* corr. to *credit* (see textual note)
222.35
54: *themselvth both both* canc. here (see
Textual Note)
229.11
54: *muth'nt* (an obvious error) corr. to *muthn't*
229.35
54: *know him?* (thus probably by mistake)
corr. to *know him!*
231.39
54: *prethnt* (thus probably by mistake) corr.
to *prethent*
235.16
54: has white line after *his men,* but see
textual note
236.05
54: *name?"* corr. to *name"?*

HARD TIMES.

Fig. 3. Thomas Gradgrind and his two children, Louisa and Tom (Harry French, wood engraving, 1870s). (London: Chapman and Hall, 1875). Engraving by Harry French. © The British Library, Board, W14/1110.(2).

Fig. 4. Copper factory in Manchester, England. Engraving, 1865.
© Leemage/Lebrecht Music & Arts.

Fig. 5. Interior view of the J & S Eyres Ltd, ironfounders, Miles Platting,
c. 1890. Courtesy of Manchester Central Library Archives.

Fig. 6. Market Court photographed in 1868, just prior to its demolition. Courtesy of the Royal Borough of Kensington and Chelsea Libraries.

Fig. 7. New Street, Vauxhall, London c. 1860. Courtesy of the Victoria & Albert Museum/The Art Archive.

Fig. 8. Stephen and Rachael in Sick Room (New York: Hurd and Houghton, 1869), vol. I, p. 116. Engraving by Fred Walker. 21446.3 Houghton Library, Harvard University.

Fig. 9. Stephen Blackpool. Frontispiece (New York: Hurd and Houghton, 1869), vol. I, p. i. Engraving by Fred Walker. 21446.3 Houghton Library, Harvard University.

"THIS, SIR," SAID BOUNDERBY, "IS MY WIFE, MRS. BOUNDERBY."

Fig. 10. "This Sir," Said Bounderby, "Is My Wife, Mrs. Bounderby"
(London: Chapman and Hall, 1875). Engraving by Harry French. ©
The British Library, Board, W14/1110.(2).

Fig. 11. Mr Harthouse Dining at the Bounderbys (New York: Hurd and Houghton, 1869), vol. I, p. 172. Engraving by Fred Walker. 21446.3 Houghton Library, Harvard University.

Fig. 12. Mr Harthouse and Tom Gradgrind in the Garden (New York: Hurd and Houghton, 1869), vol. I, p. 321. Engraving by Fred Walker. 21446.3 Houghton Library, Harvard University.

Fig. 13. The Mouth of the Pit (New York: Hurd and Houghton, 1869), vol. II, p. 22. Engraving by Fred Walker. 21446.3 Houghton Library, Harvard University.

Fig. 14. Stephen Blackpool Recovered from the Old Hell Shaft (New York: Hurd and Houghton, 1869), vol. II, p. 28. Engraving by Fred Walker. 21446.3 Houghton Library, Harvard University.

CONTEXTS

HARD TIMES CALENDAR

August 1853: Dickens finished writing *Bleak House* while residing in France.

September: Finished *A Child's History of England*.

October–December: Trip to Italy. News of strike in Preston.

Mid-December: Return to England; public reading in Birmingham.

January 23, 1854: First page of *Hard Times* written.

January 29: Visit to Preston during the strike.

April 1: First installment of *Hard Times* published in *Household Words*.

June: Moved back to France with his family.

July 19: Finished writing *Hard Times*.

August 12: Publication of final number of *Hard Times*.

Dickens' Comments on the Composition of *Hard Times*[†]

[From *Letter to W. H. Wills,*[1] *July 27, 1853*]

I have also thought of another [article], to be called *Frauds upon the Fairies—apropòs* of George Cruikshank's editing.[2] Half playfully and half seriously, I mean to protest most strongly against alteration—for any purpose—of the beautiful little stories which are so tenderly and humanly useful to us in these times when the world is too much with us early and late; *** I shall not be able to do it until after finishing "Bleak House."

[From *Letter to Angela Burdett Coutts,*[3] *September 18, 1853*]

Do you see Household Words in Paris? If not, I will send you two papers I should like you to read. The first, called *Frauds on the Fairies,* I think would amuse you, and enlist you on my side—which is for a little more fancy among children and a little less fact.

[From *Dickens' Article, "Frauds on the Fairies,"*
in Household Words, *October 1, 1853*]

In a utilitarian age *** it is a matter of grave importance that Fairy tales should be respected. *** A nation without fancy, without some romance, never did, never can, never will, hold a great place under the sun.

---

† The letters reprinted here are from the Pilgrim Edition, *The Letters of Charles Dickens,* Volume 7: *1853–1855,* ed. Graham Storey, Kathleen Tillotson, and Angus Easson (Oxford: Clarendon, 1993), pp. 121, 148, 213–14, 244–45, 250, 254, 256, 260–61, 279, 282, 284–85, 288, 290–91, 293, 294, 317, 320, 342, 351, 354, 367, 368, 369, 371, 404, 453, 492–93. Reprinted by permission of Oxford University Press.
1. Editorial assistant for *Household Words.*
2. Dickens had recently read a book review about George Cruikshank's retelling of traditional fairy tales. Because Cruikshank was an ardent teetotaller, his "editing" of *Hop o' my Thumb and the Seven League Boots* consisted of inserting warnings into the story about the dangers of alcohol and other failings such as "card-playing, betting on horse races, and all sorts of foolish gambling" (*The Examiner,* July 23, 1853, p. 469).
3. A wealthy philanthropist with whom Dickens worked closely as an adviser.

[From *Letter to Angela Burdett Coutts (from Italy)*,
November 27, 1853]

I am sorry to see that there have been some disturbances in Lancashire, arising out of the unhappy strikes. I read in an Italian paper last night, that there had been symptoms of rioting at Blackburn. The account stated that the workers of that place, supposing some of the obnoxious manufacturers of Preston to be secreted "nel palazzo Bull" assembled before that Palazzo, and demanded to have them produced *** I suppose the Palazzo Bull to be the Bull Hotel, but the paragraph gave no hint of such a thing.

(I wish you would come to Birmingham and see *those* working people on the night when I have so many of them together. I have never seen them collected in any number in that place, without extraordinary pleasure—even when they have been agitated by political events.)

[From *Dickens' Speech in Birmingham Town Hall*,
December 30, 1853]

I have no fear of being misunderstood—of being supposed to mean too much in this.[4] If there ever was a time when any one class could of itself do much for its own good, and for the welfare of society—which I greatly doubt—that time is unquestionably past. It is in the fusion of different classes, without confusion; in the bringing together of employers and employed; in the creating of a better common understanding among those whose interests are identical, who depend upon each other, and who can never be in unnatural antagonism without deplorable results, that one of the chief principles of a Mechanics' Institution should consist. In this world a great deal of the bitterness among us arises from an imperfect understanding of one another. Erect in Birmingham a great Educational Institution, properly educational; educational of the feelings as well as of the reason; to which all orders of Birmingham men can contribute; in which all orders of Birmingham men can meet; wherein all orders of Birmingham men are faithfully represented; and you will erect a Temple of Concord here which will be a model edifice to the whole of England.

[From *Letter to Angela Burdett Coutts, January 14, 1854*]

I have had a long talk with Charley[5] this morning. *** He is very gentle and affectionate *** His inclinations are all good; but I think

---

4. Dickens had been urging that working men ought to be invited to serve on the committee of the Birmingham Institute, an organization concerned with improving working men's education.
5. Dickens' eldest son, sixteen-year-old Charles, had been studying in Germany, without much success, after having left Eton.

he has less fixed purpose and energy than I could have supposed possible in my son. He is not aspiring, or imaginative in his own behalf. With all the tenderer and better qualities which he inherits from his mother, he inherits an indescribable lassitude of character— a very serious thing in a man—which seems to me to express the want of a strong, compelling hand always beside him.

[From *Letter to W. F. de Cerjat*,[6] *January 16, 1854*]

The sad affair of the Preston strike remains unsettled; and I hear, on strong authority, that if that were settled, the Manchester people are prepared to strike next. Provisions very dear, but the people very temperate and quiet in general.

[From *Letter to John Forster*,[7] *January 20, 1854*]

I wish you would look at the enclosed titles for the *H. W.* story, between this and two o'clock or so, when I will call. * * * It seems to me that there are three very good ones among them. I should like to know whether you hit upon the same. [*The enclosure reads*:]
  1. According to Cocker. 2. Prove it. 3. Stubborn Things. 4. Mr. Gradgrind's Facts. 5. The Grindstone. 6. Hard Times. 7. Two and Two are Four. 8. Something Tangible. 9. Our Hard-headed Friend. 10. Rust and Dust. 11. Simple Arithmetic. 12. A Matter of Calculation. 13. A Mere Question of Figures. 14. The Gradgrind Philosophy.

[From *Letter to Angela Burdett Coutts, January 23, 1854*]

I have fallen to work again. My purpose is among the mighty secrets of the world at present; but there is such a fixed idea on the part of my printers and copartners in *Household Words*, that a story by me, continued from week to week, would make some unheard-of-effect with it, that I am going to write one. It will be as long as five Nos. of Bleak House, and will be five months in progress. The first written page now stares at me from under this sheet of note paper. The main idea of it, is one on which you and I and Mrs. Brown have often spoken; and I know it will interest you as a purpose.

[From *Letter to John Forster, January 29, 1854*][8]

I am afraid I shall not be able to get much here. Except the crowds at the street-corners reading the placards pro and con; and the cold

---

6. A Swiss friend of Dickens'.
7. Essayist, biographer, and Dickens' close friend and literary adviser.
8. Written from Preston, a textile-manufacturing town, which Dickens was visiting to observe a strike.

absence of smoke from the mill-chimneys; there is very little in the streets to make the town remarkable. I am told that the people 'sit at home and mope.' The delegates with the money from the neighbouring places come in to-day to report the amounts they bring; and tomorrow the people are paid. When I have seen both these ceremonies, I shall return. It is a nasty place (I thought it was a model town); and I am in the Bull Hotel, before which some time ago the people assembled supposing the masters to be here, and on demanding to have them out were remonstrated with by the landlady in person. I saw the account in an Italian paper, in which it was stated that "the populace then environed the Palazzo Bull, until the padrona of the Palazzo heroically appeared at one of the upper windows and addressed them!" One can hardly conceive anything less likely to be represented to an Italian mind by this description, than the old, grubby, smoky, mean, intensely formal red brick house with a narrow gateway and a dingy yard, to which it applies.

[From *Letter to Mark Lemon*,[9] *February 20, 1854*]

Will you note down and send me any slang terms among the tumblers and Circus-people, that you can call to mind? I have noted down some—I want them in my new story—but it is very probable that you will recall several which I have not got.

[From *Letter to John Forster* (*concerning* Hard Times), *February 1854*]

The difficulty of the space is CRUSHING. Nobody can have an idea of it who has not had an experience of patient fiction-writing with some elbow-room always, and open places in perspective. In this form, with any kind of regard to the current number, there is absolutely no such thing.

[From *Letter to Bradbury & Evans*,[1] *March 7, 1854*]

Throughout Hard Times, will you arrange when you get the corrected revises back from me (I now send those of the two first parts) to have *then* pulled, for my reference copy at work, a proof folded in any easy form for reference that may not give much trouble to your people. I want to avoid the botheration, both the long slips, and of having to cut my working copy out of the Nos. week by week.

9. The founder and editor of *Punch* magazine and Dickens' close friend.
1. Dickens' publisher.

[From *Letter to Émile de la Rue*,[2] *March 9, 1854*]

It was considered, when I came home, such a great thing that I should write a story for Household Words, that I am at present up to the eyes in one. It is to be published in Household Words, weekly, through five months, and will be altogether as long as five Nos. of Copperfield or Bleak House. I did intend to be as lazy as I *could* be through the summer, but here I am with my armour on again.

[From *Letter to Peter Cunningham*,[3] *March 11, 1854*]

Being down at Dover yesterday, I happened to see the Illustrated London News lying on the table, and there read a reference to my new book[4] which I believe I am not mistaken in supposing to have been written by you.

I don't know where you may have found your information, but I can assure you that it is altogether wrong. The title was many weeks old, and chapters of the story were written, before I went to Preston or thought about the present Strike. The mischief of such a statement is twofold. First, it encourages the public to believe in the impossibility that books are produced in that very sudden and Cavalier manner (as poor Newton used to feign that he produced the elaborate drawings he made in his madness, by winking at his table); and Secondly in this instance it has this pernicious bearing: It localizes (so far as your readers are concerned) a story which has a direct purpose in reference to the working people all over England, and it will cause, as I know by former experience, characters to be fitted on to individuals whom I never saw or heard of in my life.

I do not suppose that you can do anything to set this mis-statement right, being made; nor do I wish you to set it right. But if you will, at any future time, ask me what the fact is before you state it, I will tell you, as frankly and readily as it is possible for one friend to tell another, what the truth is and what it is not.

[From *Letter to Charles Knight*,[5] *March 17, 1854*]

I earnestly entreat your attention to the point (I have been working upon it, weeks past, in Hard Times) * * * The English are, so far as I know, the hardest-worked people on whom the sun shines. Be content

2. A Swiss businessman living in Italy with whom Dickens became friendly and whose wife he had attempted to help with mesmerism.
3. British writer and friend of Dickens'.
4. See *Illustrated London News* (March 4, 1854, p. 194): "The title of Mr. Dickens's new work is 'Hard Times.' His recent inquiry into the Preston strike is said to have originated the title, and, in some respects, suggested the turn of the story."
5. British author and publisher.

if in their wretched intervals of pleasure they read for amusement and do no worse. They are born at the oar, and they live and die at it. Good God, what would we have of them!

[From *Letter to Angela Burdett Coutts, March 17, 1854*]

* * *

A lady-friend of ours broke her leg at about the same time in very much the same manner. Do you think it would be good for her to hear half an hour of my new story? It contains that dawn of the idea and is not at all distressing—yet. If you would like it, as the publication begins tomorrow fortnight, I would come up any evening in the meantime, except Wednesdays.

[From *Letter to H. W. Wills, April 18, 1854*]

I am in a dreary state, planning and planning the story of Hard Times (out of materials for I don't know how long a story), and consequently writing little.

[From *Letter to Mrs. Elizabeth Gaskell,*[6] *April 21, 1854*]

I have no intention of striking.[7] The monstrous claims at domination made by a certain class of manufacturers, and the extent to which the way is made easy for working men to slide down into discontent under such hands, are within my scheme; but I am not going to strike. So don't be afraid of me.

[From *Letter to Frank Stone,*[8] *May 30, 1854*]

I stand engaged to dine * * * with one Buckle[9] * * * a man who has read every book that ever was written * * * and is a perfect Gulf of information. Before exploding a mine of knowledge he has a habit of closing one eye and wrinkling up his nose, so that he seems to be perpetually taking aim at you and knocking you over with a terrific charge. Then he loads again, and takes another aim. So you are always on your back, with your legs in the air.

6. Elizabeth Gaskell (1810–1865), British novelist, author of *Mary Barton* (1848) and *Cranford* (1853).
7. Gaskell's novel, *North and South*, which was to be published in *Household Words*, portrays a strike. She was concerned that if Dickens were to include scenes from a strike in *Hard Times* there might be duplication.
8. A successful self-taught British painter and Dickens' close friend.
9. H. T. Buckle, author of the *History of Civilization*. His emphasis on facts and statistics and his general set of values have similarities with the point of view of Mr. Gradgrind.

[From *Letter to Mark Lemon, June (?), 1854*]

But let us go somewhere, say to the public by the Thames where those performing dogs go at night. I think the travestie may be useful to me, and I may make something out of such an expedition; it will do us good after such a blue-devilish afternoon as this has been.

[From *Letter to Henry Cole,*[1] *June 17, 1854*]

I often say to Mr. Gradgrind that there is reason and good intention in much that he does—in fact, in all that he does—but that he over-does it. Perhaps by dint of his going his way and my going mine, we shall meet at last at some halfway house where there are flowers on the carpets, and a little standing-room for Queen Mab's Chariot[2] among the Steam Engines.

[From *Letter to Thomas Carlyle,*[3] *July 13, 1854*]

I am going, next month, to publish in One Volume a story now coming out in Household Words, called Hard Times. I have constructed it patiently, with a view to its publication altogether in a compact cheap form. It contains what I do devoutly hope will shake some people in a terrible mistake of these days, when so presented. I know it contains nothing in which you do not think with me, for no man knows your books better than I. I want to put in the first page of it, that it is inscribed to Thomas Carlyle. May I?

[From *Letter to W. H. Wills (from Boulogne, France)*
July 14, 1854]

I am so stunned with work, that I really am not able * * * to answer your questions. * * * I doubt if there will not be too much of Hard Times, to admit of the conclusion all going in together. There will probably be either 14 or 15 sides of my writing. But the best thing will be for me to come over with it, the moment I have finished. *On Wednesday night* [July 19] *at a quarter past ten,* I hope to be at London Bridge. * * * The MS now sent, contains what I have looked forward to through many weeks.

[From *Letter to John Forster, July 14, 1854*]

I am three parts mad, and the fourth delirious, with perpetual rushing at *Hard Times*. I have done what I hope is a good thing with

---

1. Secretary of the government's Department of Science and Art.
2. *Romeo and Juliet* 1.4.53 and 57.
3. See p. 4.

Stephen, taking his story as a whole; and hope to be over in town with the end of the book on Wednesday night. *** I have been looking forward through so many weeks and sides of paper to this Stephen business, that now—as usual—it being over, I feel as if nothing in the world, in the way of intense and violent rushing hither and thither, could quite restore my balance.

[From *Letter to W. H. Wills, July 17, 1854*]

I am happy to say that I have finished Hard Times this morning.

[From *Letter to Henry Carey*,[4] *August 24, 1854*]

I think it possible that I may have considered the powers and purposes of Fiction, a little longer and a little more anxiously and attentively, than your lady friend. To interest and affect the general mind in behalf of anything that is clearly wrong—to stimulate and rouse the public soul to a compassionate or indignant feeling that it *must not be*—without obtruding any pet theory of cause or cure, and so throwing off allies as they spring up—I believe to be one of Fiction's highest uses. And this is the use to which I try to turn it.

Nevertheless I promise myself the pleasure of reading your books. I am much obliged to you for the orders you send me, and will not fail to use them.

[From *Letter to Mrs. Richard Watson*,[5] *November 1, 1854*]

Why I found myself so "used up," after Hard Times, I scarcely know. Perhaps because I had intended to do nothing in that way for a year, when the idea laid hold of me by the throat in a very violent manner; and because the compression and close condensation necessary for that disjointed form of publication, gave me perpetual trouble. But I really was—tired!

[From *Letter to Charles Knight, December 30, 1854*]

Indeed there is no fear of my thinking you the owner of a cold heart. *** My satire is against those who see figures and averages, and nothing else—the representatives of the wickedest and most enormous vice of this time—the men who, through long years to come, will do more to damage the real useful truths of political economy, than I could do (if I tried) in my whole life—the addled

---

4. An American publisher and political scientist.
5. An aristocratic friend whose home, Rockingham Castle, Dickens used as the model for Chesney Wold in *Bleak House*.

heads who would take the average of cold in the Crimea during twelve months, as a reason for clothing a soldier in nankeen[6] on a night when he would be frozen to death in fur—and who would comfort the labourer in travelling twelve miles a day to and from his work, by telling him that the average distance of one inhabited place from another in the whole area of England, is not more than four miles. Bah! What have you to do with these?

6. Cotton cloth.

Industrialism

During the period in which *Hard Times* was conceived and written, a topic frequently brought to Dickens' attention was that of a bitterly contested strike that had broken out in the industrial north of England. This was at Preston, a textile-manufacturing town in Lancashire that Dickens himself eventually visited in late January 1854 and about which he wrote his article "On Strike" for *Household Words*. Other newspapers and magazines also made extensive reports on this strike, for Preston was regarded as a test case of the power of the trade unions, which after having declined in influence during the 1830s had made a remarkable recovery in the 1850s. At Preston, however, the union cause suffered a severe and painful defeat following a struggle that lasted more than eight months.

In the summer of 1853, after the Preston weavers were refused a 10 percent increase in wages, strikes were called at some of the textile mills. The mill owners responded, in late October, by closing all the mills in the town, and to obtain food and clothing the Preston strikers had thereafter to rely on subscriptions collected from union members in other manufacturing towns where the factories were still operating. In addition to such subscriptions, the union leaders relied on speeches and rallies to sustain morale throughout the lock-out, but as *The Illustrated London News* noted:

> Ignorant and violent speeches may keep up a fading enthusiasm for a short time longer, but the wintry cold, the fireless grate, the empty cupboard * * * will deprive the oratory of their leaders of the power to persuade them that no bread is better than half a loaf, or that charity wrung from their fellows is pleasanter to live upon than their own honest earnings.

This prediction, made on December 10, 1853, was accurate but premature. Not until late April 1854 did the strike collapse and the dispirited participants resume work in the mills. By May 1 the *Times* reported with satisfaction that 7,700 strikers had returned to their looms. Their leaders, George Cowell and Mortimer Grimshaw, whose speeches Dickens described, had been arrested in March on charges of conspiracy (although after the failure of the strike they were never brought to trial), but the principal reason for giving in seems to have been the drying up of the funds contributed from other towns, funds on which the Preston strikers had become entirely dependent.

Dickens' interest in factory conditions, stimulated by these events at Preston, led to his concern with another controversial topic: industrial safety. A gruesome report on accidents in factories, "Ground in the Mill," submitted by one of his contributors to *Household Words*, stirred Dickens deeply as an expression of his own feelings about the alleged negligence of factory owners and mine owners. So deeply was he stirred, in fact, that he inserted into the proofsheets of *Hard Times* a footnote specifically recommending this magazine article to the attention of his readers. Just before publication he decided to delete the footnote, a decision he could have made simply for artistic reasons, inasmuch as the intrusion of this kind of documentation would distract his readers from the realities of his fictional world. A more immediate reason for the deletion, however, was that he seemingly changed his mind about how openly and prominently the topic of industrial accidents ought to be treated in his novel. As the textual note indicates, he had originally planned to feature the topic in an important exchange between Stephen Blackpool and Rachael in book I, chapter XIII. In this original version, Stephen makes a "promise" to Rachael that he will refrain from meddling in controversies about industrial problems. This promise is made after Stephen has given vent to an outburst of indignation about persons in authority who are indifferent to industrial accidents, an outburst prompted by his recalling how Rachael's angelic little sister had suffered when her arm had been torn off by a factory machine.

Although the original scene and its footnote were canceled before publication, Dickens did not altogether bury his own indignation on the score of industrial accidents. Elsewhere in his novel he let stand a number of references to them, as in his account of the Old Hell Shaft in book III, chapter VI. These implied allegations against callous mill owners prompted a reply (pp. 335–38) by the essayist and novelist, Harriet Martineau—one of the most biting attacks ever made on Dickens as a social critic. Martineau's animosity may have been engendered not only by Dickens' general satire of laissez-faire economic theories (of which she was a passionate adherent) but also by some satirical references in chapter VIII of *Hard Times* to the kind of stories she herself had written and by which she had made her mark as a popular author. Her *Illustrations of Political Economy* (1831), with its tales of how to adapt to the capitalist system, might have provided the model for Dickens' reference to "leaden little books *** showing how the good grown-up baby invariably got to the savings-bank, and the bad grown-up baby invariably got transported."

For an informative study of this topic, see K. J. Fielding and Anne Smith, "*Hard Times* and the Factory Controversy: Dickens vs. Harriet Martineau," *Dickens Centennial Essays*, ed. Nisbet and Nevius (1971), pp. 22–45, and R. D. Butterworth, "Dickens the Novelist: The Preston Strike and *Hard Times*," *Dickensian* 88 (summer 1992): 91–102 (pp. 338–51 of this volume).

ANONYMOUS
[The Preston Strike: A History]†

THE WAGES MOVEMENT.—TERMINATION OF THE PRESTON STRIKE.

In the CHRONICLE of 1853, p. 56, will be found a short account of the general movement of the operative classes to obtain an advance of wages—an attempt which originated in the extraordinary extension of manufacturers and the export trade, and the high price of provisions. The plan of the leaders of the movement was avowedly to select a particular town for their operations, and particular firms in that town; by compelling the firms to succumb individually, to accomplish their aim in that particular district, and then to enforce the same move in another; by this means also the great mass of the workmen would always be employed and able to support such portion of them as might be "out on strike." The employers, on the other hand, were fully aware of the nature of the blow designed for them, and determined to meet the attack by a correspondent movement; and refusing to be plucked leaf by leaf, whenever a strike took place in one factory, the other firms in the same district instantly closed their works.

The contest was conducted on the part of the working classes with astonishing endurance. Preston and Burnley were the places chosen for their first operations, and in consequence the whole mass of workmen in those towns were thrown out of employment, and were supported by general contributions. In many other places there were partial strikes; but for the most part they were soon terminated, either by concession on the part of the employers, or by the people being persuaded that they would hurt the general cause by persevering. The great interest of the movement centred in Preston, where between 15,000 and 16,000 idle hands were supported by weekly contributions from the employed. The committee had a

† From the *Annual Register*, May 1854.

thorough organisation for collecting the funds, which were so successful, that upwards of 3000*l*. was thus distributed weekly; equal
to about 5*s*. a-head. The amount of misery entailed by this course
of proceeding is fearful to contemplate. Of course, each person did
not receive this sum—the skilled operative received more, the girl
or boy less; and on such miserable pittances did they support life, in
utter idleness, for thirty-seven weeks. The savings of the careful
man, the deposits of the provident, the sums insured for age and
sickness, melted away in support of the struggle. Their clothes and
personal ornaments were sold for trifles, where there were none to
purchase; their food became scanty, their habits sordid, their intercourse morose—still they struggled on with surprising endurance.
Nor were the evils confined to their own class. The retail trades
of the towns fell to nothing, and the shop-keepers were ruined;
numerous poor persons who, though not operatives, lived by the
requirements induced by active business, were reduced to utter
extremity, while the sources of charity were cut off. The numerous
trades, which in all parts of the kingdom are urged into activity by
the demands of the factories, languished, and the effects were thus
indirectly felt in all quarters. Again, though the operatives in other
seats of manufacture did not share in the strike, yet they maintained
the large number who did; and their contributions were so much
deducted from their own earnings, and abstracted from their own
sustenance; if they could part with this and not feel it, the condition
of the working class is not that of oppression that they represent; if
they did feel it, the privation induced by the subtraction of a small
percentage from a scanty income is very severe. Thus, the suffering
produced by the struggle they had entered into must have been great
and widely extended. But they bore it not with patience merely,
but with enthusiasm. "Ten per cent. and no surrender!" was the
general cry. The passion produced by this abstract idea is one of the
singular phenomena of the human mind. It seemed to have possessed
the minds of the working classes, in some districts, *as a religious faith;
nay, in one place, the people assembled in a chapel and sung a hymn
to Ten per Cent.*!

An incident occurred in March which showed the perfect control
under which the operatives kept themselves, and their complete
submission to their leaders. The employers of Preston, whose mills
had been idle all this time, sought labour in markets where it was to
be had, and introduced into the town some hundreds of Irish and
others. These persons the native workmen, by a watchful obstruc-
tion, and, perhaps, by a little bribery, prevented from fulfilling their
engagements. The employers then ventured on the dangerous step
of arresting the leaders, Cowell and others, on a charge of conspiracy, and the magistrates committed them for trial. But this pro-

ceeding produced no disturbance, and the workmen persevered in their plan of impoverishing the mill-owners into submission. But this contest between capital and labour never, save under very exceptional circumstances, can terminate in favour of the latter. The capitalist loses his gains, and some of his principal; he knows, too, that if he yields he is but postponing the loss of both for a short term, when it will come upon him with accumulated ruin; he therefore holds on in diminished splendour—in anxiety, perhaps, but free from physical suffering. With the day-labourer it is different: his misery is instant and personal, and destitution is heaped upon him in his wife, his children, in every one who approaches him. The contest can terminate but one way. In the course of April it became evident that matters were tending to this result. Nearly 8000 hands were found to be employed; and although still more than 12,000 persons were relieved, their allowances were reduced to a miserable pittance—the card-room hands received but 1s. a week. The subscriptions also from other towns began to fall off; and although large sums were contributed to their fund in a very mysterious manner, they could go but a small way in the support of so many. The movement was brought to an abrupt close by a departure from the plan of campaign laid down. The operatives of Stockport threw themselves out of work to the number of 18,000; and although this movement was speedily terminated by an advance of wages, the additional burden thrown on the industrious, and the withdrawal of the large sum contributed by Stockport to the Preston fund (200l. weekly), proved fatal to the strike at that place, in the 37th week of the struggle. On the 1st of May the Committee announced that the employers had succeeded in "their unholy crusade." They denounced the most bitter reproaches on the operatives generally, for deserting them "at a time when they more than ever needed their friendly counsel and assistance to conduct them with honour to the end;" and they admitted that the large donations said to have been found in their box were in fact loans, which required to be instantly repaid.

The men could not, of course, restore themselves instantly to the position they had voluntarily abandoned, and several thousands remained unemployed and in the utmost destitution for a long period after the termination of this misguided movement.

The sums expended in maintaining the idle workmen in Preston alone amounted to 100,000l.; the amount of earnings they forewent was certainly not less than thrice that sum; and it has been computed, on good grounds, that the abortive Preston strike cost the working classes, in direct losses, not less than 500,000l.

Cowell, the leader of the workmen, was soon after thrown into gaol, for debts incurred by him in promoting the strike.

314

ANONYMOUS

[An Ostracized Workman]†

TO THE EDITOR OF THE TIMES.

Sir,—Allow a working man to thank you for your able article on "strikes" in *The Times* of yesterday, and, to avoid waste of your valuable space, I will proceed at once to give you a case in point.

I was three months ago at work for a good master in a good shop, one among 200, and quite content, as was the majority, with the remuneration received—viz., 5s. per day. About this time trade meetings were convened to discuss the propriety of demanding an advance of 10 per cent., or 5s. 6d. per day, and a few of our men attended. A deputation was appointed and waited on our employer, with an intimation that, unless their demand was complied with, a "strike" would be the result. The master plainly stated that, having contracts on hand to a very great amount, the completion of which in a few months was insured by heavy penalties, he could not, without great pecuniary loss,—indeed, not without risk of failure,—at once grant their request, but that, if his men would remain at their work on the then terms, he would endeavour to make such arrangements as would enable him to meet their demand when a portion of his present contracts were worked out,—say, in five or six months; but, no; the deputation were not inclined to entertain anything so reasonable as this. Other meetings were called, at which some half-dozen "speakers" and "grand movers" used all their eloquence to prove employers tyrants and workmen slaves. The result was a "turn-out;" the great majority going out because they were afraid to be marked men, and because they had no confidence in each other, although they were convinced they were thereby doing their employer an injustice and running a risk of gaining a questionable advantage for themselves. After remaining idle some time the contracts pressed so much that our employer was compelled to succumb, and we all returned with the advance demanded. But mark the sequel. I and a great many others were in a short time discharged, and arrangements were made to extend the time for several large contracts, thereby dispensing with our services. Another result is, that the high rate of wages in town has drawn so many hands from the country, although there was no lack of workmen before the advance, that I have not been able since to procure a job at the new rate of wages; and, Sir, my case is the case of hundreds besides. To keep myself from starving, I offered to work in a large shop at the old rate of 5s., but as soon as this

† Letter to *The Times*, October 10, 1853.

became known I was literally hunted out of the shop, and I am now, no doubt, what is so much dreaded by all my class—a marked man.

I am not allowed to work for what my own conviction tells me is a fair remuneration, and cannot procure employment at the advanced rate, as no master is inclined to set on more workmen, under present circumstances, than will just complete what he is compelled by heavy penalties to finish in a given time.

Thus, Sir, you see that numbers may remain out of employment— a burden to themselves and to society—that those who are so lucky as to be retained may exult in having obtained a trifling advantage, which they are all along afraid (and not without reason) of losing every day. At the same time it is certain that had the "supply and demand" been duly considered, a strike or a rise would not have taken place, to throw us into this uncomfortable and ruinous state of affairs.

Your willingness to give ear to a poor man's grievances, and my cause to complain, must be my apology for troubling you with so long a letter.

I am, Sir, your obedient servant,

October 8.   A SUFFERER.

JAMES LOWE

From Locked Out[†]

Preston—situated upon the banks of the Ribble, some fifteen miles from the mouth of that river—is a good, honest, work-a-day looking town, built upon a magnificent site, surrounded by beautiful country; and, for a manufacturing town, wears a very handsome and creditable face. * * *

We pass out of the station, astonished to perceive that the atmosphere, instead of being thick and smoky, is as clear here as the air upon Hampstead Heath. An intelligent Prestonian explains that now, there are fifty tall chimneys cold and smokeless, and that ought to make a difference. Forty-one firms have "locked out" their hands, and twenty-one thousand workpeople are obliged to be at play. * * *

By this time we find ourselves on a level plain of marshy ground, upon the banks of the Ribble, and below the town of Preston. This is called THE MARSH, and it is at once the Agora and the Academe of the place. Here * * * do the mob-orators appear in times of trouble and contention, to excite, with their highly spiced eloquence, the thoughtless crowd; over whom they exercise such pernicious sway. * * * On one part of the marsh an old punt has stranded, and its

† From "Locked Out," in *Household Words,* December 1853.

deck forms a convenient rostrum for the hypæthral or open-air ora-
tors of Preston. A meeting is about to take place, over which John
Gruntle is to preside, and at which Cowler, Swindle, and O'Brigger
are expected to address the people. Presently, a small knot of persons get upon the deck of the punt, the crowd thickens round them.
* * * Gruntle is voted into the chair, and one of those meetings which
thirty years ago would have been a criminal offence is formally
opened.

Gruntle is not very prolix—he is an old stager, and used to these
things. In a few words he states the object of the meeting, and
announces to the audience that their friend Cowler will address
them. At this name a shout rends the air. Cowler is evidently the
chosen of the people; rightly or wrongly, they hold him in great
regard. His appearance is very much in his favour, for he wears the
look of a straightforward honest man; a smile plays round his
mouth as he steps forward with the air of a man sure of his audience; but the feverish and anxious expression of the eyes tells of
sleepless nights and of constant agitation? "Respected friends," he
begins; and, in a trice, he has plunged into the middle of the question. He has been accused, he says, of fostering agitation, and gaining advantage from the strike. Why, how can they say that, when
his constant cry has been for the masters to open their mills, and
give the operatives their just rights? Let them only do that, and he'll
soon show them how glad he'll be to give over agitating. It's not
such very pleasant work, either, is agitating. For example, he himself hasn't been to bed for these two nights. Last night they got the
money that their good friends in the neighbouring towns had sent
them; so he sat up to take care of it, for fear some one should come
and borrow it from them. (Laughter.) The editor of the London
Thunderer had been abusing him. Well! here was a thing! Twenty
years ago such a thing was never thought of as that a working man
should be noticed by a London paper. But the editor had not been
very courteous; he had called him "a fool," because he said that it
was a shame for the wives of the cotton lords to wear silks and satins, whilst the factory lasses were forced to be contented with plain
cotton. Was he a fool for that? ("Noa! Noa!" Great excitement among
the lasses, and exclamations of "Eh! Lord!")

To Cowler succeeds Swindle, a lean and hungry Cassius, the
very example of an agitator; a man who has lived by literary garbage, without fattening upon the unwholesome stuff. He seems
half tipsy; his eyes roll, and his gesticulations are vehement. One
more glass of whisky and he would be prepared to head an insur-
rection. He rants and raves for a quarter of an hour, and we are
pleased to observe that his audience are too sensible to care much
about him.

Then comes O'Brigger, oily-tongued, and with a brogue. He complains that it has been charged against 'um that he is an Irishman. So he is, faith! and he's moighty proud av it. The manufacturers are all av them toirants. However, this toime they will learrn that the people av England are not to be opprissed; for they will get such a flogging as never they had in the course av their lives. * * *

When O'Brigger has concluded, it is the turn of a crowd of the delegates to have their say. There is the delegate from this town, and the delegate from that factory; all with marvellous stories about the tyranny of the masters, the woes of the operatives, and the determination of each particular district to stand by Preston to the last. They all end by fiercely denouncing the manufacturers, whom they term "the miserable shoddyocracy," * * *

We walk sadly from "the Marsh," and reach a locked-up and smokeless factory, at the gates of which a knot of young girls are singing and offering for sale some of the Ten Per Cent. Songs, taking their name from the origin of the strike. In eighteen hundred and forty-seven, when trade was very bad, the masters told their workpeople that they could no longer afford to pay them the wages they had been paying, and that they must take off ten per cent.; upon the understanding, as the workpeople allege, that when times got better they would give them the ten per cent. back again. Whether such a promise was, or was not, actually given, we cannot presume to determine, for the masters emphatically deny it; but it is quite certain that, at the beginning of the present year, the Stockport operatives combined successfully to force the ten per cent. from *their* masters, and the Preston operatives aided them with funds. They acted upon Napoleon's principle of combining forces upon single points in succession, and so reducing the enemy in detail. Then it was that the Preston masters, fearing that similar tactics would be turned against themselves, combined to oppose the attempt, and eventually "locked out" their operatives. * * *

Again we sally out into the dingy streets, and find that the evening is closing in over them. More knots of "lads and lasses" idling about the corners, more bands of singers, solitary famine-stricken faces, too, plead mutely for bread, and even worse expedients are evidently resorted to for the purpose of keeping body and soul together: in Preston, as elsewhere, the facilities for crime are too abundant, and we repeat to ourselves those lines of Coleridge:—

Oh I could weep to think, that there should be
Cold-bosomed lewd ones, who endure to place
Foul offerings on the shrine of misery,
And force from Famine the caress of Love.

Ignorance of the most deplorable kind is at the root of all this sort of strife and demoralizing misery. Every employer of labour should write up over his mill door, that Brains in the Operative's Head is Money in the Master's Pocket.

CHARLES DICKENS

On Strike[†]

Travelling down to Preston a week from this date, I chanced to sit opposite to a very acute, very determined, very emphatic personage, with a stout railway rug so drawn over his chest that he looked as if he were sitting up in bed with his great coat, hat, and gloves on, severely contemplating your humble servant from behind a large blue and grey checked counterpane. In calling him emphatic, I do not mean that he was warm; he was coldly and bitingly emphatic as a frosty wind is.

"You are going through to Preston, sir?" says he, as soon as we were clear of the Primrose Hill tunnel.

The receipt of his question was like the receipt of a jerk of the nose; he was so short and sharp.

"Yes."

"This Preston strike is a nice piece of business!" said the gentleman. "A pretty piece of business!"

"It is very much to be deplored," said I, "on all accounts."

"They want to be ground. That's what they want, to bring 'em to their senses," said the gentleman; whom I had already began to call in my own mind Mr. Snapper, and whom I may as well call by that name here as by any other.

I deferentially enquired, who wanted to be ground?

"The hands," said Mr. Snapper. "The hands on strike, and the hands who help 'em."

I remarked that if that was all they wanted, they must be a very unreasonable people, for surely they had had a little grinding, one way and another, already. Mr. Snapper eyed me with sternness, and after opening and shutting his leathern-gloved hands several times outside his counterpane, asked me abruptly, "Was I a delegate?"

I set Mr. Snapper right on that point, and told him I was no delegate.

"I am glad to hear it," said Mr. Snapper. "But a friend to the Strike, I believe?"

"Not at all," said I.

†   From *Household Words*, February 11, 1854.

"A friend to the Lock-out?" pursued Mr. Snapper.

"Not in the least," said I.

Mr. Snapper's rising opinion of me fell again, and he gave me to understand that a man *must* either be a friend to the Masters or a friend to the Hands.

"He may be a friend to both," said I.

Mr. Snapper didn't see that; there was no medium in the Political Economy of the subject. I retorted on Mr. Snapper, that Political Economy was a great and useful science in its own way and its own place; but that I did not transplant my definition of it from the Common Prayer Book, and make it a great king above all gods. Mr. Snapper tucked himself up as if to keep me off, folded his arms on the top of his counterpane, leaned back, and looked out of window.

"Pray what would you have, sir," enquired Mr. Snapper, suddenly withdrawing his eyes from the prospect to me, "in the relations between Capital and Labor, *but* Political Economy?"

I always avoid the stereotyped terms in these discussions as much as I can, for I have observed, in my little way, that they often supply the place of sense and moderation. I therefore took my gentleman up with the words employers and employed, in preference to Capital and Labor.

"I believe;" said I, "that into the relations between employers and employed, as into all the relations of this life, there must enter something of feeling and sentiment; something of mutual explanation, forbearance, and consideration; something which is not to be found in Mr. McCulloch's dictionary, and is not exactly stateable in figures; otherwise those relations are wrong and rotten at the core and will never bear sound fruit."

Mr. Snapper laughed at me. As I thought I had just as good reason to laugh at Mr. Snapper, I did so, and we were both contented.

"Ah!" said Mr. Snapper, patting his counterpane with a hard touch. "You know very little of the improvident and unreasoning habits of the common people, *I* see."

"Yet I know something of those people, too," was my reply. "In fact, Mr.———," I had so nearly called him Snapper! "in fact, sir, I doubt the existence at this present time of many faults that are merely class faults. In the main, I am disposed to think that whatever faults you may find to exist, in your own neighbourhood for instance, among the hands, you will find tolerably equal in amount among the masters also, and even among the classes above the masters. They will be modified by circumstances, and they will be the less excusable among the better-educated, but they will be pretty fairly distributed. I have a strong expectation that we shall live to see the conventional adjectives now apparently inseparable from the phrases working people and lower orders, gradually fall into complete disuse for this reason."

"Well, but we began with strikes," Mr. Snapper observed impatiently. "The masters have never had any share in strikes."

"Yet I have heard of strikes once upon a time in that same county of Lancashire," said I, "which were not disagreeable to some masters when they wanted a pretext for raising prices."

"Do you mean to say those masters had any hand in getting up those strikes?" asked Mr. Snapper.

"You will perhaps obtain better information among persons engaged in some Manchester branch trades, who have good memories," said I.

Mr. Snapper had no doubt, after this, that I thought the hands had a right to combine?

"Surely," said I. "A perfect right to combine in any lawful manner. The fact of their being able to combine and accustomed to combine may, I can easily conceive, be a protection to them. The blame even of this business is not all on one side. I think the associated Lock-out was a grave error. And when you Preston masters—"

"*I* am not a Preston master," interrupted Mr. Snapper.

"When the respectable combined body of Preston masters," said I, "in the beginning of this unhappy difference, laid down the principle that no man should be employed henceforth who belonged to any combination—such as their own—they attempted to carry with a high hand a partial and unfair impossibility, and were obliged to abandon it. This was an unwise proceeding, and the first defeat."

Mr. Snapper had known, all along, that I was no friend to the masters.

"Pardon me," said I, "I am unfeignedly a friend to the masters, and have many friends among them."

"Yet you think these hands in the right?" quoth Mr. Snapper.

"By no means," said I; "I fear they are at present engaged in an unreasonable struggle, wherein they began ill and cannot end well."

Mr. Snapper, evidently regarding me as neither fish, flesh, nor fowl, begged to know after a pause if he might enquire whether I was going to Preston on business?

Indeed I was going there, in my unbusiness-like manner, I confessed, to look at the strike.

"To look at the strike!" echoed Mr. Snapper, fixing his hat on firmly with both hands. "To look at it! Might I ask you now, with what object you are going to look at it?"

"Certainly," said I. "I read, even in liberal pages, the hardest Political Economy—of an extraordinary description too sometimes, and certainly not to be found in the books—as the only touchstone of this strike. I see, this very day, in a to-morrow's liberal paper, some astonishing novelties in the politico-economical way, showing how profits and wages have no connexion whatever; coupled with such references to these hands as might be made by a very irascible General to rebels and brigands in arms. Now, if it be the case that some of the highest virtues of the working people still shine through them brighter than ever in their conduct of this mistake of theirs, perhaps the fact may reasonably suggest to me—and to others besides me—that there is some little thing wanting in the relations between them and their employers, which neither political economy nor Drum-head proclamation writing will altogether supply, and which we cannot too soon or too temperately unite in trying to find out."

Mr. Snapper, after again opening and shutting his gloved hands several times, drew the counterpane higher over his chest, and went to bed in disgust. He got up at Rugby, took himself and counterpane into another carriage, and left me to pursue my journey alone.

When I got to Preston, it was four o'clock in the afternoon. The day being Saturday and market-day, a foreigner might have expected, from among so many idle and not over-fed people as the town contained, to find a turbulent, ill-conditioned crowd in the streets. But, except for the cold smokeless factory chimneys, the placards at the street corners, and the groups of working people attentively reading them, nor foreigner nor Englishman could have had the least suspicion that there existed any interruption to the usual labours of the place. The placards thus perused were not remarkable for their logic certainly, and did not make the case particularly clear; but, considering that they emanated from, and were addressed to, people who had been out of employment for three-and-twenty consecutive weeks, at least they had little passion in them, though they had not much reason. Take the worst I could find:

> "FRIENDS AND FELLOW OPERATIVES,
>
> "Accept the grateful thanks of twenty thousand struggling Operatives, for the help you have showered upon Preston since the present contest commenced.
>
> "Your kindness and generosity, your patience and long-continued support deserve every praise, and are only equalled by the heroic and determined perseverance of the outraged and insulted factory workers of Preston, who have been struggling for some months, and are, at this inclement season of the year, bravely battling for the rights of themselves and the whole toiling community.

"For many years before the strike took place at Preston, the Operatives were the down trodden and insulted serfs of their Employers, who in times of good trade and general prosperity, wrung from their labour a California of gold, which is now being used to crush those who created it, still lower and lower in the scale of civilization. This has been the result of our commercial prosperity!—*more wealth for the rich and more poverty for the Poor*! Because the workpeople of Preston protested against this state of things,—because they combined in a fair and legitimate way for the purpose of getting a reasonable share of the reward of their own labour, the *fair dealing* Employers of Preston, to their eternal shame and disgrace, *locked up* their Mills, and at one fell swoop deprived, as they thought, from twenty to thirty thousand human beings of the means of existence. Cruelty and tyranny always defeat their own object; it was so in this case, and to the honour and credit of the working classes of this country, we have to record, that, those whom the rich and wealthy sought to destroy, the poor and industrious have protected from harm. This love of justice and hatred of wrong, is a noble feature in the character and disposition of the working man, and gives us hope that in the future, this world will become what its great architect intended, not a place of sorrow, toil, oppression and wrong, but the dwelling place and the abode of peace, plenty, happiness and love, where avarice and all the evil passions engendered by the present system of fraud and injustice shall not have a place.

"The earth was not made for the misery of its people; intellect was not given to man to make himself and fellow creatures unhappy. No, the fruitfulness of the soil and the wonderful inventions—the result of mind—all proclaim that these things were bestowed upon us for our happiness and well-being, and not for the misery and degradation of the human race.

"It may serve the manufacturers and all who run away with the lion's share of labour's produce, to say that the *impartial* God intended that there should be a *partial* distribution of his blessings. But we know that it is against nature to believe, that those who plant and reap all the grain, should not have enough to make a mess of porridge; and we know that those who weave all the cloth should not want a yard to cover their persons, whilst those who never wove an inch have more calico, silks and satins, than would serve the reasonable wants of a dozen working men and their families.

"This system of giving everything to the few, and nothing to the many, has lasted long enough, and we call upon the working people of this country to be determined to establish a new and improved system—a system that shall give to all who labour, a fair share of those blessings and comforts which their toil produce;

in short, we wish to see that divine precept enforced, which says, 'Those who will not work, shall not eat.'

"The task is before you, working men; if you think the good which would result from its accomplishment, is worth struggling for, set to work and cease not, until you have obtained the *good time coming*, not only for the Preston Operatives, but for yourselves as well.

"*By Order of the Committee.*
"*Murphy's Temperance Hotel, Chapel Walks,*
"*Preston, January 24th,* 1854."

It is a melancholy thing that it should not occur to the Committee to consider what would become of themselves, their friends, and fellow operatives, if those calicoes, silks, and satins, were *not* worn in very large quantities; but I shall not enter into that question. As I had told my friend Snapper, what I wanted to see with my own eyes, was, how these people acted under a mistaken impression, and what qualities they showed, even at that disadvantage, which ought to be the strength and peace—not the weakness and trouble—of the community. I found, even from this literature, however, that all masters were not indiscriminately unpopular. Witness the following verses from the New Song of the Preston Strike:

"There's Henry Hornby, of Blackburn, he is a jolly brick,
He fits the Preston masters nobly, and is very bad to trick;
He pays his hands a good price, and I hope he will never sever,
So we'll sing success to Hornby and Blackburn for ever.

"There is another gentleman, I'm sure you'll all lament,
In Blackburn for him they're raising a monument,
You know his name, 'tis of great fame, it was late Eccles
of honour,
May Hopwood, and Sparrow, and Hornby live for ever.

"So now it is time to finish and end my rhyme,
We warn these Preston Cotton Lords to mind for future time.
With peace and order too I hope we shall be clever,
We sing success to Stockport and Blackburn for ever.
        "Now, lads, give your minds to it."

The balance sheet of the receipts and expenditure for the twenty-third week of the strike was extensively posted. The income for that week was two thousand one hundred and forty pounds odd. Some of the contributors were poetical. As,

"Love to all and peace to the dead,
May the poor now in need never want bread.

three-and-sixpence." The following poetical remonstrance was appended to the list of contributions from the Gorton district:

> "Within these walls the lasses fair
> Refuse to contribute their share,
> Careless of duty—blind to fame,
> For shame, ye lasses, oh! for shame!
> Come, pay up, lasses, think what's right,
> Defend your trade with all your might;
> For if you don't the world will blame,
> And cry, ye lasses, oh, for shame!
> Let's hope in future all will pay,
> That Preston folks may shortly say—
> That by your aid they have obtain'd
> The greatest victory ever gained."

Some of the subscribers veiled their names under encouraging sentiments, as Not tired yet, All in a mind, Win the day, Fraternity, and the like. Some took jocose appellations, as A stunning friend, Two to one Preston wins, Nibbling Joe, and The Donkey Driver. Some expressed themselves through their trades, as Cobbler Dick, sixpence, The tailor true, sixpence, Shoemaker, a shilling, The chirping blacksmith, sixpence, and A few of Maskery's most feeling coachmakers, three and threepence. An old balance sheet for the fourteenth week of the Strike was headed with this quotation from MR. CARLYLE. "Adversity is sometimes hard upon a man; but for one man who can stand prosperity, there are a hundred that will stand adversity." The Elton district prefaced its report with these lines:

> "Oh! ye who start a noble scheme,
>   For general good designed;
> Ye workers in a cause that tends
>   To benefit your kind!
> Mark out the path ye fain would tread,
>   The game ye mean to play;
> And if it be an honest one,
>   Keep stedfast in your way!
>
> "Although you may not gain at once
>   The points ye most desire;
> Be patient—time can wonders work;
>   Plod on, and do not tire:
> Obstructions, too, may crowd your path,
>   In threatening, stern array;
> Yet flinch not! fear not! they may prove
>   Mere shadows in your way.

"Then, while there's work for you to do,
   Stand not despairing by,
Let 'forward' be the move ye make,
   Let 'onward' be your cry;
And when success has crowned your plans,
   'Twill all your pains repay,
To see the good your labour's done—
   Then droop not on your way."

In this list, "Bear ye one another's burthens," sent one Pound fifteen. "We'll stand to our text, see that ye love one another," sent nineteen shillings. "Christopher Hardman's men again, they say they can always spare one shilling out of ten," sent two and six-pence. The following masked threats were the worst feature in any bill I saw:

> "If that fiddler at Uncle Tom's Cabin blowing room does not pay Punch will set his legs straight.
> "If that drawer at card side and those two slubbers do not pay, Punch will say something about their bustles.
> "If that winder at last shift does not pay next week, Punch will tell about her actions."

But, on looking at this bill again, I found that it came from Bury and related to Bury, and had nothing to do with Preston. The Masters' placards were not torn down or disfigured, but were being read quite as attentively as those on the opposite side.

That evening, the Delegates from the surrounding districts were coming in, according to custom, with their subscription lists for the week just closed. These delegates meet on Sunday as their only day of leisure; when they have made their reports, they go back to their homes and their Monday's work. On Sunday morning, I repaired to the Delegates' meeting.

These assemblages take place in a cockpit, which, in the better times of our fallen land, belonged to the late Lord Derby for the purpose of the intellectual recreation implied in its name. I was directed to the cockpit up a narrow lane, tolerably crowded by the lower sort of working people. Personally, I was quite unknown in the town, but every one made way for me to pass, with great civility, and perfect good humour. Arrived at the cockpit door, and express-ing my desire to see and hear, I was handed through the crowd, down into the pit, and up again, until I found myself seated on the topmost circular bench, within one of the secretary's tables, and within three of the chairman. Behind the chairman was a great crown on the top of a pole, made of parti-coloured calico, and strongly suggestive of May-day. There was no other symbol or orna-ment in the place.

It was hotter than any mill or factory I have ever been in; but there was a stove down in the sanded pit, and delegates were seated close to it, and one particular delegate often warmed his hands at it, as if he were chilly. The air was so intensely close and hot, that at first I had but a confused perception of the delegates down in the pit, and the dense crowd of eagerly listening men and women (but not very many of the latter) filling all the benches and choking such narrow standing-room as there was. When the atmosphere cleared a little on better acquaintance, I found the question under discussion to be, Whether the Manchester Delegates in attendance from the Labor Parliament, should be heard?

If the Assembly, in respect of quietness and order, were put in comparison with the House of Commons, the Right Honorable the Speaker himself would decide for Preston. The chairman was a Preston weaver, two or three and fifty years of age, perhaps; a man with a capacious head, rather long dark hair growing at the sides and back, a placid attentive face, keen eyes, a particularly composed manner, a quiet voice, and a persuasive action of his right arm. Now look'ee heer my friends. See what t' question is. T' question is, sholl these heer men be heerd. Then 't cooms to this, what ha' these men got t' tell us? Do they bring mooney? If they bring mooney t'ords t' expenses o' this strike, they're welcome. For, Brass, my friends, is what we want, and what we must ha' (hear hear hear!). Do they coom to us wi' any suggestion for the conduct of this strike? If they do, they're welcome. Let 'em give us their advice and we will hearken to 't. But, if these men coom heer, to tell us what t' Labor Parliament is, or what Ernest Jones's opinions is, or t' bring in politics and differences amoong us when what we want is 'armony, brotherly love, and con-cord; then I say t' you, decide for yoursel' carefully, whether these men ote to be heerd in this place. (Hear hear hear! and No no no!) Chairman sits down, earnestly regarding delegates, and holding both arms of his chair. Looks extremely sensible; his plain coarse working man's shirt collar easily turned down over his loose Belcher neckerchief. Delegate who has moved that Manchester delegates be heard, presses motion—Mr. Chairman, will that delegate tell us, as a man, that these men have anything to say concerning this present strike and lock-out, for we have a deal of business to do, and what concerns this present strike and lock-out is our business and nothing else is. (Hear hear hear!)—Delegate in question will not compromise the fact; these men want to defend the Labor Parliament from certain charges made against them.—Very well, Mr. Chairman, Then I move as an amendment that you do not hear these men now, and that you proceed wi' business—and if you don't I'll look after you, I tell you that. (Cheers and laughter)—Coom lads, prove 't then!—Two or three hands for the delegates; all the rest for the business. Motion lost, amendment carried, Manchester deputation not to be heard.

But now, starts up the delegate from Throstletown, in a dreadful state of mind. Mr. Chairman, I hold in my hand a bill; a bill that requires and demands explanation from you, sir; an offensive bill; a bill posted in my town of Throstletown without my knowledge, without the knowledge of my fellow delegates who are here beside me; a bill purporting to be posted by the authority of the massed committee sir, and of which my fellow delegates and myself were kept in ignorance. Why are we to be slighted? Why are we to be insulted? Why are we to be meanly stabbed in the dark? Why is this assassin-like course of conduct to be pursued towards us? Why is Throstletown, which has nobly assisted you, the operatives of Preston, in this great struggle, and which has brought its contributions up to the full sevenpence a loom, to be thus degraded, thus aspersed, thus traduced, thus despised, thus outraged in its feelings by un-English and unmanly conduct? Sir, I hand you up that bill, and I require of you, sir, to give me a satisfactory explanation of that bill. And I have that confidence in your known integrity, sir, as to be sure that you will give it, and that you will tell us who is to blame, and that you will make reparation to Throstletown for this scandalous treatment. Then, in hot blood, up starts Gruffshaw (professional speaker) who is somehow responsible for this bill. O my friends, but explanation is required here! O my friends, but it is fit and right that you should have the dark ways of the real traducers and apostates, and the real un-English stabbers, laid bare before you. My friends when this dark conspiracy first began—But here the persuasive right hand of the chairman falls gently on Gruffshaw's shoulder. Gruffshaw stops in full boil. My friends, these are hard words of my friend Gruffshaw, and this is not the business—No more it is, and once again, sir, I, the delegate who said I would look after you, do move that you proceed to business!—Preston has not the strong relish for personal altercation that Westminster hath. Motion seconded and carried, business passed to, Gruffshaw dumb.

Perhaps the world could not afford a more remarkable contrast than between the deliberate collected manner of these men proceeding with their business, and the clash and hurry of the engines among which their lives are passed. Their astonishing fortitude and perseverance; their high sense of honor among themselves; the extent to which they are impressed with the responsibility that is upon them of setting a careful example, and keeping their order out of any harm and loss of reputation; the noble readiness in them to help one another, of which most medical practitioners and working clergymen can give so many affecting examples; could scarcely ever be plainer to an ordinary observer of human nature than in this cockpit. To hold, for a minute, that the great mass of them were not sincerely actuated by the belief that all these qualities were bound up in what they were doing, and that they were doing right, seemed to me little short of an impossibility. As the different delegates (some in the very dress in which they had left the mill last night) reported the amounts sent from the various places they represented, this strong faith on their parts seemed expressed in every tone and every look that was capable of expressing it. One man was raised to enthusiasm by his pride in bringing so much; another man was ashamed and depressed because he brought so little; this man triumphantly made it known that he could give you, from the store in hand, a hundred pounds in addition next week, if you should want it; and that man pleaded that he hoped his district would do better before long; but I could as soon have doubted the existence of the walls that enclosed us, as the earnestness with which they spoke (many of them referring to the children who were to be born to labor after them) of "this great, this noble, gallant, godlike struggle." Some designing and turbulent spirits among them, no doubt there are; but I left the place with a profound conviction that their mistake is generally an honest one, and that it is sustained by the good that is in them, and not by the evil.

Neither by night nor by day was there any interruption to the peace of the streets. Nor was this an accidental state of things, for the police records of the town are eloquent to the same effect. I traversed the streets very much, and was, as a stranger, the subject of a little curiosity among the idlers; but I met with no rudeness or ill-temper. More than once, when I was looking at the printed balance-sheets to which I have referred, and could not quite comprehend the setting forth of the figures, a bystander of the working class interposed with his explanatory forefinger and helped me out. Although the pressure in the cockpit on Sunday was excessive, and the heat of the room obliged me to make my way out as I best could before the close of the proceedings, none of the people whom I put to inconvenience showed the least impatience; all helped me, and all cheerfully acknowledged my word of apology as I passed. It is very probable, notwithstanding, that they may have supposed from my being there at all—I and my companion were the only persons present, not of their own order—that I was there to carry what I heard and saw to the opposite side; indeed one speaker seemed to intimate as much.

On the Monday at noon, I returned to this cockpit, to see the people paid. It was then about half filled, principally with girls and women. They were all seated, waiting, with nothing to occupy their attention; and were just in that state when the unexpected appearance of a stranger differently dressed from themselves, and with his own individual peculiarities of course, might, without offence, have had something droll in it even to more polite assemblies. But I stood there, looking on, as free from remark as if I had come to be paid with the rest. In the place which the secretary had occupied yesterday, stood a dirty little common table, covered with five-penny piles of halfpence. Before the paying began, I wondered who was going to receive these very small sums; but when it did begin, the mystery was soon cleared up. Each of these piles was the change for sixpence, deducting a penny. All who were paid, in filing around the building to prevent confusion, had to pass this table on the way out; and the greater part of the unmarried girls stopped here, to change, each a sixpence, and subscribe her weekly penny in aid of the people on strike who had families. A very large majority of these girls and women were comfortably dressed in all respects, clean, wholesome and pleasant-looking. There was a prevalent neatness and cheerfulness, and an almost ludicrous absence of anything like sullen discontent.

Exactly the same appearances were observable on the same day, at a not numerously attended open air meeting in "Chadwick's Orchard"—which blossoms in nothing but red bricks. Here, the chairman of yesterday presided in a cart, from which speeches were delivered. The proceedings commenced with the following sufficiently general and discursive hymn, given out by a workman from Burnley, and sung in long metre by the whole audience:

> "Assembled beneath thy broad blue sky,
> To thee, O God, thy children cry.
> Thy needy creatures on Thee call,
> For thou art great and good to all.
>
> "Thy bounty smiles on every side,
> And no good thing hast thou denied;
> But men of wealth and men of power,
> Like locusts, all our gifts devour.
>
> "Awake, ye sons of toil! nor sleep
> While millions starve, while millions weep;
> Demand your rights; let tyrants see
> You are resolved that you'll be free."

Mr. Hollins's Sovereign Mill was open all this time. It is a very beautiful mill, containing a large amount of valuable machinery, to which some recent ingenious improvements have been added.

Four hundred people could find employment in it; there were eighty-five at work, of whom five had "come in" that morning. They looked, among the vast array of motionless power-looms, like a few remaining leaves in a wintry forest. They were protected by the police (very prudently not obtruded on the scenes I have described), and were stared at every day when they came out, by a crowd which had never been large in reference to the numbers on strike, and had diminished to a score or two. One policeman at the door sufficed to keep order then. These eighty-five were people of exceedingly decent appearance, chiefly women, and were evidently not in the least uneasy for themselves. I heard of one girl among them, and only one, who had been hustled and struck in a dark street.

In any aspect in which it can be viewed, this strike and lock-out is a deplorable calamity. In its waste of time, in its waste of a great people's energy, in its waste of wages, in its waste of wealth that seeks to be employed, in its encroachment on the means of many thousands who are laboring from day to day, in the gulf of separation it hourly deepens between those whose interests must be understood to be identical or must be destroyed, it is a great national affliction. But, at this pass, anger is of no use, starving out is of no use—for what will that do, five years hence, but overshadow all the mills in England with the growth of a bitter remembrance?— political economy is a mere skeleton unless it has a little human covering and filling out, a little human bloom upon it, and a little human warmth in it. Gentlemen are found, in great manufacturing towns, ready enough to extol imbecile mediation with dangerous madmen abroad; can none of them be brought to think of authorised mediation and explanation at home? I do not suppose that such a knotted difficulty as this; is to be at all untangled by a morning-party in the Adelphi; but I would entreat both sides now so miserably opposed, to consider whether there are no men in England, above suspicion, to whom they might refer the matters in dispute, with a perfect confidence above all things in the desire of those men to act justly, and in their sincere attachment to their countrymen of every rank and to their country. Masters right, or men right; masters wrong, or men wrong; both right, or both wrong; there is certain ruin to both in the continuance or frequent revival of this breach. And from the ever-widening circle of their decay, what drop in the social ocean shall be free!

HENRY MORLEY

From Ground in the Mill[†]

"It is good when it happens," say the children,—"that we die before our time." Poetry may be right or wrong in making little operatives who are ignorant of cowslips say anything like that. We mean here to speak prose. There are many ways of dying. Perhaps it is not good when a factory girl, who has not the whole spirit of play spun out of her for want of meadows, gambols upon bags of wool, a little too near the exposed machinery that is to work it up, and is immediately seized, and punished by the merciless machine that digs its shaft into her pinafore and hoists her up, tears out her left arm at the shoulder joint, breaks her right arm, and beats her on the head. No, that is not good; but it is not a case in point, the girl lives and may be one of those who think that it would have been good for her if she had died before her time.

She had her chance of dying, and she lost it. Possibly it was better for the boy whom his stern master, the machine, caught as he stood on a stool wickedly looking out of window at the sunlight and the flying clouds. These were no business of his, and he was fully punished when the machine he served caught him by one arm and whirled him round and round till he was thrown down dead. There is no lack of such warnings to idle boys and girls. What right has a gamesome youth to display levity before the supreme engine. "Watch me do a trick!" cried such a youth to his fellow, and put his arm familiarly within the arm of the great iron-hearted chief. *"I'll* show you a trick," gnashed the pitiless monster. A coil of strap fastened his arm to the shaft, and round he went. His leg was cut off, and fell into the room, his arm was broken in three or four places, his ankle was broken, his head was battered; he was not released alive.

Why do we talk about such horrible things? Because they exist, and their existence should be clearly known. Because there have occurred during the last three years, more than a hundred such deaths, and more than ten thousand (indeed, nearly twelve thousand) such accidents in our factories, and they are all, or nearly all, preventible.

These few thousands of catastrophes are the results of the administrative kindness so abundant in this country. They are all the fruits of mercy. A man was lime-washing the ceiling of an engine-room: he was seized by a horizontal shaft and killed immediately. A boy was brushing the dust from such a ceiling, before whitewashing: he had a cloth over his head to keep the dirt from falling on him; by that cloth the engine seized and held him to administer a chastisement

† From *Household Words*, April 22, 1854.

with rods of iron. A youth while talking thoughtlessly took hold of a strop that hung over the shaft: his hand was wrenched off at the wrist. A man climbed to the top of his machine to put the strap on the drum: he wore a smock which the shaft caught; both of his arms were then torn out of the shoulder-joints, both legs were broken, and his head was severely bruised: in the end, of course, he died. What he suffered was all suffered in mercy. He was rent asunder, not perhaps for his own good; but, as a sacrifice to the commercial prosperity of Great Britain. There are few amongst us—even among the masters who share most largely in that prosperity—who are willing, we will hope and believe, to pay such a price as all this blood for any good or any gain that can accrue to them.

These accidents have arisen in the manner following. By the Factory Act, passed in the seventh year of Her Majesty's reign, it was enacted, among other things, that all parts of the mill-gearing in a factory should be securely fenced. There were no buts and ifs in the Act itself; these were allowed to step in and limit its powers of preventing accidents out of a merciful respect, not for the blood of the operatives, but for the gold of the mill-owners. It was strongly represented that to fence those parts of machinery that were higher than the heads of workmen—more than seven feet above the ground—would be to incur an expense wholly unnecessary. Kind-hearted interpreters of the law, therefore, agreed with mill-owners that seven feet of fencing should be held sufficient. The result of this accommodation—taking only the accounts of the last three years—has been to credit mercy with some pounds and shillings in the books of English manufacturers; we cannot say how many, but we hope they are enough to balance the account against mercy made out on behalf of the English factory workers thus:—Mercy debtor to justice, of poor men, women, and children, one hundred and six lives, one hundred and forty-two hands or arms, one thousand two hundred and eighty-seven (or, in bulk, how many bushels of) fingers, for the breaking of one thousand three hundred and forty bones, for five hundred and fifty-nine damaged heads, and for eight thousand two hundred and eighty-two miscellaneous injuries. It remains to be settled how much cash saved to the purses of the manufacturers is a satisfactory and proper off-set to this expenditure of life and limb and this crushing of bone in the persons of their work-people.

For, be it strictly observed, this expenditure of life is the direct result of that good-natured determination not to carry out the full provision of the Factory Act, but to consider enough done if the boxing-off machinery be made compulsory in each room to the height of seven feet from the floor. * * *

Manufacturers are to do as they please, and cut down in their own way the matter furnished for their annual of horrors. Only of this they are warned, that they must reduce it; and that, hereafter, the friends of injured operatives will be encouraged to sue for compensation upon death or loss of limb, and Government will sometimes act as prosecutor. What do we find now in the reports? For severe injury to a young person caused by gross and cognisable neglect to fence or shaft, the punishment awarded to a wealthy firm is a fine of ten pounds twelve shillings costs. For killing a woman by the same act of indifference to life and limb, another large firm is fined ten pounds, and has to pay one guinea costs. A fine of a thousand pounds and twelve months at the treadmill would, in the last case, have been an award much nearer the mark of honesty, and have indicated something like a civilised sense of the sacredness of human life. If the same firm had, by an illegal act of negligence, caused the death of a neighbour's horse, they would have had forty, fifty, sixty pounds to pay for it. Ten pounds was the expense of picking a man's wife, a child's mother, limb from limb.

SVEN BECKERT

[One of the Saddest Sights][†]

One of the saddest sights to this day is St. Michael's Flags in Manchester, a small park where allegedly forty thousand people, most of them cotton workers, lie buried in unmarked graves, one on top of the other, "an almost industrial process of burying the dead." Ellen Hootton was one of these rare exceptions. Unlike millions of others, she entered the historical record when in June 1833 she was called before His Majesty's Factory Inquiry Commission, which was charged with investigating child labor in British textile mills. Though only ten when she appeared before the committee and frightened, she was already a seasoned worker, a two-year veteran of the cotton mill. Ellen had drawn public attention because a group of middle-class Manchester activists concerned with labor conditions in the factories sprouting in and around their city had sought to use her case to highlight the abuse of children. They asserted that she was a child slave, forced to work not just in metaphorical chains, but in real ones, penalized by a brutal overseer.[1]

† From Sven Beckert, *Empire of Cotton: A Global History* (New York: Knopf, 2014), pp. 176–78. Copyright © 2014 by Sven Beckert. Used by permission of Alfred A. Knopf, an imprint of the Knopf Doubleday Publishing Group, a division of Penguin Random House LLC and Penguin Books Ltd. All rights reserved.
1. For the quotation, see forum post by "The Longford," March 9, 2009, www.skyscrapercity .com/showthread.php?t-823790, accessed March 8, 2013: Ellen Hootton's case is documented in House of Commons Parliamentary Papers, First Report of the Central Board of His Majesty's Commissioners for Inquiring into the Employment of Children in Factories, 1833, xx, D.i. 103–15. Her history has also been beautifully analyzed by

The commission, determined to show that the girl was a "notorious liar" who could not be trusted, questioned Ellen, her mother, Mary, and her overseer William Swanton, as well as factory manager John Finch. Yet despite their efforts to whitewash the case, the accusations proved to be essentially true: Ellen was the only child of Mary Hootton, a single mother, who was herself a handloom weaver barely able to make a living. Until she turned seven, Ellen had received some child support from her father, also a weaver, but once that expired her mother brought her down to a nearby factory to add to the family's meager income. After as many as five months of unpaid labor (it was said that she had to learn the trade first), she became one of the many children working at Eccles' Spinning Mill. When asked about her workday, Ellen said it began at five-thirty in the morning and ended at eight in the evening, with two breaks, one for breakfast and one for lunch. The overseer, Mr. Swanton, explained that Ellen worked in a room with twenty-five others, three adults, the rest children. She was, in her own words, a "piecer at throstles"—a tedious job that entailed repairing and reknotting broken threads as they were pulled onto the bobbin of the mule. With constant breakage, often several times a minute, she only had a few seconds to finish her task.

It was all but impossible to keep up with the speed of the machine as it moved back and forth, so she sometimes had "her ends down"—that is, she had not attached the loose and broken ends of the thread fast enough. Such errors were costly. Ellen reported being beaten by Swanton "twice a week" until her "head was sore with his hands." Swanton denied the frequency of the beatings, but admitted using "a strap" to discipline the girl. Her mother, who called her daughter "a naughty, stupid girl," testified that she approved of such corporal punishment, and had even asked Swanton to be more severe to put an end to her habit of running away. Life was hard for Mary Hootton, she desperately needed the girl's wages, and she begged Swanton repeatedly to keep on the girl, despite all the troubles. As Mary said, "I cries many a times."

The beatings, however, were not the worst treatment Ellen experienced at Swanton's hands. One day, when she arrived late to work, Swanton penalized her even more severely: He hung an iron weight around her neck (there was no agreement about whether it weighed sixteen or twenty pounds) and made her walk up and down the factory floor. The other children heckled her, and as a result, "she fell down several times while fighting with the other hands. She fought

Douglas A. Galbi, "Through the Eyes in the Storm: Aspects of the Personal History of Women Workers in the Industrial Revolution," *Social History* 21, no. 2 (1996): 142–59.

them with the stick." Even today, nearly two hundred years later, the pain of the girl's life, from the tedium of her work to the violence of her abuse, is hard to fathom.

While the city of Manchester sports a Rylands Library, Harvard University a Lowell student dormitory, and while every grade-school student learns about Richard Arkwright and Eli Whitney, there is of course no library or school named for Ellen Hooton. No one but a handful of historians knows anything about her life. Yet when we think about the world of cotton manufacturing, we should think of Ellen Hooton. Without her labor and that of millions of children, women, and men, the empire of cotton would have never been built. Neither Rylands nor Lowell would have accumulated their riches, and Arkwright's and Eli's inventions would have collected dust in the corner of a barn. Ellen's story highlights the physical violence of punishment, but as important, the more banal violence of economic desperation, which brought ever larger numbers of people into factories, where they spent their lives, quite literally, in the service of the empire of cotton.

HARRIET MARTINEAU

From The Factory Legislation[†]

*** A good many people have wondered before that Mr. Dickens, who has such a horror of Poor-law reform, and who acted the part of sentimental philanthropist in "Oliver Twist," by charging the faults of the repealed law upon the new one, and other devices common to that order of pleaders, should have fallen foul afterwards of the prison reformers and the African missionaries,[1] and certain other philanthropic adventurers. But there was the excuse that he was a novelist; and no one was eager to call to account on any matter of doctrine a very imaginative writer of fiction. It might be a pity, as a matter of taste, that a writer of fiction should choose topics in which political philosophy and morality were involved; but the criticism was willingly restricted to this. But Mr. Dickens himself changed the conditions of his responsibilities and other people's judgments when he set up "Household Words" as an avowed agency of popular

---

[†] From Harriet Martineau, *The Factory Controversy: A Warning against Meddling Legislation* (Manchester: National Association of Factory Occupiers, 1855), pp. 35–45,
1. An allusion to Dickens' novel *Bleak House*, in which he had satirized Mrs. Jellyby's zealous philanthropic activities on behalf of an imaginary African state, Borrioboola-Gha. On the publication of *Oliver Twist* (1837) Dickens was criticized for damning Poor laws that had already been repealed in favor of somewhat more humane regulations [*editor*].

instruction and social reform. From that time, it was not only the right but the duty of good citizens to require from him some soundness of principle and some depth of knowledge in political philosophy. It is not within our scope now to show how conspicuous has been Mr. Dickens's proved failure in the department of instruction upon which he spontaneously entered. We need refer to only a single instance out of many,—as his Tale of "Hard Times." On this occasion, again, the plea of those who would plead for Charles Dickens to the last possible moment is that "Hard Times" is fiction. A more effectual security against its doing mischief is that the Tale, in its characters, conversations, and incidents, is so unlike life,—so unlike Lancashire or English life,—that it is deprived of its influence. Master and man are as unlike life in England, at present, as Ogre and Tom Thumb: and the result of the choice of subject is simply, that the charm of an ideal creation is foregone, while nothing is gained in its stead. But a much greater responsibility is incurred by Mr. Dickens, in the more recent papers in "Household Words," in which this Factory Controversy is treated of. Who wrote the papers we do not know, and it is of no importance to inquire. Mr. Dickens is responsible for them and, whoever may be his partner in the disgrace of them, he alone stands before the world as answerable for their contents ***

A very few citations will sustain our rebuke. The society of mill-occupiers is entitled, by Mr. Dickens or his contributor "The National Association for the Protection of the Right to Mangle Operatives." *** He makes the extraordinary statement that "these deadly shafts" "mangle or murder, every year, two thousand human creatures:" and, considering the magnitude of this exaggeration (our readers will remember that the average of deaths by factory shafts is twelve per year), it is no wonder that he finds fault with figures, when used in reply to charges so monstrous. When the manufacturers produced facts in answer to romance about the numbers concerned, he presents them as reading out of "Death's cyphering book," and proceeds to beg the question, as usual, in such language as this:—"As for ourselves, we admit freely that it never did occur to us that it was possible to justify, by arithmetic, a thing unjustifiable by any code of morals, civilized or savage;" this "justification" being a quoting of the coroners' returns by which "it appears that, out of 858 accidents occasioning loss of life, only 29, or 3½ per cent, had been occasioned by factory machinery" of any kind whatever. "Three and a half per cent!" exclaims Mr. Dickens or his contributor. "The argument is of a substantial character." If he assigns his number, of 2,000 a year, his opponents may surely cite theirs, of 3½ per cent, or 12 in a year. But Mr. Dickens cannot endure a comparative number which may diminish the show he makes with a positive one. He follows up, and improves upon, Mr. Homer's horror at the penalty of Ten Pounds,—adopting, of course, without a hint of there being a doubt in the case, the statement that a few hooks, costing a few shillings, would have saved the life of the poor reckless fellow Ashworth, who, as we have seen, threw it away. "When," says the writer "the mill-owner sets that price (ten pounds) on his workman's brains, who can wonder if the workman sets a price still lower on his master's heart!" The mingled levity and fustian of the style of the specimens we have quoted will neutralise their mischief to educated people; but the responsibility of presenting such pictures, and offering such sentiment, to a half-educated order of readers, is such as few writers would like to be burdened with. We do not believe that there will be any outbreak in factory districts about this matter, with or without Mr. Dickens's incitement; because the factory people understand the value of casings and hooks better than he does; and because an amendment and elucidation of the law may be considered only a question of time; but Mr. Dickens had better consider, for the sake of his own peace of mind, as well as the good of his neighbors, how to qualify himself for his enterprise before he takes up his next task of reform. If he must give the first place to his idealism and sensibilities, let him confine himself to fiction; and if he will put himself forward as a social reformer, let him do the only honest thing,—study both sides of the question he takes up. * * *

We must say that a mission to Borrioboola-Gha is an innocent enterprise, in comparison with that which Mr. Dickens has undertaken on behalf of meddling and mischievous legislation like that of the fencing clauses of the Factory Acts. If we had room, and if our object was to convict the humanity-monger in "Household Words" of all his acts of unfairness and untruth, we should go into the case of the boy in Mr. Cheetham's factory, who, in defiance of remonstrance, thrust himself into the extremity of danger, and was killed on the instant; and of the overlooker at Bury, George Hoyle, aged 50, of whom his comrades said at the inquest, "It was entirely his own fault; the shaft was quite out of the way of everybody, and unless a person wilfully did something that he ought not to do, he could not be injured by that shaft." * * * Such cases as these, set off with ironical descriptions of split brain, puddles of blood, crushed bones, and torn flesh, are exhibited as spectacles for which the masters are answerable, and which they obstinately prefer to an expenditure of a few shillings to make all safe. If Mr. Dickens really believes in such a state of things as he describes, he should not meddle with affairs in which rationality of judgment is required; and if he can be satisfied to represent the great class of manufacturers—unsurpassed for intelligence, public spirit, and

beneficence—as the monsters he describes, without seeking knowledge of their actual state of mind and course of life, we do not see
how he can complain of being himself classed with the pseudo-
philanthropists whom he delights to ridicule. He has exposed philo-
criminal, and philo-heathen cant; but his own philo-operative cant
is quite as irrational as either, while it has the distinction of being
far more mischievous. The danger is less than it was. In Luddite
times, Mr. Dickens might have been answerable for the burning of
mills and the assassination of masters; and if no deadly mischief
follows now, it will be because the workers understand their own
case better than he does. The benevolence of their employers, educating them long before the Factory Law made education compulsory, and feeding them in times of hardship, has generated a mutual
understanding, and a common intelligence, which go far to render
Mr. Dickens's representations harmless; but not for this is his
responsibility the less. If the names of Dickens and Jellyby are
joined in a firm as humanity-mongers in the minds of his readers,
the gentleman may resent being so yoked with a noodle; but the
lady might fairly plead that her mission had no mischief in it, if no
good,—no exciting fierce passions and class hostilities through
false principles and insufficient knowledge. In conceit, insolence,
and wilful one-sidedness, the two mission-managers may compare
with each other; but the people of Borrioboola-Gha could hardly be
so lowered and insulted by any ministrations of Mrs. Jellyby as the
Lancashire operatives would be if Mr. Dickens could succeed in
reviving on their behalf the legislation which their ancestors out-
grew some centuries ago.

✳   ✳   ✳

R. D. BUTTERWORTH

Dickens the Novelist: The Preston Strike
and *Hard Times*[†]

Dickens's visit to Preston in January 1854 was made as he was planning the novel which began to be serialised in *Household Words* in
April of the same year as *Hard Times*. It remains contentious, however, whether he eventually made much direct use of his Preston
visit in *Hard Times*; and it is questionable how much he could have
hoped to get out of a visit of a bare forty-eight hours. He could
remind himself, but little more, of the general cast of life in the

† From *Dickensian* 88.2 (Summer 1992): 91–102. Reprinted by permission of the author.

industrial North, his depiction of which remains that of an outsider. His descriptions of Coketown lack the intimacy of someone
who had lived in industrial Lancashire rather than merely visited it:
the two extended descriptions of Coketown, in *Hard Times* I,5 and
II, I, are mainly of the outsides of the buildings, and in the latter
case, of the town seen from a distance. His brief and vague description of the inside of Stephen Blackpool's lodgings—'A few books
and writings were on an old bureau in a corner, the furniture was
decent and sufficient, and though the atmosphere was tainted, the
room was clean' (I,10)[1]—contrasts starkly with, for instance, Elizabeth Gaskell's very detailed description of the interior of the Barton
household in chapter two of *Mary Barton*; and the bitterly ironic
key image of the factories as 'Fairy Palaces' is significantly that of
'travellers by express-train' (I,10), who have not lingered in Coketown, have not seen the factories close up, and know little of conditions inside them.

What Dickens could hope to gain, however, was some first-hand
experience of what unions were like and of the temper of a town
on strike. Such experience was indeed what interested Dickens
in Preston, as his article 'On Strike[2] reveals, and it has usually been
assumed that it is the chapters in *Hard Times* dealing with the union
that are most directly derived from what he saw during his Preston
visit.

It has often been pointed out, however, that the picture of Slackbridge and the United Aggregate Tribunal does not accurately
reflect what is known about George Cowell and the activities of the
Preston weavers' union;[3] even the account in 'On Strike' gives a very
different, much more sympathetic picture than the hostile portrait
in *Hard Times*. Dickens's surprising portrayal of the union has furthermore become, at least since F. R. Leavis's important essay on
the novel, the major crux of the novel; for as Leavis comments,
'Dickens has no glimpse of the part to be played by Trade Unionism
in bettering the conditions he deplored'.[4] In essence this is perhaps
an argument from history. Unions were later to play a very important
role in improving the lot of working people, and were not to be the
mere instruments of demagogues for causing civil strife that seems
to be Dickens's version of them. This in turn raises the question of
how Dickens could be so wrong about the nature and intentions of

1. All quotations from *Hard Times* are from the Oxford Illustrated Dickens edition
(Oxford, 1955).
2. *Household Words*, 8, 11 Feb. 1854.
3. This problem has been discussed in, for instance, 'Dickens, Mrs. Gaskell, and the Preston Strike'—G. Carnall, *Victorian Studies*, vol. 13, 1964, pp. 31–48 and '*Hard Times*
and the *Times* Newspaper'—A. Smith, *Dickensian*, vol. 69, 1973, pp. 153–62.
4. F. R. Leavis, *The Great Tradition* (London, 1948), p. 246.

unions, especially after observing the Preston weavers' union at first hand.

The matter is more complicated than might be imagined. One of the bases on which it has been contended that Dickens deliberately falsified his own experience in creating his fictional union has been the character of George Cowell. For Cowell, a Methodist and teetotaler[5] who became pre-eminent among the union leaders in the Preston Strike, was upright, restrained and reasonable, and not at all of the same mettle as Dickens's Slackbridge. Initially Cowell had been antipathetic to the idea of striking.[6] In July 1853, strikes at two Preston mills were ended when Cowell persuaded the operatives to return to work and not long after he was associated with a view that 'extreme measures in the shape of a strike should not be resorted to.'[7] After the Masters' Association announcement on 15 September 1853 that a general lock-out would begin one month later, he urged the opening of negotiations so that a peaceful settlement could be reached.[8] His attitude during the strike itself remained conciliatory. In January 1854 he made a major concession in expressing a willingness that negotiations should proceed mill by mill, the masters holding discussions with their own employees rather than with the delegates' committee,[9] and at the very time of Dickens's visit to Preston, Cowell was declaring that the strike could be ended by a meeting of equal numbers of masters and operatives 'to discuss the question calmly with a view to an amicable settlement' or by submitting the matter to arbitration.[1] Even as antagonistic an observer as the industrialist Henry Ashworth was to acknowledge that 'he may be pronounced a man who would do honour to a juster cause'.[2]

Cowell, however, seems to have played no prominent part at the Sunday delegates' meeting that Dickens attended, and may not even have been present,[3] certainly he was not present at the Mon-

5. H. I. Dutton and J. E. King, 'Ten Per Cent and No Surrender': The Preston Strike 1853–1854 (Cambridge, 1981), vol. 1. p. 46.
6. Dutton and King, I, p. 31.
7. "'A fallacy, a delusion, and a snare': Arbitration and Conciliation in the Preston Strike, 1853–4"—H. I. Dutton and J. E. King, Transactions of the Historic Society of Lancashire and Cheshire, vol. 131. Dutton and King, II, p. 70.
8. Dutton and King I, p. 42. See also Dutton and King II, p. 70.
9. Dutton and King II, p. 71.
1. In addressing the Society of Arts' Conference on Strikes and Lockouts: cf. Supplement to the Journal of the Society of Arts, vol. 2, 1854, p. 204.
2. Henry Ashworth, The Preston Strike, An Enquiry into its Causes and Consequences (Manchester, 1854), p. 27. Ashworth later acknowledges (p. 29) that the leaders of the strike 'exerted, upon the whole, a useful influence in repressing violence, and restraining the operatives within the limits of moral force'.
3. The reports of the Sunday meeting in the Preston Chronicle (4 Feb. 1854), Preston Guardian (4 Feb. 1854), Preston Pilot (4 Feb. 1854), The Times (31 Jan. 1854), Manchester Guardian (1 Feb. 1854) and Reynolds's Newspaper (5 Feb. 1854) make no mention of Cowell, though it should be noted that some of these reports are very brief.

day meeting for he was in London on that day attending the Society of Arts' conference on strikes. Furthermore, the Sunday meeting was, as H. I. Dutton and J. E. King comment, 'more than usually fractious',[4] full of what the *Preston Chronicle* called 'wordy wars'.[5] In the course of the meeting, Mortimer Grimshaw (Dickens's Gruffshaw), on whom Slackbridge seems to be based, 'poured out a volley of invective',[6] or in the words of the *Manchester Guardian*, 'poured out the vials of his wrath upon the committee and the operatives' of Warrington.[7]

Grimshaw, prominent at both the Sunday and Monday meetings Dickens attended (though his contribution to the latter meeting was probably after Dickens's departure), had something of the firebrand about him. Known as the 'Thunderer of Lancashire', Mortimer Grimshaw was a weaver who, by his own account, was blacklisted in every mill in Lancashire. He had been involved in earlier campaigning in the industrial field, both the strengthening and full enforcement of the Factory Acts, and against the victimisation of political activists at a mill in Royton, where he had lived: and he had taken part in the 'Ten per cent' campaign from as early as March 1853 in Stockport.[8] At the end of the strike, Charles Hardwick recorded some impressions of Grimshaw in an article in *Eliza Cook's Journal*:

> He was well known by his white hat, which, I suppose, he wore after the fashion of Hunt and Cobbett, to indicate the depth of his 'Radical' propensities. . . . Mortimer Grimshaw advocates liberty to the oppressed 'factory slaves' with a dogmatical invective . . . more worthy of a Russian despot than an English patriot. I do not assert that he is insincere. . . . He appears to me to be an enthusiast, and that the warmth of his feelings, when excited, overpowers his judgment.[9]

Henry Ashworth, as might be expected, gives a less sympathetic account.

> Of Mr. Grimshaw, the less that is said the better. We have heard it alleged, that every wild and violent sentiment which was uttered during the Preston strike came from his lips. He was commonly introduced as the 'Thunderer of Lancashire'. In his speeches we find the perfection of mob oratory. 'He's a stunner,' exclaimed an old woman at the close of one of his

4. Dutton and King I, p. 111.
5. *Preston Chronicle*, 4 Feb. 1854.
6. *Ibid.*
7. *Manchester Guardian*, 1 Feb. 1854.
8. Dutton and King I, p. 46.
9. *Eliza Cook's Journal*, 227, 19 August, 1854: cited in Dutton and King I, p. 47.

perorations; to which an admiring operative who had heard
her, replied, perhaps truthfully,—'he's nowt else.'[1]

How Grimshaw earned his living was something of a mystery, and
this gave rise to accusations that he was a 'self-interested professional agitator.[2] He can thus be seen as a clear source for much of
the character of Slackbridge; and to this extent, given the prominence
of Grimshaw rather than Cowell at these meetings, Dickens's portrait might be said to be a reflection of what he saw.

Nevertheless, other strike leaders Dickens observed were quite
unlike Grimshaw. The chairman of the two meetings Dickens
attended, Kinder Smith, a man of similar ilk to Cowell, is described
sympathetically by Dickens as a man with 'a placid attentive face,
keen eyes, a particularly composed manner, a quiet voice', who
glances at other delegates 'earnestly' and 'Looks extremely sensible'.[3]
His is a successfully restraining influence on wilder men: 'the persuasive right hand of the chairman falls gently on Gruffshaw's
shoulder. Gruffshaw stops in full boil.'[4] The whole meeting, indeed,
is commended for its 'quietness and order.'[5]

Such pieces of description also indicate that Dickens's perception of unions was not blinkered by the sort of prejudices which
Humphry House identifies as common at the time, such as that 'the
leaders of such unions were bound to be demagogic frauds',[6] though
such attitudes are not hard to find reflected in accounts of the
Preston Strike. A letter in the *Preston Chronicle* of the weekend of
Dickens's visit for instance refers to 'these paid demagogues' and
'the vagabond banditti styling themselves delegates, who, with the
basest effrontery, are sucking to the very heart's-core the life's-
blood of their deluded victims'.[7] In similar vein, Henry Ashworth
writes of the workers' 'ignorance', which makes them 'the more
docile', for 'where they do not see clearly, they submit to be led'; and
'a mass of operatives of this character offers a fine field for the
demagogue'.[8] Dickens, however, was hardly a natural ally of men
like Henry Ashworth, and it is questionable whether their views
would coincide very much. Indeed, as P. Brantlinger points out,
Dickens scorns such attitudes through Stephen Blackpool's rejection
of Bounderby's theory of 'mischievous strangers',[9] and the evidence

1. Ashworth, *op.cit.*, pp. 28–9. On the personalities and behaviour of Cowell and Grimshaw, see also Carnall, *op.cit.* esp. pp. 34ff, 40f.
2. Dutton and King I, p. 46.
3. 'On Strike', *op.cit.*
4. *Ibid.*
5. *Ibid.*
6. H. House, *The Dickens World* (Oxford, 1960 edition), p. 209.
7. *Preston Chronicle*, 28 Jan. 1854.
8. Ashworth, *op.cit.*, pp. 26–7.
9. P. Brantlinger, 'The Case Against Trade Unions in Early Victorian Fiction', *Victorian
Studies*, vol. 13, 1969, p. 48.

of 'On Strike' is that Dickens sees the strikers and their union in a rather different light.

It is, then, not easy to explain Dickens's attitude to the unions on the basis of his visit to Preston; and an explanation is perhaps to be found rather in considering the broader background to the writing of the novel. For, if 'On Strike' is an impressionistic account of the Preston Strike, it can be argued that *Hard Times* is also impressionistic—this time about the state of England—and that it is a novel to which Dickens's visit to Preston was in some ways incidental. It does not concern itself with a particular real-life union, let alone a particular strike (there is, of course, no strike in the novel); Dickens is concerned no more than in 'On Strike' with minutiae, but rather with a perception of a diseased society. Part of the context is that of other 'Condition of England' novels. There are, however, some specific features of the background to the novel that are particularly important to *Hard Times*.

The period of the Preston Strike was a time of considerable industrial unrest. Though none of them was epoch-making, strikes were rampant:

> In the spring of 1853 there developed throughout the country a movement for higher wages. . . . The Manchester brickmakers struck in January, followed in February by masons and joiners at Ashton, and by farm labourers near Salisbury. March saw strikes in several Liverpool crafts, in the Batley and Dewsbury woollen mills, and on the land in Oxfordshire. In April boys struck at a Liverpool engine works and a shipyard at Birkenhead, and strikes broke out among waggonwrights and bricklayers at South Shields, seamen at Ipswich, Liverpool shoemakers, brickmakers and joiners at Wigan, and the joiners of Sutherland and Hartlepool.[1]

Henry Ashworth recalled industrial unrest over wages running through 'the whole of 1852 and the first half of 1853', agitation which, he noted, 'was not confined to those northern districts, or indeed to any particular trade, but spread pretty equally throughout the kingdom':

> Commencing with those employed in the production of iron and coal, it passed through most of the building trades, affected the branches of industry which are connected with Nottingham and Leicester, and even extended to the porters and dock labourers of such towns as Liverpool, Bristol and Hull. In some places, as in Manchester and Liverpool, the police struck for an advance of wages. . . . Agricultural strikes

1. Dutton and King I, p. 27.

were now heard of. . . . A rise of wages was also universal in
the ship-yards of the Clyde and the Wear, the Mersey and the
Thames.[2]

It is little wonder that an article which appeared in the same issue
of the *Illustrated London News* as a piece on the Preston Strike
adopted a tone intended to be reassuring. 'Sketches of Strikes and
Riots in the Cotton Districts' sought to calm any anxieties the
reader may have had about the spate of strikes by emphasising that
strikes, far from being a worrying new phenomenon, pre-dated the
Industrial Revolution:

> though most persons who have written of them date their com-
> mencement at the period when spinning mills arose—namely,
> between 1765 and 1769. Strikes were as frequent before the
> invention of the jenny in 1765 as since; but they affected fewer
> persons.[3] It was in the context of a society in this state that
> Dickens came to write about the industrial world and to por-
> tray an England splitting into contentious factions willing to
> use their collective power to gain the ends of their members.[4]

Contemporary views of industrial relations, unions and strikes, furthermore, included certain elements somewhat uncommon in later
views. 'On Strike' itself raises the issue of whether terms like 'Capital' and 'Labour' should be used in preference to 'employers' and
'employed' and the phenomenon of contemporary documents,
which sometimes use the one set of terms and sometimes the other,
indicates that this was a period of transition in the public's perception of the industrial world.[5] To use words like 'Capital' and 'Labour'
in connection with industrial relations is to see them from what
may be very broadly called a political point of view; and this is probably the most common view of industrial relations today. In the
1850s, however, many people's perspective on them was rather, the
evidence suggests, moral, and religious. It is necessary to go no
further than 'On Strike' to find evidence of this. The placard tran-
scribed by Dickens refers to

2. Ashworth, *op.cit.*, pp. 5–6.
3. *Illustrated London News*, 12 Nov. 1853.
4. Preston itself formed a good example of the factionalism Dickens attacks in *Hard Times*, and not only because the workers had become organised into unions. The Preston employers had long had an association: 'As early as the 1820s the Masters' Association in Preston was regarded as one of the strongest in Lancashire' (Dutton and King I, p. 21). Its history went back continuously, however, 'no further than the great strike of 1836' (*Ibid*. p. 20). Nevertheless, as such, it was one of the oldest Masters' Associations. In 1853, the Masters' Association was revived before the Preston spinners' union began its agitation; the Preston weavers only formed a combination a couple of months later: cf. Dutton and King I, pp. 28–31.
5. Cf. the vacillation between the two sets of terms among speakers at the Society of Arts' Conference on Strikes and Lockouts in the account given in *Supplement to the Journal of the Society of Arts*, *op.cit.*, pp. 189–207.

> This love of justice and hatred of wrong . . . a noble feature in the character and disposition of the working man . . . gives us hope that in the future this world will become what its great architect intended, not a place of sorrow, toil, oppression and wrong, but the dwelling place and abode of peace, plenty, happiness and love, where avarice and all the evil passions engendered by the present system of fraud and injustice shall not have a place.

The manufacturers, furthermore, are attacked for their contention that 'the *impartial* God intended that there should be a *partial* distribution of his blessings'. Much Biblical or pseudo-Biblical phraseology and imagery—'the fruitfulness of the soil', 'plant and reap all the grain', 'a mess of porridge'—is used, and the Biblical precept 'Those who will not work, shall not eat' is cited. Soubriquets on a balance-sheet include 'Bear ye one another's burthens' and 'We'll stand to our text, see that ye love one another'. A hymn sung—at the Monday meeting of the strikers is quoted:

> To thee, O God, thy children cry
> Thy needy creatures on thee call
> . . . no good thing hast thou denied
> But men of wealth and men of power
> Like locusts, all our gifts devour.

The hymn ends with an exhortation to 'ye sons of toil' to

> Demand your rights; let tyrants see
> You are resolved that you'll be free.

Many similar references may be cited. Around the time of Dickens's visit, a correspondent of the *Preston Pilot*, deploring 'these ruinous and devastating "strikes" which are the order of the day, and which rage like a pestilence around us', averred that 'In that blessed curse,—"By the sweat of thy brow thou shalt eat bread", we have politics in perfection.[6] A letter to the *Preston Chronicle* refers to the strike as 'the present unfortunate, un-English, anti-Christian struggle[7] and one to the *Preston Guardian* to 'the present unchristian warfare.[8] In the same week's issue of the *Preston Pilot*, a correspondent bemoaned that 'It will require many years of prosperity, unity and peace to remedy the sad evils, both temporal and spiritual' resulting from the strike. The writer, 'Clericus', went on to suggest that ministers of religion might act as mediators between the two sides. He expressed the hope that the masters 'as God has been pleased to bless many of them with great and long-continued prosperity . . . will

6. *Preston Pilot; and County Advertiser,* 4 Feb. 1854.
7. *Preston Chronicle,* 28 Jan. 1854.
8. *Preston Guardian,* 28 Jan. 1854.

be induced, in a kind, conciliatory spirit, to make as large concessions as they possibly can'. From the workers, Clericus asked for 'A disposition to meet their employers in a friendly manner', which 'would . . . contribute much to their future happiness and welfare, and, above all, it would be pleasing and acceptable to Him whose name is LOVE'.[9]

The leaders of the strike too viewed matters from a religious perspective. Geoffrey Carnall noted a speech made by George Cowell which is echoed in *Hard Times*,[1] and which appeared in print in the *Preston Guardian* on the very day Dickens arrived in Preston.

> Political economy! What is it? The doctrine of buying cheap and selling dear—a doctrine utterly irreconcilable with the divine precept, 'Do unto others as you would that they should do unto you.' The sooner we can rout political economy from the world, the better it will be for the working classes of this country.[2]

Mortimer Grimshaw picked up this idea, and extended it in a lecture given at Accrington soon after, in which, in addition to arguing from the text 'the labourer is worthy of his hire', he maintained political economy to be 'at variance with Christianity, true reason, equity, and justice':

> Christianity is either false or political economy is false. Buy cheap and sell dear! The great founder of Christianity said— 'Love thy neighbour as thyself. Do unto others as you would have others do to you.' The 'buy cheap and sell dear' principle says no such thing.[3]

The chairman of that same meeting, the Baptist minister, Rev. Charles Williams, made an interesting qualification when acknowledging the cogency of Grimshaw's argument:

> I have no hesitation in saying that I think buying cheap and selling dear, when carried on rigorously and without mercy, is unchristian in its character. Both parties, however, act upon it, and what is wanted, in my opinion, is this, the introduction of a moral principle to modify the working of this hard maxim, and except there be the moral principle of justice, love and brotherhood, that principle will prove the ruin of Lancashire and of England. I wish there were a little less of selfishness; to fill a man's pockets appears to be the order of the day . . . Political

9. *Preston Pilot*, 28 Jan. 1854.
1. Carnall, *op.cit.*, pp. 41–2.
2. *Preston Guardian*, 28 Jan. 1854. These sentiments were also reported in the other local newspapers, the *Preston Chronicle* and the *Preston Pilot*, of the same date.
3. *Preston Guardian*, 4 Feb. 1854.

> economy must ever have its place in political life . . . but there
> are higher considerations, and when the lower considerations
> are found to clash with the higher, then I say you ought to
> make interest give way to principle and morality.[4]

Much of this reflects Dickens's views as presented in the novel, in
particular the argument that both sides act upon the same unholy
precepts, with workers following the example set by industrialists
('Both sides, however, act upon it') and the emphasis on the need
for the Christian virtues of 'justice, love and brotherhood'. For if
the widespread use of the strike weapon in the years immediately
preceding the writing of the novel forms part of the background to
Hard Times, the Victorian religious perspective on the industrial
world greatly influences Dickens's novel. The Britain he depicts in
Hard Times is a nation splitting into factions, a society in which
men no longer recognise all other men as their fellows. The concept
of the brotherhood of man has been lost as the powerful in this
society have in effect ceased to recognise ordinary workers as fully
human. Instead, conceived of not as individuals but 'generically',
they are merely 'the Hands' and are 'a race who would have found
more favour with some people, if Providence had seen fit to make
them only hands, or, like the lower creatures of the seashore,
only hands and stomachs' (I,10) [45]. Once the powerful no longer
acknowledge their common humanity with working people, they
have little conscience about the suffering their deeds or negligence
cause to their fellow human beings; it is vain that miners, themselves, as Stephen points out, 'fathers, sons, brothers, dear to
thousands an' thousands, an' keeping 'em fro' want and hunger'
have in vain

> pray'n and pray'n the lawmakers for Christ's sake not to let
> their work be murder to 'em, but to spare 'em for th' wives and
> children that they loves as well as gentlefok loves theirs (III,6).

Without a sense of identification with the workers and lacking a
sense of their Christian obligation to them, the industrialists appear
undisturbed by the deaths of such as Rachael's sister whose demise
'young and misshapen' was 'awlung o' sickly air as had'n no need to
be' (III,6). It is, of course, this trend that Stephen Blackpool is
deploring when he describes what he pathetically expresses as a
lack of 'drawin nigh to fok' which is accompanied by

> rating 'em as so much Power, and reg'latin' 'em as if they was
> figures in a soom, or machines: wi'out loves and likens, wi'out
> memories and inclinations, wi'out souls to weary and souls to

> hope—when aw goes quiet, draggin on wi' 'em as if they'd
> nowt o' th' kind, and when aw goes onquiet, reproachin 'em for
> their want o' sitch humanly feelins in their dealins wi' yo (II,5)

Hence, also, his dying wish 'that aw the world may on'y coom toogether
more, an' get a better unnerstan'in o' one another' (III,6).

Against this perspective; unions, far from providing a cure for
society's ills, are merely another symptom of the disease. In an
article published in 1851 on 'Railway Strikes[5] it was precisely the
tendency to factionalism—to identifying only with a sector of
the community, rather than with all one's fellow men—that made
Dickens deplore the railmen's strike, even though he had 'friendly
feelings' towards the railmen. He there emphasised the interlock-
ing nature of the work of all the people who had contributed to the
establishment of the railway, and then bade them not to identify
only with their fellow railwaymen, and thus feel it their duty to
show solidarity with them, but to give regard to a much wider con-
stituency of their fellow citizens. Each should think, Dickens wrote,
of 'my duty to the public' and 'my duty to my fellow workmen of all
denominations: not only here, upon this Railway, but all over
England'. His fictional mouthpiece among the railwaymen sums up
the issue:

> I leave you to judge how it serves the workman's case, at such a
> time, to show a small body of his order, combined, in a misuse
> of power, against the whole community!

To identify oneself with only one restricted group is to deny the
brotherhood of all men; and as such, it is unchristian. The world of
Hard Times is one in which Christianity and Christian values count
for little: the Good Samaritan is 'a bad Economist' (II,12); right-
headed people like Sissy are scorned for thinking that the first
principle of political economy, as of everything in the human sphere,
is 'To do unto others as I would that they should do unto me'. (I,9);
only at the very end does Mr Gradgrind come to make 'his facts and
figures subservient to Faith, Hope, and Charity' (III,9).

Unions, in Dickens's view, augment the evil in the industrial world
by following, in their proceedings, the agenda set by the masters.[6]
If the masters do not acknowledge the workers as fellow men, but
only as 'hands', the union encourages the workers to regard the
masters as enemies, 'the oppressors' that workers are to 'crumble into
dust' (I,4). It creates division even among the workers: each man
either becomes a unionist or is treated as an outcast, and no longer

5. *Household Words*, 2, 11 Jan. 1851.
6. In the novel the formation of a union by the workers is directly following the example
   of the employers who are, as Bitzer points out, 'united' (II, 1).

a brother. The unchristian nature of this is reflected in the rejection of the philosophy and behaviour of the Good Samaritan; as Stephen comments,

> if I was a lyin parisht i' th' road, yo'd feel it right to pass me by, as a forrenner and stranger. (II,4)

Union leaders like Slackbridge speak the language of brotherhood and Christian principles, urging 'my friends and fellow-sufferers, and fellow-workmen, and fellow-men' to fight for 'the God-created glorious rights of Humanity' and 'the holy and eternal privileges of Brotherhood' (II,4)—but they do not adhere to the values embodied in the words. As the case of Stephen and his workmates, in which 'private feeling must yield to the common cause' (II,4), shows, they encourage workers to regard each other not as individuals and fellow men, but as members, or not, of the faction that makes up the union.

A fundamental question Dickens raises in *Hard Times* is whether an industrial society, or, at least, one based on the principles of that he observes around him, is compatible with Christianity; and if those acting on the principles on which this society is founded are in effect being anti-Christian, this in turn raises the question of how a man should face the evil of the world in which he finds himself. At root, it is a matter of either dealing pragmatically with an evil world and making accommodations to it or of making a stand for the principles in which he believes and which he knows to be right. Even in his journalistic pieces, Dickens's position is uncompromising. He insists on an adherence to moral principle no matter what the particular circumstances. 'We dismiss from consideration, the merits of the case' is his starting point in his article about the 1851 railways dispute,[7] in 'On Strike', he is interested in depicting the character of the strike but not in arguing the rights and wrongs of the workers' or the masters' cases:

> Masters right, or men right; masters wrong, or men wrong; both right, or both wrong; there is certain ruin to both in the continuance of or frequent revival of this breach.[8]

It is thus that Dickens can call the strike 'this mistake' even as he praises the operatives as motivated to persist in their strike by 'the good that is in them, and not by the evil.[9]

The position he adopts reflects his philosophy: refusing to take part in the factionalism of Mr Snapper—'a man *must* either be a friend to the Masters or a friend to the Hands'—he declares himself

7. 'Railway Strikes', *op.cit.*
8. 'On Strike', *op.cit.*
9. *Ibid.*

'a friend to both.'[1] Consistent with this, he rejects as a fallacy that there are real differences between people in different sections of society:

> I doubt the existence at this present time of many faults that are merely class faults. In the main, I am disposed to think that whatever faults you may find to exist, in your own neighbourhood for instance, among the hands, you will find tolerably equal in amount among the masters also, and even among the class above the masters.[2]

Dickens does not pretend that for those immediately involved, it is easy to take such a stance. In the novel Dickens does not shirk, in his presentation of Stephen Blackpool as adopting this position, the difficulties and suffering entailed in it. In a society in which the concept of brotherhood has been debased or rejected, the man who refuses to join one faction or the other in the industrial world, is cast out by, and suffers at the hands of both. The suffering is very real: on the one hand, in the wake of the workers' refusal to speak to Stephen, he finds that he 'had never known before the strength of the want in his heart for the frequent recognition of a nod, a look, a word' and he finds the experience 'appalling' (II,4); on the other hand, Bounderby's displeasure leads to dismissal, which deprives Stephen not only of his livelihood, but also, with the resulting need to leave Coketown, of the company of Rachael. Ultimately, of course, the consequence of his refusal to join the union, is, at the end of a long chain of events, his death. There is indeed a price to be paid for refusing to compromise with the evil of the world.

In 'On Strike', Dickens eventually identifies the 'some little thing wanting in the relations between them [working people] and their employers' as a recognition by all of the humanity of those they are dealing with and a consequent modification of behaviour, with the introduction of 'a little human covering', 'a little human bloom', 'a little human warmth' to transform the 'skeleton' of political economy.[3] It is this, rather than what Stephen Blackpool calls 'Vict'ry and triumph' (II,5) by either side, that will set society on a better foundation.

Viewed from this perspective, Dickens's view of unions, if still controversial, can be seen to be more than merely naive or ill-informed. And as an historical perspective can be used to criticise Dickens's stance over unions, it can be used as well to vindicate it, as witness all those industrial disputes in which class conflict has formed a text or unacknowledged sub-text to the actions of employers and

1. *Ibid.*
2. *Ibid.*
3. *Ibid.*

employed, If unions have been responsible for much in the improvement in the lot of workers, it has inevitably been at the price of
contributing to the fragmentation of British society, particularly
along class lines.

Hard Times, then, seems to have been influenced in a relatively
marginal way by Dickens's stay in Preston. He may have derived
some of the religious ideas in the novel from his visit. The union
figures he observed in Preston—the firebrand, the more restrained
chairman—are recreated in the novel. The character of the meeting has been changed, however, from one dominated by 'quietness
and order' in real life to one dominated by the rabble-rousing
rhetoric of a professional agitator in the novel. Partly this is to be
explained by Dickens's stance, for reasons already explained, of
remaining neutral, the unsympathetic master, Bounderby, is balanced by the unsympathetic workers' leader, Slackbridge. But it is
also perhaps to be explained by reference to the difference between
journalism and fiction. In his journalism, derived directly from real
life, Dickens makes some acknowledgement that unions may serve
in the immediate term a valid purpose—'The fact of their being able
to combine may, I can easily conceive, be a protection to them'[4] and
that the strikers are sincere. Fiction, on the other hand, is no place in
which to make compromises, but to argue what the writer thinks is
right. It is a place for vision and analysis; and in the process of conveying his vision of a society in the very throes of being riven into
fragments, Dickens looks not to the short-term but argues rather for
the fundamental reform of society on the basis of principles which
will, he thinks, ensure its long-term health and happiness.

4. *Ibid.*

Education

J. M. M'CULLOCH

From Preface to *A Series of Lessons*†

Till within the last few years, the system of Education which prevailed in the majority of our initiatory schools was in the highest degree artificial. The qualification most highly valued in a Teacher was a practical acquaintance with some popular theory of Elocution; and the chief, and, in some instances, the sole end aimed at in Teaching, seems to have been—to burden the memory of the pupil with "Rules" and "Extracts" utterly unsuited to his capacity. No one who has escaped the misfortune of toiling through the works of the fashionable Teachers of the last generation,—their "Speakers," "Rhetorical Readers," "Pronouncing Vocabularies," &c.—can form any conception of the ingenuity that has been expended in rearing up barriers in the Scholar's way to the temple of learning.—But a better order of times has now dawned; and the increased demand which has arisen, within the last few years, for Class-books compiled on more simple and natural principles, seems to justify the hope,—that the artificial system is on the wane,—that the success of the experiments recently made in such admirable institutions as the Edinburgh Sessional School, Circus-Place School, &c. is beginning to be admitted,—and that the time is nearly gone by, when children of seven and eight years of age are to be compelled to waste their time and their faculties on such preposterous and unsuitable

---

† One of the most popular writers of textbooks in Dickens' lifetime was J. M. M'Culloch, whose *A Series of Lessons in Prose and Verse* went through fifty printings after its first appearance in 1831. M'Culloch (1801–1883) is described on the title page of his text as having been "formerly Head Master of Circus-Place School, Edinburgh," and it is tempting to speculate whether such a title page might, by association, have inspired the creation not only of M'Choakumchild but of Mr. Sleary of the circus.

Being a clergyman as well as a schoolmaster, M'Culloch was the author of some volumes of sermons and also a manual of devotion for schools, *Pietas Juvenilis*, but his fame rested primarily on the success of his textbooks, in particular, *A Series of Lessons*. In his revised "Preface" to the thirty-seventh reprinting of this work, M'Culloch pointedly restated the principle on which his success was based: that the readings he had selected were designed to "enrich the mind with the knowledge of useful and interesting facts."

exercises as enacting dramatic scenes, reciting parliamentary speeches, and reading the latest sentimental poetry. The change of system is the more deserving of gratulation, as it is as decidedly favorable to the morals as it is to the mental culture of our youth. It is truly deplorable to think of the amount of bad morality and false religion that must have been disseminated among the youth of this country, through the medium of school-books which were mainly compiled from such writers as Shakespeare, Chesterfield, and Hume.

The following little Work has been compiled in adaptation to the Improved System of Teaching, and belongs to the same class of books with the "Lessons for Schools" of Dr. Thomson, the Edinburgh Sessional School Books, and the Author's "Course of Elementary Reading"—to which last it is meant to be introductory. Being intended for schools, where the Teacher makes it his business to instruct his Pupils in the *meaning* of what is read, as well as in the "art of reading," it has been compiled on the principle of admitting only such lessons as appeared well adapted to stimulate juvenile curiosity, and store the mind with useful knowledge. Simple extracts, relating to Natural History, Elementary Science, Religion, &c. have taken the place of Dramatic Scenes, Sentimental Poetry, and Parliamentary Orations. And while only such pieces have been admitted as seemed likely to form and interest the youthful mind, care has been taken so to abridge and otherwise alter them, as to adapt their style as well as their sentiments to the juvenile capacity.

* * *

CHARLES DICKENS

[A Conference of Statisticians]†

"MR. SLUG stated to the section the result of some calculations he had made with great difficulty and labour, regarding the state of infant education among the middle classes of London. He found that, within a circle of three miles from the Elephant and Castle, the following were the names and numbers of children's books principally in circulation:—

† From *Full Report of the First Meeting of the Mudfog Association for the Advancement of Everything*, 1837. Among Dickens' earliest writings is a series of satirical sketches portraying events in the town of Mudfog. The following, from his account of a conference of statisticians in Mudfog, features a report by Mr. Slug, "so celebrated for his statistical researches."

"Jack the Giant-killer.............................. 7,943
Ditto and Bean-stalk............................. 8,621
Ditto and Eleven Brothers....................... 2,845
Ditto and Jill.. 1,998
Total.............................. 21,407

"He found that the proportion of Robinson Crusoes to Philip Quarlls was as four and a half to one. * * * The ignorance that prevailed, was lamentable. One child, * * * a little boy of eight years old, was found to be firmly impressed with a belief in the existence of dragons, and openly stated that it was his intention when he grew up, to rush forth sword in hand for the deliverance of captive princesses, and the promiscuous slaughter of giants. Not one child among the number interrogated had ever heard of Mungo Park,— some inquiring whether he was at all connected with the black man that swept the crossing; and others whether he was in any way related to the Regent's Park. They had not the slightest conception of the commonest principles of mathematics and considered Sinbad the Sailor the most enterprising voyager that the world had ever produced.

"A Member strongly deprecating the use of all the other books mentioned, suggested that Jack and Jill might perhaps be exempted from the general censure, inasmuch as the hero and heroine, in the very outset of the tale, were depicted as going *up* a hill to fetch a pail of water, which was a laborious and useful occupation,—supposing the family linen was being washed, for instance.

"MR. SLUG feared that the moral effect of this passage was more than counterbalanced by another in a subsequent part of the poem, in which very gross allusion was made to the mode in which the heroine was personally chastised by her mother

"'For laughing at Jack's disaster;'

besides, the whole work had this one great fault, *it was not true*.

"THE PRESIDENT complimented the honourable member on the excellent distinction he had drawn. Several other Members, too; dwelt upon the immense and urgent necessity of storing the minds of children with nothing but facts and figures; which process the President very forcibly remarked, had made them (the section) the men they were."

* * *

[Joe Whelks and Education]†

As one half of the world is said not to know how the other half lives, so it may be affirmed that the upper half of the world neither knows nor greatly cares how the lower half amuses itself. Believing that it does not care, mainly because it does not know, we purpose occasionally recording a few facts on this subject.

The general character of the lower class of dramatic amusements is a very significant sign of a people, and a very good test of their intellectual condition. We design to make our readers acquainted in the first place with a few of our experiences under this head in the metropolis.

It is probable that nothing will ever root out from among the common people an innate love they have for dramatic entertainment in some form or other. It would be a very doubtful benefit to society, we think, if it could be rooted out. The Polytechnic Institution in Regent Street, where an infinite variety of ingenious models are exhibited and explained, and where lectures comprising a quantity of useful information on many practical subjects are delivered, is a great public benefit and a wonderful place, but we think a people formed *entirely* in their hours of leisure by Polytechnic Institutions would be an uncomfortable community. We would rather not have to appeal to the generous sympathies of a man of five-and-twenty, in respect of some affliction of which he had had no personal experience, who had passed all his holidays, when a boy, among cranks and cog-wheels. We should be more disposed to trust him if he had been brought into occasional contact with a Maid and a Magpie; if he had made one or two diversions into the Forest of Bondy; or had even gone the length of a Christmas Pantomime. There is a range of imagination in most of us, which no amount of steam-engines will satisfy; and which The-great-exhibition-of-the-works-of-industry-of-all-nations, itself, will probably leave unappeased. The lower we go, the more natural it is that the best-relished provision for this should be found in dramatic entertainments; as at once the most obvious, the least troublesome, and the most real, of all escapes out of the literal world. Joe Whelks, of the New Cut, Lambeth, is not much of a reader, has no great store of books, no very commodious room to read in, no very decided inclination to read, and no power at all of presenting vividly before his mind's eye what he reads about. But put Joe in the gallery of the Victoria Theatre; show

---

† From "The Amusements of the People," in *Household Words*, March 30 and April 30, 1850. Joe Whelks is the name of a person invented by Dickens to be representative of a working-class Cockney living in "New Cut," a street in London.

him doors and windows in the scene that will open and shut, and that people can get in and out of; tell him a story with these aids, and by the help of live men and women dressed up, confiding to him their innermost secrets, in voices audible half a mile off; and Joe will unravel a story through all its entanglements, and sit there as long after midnight as you have anything left to show him. Accordingly, the Theatres to which Mr. Whelks resorts, are always full; and whatever changes of fashion the drama knows elsewhere, it is always fashionable in the New Cut.

The question, then, might not unnaturally arise, one would suppose, whether Mr. Whelks's education is at all susceptible of improvement, through the agency of his theatrical tastes. How far it is improved at present, our readers shall judge for themselves.

In affording them the means of doing so, we wish to disclaim any grave imputation on those who are concerned in ministering to the dramatic gratification of Mr. Whelks. Heavily taxed, wholly unassisted by the State, deserted by the gentry, and quite unrecognised as a means of public instruction, the higher English Drama has declined. Those who would live to please Mr. Whelks, must please Mr. Whelks to live. It is not the Manager's province to hold the Mirror up to Nature, but to Mr. Whelks—the only person who acknowledges him. If, in like manner, the actor's nature, like the dyer's hand, becomes subdued to what he works in, the actor can hardly be blamed for it. He grinds hard at his vocation, is often steeped in direful poverty, and lives, at the best, in a little world of mockeries. It is bad enough to give away a great estate six nights a-week, and want a shilling; to preside at imaginary banquets, hungry for a mutton chop; to smack the lips over a tankard of toast and water, and declaim about the mellow produce of the sunny vineyard on the banks of the Rhine; to be a rattling young lover, with the measles at home; and to paint sorrow over, with burnt cork and rouge; without being called upon to despise his vocation too. If he can utter the trash to which he is condemned, with any relish, so much the better for him, Heaven knows; and peace be with him!

A few weeks ago, we went to one of Mr. Whelks's favourite Theatres, to see an attractive Melo-Drama called *May Morning*, or *The Mystery of 1715, and the Murder!* We had an idea that the former of these titles might refer to the month in which either the mystery or the murder happened, but we found it to be the name of the heroine, the pride of Keswick Vale; who was "called May Morning" (after a common custom among the English Peasantry) "from her bright eyes and merry laugh." Of this young lady, it may be observed, in passing, that she subsequently sustained every possible calamity of human existence, in a white muslin gown with blue tucks; and that she did every conceivable and inconceivable thing with a pistol, that could anyhow be effected by that description of fire-arms.

The Theatre was extremely full. The prices of admission were, to the boxes, a shilling; to the pit, sixpence, to the gallery, threepence. The gallery was of enormous dimensions (among the company, in the front row, we observed Mr. Whelks); and overflowing with occupants. It required no close observation of the attentive faces, rising one above another, to the very door in the roof, and squeezed and jammed in, regardless of all discomforts, even there, to impress a stranger with a sense of its being highly desirable to lose no possible chance of effecting any mental improvement in that great audience.

The company in the pit were not very clean or sweet-savoured, but there were some good-humoured young mechanics among them, with their wives. These were generally accompanied by "the baby," insomuch that the pit was a perfect nursery. No effect made on the stage was so curious, as the looking down on the quiet faces of these babies fast asleep, after looking up at the staring sea of heads in the gallery. There were a good many cold fried soles in the pit, besides; and a variety of flat stone bottles, of all portable sizes.

The audience in the boxes was of much the same character (babies and fish excepted) as the audience in the pit. A private in the Foot Guards sat in the next box; and a personage who wore pins on his coat instead of buttons, and was in such a damp habit of living as to be quite mouldy, was our nearest neighbour. In several parts of the house we noticed some young pickpockets of our acquaintance; but as they were evidently there as private individuals, and not in their public capacity, we were little disturbed by their presence. For we consider the hours of idleness passed by this class of society as so much gain to society at large; and we do not join in a whimsical sort of lamentation that is generally made over them, when they are found to be unoccupied.

* * *

We will add that we believe these people have a right to be amused. A great deal that we consider to be unreasonable, is written and talked about not licensing these places of entertainment. We have already intimated that we believe a love of dramatic representations to be an inherent principle in human nature. In most conditions of human life of which we have any knowledge, from the Greeks to the Bosjesmen, some form of dramatic representation has always obtained. We have a vast respect for county magistrates, and for the Lord Chamberlain; but we render greater deference to such extensive and immutable experience, and think it will outlive the whole existing court and commission. We would assuredly not bear harder on the fourpenny theatre, than on the four shilling theatre, or the four guinea theatre; but we would decidedly interpose to turn to some wholesome account the means of instruction which it has at command, and we would make that office of Dramatic Licenser, which, like many other offices, has become a mere piece of Court favour and dandy conventionality, a real, responsible, educational trust. We would have it exercise a sound supervision over the lower drama, instead of stopping the career of a real work of art, as it did in the case of Mr. Chorley's play at the Surrey Theatre, but a few weeks since, for a sickly point of form.

* * *

Ten thousand people, every week, all the year round, are estimated to attend this place of amusement. If it were closed to-morrow—if there were fifty such, and they were all closed to-morrow—the only result would be to cause that to be privately and evasively done, which is now publicly done; to render the harm of it much greater, and to exhibit the suppressive power of the law in an oppressive and partial light. The people who now resort here, *will be* amused somewhere. It is of no use to blink that fact, or to make pretences to the contrary. We had far better apply ourselves to improving the character of their amusement. It would not be exacting much, or exacting anything very difficult, to require that the pieces represented in these Theatres should have, at least, a good, plain, healthy purpose in them.

* * *

JANE SINNETT

[Dickens as a Critic of Education]†

"Hard Times" decidedly reads better in a volume than it did in detached chapters; we can hasten over those parts which are painful to dwell upon towards those of more pleasing interest.

When it was announced, amid the strikes and consequent derangements of commerce, that Mr. Dickens was about to write a tale in "Household Words" to be called "Hard Times," the general attention was instantly arrested. It was imagined the main topic of the story would be drawn from the fearful struggle which was being then enacted in the north, in which loss of money on the one side

† From a review of *Hard Times*, by Jane Sinnett, published anonymously in *The Westminster Review*, October 1854.

and the pangs of hunger on the other, were the weapons at command. The inner life of those great movements would, it was thought, be exhibited, and we should see the results of the wrongs and the delusions of the workman, and the alternations of hope and fear which must from day to day have agitated him at the various crises of the conflict, delineated in many a moving scene. Mr. Dickens—if any one—it was considered, could be intrusted with this delicate task, and would give us a true idea of the relations of master and workman, both as they are and as they might be. Some of this is done in the book now before us, only this purpose is subordinated and made incidental to another, which is to exhibit the evil effects of an exclusive education of the intellect, without a due cultivation of the finer feelings of the heart and the fancy. We suppose it is in anticipation of some change of the present educational system for one that shall attempt to kill "outright the robber Fancy," that Mr. Dickens launches forth his protest, for we are not aware of such a system being in operation anywhere in England. On the contrary, it is the opinion of various continental professors, very competent to form a judgment on this subject, that more play is given to the imagination and will by the English system of instruction than by any other. If we look to our public schools and universities, we find great part, too great part, we think, of the period of youth and adolescence devoted to the study of the mythology, literature, and history of the most poetic people of all time. The "gorgeous Tragedies" of Athens,

> "Presenting Thebes' or Pelops' line.
> Or the tale of Troy divine,"

under the name of Greek Play, have produced no slight consumption of birch-rod in this country. In almost every school in the kingdom, passages of our finest poets are learned by heart; and Shakespeare and Walter Scott are among the Penates of every decent family. If there are Gradgrind schools, they are not sufficiently numerous to be generally known. Now, at the very commencement of "Hard Times," we find ourselves introduced to a set of hard uncouth personages, of whose existence as a class no one is aware, who are engaged in cutting and paring young souls after their own ugly pattern, and refusing them all other nourishment but facts and figures. The unpleasant impression caused by being thus suddenly introduced into this cold and uncongenial atmosphere, is never effaced by the subsequent charm of narrative and well-painted characters of the tale. One can have no more pleasure in being present at this compression and disfigurement than in witnessing the application of the boot—nor in, following these poor souls, thus intellectually halt and maimed, through life, than in

seeing Chinese ladies hobbling through a race. It is not then with
the truth Mr. Dickens wishes to enforce, but with the manner in
which it is enforced, that we find fault. It was possible to have done
this in a less forbidding form, with actors whom we should have
recognised as more natural and less repulsive than the Gradgrinds,
Bounderbys, and Crakemchilds; to have placed in contrast persons
educated after an ordinary and *practicable* plan, and persons of higher
aesthetic training; but, at the same time, the task would have required
a deeper acquaintance with human nature. The most successful
characters in "Hard Times," as is usual with Mr. Dickens, are those
which are the *simplest* and least cultivated. Stephen Blackpool,
Rachel and Sissy, Mr. Thleary of the 'horth-riding,' and his single-
hearted troupe, all act and talk with such simplicity of heart and
nobleness of mind, that their appearance on the stage is a most
welcome relief from the Gradgrinds, Bounderbys, Sparsits, &c., who
are all odd characters portrayed in a quaint style; and we regret
that more of the story is not devoted to objects who are so much
more within Mr. Dickens's power of representation.

* * *

CHARLES DARWIN

[Atrophy of Imagination in a Scientist]†

*** I have said that in one respect my mind has changed during the
last twenty or thirty years. Up to the age of thirty, or beyond it,
poetry of many kinds, such as the works of Milton, Gray, Byron,
Wordsworth, Coleridge, and Shelley, gave me great pleasure, and
even as a schoolboy I took intense delight in Shakespeare, especially in the historical plays. I have also said that formerly pictures
gave me considerable, and music very great delight. But now for
many years I cannot endure to read a line of poetry: I have tried
lately to read Shakespeare, and found it so intolerably dull that it
nauseated me. I have also almost lost any taste for pictures or music.—
Music generally sets me thinking too energetically on what I have
been at work on, instead of giving me pleasure. ***

This curious and lamentable loss of the higher aesthetic tastes is
all the odder, as books on history, biographies and travels (indepen-
dently of any scientific facts which they may contain), and essays on
all sorts of subjects interest me as much as ever they did. My mind

† From *The Life and Letters of Charles Darwin: Including an Autobiographical Chapter:
Edited by His Son, Francis Darwin. In Three Volumes: Vol. 1* (London: John Murray,
Albemarle Street, 1887), pp. 100–02.

seems to have become a kind of machine for grinding general laws out of large collections of facts, but why this should have caused the atrophy of that part of the brain alone, on which the higher tastes depend, I cannot conceive. A man with a mind more highly organised or better constituted than mine, would not I suppose have thus suffered; and if I had to live my life again I would have made a rule to read some poetry and listen to some music at least once every week; for perhaps the parts of my brain now atrophied could thus have been kept active through use. The loss of these tastes is a loss of happiness, and may possibly be injurious to the intellect, and more probably to the moral character, by enfeebling the emotional part of our nature.

* * *

Utilitarianism and the Science of Political Economy

Of the three aspects of the Victorian age that Dickens represents most often in *Hard Times*—industrialism, education, and
Utilitarianism—the third is much the most difficult to illustrate
or describe. Such critics as E. P. Whipple, whose *Atlantic Monthly*
article on *Hard Times* as appears on page 374, have argued that
Dickens did not understand Utilitarianism and that the "Gradgrind
philosophy" misrepresents the philosophical position of Jeremy
Bentham (1748–1832), the founder of the Utilitarian school. In
defense of Dickens it could be said that even if his understanding
of Utilitarian philosophy was incomplete, he nevertheless had a
shrewd understanding of the Utilitarian temperament as illustrated by his creation of Mr. Gradgrind. Bentham himself, as he
appears in J. S. Mill's portrait of him (p. 365), has much in common with Dickens' Gradgrind (at least in the first half of the
novel).

Also in defense of Dickens it could be argued that the philosophy of Utilitarianism was itself such a complicated one that it is
no wonder if the novelist did not understand it. Bentham was primarily a legal reformer, "the great questioner of things established,"
as Mill described him. He and his followers were responsible for
many of the most important reforms in the nineteenth century,
fearlessly investigating traditional procedures in law or government and, on the basis of statistical evidence, pushing through
drastic changes. Theoretically, on the other hand, Bentham and
his followers were committed to the economic point of view of
Adam Smith, that man is a self-seeking creature who thrives best
when no one interferes to regulate his activities. As G. D. Klin-
gopulos writes:

> Utilitarianism itself was full of paradoxes. *** Though it theo-
> retically favoured *laissez-faire* it, nevertheless, came to stand
> for efficient centralized administration and a strong civil ser-
> vice. Though in some matters, such as the agitation for cheap
> bread, the utilitarians were friends of the working man, in

others, such as the regulation of conditions in the factories, they were his enemies.[1]

In *Hard Times* (unlike his earlier attacks on Utilitarianism in *Oliver Twist* and *The Chimes*) Dickens is little concerned with the Utilitarians as reformers. Instead he concentrates on the basic Utilitarian views of human nature and of economic drives, views widely shared in the world of Victorian commerce. Included in the following selections are some more theoretical demonstrations of the values of unrestricted self-help as favored by both the Utilitarians and a larger group of Victorian economists. Typical of such writers was John Ramsey McCulloch, (1789–1864), a statistician and at one time a professor of political economy at the University of London, whose popular and influential books (such as his *Principles of Political Economy*) summed up the economic theories of Adam Smith, Malthus, and Ricardo—theories echoed or caricatured in some of Mr. Bounderby's speeches in *Hard Times*. For this J. R. McCulloch (not to be confused with his fellow countryman, J. M. M'Culloch, the schoolteacher), Dickens seems to have had nothing but scorn. In 1853, to express his dissatisfaction with some articles submitted to *Household Words* that impressed him as dull and lacking in "fancy," Dickens told his assistant editor that they sounded as if they had been written by McCulloch. Some months later, in his article on the strike at Preston, he wrote of the "forbearance and consideration" that ought to characterize the relations of employers and employed, "something," he added, "which is not to be found in Mr. McCulloch's dictionary" (an allusion to McCulloch's *Dictionary, Practical, Theoretical, and Historical of Commerce*, originally published in 1832). And in 1855 Dickens once more aired his dislike of these laissez-faire economic principles. Of McCulloch's activities on a committee, he wrote to his friend, John Forster:

> O what a fine aspect of political economy it is, that the noble professors of the science on the adulteration committee should have tried to make Adulteration a question of Supply and Demand! We shall never get to the Millennium, sir, by the rounds of that ladder; and I, for one won't hold by the skirts of that Great Mogul of impostors, Master McCulloch!

1. In *From Dickens to Hardy*, ed. Boris Ford (Penguin Books, 1958), pp. 30–31 [vol. 6 of *The Pelican Guide to English Literature*].

JOHN STUART MILL

[The Mind and Character of Jeremy Bentham]†

Bentham's contempt, then, of all other schools of thinkers; his determination to create a philosophy wholly out of the materials furnished by his own mind, and by minds like his own; was his first
disqualification as a philosopher. His second, was the incomplete-
ness of his own mind as a representative of universal human nature.
In many of the most natural and strongest feelings of human nature
he had no sympathy; from many of its graver experiences he was
altogether cut off; and the faculty by which one mind understands
a mind different from itself, and throws itself into the feelings of
that other mind, was denied him by his deficiency of Imagination.

With Imagination in the popular sense, command of imagery
and metaphorical expression, Bentham was, to a certain degree,
endowed. For want, indeed, of poetical culture, the images with
which his fancy supplied him were seldom beautiful, but they were
quaint and humorous, or bold, forcible, and intense: passages might
be quoted from him both of playful irony, and of declamatory eloquence, seldom surpassed in the writings of philosophers. The
Imagination which he had not, was that to which the name is generally appropriated by the best writers of the present day; that
which enables us, by a voluntary effort, to conceive the absent as if
it were present, the imaginary as if it were real, and to clothe it in
the feelings which, if it were indeed real, it would bring along with
it. This is the power by which one human being enters into the
mind and circumstances of another. This power constitutes the
poet, in so far as he does anything but melodiously utter his own
actual feelings. It constitutes the dramatist entirely. It is one of the
constituents of the historian; by it we understand other times; by it
Guizot interprets to us the middle ages; Nisard, in his beautiful
Studies on the later Latin poets, places us in the Rome of the
Cæsars; Michelet disengages the distinctive characters of the different races and generations of mankind from the facts of their
history. Without it nobody knows even his own nature, further
than circumstances have actually tried it and called it out; nor the
nature of his fellow-creatures, beyond such generalizations as he may
have been enabled to make from his observation of their outward
conduct.

By these limits, accordingly, Bentham's knowledge of human
nature is bounded. It is wholly empirical; and the empiricism of one

† From *The Westminster Review* (1838).

who has had little experience. He had neither internal experience nor external; the quiet, even tenor of his life, and his healthiness of mind, conspired to exclude him from both. He never knew prosperity and adversity, passion nor satiety: he never had even the experiences which sickness gives; he lived from childhood to the age of eighty-five in boyish health. He knew no dejection, no heaviness of heart. He never felt life a sore and a weary burthen. He was a boy to the last. Self-consciousness, that dæmon of the men of genius of our time, from Wordsworth to Byron, from Goethe to Chateaubriand, and to which this age owes so much both of its cheerful and its mournful wisdom, never was awakened in him. How much of human nature slumbered in him he knew not, neither can we know. He had never been made alive to the unseen influences which were acting on himself, nor consequently on his fellow-creatures. Other ages and other nations were a blank to him for purposes of instruction. He measured them but by one standard; their knowledge of facts, and their capability to take correct views of utility, and merge all other objects in it. His own lot was cast in a generation of the leanest and barrenest men whom England had yet produced, and he was an old man when a better race came in with the present century. He saw accordingly in man little but what the vulgarest eye can see; recognised no diversities of character but such as he who runs may read. Knowing so little of human feelings, he knew still less of the influences by which those feelings are formed: all the more subtle workings both of the mind upon itself, and of external things upon the mind, escaped him; and no one, probably, who, in a highly instructed age, ever attempted to give a rule to all human conduct, set out with a more limited conception either of the agencies by which human conduct *is*, or of those by which it *should* be, influenced.

This, then, is our idea of Bentham. He was a man both of remarkable endowments for philosophy, and of remarkable deficiencies for it: fitted, beyond almost any man, for drawing from his premises, conclusions not only correct, but sufficiently precise and specific to be practical: but whose general conception of human nature and life, furnished him with an unusually slender stock of premises. It is obvious what would be likely to be achieved by such a man; what a thinker, thus gifted and thus disqualified, could do in philosophy. He could, with close and accurate logic, hunt half-truths to their consequences and practical applications, on a scale both of greatness and of minuteness not previously exemplified; and this is the character which posterity will probably assign to Bentham.

* * *

J. R. McCULLOCH

[On Adam Smith and Laissez-Faire]†

At length, in 1776, our illustrious countryman, Adam Smith, published the "Wealth of Nations"—a work which has done for Political Economy what the Essay of Locke did for the philosophy of mind. In this work the science was, for the first time, treated in its fullest extent; and the fundamental principles on which the *production* of wealth depends, established beyond the reach of cavil and dispute. In opposition to the *Economists*, Dr. Smith has shewn that *labour* is the only source of wealth, and that the wish to augment our fortunes and to rise in the world—a wish that comes with us from the womb, and never leaves us till we go into the grave—is the cause of wealth being saved and accumulated: he has shewn that labour is productive of wealth when employed in manufactures and commerce, as well as when it is employed in the cultivation of the land; he has traced the various means by which labour may be rendered most effective; and has given a most admirable analysis and exposition of the prodigious addition made to its powers by its *division* among different individuals and countries, and by the employment of accumulated wealth, or *capital*, in industrious undertakings. He has also shewn, in opposition to the commonly received opinions of the merchants, politicians, and statesmen of his time, that wealth does not consist in the abundance of gold and silver, but in the abundance of the various necessaries, conveniences, and enjoyments of human life; that it is in every case sound policy to leave individuals to pursue their own interest in their own way; that, in prosecuting branches of industry advantageous to themselves, they necessarily prosecute such as are, at the same time, advantageous to the public; and that every regulation intended to force industry into particular channels, or to determine the species of commercial intercourse to be carried on between different parts of the same country, or between distant and independent countries, is impolitic and pernicious—injurious to the rights of individuals— and adverse to the progress of *real* opulence and lasting prosperity.

*   *   *

---

† From *The Principles of Political Economy* (Edinburgh: William and Charles Tait, 1825), pp. 52–54. For Adam Smith, see p. 22, n. 6.

[Malthus and Population]†

Mr. Malthus was probably the first who conclusively showed that, speaking generally, the tendency of population is not merely to keep on a level with the means of subsistence, but to exceed them; and the object of his "Essay on the Principles of Population," is to illustrate this principle, by pointing out the pernicious consequences resulting from a redundant population, improvident unions, and the bringing of human beings into the world without being able to provide for their subsistence and education. And instead of this doctrine being, as has been often stated, unfavourable to human happiness, a material change for the better would undoubtedly be effected in the condition of society, were its justice generally acknowledged, and a vigorous effort made to give it a practical bearing and real influence. It is evident, on the least reflection, that poverty is the source of the greater portion of the ills which afflict humanity; and there can be no manner of doubt, that a too great increase of population, by occasioning a redundant supply of labour, an excessive competition for employment, and low wages, is the most efficient cause of poverty. It is now too late to contend that a crowded population is a sure symptom of national prosperity. The population of the United States is not nearly so dense as that of Ireland; but will any one say that they are less flourishing and happy? The truth is, that the prosperity of a nation depends but little on the number of its inhabitants, but much on their industry, their intelligence, and their command over necessaries and conveniences. The earth affords room only, with the existing means of production, for a certain number of human beings to be trained to any degree of perfection. And "every real philanthropist would rather witness the existence of a thousand such beings, than that of a million of millions of creatures, pressing against the limits of subsistence, burdensome to themselves, and contemptible to each other." Wherever the labouring classes continue to increase more rapidly than the fund which has to support and employ them, their wages are gradually reduced till they reach the lowest possible limit. When placed under such unfortunate circumstances, they are cut off from all expectation of rising in the world, or of improving their condition. Their exertions are neither inspired by hope nor by ambition. Unable to save, or to acquire a stake in society, they have no inducement to make any unusual exertions. They consequently become indolent and dispirited; and, if not pressed by hunger would be always idle.

† From *A Treatise on the Circumstances which Determine the Rate of Wages and the Condition of the Labouring Classes* (Edinburgh: Black and Tait, 1826, rev. ed. 1854). For Malthus, see p. 22, n. 6.

It is thus apparent that the ratio which the progress of capital bears to the progress of population, is the pivot on which the comfort and well-being of the great bulk of society must always turn. If capital, as compared with population, be increased, the population will be better provided for; if it continue the same, the condition of the population will undergo no change; and if it be diminished, that condition will be changed for the worse.

The principles thus briefly elucidated render it apparent, on a little reflection, that the condition of the bulk of every people must usually depend much more on their own conduct than on that of their rulers. Not that we mean to insinuate that the influence of governments over their subjects is not great and powerful, or that the latter should not be governed in the best possible manner. A people who have the misfortune to be subjected to arbitrary and intolerant rulers, though otherwise possessed of all the powers and capacities necessary for the production of wealth, will, from the want of security and freedom, be most probably sunk in poverty and wretchedness. But wherever property is secure, industry free, and the public burdens moderate, the happiness or misery of the labouring classes depends almost wholly on themselves. Government has there done for them all that it should, and all in truth that it can do. It has given them security and freedom. But the use or abuse of these inestimable advantages is their own affair. They may be either provident on improvident, industrious or idle; and being free to choose, they are alone responsible for the consequences of their choice. * * *

What others can do for them is, in truth, but as the small dust of the balance compared with what they may do for themselves. The situation of most men not born to affluence, is always in great measure dependent on their own exertions. And this is most especially true of the labouring classes, the great majority of whom can owe nothing to patronage or favour. Industry, frugality, and forethought, are their only friends. But, happily, they are all-powerful. And how unpromising soever their situation, those who avail themselves of their willing assistance, are never disappointed, but secure in the end their own comfort and that of their families. Those, on the contrary, who neglect their aid, though otherwise placed under the most favourable circumstances, inevitably sink into a state of misery. The contrast between a well cultivated field and one that is neglected and overrun with thorns and brambles, is not greater than the contrast between the condition of the diligent and slothful, the careful and the wasteful labourers. The cottages of the former are clean, neat, and comfortable, their children well clothed and well instructed; whereas the cottages of the latter are slatternly and uncomfortable, being often little better than pig-styes, and their children in rags and ignorant. No increase of wages can be of any permanent advantage to the one class, while the smallest increase conduces to the well-being of the other.

[Useful Education for the Working Classes]†

Of all the means of providing for the permanent improvement of the poor hitherto suggested, few, if any, seem to promise to be so effectual as the establishment of a really useful system of public education. Much of the misery and crime which afflict and disgrace society have their sources in ignorance—in the ignorance of the poor with respect to the circumstances which really determine their condition. Those who have laboured to promote their education seem, generally speaking, to be satisfied, provided they succeed in making them able to read and write. But the education which stops at this point omits those parts that are really the most important. A knowledge of the arts of reading, writing, and arithmetic may, and indeed very often does, exist in company with an all but entire ignorance of those principles with respect to which it is most for the interest of the poor themselves, as well as the other portions of the community, that they should be well informed. To render education productive of all the utility that may be derived from it, the poor should, in addition to the elementary instruction now communicated to them, be made acquainted with the duties enjoined by religion and morality; and with the circumstances which occasion that gradation of ranks and inequality of fortunes which are of the essence of society. And they should be impressed, from their earliest years, with a conviction of the important truth, which it has been the main object of this work to establish and illustrate, that they are in great measure the arbiters of their own fortune—that what others can do for them is but trifling compared with what they can do for themselves—and that the most liberal government, and the best institutions, cannot shield them from poverty and misery, without the exercise of a reasonable degree of forethought and good conduct on their part. It is a proverbial expression, that man is the creature of habit; and no education can be good for much in which the peculiar and powerful influence of different habits and modes of acting over the happiness and comfort of individuals is not traced and exhibited in the clearest light, and which does not show how those productive of advantage may be most easily acquired, and

† From *A Treatise on the Circumstances which Determine the Rate of Wages and the Condition of the Labouring Classes* (Edinburgh: Black and Tait 1826, rev. ed. 1854).

those having a contrary effect most easily guarded against. The grand object in educating the lower classes should be to teach them to regulate their conduct with a view to their well-being, whatever may be their employments. The acquisition of scientific information, or even of the arts of reading or writing, though of the greatest importance, is subordinate and inferior to an acquaintance with the great art of "living well;" that is, of living so as to secure the greatest amount of comfort and respectability to individuals, under whatever circumstances they may be placed. That the ultimate effect of an education of this sort would be most advantageous, there can be little doubt. Neither the errors nor the vices of the poor are incurable. They investigate the practical questions which affect their immediate interests with the greatest sagacity and penetration, and do not fail to trace their remote consequences. And if education were made to embrace objects of real utility—if it were made a means of instructing the poor with respect to the circumstances which elevate and depress the rate of wages, and which improve and deteriorate their individual condition, the presumption is, that numbers would endeavour to profit by it. The harvest of good education may he late, but in the end it can hardly fail to be luxuriant. And it will amply reward the efforts of those who are not discouraged, in their attempts to make it embrace such objects as we have specified, by the difficulties they may expect to encounter at the commencement, and during the progress of their labours.

* * *

THOMAS CARLYLE

[The Condition of the Working Class]†

A feeling very generally exists that the condition and disposition of the Working Classes is a rather ominous matter at present; that something ought to be said, something ought to be done, in regard to it. And surely, at an epoch of history when the 'National Petition' carts itself in wagons along the streets, and is presented 'bound with iron hoops, four men bearing it,' to a Reformed House of Commons; and Chartism numbered by the million and half, taking nothing by its iron-hooped Petition, breaks out into brickbats, cheap pikes, and even into sputterings of conflagration, such very general feeling cannot be considered unnatural! To us individually this matter appears, and has for many years appeared, to be the

† From *Chartism* (London and Boston, 1839), chapter 1.

most ominous of all practical matters whatever; a matter in regard to which if something be not done, something will *do* itself one day, and in a fashion that will please nobody. The time is verily come for acting in it; how much more for consultation about acting in it, for speech and articulate inquiry about it!

* * *

What are the rights, what are the mights of the discontented Working Classes in England at this epoch? He were an Œdipus, and deliverer from sad social pestilence, who could resolve us fully! For we may say beforehand, The struggle that divides the upper and lower in society over Europe, and more painfully and notably in England than elsewhere, this too is a struggle which will end and adjust itself as all other struggles do and have done, by making the right clear and the might clear; not otherwise than by that. Meantime, the questions, Why are the Working Classes discontented; what is their condition, economical, moral, in their houses and their hearts, as it is in reality and as they figure it to themselves to be; what do they complain of; what ought they, and ought they not to complain of?—these are measurable questions; on some of these any common mortal, did he but turn his eyes to them, might throw some light. Certain researches and considerations of ours on the matter, since no one else will undertake it, are now to be made public. The researches have yielded us little, almost nothing; but the considerations are of old date, and press to have utterance. We are not without hope that our general notion of the business, if we can get it uttered at all, will meet some assent from many candid men.

[Selling Cheap]†

The Continental people, it would seem, are 'exporting our machinery, beginning to spin cotton and manufacture for themselves, to cut us out of this market and then out of that!' Sad news indeed; but irremediable;—by no means the saddest news. The saddest news is, that we should find our National Existence, as I sometimes hear it said, depend on selling manufactured cotton at a farthing an ell[1] cheaper than any other People. A most narrow stand for a great Nation to base itself on! A stand which, with all the Corn-Law Abrogations conceivable, I do not think will be capable of enduring.

My friends, suppose we quitted that stand; suppose we came honestly down from it, and said: "This is our minimum of cotton-prices. We care not, for the present, to make cotton any cheaper. Do you, if

---

† From *Past and Present* (London and New York, 1843), book III, chapter 9.
1. An ell is a unit of measurement equal to 1.25 yards.

it seem so blessed to you, make cotton cheaper. Fill your lungs with cotton-fuz, your hearts with copperas-fumes, with rage and mutiny; become ye the general gnomes of Europe, slaves of the lamp!"—I admire a Nation which fancies it will die if it do not undersell all other Nations, to the end of the world. Brothers, we will cease to *under*sell them; *we* will be content to *equal*-sell them; to be happy selling equally with them! I do not see the use of underselling them. Cotton-cloth is already two-pence a yard or lower; and yet bare backs were never more numerous among us. Let inventive men cease to spend their existence incessantly contriving how cotton can be made cheaper; and try to invent, a little, how cotton at its present cheapness could be somewhat justlier divided among us. Let inventive men consider, Whether the Secret of this Universe, and of Man's Life there, does, after all, as we rashly fancy it, consist in making money? There is One God, just, supreme, almighty: but is Mammon the name of him?—With a Hell which means 'Failing to make money,' I do not think there is any Heaven possible that would suit one well; nor so much as an Earth that can be habitable long! In brief, all this Mammon-Gospel, of Supply-and-demand, Competition, Laissez-faire, and Devil take the hindmost, begins to be one of the shabbiest Gospels ever preached; or altogether the shabbiest. Even with Dilettante partridge-nets, and at a horrible expenditure of pain, who shall regret to see the entirely transient, and at best somewhat despicable life strangled out of *it*? At the best, as we say, a somewhat despicable, unvenerable thing, this same 'Laissez-faire;' and now, at the *worst*, fast growing an altogether detestable one!

"But what is to be done with our manufacturing population, with our agricultural, with our ever increasing population?" cry many.—Aye, what? Many things can be done with them, a hundred things, and a thousand things,—had we once got a soul, and begun to try. This one thing, of doing for them by 'underselling all people,' and filling our own bursten pockets and appetites by the road; and turning over all care for any 'population,' or human or divine consideration except cash only, to the winds, with "Laissez-faire" and the rest of it: this is evidently not the thing. Farthing cheaper per yard? No great Nation can stand on the apex of such a pyramid; screwing itself higher and higher; balancing itself on its great-toe! Can England not subsist without being *above* all people in working? England never deliberately purposed such a thing. If England work better than all people, it shall be well. England, like an honest worker, will work as well as she can; and hope the gods may allow her to live on that basis. Laissez-faire and much else being once well dead, how many 'impossibles' will become possible! They are impossible, as cotton-cloth at two-pence an ell was—till men set about making it. The inventive genius of great England will not forever sit patient with mere wheels and pinions, bobbins, straps and billy-rollers whir-ring in the head of it. The inventive genius of England is not a Bea-ver's, or a Spinner's or Spider's genius: it is a *Man's* genius, I hope, with a God over him!

E. P. WHIPPLE

[On the Economic Fallacies of *Hard Times*]†

Dickens established a weekly periodical, called Household Words, on the 30th of March, 1850. On the 1st of April, 1854, he began in it the publication of the tale of Hard Times, which was continued in weekly installments until its completion in the number for the 12th of August. The circulation of Household Words was doubled by the appearance in its pages of this story. When published in a separate form, it was appropriately dedicated to Thomas Carlyle, who was Dickens's master in all matters relating to the "dismal sci-ence" of political economy.

During the composition of Hard Times the author was evidently in an embittered state of mind in respect to social and political questions. He must have felt that he was in some degree warring against the demonstrated laws of the production and distribution of wealth; yet he also felt that he was putting into prominence some laws of the human heart which he supposed political economists had studiously overlooked or ignored. He wrote to Charles Knight that he had no design to damage the really useful truths of political economy, but that his story was directed against those "who see figures and averages, and nothing else; who would take the average of cold in the Crimea during twelve months as a reason for clothing a soldier in nankeen on a night when he would be frozen to death in fur; and who would comfort the labourer in traveling twelve miles a day to and from his work by telling him that the average distance of one inhabited place from another, on the whole area of England, is only four miles." This is, of course, a caricatured statement of what statisticians propose to prove by their "figures and averages." Dickens would have been the first to laugh at such an economist and statistician as Michael Thomas Sadler, who mixed up figures of arithmetic and figures of rhetoric, tables of population and gushing sentiments, in one odd jumble of doubtful calculations and bombas-tic declamations; yet Sadler is only an extreme case of an investiga-tor who turns aside from his special work to introduce considerations which, however important in themselves, have nothing to do with

† From *The Atlantic Monthly* (1877).

the business he has in hand. Dickens's mind was so deficient in the power of generalization, so inapt to recognize the operation of inexorable law, that whatever offended his instinctive benevolent sentiments he was inclined to assail as untrue. Now there is no law the operation of which so frequently shocks our benevolent sentiments as the law of gravitation; yet no philanthropist, however accustomed he may be to subordinate scientific truth to amiable impulses, ever presumes to doubt the certain operation of that law. The great field for the contest between the head and the heart is the domain of political economy. The demonstrated laws of this science are often particularly offensive to many good men and good women, who wish well for their fellow-creatures, and who are pained by the obstacles which economic maxims present to their diffusive benevolence. The time will come when it will be as intellectually discreditable for an educated person to engage in a crusade against the established laws of political economy as in a crusade against the established laws of the physical universe; but the fact that men like Carlyle, Ruskin, and Dickens can write economic nonsense without losing intellectual caste shows that the science of political economy, before its beneficent truths come to be generally admitted, must go through a long struggle with benevolent sophisms and benevolent passions. * * *

It is curious to note the different opinions of two widely differing men regarding the story itself.

In judging the work, neither Ruskin nor Macaulay seems to have made any distinction between Dickens as a creator of character and Dickens as a humorous satirist of what he considers flagrant abuses. As a creator of character he is always tolerant and many-sided; as a satirist he is always intolerant and one-sided; and the only difference between his satire and that of other satirists consists in the fact that he has a wonderful power in individualizing abuses in persons. Juvenal, Dryden, and Pope, though keen satirists of character, are comparatively ineffective in the art of concealing their didactic purpose under an apparently dramatic form. So strong is Dickens's individualizing faculty, and so weak his faculty of generalization, that as a satirist he simply personifies his personal opinions. These opinions are formed by quick-witted impressions intensified by philanthropic emotions; they spring neither from any deep insight of reason nor from any careful processes of reasoning; and they are therefore contemptuously discarded as fallacies by all thinkers on social problems who are devoted to the investigation of social phenomena and the establishment of economic laws; but they are so vividly impersonated, and the classes satirized are so felicitously hit in some of their external characteristics and weak points, that many readers fail to discover the essential difference between such realities of character as Tony Weller and Mrs. Gamp, and such semblances of character as Mr. Gradgrind and Mr. Bounderby. Whatever Dickens understands he humorously represents; whatever he does not understand he humorously misrepresents; but in either case, whether he conceives or misconceives, he conveys to the general reader an impression that he is as great in those characters in which he personifies his antipathies as in those in which he embodies his sympathies.

The operation of this satirical as contrasted with dramatic genius is apparent in almost every person who appears in Hard Times, except Sleary and his companions of the circus combination. Mr. Gradgrind and Mr. Bounderby are personified abstractions, after the method of Ben Jonson; but the charge that Macaulay brings against them, that they have little of Dickens's humor, must be received with qualifications. Mr. Bounderby, for example, as the satirical representative of a class, and not as a person who could have had any real existence—as a person who gathers into himself all the vices of a horde of English manufacturers, without a ray of light being shed into his internal constitution of heart and mind,—is one of the wittiest and most humorous of Dickens's embodied sarcasms. Bounderby becomes a seeming character by being looked at and individualized from the point of view of imaginative antipathy. So surveyed, he seems real to thousands who observe their employers from the outside, and judge of them, not as they are, but as they appear to their embittered minds and hearts. Still, the artistic objection holds good that when a man resembling Mr. Bounderby is brought into the domain of romance or the drama, the great masters of romance and the drama commonly insist that he shall be not only externally represented but internally known. There is no authorized, no accredited way of exhibiting character but this, that the dramatist or novelist shall enter into the soul of the personage represented, shall sympathize with him sufficiently to know him, and shall represent his passions, prejudices, and opinions as springing from some central will and individuality. This sympathy is consistent with the utmost hatred of the person described; but characterization becomes satire the moment that antipathy supersedes insight and the satirist berates the exterior manifestations of an individuality whose interior life he has not diligently explored and interpreted. Bounderby, therefore, is only a magnificent specimen of what satirical genius can do when divorced from the dramatist's idea of justice, and the dramatist's perception of those minute peculiarities of intellect, disposition, and feeling which distinguish one "bully of humility" from another.

It is ridiculous to assert, as Ruskin asserts, that Hard Times is Dickens's greatest work; for it is *the* one of all his works which should be distinguished from the others as specially wanting in that power of real characterization on which his reputation as a vivid delineator of human character and human life depends. The whole effect of the story, though it lacks neither amusing nor pathetic incidents, and though it contains passages of description which rank with his best efforts in combining truth of fact with truth of imagination, is ungenial and unpleasant. Indeed, in this book, he simply intensified popular discontent; he ignored or he was ignorant of those laws the violation of which is at the root of popular discontent; and proclaimed with his favorite ideal workman, Stephen Blackpool, that not only the relation between employers and employed, but the whole constitution of civilized society itself, was a hopeless "muddle," beyond the reach of human intelligence or humane feeling to explain and justify. It is to be observed here that all cheering views of the amelioration of the condition of the race come from those hard thinkers whose benevolent impulses push them to the investigation of natural and economic laws. Starting from the position of sentimental benevolence, and meeting unforeseen intellectual obstacles at every step in his progress, Dickens ends "in a muddle" by the necessity of his method. Had he been intellectually equipped with the knowledge possessed by many men to whom in respect to genius he was immensely superior, he would never have landed in a conclusion so ignominious, and one which the average intellect of well-informed persons of the present day contemptuously rejects. If Dickens had contented himself with using his great powers of observation, sympathy, humor, imagination, and characterization in their appropriate fields, his lack of scientific training in the austere domain of social, legal, and political science would have been hardly perceptible; but after his immense popularity was assured by the success of The Pickwick Papers, he was smitten with the ambition to direct the public opinion of Great Britain by embodying, in exquisitely satirical caricatures, rash and hasty judgments on the whole government of Great Britain in all its departments, legislative, executive, and judicial. He overlooked uses, in order to fasten on abuses. His power to excite, at his will, laughter, or tears, or indignation was so great, that the victims of his mirthful wrath were not at first disposed to resent his debatable fallacies while enjoying his delicious fun. His invasion of the domain of political science with the palpable design of substituting benevolent instincts for established laws was carelessly condoned by the statesmen, legists, and economists whom he denounced and amused.

*   *   *

CRITICISM

HIPPOLYTE TAINE

[The Two Classes of Characters in *Hard Times*][†]

Take away the grotesque characters, who are only introduced to fill up and to excite laughter, and you will find that all Dickens' characters belong to two classes—people who have feelings and emotions, and people who have none. He contrasts the souls which nature creates with those which society deforms. One of his last novels, *Hard Times*, is an abstract of all the rest. He there exalts instinct above reason, intuition of heart above positive science; he attacks education built on statistics, figures, and facts; overwhelms the positive and mercantile spirit with misfortune and ridicule; combats the pride, hardness, selfishness of the merchant and the aristocrat; falls foul of manufacturing towns, towns of smoke and mud, which fetter the body in an artificial atmosphere, and the mind in a factitious existence. He seeks out poor artisans, mountebanks, a foundling, and crushes beneath their common sense, generosity, delicacy, courage, and sweetness, the false science, false happiness, and false virtue of the rich and powerful who despise them. He satirises oppressive society; praises oppressed nature; and his elegiac genius, like his satirical genius, finds ready to his hand in the English world around him, the sphere which it needs for its development.

JOHN RUSKIN

A Note on *Hard Times*[‡]

The essential value and truth of Dickens's writing have been unwisely lost sight of by many thoughtful persons merely because he presents his truth with some colour of caricature. Unwisely, because Dickens's caricature, though often gross, is never mistaken. Allowing for his manner of telling them, the things he tells us are always true. I wish that he could think it right to limit his brilliant exaggeration to works written only for public amusement; and when he takes up a subject of high national importance, such as that which he handled in *Hard Times*, that he would use severer and more accurate analysis. The usefulness of that work (to my mind, in several respects, the greatest he has written) is with many

† From an 1856 essay incorporated into Hippolyte Taine, *History of English Literature: Vol. II*, trans. H. Van Laun (Edinburgh: Edmonston and Douglas, 1871), pp. 358–59.
‡ From *Cornhill Magazine*, II (1860), and also in *Unto This Last: Four Essays on the First Principles of Political Economy* (London: Smith, Elder and Co., 1862).

persons seriously diminished because Mr. Bounderby is a dramatic monster, instead of a characteristic example of a worldly master; and Stephen Blackpool a dramatic perfection, instead of a characteristic example of an honest workman. But let us not lose the use of Dickens's wit and insight, because he chooses to speak in a circle of stage fire. He is entirely right in his main drift and purpose in every book he has written; and all of them, but especially *Hard Times*, should be studied with close and earnest care by persons interested in social questions. They will find much that is partial, and, because partial, apparently unjust; but if they examine all the evidence on the other side, which Dickens seems to overlook, it will appear, after all their trouble, that his view was the finally right one, grossly and sharply told.

GEORGE GISSING

[Dickens' Portrayal of the Working Class in *Hard Times*]†

* * *

We do not nowadays look for a fervent Christianity in leaders of the people. In that, as in several other matters, Dickens was by choice retrospective. Still writing at a time when "infidelity"—the word then used—was becoming rife among the populace of great towns, he never makes any reference to it, and probably did not take it into account; it had no place in his English ideal. I doubt, indeed, whether he was practically acquainted with the "free-thinking" workman. A more noticeable omission from his books (if we except the one novel which I cannot but think a failure) is that of the workman at war with capital. This great struggle, going on before him all his life, found no place in the scheme of his fiction. He shows us poor men who suffer under tyranny, and who exclaim against the hardship of things; but never such a representative wage-earner as was then to be seen battling for bread and right. One reason is plain; Dickens did not know the north of England. With adequate knowledge of a manufacturing town, he would never have written so unconvincingly as in his book *Hard Times*—the opportunity for dealing with this subject. Stephen Blackpool represents nothing at all; he is a mere model of meekness, and his great misfortune is such as might befall any man anywhere, the curse of a drunken wife. The book is a crude attack on materialism, a theme which might, of course,

† From George Gissing, *Charles Dickens: A Critical Study* (London: Blackie and Son, 1898), pp. 201–02.

have entered very well into a study of the combatant working-class. But, as I have already pointed out, the working-class is not Dickens's field, even in London. For the purposes of fiction, it is a class still waiting its portrayer; much has been written about it in novels, but we have no work of the first order dealing primarily with that form of life. Mrs. Gaskell essayed the theme very faithfully, and with some success; but it was not her best work. I can recall no working-class figures in English novels so truly representative as those in Charlotte Brontë's second book. Given a little wider experience, the author of *Shirley* might have exhibited this class in a masterpiece such as we vainly look for.

* * *

GEORGE BERNARD SHAW

Hard Times[†]

John Ruskin once declared *Hard Times* Dickens's best novel. It is worthwhile asking why Ruskin thought this, because he would have been the first to admit that the habit of placing works of art in competition with one another, and wrangling as to which is the best, is the habit of the sportsman, not of the enlightened judge of art. Let us take it that what Ruskin meant was that *Hard Times* was one of his special favorites among Dickens's books. Was this the caprice of fancy? or is there any rational explanation of the preference? I think there is.

Hard Times is the first fruit of that very interesting occurrence which our religious sects call, sometimes conversion, sometimes being saved, sometimes attaining to conviction of sin. Now the great conversions of the XIX century were not convictions of individual, but of social sin. The first half of the XIX century considered itself the greatest of all the centuries. The second discovered that it was the wickedest of all the centuries. The first half despised and pitied the Middle Ages as barbarous, cruel, superstitious, ignorant. The second half saw no hope for mankind except in the recovery of the faith, the art, the humanity of the Middle Ages. In Macaulay's *History of England*, the world is so happy, so progressive, so firmly set in the right path, that the author cannot mention even the National Debt without proclaiming that the deeper the country goes into debt, the more it prospers. In Morris's *News from*

† From George Bernard Shaw, *Introduction to Hard Times* (London: Waverley, 1912). Reprinted by permission of The Society of Authors on behalf of the George Bernard Shaw Estate.

Nowhere there is nothing left of all the institutions that Macaulay glorified except an old building, so ugly that it is used only as a manure market, that was once the British House of Parliament. *Hard Times* was written in 1854, just at the turn of the half century; and in it we see Dickens with his eyes newly open and his conscience newly stricken by the discovery of the real state of England. In the book that went immediately before, *Bleak House*, he was still denouncing evils and ridiculing absurdities that were mere symptoms of the anarchy that followed the industrial revolution of the XVIII and XIX centuries, and the conquest of political power by Commercialism in 1832. In *Bleak House* Dickens knows nothing of the industrial revolution: he imagines that what is wrong is that when a dispute arises over the division of the plunder of the nation, the Court of Chancery, instead of settling the dispute cheaply and promptly, beggars the disputants and pockets both their shares. His description of our party system, with its Coodle, Doodle, Foodle, etc., has never been surpassed for accuracy and for penetration of superficial pretence. But he had not dug down to the bed rock of the imposture. His portrait of the ironmaster who visits Sir Leicester Dedlock, and who is so solidly superior to him, might have been drawn by Macaulay: there is not a touch of Bounderby in it. His horrible and not untruthful portraits of the brickmakers whose abject and battered wives call them "master," and his picture of the now vanished slum between Drury Lane and Catherine Street which he calls Tom All Alone's, suggest (save in the one case of the outcast Jo, who is, like Oliver Twist, a child, and therefore outside the old self-help panacea of Dickens's time) nothing but individual delinquencies, local plague-spots, negligent authorities.

In *Hard Times* you will find all this changed. Coketown, which you can see to-day for yourself in all its grime in the Potteries (the real name of it is Hanley in Staffordshire on the London and North Western Railway), is not, like Tom All Alone's, a patch of slum in a fine city, easily cleared away, as Tom's actually was about fifty years after Dickens called attention to it. Coketown is the whole place; and its rich manufacturers are proud of its dirt, and declare that they like to see the sun blacked out with smoke, because it means that the furnaces are busy and money is being made; whilst its poor factory hands have never known any other sort of town, and are as content with it as a rat is with a hole. Mr. Rouncewell, the pillar of society who snubs Sir Leicester with such dignity, has become Mr. Bounderby, the self-made humbug. The Chancery suitors who are driving themselves mad by hanging about the Courts in the hope of getting a judgment in their favor instead of trying to earn an honest living, are replaced by factory operatives who toil miserably and incessantly only to see the streams of gold they set flowing slip through their fingers into the pockets of men who revile and oppress them.

Clearly this is not the Dickens who burlesqued the old song of the Fine Old English Gentleman, and saw in the evils he attacked only the sins and wickednesses and follies of a great civilization. This is Karl Marx, Carlyle, Ruskin, Morris, Carpenter, rising up against civilization itself as against a disease, and declaring that it is not our disorder but our order that is horrible; that it is not our criminals but our magnates that are robbing and murdering us; and that it is not merely Tom All Alone's that must be demolished and abolished, pulled down, rooted up, and made for ever impossible so that nothing shall remain of it but History's record of its infamy, but our entire social system. For that was how men felt, and how some of them spoke, in the early days of the Great Conversion which produced, first, such books as the *Latter Day Pamphlets* of Carlyle, Dickens's *Hard Times*, and the tracts and sociological novels of the Christian Socialists, and later on the Socialist movement which has now spread all over the world, and which has succeeded in convincing even those who most abhor the name of Socialism that the condition of the civilized world is deplorable, and that the remedy is far beyond the means of individual righteousness. In short, whereas formerly men said to the victim of society who ventured to complain, "Go and reform yourself before you pretend to reform Society," it now has to admit that until Society is reformed, no man can reform himself except in the most insignificantly small ways. He may cease picking your pocket of half crowns; but he cannot cease taking a quarter of a million a year from the community for nothing at one end of the scale, or living under conditions in which health, decency, and gentleness are impossible at the other, if he happens to be born to such a lot.

You must therefore resign yourself, if you are reading Dickens's books in the order in which they were written, to bid adieu now to the lighthearted and only occasionally indignant Dickens of the earlier books, and get such entertainment as you can from him now that the occasional indignation has spread and deepened into a passionate revolt against the whole industrial order of the modern world. Here you will find no more villains and heroes, but only oppressors and victims, oppressing and suffering in spite of themselves, driven by a huge machinery which grinds to pieces the people it should nourish and ennoble, and having for its directors the basest and most foolish of us instead of the noblest and most farsighted.

Many readers find the change disappointing. Others find Dickens worth reading almost for the first time. The increase in strength and intensity is enormous: the power that indicts a nation so terribly is much more impressive than that which ridicules individuals. But it cannot be said that there is an increase of simple pleasure for the reader, though the books are not therefore less attractive. One cannot say that it is pleasanter to look at a battle than at a merry-go-round; but there can be no question which draws the larger crowd.

To describe the change in the readers' feelings more precisely, one may say that it is impossible to enjoy Gradgrind or Bounderby as one enjoys Pecksniff or the Artful Dodger or Mrs. Gamp or Micawber or Dick Swiveller, because those earlier characters have nothing to do with us except to amuse us. We neither hate nor fear them. We do not expect ever to meet them, and should not be in the least afraid of them if we did. England is not full of Micawbers and Swivellers. They are not our fathers, our schoolmasters, our employers, our tyrants. We do not read novels to escape from them and forget them: quite the contrary. But England is full of Bounderbys and Podsnaps and Gradgrinds; and we are all to a quite appalling extent in their power. We either hate and fear them or else we are them, and resent being held up to odium by a novelist. We have only to turn to the article on Dickens in the current edition of the *Encyclopedia Britannica* to find how desperately our able critics still exalt all Dickens's early stories about individuals whilst ignoring or belittling such masterpieces as *Hard Times, Little Dorrit, Our Mutual Friend*, and even *Bleak House* (because of Sir Leicester Dedlock), for their mercilessly faithful and penetrating exposures of English social, industrial, and political life; to see how hard Dickens hits the conscience of the governing class; and how loth we still are to confess, not that we are so wicked (for of that we are rather proud), but so ridiculous, so futile, so incapable of making our country really prosperous. *The Old Curiosity Shop* was written to amuse you, entertain you, touch you; and it succeeded. *Hard Times* was written to make you uncomfortable; and it will make you uncomfortable (and serve you right) though it will perhaps interest you more, and certainly leave a deeper scar on you, than any two of its forerunners.

At the same time you need not fear to find Dickens losing his good humor and sense of fun and becoming serious in Mr. Gradgrind's way. On the contrary, Dickens in this book casts off, and casts off for ever, all restraint on his wild sense of humor. He had always been inclined to break loose: there are passages in the speeches of Mrs. Nickleby and Pecksniff which are impossible as well as funny. But now it is no longer a question of passages: here he begins at last to exercise quite recklessly his power of presenting a character to you in the most fantastic and outrageous terms, putting into its mouth from one end of the book to the other hardly one word which could conceivably be uttered by any sane human being, and yet

leaving you with an unmistakable and exactly truthful portrait of
a character that you recognize at once as not only real but typical.
Nobody ever talked, or ever will talk, as Silas Wegg talks to Boffin
and Mr. Venus, or as Mr. Venus reports Pleasant Riderhood to have
talked, or as Rogue Riderhood talks, or as John Chivery talks. They
utter rhapsodies of nonsense conceived in an ecstasy of mirth. And
this begins in *Hard Times*. Jack Bunsby in *Dombey and Son* is
absurd: the oracles he delivers are very nearly impossible, and yet
not quite impossible. But Mrs. Sparsit in this book, though Rem-
brandt could not have drawn a certain type of real woman more
precisely to the life, is grotesque from beginning to end in her way
of expressing herself. Her nature, her tricks of manner, her way of
taking Mr. Bounderby's marriage, her instinct for hunting down
Louisa and Mrs. Pegler, are drawn with an unerring hand; and she
says nothing that is out of character. But no clown gone suddenly
mad in a very mad harlequinade could express all these truths in
more extravagantly ridiculous speeches. Dickens's business in
life has become too serious for troubling over the small change of
verisimilitude, and denying himself and his readers the indulgence of his humor in inessentials. He even calls the schoolmaster
McChoakumchild, which is almost an insult to the serious reader.
And it was so afterwards to the end of his life. There are moments
when he imperils the whole effect of his character drawing by some
overpoweringly comic sally. For instance, happening in *Hard Times*
to describe Mr. Bounderby as drumming on his hat as if it were a
tambourine, which is quite correct and natural, he presently says that
"Mr. Bounderby put his tambourine on his head, like an oriental
dancer." Which similitude is so unexpectedly and excruciatingly
funny that it is almost impossible to feel duly angry with the odious
Bounderby afterwards.

This disregard of naturalness in speech is extraordinarily entertaining in the comic method; but it must be admitted that it is not
only not entertaining, but sometimes hardly bearable when it does
not make us laugh. There are two persons in *Hard Times*, Louisa
Gradgrind and Cissy Jupe, who are serious throughout. Louisa is a
figure of poetic tragedy; and there is no question of naturalness in
her case: she speaks from beginning to end as an inspired prophet-
ess, conscious of her own doom and finally bearing to her father the
judgment of Providence on his blind conceit. If you once consent to
overlook her marriage, which is none the less an act of prostitution
because she does it to obtain advantages for her brother and not for
herself, there is nothing in the solemn poetry of her deadly speech
that jars. But Cissy is nothing if not natural; and though Cissy is as
true to nature in her character as Mrs. Sparsit, she "speaks like a
book" in the most intolerable sense of the words. In her interview

with Mr. James Harthouse, her unconscious courage and simplicity, and his hopeless defeat by them, are quite natural and right; and the contrast between the humble girl of the people and the smart sarcastic man of the world whom she so completely vanquishes is excellently dramatic; but Dickens has allowed himself to be carried away by the scene into a ridiculous substitution of his own most literary and least colloquial style for any language that could conceivably be credited to Cissy.

> "Mr. Harthouse: the only reparation that remains with you is to leave her immediately and finally. I am quite sure that you can mitigate in no other way the wrong and harm you have done. I am quite sure that it is the only compensation you have left it in your power to make. I do not say that it is much, or that it is enough; but it is something, and it is necessary. Therefore, though without any other authority than I have given you, and even without the knowledge of any other person than yourself and myself, I ask you to depart from this place to-night, under an obligation never to return to it."

This is the language of a Lord Chief Justice, not of the dunce of an elementary school in the Potteries.

But this is only a surface failure, just as the extravagances of Mrs. Sparsit are only surface extravagances. There is, however, one real failure in the book. Slackbridge, the trade union organizer, is a mere figment of the middle-class imagination. No such man would be listened to by a meeting of English factory hands. Not that such meetings are less susceptible to humbug than meetings of any other class. Not that trade union organizers, worn out by the terribly wearisome and trying work of going from place to place repeating the same commonplaces and trying to "stoke up" meetings to enthusiasm with them, are less apt than other politicians to end as windbags, and sometimes to depend on stimulants to pull them through their work. Not, in short, that the trade union platform is any less humbug-ridden than the platforms of our more highly placed political parties. But even at their worst trade union organizers are not a bit like Slackbridge. Note, too, that Dickens mentions that there was a chairman at the meeting (as if that were rather surprising), and that this chairman makes no attempt to preserve the usual order of public meeting, but allows speakers to address the assembly and interrupt one another in an entirely disorderly way. All this is pure middleclass ignorance. It is much as if a tramp were to write a description of millionaires smoking large cigars in church, with their wives in low-necked dresses and diamonds. We cannot say that Dickens did not know the working classes, because he knew humanity too well to be ignorant of any class. But this sort of knowledge is as

compatible with ignorance of class manners and customs as with
ignorance of foreign languages. Dickens knew certain classes of
working folk very well: domestic servants, village artisans, and
employees of petty tradesmen, for example. But of the segregated
factory populations of our purely industrial towns he knew no more
than an observant professional man can pick up on a flying visit in
Manchester.

It is especially important to notice that Dickens expressly says in
this book that the workers were wrong to organize themselves in
trade unions, thereby endorsing what was perhaps the only practical
mistake of the Gradgrind school that really mattered much. And
having thus thoughtlessly adopted, or at least repeated, this error,
long since exploded, of the philosophic Radical school from which
he started, he turns his back frankly on Democracy, and adopts the
idealized Toryism of Carlyle and Ruskin, in which the aristocracy
are the masters and superiors of the people, and also the servants of
the people and of God. Here is a significant passage.

> "Now perhaps," said Mr. Bounderby, "you will let the gentle-
> man know how you would set this muddle (as you are so fond
> of calling it) to rights."
> "I donno, sir. I canna be expecten to't. Tis not me as should
> be looken to for that, sir. Tis they as is put ower me, and ower
> aw the rest of us. What do they tak upon themseln, sir, if not to
> do it?"

And to this Dickens sticks for the rest of his life. In *Our Mutual
Friend* he appeals again and again to the governing classes, asking
them with every device of reproach, invective, sarcasm, and ridicule of which he is master, what they have to say to this or that evil
which it is their professed business to amend or avoid. Nowhere
does he appeal to the working class to take their fate into their
own hands and try the democratic plan.

Another phrase used by Stephen Blackpool in this remarkable
fifth chapter is important. "Nor yet lettin alone will never do it." It
is Dickens's express repudiation of *laissez-faire*.

There is nothing more in the book that needs any glossary, except,
perhaps, the strange figure of the Victorian "swell," Mr. James Harthouse. His pose has gone out of fashion. Here and there you may
still see a man—even a youth—with a single eyeglass, an elaborately
bored and weary air, and a little stock of cynicisms and indifferent-
isms contrasting oddly with a mortal anxiety about his clothes.
All he needs is a pair of Dundreary whiskers, like the officers in
Desanges' military pictures, to be a fair imitation of Mr. James Harthouse. But he is not in the fashion: he is an eccentric, as Whistler
was an eccentric, as Max Beerbohm and the neo-dandies of the *fin*

de siècle were eccentrics. It is now the fashion to be energetic, to hustle as American millionaires are supposed (rather erroneously) to hustle. But the soul of the swell is still unchanged. He has changed his name again and again, become a Masher, a Toff, a Johnny and what not; but fundamentally he remains what he always was, an Idler, and therefore a man bound to find some trick of thought and speech that reduces the world to a thing as empty and purposeless and hopeless as himself. Mr. Harthouse reappears, more seriously and kindly taken, as Eugene Wrayburn and Mortimer Lightwood in *Our Mutual Friend*. He reappears as a club in The Finches of the Grove of *Great Expectations*. He will reappear in all his essentials in fact and in fiction until he is at last shamed or coerced into honest industry and becomes not only unintelligible but inconceivable.

Note, finally, that in this book Dickens proclaims that marriages are not made in heaven, and that those which are not confirmed there, should be dissolved.

F. R. LEAVIS

Hard Times: An Analytic Note[†]

Hard Times is not a difficult work; its intention and nature are pretty obvious. If, then, it is the masterpiece I take it for, why has it not had general recognition? To judge by the critical record, it has had none at all. If there exists anywhere an appreciation, or even an acclaiming reference, I have missed it. In the books and essays on Dickens, so far as I know them, it is passed over as a very minor thing; too slight and insignificant to distract us for more than a sentence or two from the works worth critical attention. Yet, if I am right, of all Dickens's works it is the one that has all the strength of his genius, together with a strength no other of them can show— that of a completely serious work of art.

The answer to the question asked above seems to me to bear on the traditional approach to 'the English novel'. For all the more sophisticated critical currency of the last decade or two, that approach still

† From F. R. Leavis, *The Great Tradition* (London: Chatto & Windus, 1948), pp. 227–48. Copyright 1960. Reprinted by permission of Faber & Faber Ltd. In 1970 this "Analytic Note" became a chapter in Leavis's book, *Dickens the Novelist* (of which Q. D. Leavis was co-author). The 1970 version is virtually identical to the 1948 version except for a modification of the final sentence of the first paragraph. The revised version is as follows: "Yet, if I am right, of all Dickens's works it is the one that, having the distinctive strength that makes him a major artist, has it in so compact a way, and with a concentrated significance so immediately clear and penetrating, as, one would have thought, to preclude the reader's failing to recognize that he had before him a completely serious, and, in its originality, a triumphantly successful work of art" (London: Chatto and Windus, 1970), p. 147.

prevails, at any rate in the appreciation of the Victorian novelists. The business of the novelist, you gather, is to 'create a world', and the mark of the master is external abundance—he gives you lots of 'life'. The test of life in his characters (he must above all create 'living' characters) is that they go on living outside the book. Expectations as unexacting as these are not, when they encounter significance, grateful for it, and when it meets them in that insistent form where nothing is very engaging as 'life' unless its relevance is fully taken, miss it altogether. This is the only way in which I can account for the neglect suffered by Henry James's *The Europeans*, which may be classed with *Hard Times* as a moral fable—though one might have supposed that James would enjoy the advantage of being approached with expectations of subtlety and closely calculated relevance. Fashion, however, has not recommended his earlier work, and this (whatever appreciation may be enjoyed by *The Ambassadors*) still suffers from the prevailing expectation of redundant and irrelevant 'life'.

I need say no more by way of defining the moral fable than that in it the intention is peculiarly insistent, so that the representative significance of everything in the fable—character, episode, and so on—is immediately apparent as we read. Intention might seem to be insistent enough in the opening of *Hard Times*, in that scene in Mr. Gradgrind's school. But then, intention is often very insistent in Dickens, without its being taken up in any inclusive significance that informs and organizes a coherent whole; and, for lack of any expectation of an organized whole, it has no doubt been supposed that in *Hard Times* the satiric irony of the first two chapters is merely, in the large and genial Dickensian way, thrown together with melodrama, pathos and humour—and that we are given these ingredients more abundantly and exuberantly elsewhere. Actually, the Dickensian vitality is there, in its varied characteristic modes, which have the more force because they are free of redundance: the creative exuberance is controlled by a profound inspiration.

The inspiration is what is given in the grim clinch of the title, *Hard Times*. Ordinarily Dickens's criticisms of the world he lives in are casual and incidental—a matter of including among the ingredients of a book some indignant treatment of a particular abuse. But in *Hard Times* he is for once[1] possessed by a comprehensive vision, one in which the inhumanities of Victorian civilization are seen as fostered and sanctioned by a hard philosophy, the aggressive formulation of an inhumane spirit. The philosophy is represented by Thomas Gradgrind, Esquire, Member of Parliament for Coketown, who has brought up his children on the lines of the experiment recorded by John Stuart Mill as carried out on himself.

---

1. In 1970 "for once possessed" was changed to "unmistakably possessed" [*editor*].

What Gradgrind stands for is, though repellent, nevertheless respectable; his Utilitarianism is a theory sincerely held and there is intellectual disinterestedness in its application. But Gradgrind marries his eldest daughter to Josiah Bounderby, 'banker, merchant, manufacturer', about whom there is no disinterestedness whatever, and nothing to be respected. Bounderby is Victorian 'rugged individualism' in its grossest and most intransigent form. Concerned with nothing but self-assertion and power and material success, he has no interest in ideals or ideas—except the idea of being the completely self-made man (since, for all his brag, he is not that in fact). Dickens here makes a just observation about the affinities and practical tendency of Utilitarianism, as, in his presentment of the Gradgrind home and the Gradgrind elementary school, he does about the Utilitarian spirit in Victorian education.

All this is obvious enough. But Dickens's art, while remaining that of the great popular entertainer, has in *Hard Times*, as he renders his full critical vision, a stamina, a flexibility combined with consistency, and a depth that he seems to have had little credit for. Take that opening scene in the school-room:

> "'Girl number twenty,' said Mr. Gradgrind, squarely pointing with his square forefinger, "I don't know that girl. Who is that girl?"
>
> "'Sissy Jupe, sir,' explained number twenty, blushing, standing up, and curtsying.
>
> "'Sissy is not a name,' said Mr. Gradgrind. "Don't call yourself Sissy. Call yourself Cecilia."
>
> "'It's father as calls me Sissy, sir,' returned the young girl in a trembling voice, and with another curtsy.
>
> "'Then he has no business to do it,' said Mr. Gradgrind. "Tell him he mustn't. Cecilia Jupe. Let me see. What is your father?"
>
> "'He belongs to the horse-riding, if you please, sir.'
>
> 'Mr. Gradgrind frowned, and waved off the objectionable calling with his hand.
>
> "'We don't want to know anything about that here. You mustn't tell us about that here. Your father breaks horses, don't he?"
>
> "'If you please, sir, when they can get any to break, they do break horses in the ring, sir.'
>
> "'You mustn't tell us about the ring here. Very well, then. Describe your father as a horse-breaker. He doctors sick horses, I dare say?"
>
> "'Oh, yes, sir!'
>
> "'Very well, then. He is a veterinary surgeon, a farrier, and horse-breaker. Give me your definition of a horse.'"

> (Sissy Jupe thrown into the greatest alarm by this demand.)
> '"Girl number twenty unable to define a horse!" said
> Mr. Gradgrind, for the general benefit of all the little pitchers.
> "Girl number twenty possessed of no facts in reference to one
> of the commonest animals! Some boy's definition of a horse.
> Bitzer, yours."
>
> . . . .
>
> '"Quadruped. Graminivorous. Forty teeth, namely, twenty-
> four grinders, four eye-teeth, and twelve incisive. Sheds coat in
> the spring; in marshy countries, sheds hoofs too. Hoofs hard,
> but requiring to be shod with iron. Age known by marks in
> mouth." Thus (and much more) Bitzer.'

Lawrence himself, protesting against harmful tendencies in education, never made the point more tellingly. Sissy has been brought
up among horses, and among people whose livelihood depends
upon understanding horses but 'we don't want to know anything
about that here'. Such knowledge isn't real knowledge. Bitzer, the
model pupil, on the button's being pressed, promptly vomits up the
genuine article, 'Quadruped. Graminivorous', etc.; and 'Now, girl
number twenty, you know what a horse is'. The irony, pungent
enough locally, is richly developed in the subsequent action. Bitzer's
aptness has its evaluative comment in his career. Sissy's incapacity
to acquire this kind of 'fact' or formula, her unaptness for education, is manifested to us, on the other hand, as part and parcel of
her sovereign and indefeasible humanity: it is the virtue that makes
it impossible for her to understand, or acquiesce in, an ethos for
which she is 'girl number twenty', or to think of any other human
being as a unit for arithmetic.

This kind of ironic method might seem to commit the author to
very limited kinds of effect. In *Hard Times*, however, it associates
quite congruously, such is the flexibility of Dickens's art, with very
different methods; it co-operates in a truly dramatic and profoundly
poetic whole. Sissy Jupe, who might be taken here for a merely conventional *persona*, has already, as a matter of fact, been established
in a potently symbolic rôle: she is part of the poetically-creative
operation of Dickens's genius in *Hard Times*. Here is a passage I
omitted from the middle of the excerpt quoted above:

> 'The square finger, moving here and there, lighted suddenly
> on Bitzer, perhaps because he chanced to sit in the same ray of
> sunlight which, darting in at one of the bare windows of the
> intensely white-washed room, irradiated Sissy. For the boys
> and girls sat on the face of an inclined plane in two compact
> bodies, divided up the centre by a narrow interval; and Sissy,
> being at the corner of a row on the sunny side, came in for the

beginning of a sunbeam, of which Bitzer, being at the corner of a row on the other side, a few rows in advance, caught the end. But, whereas the girl was so dark-eyed and dark-haired that she seemed to receive a deeper and more lustrous colour from the sun when it shone upon her, the boy was so light-eyed and light-haired that the self-same rays appeared to draw out of him what little colour he ever possessed. His cold eyes would hardly have been eyes, but for the short ends of lashes which, by bringing them into immediate contrast with something paler than themselves, expressed their form. His short-cropped hair might have been a mere continuation of the sandy freckles on his forehead and face. His skin was so unwholesomely deficient in the natural tinge, that he looked as though, if he were cut, he would bleed white.'

There is no need to insist on the force—representative of Dickens's art in general in *Hard Times*—with which the moral and spiritual differences are rendered here in terms of sensation, so that the symbolic intention emerges out of metaphor and the vivid evocation of the concrete. What may, perhaps, be emphasized is that Sissy stands for vitality as well as goodness—they are seen, in fact, as one; she is generous, impulsive life, finding self-fulfilment in self-forgetfulness—all that is the antithesis of calculating self-interest. There is an essentially Laurentian suggestion about the way in which 'the dark-eyed and dark-haired' girl, contrasting with Bitzer, seemed to receive a 'deeper and more lustrous colour from the sun', so opposing the life that is lived freely and richly from the deep instinctive and emotional springs to the thin-blooded, quasi-mechanical product of Gradgrindery.

Sissy's symbolic significance is bound up with that of Sleary's Horse-riding where human kindness is very insistently associated with vitality.

The way in which the Horse-riding takes on its significance illustrates beautifully the poetic-dramatic nature of Dickens's art. From the utilitarian schoolroom Mr. Gradgrind walks towards his utilitarian abode, Stone Lodge, which, as Dickens evokes it, brings home to us concretely the model regime that for the little Gradgrinds (among whom are Malthus and Adam Smith) is an inescapable prison. But before he gets there he passes the back of a circus booth, and is pulled up by the sight of two palpable offenders. Looking more closely, 'what did he behold but his own metallurgical Louisa peeping through a hole in a deal board, and his own mathematical Thomas abasing himself on the ground to catch but a hoof of the graceful equestrian Tyrolean flower act!' The chapter is called 'A Loophole', and Thomas 'gave himself up to be taken home like a machine'.

Representing human spontaneity, the circus-athletes represent at the same time highly-developed skill and deftness of kinds that bring poise, pride and confident ease—they are always buoyant, and ballet-dancer-like, in training:

> 'There were two or three handsome young women among them, with two or three husbands, and their two or three mothers, and their eight or nine little children, who did the fairy business when required. The father of one of the families was in the habit of balancing the father of another of the families on the top of a great pole; the father of the third family often made a pyramid of both those fathers; with Master Kidderminster for the apex, and himself for the base; all the fathers could dance upon rolling casks, stand upon bottles, catch knives and balls, twirl hand-basins, ride upon anything, jump over everything, and stick at nothing. All the mothers could (and did) dance upon the slack wire and the tight-rope, and perform rapid acts on bare-backed steeds; none of them were at all particular in respect of showing their legs; and one of them, alone in a Greek chariot, drove six-in-hand into every town they came to. They all assumed to be mighty rakish and knowing, they were not very tidy in their private dresses, they were not at all orderly in their domestic arrangements, and the combined literature of the whole company would have produced but a poor letter on any subject. Yet there was a remarkable gentleness and childishness about these people, a special inaptitude for any kind of sharp practice, and an untiring readiness to help and pity one another, deserving often of as much respect, and always of as much generous construction, as the every-day virtues of any class of people in the world.'

Their skills have no value for the Utilitarian calculus, but they express vital human impulse, and they minister to vital human needs. The Horse-riding, frowned upon as frivolous and wasteful by Gradgrind and malignantly scorned by Bounderby, brings the machine-hands of Coketown (the spirit-quenching hideousness of which is hauntingly evoked) what they are starved of. It brings to them, not merely amusement, but art, and the spectacle of triumphant activity that, seeming to contain its end within iself, is, in its easy mastery, joyously self-justified. In investing a travelling circus with this kind of symbolic value Dickens expresses a profounder reaction to industrialism than might have been expected of him. It is not only pleasure and relaxation the Coketowners stand in need of; he feels the dreadful degradation of life that would remain even if they were to be given a forty-four hour week, comfort, security and fun. We recall a characteristic passage from D. H. Lawrence.

'The car ploughed uphill through the long squalid straggle of Teckhall, the blackened brick dwellings, the black slate roofs, glistening their sharp edges, the mud black with coal-dust, the pavements wet and black. It was as if dismalness had soaked through and through everything. The utter negation of natural beauty, the utter negation of the gladness of life, the utter absence of the instinct for shapely beauty which every bird and beast has, the utter death of the human intuitive faculty was appalling. The stacks of soap in the grocers' shops, the rhubarb and lemons in the greengrocers'! the awful hats in the milliners all went by ugly, ugly, ugly, followed by the plaster and gilt horror of the cinema with its wet picture anouncements, "A Woman's Love," and the new big Primitive chapel, primitive enough in its stark brick and big panes of greenish and raspberry glass in the windows. The Wesleyan chapel, higher up, was of blackened brick and stood behind iron railings and blackened shrubs. The Congregational chapel, which thought itself superior, was built of rusticated sandstone and had a steeple, but not a very high one. Just beyond were the new school buildings, expensive pink brick, and gravelled playground inside iron railings, all very imposing, and mixing the suggestion of a chapel and a prison. Standard Five girls were having a singing lesson, just finishing the la-me-do-la exercises and beginning a "sweet children's song." Anything more unlike song, spontaneous song, would be impossible to imagine: a strange bawling yell followed the outlines of a tune. It was not like animals: animals *mean* something when they yell. It was like nothing on earth, and it was called singing. Connie sat and listened with her heart in her boots, as Field was filling petrol. What could possibly become of such a people, a people in whom the living intuitive faculty was dead as nails, and only queer mechanical yells and uncanny willpower remained?'

Dickens couldn't have put it in just those terms, but the way in which his vision of the Horse-riders insists on their gracious vitality implies that reaction.

Here an objection may be anticipated—as a way of making a point. Coketown, like Gradgrind and Bounderby, is real enough; but it can't be contended that the Horse-riding is real in the same sense. There would have been some athletic skill and perhaps some bodily grace among the people of a Victorian travelling circus, but surely so much squalor, grossness and vulgarity that we must find Dickens's symbolism sentimentally false? And 'there was a remarkable gentleness and childishness about these people, a special inaptitude for any kind of sharp practice'—that, surely, is going ludicrously too far?

If Dickens, intent on an emotional effect, or drunk with moral enthusiasm, had been deceiving himself (it couldn't have been innocently) about the nature of the actuality, he would then indeed have been guilty of sentimental falsity, and the adverse criticism would have held. But the Horse-riding presents no such case. The virtues and qualities that Dickens prizes do indeed exist, and it is necessary for his critique of Utilitarianism and industrialism, and for (what is the same thing) his creative purpose, to evoke them vividly. The book can't, in my judgment, be fairly charged with giving a misleading representation of human nature. And it would plainly not be intelligent criticism to suggest that anyone could be misled about the nature of circuses by *Hard Times*. The critical question is merely one of tact: was it well-judged of Dickens to try to do *that*—which had to be done somehow—with a travelling circus?

Or, rather, the question is: by what means has he succeeded? For the success is complete. It is conditioned partly by the fact that, from the opening chapters, we have been tuned for the reception of a highly conventional art—though it is a tuning that has no narrowly limiting effect. To describe at all cogently the means by which this responsiveness is set up would take a good deal of 'practical criticism' analysis—analysis that would reveal an extraordinary flexibility in the art of *Hard Times*. This can be seen very obviously in the dialogue. Some passages might come from an ordinary novel. Others have the ironic pointedness of the school-room scene in so insistent a form that we might be reading a work as stylized as Jonsonian comedy: Gradgrind's final exchange with Bitzer (quoted below) is a supreme instance. Others again are 'literary', like the conversation between Gradgrind and Louisa on her flight home for refuge from Mr. James Harthouse's attentions.

To the question how the reconciling is done—there is much more diversity in *Hard Times* than these references to dialogue suggest—the answer can be given by pointing to the astonishing and irresistible richness of life that characterizes the book everywhere. It meets us everywhere, unstrained and natural, in the prose. Out of such prose a great variety of presentations can arise congenially with equal vividness. There they are, unquestionably 'real'. It goes back to an extraordinary energy of perception and registration in Dickens. 'When people say that Dickens exaggerates', says Santayana, 'it seems to me that they can have no eyes and no ears. They probably only have *notions* of what things and people are; they accept them conventionally, at their diplomatic value'. Settling down as we read to an implicit recognition of this truth, we don't really and confidently apply any criterion we suppose ourselves to hold for distinguishing varieties of relation between what Dickens gives us and a normal 'real'. His flexibility is that of a richly poetic art of the word. He doesn't write 'poetic prose'; he writes with a poetic force of evocation, registering with the responsiveness of a genius of verbal expression what he so sharply sees and feels. In fact, by texture, imaginative mode, symbolic method, and the resulting concentration, *Hard Times* affects us as belonging with formally poetic works.

There is, however, more to be said about the success that attends Dickens's symbolic intention in the Horse-riding; there is an essential quality of his genius to be emphasized. There is no Hamlet in him, and he is quite unlike Mr. Eliot.

> *The red-eyed scavengers are creeping*
> *From Kentish Town and Golders Green*

—there is nothing of that in Dickens's reaction to life. He observes with gusto the humanness of humanity as exhibited in the urban (and suburban) scene. When he sees, as he sees so readily, the common manifestations of human kindness, and the essential virtues, asserting themselves in the midst of ugliness, squalor and banality, his warmly sympathetic response has no disgust to overcome. There is no suggestion for instance, of recoil—or of distance-keeping— from the game-eyed, brandy-soaked, flabby-surfaced Mr. Sleary, who is successfully made to figure for us a humane, anti-Utilitarian positive. This is not sentimentality in Dickens, but genius, and a genius that should be found peculiarly worth attention in an age when, as D. H. Lawrence (with, as I remember, Wyndham Lewis immediately in view) says, 'My God! they stink' tends to be an insuperable and final reaction.

Dickens, as everyone knows, is very capable of sentimentality. We have it in *Hard Times* (though not to any seriously damaging effect) in Stephen Blackpool, the good, victimized working-man, whose perfect patience under infliction we are expected to find supremely edifying and irresistibly touching as the agonies are piled on for his martyrdom. But Sissy Jupe is another matter. A general description of her part in the fable might suggest the worst, but actually she has nothing in common with Little Nell: she shares in the strength of the Horse-riding. She is wholly convincing in the function Dickens assigns to her. The working of her influence in the Utilitarian home is conveyed with a fine tact, and we do really feel her as a growing potency. Dickens can even, with complete success, give her the stage for a victorious *tête-à-tête* with the well-bred and languid elegant, Mr. James Harthouse, in which she tells him that his duty is to leave Coketown and cease troubling Louisa with his attentions:

'She was not afraid of him, or in any way disconcerted; she seemed to have her mind entirely preoccupied with the occasion of her visit, and to have substituted that consideration for herself.'

The quiet victory of disinterested goodness is wholly convincing.

At the opening of the book Sissy establishes the essential distinction between Gradgrind and Bounderby. Gradgrind, by taking her home, however ungraciously, shows himself capable of humane feeling, however unacknowledged. We are reminded, in the previous school-room scene, of the Jonsonian affinities of Dickens's art, and Bounderby turns out to be consistently a Jonsonian character in the sense that he is incapable of change. He remains the blustering egotist and braggart, and responds in character to the collapse of his marriage:

"'I'll give *you* to understand, in reply to that, that there unquestionably is an incompatibility of the first magnitude— to be summed up in this—that your daughter don't properly know her husband's merits, and is not impressed with such a sense as would become her, by George! of the honour of his alliance. That's plain speaking, I hope.'"

He remains Jonsonianly consistent in his last testament and death. But Gradgrind, in the nature of the fable, has to *experience* the confutation of his philosophy, and to be capable of the change involved in admitting that life has proved him wrong. (Dickens's art in *Hard Times* differs from Ben Jonson's not in being inconsistent, but in being so very much more flexible and inclusive—a point that seemed to be worth making because the relation between Dickens and Jonson has been stressed of late, and I have known unfair conclusions to be drawn from the comparison, notably in respect of *Hard Times*.)

The confutation of Utilitarianism by life is conducted with great subtlety. That the conditions for it are there in Mr. Gradgrind he betrays by his initial kindness, ungenial enough, but properly rebuked by Bounderby, to Sissy. 'Mr. Gradgrind', we are told, 'though hard enough, was by no means so rough a man as Mr. Bounderby. His character was not unkind, all things considered; it might have been very kind indeed if only he had made some mistake in the arithmetic that balanced it years ago'. The inadequacy of the calculus is beautifully exposed when he brings it to bear on the problem of marriage in the consummate scene with his eldest daughter:

'He waited, as if he would have been glad that she said something. But she said never a word.

'"Louisa, my dear, you are the subject of a proposal of marriage that has been made to me."

'Again he waited, and again she answered not one word. This so far surprised him as to induce him gently to repeat, "A proposal of marriage, my dear." To which she returned, without any visible emotion whatever:

'"I hear you, father. I am attending, I assure you."

'"Well!" said Mr. Gradgrind, breaking into a smile, after being for the moment at a loss, "you are even more dispassionate than I expected, Louisa. Or, perhaps, you are not unprepared for the announcement I have it in charge to make?"

'"I cannot say that, father, until I hear it. Prepared or unprepared, I wish to hear it all from you. I wish to hear you state it to me, father."

'Strange to relate, Mr. Gradgrind was not so collected at this moment as his daughter was. He took a paper knife in his hand, turned it over, laid it down, took it up again, and even then had to look along the blade of it, considering how to go on.

'"What you say, my dear Louisa, is perfectly reasonable. I have undertaken, then, to let you know that—in short, that Mr. Bounderby . . ."'

His embarrassment—by his own avowal—is caused by the perfect rationality with which she receives his overture. He is still more disconcerted when, with a completely dispassionate matter-of-factness that does credit to his *régime*, she gives him the opportunity to state in plain terms precisely what marriage should mean for the young Houyhnhnm:

'Silence between them. The deadly statistical clock very hollow. The distant smoke very black and heavy.

'"Father," said Louisa, "do you think I love Mr. Bounderby?"

'Mr. Gradgrind was extremely discomforted by this unexpected question. "Well, my child," he returned, "I—really—cannot take upon myself to say."

'"Father," pursued Louisa in exactly the same voice as before, "do you ask me to love Mr. Bounderby?"

'"My dear Louisa, no. I ask nothing."

'"Father," she still pursued, "does Mr. Bounderby ask me to love him?"

'"Really, my dear," said Mr. Gradgrind, "it is difficult to answer your question—"

'"Difficult to answer it, Yes or No, father?"

'"Certainly, my dear. Because"—here was something to demonstrate, and it set him up again—"because the reply depends so materially, Louisa, on the sense in which we use the expression. Now, Mr. Bounderby does not do you the injustice, and does not do himself the injustice, of pretending to anything fanciful, fantastic, or (I am using synonymous terms) sentimental. Mr. Bounderby would have seen you grow up under his eye to very little purpose, if he could so far forget what is due to your good sense, not to say to his, as to address you from any such ground. Therefore, perhaps, the expression itself—I merely suggest this to you, my dear—may be a little misplaced."

'"What would you advise me to use in its stead, father?"

'"Why, my dear Louisa," said Mr. Gradgrind, completely recovered by this time, "I would advise you (since you ask me) to consider the question, as you have been accustomed to consider every other question, simply as one of tangible Fact. The ignorant and the giddy may embarrass such subjects with irrelevant fancies, and other absurdities that have no existence, properly viewed—really no existence—but it is no compliment to say that you know better. Now, what are the Facts of this case? You are, we will say in round numbers, twenty years of age; Mr. Bounderby is, we will say in round numbers, fifty. There is some disparity in your respective years, but . . ."'

—And at this point Mr. Gradgrind seizes the chance for a happy escape into statistics. But Louisa brings him firmly back:

'"What do you recommend, father?" asked Louisa, her reserved composure not in the least affected by these gratifying results, "that I should substitute for the term I used just now? For the misplaced expression?"

'"Louisa," returned her father, "it appears to me that nothing can be plainer. Confining yourself rigidly to Fact, the question of Fact you state to yourself is: Does Mr. Bounderby ask me to marry him? Yes, he does. The sole remaining question then is: Shall I marry him? I think nothing can be plainer than that."

'"Shall I marry him?" repeated Louisa with great deliberation.

'"Precisely."'

It is a triumph of ironic art. No logical analysis could dispose of the philosophy of fact and calculus with such neat finality. As the issues are reduced to algebraic formulation they are patently emptied of all real meaning. The instinct-free rationality of the emotionless Houyhnhnm is a void. Louisa proceeds to try and make him understand that she is a living creature and therefore no Houyhnhnm, but in vain ('to see it, he must have overleaped at a bound the artificial barriers he had for many years been erecting between himself and all those subtle essences of humanity which will elude the utmost cunning of algebra, until the last trumpet ever to be sounded will blow even algebra to wreck').

'Removing her eyes from him, she sat so long looking silently towards the town, that he said at length: "Are you consulting the chimneys of the Coketown works, Louisa?"

'"There seems to be nothing there but languid and monotonous smoke. Yet, when the night comes, Fire bursts out, father!" she answered, turning quickly.

'"Of couse I know that, Louisa. I do not see the application of the remark." To do him justice, he did not at all.

'She passed it away with a slight motion of her hand, and concentrating her attention upon him again, said, "Father, I have often thought that life is very short"—This was so distinctly one of his subjects that he interposed:

'"It is short, no doubt, my dear. Still, the average duration of human life is proved to have increased of late years. The calculations of various life assurance and annuity offices, among other figures which cannot go wrong, have established the fact."

'"I speak of my own life, father."

'"Oh, indeed! Still," said Mr. Gradgrind, "I need not point out to you, Louisa, that it is governed by the laws which govern lives in the aggregate."

'"While it lasts, I would wish to do the little I can, and the little I am fit for. What does it matter?"

'Mr. Gradgrind seemed rather at a loss to understand the last four words; replying, "How, matter? What matter, my dear?"

'"Mr. Bounderby," she went on in a steady, straight way, without regarding this, "asks me to marry him. The question I have to ask myself is, shall I marry him? That is so, father, is it not? You have told me so, father. Have you not?"

'"Certainly, my dear."

'"Let it be so."'

The psychology of Louisa's development and of her brother Tom's is sound. Having no outlet for her emotional life except in her love for her brother, she lives for him, and marries Bounderby—under pressure from Tom—for Tom's sake ('What does it matter?'). Thus, by the constrictions and starvations of the Gradgrind *régime*, are natural affection and capacity for disinterested devotion turned to ill. As for Tom, the *régime* has made of him a bored and sullen whelp, and 'he was becoming that not unprecedented triumph of calculation which is usually at work on number one'—the Utilitarian philosophy has done that for him. He declares that when he goes to live with Bounderby as having a post in the bank, 'he'll have his revenge'—'I mean, I'll enjoy myself a little, and go about and see something and hear something. I'll recompense myself for the way in which I've been brought up'. His descent into debt and bank-robbery is natural. And it is natural that Louisa, having sacrificed herself for this unrepaying object of affection, should be found not altogether unresponsive when Mr. James Harthouse, having sized up the situation, pursues his opportunity with well-bred and calculating tact. His apologia for genteel cynicism is a shrewd thrust at the Gradgrind philosophy:

> '"The only difference' between us and the professors of virtue or benevolence, or philanthropy—never mind the name—is, that we know it is all meaningless, and say so; while they know it equally; and will never say so."
>
> 'Why should she be shocked or warned by this reiteration? It was not so unlike her father's principles, and her early training, that it need startle her.'

When, fleeing from temptation, she arrives back at her father's house, tells him her plight, and, crying, 'All I know is, your philosophy and your teachings will not save me', collapses, he sees 'the pride of his heart and the triumph of his system lying an insensible heap at his feet'. The fallacy now calamitously demonstrated can be seen focused in that 'pride', which brings together in an illusory oneness the pride of his system and his love for his child. What that love is Gradgrind now knows, and he knows that it matters to him more than the system, which is thus confuted (the educational failure as such being a lesser matter). There is nothing sentimental here; the demonstration is impressive, because we are convinced of the love, and because Gradgrind has been made to exist for us as a man who has 'meant to do right':

> 'He said it earnestly, and, to do him justice, he had. In gauging fathomless deeps with his little mean excise rod, and in staggering over the universe with his rusty stiff-legged compasses, he had meant to do great things. Within the limits of his short tether he had tumbled about, annihilating the flowers of existence with greater singleness of purpose than many of the blatant personages whose company he kept.'

The demonstration still to come, that of which the other 'triumph of his system', Tom, is the centre, is sardonic comedy, imagined with great intensity and done with the sure touch of genius. There is the pregnant scene in which Mr. Gradgrind, in the deserted ring of a third-rate travelling circus, has to recognize his son in a comic negro servant; and has to recognize that his son owes his escape from Justice to a peculiarly disinterested gratitude—to the opportunity given him to assume such a disguise by the non-Utilitarian Mr. Sleary, grateful for Sissy's sake:

'In a preposterous coat, like a beadle's, with cuffs and flaps exaggerated to an unspeakable extent; in an immense waist-coat, knee breeches, buckled shoes, and a mad cocked-hat; with nothing fitting him, and everything of coarse material, moth-eaten, and full of holes; with seams in his black face, where fear and heat had started through the greasy composition daubed all over it; anything so grimly, detestably, ridiculously shameful as the whelp in his comic livery, Mr. Gradgrind never could by any other means have believed in, weighable and mea-surable fact though it was. And one of his model children had come to this!

'At first the whelp would not draw any nearer but persisted in remaining up there by himself. Yielding at length, if any con-cession so sullenly made can be called yielding, to the entreaties of Sissy—for Louisa he disowned altogether—he came down, bench by bench, until he stood in the sawdust, on the verge of the circle, as far as possible, within its limits, from where his father sat.

'"How was this done?" asked the father.

'"How was what done?" moodily answered the son.

'"This robbery," said the father, raising his voice upon the word.

'"I forced the safe myself overnight, and shut it up ajar before I went away. I had had the key that was found made long before. I dropped it that morning, that it might be supposed to have been used. I didn't take the money all at once. I pretended to put my balance away every night, but I didn't. Now you know all about it."

'"If a thunderbolt had fallen on me," said the father, "it would have shocked me less than this!"

'"I don't see why," grumbled the son. "So many people are employed in situations of trust; so many people, out of so many, will be dishonest. I have heard you talk, a hundred times, of its being a law. How can I help laws? You have comforted others with such things, father. Comfort yourself!"

'The father buried his face in his hands, and the son stood in his disgraceful grotesqueness, biting straw: his hands, with the black partly worn away inside, looking like the hands of a mon-key. The evening was fast closing in; and, from time to time, he turned the whites of his eyes restlessly and impatiently towards his father. They were the only parts of his face that showed any life or expression, the pigment upon it was so thick.'

Something of the rich complexity of Dickens's art may be seen in this passage. No simple formula can take account of the various

elements in the whole effect, a sardonic-tragic in which satire con-
sorts with pathos. The excerpt in itself suggests the justification for
saying that *Hard Times* is a poetic work. It suggests that the genius
of the writer may fairly be described as that of a poetic dramatist,
and that, in our preconceptions about 'the novel', we may miss, within
the field of fictional prose, possibilities of concentration and flexibility in the interpretation of life such as we associate with Shake-
spearean drama.

The note, as we have it above in Tom's retort, of ironic-satiric discomfiture of the Utilitarian philosopher by the rebound of his formulae upon himself is developed in the ensuing scene with Bitzer, the
truly successful pupil, the real triumph of the system. He arrives to
intercept Tom's flight:

> 'Bitzer, still holding the paralysed culprit by the collar, stood
> in the Ring, blinking at his old patron through the darkness of
> the twilight.
> '"Bitzer," said Mr. Gradgrind, broken down and miserably
> submissive to him, "have you a heart?"
> '"The circulation, sir," returned Bitzer, smiling at the oddity
> of the question, "couldn't be carried on without one. No man,
> sir, acquainted with the facts established by Harvey relating to
> the circulation of the blood, can doubt that I have a heart."
> '"Is it accessible," cried Mr. Gradgrind, "to any compassion-
> ate influence?"
> '"It is accessible to Reason, sir," returned the excellent young
> man. "And to nothing else."
> 'They stood looking at each other; Mr. Gradgrind's face as
> white as the pursuer's.
> '"What motive—even what motive in reason—can you
> have for preventing the escape of this wretched youth," said
> Mr. Gradgrind, "and crushing his miserable father? See his
> sister here. Pity us!"
> '"Sir," returned Bitzer in a very business-like and logical
> manner, "since you ask me what motive I have in reason for
> taking young Mr. Tom back to Coketown, it is only reasonable
> to let you know . . . I am going to take young Mr. Tom back to
> Coketown, in order to deliver him over to Mr. Bounderby. Sir,
> I have no doubt whatever that Mr. Bounderby will then pro-
> mote me to young Mr. Tom's situation. And I wish to have his
> situation, sir, for it will be a rise to me, and will do me good."
> '"If this is solely a question of self-interest with you—"
> Mr. Gradgrind began.
> '"I beg your pardon for interrupting you, sir," returned
> Bitzer, "but I am sure you know that the whole social system is
> a question of self-interest. What you must always appeal to is a
> person's self-interest. It's your only hold. We are so constituted.

I was brought up in that catechism when I was very young, sir, as you are aware."

'"What sum of money," said Mr. Gradgrind, "will you set against your expected promotion?"

'"Thank you, sir," returned Bitzer, "for hinting at the proposal; but I will not set any sum against it. Knowing that your clear head would propose that alternative, I have gone over the calculations in my mind; and I find that to compound a felony, even on very high terms indeed, would not be as safe and good for me as my improved prospects in the Bank."

'"Bitzer," said Mr. Gradgrind, stretching out his hands as though he would have said, See how miserable I am! "Bitzer, I have but one chance left to soften you. You were many years at my school. If, in remembrance of the pains bestowed upon you there, you can persuade yourself in any degree to disregard your present interest and release my son, I entreat and pray you to give him the benefit of that remembrance."

'"I really wonder, sir," rejoined the old pupil in an argumentative manner, "to find you taking a position so untenable. My schooling was paid for; it was a bargain; and when I came away, the bargain ended."

'It was a fundamental principle of the Gradgrind philosophy, that everything was to be paid for. Nobody was ever on any account to give anybody anything, or render anybody help without purchase. Gratitude was to be abolished, and the virtues springing from it were not to be. Every inch of the existence of mankind, from birth to death, was to be a bargain across the counter. And if we didn't get to Heaven that way, it was not a politico-economical place, and we had no business there.

'"I don't deny," added Bitzer, "that my schooling was cheap, But that comes right, sir. I was made in the cheapest market, and have to dispose of myself in the dearest."'

Tom's escape is contrived, successfully in every sense, by means belonging to Dickensian high-fantastic comedy. And there follows the solemn moral of the whole fable, put with the rightness of genius into Mr. Sleary's asthmatic mouth. He, agent of the artist's marvellous tact, acquits himself of it characteristically:

'"Thquire, you don't need to be told that dogth ith wonderful animalth."

'"Their instinct," said Mr. Gradgrind, "is surprising."

'"Whatever you call it—and I'm bletht if I know what to call it"—said Sleary, "it ith athtonithing. The way in which a dog'll find you—the dithtanthe he'll come!"

'"His scent," said Mr. Gradgrind, "being so fine."

'"I'm bletht if I know what to call it," repeated Sleary, shaking his head, "but I have had dogth find me, Thquire . . ."'

—And Mr. Sleary proceeds to explain that Sissy's truant father is certainly dead because his performing dog, who would never have deserted him living, has come back to the Horse-riding:

'"he wath lame, and pretty well blind. He went to our children, one after another, ath if he wath a theeking for a child he knowed; and then he come to me, and throwd hithelf up behind, and thtood on hith two fore-legth, weak as he wath, and then he wagged hith tail and died. Thquire, that dog was Merrylegth."

The whole passage has to be read as it stands in the text (Book III, Chapter VIII). Reading it there we have to stand off and reflect at a distance to recognize the potentialities that might have been realized elsewhere as Dickensian sentimentality. There is nothing sentimental in the actual effect. The profoundly serious intention is in control, the touch sure, and the structure that ensures the poise unassertively complex. Here is the formal moral:

'"Tho, whether her father bathely detherted her; or whether he broke hith own heart alone, rather than pull her down along with him; never will be known now, Thquire, till—no, not till we know how the dogth findth uth out!"

'"She keeps the bottle that he sent her for, to this hour; and she will believe in his affection to the last moment of her life," said Mr. Gradgrind.

'"It theemth to prethent two thingth to a perthon, don't it, Thquire?" said Mr. Sleary, musing as he looked down into the depths of his brandy-and-water: "one, that there ith a love in the world, not all Thelf-interetht after all, but thomething very different; t'other, that it hath a way of ith own of calculating or not calculating, whith thomehow or another ith at leatht ath hard to give a name to, ath the wayth of the dogth ith!"

'Mr. Gradgrind looked out of the window, and made no reply. Mr. Sleary emptied his glass and recalled the ladies.'

It will be seen that the effect (I repeat, the whole passage must be read), apparently so simple and easily right, depends upon a subtle interplay of diverse elements, a multiplicity in unison of timbre and tone. Dickens, we know, was a popular entertainer, but Flaubert never wrote anything approaching this in subtlety of achieved art. Dickens, of course, has a vitality that we don't look for in Flaubert. Shakespeare was a popular entertainer, we reflect—not too extravagantly, we can surely tell ourselves, as we ponder passages of this characteristic quality in their relation, a closely organized one, to the poetic whole.

Criticism, of course, has its points to make against *Hard Times*. It can be said of Stephen Blackpool, not only that he is too good and qualifies too consistently for the martyr's halo, but that he invites an adaptation of the objection brought, from the negro point of view, against Uncle Tom, which was to the effect that he was a white man's good nigger. And certainly it doesn't need a working-class bias to produce the comment that when Dickens comes to the Trade Unions his understanding of the world he offers to deal with betrays a marked limitation. There were undoubtedly professional agitators, and Trade Union solidarity was undoubtedly often asserted at the expense of the individual's rights, but it is a score against a work so insistently typical in intention that it should give the representative rôle to the agitator, Slackbridge, and make Trade Unionism nothing better than the pardonable error of the misguided and oppressed, and, as such, an agent in the martyrdom of the good working man. (But to be fair we must remember the conversation between Bitzer and Mrs. Sparsit:

> '"It is much to be regretted," said Mrs. Sparsit, making her nose more Roman and her eyebrows more Coriolanian in the strength of her severity, "that the united masters allow of any such class combination."
>
> '"Yes, ma'am," said Bitzer.
>
> '"Being united themselves, they ought one and all to set their faces against employing any man who is united with any other man," said Mrs. Sparsit.
>
> '"They have done that, ma'am," returned Bitzer; "but it rather fell through, ma'am."
>
> '"I do not pretend to understand these things," said Mrs. Sparsit with dignity. ". . . I only know that these people must be conquered, and that it's high time it was done, once and for all."')

Just as Dickens has no glimpse of the part to be played by Trade Unionism in bettering the conditions he deplores, so, though he sees there are many places of worship in Coketown, of various kinds of ugliness, he has no notion of the part played by religion in the life of nineteenth-century industrial England. The kind of self-respecting steadiness and conscientious restraint that he represents in Stephen did certainly exist on a large scale among the working-classes, and this is an important historical fact. But there would have been no such fact if those chapels described by Dickens had had no more relation to the life of Coketown than he shows them to have.

Again, his attitude to Trade Unionism is not the only expression of a lack of political understanding. Parliament for him is merely the 'national dust-yard', where the 'national dustmen' entertain one another 'with a great many noisy little fights among themselves', and appoint commissions which fill blue-books with dreary facts and futile statistics—of a kind that helps Gradgrind to 'prove that the Good Samaritan was a bad economist'.

Yet Dickens's understanding of Victorian civilization is adequate for his purpose; the justice and penetration of his criticism are unaffected. And his moral perception works in alliance with a clear insight into the English social structure. Mr. James Harthouse is necessary for the plot; but he too has his representative function. He has come to Coketown as a prospective parliamentary candidate, for 'the Gradgrind party wanted assistance in cutting the throats of the Graces', and they 'liked fine gentlemen; they pretended that they did not, but they did'. And so the alliance between the old ruling class and the 'hard' men figures duly in the fable. This economy is typical. There is Mrs. Sparsit, for instance, who might seem to be there merely for the plot. But her 'husband was a Powler', a fact she reverts to as often as Bounderby to his mythical birth in a ditch; and the two complementary opposites, when Mr. James Harthouse, who in his languid assurance of class-superiority doesn't need to boast, is added, form a trio that suggests the whole system of British snobbery.

But the packed richness of *Hard Times* is almost incredibly varied, and not all the quoting I have indulged in suggests it adequately. The final stress may fall on Dickens's command of word, phrase, rhythm and image: in ease and range there is surely no greater master of English except Shakespeare. This comes back to saying that Dickens is a great poet: his endless resource in felicitously varied expression is an extraordinary responsiveness to life. His senses are charged with emotional energy, and his intelligence plays and flashes in the quickest and sharpest perception. That is, his mastery of 'style' is of the only kind that matters—which is not to say that he hasn't a conscious interest in what can be done with words; many of his felicities could plainly not have come if there had not been, in the background, a habit of such interest. Take this, for instance:

> 'He had reached the neutral ground upon the outskirts of the town, which was neither town nor country, but either spoiled . . .'

But he is no more a stylist than Shakespeare; and his mastery of expression is most fairly suggested by stressing, not his descriptive evocations (there are some magnificent ones in *Hard Times*—the varied *décor* of the action is made vividly present, you can feel the

velvety dust trodden by Mrs. Sparsit in her stealth, and feel the
imminent storm), but his strictly dramatic felicities. Perhaps, however, 'strictly' is not altogether a good pointer, since Dickens is a master of his chosen art, and his mastery shows itself in the way in which
he moves between less direct forms of the dramatic and the direct
rendering of speech. Here is Mrs. Gradgrind dying (a cipher in the
Gradgrind system, the poor creature has never really been alive):

> 'She had positively refused to take to her bed; on the ground
> that, if she did, she would never hear the last of it.
> 'Her feeble voice sounded so far away in her bundle of shawls,
> and the sound of another voice addressing her seemed to take
> such a long time in getting down to her ears, that she might have
> been lying at the bottom of a well. The poor lady was nearer
> Truth than she had ever been: which had much to do with it.
> 'On being told that Mrs. Bounderby was there, she replied,
> at cross purposes, that she had never called him by that name
> since he had married Louisa; and that pending her choice of
> an objectionable name, she had called him J; and that she could
> not at present depart from that regulation, not being yet pro-
> vided with a permanent substitute. Louisa had sat by her for
> some minutes, and had spoken to her often, before she arrived
> at a clear understanding who it was. She then seemed to come
> to it all at once.
> '"Well, my dear," said Mrs. Gradgrind, "and I hope you are
> going on satisfactorily to yourself. It was all your father's doing.
> He set his heart upon it. And he ought to know."
> '"I want to hear of you, mother; not of myself."
> '"You want to hear of me, my dear? That's something new,
> I am sure, when anybody wants to hear of me. Not at all well,
> Louisa. Very faint and giddy."
> '"Are you in pain, dear mother?"
> '"I think there's a pain somewhere in the room," said
> Mrs. Gradgrind, "but I couldn't positively say that I have got it."
> 'After this strange speech, she lay silent for some time.
>   •   •   •   •   •   •   •
> '"But there is something—not an Ology at all—that your
> father has missed, or forgotten, Louisa. I don't know what it is.
> I have often sat with Sissy near me, and thought about it. I
> shall never get its name now. But your father may. It makes me
> restless. I want to write to him, to find out, for God's sake,
> what it is. Give me a pen, give me a pen."
> 'Even the power of restlessness was gone, except from the
> poor head, which could just turn from side to side.
> 'She fancied, however, that her request had been complied
> with, and that the pen she could not have held was in her
> hand. It matters little what figures of wonderful no-meaning

she began to trace upon her wrappers. The hand soon stopped in the midst of them; the light that had always been feeble and dim behind the weak transparency, went out; and even Mrs. Gradgrind, emerged from the shadow in which man walketh and disquieteth himself in vain, took upon her the dread solemnity of the sages and patriarchs.'

With this kind of thing before us, we talk not of style but of dramatic creation and imaginative genius.

MARTHA C. NUSSBAUM

From The Literary Imagination in Public Life†

I. Nothing but Facts

Dickens's *Hard Times*[1] contains a normative vision of a scientific political economy and of the scientific political imagination. It presents this norm, to be sure, as a target of withering satirical attack, a goal that cannot be truly described without being made to appear both ridiculous and sinister. But since the attack is a deep attack, the satirical target itself is described with insight, as the novel both depicts and shows the deeper significance of what is still today very often taught as normative in public policy-making, in welfare and development economics—and, recently, even in the law. What makes this norm appear so odd to the reader of the novel is that it is taken seriously all the way down, so to speak; understood not just as a way of writing up reports, but as a way of dealing with people in daily encounters; not just as a way of doing economics, but a way of defining a horse or talking to a child; not just as a way of appearing professionally respectable, but as a commitment that determines the whole content of one's personal and social life. But since this norm does in fact claim to be a norm of rationality, and not just a handy professional tool, and since, if it is really a norm, it seems fair to ask people to abide by it consistently, it seems perfectly fair to examine it in this way, asking what people who really and thoroughly saw the world in the way this norm recommends would be like, and whether such a vision does really seem to be a complete one. (And it seems reasonable, too, to suppose that the personal vision and conduct of committed social scientists is actually influenced at least to some extent by the content of the norm their science upholds, by

† From *New Literary History* 22.4 (Autumn 1991): 877–910. © 1991 *New Literary History*, The University of Virginia. Reprinted with permission of Johns Hopkins University Press.
1. Nussbaum used Penguin's 1969 edition edited by David Craig; page citations here refer to this Norton Critical Edition [*editor*].

the habits of perception and recognition it encourages. So in examining it this way we can expect to learn something about what we do *to* people by holding it up as a norm, and what we can expect *from* people so treated.) Dickens pays the economic utilitarian the tribute of taking him at his word and holding him to his word; of this treatment he can hardly, it seems to me, complain. Later I shall draw some explicit connections between the Gradgrind philosophy and some aspects of contemporary economic thought and practice. But for now I need to set out the features of this norm, as the novel dissects it. (This will mean beginning to speak of its limitations as well: for in seeing it we see what the novel sees.)

What I am about to say here may seem in some respects obvious. For it is part of the novel's design that the economist's way of thinking, seen in the full context of daily life, should look extremely strange, and the opposing way natural. What I hope to bring out here, however, is that the economic opponent is not a straw man: it is a conception that even now dominates much of our public life, in a form not very different from the form presented in this novel. Once, focusing on the subtle modifications of utilitarianism that one finds in recent philosophy,[2] I felt that the satire of *Hard Times* was unfair. But now that I have spent time in the world of economics, reading the prose and following the arguments, I am convinced that the criticisms in the novel are both fair and urgent. The simple utilitarian idea of what rational choice consists in dominates not only economic thought and practice, but also—given the prestige of economics within the social sciences—a great deal of writing in other social sciences as well, where "rational choice theory" is taken to be equivalent to utilitarian rational choice theory as practiced in neoclassical economics. Public policy-makers turn to these norms to find a principled, orderly way of making decisions. And the allure of the theory's elegant simplicity is so great that it is having an increasing influence even in the law, which has traditionally reasoned in a very different way, using a different norm of the rational.[3] Recently the theory has even made its way into literary studies, where the prestige of neoclassical economics, Chicago style, is evoked in defense of a broad application of its behavioral theory to all areas of human life.[4] To the reader who has no familiarity with

2. For example, see James Griffin, *Well-Being* (Oxford, 1986), and Richard B. Brandt, *A Theory of the Good and Right* (Oxford, 1979).
3. See all the writings of Richard Posner, including *Economic Analysis of Law* (Boston, Mass., 1977), *The Economics of Justice* (Cambridge, Mass., 1981), and *Law and Literature: A Misunderstood Relation* (Cambridge, Mass., 1988). In *The Problems of Jurisprudence* (Cambridge, Mass., 1990) Posner has modified his approach, espousing a kind of "pragmatism." For a good general critique of economic reasoning in public life generally, see the introduction to *Utilitarianism and Beyond*, ed. Amartya Sen and Bernard Williams (Cambridge, 1988).
4. See Barbara Herrnstein Smith, *Contingencies of Value* (Cambridge, Mass., 1988).

the opposing position and the prose in which it is expressed, a short course in the writings of Gary Becker or Richard Posner might be recommended. (For their views are extreme—but only in the sense that, like this novel, they apply across the board a theory that economics treats as normative for rational choice in general. If it is indeed a norm of rationality, they are right to do so: and we are justified in examining their works as tests of the theory's normative appropriateness.[5] To the reader I leave, then, the further investigation of the economist's position in contemporary life. For now I myself shall turn to Mr. Gradgrind—who at least ends the novel by expressing remorse, and revealing, in the process, a certain human complexity.

"'In this life, we want nothing but Facts, sir; nothing but Facts'" [7]. This famous demand, announced in the Gradgrind schoolroom in the opening chapter of the novel (a chapter entitled "The One Thing Needful"), states the essence of the Gradgrind philosophy. And the novel shortly characterizes it further, speaking for Mr. Gradgrind in the hard blunt confrontational sentences that seem well suited to express the quality of his mind: "Thomas Gradgrind, sir. A man of realities. A man of fact and calculations. A man who proceeds upon the principle that two and two are four, and nothing over, and who is not to be talked into allowing for anything over. Thomas Gradgrind, sir—peremptorily Thomas—Thomas Gradgrind. With a rule and a pair of scales, and the multiplication table always in his pocket, sir, ready to weigh and measure any parcel of human nature, and tell you exactly what it comes to. It is a mere question of figures, a case of simple arithmetic" [8]. Gradgrind's political economy claims to be a science, to offer facts in place of idle fancy, objectivity in place of mere subjective impressions, the precision of mathematical calculation instead of the intractable elusiveness of qualitative distinctions. "The reason is (as you know)," he remarks to Bounderby, "the only faculty to which education should be addressed" [21]. And Gradgrind economics claims proudly to approach the world with reason rather than sentiment—and with the detached theoretical and calculative power of the mathematical intellect, rather than any more qualitative type of reasoned deliberation. Gradgrind intellect

5. See Posner, *Economic Analysis of Law* and *The Economics of Justice*; Gary Becker, *The Economic Approach to Human Behavior* (Chicago, 1976), and *A Treatise on the Family* (Cambridge, Mass., 1981). Especially instructive is the opening of Posner's *The Economics of Justice*, where he first introduces the "assumption that people are rational maximizers of their satisfactions," noting that "the principles of economics are deductions from this assumption"—and then goes on to use the word "rational," without further philosophical argument, as if it just *meant* "maximizers of satisfactions." (See pp. 1–2.) One trenchant critique of Posner, with regard to the worth of one's personal integrity, is Margaret Jane Radin, "Market-Inalienability," *Harvard Law Review*, 100 (1987), 1849 ff.

sees the heterogeneous furniture of the world, human beings
included, as so many surfaces or "parcels" to be weighed and
measured.

In this brief description we see four aspects of the economic-
utilitarian mind, neatly encapsulated.[6] First, it reduces qualitative
differences to quantitative differences. Instead of Louisa, Tom,
Stephen, Rachael, in all of their complex qualitative diversity, their
historical particularity, we have simply so and so many quantifiable
"parcels of human nature." This effacement of qualitative difference is accomplished, we see, by a process of abstraction from all in
people that is not easily funneled into mathematical formulae; so
this mind, in order to measure what it measures, attends only to an
abstract and highly general version of the human being, rather than
to the diverse concreteness with which the novel confronts us. We
see this abstracting mathematical mind at work in the Gradgrind
school's treatment of its students, called by number ("Girl number
twenty") rather than by name, and seen as an "inclined plane of
little vessels then and there arranged in order, ready to have imperial gallons of facts poured into them until they were full to the
brim" [7–8]. We see it at work in the treatment of the workers of
Coketown as so and so many "hands and stomachs" [56], as "teeming
myriads" whose destinies could be reckoned on a slate [81], their
qualitative differences as irrelevant as those of "ants and beetles"
"passing to and from their nests" [128].[7]

Second, the Gradgrind mind, bent on calculation, is determined
to aggregate the data gained about and from individual lives, arriving at a picture of total or average utility that effaces personal separateness as well as qualitative difference.[8] The individual is not
even as distinct as a distinct countable insect; for in Mr. Gradgrind's
calculation it becomes simply an input into a complex mathematical
operation that treats the social unit as a single large system in which
the preferences and satisfactions of all are combined and melded.
Thus, in Louisa's education, the working classes become:

> Something to be worked so much and paid so much, and there
> ended; something to be infallibly settled by laws of supply and
> demand; something that blundered against those laws, and

6. Some of these criticisms do apply, as well, to philosophical utilitarians, many of whom
do treat values as commensurable by a single quantitative standard. See, for example,
James Griffin, "Are There Incommensurable Values?" *Philosophy and Public Affairs*, 7
(1977), 34–59, criticized in Martha C. Nussbaum, "The Discernment of Perception,"
Love's Knowledge: Essays on Philosophy and Literature (New York, 1990), pp. 54–105.
7. The workers complain that their lives are constrained by an enforced "sameness" (180),
an absence of qualitative variation. It is no wonder that a theory bent on eliminating
qualitative distinctions would treat them in this way.
8. See the good account of this feature in Sen and Williams, Introduction to *Utilitarianism and Beyond*.

floundered into difficulty; something that was a little pinched when wheat was dear, and over-ate itself when wheat was cheap; something that increased at such a rate of percentage, and yielded such another percentage of crime, and such another percentage of pauperism; something wholesale, of which vast fortunes were made; something that occasionally rose like the sea, and did some harm and waste (chiefly to itself), and fell again; this she knew the Coketown hands to be. But, she had scarcely thought more of separating them into units, than of separating the sea itself into its component drops. [128–29]

Lives are drops in an undermarcated ocean; and the question how the group is doing is a question whose economic resolution requires effacing the separate life and agency of each.[9]

Mr. Gradgrind does not achieve this goal perfectly in his school, where students, though numbered rather than named, retain their distinct levels of performance, their abilities to think and speak as separate centers of choice, and even some measure of qualitative distinctness. He does not achieve this goal perfectly, we are bound to observe, in his relation to himself: for his internal rhetoric, in the passage cited, insists on the separateness and the qualitative difference of his own mind from those of others: "You might hope to get some other nonsensical belief into the head of George Gradgrind, or Augustus Gradgrind, or John Gradgrind, or Joseph Gradgrind (all supposititious, nonexistent persons), but into the head of Thomas Gradgrind—no sir!" [8]. It is a subtle point in the novel that the measure of personal autonomy and self-respect that Mr. Gradgrind wishes to claim for himself requires him to view himself with a distinctness denied in his calculations—and even to indulge in a rare bit of (however crude) fiction-making.[1]

But within his immediate family, he fares better. For he does manage, most of the time, to perceive his own children in more or less the way that political economy recommends.[2] When Louisa, in inner agony about her impending marriage to Bounderby, bursts out: "'Father, I have often thought that life is very short,'" her baffled father replies:

"It is short, no doubt, my dear. Still, the average duration of human life is proved to have increased of late years. The calcu-

9. Shortly after this, hearing of Stephen's misfortunes, Louisa remark that she had previously heard them mentioned, "though I was not attending to the particulars at the time" (188).
1. For another example of crude economic fiction-making, see the account of the "leaden little books . . . showing how the good grown-up baby invariably got to the Savings-bank, and the bad grown-up baby invariably got transported" (90).
2. That this is no mere fiction can be confirmed by reading Becker's A *Treatise on the Family*.

lations of various life assurance and annuity offices, among
other figures which cannot go wrong, have established the fact."
"I speak of my own life, father."
"O indeed? Still," said Mr. Gradgrind, "I need not point out to
you, Louisa, that it is governed by the laws which govern lives
in the aggregate." [84].[3]

And in one of the novel's most chilling and brilliant moments, we
see what it can be like to see one's own self through the eyes of
political economy. Mrs. Gradgrind, subservient and with an always
fragile sense both of her own qualitative distinctness and of her
separate boundaries, her separate agency, lies on what will soon be
her deathbed. "'Are you in pain, dear mother?'" asks Louisa. The
answer comes back. "'I think there's a pain somewhere in the room,'
said Mrs. Gradgrind, 'but I couldn't positively say that I have got
it'" [160]. Political economy sees only pains and satisfactions and
their general location: it does not see persons as distinctly bounded
centers of satisfaction, far less as agents whose active planning is
essential to the humanness of whatever satisfaction they will
achieve. Mrs. Gradgrind has learned her lesson well.

If we return now to the initial description of Mr. Gradgrind, we
see in it a third feature of the political-economical mind: its determination to find a clear and precise solution for any human problem.[4]
Mr. Gradgrind, we recall, is prepared "to weigh and measure any
parcel of human nature, and tell you exactly what it comes to" [8].
And his study, later on, is described as a "charmed apartment" in
which "the most complicated social questions were cast up, got into
exact totals, and finally settled" [81]. Because it has from the start
cast the human data into "tabular form," the economic mind finds
it easy to view the lives of human beings as a problem in (relatively
elementary) mathematics that has a definite solution—ignoring the
mystery and complexity that are within each life, in its puzzlement
and pain about its choices, in its tangled loves, in its attempt to grap-
ple with the mysterious and awful fact of its own mortality.[5] The
cheerful fact-calculating mind plays round the surfaces of these

---

3. Contrast p. 175, where Louisa now sees that her marriage failed because of "all those
   causes of disparity which arise out of our two individual natures, and which no general
   laws shall ever rule or state for me, father, until they shall be able to direct the anatomist where to strike his knife into the secrets of my soul."
4. This lies very deep in the motivation behind utilitarianism in general, and inspires
   some of its deliberate departures from ordinary belief. Henry Sidgwick, for example,
   conceding that to adopt a single metric of choice is to depart from ordinary belief,
   writes, "If we are not to systematize human activities by taking Universal Happiness as
   their common end, on what other principles are we to systematize them?"—and
   remarks that such departures are always found when a science is born (Methods of Ethics,
   7th ed. [London, 1907], pp. 401, 406, 425).
5. Just before we hear of the "leaden books," the narrator himself describes the people of
   Coketown as "walking against time towards the infinite world" [45].

lives, as if it had no need to look within, as if, indeed, it "could settle all their destinies on a slate" [81]. Gradgrind children are taught from an early age to approach the world of nature without any sense of mystery, awe, and depth. Thus Bitzer's definition of a horse, which gives a remarkably flat and abstract description of the surface features of that animal, refusing to imagine either its own complex form of life or its significances in the lives of humans who love and care for horses. So too with human lives. Mr. Gradgrind does not even understand the significance of his own child's outburst, when she speaks obscurely of a fire that bursts forth at night, and wonders about the shortness of her life [84]. How much less, then, does he feel a sense of mystery and wonder before the distant human beings who work in the factories of Coketown. In one of the most striking incursions of a first-person voice into this novel *** this habit of mind is described, and criticized:

> So many hundred Hands in this Mill; so many hundred horse Steam Power. It is known, to the force of a single pound weight, what the engine will do; but, not all the calculators of the National Debt can tell me the capacity for good or evil, for love or hatred, for patriotism or discontent, for the decomposition of virtue into vice, or the reverse, at any single moment in the soul of one of these its quiet servants, with the composed faces and the regulated actions. There is no mystery in it; there is an unfathomable mystery in the meanest of them, for ever.— Supposing we were to reserve our arithmetic for material objects, and to govern these awful unknown quantities by other means! [61]

If political economy does not include the complexities of the inner moral life of each human being, its strivings and perplexities, its complicated emotions, its perplexity and terror, if it does not distinguish in its descriptions between a human life and a machine, then we should regard with suspicion its claim to govern a nation of human beings; and we should ask ourselves whether, having seen us as little different from inanimate objects, it might not be capable of treating us with a certain lack of tenderness.

And this brings us directly to the fourth characteristic of economic rationality with which the novel acquaints us. Seeing human beings as counters in a mathematical game, and refusing to see their mysterious inner world, the Gradgrind philosophy is able to adopt a theory of human motivation that is elegant and simple, well suited for the game of calculation, but whose relation to the more complicated laws that govern the inner world of a human being should be viewed with skepticism. In accordance with Gradgrind's view of himself as a down-to-earth realistic man, a man of cold, hard fact rather than airy fancy, the theory has an air of hard-nosed realism about it, suggesting the unmasking of pleasant but airy fiction. Human beings, this unsentimental view teaches, are all motivated by self-interest in all of their actions.[6] The all-too-perfect Gradgrind pupil Bitzer, at the novel's end, reveals the principle on which he was raised. As the chastened Mr. Gradgrind attempts to appeal to his gratitude and love, Bitzer cuts in:

> "I beg your pardon for interrupting you, sir," returned Bitzer; "but I am sure you know that the whole social system is a question of self-interest. What you must always appeal to, is a person's self-interest. It's your only hold. We are so constituted. I was brought up in that catechism when I was very young, sir, as you are aware." [228].

Bitzer, the perfect product of political economy, refuses to acknowledge even those residual motivations of love and altruism that now deeply grip the heart of Mr. Gradgrind himself. For that is the philosophy on which he was raised. And this philosophy leads to odd and implausible interpretations of the world.

Earlier in the novel, when Sissy Jupe's father has left her, and her own first tendency is to impute to him altruistic motives, projects for her good, Bounderby will have none of it. She had better know, he says, the hard bad facts of her situation: she has simply been abandoned, her father has simply pleased himself and run off. The novel pointedly leaves this particular case unresolved; its function is to point up different behavioral assumptions, different ways of construing the world. The novel as a whole convinces the reader (and Mr. Gradgrind) that Gradgrind is wrong to deny the possibility of genuinely altruistic and other-regarding action. But if there exists this other possibility, then Bounderby has construed Sissy's situation hastily, and also ungenerously. The suggestion is that the economist's habit of reducing everything to calculation, combined with the need for an extremely simple theory of human action, produces a tendency to see calculation everywhere, rather than commitment and sympathy. "Every inch of the existence of mankind, from birth to death, was to be a bargain across a counter" [228]. This tendency leads to crude analysis, and frequently to error. Even when it does not lead to error, it leads to an ungenerous perception of people and events. And, worst of all, taught from an early age, it produces pupils in its own image.

In short, the claim of political economy to present all and only the facts of human life needs to be viewed with skepticism, if by "facts" we mean "truths." And its claim to stand for "reason" must

6. For a trenchant documentation and critique of these behavioral assumptions, see Amartya Sen, "Rational Fools," *Philosophy and Public Affairs*, 6 (1976–77), 317–44.

also be viewed with skepticism, if by "reason" we mean a faculty that is self-critical and committed to truth. For the "facts" of political economy are actually reductive and incomplete perceptions, and to "reason" is a dogmatic operation of intellect that looks, frequently, both incomplete and unreliable. The fact-finding intellect plays around the surfaces of objects, not even obtaining very adequate perceptual data—Mr. Gradgrind's study is compared to an astronomical observatory without windows, where the astronomer arranges the world "solely by pen, ink, and paper" [81], determined to perceive only those abstract features of people and situations that can easily be translated into economic calculations. From its own point of view it has positive motivations for this way of proceeding in its determination to be realistic and not sentimental, its determination to be exact, and even its determination not to be biased in favor of what is near at hand. (For Mr. Gradgrind reflects that Louisa "Would have been self-willed . . . but for her bringing-up" [16].) The novel permits us to see these positive goals.[7] Its very sentences express a commitment to be detached, and realistic, and unbiased—in their blunt square shape, their syntactical plainness, their hard sound and rhythm. (We must, however, note that the prose the novel imputes to the Gradgrind imagination is far more expressive, more succinct, more rhythmical, more *pleasing* in its odd squareness, than the flat unexpressive jargon-laden prose that is actually used by most economists of the Gradgrind type. Dickens has been able to make Mr. Gradgrind a lively character in a readable novel only by to this extent changing him.)

But, the novel shows, in its determination to see only what can enter into utilitarian calculations, the economic mind is blind: blind to the qualitative richness of the perceptible world; to the separateness of its people, to their inner depths, their hopes and loves and fears; blind to what it is like to live a human life and to try to endow it with a human meaning. Blind, above all, to the fact that human life is something mysterious and not altogether fathomable, something that demands to be approached with faculties of mind and resources of language that are suited to the expression of that complexity. In the name of science, the wonder that illuminates and prompts the most creative and deepest science has been jettisoned.[8] And we have, simply, a reductive charade of science in which some small part of human life appears, as figures on slate.

7. Indeed, if we bear in mind that one of utilitarianism's central claims on its own behalf is that it can take seriously the pain of the poor, we see the novel as offering, in addition, a devastating *internal* critique.

8. At the same time, the utilitarian's particular conception of science owes something to the Cartesian conception of nature as a machine: this shows up especially clearly in the attitudes to animals in the Gradgrind schoolroom.

＊   ＊   ＊

I must now insist that in this novel—and in my own view—there is no disparagement of reason or of the scientific search for truth. What I am criticizing is a pseudo-science that claims to stand for truth and for reason. What I am saying about it is that it fails to stand for truth insofar as it dogmatically misrepresents the complexity of human beings and human life. It fails to stand for reason when it uncritically trusts half-baked perceptions and crude psychological theories in order not to complicate its elegant models. The novel speaks not of dismissing reason, but of coming upon it in a way illuminated by fancy, which is here seen as a faculty at once both creative and veridical. The alternative I am proposing is not Sleary's circus. The circus offers the reader essential metaphors of art, discipline, play, and love; but even within the novel its attitudes are shown as politically incomplete, too ill-educated and whimsical to govern a nation. The novel offers us an alternative: itself, its complex combination of qualitatively rich description with critical social reflection. And it indicates that political and economic treatises of a more abstract and mathematical sort would be perfectly consistent with its purpose—so long as the view of the human being underlying the treatises was the richer view available in the novel; so long as they do not lose sight of what they are, for efficiency, omitting. Government cannot investigate the life story of every citizen in the way a novel does with its characters; it can, however, know *that* each citizen has a complex history of this sort, and it can remain aware that the norm in principle would be to acknowledge the separateness and qualitative difference of each in the manner of the novel.

In one particular way the novel, as genre, is strongly in league with a certain norm of rationality: namely, in its insistence on the fundamental role, in its own construction, of a general notion of the *human being*. The description of the Coketown library speaks of "human nature, human passions, human hopes and fears," the subject matter of the novel. In so doing it reminds us that the novel does not purchase its attention to social context and to individual variety at the price of jettisoning a sense of human community. It forges a complex relationship with its reader in which, on the one hand, the reader is urged to care about concrete features of circumstance and history, and to see these as relevant for social choice; but is, on the other hand, urged always to recognize that human beings in different spheres do have common passions, hopes, and fears, the need to confront the mystery of death, the desire for learning, the deep bonds of the family. Its hypothetical reader is explicitly addressed as one whose sphere of life is different from that of the author—with different concrete choices and possibilities. And yet it is assumed that the reader can still identify with the characters and events of the novel as with possibilities for human life in general, and think how "such things" can be instantiated in his or her own concrete life.[9] This complex movement of imagination and reason, from the concrete to the general back to the concrete, through both sympathy and identification, is built into the genre, as *Hard Times* correctly states. And in real life one does find that works of imaginative literature are frequently far more supple and versatile deliberative agents across cultural boundaries than are philosophical treatises, with their time-bound and culture-bound terms of art, their frequent lack of engagement with common hopes and fears.

In its engagement with a general notion of the human being, this novel (like many novels) is, I think, while particularistic, not relativistic. That is, it recognizes human needs that transcend boundaries of time, place, class, religion, and ethnicity, and it makes the focus of its moral deliberation the question of their adequate fulfillment. Its criticism of concrete political and social situations relies on a notion of what it is for a human being to flourish, and this notion itself, while extremely general and in need of further specification, is neither local nor sectarian. On the other hand, part of the content of the idea of flourishing is a deep respect for qualitative difference—so the norm enjoins that governments, wherever they are, should attend to citizens in all their concreteness and variety, and should respond in a sensitive way to particular historical and personal contingencies. But the point is, that is itself a universal injunction, and part of a universal picture of humanness. And it is by relying on this universal ideal that the novel, so different from a guidebook or even an anthropological field report, makes the reader a participant in the lives of people very different from herself and also a critic of the class distinctions that give people similarly constructed an unequal access to flourishing.[1] Thus the novel, in its structure and aspiration, is, I think, a defender of enlightenment ideals of the equality and dignity of all human life—not of traditionalism or parochialism. It is opposed to the perversion of that ideal in the name of the pseudo-science of economics, and also to

9. For more on this, see Martha C. Nussbaum, "Aristotelian Social Democracy," in *Liberalism and the Good*, ed. R. Bruce Douglass, Gerald M. Mara, and Henry S. Richardson (New York, 1990), pp. 203–52: "Aristotle on Human Nature and the Foundations of Ethics," in a volume in honor of Bernard Williams, ed. Ross Harrison and J. E. G. Altham (Cambridge, 1991); and "Human Functioning and Social Justice: In Defense of Aristotelian Essentialism," read at the Institute for Humanities at the University of Chicago (in *Political Theory*).

1. See Amartya Sen, *Choice, Welfare, and Measurement* (Oxford, 1982); *Resources, Value, and Development* (Oxford, 1984); *Commodities and Capabilities* (North-Holland, 1985); *The Standard of Living* (Cambridge, 1987).

its insensitive application with insufficient respect for stories told within a concrete historical context—not to the ideal itself.

PAULETTE KIDDER

From Martha Nussbaum on Dickens's *Hard Times*†

At the heart of Martha Nussbaum's work in capability ethics is a rejection of utilitarianism. Nussbaum has repeatedly recounted a pivotal moment in Dickens's *Hard Times* (1854), in which the young Sissy Jupe delivers an innocent but devastating critique of the utilitarian system.[1] Nussbaum's most extended and compelling reading of *Hard Times* appears in *Poetic Justice: The Literary Imagination and Public Life*.[2] Nussbaum convincingly shows that Dickens's novel is a "deep attack" on utilitarianism, going to the heart of the assumption that the human good consists in maximizing the satisfaction of preferences of the greatest aggregate of persons.

* * *

Gradgrind's system, Nussbaum argues, is blind, "blind to the qualitative richness of the perceptible world, to the separateness of its people, to their inner depths, their hopes and loves and fears; blind to what it is like to live a human life and to try to endow it with a human meaning" [419]. In both form and content, she argues, Dickens's novel explicitly proposes a remedy for the blindness of Gradgrind, in the cultivation of "Fancy," or what Nussbaum terms the metaphorical imagination. *Hard Times*, she argues, shows that the ability to imagine one thing as another is "morally crucial," linking the ability to imagine charitably the inner lives of others to the desire to behave compassionately toward them.

Nussbaum's reading of Dickens's novel focuses on the eclipse of those complexities of human life that fail to fit the Gradgrind philosophy. However, it may be argued that despite her sensitivity to these dimensions of Dickens's critique of utilitarianism, Nussbaum's own reading of the novel fails to include at least one important dimension of human motivation: that of spiritual longing toward a dimension of transcendent mystery.

---

† From *Philosophy and Literature* 33.2 (2009), pp. 417–26. © 2009 The Johns Hopkins University Press. Reprinted with permission of Johns Hopkins University Press. Nussbaum used Penguin's 1969 edition edited by David Craig; page references here refer to this Norton Critical Edition.
1. See, for example, Martha C. Nussbaum, *Frontiers of Justice: Disability, Nationality, Species Membership* (Cambridge: Harvard University Press, 2006), p. 282.
2. Martha C. Nussbaum, *Poetic Justice: The Literary Imagination and Public Life* (Boston: Beacon Press, 1995); hereafter abbreviated *PJ*.

In her own work in capabilities ethics, Nussbaum makes a case that human beings have capacities that cry out for support and development. For example, a being with senses, imagination, and thought, she argues, ought to be able to use these abilities in "a way informed and cultivated by an adequate education," and "to search for the ultimate meaning of life in one's own way."[3] Historically, this search for ultimate meaning has taken the form of spiritual questioning, a turning toward a dimension of mystery that is experienced as the hidden ground of human life and of the whole of being. In her reading of *Hard Times* and its critique of utilitarian thought, Nussbaum has explicitly appealed to a number of the other capabilities that are important in her ethical system, but has not specifically alluded to the way the search for ultimate meaning is at play in the novel's polemical argument.

If we were to approach *Hard Times* again with the question of whether the search for ultimate meaning is at play in the novel, we would find that Dickens indeed shows an awareness that the resistance to utilitarianism is grounded in a spiritual longing for meaning and that specifically Christian and Biblical symbols provide powerful resistance to the utilitarian version of human motivation. Pursuing this line of inquiry, I would note, first, that several of Dickens's characters, in their dissatisfaction with the limited vision of Reason of Gradgrind's system, reflect a sense that there are deeper questions to be asked, and that they are missing the direction their lives ought to take. Louisa, dissatisfied early on by her education, spends an evening staring into the fire, and remarks to her mother, "I have such unmaneageable thoughts, . . . that they *will* wonder," a claim that her mother says is "morally and physically impossible," unless someone has encouraged Louisa to "wonder" against her father's instructions.

Mrs. Gradgrind, on her deathbed, pathetically attempts to write down "something—not an Ology at all—that your father has missed, or forgotten, Louisa. I don't know what it is. I have often sat with Sissy near me, and thought about it. I shall never get its name now. But your father may. It makes me restless. I want to write to him, to find out for God's sake, what it is. Give me a pen, give me a pen" [161]. Thus both she and her daughter feel the absence of something crucial in their lives that has been left aside in Gradgrind's version of Reason.

Nussbaum, as we have seen, argues that the missing "something," for Dickens, is Fancy, or what Nussbaum has termed the metaphorical imagination, the ability to see one thing as another. In

---

3. Martha C. Nussbaum, *Women and Human Development: The Capabilities Approach* (Cambridge: Cambridge University Press, 2000), p. 79.

PAULETTE KIDDER

this, she is clearly correct as far as she goes. However, the novel gives strong indications that Fancy has a deep source of support in the tradition of Judeo-Christian symbols that take us into a realm of questioning our relationship to a divine mystery or ground of being.

To see how *Hard Times* invokes Judeo-Christian symbols in support of its resistance to utilitarianism, let us first note that *Hard Times* stands out among Dickens's novels for its many references to Biblical texts and to well known prayers. The titles of the three parts of the book, "Sowing," "Reaping," and "Garnering," recall New Testament parables that emphasize the choices that lead to one's being saved or damned.[4] The title of the first chapter, "One Thing Needful," is an ironic comment on the contrast between Gradgrind's reliance on "facts" alone and Jesus' rebuke to Martha (*Luke* 10:38–42). Jesus tells her that her sister Mary has chosen the "better part," and the "one thing needful," when she stays and listens to him rather than helping Martha with the work of the household. In Book 3, Dickens titles his first chapter "Another Thing Needful"; in this chapter, Gradgrind has understood at last that Louisa's education was a disaster for her, and begins to look for an alternative to his system, in a "wisdom of the Heart" [179].

Dickens's use of biblical language and images throughout the book moves between passages in which the Gradgrind system and its allies are represented ironically as a substitute for Christianity, and passages in which Christianity is pitted against the Gradgrind system as its antithesis. The ironic substitution of utilitarianism for Christianity is seen in the early description of Coketown: "Fact, fact, everywhere in the material aspect of the town: fact, fact, fact, everywhere in the immaterial . . . and what you couldn't state in figures, or show to be purchaseable in the cheapest market and saleable in the dearest, was not, and never should be, world without end, Amen" [24]. The Coketown property owners' tender care for their property, which increases at the expense of the quality of the air of Coketown, is also ironically couched in Biblical language: "So there it was, in the haze yonder, and it increased and multiplied" [92].[5]

The churches of Coketown might be thought to represent an alternative to the Gradgrind faith in facts, but Dickens portrays the churches as reinforcing the system that presses upon the working people, supporting the landowners and strengthening, for example,

4. See, for example, *Matthew* 3:11–12, *Luke* 3:16–17, *Matthew* 13:24–30, *Luke* 8:4–15, and *Matthew* 6:24–34. I am indebted for this point to Graham Law; see his introduction to *Hard Times*, ed. Graham Law (Toronto: Broadview Press, 1996), p. 21. Law points out that Dickens's use of Biblical references and references to the Book of Common Prayer in this novel is unusually frequent.
5. Compare to *Genesis* 9:1.

the marriage laws that apply so unequally to the rich and poor.[6] But although the churches are of no help to the working people of Coketown, the Christian teachings that some of them still live by are a crucial counterpoint to the self-centered motivations of Bounderby and his like. Stephen and his friend Rachael explicitly invoke Christian principles of forgiveness and of comfort in the face of death [217], and both are metaphorically associated with Jesus.

At important points in the novel, Dickens explicitly sets up an opposition between Gradgrind and his allies on the one hand and Biblical exemplars on the other. Book I, Chapter 2 refers to Gradgrind's system of education as "Murdering the Innocents," invoking Herod's killing of young children in an attempt to murder the infant Jesus [8]. Sissy, asked in class for the first principle of Political Economy, answers, "To do unto others as I would that they should do unto me," an answer that her teachers acknowledge is absurd [50]. And Gradgrind is described in one scene as busy "proving something no doubt—probably, in the main, that the Good Samaritan was a Bad Economist" [173].

Dickens hints at the power of divinity to overcome the utilitarians and industrialists, when he mentions the time when "the last trumpet ever to be sounded shall blow even algebra to wreck" [84]. Yet in other passages, Dickens is more ambiguous regarding the ultimate success or failure of the utilitarian vision. Dickens sets out the opposition between the works of modernity and the works of God in a passage we looked at previously:

> Stephen bent over his loom, quiet, watchful, and steady. A special contrast, as every man was in the forest of looms where Stephen worked, to the crashing, smashing, tearing piece of mechanism at which he laboured. Never fear, good people of an anxious turn of mind, that Art will consign Nature to oblivion. Set anywhere, side by side, the work of God and the work of man; and the former, even though it be a troop of Hands of very small account, will gain in dignity from the comparison.
>
> So many hundred Hands in this Mill; so many hundred horse Steam Power. It is known, to the force of a single pound weight, what the engine will do; but, not all the calculators of the National Debt can tell me the capacity for good or evil, for love or hatred, for patriotism or discontent, for the decomposition of virtue into vice, or the reverse, at any single moment in the soul of one of these its quiet servants, with the composed faces and the regulated actions. There is no mystery in it; there

---

6. See, for example, Charles Dickens, *Hard Times*, ed. Fred Kaplan and Sylvère Monod (New York: W.W. Norton and Company, 2001), pp. 21, 68, 168.

is an unfathomable mystery in the meanest of them, forever.—
Supposing we were to reserve our arithmetic for material
objects, and to govern these awful unknown quantities by other
means! [61]

In this passage, Dickens draws a contrast between the work of
Man and the work of God, calling for a respect for the mysterious
motivations of human beings and asserting the inherent dignity of
human beings as works of God. The opposition between the work
of God and that of Man is continued in the next paragraph, as the
daylight is contrasted to the artificial lights of the factory, the rain
and mist to the "submissive" and "cursed" Smoke serpents (identified here with the serpent of Genesis).

In light of the opposition Dickens portrays between Christian
faith and utilitarian economics, Sissy Jupe's patient waiting for the
return of her father takes on added meaning (*PJ*, p. 25). In the
course of the novel, her father never returns, and the reader, along
with the characters in the novel, is left to wonder what his motives
were for leaving. Bounderby, as Nussbaum notes, imputes selfish
motives to Sissy's father, as he does to everyone. Sissy, on the other
hand, never wavers in her belief that her father will return to her.
In the hope of his return, Sissy preserves for years a bottle of "nine
oils" to massage her father's aching muscles [27].

Sissy's faith in her father, despite his unexplained absence, reso-
nates symbolically with the New Testament story of Mary, criticized by Jesus' disciples for using expensive ointment to wash Jesus'
feet (*John* 12:1–8), and with parables such as that of the wise and
foolish virgins, waiting for the bridegroom's arrival (*Matthew* 25).
Sissy is symbolically linked with those who preserve faith in what
cannot be seen, despite criticism by those who claim to have rational explanations that would reduce their faith to a delusion.

The belief in "something" that is not reducible to self-interest and
cannot be captured by the quantitative methods of Gradgrind or the
self-interest of Bounderby is put, as is fitting for a Christian vision,
into the mouths of the disadvantaged: the workers, the lisping
Sleary, and the timid Mrs. Gradgrind. It is identified with children
and with the childlike Sissy. Dickens shows a hidden power in these
apparently helpless characters, when Sissy demonstrates the ability
to persuade Harthouse, who is frequently identified symbolically
with Lucifer, to leave Coketown.[7]

In reviewing these passages, I have shown, first, that Dickens
indicates through his characters that the dissatisfaction with the

---

7. For passages identifying Harthouse with a devil, see pp. 110, 143, 144, 145, and 146 in
   this edition.

limits of utilitarian accounts of human reason has roots in a spiritual longing. In addition, I have shown that for Dickens, the resistance to utilitarianism is articulated largely in Christian terms. The critique of the four aspects of utilitarianism singled out by Nussbaum are all deepened by the resonance of these symbols. How can one more pointedly oppose the notion that all goods are reducible to pleasure and pain, that the goal of life is to maximize self-interest, that one individual is interchangeable with any other, or that one ought to trust unquestioningly one's possibly corrupt desires, than by contrasting these claims to a Biblical view of the meaning of a human life? * * * One is left wondering, if Dickens's critique of utilitarianism draws so much of its depth and power from the use of Judeo-Christian symbols, why are these symbols completely absent from Nussbaum's reading of the novel?

In Nussbaum's defense, a reader may point out that *every* reading of a work of literature has to use one lens and not another. In response, I would argue that in this novel the religious symbols are so pervasive, and so integral to the very themes that Nussbaum highlights, that to omit them is an oddity that calls for an explanation.

One such explanation is that Nussbaum is influenced by John Rawls's notion of an "overlapping consensus"—a set of ethical arguments that can be agreed to by any rational and reasonable person despite differences in their "comprehensive" views of human nature. Religious systems, by this account, fall outside the realm of what every reasonable person can agree to. By avoiding discussion of the religious dimension of the novel, Nussbaum has restricted herself to those aspects of its argument that both religious and nonreligious readers can resonate with.

Another reason that may explain Nussbaum's overlooking Dickens's use of symbols of transcendence is her own longstanding critique of the misuse of those symbols in the work of Plato and in Christian thinkers such as Augustine and Dante.

Nussbaum has written extensively of the ways that those who seek the meaning of human existence in an otherworldly realm end up betraying the significance of the world of finite and fragile human beings. Of Dante, she writes, "The image of Heaven as a place of self-sufficiency, and a place of beatitude in the sense of an end to mourning, cannot ultimately be reconciled with the idea of ongoing compassion for human life. Compassion is incomprehensible without mourning; if these things are important, they are important. [One] must ultimately choose between regarding this world as merely provisional and regarding it as a scene of significant struggles. . . ."[8]

8. Martha C. Nussbaum, *Upheavals of Thought: The Intelligence of Emotions* (Cambridge: Cambridge University Press, 2001), p. 590.

My own view is that to long for transcendence need not lead—
as Nussbaum believes it does—to a belief that the struggles of
this world are unimportant. While it is well to bear in mind Nussbaum's reasons to be wary of our longing for transcendence, I
think that something irreplaceable is lost in Nussbaum's trun-
cated version of Dickens's narrative and symbolic resistance to
the utilitarian reduction of human beings to a few simple desires.
The spiritual traditions of the past, for all their capacity to be
abused, are carriers of insights that some of the intellectual movements of the modern period have all but erased from view. Among
these are the faith in a source of love that grounds our longing for
a better world, and the grace that supports our capacity for hope
and forgiveness.

DAVID M. LEVY

From *Hard Times* and the Moral Equivalence of Markets and Slavery[†]

The Novelist as Rational Chooser

Charles Dickens's novel *Hard Times* gives definitive form to Thomas
Carlyle's opposition to the "cash nexus" of market exchange. As
we have seen, when Carlyle coined the term *dismal science* he jux-
taposed it to the "gay science" of poetry. The debate to which he
pointed, economics versus poetry, continues in our own time. The
literary critics and philosophers influenced by these literary critics,
whom we shall encounter soon, seem to take it for granted, as befits
such a great work of art as *Hard Times*, that the story Dickens told
is "true" and so can serve as opposition to the truth claims of economic models.

The truth claims on behalf of *Hard Times* are twofold. Not only
are claims about the world outside the novel a serviceable approx-
imation of that reality (first), but (second) the acts described in
the story are consistent with the laws of the world imagined. I
propose to question this tradition root and branch. I shall venture
the claim that it is precisely where the novel is "false" in both of
these directions—one critical claim about the world outside the
story is a transparent falsification and the characters's actions
deviate from the laws of Dickens's world to serve Dickens's

[†] From David M. Levy, *How the Dismal Science Got Its Name: Classical Economics and
the Ur-Text of Racial Politics* (Ann Arbor: University of Michigan Press, 2001), pp. 158–
97. Reprinted by permission of the University of Michigan Press.

polemic purpose—that we can see what message *Hard Times* has to convey.

To make my case that we can observe false choices in *Hard Times*, I need to identify a law of Dickens's world independent of the acts of the agents. But in *Hard Times* this is easy. The law of the world is that the self-described economic-Utilitarian agents seek to maximize their happiness without regard for the happiness of others. The problem with Utilitarianism is its hardness and inhumanity. This is the first of many things that F. R. Leavis, the modern scholar most responsible for *Hard Times'* contemporary fame, writes:

> But in *Hard Times* he is for once possessed by a comprehensive vision, one in which the inhumanities of Victorian civilization are seen as fostered and sanctioned by a hard philosophy, the aggressive formulation of an inhumane spirit. The philosophy is represented by Thomas Gradgrind, Enquire, Member of Parliament for Coketown, who has brought up his children on the lines of the experiment recorded by John Stuart Mill as carried out on himself. What Gradgrind stands for is, though repellent, nevertheless respectable.

Attacking Modern Economics by Means of Victorian Novels

It is in the spirit of the doctrine of authorial infallibility in great works of art that we might read Martha Nussbaum's recent lecture on economics past and present in light of *Hard Times*. Here she contrasts economic with novelistic accounts:

> Mr. Gradgrind knows that storybooks are not simply decorative, not simply amusing—though this already would be enough to cause him to doubt their utility. Literature, he sees, is subversive. It is the enemy of political economy, as Mr. Gradgrind knows that science. It expresses, in its structures and its ways of speaking, a sense of life that is incompatible with the vision of the world embodied in the texts of political economy; and engagement with it forms the imagination and the desires in a manner that subverts that science's norm of rationality.[1]

Nussbaum asserts—on the basis of her personal experience of life among "the econ"—that the criticism of economics in *Hard Times*

---

1. Martha C. Nussbaum, "Literary Imagination in Public Life," *New Literary History* 22 (1991): 907.

is fundamentally fair. The novel is more nearly true than the competing economic models with which it contends.[2]

While Nussbaum's conflation of the target of *Hard Times*, early- and mid-nineteenth-century economics, with that with which she has personal knowledge might seem to be debatable essentialism, I have no quarrel with at least one central theme in her argument. ChicagoSchool economics does indeed assume a fixed human nature of a fairly simple form. Change incentives, change behavior. That's rational choice theory. Obviously, there are technical details to fuss over, but indeed the critical step is the assumption that human nature is fixed. And the economic teaching that provoked Dickens made a similarly simple claim about human rationality in terms of fixed human nature.

It is the next step I worry about. Nussbaum makes the following claims against modern economics:

> It does not even tell us about life expectancy and infant mortality—far less about health, education, political functioning, the quality of ethnic and racial and gender relations.

And this bears on the target of Dickens how? Nussbaum is vague here, and since she does not cite the texts of past economists I shall attempt to reconstruct an argument to fill the gap. She writes as if one need not actually read the past to know what cannot be found there. This seems to me to be as pure an instance of presentism as one could hope to find. This surely means to say that if a concept is not found in modern economics—that economics she knows, with all its high mathematical and statistical technology—it cannot be found in the past. If modern economists do not worry about life expectancy, such concerns are not found in the past. If modern economists of undoubtedly respectable views on race and politics are not concerned in their technical work about "the quality of ethnic and racial and gender relations," surely those blasted souls of economics past could not have been so concerned. Economics present is an upper bound to economics past.

---

2. "What I am about to say here may seem in some respects obvious. For it is part of the novel's design that the economist's way of thinking, seen in the full context of daily life, should look extremely strange, and the opposing way natural. What I hope to bring out here, however, is that the economic opponent is not a straw man: it is a conception that even now dominates much of our public life, in a form not very different from the form presented in this novel. Once, focusing on the subtle modifications of utilitarianism that one finds in recent philosophy, I felt that the satire of *Hard Times* was unfair. But now that I have spent time in the world of economics, . . . reading the prose and following the arguments, I am convinced that the criticisms in the novel are both fair and urgent. The simple utilitarian idea of what rational choice consists in dominates not only economic thought and practice, but also—given the prestige of economics within the social sciences—a great deal of writing in the other social sciences as well, where 'rational choice theory' is taken to be equivalent to utilitarian rational choice theory as practiced in neoclassical economics" (Nussbaum 1991, 882).

On the contrary, I should argue that the content of economics past serves as a lower bound to economics future. If it was in the past, then as long as we persist in holding to our rational choice vision it can be in our future. Thus, while I think some of Nussbaum's criticisms of economics present are sensible, the defects she points out are not inevitable in a rational choice model of the future precisely because they were dealt by those who worked in the rational choice tradition of the past.

The quarrel I have with Nussbaum is that by using economics present to bound economics past she completely misses the context of the larger debate in which *Hard Times* is but one set piece. A vast amount of classical economics is intertwined with controversies over racial slavery. And, as economic theory is a public good, it was seized upon by noneconomists in the antislavery movement and so entered a great public debate.

* * *

Sissy Jupe Passes Her Exam

When Nussbaum writes about Dickens's attack on economics, she does not consider his attacks on the Christian evangelicals. That these groups ought to be taken as one target is the considered judgment of a modern specialist:

> If Dickens was in the main an environmentalist, he could number among the moralists, two of his least favorite groups: evangelicals and political economists. Indeed, these two groups often overlapped in the nineteenth century to produce writers who, in the tradition of Malthus, "preached what might be called evangelical economics."[3]

We know from the Carlyle-Mill exchange that the cause of black emancipation united Utilitarian and evangelical. As we have seen, the antislavery coalition between Utilitarians and evangelical Christians functioned because in part it was agreed that there is a formal identity between the Golden Rule of Christianity and the Greatest Happiness Principle of Utilitarianism, thus forging what one might label "broad utilitarianism."

This agreement on foundations requires a further stipulation to turn it into an effective antislavery coalition; that is, the agreement among the partners that black slaves are at the bottom of the distribution of happiness and that their lot deserves immediate attention. Lord Denman's attack on Dickens's views on slavery, as revealed

3. Paul Schact, "Dickens and the uses of Nature," *Victorian Studies* 34 (1990): 78.

in the *Household Words* review of *Uncle Tom's Cabin*, comes from the point of view of a biblical literalism raging against the coming of progressive religion, which would, by denying the imperative to raise the worst off, deny the Gospel:

> But it is only of late years that small wits have found the senti-ment a proper theme of ridicule. They have all become ashamed of their dark-complexioned brother, and would fain disclaim the relationship. They cannot do so without renounc-ing that of Him who spoke of the whole family of man as one brotherhood, without distinction of class or colour, and pro-claimed eternal happiness or misery to the great ones of the earth, according to the deeds that they shall have done to the least of His brethren.[4]

Now this raises a series of interesting questions about what to make of *Hard Times* and Leavis's interpretation of that text, pre-cisely the inconsistency between Utilitarianism and Christianity that forms the philosophical claim in the text for which Leavis vouches "finality." Consider that celebrated passage in which Sissy Jupe first encounters political economy:

> [A]fter eight weeks of induction into the elements of Political Economy, she had only yesterday been set right by a prattler three feet high, for returning to the question "What is the first principle of this science?" the absurd answer, "To do unto others as I would that they should do unto me."

Since the economists in *Hard Times* are supposedly Utilitarian, the "absurd" answer is nothing of the kind. Among those qualified to grade such an examination—the founders of Utilitarianism and the opponent they took with most seriousness, as we have seen—her answer has been certified as the correct answer. The Golden Rule of Christianity is an equivalence of the Greatest Hap-piness Principle of Utilitarianism. Nonetheless, as far as I know, professional students of *Hard Times* follow Leavis in accepting Dickens's claim of the inexorable opposition of Utilitarianism and Christianity.

* * *

DICKENS ON UNCLE TOM'S CABIN *AND THE* "*REFORM*" *OF SLAVERY.*

Fortunately for later scholars, many of the basic facts connecting Dickens and *Uncle Tom's Cabin* have been reported by Harry

---

4. Matthew 25:40: "And the King shall answer and say unto them, Verily I say unto you, Inasmuch as ye have done [it] unto one of the least of these my brethren, ye have done [it] unto me."

Stone.[5] In particular, Stone draws attention to the newspaper attack on Dickens's views on slavery by Lord Denman—some of which has been quoted—which was quickly republished under the title *Uncle Tom's Cabin, Bleak House, Slavery, and Slave Trade*. Denman distinguished between those who favored slavery and those who opposed the attempts to abolish it. Dickens he put in the camp of what we might consider the anti-antislavers:

> We have a still heavier charge against Mr. Dickens. In one particular instance, but the most important of all at this crisis, he exerts his powers to obstruct the great cause of human improvement—that cause which in general he cordially advocates. He does his best to replunge the world into the most barbarous abuse that ever afflicted it. We do not say that he actually defends slavery or the slave-trade; but he takes pains to discourage, by ridicule, the effort now making to put them down. We believe, indeed, that in general terms he expresses just hatred for both; but so do all those who profit or wish to profit by them, and who, by that general profession, prevent the detail of particulars too atrocious to be endured. The disgusting picture of a woman who pretends zeal for the happiness of Africa, and is constantly employed in securing a life of misery to her own children, is a laboured work of art in his present exhibition. (1853, 9)

Denman characterized the program of those who would use slavery for "education" of the slave and compares this with the real antislavery of the evangelical Clapman sect variety:

> The "Times" Reviewer is quite justified in comparing the relation which the present slaveholders in America bear to this question to that of the planters in Jamaica before the great act of emancipation. But those planters and their advocates against the natural rights of the negro were loud in denouncing the experiment of giving freedom to the slave. They declared him unfitted to receive that blessing, urged that he be required to be educated into that capacity. . . . These views were . . . discussed by Mr. Macaulay (as we understood) in an able paper which appeared in the "Edinburgh Review." He ridiculed the notion that such preparation was requisite, comparing it to the prudence of the father who advised his son not to bathe until he could swim.

Can slavery make one fit for freedom? Here is where the assumption of a fixed human nature becomes a weapon in the war against human bondage. Thirty years had passed, but Denman recalls

5. Harry Stone, "Charles Dickens and Harriet Beecher Stowe," *Nineteenth-Century Fiction* 12 (1957): 188–202.

T. B. Macaulay's argument against the delay of emancipation. There is no harder rationality principle than that which Macaulay learned from Smith. The institution of slavery cannot remake one's nature, not for good nor for ill. Here is evangelical-economics policy in one lesson: release the slaves and they grope in freedom to become the same as their masters. This is so even though the masters are white and the slaves are black. Human nature is one and the same everywhere.

Macaulay and his parliamentary associates were unable to effect immediate emancipation. Even with a 20 million pound ransom paid to the West Indian slaveholders by the British taxpayers, emancipation required an additional "apprenticeship" on the part of the slaves. Macaulay himself seems to bear personal responsibility for shortening the period of transition.

Stone, who draws our attention to Denman on Dickens and slavery, also points out the importance of Henry Morley and Dickens's review of *Uncle Tom's Cabin* in an 1852 issue of *Household Words*. Several things are made clear in this review. First, just as Denman suggested, Morley and Dickens propose to reform slavery, to delay emancipation until the black slaves are "suited" for freedom. Slavery, which has mutilated black people, can also, when suitably reformed, heal them. Morley and Dickens describe in detail the hideously cruel treatment visited upon slaves. Cruelty is bad, but intellectual development is good. How shall we choose when the two goals might conflict?

> We think, too, that it is possible to combine with the duty of emancipation the not less important duty of undoing the evil that has been done to the slaves' minds and of doing them some good service by way of atonement. When we have clipped men's minds and made them slavish, it is poor compensation that their bodies should be set at large.

Morley and Dickens appeal to the importance of kind masters; those who would guide by words and not the lash.[6] The reformed slavery would be one without cruelty:

> The stripes! Though slavery be not abolished promptly, there can be no reason why stripes should not cease. Though there *may* be little of lashing and wailing in the slave system, as it is commonly administered in North America, yet men are degraded by being set to work by a coarse action of their fears,

---

6. And just where are these kind, new model masters supposed to come from to replace the really existing masters? The fundamental nonseriousness of Dickens as a social reformer is remarked upon by an unknown reviewer in the *Dublin Review* of 1871. The "stupidity" interpretation of Dickens is there pressed ("Two English Novelists: Dickens and Thackery" 1871).

when the same men are far more capable of being stimulated by an excitement of their love of honour and reward.

Then Morley and Dickens reflect upon innate racial differences and how the newly reformed slavery could make blacks nearly white. The educational prospects of the new model slavery are compared in detail to those of the existing model of slavery. In the existing system, the slaves are too stupid to figure out that they ought to resent their situation. This is why Christianity cannot be preached in full:

> The negro has what the phrenologists would call love of approbation very strongly marked. Set him to work for the hope of distinction, instead of the fear of blows. No doubt it has been true that negroes, set to work by any motive which called out their higher feelings as men, would become ambitious and acquire a thirst for freedom in the end. So it is, so let it be. Educate the negroes on plantations, make them intelligent men and women, let them imbibe in their full freedom the doctrines of Christianity. It has been true that it was not safe to give knowledge to men who were placed in a position which the faintest flash of reason would resent.

Under reformed slavery, this defect will be mended and with it the slaves will be remade:

> We have been told by a Christian minister, who laboured in his way to elevate the minds of negroes in some North American plantations, that his permission to preach was clogged with many stipulations that he was expressly forbidden to teach anything which might induce a slave to question his position or wish to be free; and that, in consequence, he found himself unable to preach even man's duty to his neighbour. So it has been and must be; the slave who acquires education and religious principle must desire to be free: let it be so.

As a matter of racial destiny, blacks could never really compete with whites, so after the period of beneficent slavery they would leave for lands for which their nature is suitable. Slavery is not essential, Morley and Dickens assure us, *if*:

> The time is not far distant when the demand for negroes will be confined wholly to those districts in which the climate appears to be unsuited for field labour by white men: even to those districts whites will become acclimatised, but in those, for some time at any rate, negroes will be needed. *It is not essential that the negroes should be slaves. If, step by step, the degraded race be raised, their higher impulses awakened, their minds developed, their moral ties religiously respected, there will arise out of the*

436 DAVID M. LEVY

present multitude of slaves, by slow degrees, a race of free labourers far more efficient than the present gangs, while the yearly increasing surplus of black population educated into love of freedom would pass over to Liberia.[7]

As we reflect upon how one is supposed to "reform" slavery—by means of what magic wand are the whips to be banished and the Bible uncensored?—it is helpful to recall George Orwell's reading of the Dickens program to "reform" capitalism:

> Bounderby is a bullying windbag and Gradgrind has been morally blinded, but if they were better men, the system would work enough—that, all through, is the implication. And so far as social criticism goes, one can never extract much more from Dickens than this, unless one deliberately reads meaning into him. His whole "message" is one that at first glance looks like an enormous platitude: If men would behave decently the world would be decent.
>
> Naturally this calls for a few characters who are in positions of authority and who *do* behave decently. Hence that recurrent Dickens figure, the Good Rich Man. This character belongs especially to Dickens's early optimistic period. He is usually a "merchant" (we are not necessarily told what merchandise he deals in), and he is always a superhumanly kind-hearted old gentleman who "trots" to and fro, raising his employees' wages, patting children on the head, getting debtors out of jail and, in general, acting the fairy godmother.[8]

In a competitive market economy, why does the kindness of masters especially matter? If one's conditions of employment can be raised by seeking alternatives, then what is so special about the kindness of one's employer in comparison, say, to the cleanliness of the workplace? There is an enormous number of nonpecuniary forms of compensation that one weighs in considering the net advantages of different employment.[9] If one's master is unkind and there is nothing offered by way of compensation, move across the street. What if

---

7. I have added the emphasis. One of the issues in Dickens's continual sniping at Harriet Beecher Stowe was her treatment of blacks as members of a rather superior race. Blacks, in her account, are noticeably closer to God than are whites. Stone (1957) gives the references to Dickens's correspondence. Stowe's eccentric racism—inconsequential in terms of the contemporary policy debates—was duly noted as a matter of amusement by Nassau Senior, who reviewed *Uncle Tom's Cabin* for the *Edinburgh Review*.

8. George Orwell, *The Collected Essays, Journalism, and Letters of George Orwell*, ed. Sonia Orwell and Ian Angus (New York: Harcourt, Brace, and World, 1968), p. 417.

9. The canonical treatment is found in *Wealth of Nations* (London: W. Strahan and T. Cadell, 1776), book 1, chapter 10, in which the equalization of the net advantages of employment within a labor market are described. In this chapter, Smith describes in detail how the desire for approbation of all people influences their calculation of individual agents. Dickens's falsification works by ignoring such elements in the economist's bag of tools. Chapters 9 and 11 demonstrate how they work.

there is no one across the street? Then we question the competitive assumption and need to think hard.

By contrast, in a system of slavery, surely, the kindness of one's master is of overwhelming importance. And in Dickens's *Household Words*, both in what he himself wrote and in what he published that was written by others, he emphasizes over and over again the dreadful fate of slaves who are cursed with unkind masters.[1] But still the question is: what shall be done? The choices Dickens seems to imagine are freeing the slaves or removing the cruel masters. In *Uncle Tom's Cabin*, the rational slave is seen as preferring freedom to slavery under the most benevolent master because one never knows who the next master might be. The reading of *Hard Times* for which I shall argue next is that Dickens responds to this by making the case that there is no difference between markets and slavery—everything is just a question of the kindness of the masters.

* * *

SELLING WOMEN INTO SEXUAL SERVICE

Recent attention paid by scholars to the sexual aspects of *Hard Times* seems to be responsible for some interpretative instability in the commentary on the novel. * * *

The impossibility of a stable Christian marriage among slaves is a standard trope of the antislavery evangelicals. What kind of a marriage could one expect under an institution in which, whenever it suited their master's interests, husband and wife might be sold separately? Is Dickens asserting that marital instability is no different in markets than in slavery?

Marital instability is a hopelessly broad topic. Consequently, I consider only the most narrow aspect of the sexual issues in *Hard Times*, Tom's pandering of Louisa. It is completely nonobvious just how Tom manages to pander his sister to Mr. Bounderby. Here is the transaction:

> What a game girl you are, to be such a first-rate sister, Loo!" whispered Tom.

1. The evils of slavery seem easier to appreciate when the slave owners are not British. "A shriek was heard, suddenly, and horrible; another yet more frightful pierced the thunder of the breakers; the sea-water became purple. Those unhappy wretches had made their choice between the Spaniards and the ground-sharks" (Von Goetznitz, 1858. "A Negro-Hunt," *Household Words. A Weekly Journal Conducted by Charles Dickens* 18 [July 17, 1858]: 112). On the other hand, when are the masters kind? John Hollingshead's (1858) treatment of the kindly slave ship captain reads like *Springtime on the Middle Passage*. Lohrli quotes Dickens's policy on some topics. "Let Hollingshead do it. . . . He's the most ignorant man on the staff, but he'll cram up the facts, and won't give us an encyclopaedical article" (Anne Lohrli, *Household Words: A Weekly Journal, 1850–1859, Conducted by Charles Dickens* [Toronto: U of Toronto P 1973]).

> She clung to him, as she should have clung to some far bet-
> ter nature that day, and was a little shaken in her reserved
> composure for the first time.
> "Old Bounderby's quite ready," said Tom. "Time's up. Good-
> bye! I shall be on the look-out for you, when you come back. I
> say, my dear Loo! AN'T it uncommonly jolly now!"

This is Tom's explanation of the episode later in the story:

> "You know our governor, Mr. Harthouse," said Tom, "and
> therefore you needn't be surprised that Loo married old Bound-
> erby. She never had a lover, and the governor proposed old
> Bounderby, and she took him."
> "Very dutiful in your interesting sister," said Mr. James
> Harthouse.
> "Yes, but she wouldn't have been as dutiful, and it would not
> have come off as easily," returned the whelp, "if it hadn't been
> for me."
> The tempter merely lifted his eyebrows; but the whelp was
> obliged to go on.
> "*I* persuaded her," he said, with an edifying air of superiority.
> "I was stuck in old Bounderby's bank (where I never wanted to
> be), and I knew I should get into scrapes there, if she put old
> Bounderby's pipe out; so I told her my wishes, and she came
> into them. She would do anything for me. It was very game of
> her, wasn't it?"

Of course, Harthouse attempts to buy her from Tom, but that
transaction does not work so smoothly.

Is Dickens making the claim that all Utilitarians would prosti-
tute their family members if the price were right? Of course not.
Mr. Gradgrind—who was not raised as a Utilitarian—passes on
Bounderby's proposal of marriage to his daughter, reviews the costs
and benefits of the transaction, and encourages her to make the
decision *she* thinks best. Gradgrind is a creditable feminist, so the
same *choice* that was given to him will be given to her. He treats his
daughter as a competent optimizing agent, but as both a caring
father and an experienced economist he wants to verify the solution
by means of standard algorithms:

> "I now leave you to judge for yourself," said Mr. Gradgrind. "I
> have stated the case, as such cases are usually stated among
> practical minds; I have stated it, as the case of your mother
> and myself was stated in its time. The rest, my dear Louisa, is
> for you to decide."

Moreover, upon discovering the truth about the marriage, he pro-
tects his daughter with a quiet fierceness that puts the fright in
Bounderby.

The weirdness of a woman making this critical sexual decision on the basis of what best suits her brother's pecuniary interest— and her brother's evident belief that even after she was married he can repander her—evaporates if one supposes that *Hard Times* was written in opposition to *Uncle Tom's Cabin*. Stowe opens her book with a portrait of two slave owners—the decent Shelby and the loutish Haley. When Haley catches sight of the fetching Eliza, guess what transaction first pops into his mind?

> "By Jupiter," said the trader, turning to him in admiration, "there's an article now! You might make your fortune on that ar gal in Orleans, any day. I've seen over a thousand in my day, paid down for gals not a bit handsomer."

Shelby, motivated by fear of his wife's reaction, refuses to discuss such a trade. Here and elsewhere, Stowe seems to propose this test for the morals of slave owners: will they sell or buy a woman for sexual service? Some pass, some fail. In all institutions there are good people and bad people. What is important is how institutions bend behavior. Or at least that is how the promarket abolitionists saw the case, as they proposed to end the possibility of such sales by ending the ownership of other humans.

I read Dickens as posing the Martineau-Stowe test in market capitalism. Those who would sell or buy a woman for sexual service are moral monsters; those who would not live in hope of their redemption. Gradgrind Sr. is an unlucky man saved by his pre-Utilitarian upbringing. Dickens seems to make the case that institutions like market capitalism or slavery are neither good not bad; all that matters is the quality of the people inside the institutions. Thus capitalism and slavery are morally equivalent, morally neutral.

* * *

Human Malleability—Deformed by Choice

After a lengthy detour, we return to the question of rational choice models and their presupposition of a fixed human nature. If the antislavery coalition held to a fixed nature for all humans, what did those who wrote against them hold?

Not surprisingly, the answer is human malleability. Of course, humans can be remade for the worse as well as for the better. Perhaps the most dramatic example of Dickens's belief in the ability of slavery to remake human nature for the worse is the following passage from *American Notes*. The cruelty of their masters has turned slaves in America into beasts more closely resembling Swift's "humans":

To those who are happily unaccustomed to them, the countenances in the streets and labouring places, too, are shocking.
All men who know that there are laws against instructing
slaves, of which the pains and penalties greatly exceed in their
amount, the fines imposed on those who main and torture
them, must be prepared to find their faces very low in the scale
of intellectual expression. But the darkness—not of skin, but
mind—which meets the stranger's eye at every turn; the bru-
talizing and blotting out of all fairer characters traced by
Nature's hand; immeasurably outdo his worst belief. That travelled creation of the great satirist's brain, who fresh from living among horses, peered from a high casement down upon
his own kind with trembling horror, was scarcely more repelled
and daunted by the sight, than those who look upon some of
these faces for the first time must surely be.

Capitalism remakes humans for the worse, too. Here is one of
Dickens's accounts of Coketown, where human nature is again
remade:

You saw nothing in Coketown but what was severely workful. If the members of a religious persuasion built a chapel
there—as the members of eighteen religious persuasions
had done—they made it a pious warehouse of red brick, with
sometimes (but this only in highly ornamented examples) a
bell in a bird-cage on the top of it. . . . All the public inscriptions in the town were painted alike, in severe characters of
black and white. The jail might have been the infirmary, the
infirmary might have been the jail, the town-hall might have
been either, or both, or anything else, for anything that
appeared to the contrary in the graces of their construction.
Fact, fact, fact, everywhere in the material aspect of the
town; fact, fact, fact, everywhere in the immaterial. The
M'Choakumchild school was all fact, and the school of design
was all fact, and the relations between master and man were
all fact. . . .
    A town so sacred to fact, and so triumphant in its asser-
tion, of course got on well? Why no, not quite well. No? Dear
me!

And how is human nature remade? We read in Morley and Dickens's discussion of American slavery how slave owners operating on
the *supply* side prevent the dissemination of Christianity and so
deform the slaves. Somehow British industrial capitalism operating
on the *demand* side prevents the dissemination of Christianity and
so deforms the workers. Dickens's workers have a choice of eighteen denominations; Adam Smith's vision of religion as a competitive industry is alive outside of America:

No. Coketown did not come out of its own furnaces, in all respects like gold that had stood the fire. First, the perplexing mystery of the place was, Who belonged to the eighteen denominations? Because, whoever did, the labouring people did not. It was very strange to walk through the streets on a Sunday morning, and note how few of *them* the barbarous jangling of bells that was driving the sick and nervous mad, called away from their own quarter, from their own close rooms, from the corners of their own streets, where they lounged listlessly, gazing at all the church and chapel going, as at a thing with which they had no manner of concern.

Dickens's workers cannot select among the eighteen denominations. Like stories of the reaction of Soviet refugees to American supermarkets, his workers are frozen by choice:

Nor was it merely the stranger who noticed this, because there was a native organization in Coketown itself, whose members were to be heard of in the House of Commons every session indignantly petitioning, for acts of parliament that should make these people religious by main force. Then, came the Teetotal Society, who complained that these same people *would* get drunk, and showed in tabular statements that they did get drunk, and proved at tea parties that no inducement, human or Divine (except a medal), would induce them to forgo their custom of getting drunk. Then, came the chemist and druggist, with other tabular statements, showing that when they didn't get drunk, they took opium.

Surely there never was such fragile china-ware as that of which the millers of Coketown were made.

Decades after *Culture and Society*, [Raymond] Williams returned to *Hard Times* and noticed something interesting about these and other related passages:

For at its deepest, most formative level, *Hard Times* is composed from two incompatible ideological positions, which are unevenly held both by Dickens and by many of his intended readers. Put broadly, these positions are: first, that environment influences and in some sense determines character; second, that some virtues and vices are original and both triumph over and in some cases can change any environment.[2]

Perhaps there is a simple solution to Williams's puzzle. The masters of mankind are outside the chain of cause and effect. The higher orders can—for good or evil—remake the lower orders. They

2. Raymond Williams, *Writing in Society* (London: Verso, 1983), p. 169.

are like our parents would be if we never grew up. And if these lower orders object to their remaking? As we learn from the Eyre Controversy, that only proves that they are not fit to be human and are outside the rule of law.

In this context, perhaps, we might wish to reread Dickens's famous letter of June 17, 1854, about his quarrel with Mr. Gradgrind:

> I often say to Mr. Gradgrind that there is reason and good intention in much that he does—in fact, in all that he does— but that he over-does it. Perhaps by dint of his going his way and my going mine, we shall meet at last at some halfway house where there are flowers on the carpets, and a little standing-room for Queen Mab's Chariot among the Steam Engines.

As I read this, Dickens renounces any deep quarrel with the market economy; he just wants to have a hand in the mastering.

Conclusion

There are three mistakes that I find scholars making in reading *Hard Times*. The first is to assume that what Dickens said about his opponents is always an accurate statement of their views. The charge of misrepresentation was made while he lived. The second mistake is to read midcentury antimarket British works in isolation from antislavery American works of the same period. The charge of anti-antislavery was made while Dickens lived.

In my view, whatever theorists might argue about a possible socialism, the material world of the 1850s was divided between people who believed in markets and people who believed in slavery. What made one less attractive made its alternative more attractive. The third and final mistake—the one my fellow economists often commit—is to fail to treat Dickens with all due seriousness, to assume that his opinions are the result of some drab combination of ignorance and stupidity. I find it most fitting that I close on a point of full agreement with F. R. Leavis, who first taught the world that *Hard Times* is worthy of the most serious study.

CHRISTOPHER BARNES

From Hard Times: Fancy as Practice[†]

* * *

The critical history of *Hard Times* is well known. To summarize: most contemporary reviewers dismissed it as a didactic novel unrelated to Dickens's "better" work.[1] Leftist critics—Gissing, Shaw, G. K. Chesterton, and Raymond Williams—blast his unsympathetic and frankly false depiction of mid-century trades unions; F. R. Leavis in *The Great Tradition* constructed a more positive critical reputation for *Hard Times*, calling it a "moral fable," a "masterpiece," and Dickens's only "completely serious work of art" (227). With notable exceptions,[2] critics in the second half of the twentieth century tend to use the novel in passing to illustrate a thesis about another of Dickens's works. Most recently, Alexander Welsh has found *Hard Times* to be a sequel in theme and style to the novel immediately preceding, *Bleak House*. Countless undergraduate students, meanwhile, have read *Hard Times* in introductory classes primarily because of its (lack of) length.

An interpretation of *Hard Times* on its own terms, however, and in light of the other industrial novels with which it is grouped finds that Dickens is interested, not just in respite or contrast or solely in the industrial problem, but in relations of power across society: relationships between teacher and pupil, parent and child, husband and wife, mill owner and laborer, union leader and union members, governor and governed, and ultimately between the middle and working classes.[3]

---

† From *Dickens Studies Annual* 34 (2004): 234–40, 248–50, 252–53. Reprinted by permission of AMS Press, Inc.

1. Notwithstanding, Ruskin found the novel aesthetically pleasing and thought it the greatest Dickens had written (48). (John Ruskin, "Unto This Last," *Cornhill Magazine* 2 [August 1860]: 47–55.)

2. Edgar Johnson praises *Hard Times* as a stark, formalized, and allegorical moral drama. (Edgar Johnson, *Charles Dickens: His Tragedy and Triumph*, 2 vols. [New York: Simon & Schuster, 1952].) John Holloway argues that the novel can retain our attention if we are "enticed by problems but indifferent to art" (171). (John Holloway, "*Hard Times*: A History and Criticism," *Dickens and the Twentieth Century*, ed. John Gross and Gabriel Pearson [Toronto: U of Toronto P, 1962].) In an attempt to explain away the book's faults by making them virtues, A. E. Dyson writes that Dickens emphasized Fact by de-emphasizing his art (187). (A. E. Dyson, *The Inimitable Dickens: A Reading of the Novels* [London: Macmillan, 1970].)

3. Philip Collins persuasively makes the case that Dickens was not intimately knowledgeable of industrial areas of the country (652–53). (Philip Collins, "Dickens and Industrialism," *Studies in English Literature* 20 [1980]: 651–73.) Dickens had for years been promising to address the industrial question, but *Hard Times* neglects many of the central issues surrounding industrialism: child labor, the ten-hours bill, worker safety. Interestingly, before publication, Dickens deleted a passage from chapter 13 of book one of *Hard Times* in which Stephen graphically alludes to the maiming of Rachael's sister by having "her child arm tore off afore thy [Rachael's] face." Editor Kate Flint reproduces the omitted passage in the Penguin edition of the novel. In the scene, Stephen also criticizes the millowners for resisting government-mandated safety measures they deem too expensive (309).

Subaltern characters determinedly, yet indirectly, fight to modify the representations of themselves assumed and imposed by the hegemonic force, whether that force is the middle class, one's teacher, one's father, one's husband, or one's employer. In "fancy," Dickens recognizes these more subtle forms of resistance, though his critics have not often given him credit for this level of subtlety.[4]

* * *

Many critics find the opposition in *Hard Times* between fact and fancy problematic or simplistic. Patricia Johnson concludes that fancy "can do little more than decorate" the drabness represented by facts. Cynthia Malone finds the "rhetoric of opposition in *Hard Times . . .* misleading." She finds the novel's thrust, not in opposition to, but supporting the values consistent with middle-class reform. Dickens does not, Sylvère Monod believes, put forward a "clear, coherent, persuasive thesis," but rather a "kind of sentimental socialism."[5]

Because these critics and reviewers concentrate on the strategic (profound and direct) resistance embodied in fancy, they interpret the resistance in the novel to be, at best, unrealistic, as in Sissy's confrontation with Harthouse, or ineffective, as in the workers' confrontations with their employers. These are important forms of resistance, but they are all strategic (direct) forms of resistance. When tactical (hidden, non-confrontational) resistance is added to our definition of fancy, a more cogent and coherent opposition to the authority of the world symbolized by "fact" emerges.

Fact

The ethos of *fact* that dominates *Hard Times* is a disciplinary force within the novel, representing those subject to its domination in ways that encourage conformity and enforce hegemony. The elder Gradgrind, Thomas, is a comical exaggeration of utilitarianism, emphasizing fact and rationality—the head—above all things. He is inflexible, dry, emphatic, dictatorial, hard set, obstinate, and

---

4. Razak Dahmane demonstrates that Dickens also endorses fancy in his manipulation of metaphorical language. Dickens "articulate[s] his alternative to the hard-fact faction" by emphasizing the imaginative and figurative abilities of, especially, the narrator while denying figurative license to those opposed to fancy. The literal-mindedness of Gradgrind, Bounderby, and Bitzer weakens the philosophy to which they attach so much significance. "[M]etaphorical proficiency," Dahmane writes, is a "linguistic badge of moral decency and imaginative health" (137–38). (Razak Dahmane, "'A Mere Question of Figures': Measures, Mystery, and Metaphor in *Hard Times*," *Dickens Studies Annual* 23 [1994]: 137–62.)

5. Dickens's contemporary critics agreed. See, for instance, reviews in *Athenaeum* 1398 (12 August 1854): 992; *Gentlemen's Magazine* 42 (September 1854): 276–78; *British Quarterly Review* 20.40 (October 1854): 581–82; *Rambler* 2.10 (October 1854): 361–62; *Westminster Review* 6.12 (October 1854): 604–06; and *Blackwood's Edinburgh Magazine* 77.474 (April 1855): 453–54.

stubborn. He is the kind of man who confidently reduces any aspect of human nature to "figures, a case of simple arithmetic" (2), but as one critic puts it, "The crude but forceless simplicity of Gradgrind can scarcely be said to represent the complexity and solidity of Bentham's influential contributions to English thought." Nevertheless, the grounds upon which Dickens attacks utilitarianism are the same grounds which John Stuart Mill addresses in his *Autobiography*, where he attributes his breakdown at the age of twenty-one to the one-sided nature of his education. Mill comes to understand a need to enrich "the internal culture of the individual" with an attention to one's own emotions and to the enjoyment of poetry, art, and music.

✳ ✳ ✳

Systems as Power

Hard Times, however, is not just an examination of utilitarianism; it is a critique of systems in general as forms of power. In *Hard Times*, those in authority—employers, teachers, parents, and the middle class as a whole—have a simplified and caricatured understanding of their subalterns. Both Bounderby and Gradgrind believe that the working classes are "a bad lot altogether." They believe laborers are ungrateful and disloyal, and "that they lived upon the best, and bought fresh butter; and insisted on Mocha coffee, and rejected all but prime parts of meat, and yet were eternally dissatisfied and unmanageable." Though Bounderby believes that the workers only want to be "set up in a coach and six, and to be fed on turtle soup and venison, with a gold spoon," the reality is that working-class characters are never shown eating at all.

Louisa is similarly ignorant of the working class. Upon visiting Blackpool's room, "for the first time in her life she was face to face with anything like individuality in connection with [the workers]." For Louisa, the working class is an abstraction: they are the sum of the statistical evidence she has been given about them, a single mass unit without component parts. Louisa's attitudes emphasize the miscommunication and ignorance resulting from partial, general, and abstract knowledge, from not exploring the specifics and the individuality of the "other." Rachael notes the separate worlds the working and middle classes inhabit: "'The like of you don't know us, don't care for us, don't belong to us,'" she tells Louisa.

The various religious denominations or societies for improving social conditions in Coketown also delude themselves with these partial, reductive, and paternalistic attitudes toward labor. E. P. Thompson lists a sample from the late eighteenth and early nineteenth

centuries of those who desire to put the "houses of the poor in
order," and Dickens must have had in mind very similar sorts of
groups. Thompson lists "Hannah More, with her halfpenny tracts
and Sunday Schools, the Methodists with their renewed emphasis
upon order and submissiveness, Bishop Barrington's more humane
Society for Bettering the Condition of the Poor, and William Wil-
berforce and Dr. John Bowdler, with their Society for the Suppression of Vice and Encouragement of Religion." Add to these the
Independents, the Baptists, the Congregationalists, and the Uni-
tarians. The bells from the chapels of these denominations, rather
than providing comfort, are a "barbarous jangling" that drives the
"sick and nervous mad." The laborers, Dickens asserts, avoid these
organizations because they treat the workers as if they are infants,
as if they are "twenty, thirty, forty, or fifty" -year-old "babies." The
laborers are told by these groups, as Louisa is told by her father,
never to wonder, but to trust in the reasoning of those in authority.
These religious denominations and societies all seek to define narrowly, to represent narrowly, members of the working class in order
to simplify, understand, and ultimately control them. The Christian Socialism Charles Kingsley puts forward in *Alton Locke* is an
analogously authoritarian system. As a Unitarian, Elizabeth Gaskell in *Mary Barton* opposes the independence and anarchy she
finds in the more enthusiastic brands of religion. In order to reinforce middle-class ideals of religious and social conformity, she
criticizes the Methodist church—which was widely seen as addressing itself to the needs and point of view of the working class—at a
point in history when, in fact, in Manchester at the middle of the
century, Methodists comprised a majority of the citizenry:[6]

Because Dickens's primary theme is authority, to the eighteen
denominations or improvement societies that vie for control of
the Coketown citizenry, one more could be added: the United
Aggregate Tribunal. Dickens has Slackbridge deliver to the laborers what Dickens's middle-class readers would understand to be
a simplification and an abstraction of the middle and owning
class. * * *

*   *   *

Like Gradgrind, Slackbridge and the United Aggregate Tribunal
insist on conformity. Though George Bernard Shaw, F. R. Leavis,
George Gissing, Sylvère Monod, and Raymond Williams all point

6. In *Manchester in 1844: Its Present Condition and Future Prospects* (London: Simpkin,
  Marshal, and Co., 1844. Rpt. 1969. Frank Cass), Léon Faucher notes that Methodists
  were the largest religious group in Manchester at midcentury. Of the 137 places of worship in Manchester in 1844, only thirty-nine belonged to the Church of England while
  forty-three were Methodist. Only five were Unitarian (23).

out that Dickens's depiction of trade unions in *Hard Times* is simplistic caricature,[7] from Dickens's perspective the world-view of labor organizations is simply another representation of the social, and is hence partial, prejudiced, and limited. Slackbridge subverts and manipulates truth (much as Gradgrind did with Sissy's father) to make Blackpool a scapegoat and creates an atmosphere of crisis where before had existed only difference, ignorance, and lack of experience. Because Blackpool is represented by Slackbridge as a "'traitor and a craven and a recreant'" standing against "'Freedom'" and "'Right,'" the union feels compelled to shun Blackpool rather than incorporate his objections or simply to acknowledge and tolerate his refusal to join with them. These consequences are the result of decisions based on partial and antagonistic points of view. * * *

In the manipulative and partisan Slackbridge, Dickens reproduces the middle-class fear of an organized working class. Brantlinger notes that the "Humanitarian perspective" of many Victorian writers "was flexible enough to include sympathy for the Ten Hours Movement, the agitation against the New Poor Law, cooperative associations, and even 'moral force' Chartism, but it did not include much sympathy for trade unions and strikes." In the guise of fiction, Dickens echoes Carlyle's denunciation of unions in *Chartism* as dogmatic and intolerant fraternities: "What kind of 'wild-justice' must it be in the hearts of these men that prompts them, with cold deliberation, in conclave assembled, to doom their brother workman, as the deserter of his order and his order's cause, to die as a traitor and deserter." In Gaskell's *North and South*, a workman with eight children to feed who is thrown out of work because of a strike, says to a fellow workman, "'Yo' may be kind hearts, each separate; but, once banded together, yo've no more pity for a man than a wild hunger-maddened wolf." The riots in Kingsley's *Alton Locke*, George Eliot's *Felix Holt*, and Disraeli's *Sybil* all depict labor's efforts to combine as existing dangerously on the edge of violence. The difference is that these other middle-class writers cast the middle class in opposition to the working class. The middle class provides a rational corrective. Dickens depicts all systems as partial and reductive.

For Dickens, social change led by an authoritarian group, howsoever well-meaning, cannot be widespread or meaningful unless it is in continuous dialogue with the working class. From Dickens's

---

7. Sylvère Monod, *Dickens the Novelist* (Norman: U of Oklahoma P, 1968), p. 470; George Gissing, *Charles Dickens* (Port Washington, NY: Kennikat, 1966), p. 18; F. R. Leavis, *The Great Tradition* (New York: New York UP, 1964), pp. 245–46, 248; Frank Smith, "Perverted Balance: Expressive Form in *Hard Times*," *Dickens Studies Annual* 6 (1977): 108; and Raymond Williams, *The English Novel from Dickens to Lawrence* (London: Chatto and Windus, 1970), pp. 93, 96.

middle-class point of view, Slackbridge and his union represent such a powerful minority, and in that sense his depiction of them is a caricature, but his point still remains that power impervious to critique represents the working class to be plastic and passive rather than active and intelligent. From Dickens's perspective, Slackbridge is just as impervious to critique as Gradgrind and Bounderby. Slackbridge might as well be saying, in echo of Gradgrind, "'No. The course we pursue, we pursue according to the system—the system—and there is no more to be said about it." *** Slackbridge is the outsider, a man of words and theories in a world of experience, practice, and action.

* * *

Blackpool's Muddle

Stephen Blackpool functions in the novel to define himself in opposition to both the alienating, inhumane policies of Bounderby and the factory and to the unthinking loyalty demanded by Slackbridge and the union. His function is parallel to Sissy's opposition to Gradgrind's utilitarian family and school, with one significant difference: Blackpool predominantly engages in direct, strategic actions, not in disguised tactical practice. His confrontations with the trade union and with Bounderby demonstrate the bankruptcy of the bourgeois ideal of the autonomous individual.

* * *

Dickens's description of the union meeting and the subsequent decisions of the workers is a good example both of his middle-class perspective and of working-class resistance to such a middle-class representation. The result is an ambiguity that attempts to depict both sides honestly. Though Dickens cannot explain the workers' attraction to the union, except to point out that working conditions must be bad for such a man to be persuasive, he allows room for such actions on their part. This contradiction between Slackbridge's message, which rings true for his audience, and his personal absence of authority is resolved if one understands that Dickens's object of satire is neither the working class nor the middle class, but rather those who would simplify, those who would substitute the abstraction of a prejudice, a tabular conclusion, or the mandates of a system for the specificity of individual relationships. Subalterns, when confronted with a representation of themselves and forced to articulate their objection, respond by pointing to the disjunction between the representation that the powerful group operates from and the experience in which the subaltern group is immersed.

Dickens posits Stephen Blackpool as a subaltern figure who is able to criticize this simplifying tendency of the owning class. He obviously is not interested in venison and gold spoons. He says to Bounderby,

> "Deed we are in a muddle, sir. Look round town—so rich as 'tis—and see the numbers o' people as has been broughten into bein heer, fur to weave, an' to card, an' to piece out a livin', aw the same one way, somehows, 'twixt their cradles and their graves. Look how we live, an' wheer we live, an' in what numbers, an' by what chances, and wi' what sameness; and look how the mills is awlus a goin, and how they never works us no nigher to ony dis'ant object—ceptin awlus, Death. Look how you considers of us, and writes of us, and talks of us, and goes up wi' yor deputations to Secretaries o' State 'bout us, and how yo are awlus right, and how we are awlus wrong, and never had'n no reason in us sin ever we were born."

Blackpool is not confused. He does not throw up his hands and say defeatedly that all is a muddle. He is not, as Sylvère Monod insists, possessed of an "ignorant mind and a muddled brain." Instead, as a close examination of the above passage will demonstrate, he understands that social relations are contradictory. He understands that ideologies reinforcing the value and rewards of hard work and loyalty as well as paternalistic claims of the industrialist and of the government to see to the welfare of the common man are in conflict with practices. Blackpool understands, as demonstrated in his preceding speech, the concept of surplus labor as industry attracts a labor pool that it cannot support during down market cycles; he understands the alienation of the repetitive labor demanded of them; he understands that labor is consumed and cast aside when no longer useful; he understands the demands of capitalism to increase productivity and the hours worked to increase its accumulation of wealth; he understands the hegemony and egotism of the bourgeoisie believing itself to be the universal class; and finally, he understands the paternalism of the middle class that treats the working class as devoid of reason. These contradictions between the bourgeois cant and the reality he lives are what he summarizes in the term *muddle*. Consequently, his recognition of the muddle is not a sign of his "ignorant mind and a muddled brain" but is instead a cogent analysis and a call for reform.

* * *

THEODORE DALRYMPLE

Hard Times Again[†]

We live in hard times, and all the indications are that they may get much, even very much, harder. No one, at any rate, would take a bet that they won't.

The number of children in America claiming subsidized meals in school has shot up; the homeless are increasing by the hour; the formerly prosperous are laid off without so much as a thank you; the young struggle to find any work at all; beggars are making a comeback on the streets of cities as if they had been hiding all these years, waiting for the right moment to emerge from their sub-terranean lairs into the world above.

The February bicentenary of the birth of Charles Dickens, then, could hardly come at a more appropriate moment in economic history, for Dickens was the revealer, the scourge, the prose poet, of urban destitution—a destitution that, in our waking nightmares, we fear may yet return.

Dickens knew whereof he wrote. It was his habit to walk miles through the streets of London, and no man—except perhaps Henry Mayhew—was more observant than he. Often accused by his detractors of exaggerating reality, he claimed in the preface to *Martin Chuzzlewit* that he merely saw what others did not see, or chose not to see, and put it into plain words. What was caricature to some was to him no more than the unvarnished truth. He held up a mirror to his age.

The adjective "Dickensian" is more laden with connotation than the adjective that pertains to any other writer: Jamesian, for example, or Joycean, even Shakespearian. We think of workhouses, of shabby tenements with bedding of rags, of schools where sadistic and exploitative schoolmasters beat absurdities into the heads of hungry children, of heartless proponents of the cold charity, of crooked lawyers spinning out their cases in dusty, clerk-ridden chambers. We think of Oliver Twist asking for more, of Wackford Squeers exclaiming, "Here's richness for you!", as he tastes the thin slops his school doles out to his unfortunate pupils, of Mrs. Gamp looking at her patient and saying, "He'd make a lovely corpse!"

If he had been only a social commentator, though, Dickens would have been forgotten by all except specialist historians of his age. But he is not forgotten; he survives the notorious defects of his

† From *The American Conservative* (January 2012): 12–14. Copyright *The American Conservative*. Reprinted by permission of the publisher. All rights reserved.

books—their sometimes grotesque sentimentality, their sprawling lack of construction, their frequent implausibility—to achieve whatever immortality literature can confer. Over and over again, in passage after passage, the sheer genius of his writing shines from the page and is the despair of all prose writers after him.

When Dickens called himself "the Inimitable," he was speaking no more than the truth; he was the greatest comic writer in his, or perhaps in any other, language. And the comedy runs deep: it is not trivial, for while it depicts absurdity, pomposity, and even cruelty, it has the curious effect of reconciling us to life even as it lays human weaknesses out for our inspection.

Sairey Gamp, for example, the drunken, slatternly nurse in *Martin Chuzzlewit*, is as undesirable a creature as it is possible to be. Who would want to be nursed by her? She is, in effect, the exemplar of the need for the reform of an entire profession. Yet by a peculiar kind of alchemy Dickens makes us glad that there is a world in which a Mrs. Gamp can exist. A world without characters such as she would be the poorer for their absence.

When, gloriously, she says of the gin in the teapot, "Don't ask me to take none, but put it on the chimbley piece, and let me put my lips to it when I feel so dispoged," our hearts leap with an indefinable joy. The verbal genius of the simple replacement of the *s* in *disposed* by the *g* delights us. (Though no doubt Dickens would have told us that he actually had heard such a transposition rather than invented it, so that his genius was in noticing and remembering, not in inventing, which is a reproach to our own lack of observation.) The slattern's ridiculous pretension to gentility and refinement, while maintaining her slovenliness, incites us to reflect upon our own pretensions—pretense being the permanent condition of mankind.

And while our love of Mrs. Gamp, tinged as it no doubt is by guilt that we can feel any affection for so disgraceful a being, does not prevent us from recognizing the obvious need for nursing to be placed on a more respectable footing, it also performs the function of restraining our wish for soulless perfection. A perfect world, or rather an attempted perfect world, in which there were no Dickensian characters would be a living hell.

I think this is what a student of English at the North Korean Foreign Languages Institute was driving at when he sidled up to me in Pyongyang and said, quickly and *sotto voce* (for unscripted communication with foreigners was dangerous for North Koreans), "Reading Shakespeare and Dickens is the greatest, the only, joy of my life." I was, of course, in great admiration of the feat of his having learned English of such proficiency that he could appreciate the two authors while never having left his hermetic native hell and communicate his enthusiasm for them so elegantly. No doubt Dickens had been taught to him as a means of demonstrating the diabolical nature of capitalist society; but the lesson he had drawn from Dickens was quite otherwise, that Mrs. Gamp (for example), impoverished and degraded as she was, at least spoke in what was unmistakably her own voice and not that compelled by any political master. She was free as no North Korean was free.

As we live in hard times, it is worth considering Dickens's novel of that title, especially as political economy is one of its most important themes. Has this book, published more than a century and a half ago, anything to say to us about our present predicament, beyond young Tom Gradgrind's exclamation, "For God's sake, don't talk about bankers"?

Dickens is often reproached for his absence of firm and unequivocal moral, political, and philosophical outlook. He veers crazily between the ferociously reactionary and the mushily liberal. He lampoons the disinterested philanthropy of Mrs. Jellyby (in *Bleak House*) with the same gusto or ferocity as he excoriates the egotism of Mr. Veneering (in *Our Mutual Friend*). He suggests that businessmen are heartless swine (Bounderby in *Hard Times*) or disinterestedly charitable (the Cheeryble brothers in *Nicholas Nickleby*). He satirizes temperance (in *The Pickwick Papers*) as much as he derides drunkenness (in *Martin Chuzzlewit*). The evil Jew (in *Oliver Twist*) is matched by the saintly Jew (in *Our Mutual Friend*). As Stephen Blackpool, the working-class hero of *Hard Times* says, "it's aw a muddle."

George Orwell, in his famous essay on Dickens, saw in this philosophical and moral muddle not a weakness but a strength, a generosity of spirit, an openness to the irreducible complexity of mankind's moral situation, an immunity to what he called "the smelly little orthodoxies that are now contending for our souls." And indeed, the principal target of *Hard Times* is such an orthodoxy, namely a hardnosed utilitarianism combined with an unbending liberalism. (Liberal in the economic, not cultural, sense.)

The principal bearers of the doctrine are Mr. Gradgrind and Mr. Bounderby. Gradgrind is a teacher whose statement of pedagogical philosophy is surely one of the greatest opening passages of any novel ever written:

> Now what I want is, Facts. Teach these boys and girls nothing but Facts. Facts alone are wanted in life. Plant nothing else and root out everything else. You can only form the minds of reasoning animals upon Facts: nothing else will ever be of any service to them. This is the principle on which I bring up my own children, and this is the principle on which I bring up these children. Stick to Facts, sir!

By the end of the novel, Gradgrind has learned the insufficiency of facts for the conduct of human life, as he might have done merely by a little self-examination or reflection on the nature of moral and aesthetic judgment. It cannot be said that Gradgrind is a caricature, a character so exaggerated that he never did or could exist: passage after passage in *Hard Times* parallels almost exactly the account of John Stuart Mill's education in his *Autobiography,* published 19 years after the novel. Furthermore, "the minds of reasoning animals" exactly captures the flavor of much recent scientistic writing about the human condition. Like hope in the human breast, scientism springs eternal in the human mind.

Josiah Bounderby of Coketown, the mill owner, claims to have come up in the world the hard way:

> My mother left me to my grandmother, and, according to the best of my remembrance, my grandmother was the wickedest and the worst old woman that ever lived. If I got a little pair of shoes by any chance, she would take 'em off and sell 'em for drink . . . She kept me in an egg-box. As soon as I was big enough to run away, of course I ran away. Then I became a young vagabond; and instead of one old woman knocking me about and starving me, everybody of all ages knocked me about and starved me.

This turns out to be quite untrue. In fact, his parents made sacrifices on his behalf, but the lie justifies his philosophy, that workers who ask for higher pay want turtle soup to be fed them from a golden spoon, that the slightest regulation of child labor will drive employers into bankruptcy and force them to abandon their factories, that the smoke belching from the mills not only cannot be reduced but is actually healthful for the lungs, that any form of collective action by the "hands" is the first stage of violent revolution, that any form of charity is the encouragement of idleness. In short: "What you couldn't show to be purchasable in the cheapest market and salable in the dearest, was not, and never should be, world without end, Amen."

Again, this is scarcely caricature. During the Irish famine, liberals like Charles Trevelyan—at the time to the left of the political spectrum—argued that to provide any form of relief to the starving was to encourage the very habits and practices, to say nothing of the overpopulation, that caused the famine in the first place. An abstract truth, as they believed it to be, overrode all considerations of humanity. True compassion consisted of letting events take their course.

One might have supposed, then, that Dickens would be much in favor of the unions; but in fact his depiction of the union leader,

Slackbridge, in *Hard Times* is very unfavorable. He realized that demagogic leaders were perfectly capable of ensnaring good men *en masse*:

> Slackbridge was not so honest, he was not so manly, he was not so good-humored [as his audience]; he substituted cunning for their simplicity, and passion for their safe solid sense. . . . Strange as it always is to consider any assembly in submissively resigning itself to the dreariness of any complacent person . . . it was even particularly affecting to see this crowd or honest faces, whose honesty in the main no competent observer free from bias could possibly doubt, agitated by such a leader.

Under the impact of today's economic crisis, the shrillness of opposing camps, of diagnosers, prognosticators, and curers, has increased. Even the same financial page of the same newspaper may have articles proposing diametrically opposed solutions, the only thing in common between them being the certainty with which they are offered. Each has a single simple principle, Gradgrindian or not, that is the supposed key to happiness, prosperity, economic growth. But now more than ever it is necessary to suppress our inherent tendency to seek the key to all questions, and reading Dickens may help us to do it.

CHRISTINA LUPTON

From Walking on Flowers: The Kantian Aesthetics of *Hard Times*†

The opening pages of Charles Dickens's *Hard Times* make a distinction between two forms of knowledge: rationally knowing and subjectively sensing—long-standing twin sentinels for the epistemological project of modernity—appear as enemies from the very outset of this novel. In the schoolroom of M'Choakcumchild and Gradgrind, the overseer "with a rule and pair of scales, and the multiplication table always in his pocket," the possibility of measuring the world is dramatically staged as the opposite to knowing it sensually. On the one hand, there is the soulless student Bitzer, protégé of his utilitarian pedagogues and author of the bloodless definition of a horse as a "graminivorous quadruped" with "forty teeth, namely twenty-four grinders, four eye-teeth, and twelve incisive"; and on the other, there is the circus child, Sissy Jupe, whose emotional involvement with the world of horses and horseriding

† From *ELH* 70 (2003): 151–52, 154–58, 160–61, 166–69. © 2003 The Johns Hopkins University Press. Reprinted with permission of Johns Hopkins University Press.

proves useless in meeting this educational system's demand for facts about horses. Facts, to use Dickens's term, cleave away from fancy; the intuitive world of subjective experience contradicts the forms of reckoning which set human beings to work instrumentally and inhumanly against themselves.

The idea that a nonrational way of knowing might challenge the results of quantitative reason is of course not original to Dickens. For at least as long as reason itself has been held up as an ideal, the nonrational has presented an alternative measure of truth. We need only to think of the modes of feeling represented in eighteenth-century literature—of Laurence Sterne's Uncle Toby, so sensitive to the world that he is unable to raise his hand against a fly, of Tobias Smollet's "man without a skin," or of Henry MacKenzie's man of feeling—to find counterparts to the rational history-writing of Edward Gibbon, the economic calculations of Adam Smith, or the rhyming couplets of Alexander Pope.[1] Set against the complexity of this doubling, the Sissy-Bitzer debate seems little more than a poor attempt to separate two ways of seeing which have long constituted each other's field of meaning. The simplicity of this sketch is, however, itself a telling site of contrast to the complex early and mid-eighteenth century attempts to account for the relationship between fact and feeling. Until late in the century, subjective feeling served in various capacities as the hub of moral and political discourse, as a unit in a system of social organization rather than its counter-point. While David Hume privileges "taste" or [Adam] Smith "sentiment," in both cases the terms serve as proof of the individual being suited to social agreement. The arguments of Hume, Smith, and their predecessors in the discourse of individual taste and feeling, Joseph Addison and Richard Steele, all present the cultivated possibility of subjective judgment as the means of establishing and sustaining common ground for social existence and prosperity.

It was only with Imannuel Kant's three-part *Critique*, finished in 1790, that the possibility of subjective judgment became explicitly associated with an ostensible *lack* of social purpose. Here for the first time the reason-feeling dichotomy became a potential site of contradiction. Although in Kant's own system it is crucial that the subject-driven terms of aesthetic judgment actually do coincide with reason *per se*, it is significant for the dialectical theories of subject and object which follow that this Kantian subjectivity does

---

1. The three sentimental novels to which I am here referring are Tobias Smollett's *Humphry Clinker*, Henry Mackenzie's *Man of Feeling*, and Laurence Sterne's *Tristram Shandy*. In addition to the eighteenth-century literature of sentiment, one might also consider the religion of Samuel Johnson, the poetry of Edward Thompson, or the writings of Ossian as part of this counter-Enlightenment that extends throughout the century.

not depend for its validity on this coincidence of reason and feeling. Kant's discussion of beauty makes it clear that there are two distinct ways of knowing. While "the mental attunement that sustains itself and has subjective, universal validity may serve as a basis for that other way of thinking that can be sustained only by laborious resolve," his metaphysics relies on these forms of experience being by definition irreducible to one another.[2] In the Kantian subject, the capacity to experience the world nonconceptually and nonpurposively comes to the fore as an autonomous mode of discerning the truth. The fact that this mode coincides with reason is crucial for Kant, but it cannot be taken for granted.

* * *

The title of this paper, "Walking on Flowers," refers to one of the strongest moments of dialogue in *Hard Times*. Standing up to her utilitarian schoolmaster, Sissy Jupe defends the desirability of floral carpets in the world.

> Sissy blushed and stood up.
> "So you would carpet your room—or your husband's room, if you were a grown woman, and had a husband—with representations of flowers, would you?" said the gentleman. "Why would you?"
> "If you please Sir, I am very fond of flowers," returned the girl.
> "And is that why you would put tables and chairs upon them, and have people walking over them with heavy boots?"
> "It wouldn't hurt them, sir. They wouldn't crush and wither, if you please, sir. They would be pictures of what was very pretty and pleasant and I would fancy."

From the utilitarian perspective which is so well caricatured in *Hard Times*, the question of representing flowers brings Sissy quickly into contentious territory: "You don't walk upon flowers in fact; you cannot be allowed to walk upon flowers in carpets," replies the school inspector once Sissy's moment of objection is over. Nor, he continues, do you, he goes on, have china decorated with foreign butterflies, wallpaper representing quadrupeds walking up and down walls, or any place for the cosmological questions of taste, except for those which can be reduced to fact.

In this context, Sissy's defense of floral carpet is complicated. Obviously Dickens emphasizes the fact that Sissy likes flowers while her utilitarian pedagogues do not: she likes representations of flowers, because she is "very fond of flowers." This is reinforced

---

2. Kant, *Critique of Judgment*, trans. Werner Pluhar (Cambridge: Hackett Publishing Company, 1987), 78. Hereafter abbreviated *CJ* and cited parenthetically by page number.

later in the book when Sissy becomes the only character in the novel to initiate a foray into the countryside. As she and Rachel walk on the outskirts of Coketown, careful to avoid the disused mineshafts and dilapidated fences, we find proof of Sissy's capacity to take pleasure in something like landscape. More than any other character in the novel, Sissy is clearly in a position to claim simply to like flowers.

And yet to take Dickens at his word—or Sissy at her's—on this count runs the risk of ascribing a simple sensitivity to Sissy which can be no more than a weak alternative to the facts of industry. If flowers are destined to grow between mineshafts, the preference for flowers is destined to survive only in the interstices of modern life. To read *Hard Times* staging the opposition between coal mines and flowers means * * * that the hardened terms of this opposition already relegate Sissy's fancy to a compensatory role in a modern world. From this perspective, Dickens's glimpse of aesthetic pleasure has little depth; peering literally through the flaps of the circus tent to which Sissy once belonged, we are left with only the general sense of the realm of pleasure as the necessary supplement to a life of industrial progress. Although Sissy's statement in favor of flowers can emphasize the individual need for pleasure, and can even bolster the category of subjective experience, it does not set up Sissy's point of view as one which could come into effective conflict with the world of fact.

This, however, does not exhaust the question of representation raised by Sissy's taste in furnishing. Curiously enough, floral carpet also appears in Kant's *Critique of Judgment*. And this time there is no doubt that it has a distinct and structural role to play in explaining the importance of the beautiful. *The Critique of Judgment* describes "designs *à la grecque*, the foliage on borders, or on wallpaper" as nothing less than paragons of that "free beauty" which allow judgment to arise spontaneously (*CJ*, 76). Free from any instrumental relation to pleasure as well as from any prior or mimetic form, floral design provides Kant with an idealized aesthetic space: "flowers, free designs, lines aimless intertwined and called foliage: these have no significance, depend on no determinate concept, and yet we like them" (*CJ*, 49). Such purposeless (their being *ohne Zweck*) makes these objects of pleasure in ways distinct from the things we like because they are good or useful. Flowers growing on the edge of mineshafts, Kant might argue, work powerfully enough as concepts of the good or the agreeable, but they are actually much less significant in their implication than the "free beauties" of textile design.

* * *

*** Here the conflict is not between flowers and factories but between the subject who knows the difference between reality and representation in the world, and the school inspector who does not. Sissy wins, not as someone who knows flowers better, but as someone who states her preference at the point where it cannot be associated with, or measured in, conceptual terms. ***

Once it becomes clear that Sissy likes the effect of beauty because it is not representational, the idea of a binary opposition between fact and fancy turns out to be much less significant than it initially seems in *Hard Times*. In spite of what both Gradgrind and Eagleton suggest, Dickens's argument about carpet does not actually insist on the dyad of fact and fancy which would be implied in the distinction between real flowers (or horses) and the imaginative life of their observer. Rather, the role of carpet makes this a triad, with real flowers, carpet flowers, and the character who knows the difference between the two all coming into play around the moment of aesthetic contemplation where they can only finally be centered through the effect of Sissy's pleasure.

II.

What does it really mean, though, to think of Dickens as offering up aesthetic experience as an alternative both to the industrial system and the emotional life of his nonutilitarian characters? For Kant this third way can be connected to relatively concrete social advantages. Precisely because it pares experience down to an individual standard of enjoyment, the power Kant attributes to the beautiful is that it allows access to a truth unlimited by human thought. ***

* * *

Hard Times, to be sure, presents the subjectively universal in much more restricted terms. Yet if it is pictures of flowers, rather than flowers themselves, in which Dickens's hope for Sissy is vested, there are several points which can be made about the novel's aesthetic cause. We have already seen that the real opposition set up in the opening pages of *Hard Times* is between the kind of fully fledged subjectivity which acts to interpret the world, and the flat perspective of the Gradgrinds, which cannot distinguish between reality and representation. The nature of this interpretive subjectivity is partly an Enlightenment innovation and, as such, is connected both directly and indirectly to an ideal of freedom which sets itself up against the strictures of belief or conformity. In many works of the early eighteenth century, it is already clear that, while the subjective realm of experience may be ultimately modified by rational self-relation, it can no longer be seen as secondary to a larger set of cosmological certainties. Instead it has a structural role to play in discerning these certainties: in the secular terms of modernity, true beauty, reason, or judgment cannot be shown to be true unless the individual feels it to be so.

In terms of this genealogy, *Hard Times* is not particularly innovative in presenting the emotional sensibility of a character as its largest truth. Yet what makes the case of Sissy interesting is that Dickens can elect a female character of Sissy's complex, lower-class position to make the distinction between art and life. For Sissy to know that seemingly slight category of carpet flowers, she must know herself as many other worthier literary figures do not. ***

*   *   *

*** Dickens is *** well aware of where such aesthetic prowess may reinforce, rather than challenge, existing power structures. Sissy's particular incarnation as the universal subject goes a long way to explain why *Hard Times*'s revolutionary scope as a novel shrinks as well as opens-up around this question of aesthetic judgment. Understood as a site of access to the realm of subjective objectivity which eludes the novel's utilitarian characters, floral carpet frees Sissy to discover her own will, but it also recaptures her will as the stuff of not altogether unusual agreement. ***

Undoubtedly what Sissy likes about the carpet flowers as a child makes her part of this "subjective communal context," from within which Dickens imagines himself and his readers protesting against the world of sheer fact. Insofar as proof of Sissy's free will within the novel relies on this appeal to a community of aesthetically attuned novel-readers outside the world of the novel, it suggests a form of resistance that makes most sense when it strikes us as the voice of agreement. In uncannily Kantian terms, this becomes clear when we discover that Sissy's childlike free will is also what defines her line of social duty. As she becomes a young woman, Sissy's childhood claim to fancy expresses itself as an almost priestly moral certitude. Her "modest fearlessness, her truthfulness which put all artifice aside, her entire forgetfulness of herself in her earnest quiet holding to the object with which she had come" are listed as the qualities that make Sissy able to overpower and correct Mr. Harthouse, Louisa Gradgrind's amoral seducer.

If Dickens had been even more committed to the moral value of the aesthetic he might have led the fanciful Sissy much farther down this avenue of superiority. Her form of understanding might have confirmed, not just to the connoisseur of floral carpet, but also to the reader of novels, a certain level of transcendence that the subjective-objective experience of taste implies. But in the end, this is not Dickens's project: *Hard Times* makes its final appeal to the aesthetic by separating it, once again, from the language of truth. We are left at the conclusion of the novel with the image of a maternally bountiful Sissy "trying hard to know her humbler fellow creatures and to beautify their lives of machinery and reality with those imaginative graces and delights, without which the heart of infancy will wither up." Whatever the powers of imagination venerated in this description of Sissy, they lay a timorous claim to affect the social totality. Sissy's moral powers of persuasion retreat as the beautification of life's machinery is presented as a mere supplement to reality. In advocating this as a *necessary* supplementarity, Dickens makes the worlds of both fact and fancy secondary to the transcendent position of the subject who holds the two modes in view. This move also couples flowers and carpets, novels and industrial society, more securely than ever to each other via the position of a quietly knowing observer. A true Kantian to the end, Sissy is an aesthetically astute subject whose role is to accommodate rather than eliminate the contradictions she observes.

* * *

At the outset of this discussion, I pointed out that the unfavorable reception of *Hard Times* has been largely based on the view that, for a novel which claims to be in favor of imagination, its formula for knowledge is one of the least fanciful and most factual of all Dickens's literary achievements. Rather than defend *Hard Times* against the general accusation that it seems only to entertain one way of seeing, what I would now posit is that the novel's ultimate fact is not something to behold, but a way of beholding. This gesture of transcendence, which is characterized in Sissy Jupe and repeated in Dickens's approach to the question of alienated labor, cannot be dismissed simply as unimaginative objectivity. The possibility of objectivity could not have held court for so long were it not also able to account for subjective experience. If the subjective-objective project of modernity asks us to imagine walking on flowers, this is not because it returns us to an organic or imaginative relationship to the world, but because it suggests a form of understanding by which individuals are given a conscious and imaginative, though class and culture specific, role in the equation by which both flowers and factories are maintained as fact.

Postscript: Carpets and History

In 1899, twenty years after *Hard Times* was published and 100 years after Kant's celebration of patterns, William Morris gave a lecture to the working men of East London called "Some Hints on Pattern Designing." In it Morris addressed carpet making as the special province of the pattern designer. In carpet patterns, he stressed, flat and subtle designs were crucial—both because of what he called "the obvious reason that we don't feel comfortable in walking over what simulates high relief," and because "in carpet we especially desire quality in material and color: that is, every little bit of surface must have its own individual beauty of material and color."[3] Coming in the wake of Dicken's insistence that Sissy would, in fact, have little problem in walking across a simulation of high relief, there is something conspicuously guarded about Morris's desire to protect us from such confusion.

Yet carpets, in this very non-Kantian context, serve what is perhaps a more convincing function as the alternative to sheer utility and realistic representation. A symbiotic relationship between social revolution and floral carpets becomes more probable in Morris's union of art and socialism. The patterning he calls practical art—art that does not require history or education to make it interpretable—finds its ideal in the democratically accessible aesthetic of the woven textile. In Kantian terms this aesthetic is corrupt because the virtues Morris attributes to the patterned carpet disqualify it from being the pure object of contemplation:

> The purpose of applying art to articles of utility is twofold: first to add beauty to the results of the work of man, which would otherwise be ugly; and secondly to add pleasure to the work itself, which would otherwise be painful and disgusting.[4]

This fall into the world of purpose suggests the kind of fall which the aesthetic moments within *Hard Times* steadily resist. Once the Kantian dualism becomes the basis of nineteenth-century dialectical praxis, carpet flowers might remain important to that individual who has both subjective and objective understanding on her side (if Morris's carpet weavers are empowered in their relation to the beautiful, it is because it puts into practice that relation to the whole which characterizes the unalienated life of the individual), but they can no longer operate as mere supplements to the reality in which they are woven and enjoyed.

In these terms, the fact that *Hard Times* does not more radically overcome the problems it represents might still be a question of too little carpet. The radical potential of walking on flowers is, after all, something feared by Mr. Bounderby himself:

3. William Morris, "Some Hints on Pattern Designing. A Lecture Delivered by William Morris at the Working Men's Cottage, London December 10 1881" (London: Longmans and Co. 1889), 29.
4. Morris, *On Art and Socialism* (London: Purnell and Sons, 1947), 229.

Now you have heard a lot of talk about the work in our mills, no doubt. You have? Very good. I'll state the fact of it to you. It's the pleasantest work there is, and it's the lightest work there is, and it's the best-paid work there is. More than that, we couldn't improve the mills themselves, unless we laid down Turkey carpets on the floors. Which we're not a-going to do.

EFRAIM SICHER

From Dickens and the Pleasure of the Text: The Risks of *Hard Times*†

> Although our productions have afforded more extensive and unaffected pleasure than those of any other literary corporation in the world, no species of composition has been so much decried.
> Jane Austen, *Northanger Abbey*, ch. 5

Hard Times (1854) was for many years one of Dickens's less popular novels, until F. R. Leavis's discovery in it of serious art and a "comprehensive vision" [391]. Critics have often dismissed the novel as tending to caricature or denigrated it for its overdetermined depiction of the "opposition" between Fact and Fancy, misreading it as an attack on "Coketown" or on utilitarianism. Critics and scholars * * * either lament or applaud *Hard Times* according to their evaluation of how much "reality" it represents or of the author's political position; they tend to ignore questions of aesthetics or readership. * * * However, such readings of *Hard Times* obscure a more complex struggle of the novel not only to make a case for Fancy in an industrial society ruled by the dominant ideology of utilitarianism but also to stage a performance of its own usefulness in a world of Facts. This struggle raises the stakes for the role of the novel in social criticism as something more than a force for policing discipline—as establishing an aesthetics which reconciles the work ethic with the pursuit of pleasure. Aesthetics was not an uncommon preoccupation of the Victorians, and the idea of play performed a "critical, connective function within the discursive infrastructure of Victorian culture."[1] And yet little room has been found in analysis of that discourse for Dickens's playfulness, his theme of children's play, and the obvious theatricality of his writing.

† From *Partial Answers* 9.2 (2011): 311–13, 316–21, 325–27. © 2011 The Johns Hopkins University Press. Reprinted with permission of Johns Hopkins University Press. Page numbers in brackets refer to this Norton Critical Edition.
1. Jeffrey Franklin, *Serious Play: The Cultural Form of the Nineteenth-Century Realist Novel* (Philadelphia: U of Pennsylvania P, 1999), p. 5.

Hard Times is actually in keeping with the programmatic commitment made in Dickens' opening editorial in his journal *Household Words*—to bridge the gap between Masters and Laborers through the imagination and to vindicate the usefulness of literature in an industrial society governed by a utilitarian ideology. In contrast to "a mere utilitarian spirit" which binds minds to grim realities, Dickens makes the following promise:

> In the bosoms of the young and old, of the well-to-do and of the poor, we would tenderly cherish that light of Fancy which is inherent in the human breast; which, according to its nurture, burns with an inspiring flame, or sinks into a sullen glare, but which (or woe betide that day!) can never be extinguished. To show to all, that in all familiar things, even in those which are repellent on the surface, there is Romance enough, if we will find it out:—to teach the hardest workers at this whirling wheel of toil, that their lot is not necessarily a moody, brutal fact, excluded from the sympathies and graces of imagination.

Nevertheless, in vindicating its own usefulness and efficient production, Dickens's novel runs no small epistemological risk if the pleasure it gives is not taken seriously or if, like the circus, the conceit and illusion on which the plot depends do not work for all readers. If the reader does not experience pleasure or does not respond with imaginative empathy with the laboring classes, the argument may collapse into a futile battle of Fancy versus Facts. * * *

*   *   *

In mid-nineteenth century Britain pleasure was literally at risk in many factory towns, where popular culture, amusement, and even singing were regulated and policed. Employers wished to wean laborers away from the amusements and pranks that were part of the old craft manufacture that distracted them from reliable diligence in the new factories: they used their influence to maintain surveillance of their workers' activities outside the long working hours, while local clergy, temperance campaigners, and sabbatarians clamped down with evangelical zeal on frivolous and immoral amusement. Local authorities curtailed some folk festivities on the grounds that they constituted a public nuisance and encouraged drunken behavior and disorder. Music and dancing were strictly licensed at public houses, the chief recreational meeting place for the working classes and artisans (the latter often associated with the Chartist movement).

*   *   *

I want to suggest that the pleasure Dickens takes in his satire of Gradgrindery carries risks, but these too are part of the pleasure of reading, rather like the risk of ballooning, as in the depiction of Dickens and Cruikshank in the frontispiece of *Sketches by Boz* going up on a pilot trip, a common entertainment at pleasure gardens that offered a spectacle for those on the ground and a panoramic view (as well as a bumpy landing) for the middle-class gentlemen who paid for the thrills of the hazardous ride. ***

* * *

The tension between bliss and pleasure is evident in Dickens's literal performance of "the text of pleasure," when serialized parts of his work were read aloud or he gave exhaustingly dramatic readings of his work. We can readily picture ladies feeling faint when Dickens performed Sikes's murder of Nancy, and he must have been only too well aware that his popularity fed on the taste for sensationalist melodrama.[2]

The text's own performance shows that what Dickens calls Fancy is doing its work and doing it usefully. Far from merely subscribing to a status quo sugared by compassion, it shows through exemplary stories that *** a Benthamite rational egoism cannot be a fit training for life and that there are other elements left out of Bentham's sum of human motivation, foremost among them, as J. S. Mill had also noted, the role of the imagination in the formation of moral personality. The fallacious opposition of Fact and Fancy is recognizable in Mill's acknowledgment in his *Autobiography* that poetry helped him through his mental crisis after an upbringing in Facts and made the "cultivation of the feelings . . . one of the cardinal points in [his] ethical and philosophical cal creed." The opposition nevertheless obscures the more significant debate between organicism or idealism and empiricism in philosophy, not to mention the competing methodologies in science itself.

In his often cited article "Fraud on the Fairies" (*Household Words*, 1 October 1853) Dickens blasted Cruikshank, the illustrator of *Oliver Twist*, for altering fairy tales for use as a propaganda tool in favor of teetotalism (not his favorite cause). For one thing, the conscription of children's stories for any agenda was unjustifiable and sounded like the didactic utilitarian literature of the sort Dickens proceeded to satirize in an updated parody of "Cinderella"

---

2. See also Linda K. Hughes and Michael Lund, "Textual/Sexual Pleasure and Serial Publication," in *Literature in the Marketplace: Nineteenth-Century British Publishing and Reading Practices*, ed. John O. Jordan and Robert L. Patten (Cambridge: Cambridge U P, 1995), pp. 143–64; and Jennifer Hayward, *Consuming Passions: Active Audiences and Serial Fictions from Dickens to Soap Operas* (Lexington: U P of Kentucky, 1997).

which distorted the time-honored originals. Among the reports of the Mudfog Association there is a similar satire of utilitarian attacks on children's ignorance of Fact arising from their indulgence in Fancy: the story of Jack and Jill might be laudable if the children were toiling uphill on a domestic errand, but it was inexcusable that Jill should laugh at Jack's disaster. However, this was also an occasion, as Dickens explained to Angela Burdett-Coutts in a letter of September 18, 1853, to launch a plea for "a little more fancy among children and a little less fact." He believed that, in a utilitarian age in particular, "it is a matter of grave importance that Fairy Tales should be respected. Our English red tape is too magnificently red to ever be employed in the tying up of such trifles, but every one who has considered the subject knows full well that a nation without fancy, without some romance, never did, never can, never will, hold a great place under the sun. This appeal to empire-building is a way of arguing for capitalism with a human face, for only Fancy can introduce "gentleness and mercy" into working lives; it is a defense of literature as a moral agent indispensable to a humane society that abhors tyranny and brute force.

Dickens knew that Science had banished the fairies in its reading of the Book of Nature, but, as he wrote in an 1848 review of Robert Hunt's appropriately entitled *The Poetry of Science*,

> To show that Science, truly expounding nature, can, like nature herself, restore in some new form whatever she destroys; that, instead of binding us, as some would have it, in stern utilitarian chains, when she has freed us from a harmless superstition, she offers to our contemplation something better and more beautiful, something which, rightly considered, is more elevating to the soul, nobler and more stimulating to the soaring fancy; is a sound, wise wholesome object.

The plea that fantasy be left inviolate is not just a way of asking for respect for the fairy tales of childhood; it is a plea for imagination in literature and in the workplace. A literature which is neither utilitarian nor instrumental recognizes the true poetry of the "fairy-tales of Science" (to use Tennyson's phrase) by showing that the wonders of Nature can be appreciated only through the imagination and reminding us that if there had been less wondering and wonderment there might have been fewer inventions. James Watt would have been poorer by a penny for his thoughts in that apocryphal tale of his improvement of the steam engine, and Sol Gills would have had no marvelous tales to tell. For both Tennyson and Dickens, the discoveries in geology, anthropology, archeology, and evolution theory that had transformed intellectual horizons, as advances in optics and physics had done in the late seventeenth century, revealed the poetry of science, though not every statistician could see the science in poetry.

What *Hard Times* shows, however, is that Gradgrind's statistical account of society contradicts the lived life of individuals, which it is the business of fiction to show not by policing the poor, as Martineau urged Dickens in her attacks on *Hard Times*, but by exciting the middle-class readers into pleasurable empathy. At the end of the "key-note" description of Coketown in ch. 5 of Book I, in the transition to the introduction of the circus people, the narrator wonders whether there was not in the employers' stereotype of the ungrateful laborers and the Political Economists' statistical tables one thing that had been

> deliberately set at nought? That there was any Fancy in them demanding to be brought into healthy existence instead of struggling on in convulsions? That exactly in the ratio as they worked long and monotonously, the craving grew within them for some physical relief—some relaxation, encouraging good humour and good spirits, and giving them a vent—some recognized holiday, though it were but for an honest dance to a stirring band of music—some occasional light pie in which even M'Choakumchild had no finger—which craving must and would be satisfied aright, or must and would inevitably go wrong, until the laws of Creation were repealed?

Immediately following this plea, Gradgrind and Bounderby repair to the Pegasus's Arms, a pub which is an appropriate "home" to Sleary's horseriders—it was Pegasus's kick which brought out of the mountain the soul-inspiring waters of Hippocrene that came to be associated with poetic inspiration. Of course the winged horse behind the bar displays a low form of theatrical entertainment, but that is without doubt a deliberate choice: Pegasus was an emblem inevitably linked with the equestrian circus, and very different from Bitzer's definition of a horse. Yet it is not a matter of circus "philothopy" pitted against Gradgrindery—the circus people have a poor view of education and are mostly illiterate—but a question of what is wrong with Gradgrind's definition of social function and of precisely what is at fault in urban industrial civilization. In a passage opening the chapter "Stephen Blackpool" that has apparently nothing to do with the subject, Dickens writes sarcastically: "I entertain a weak idea that the English people are as hard-worked as any people upon whom the sun shines. I acknowledge to this ridiculous idiosyncracy, as a reason why I would give them a little more play."

As Sleary advises Gradgrind and Bounderby, people must be amused, and in a metafictional parallel to the theme of bridging the gap between the Two Nations the novel performs such playfulness

with a spectacle of burlesque exposures, fantasized parodies of utilitarianism, and a comic plot that is resolved by a performing horse,
no less, proving Bitzer wrong on more than one count about the
definition of that particular creature. The story of Sissy Jupe and
the dog Merrylegs shows, in Sleary's endearing lisp, "that there ith
a love in the world, not all Thelf-interetht after all, but thomething
very different; t'other, that it hath a way of calculating or not calculating, whith thomehow or another ith at leatht ath hard to give a
name to, ath the wayth of the dogth ith!" The circus is not a model
society, for all the toleration of its loose morals and bare legs and its
carnivalized display of the body,[3] an admittedly licensed exposure
that afforded pleasure to middle-class adult spectators attracted to
the theatricality of the spectacle. Yet the circus people represent a
childlike sincerity, honesty, and spontaneous compassion that is
missing in the calculating language of Gradgrindery:

> They all assumed to be mighty rakish and knowing, they were
> not very tidy in their private dresses, they were not at all orderly
> in their domestic arrangements, and the combined literature
> of the whole company would have produced but a poor letter
> on any subject. Yet there was a remarkable gentleness and child-
> ishness about these people, a special inaptitude for any kind of
> sharp practice, and an untiring readiness to help and pity one
> another, deserving, often of as much respect, and always of as
> much generous construction, as the every-day virtues of any
> class of people in the world.

This natural compassion, in contradiction of Gradgrind's class prejudice, is "one thing needful," like the faith missing in the hedonis-
tic calculus of pleasure of the Motive-Grinders and Profit-and-Loss
Philosophers in the Mill of Logic in [Carlyle's] *Sartor Resartus*. It is
in their deeds as well as in performance that the circus people must
show compassion in order to refute Gradgrindery which allows for
it neither in its arithmetic nor in its language. Emma Gordon,
herself in the family way, nurtures Sissy Jupe when her father
runs away, and Bounderby can only offer her the brutal plain Facts
of the case—much to the violent indignation of the circus people.
As Sleary warns Gradgrind after the circus people have persuaded
him to do the right thing and take in Sissy, "People mutht be
amuthed, . . . they can't be alwayth a working, nor yet they can't
be alwayth a learning." Rachael's caring affection for Stephen, too,
is testimony of innate compassion among the lower classes. Stephen performs the role of neo-Christian saint of forbearance and

3. On the "qualified eroticism" of the female body in performance that attracted a
middle-class audience see Helen Stoddart, *Rings of Desire: Circus History and Representation* (Manchester: Manchester U P, 2000), pp. 175–79.

kindness, a martyr to the Masters' hardheartedness and criminal negligence, who maintains an all-too perfect moral integrity in the muddle of hypocritical laws made for the wealthy and privileged members of society. But whereas Stephen's labor reduces him to part of the larger machine of Coketown, the performance of the circus must work as pleasure for their audience.

For all the emphasis on the illusion of art and the playful comic representation of the circus (as in *Nicholas Nickleby*), Dickens is not simply advocating the merits of popular culture, and we cannot ignore unstable meanings in his argument or paradoxes such as Sleary's role as a self-made man who collects money in the niche of his capitalist temple. Dickens is pleading for the necessity of art within the industrial city as recreation in the sense of both leisure and creativity. ***

                              *   *   *

For Carlyle, as for Dickens, the light or flame of imagination must resist the choking of the human spirit by a totalizing utilitarian discourse. Without imaginative sympathy, there can be no altruism or charity, no understanding of the Other. According to J. S. Mill, Bentham lacked that Romantic faculty of imagination

> which enables us, by a voluntary effort, to conceive the absent as if it were present, the imaginary as if were real, and to clothe it in the feelings which, if it were indeed real, it would bring along with it. This is the power by which one human being enters into the mind and circumstances of another. . . . Without it nobody knows even his own nature, further than circumstances have actually tried it and called it out; nor the nature of his fellow-creatures, beyond such generalizations as he may have been enabled to make from his observation of their outward conduct. (1962: 61–62) [365].

Dickens's novel is itself resisting the texts of Gradgrindery, just as among Coketown's library readers Defoe resists Euclid and Goldsmith resists Cocker, despite the fact that by mid-century anyone denying the principle of the happiness of the greatest number or the principle of profit-and-loss might be thought insane.

In *Hard Times*, Dickens is in effect carrying out the program of *Household Words*, to apply Fancy to knowledge of current affairs and the state of the nation. In a rehearsal of the *Bleak House* romance of familiar things, this novel brings the middle-class Victorian reader journeying through the industrial landscape into imaginative sympathy with the worker. The result is not quantifiable knowledge of collected facts that one may expect from the novel as representation, but representation through the imagination, with the pleasure of the text invoking the sense of the life of another through the workings of empathetic play.

* * *

Its fables are not "idle" (as Bounderby and Grindgrind would have it), but represent the lived lives of men and women. Because imagination serves as mode as well as metaphor for the vision of the novel, the novel must be instructive as well as entertaining, in the tradition of Defoe and Richardson, but with a modern consciousness of the illusion of art. If the novelist fails to entertain us with his verbal acrobatics, what chance for literature in an age of utilitarian conformity, let alone in our hedonist culture, where leisure is privileged over work and expects only pleasure from the text? Certainly, in *Our Mutual Friend* Dickens showed his disdain for the Wildean wit of aesthetes and cynics such as Eugene Wrayburn before he is reformed through love.

As R. H. Home noted in his *A New Spirit of the Age* (1844): Dickens's "influence upon his age is extensive—pleasurable, instructive, healthy, reformator." * * * Indeed, *Hard Times* argues that reading for pleasure *is* an agent of change. How far such agency worked beyond the middle-class reader, how many laborers read *Hard Times* or how many preferred it to Harriet Martineau's *Illustrations of Political Economy* (1833), must remain a matter of speculation. Moreover, the pleasure of the text must be contextualized within the debate over the dignity of literature that raged at mid-century, against the background of the acrimonious exchange between Thackeray (in *Pendennis*) and Dickens (in *David Copperfield*), as well as the inclusion of Carlyle in Ford Madox Ford's painting *Work* (1852–1863). Paradoxically, if the novel seduces the reader into desire, then it too has become a fetishized product, but if it successfully competes with the control and repression of desire, represented by Dombey or Gradgrind, its resistance to commodification of the body becomes a claim also for a ludic celebration of pleasure that allows Dickens to ride both Pegasus and the steam-engine.

DAVID L. COWLES

Having It Both Ways:
Gender and Paradox in *Hard Times*[†]

Hearing that her husband has apprehended Tom and Louisa peeping into Sleary's circus, Mrs. Gradgrind exclaims: "'I declare you're

† From *Dickens Quarterly* 8.2 (June 1991): 79–84. © 1991 The Dickens Society. Reprinted with permission of Johns Hopkins University Press. Page numbers in brackets refer to this Norton Critical Edition.

enough to make one regret ever having had a family at all. I have a
great mind to say I wish I hadn't. *Then* what would you have done,
I should like to know'" [20]. Dickens obviously intends us to laugh
at this obvious paradox: Mrs. Gradgrind could only prove her suffering *to* her wayward children if they did not exist. Yet such self-
contradiction typifies Dickens's own dependence on paradox in *Hard
Times*, particularly regarding gender issues.

Throughout Dickens's works, treatments of women probably engen-
der more unintentional self-contradiction than any other topic. Like
all great artists, Dickens typifies as much as he transcends the
conceptual languages of his age, and for the mid-Victorians "the
woman question" was a linguistic Tower of Babel. Examining
aspects of gender in *Hard Times,* especially as they relate to Louisa
Gradgrind/Bounderby, reveals irreconcilable contradictions in Dickens's treatment of women and suggests other crucial ways in which
the text differs from itself.

Hard Times provides two portraits of idealized Dickensian women:
Sissy Jupe and Rachael. Both characters exhibit standard Victorian
feminine virtues: extraordinary devotion (especially to a needy
male), remarkable love-based powers of intuition, firm but modest
assertion of heart-felt values, great spiritual strength and endurance. Throughout his novels, Dickens identifies these traits as
inherently feminine, natural to all good-hearted women. The sensitive male gratefully admires a woman's natural devotion to him,
and does not stand between her and self-sacrificing feminine fulfillment. This obvious projection of male desire, of course, conve-
niently excuses men for using the women who love them. The man's
own worthiness in the formula is largely irrelevant—especially if
he is a father or brother. Indeed, as with Nancy, Florence Dombey,
Little Dorrit, and Lizzie Hexam, the worse the man, the more
admirable the woman's loyalty. Such devotion is a sure sign of inner
goodness, even in otherwise wicked or insensitive female characters like Nancy and Pleasant Riderhood. Sissy and Rachael, sensitive to their own hearts and to others' needs, clearly exhibit all
these characteristics.

Louisa, too, feels intimations of these "natural" womanly traits,
especially as she functions as daughter, sister, and wife—roles that
always call for selfless devotion in Dickens. Yet Louisa's Utilitarian
education—normally reserved for boys and particularly hostile to
the traditional female virtues so essential to her "real" nature—
has largely incapacitated her for these all-important relationships.
Moreover, in Louisa's case these roles require simultaneous loyalty
and disloyalty to the particular males involved. She can exhibit
"natural" loving loyalty to her father only by rejecting everything he
sincerely stands for. Sacrificing herself for Tom means marrying a

man to whom she cannot offer loving devotion. And wifely loyalty to Bounderby—a man embodying the opposite of all her inner yearnings—is unthinkable. Indeed, Dickens places Louisa in an impossible position, and in the end he punishes her for her inability to bridge gaps inherent in his own contradictory beliefs about women.

These contradictions reveal themselves whenever gender issues arise. Consider, for example, Tom's attitude about his sister's female duty toward him. In an early conversation with Tom, Louisa laments that she cannot make his life comfortable in traditionally feminine ways. Clearly Tom considers this desire perfectly natural. After all, he points out, " 'You are a girl, too, and a girl comes out of it better than a boy does'" [47]. 'But Tom selfishly trades on Louisa's devotion without proper appreciation for her sacrifices. He later calls her a "capital girl" [80], indicating the economic (mis)use to which he puts her. Tom explains to Harthouse why Louisa married Bounderby: "'Not that it was altogether so important to her as it was to me, . . . because my liberty and comfort, and perhaps my getting on, depended on it. . . . A girl can get on anywhere. . . . Girls can always get on, somehow'" [112].

Dickens unquestionably condemns Tom for his insensitive, gender-based demands on Louisa's devoted service as his natural male right, as well as for his repeated statements that her loving sensitivity is just "another of the advantages . . . of being a girl" [48]. In fact, Dickens blames Tom for not being more like Louisa. On the other hand, Dickens has taken pains to show that Tom and Louisa have had identical educational and family experiences, and that the primary differences between the siblings are gender-determined. Further, though he shows disdain for Tom's attitude, Dickens clearly approves of Louisa's desire to serve Tom in the ways he expects—and certainly because Dickens, too, sees female self-sacrifice as natural. In effect, Dickens puts himself exactly in Tom's position by praising Louisa, Rachael, and Sissy for doing just the sort of things Tom desires. Like Tom, Dickens believes that through unselfish devotion "girls can always get on, somehow." Dickens simultaneously uses the same attitude, in effect, to condemn Tom and praise Louisa.

In another telling passage, when Gradgrind catches young Louisa and Tom at the forbidden circus, he blames Tom for instigating the venture, assuming that the boy, though younger, naturally leads. But Gradgrind is mistaken. Louisa haughtily insists she led Tom. Indeed, "Louisa looked at her father with more boldness," and the children's "air of jaded sullenness" was evident "particularly in the girl" [16]. Once again Dickens plays both sides of the gender issue. First, he clearly shows that Gradgrind really *is* wrong in assuming that the boy naturally leads. Louisa, Tom tells her afterward, "can always lead me as you like" through her deeply-buried but irrepressible feminine instincts [47]. Dickens wants us to admire Louisa for confidently following her heart beyond Gradgrind's limited teachings and for bringing Tom along after her. At the same time, however, Dickens *condemns* Louisa's unladylike and disobedient independence. Her unfeminine disloyalty to her father must be ascribed to her unfortunate education. So Dickens asks us simultaneously to approve Louisa's independence from her father's system, while blaming that same system for it. Similarly, we must respect Louisa's intellectual capacities even as we blame Gradgrind's system for forcing her to develop them instead of the natural womanly skills involved in making men comfortable. Further, Louisa's haughty reply to her father is itself a loyal defense of her younger brother, whelp though he is. Yet this very loyalty to Tom requires equal disloyalty to her father, toward whom she holds the same womanly duty. Again, Dickens plays both sides at once: We are to respect Louisa's natural womanly feelings in her loyalty to her brother; while simultaneously blaming Gradgrind's system for her disloyalty to him.

Ultimately, Louisa manages to resolve the conflict between father and brother. She returns to her father—who now needs and deserves her affectionate care. Louisa, increasingly "feminine" in outlook, now separates her father from his system: "'I have never blamed you, and I never shall'" [178]. She also remains faithful to Tom—even protecting him from justice. Unlike Bounderby's betrayed mother, Mrs. Pegler (who is correspondingly less admirable), Louisa has no illusions about Tom's guilt; she senses it intuitively from the start. Dickens clearly presents Louisa's loyalty despite Tom's unworthiness as admirably feminine. Ironically, however, this very faithfulness causes her inappropriate relationship with Harthouse—both because Harthouse manipulates her through it, and because it motivates her decision to enter an unsatisfying marriage. More importantly, in order to achieve loyalty to father and brother and attain partial feminine fulfillment, Louisa must actually abandon her husband. Dickens asks us to blame Bounderby, who is made to reject her—though not until after she has already left him. Bounderby's unworthiness somehow excuses Louisa for violating her womanly duty to support her husband. Dickens makes us feel that her mistake was marrying Bounderby in the first place, largely under her father and brother's near-criminal influence. Her loyalty to them, despite the limitations and suffering they impose on her, seems even more admirable because they do not deserve it. Yet her disloyalty to Bounderby is made to appear equally admirable, precisely *because* she must escape the same kinds of insensitive limitations and suffering from him.

Moreover, despite Dickens's clear efforts to excuse Louisa, in the end he punishes her for her unfeminine actions and attributes, but mitigates her suffering because she has a naturally loving feminine heart after all. Part of Louisa's sin against her woman's nature is clearly sexual. She has desired a man who is not her husband. Further, she has married a man she despises, who is old enough to be her father—a near-incestuous fate Esther Summerson narrowly avoids in *Bleak House*, written just before *Hard Times*. In the moral system of Dickens's novels, a woman who has sold herself sexually, for whatever reason, is forever denied the comfort and fulfillment of husband and family. Typical of Dickens's goodhearted but fallen women, Louisa must live a life dedicated to serving her father, separated forever from her beloved brother. Though her fate is less harsh than those of Nancy, Little Em'ly, or, more to the point, Edith Dombey, Dickens describes what is denied Louisa in such desirable terms that it is difficult not to see her state as a punishment.

> Herself again a wife—a mother—lovingly watchful of her children, ever careful that they should have a childhood of the mind no less than a childhood of the body, as knowing it to be even a more beautiful thing, and a possession, any hoarded scrap of which, is a blessing and happiness to the wisest? Did Louisa see this? Such a thing was never to be. [236].

Dickens attempts to mitigate Louisa's suffering by assuring us that other people's children will love her, but the elements of punishment are unmistakable.

Other characters reflect and complicate Dickens's treatment of Louisa. Indeed, nearly every important character functions as part of a large pattern of abandonment. Some desert loved ones for admirable, unselfish purposes. Sissy Jupe's father runs away from her, but, as the eternally loyal Sissy asserts, "'he left me for my good—he never would have left me for his own'" [53]. Stephen rejects his fellow workers, but in doing so maintains a higher loyalty to Rachael. Stephen must also leave Rachael, "thinking unselfishly that at least his being obliged to go away was good for her" [126]. Other characters abandon duty to others for selfish reasons. Tom largely ignores his sister as soon as he escapes his father's house—except when he needs her to sacrifice something for him. Stephen's fellow Hands reject his honest refusal to join their union. Bounderby fires Stephen and later Mrs. Sparsit for egocentric reasons. Bitzer denies all loyalty toward Gradgrind. Even Mrs. Sparsit's late husband abandoned her shortly after their marriage.

Several cases of abandonment warrant special consideration in relation to Louisa leaving Bounderby. First, Dickens clearly condemns

Stephen's wife for leaving him, something similar to what he approves in Louisa. Here the main difference is that the longsuffering Stephen deserves better while Bounderby does not. Dickens also emphasizes distinctions between the two women. Louisa marries Bounderby as an unselfish sacrifice for Tom and manages to evade at least the consummation of her dubious relationship with Harthouse. Stephen's wife is "foul" in her "moral infamy" and confronts Stephen with the threat that she will "'sell thee off agen . . . a score of times'" [60]. Consequently, we blame Stephen's wife in ways we do not blame Louisa, and we also recognize Stephen's need for divorce—though Louisa's desire for separation hardly fits into the same class.

Dickens also emphasizes Bounderby's disloyalty to Louisa—and to anyone else. His marriage, like his relationships with Mrs. Sparsit, his mother, and even Gradgrind, is intended to enhance his self-image and social position as self-made man. Despite what he tells Stephen about "a sanctity in this relation of life" that "must be kept up" [65], when Stephen describes his patience toward his wayward wife, Bounderby thinks, "The more fool you"—foreshadowing the policy he later adopts toward Louisa. In discussing Louisa's flight with Gradgrind, Bounderby complains that he has not been "'as dutifully and submissively treated by your daughter, as Josiah Bounderby of Coketown ought to be treated by his wife'" [191]. Indeed, Bounderby remarks that he does not wish to quarrel about Louisa, because "'to tell you the truth, I don't think it would be worthy of my reputation to quarrel on such a subject'" [195]. Bounderby's rejection of Louisa is unquestionably the best thing that could happen to her. She cannot go back to him; womanly loyalty to her husband is now impossible. But because Dickens makes Bounderby reject *her* (an act aggravated by his treatment of his mother), Louisa's desertion is presented as one more count against *him*, and actually becomes a point in her favor, despite violating a central tenet of the Dickensian female code.

Finally, Dickens's treatment of disempowered workers like Stephen and Rachael parallels his contradictory attitude toward disempowered women. As Dickens condemns Tom's selfish wishes regarding Louisa while simultaneously approving Louisa's desire to gratify them, so Dickens criticizes the mill owners' view of their workers as mere Hands, but asks us to admire those willing to act as little else. Like the owners, Dickens essentially treats workers in *Hard Times* as Hands. When Louisa visits Stephen's home, Dickens remarks that "for the first time in her life, Louisa had come into one of the dwellings of the Coketown Hands; for the first time in her life, she was face to face with anything like individuality in connexion with them" [128]. Dickens himself never manages this in the novel. He even identifies them primarily as "men and brothers" [113], despite the many female workers. As with Louisa, Dickens's "good" workers inhabit both sides of crucial divisions, as when Stephen addresses Bounderby: "He spoke with the rugged earnestness of his place and character—deepened perhaps by a proud consciousness that he was faithful to his class under all their mistrust; but he fully remembered where he was, and did not even raise his voice" [121].

Moreover, Dickens expects both Stephen and Louisa to endure injustice and limited opportunities for growth and self-fulfillment by taking whatever happiness (or solace) they can in self-sacrifice for others who are unworthy of their efforts, and who are clearly incapable of setting the agendas in question fairly. Dickens appears to suggest that workers, like wives, daughters, mothers, and sisters, should merely put faith in their oppressors, represented in *Hard Times* by Bounderby—hardly a rational way to improve their situation. In his ending portraits, Dickens admiringly describes Rachael as "a woman working, ever working, but content to do it, and preferring to do it as her natural lot, until she should be too old to labour any more" [235], at which time presumably she should do the proper thing and die—not that she would have other options. Do your duty, Dickens urges. Take joy or solace there. Meanwhile, I will work to make the owners more sympathetic. This is precisely what he recommends to women. That, too, is why Louisa's bolting from Bounderby seems so uncharacteristic.

In unconsciously playing both sides of irreconcilable contradictions, especially regarding gender issues, Dickens undermines many of his own thematic assertions. Yet he does so in ways harmonious with his time, sex, and class (and therefore largely invisible to his contemporary readers) through conceptual languages he could not escape any more than we can escape our own linguistic and interpretive limitations. As much as any other Dickens novel, *Hard Times* reveals the kinds of cover-ups empowered mid-Victorians needed to hide essential contradictions inherent in pat answers to "the woman question."

NILS CLAUSSON

From Dickens's *Genera Mixta*:
What Kind of a Novel Is *Hard Times*?[†]

I

The genre of *Hard Times* (1854) has seemed more or less self-evident at least since 1958, when Raymond Williams grouped together a number of early and mid-Victorian novels, including *Hard Times*, under the name "industrial novels" in his influential *Culture and Society*, and when Arnold Kettle classified the same group of novels as "social-problem novels" in an essay in the new *Penguin Guide to English Literature*.[1] Williams and Kettle did more than identify a subgenre of the Victorian novel; they also defined the terms in which these novels would be discussed for the next half century, beginning with David Lodge's 1966 essay on H. G. Wells's *Tono-Bungay* in his *Language of Fiction*, and followed by Catherine Gallagher's *The Industrial Reformation of English Fiction* (1985), Joseph W. Childer's *Novel Possibilities: Fiction and the Formation of Early Victorian Culture* (1995), and Josephine M. Guy's *The Victorian Social-Problem Novel* (1996). This classification has recently been reconfirmed by Richard Simmons Jr.'s essay "Industrial and 'Condition of England' Novels" in Blackwell's *Companion to the Victorian Novel* (2003):

> From the late 1830s on, with issues such as the "factory question," the "hungry forties," the repeal of the Corn Laws, and the Chartist uprising as rich ground from which to mine subject matter, novels about problems of class conflict and capitalism became one of the most significant subgenres of Victorian liter-

---

† From *Texas Studies in Literature and Language* 52.2 (2010): 157–58, 161–64, 173–75, 178–9. Copyright © 2010 by the University of Texas Press. Used by permission of the publisher. All rights reserved.
1. See chapter 5, "The Industrial Novels," of Raymond Williams's *Culture and Society 1780–1950* (London: Chatto & Windus, 1958), and Arnold Kettle's "The Early Victorian Social-Problem Novel," in Boris Ford, ed., *The Penguin Guide to English Literature*, vol. 6, (Harmondsworth: Penguin Books, 1958). The same group of novels was the subject of Louis Cazamian's *Roman social en Angleterre, 1830–1850*, which was published in France in 1903, but not translated into English until 1973, under the title *The Social Novel in England, 1830–1850: Dickens, Disraeli, Mrs. Gaskell, Kingsley* (London: Routledge and Kegan Paul), fifteen years after Williams and Kettle grouped these novels as social-problem, or industrial, novels. The appearance in the early 1970s of Martin Fido's translation of Cazamian's pioneering study is indicative of the renewed interest in these novels sparked by Williams and Kettle, and its publication no doubt helped solidify the generic identity of the condition-of-England novel. (From 1966 to 1973, Fido taught at the University of Leeds, where Kettle was a senior lecturer in the School of English.)

ature. Such fiction has been variously labeled, but the "condition of England" novel seems most inclusive.

While this approach has produced illuminating readings of this group of novels, it has also ensured that these novels, including *Hard Times*, have been discussed almost exclusively in terms of their intervention in the condition-of-England debate of the 1840s and 1850s, and especially debates about industrialization and the class conflict it produced. * * *

Although explicit questions about the genre of *Hard Times* have not figured prominently in criticism of it, the debates about its social and political engagements, as well as its artistic success, have, as I hope to show, been inseparable from an implicit debate about what kind of novel it should be read as. The question posed by David Lodge in his essay on the novel in *Working with Structuralism* (1981)—"what kind of novel is *Hard Times*" * * *—has, in my view, never been satisfactorily answered, although the designation of it as a condition-of-England novel has tended to mask this failure. * * *

* * * I want to suggest that reading *Hard Times* exclusively as a social-problem, or industrial, novel is an unhelpful way of trying to get beyond the debates that have dominated criticism of the novel for the last half century. The criticisms of Dickens for his inadequate response to the social problems he raises in *Hard Times* are, I shall argue, the misguided result of the attempt to read it as a single genre, the social-problem novel, instead of the *Genera Mixta* I take it to be. The way out of this critical stalemate, in my view, is to recognize that the generic dissonances and inconsistencies in *Hard Times* are not peculiar to this particular novel but are generic characteristics of the other (so-called) condition-of-England novels in whose company it is regularly placed. In short, *Hard Times* is a *genera mixta* because the condition-of-England novel is a *Genera Mixta*.

II

Like so much of modern criticism of *Hard Times*, the debate over its genre begins with F. R. Leavis's seminal essay on it in *The Great Tradition*. Leavis's generic designation of the novel as a "moral fable" is the key both to his reinterpretation and to his revaluation of it. For Leavis *Hard Times* is a "masterpiece" and "a completely serious work of art," and its artistic seriousness and success are for him inseparable from the deep moral insight he finds in the story: namely, its attack, in the name of "life," on the poverty and immorality of utilitarianism. All this is well known, but what has been overlooked is the extent to which Leavis's judgment of both the novel's moral seriousness and its artistic success is inseparable from his assumption of its genre. For Leavis, the novel's "intention and nature are pretty obvious," and what makes Dickens's "intention" so "immediately apparent" to the reader is Leavis's immediately apparent sense that *Hard Times* is a moral fable, concluding with the generically inevitable "solemn moral." "I need say no more by way of defining the moral fable than that in it the intention is peculiarly insistent, so that the representative significance of everything in the fable— characters, episode, and so on—*is immediately apparent as we read*" (italics added).

Leavis's certainty that he is reading a moral fable leads him to expect certain things in the text rather than others, and to ignore, or at least to downplay, those elements, such as Dickens's representation of trade unions and Parliament, which seem unimportant, or even irrelevant, if *Hard Times* is read as a moral fable. The moral fable is most insistently present in those scenes exposing the failure of Gradgrind's utilitarian-Benthamite system for educating his children, and so Leavis understandably concentrates his analysis on the scenes that demonstrate for him "the confutation of Utilitarianism by life." Thus the three key scenes for Leavis are "the consummate scene" in which Gradgrind conveys Bounderby's marriage proposal to Louisa, the one in which Louisa returns to her father, and the one in which Sissy Jupe persuades Harthouse to leave Coketown. Leavis (to his credit) acknowledges that "Dickens has no glimpse of the part to be played by Trade Unionism in bettering the condition he deplores," and that this blindness is evidence of "a lack of political understanding" on Dickens's part. But since the moral fable is concerned with "the confutation of Utilitarianism by life," and Slackbridge's role does not affect that intention, Leavis does not consider this acknowledged deficiency as a serious fault, since overall "the justice and penetration of [Dickens's] criticism [of Victorian civilization] are unaffected" by it. And so Leavis can confidently conclude that "Dickens's understanding of Victorian civilization is adequate for his purpose," a purpose that is intuited mainly from the directions provided to the reader by the genre of the moral fable. Thus both Leavis's interpretation and his radical revaluation of *Hard Times* are inseparable from, because underwritten by, his designation of it as a moral fable, a genre that for Leavis is so self-evident, so "peculiarly insistent" and "immediately apparent as we read," that it does not have to be argued for.

* * *

Reading *Hard Times* as a condition-of-England novel had two consequences. First, it has led critics to expect, in accordance with their definition of the genre, that it will not only represent the historical facts accurately but also offer a solution to the problems it has raised, or at least point in the direction that modern critics believe a feasible solution grounded in history must lie. "Dickens and Gaskell," as David remarks, "have been criticized for not providing remedies for the problems they present, and the perfect industrial novel, we are led to believe, is one in which we find both the logical exposition of a social problem and its feasible resolution." "The so-called industrial novels of the Victorian period, like *Hard Times*," says Lodge, "offer a special problem, or trap, for literary criticism. Because these novels comment directly upon contemporary social issues, they open themselves to evaluation according to the 'truthfulness' with which they reflect the 'facts' of social history. Modern criticism of *Hard Times* shows this tendency very clearly."

The second consequence of reading *Hard Times* as a condition-of-England novel, one that has not been sufficiently noticed, is that doing so has imposed on the novel a generic uniformity that ignores the two principal literary genres that comprise the novel and that, I would argue, ought to play a decisive role in both our interpretation and evaluation of it. These two genres, the Jonsonian comedy of humors and Menippean satire, are in fact incompatible with the polemical thrust of the social-problem novel, for the first two and the last are pulling the novel in contradictory directions. And it is these generic contradictions, I believe, rather than Dickens's lack of political and historical insight, that explain the "unresolved tensions" that Lodge and other critics find in the novel. In response to Lodge's comment that a novel like *Hard Times* offers a trap to literary criticism, I would ask: But is it really these novels that, by "comment[ing] directly upon contemporary social issues," open themselves to adverse evaluation, or is it the critics' decision to read them *as* industrial or social-problem novels that, by creating the expectation that they should accurately reflect the empirical facts of social history and offer feasible solutions to social problems, actually lays the trap for the unwary critic? The genre of the moral fable creates no such expectations since moral fables do not offer solutions to social problems: they reconfirm moral truths that are taken to be self-evident.

*** The two earlier genres of fiction that Dickens transforms and combines in *Hard Times* are, as Northrop Frye pointed out forty years ago, the comedy of humours in the tradition of Ben Jonson and Henry Fielding, and Menippean satire (which Frye renames the anatomy) in the tradition of Swift's *Gulliver's Travels*, Thomas Love Peacock's *Nightmare Abbey* (1818) and *Crotchet Castle* (1831) and, more recently, Carlyle's *Sartor Resartus* (1831). *Hard Times* transforms and combines these two earlier genres, and if it is read in these generic contexts, not only will the difficulties created by reading it exclusively as a social-problem novel become apparent, but the criticism of Dickens's lack of political understanding will also seem to carry much less force.

* * *

III

Identifying *Hard Times* as a condition-of-England novel has imposed on it a greater generic uniformity and consistency than it actually possesses. *Hard Times* is, in fact, a *Genera Mixta* that resembles the incongruous mixture of styles comprising Sleary's circus. In chapter VII of the third book, "Whelp Hunting," Sissy, Louisa, and Gradgrind set out to find young Tom, who has been concealed by Sleary in his travelling circus. When Sissy and Louisa arrive at the entrance booth to the circus, "[t]he flag with the inscription SLEARY'S HORSERIDING, was there; and the Gothic niche was there." Inside,

> The Emperor of Japan, on a steady old white horse stencilled with black spots, was twirling five wash-hand basins at once, as it is the favourite recreation of that monarch to do . . . Miss Josephine Sleary, in her celebrated graceful Equestrian Tyrolean Flower-Act, is then announced by a new clown (who humorously says Cauliflower Act), and Mr. Sleary appears, leading her in.

The Clown tells Sleary "an ingenious Allegory relating to a butcher, a three-legged stool, a dog, and a leg of mutton." After the performance, Sleary tells Sissy that Emma Gordon, who had been like a mother to Sissy, lost her husband: "He wath throw'd a heavy back-fall off a Elephant in a thort of a Pagoda thing ath the Thultan of the Indieth, and he never got the better of it." At the Gothic ticket booth patrons buy a ticket that will enable them to see the Emperor of Japan, Tyrolean Flower-Acts, and a sort of Pagoda thing housing the Sultan of the Indies. This incongruous mixture of Gothic, Tyrolean, Japanese and Indian people and architectural styles is all part of what opposes the circus to the uniformity of Coketown, where everything is like everything else: "All the public inscriptions in the town were painted alike, in severe characters of black and white. The jail might have been the infirmary, the infirmary might have been the jail, the town-hall might have been either, or both, or anything else, for anything that appeared to the contrary in the graces of their construction." The diversity and the disregard for consistency embodied in the circus—with Tyrolean flower acts on horseback next to the Sultan of the Indies perched atop an elephant while the Emperor of Japan twirls wash-hand basins—humorously mirror the equally incongruous literary and popular genres that, mixing but never blending, constitute Dickens's satirical-comical-polemical-allegorical-melodramatic-fairy-tale-pantomime *cum* social-problem novel.

IV

The mixture of incompatible genres in *Hard Times* provides, in my view, an illuminating perspective on the perennial debate of Dickens's uncertain status as a serious writer, a problem that Martin Amis, in a perceptive review of John Carey's *The Violent Effigy: A Study of Dickens' Imagination*, has nicely summed up:

> While assured of his status as a great writer, Dickens is still uncertain of his status as a serious one. He insists on being romantic, melodramatic, and unrepresentational (like his trashier contemporaries), and will not be adult, introspective, mimetic (like the major Victorians). Criticism is traditionally nervous about such discrepancies and, accordingly, most of the recent work on Dickens has urged him back into what we invidiously imagine to be "the tradition"—i.e., the social-realist tradition. Robert Garis's *The Dickens Theatre*, stressing Dickens's gift for "social prophecy," explained that he's unrealistic because he is shrewdly deploying theatrical conventions [cf. Lodge]. John Lucas's *The Melancholy Man*, stressing Dickens's social criticism and symbolic structures, explained that he's unrealistic because society is too. The Leavises' *Dickens the Novelist*, stressing Dickens's moral intelligence, erudition, and likenesses to James, Conrad and George Eliot, explained that he's realistic. When asked about the large stretches of implausibility, mawkishness and exaggeration to be found throughout his work, these critics tend to reply that Dickens put them in to beguile his Victorian public.

Though written over thirty years ago, this trenchant diagnosis of "the Dickens problem" is particularly relevant to my argument. Amis's critical vocabulary—"romantic," "melodramatic," "unrepresentational," "mimetic," "theatrical conventions," "unrealistic," "realistic," "social-realist tradition"—reveals that the debate about Dickens's novels in general and *Hard Times* in particular needs to be seen as part of a not fully articulated debate about what kind of novels he wrote. The history of much of the criticism of *Hard Times* is the history of an effort, in the name of the romantic-modernist desideratum of organic unity, to tame the "menagerie of genres" comprising the novel by elevating one genre to the "keynote" that will impose artistic unity and consistency—and hence moral seriousness—on a novel that resists critics' efforts to limit the free play within Dickens's menagerie, much as Sissy Jupe wisely and successfully resists M'Choakumchild's call for a reductionist definition of a horse. And since none of the genres in Dickens's undisciplined menagerie will keep the others in place, some critics have, reluctantly, had no choice but to judge the work an artistic failure. The debate over whether the novel is an artistic success and whether it adequately responds to the historical condition of England has blinded us to the reason Dickens feels compelled to mix genres much more in *Hard Times* than in his other novels. Dickens's exuberantly promiscuous mixing of genres in *Hard Times* is best understood not as an artistic problem unique to this novel but instead in the wider context of the efforts of social critics such as Carlyle and other condition-of-England novelists, such as Gaskell and Disraeli, to find a narrative form commensurate with the new social realities they were trying to incorporate within the existing conventions of the novel, conventions that were never designed to do the work of political and social analysis. And since no single narrative form would suit their purpose, they understandably were forced to mix genres.

*   *   *

*** Rarely if ever do writers produce original genres. That is not how literary history happens. New (as distinct from original) genres do of course regularly emerge, but not *ex nihilo*; they are re-formed out of earlier genres. A new genre, such as the condition-of-England novel, is always the transformation of one or more antecedent genres. "From where do genres come?" asks Todorov. "Why, quite simply, from other genres. A new genre is always the transformation of one or several old genres, by inversion, by displacement, by combination." The generic label social-problem novel or condition-of-England novel has imposed on texts like *Hard Times* a generic unity that they do not in fact possess. And once this fact is recognized we should be able to understand what Dickens and his fellow condition-of-England novelist were trying to do rather than interpret and judge their works as failed attempts at realism.

Works Cited

Amis, Martin. *The War Against Cliché: Essays and Reviews 1971–2000*. Toronto: Vintage Canada, 2002.

Bakhtin, Mikhail. *Problems in Dostoevsky's Poetics*. Trans. Caryl Emerson. Minneapolis: U of Minnesota P, 1984.

Bodenheimer, Rosemarie. *The Politics of Story in Victorian Social Fiction*. Ithaca, NY: Cornell UP, 1988.

Childers, Joseph W. "Industrial Culture and the Victorian Novel." *The Cambridge Companion to the Victorian Novel.* Ed. Deirdre David. Cambridge: Cambridge UP, 2001: 77–98.

David, Deirdre. *Fictions of Resolution in Three Victorian Novels.* New York: Columbia UP, 1981.

Dickens, Charles. *Hard Times: An Authoritative Text, Contexts, Criticism,* 3rd ed. Ed. Fred Kaplan and Sylvère Monod. New York: W. W. Norton, 2001.

Frye, Northrop. "Dickens and the Comedy of Humors." *Experience in the Novel: Selected Papers from the English Institute.* Ed. Roy Harvey Pearce. New York: Columbia UP, 1968.

Gardner, Peter. "The Seductive Politics of Mary Barton." *Victorians Institute Journal* 33 (2005): 45–67.

Hodgart, Matthew. *Satire.* London: Weidenfeld and Nicolson, 1969.

Howe, Irving. "The Fiction of Anti-Utopia." *A World More Attractive: A View of Modern Literature and Politics.* New York: Horizon Press, 1963.

Jackson, Leon. "The Reader Retailored: Thomas Carlyle, His American Audiences, and the Politics of Evidence." *Books History* 2.1 (1999): 146–72.

Leavis, F. R. *The Great Tradition.* London: Chatto & Windus, 1948.

Lodge, David. *Language of Fiction.* London: Routledge and Kegan Paul, 1966.

———. *Working with Structuralism.* London: Routledge and Kegan Paul, 1981.

Rabinowitz, Peter J. *Before Reading: Narrative Conventions and the Politics of Interpretation.* Ithaca: Cornell UP, 1987.

Ryals, Clyde de L. "Carlyle's *The French Revolution*: A 'True Fiction.'" *ELH* 54.4 (Winter 1987): 925–40.

Schwarzbach, F. S. "Newgate Novel to Detective Fiction." *A Companion to the Victorian Novel.* Ed. Patrick Brantlinger and William B. Thesing. Oxford: Blackwell, 2003: 227–43.

Simmons, James Richard Jr. "Industrial and 'Condition of England Novels'" *A Companion to the Victorian Novel.* Ed. Patrick Brantlinger and William B. Thesing. Oxford: Blackwell, 2003: 336–52.

Tillotson, Kathleen. *Novels of the Eighteen-Forties.* Oxford: Oxford UP, 1954.

Todorov, Tzvetan. *Genres in Discourse.* Trans. Catherine Porter. Cambridge: Cambridge UP, 1990.

Williams, Raymond. *Culture and Society 1780–1950.* Harmondsworth: Penguin Books, 1971.

KENT GREENFIELD AND JOHN E. NILSSON

From Gradgrind's Education: Using Dickens and Aristotle to Understand (and Replace?) The Business Judgment Rule[†]

Charles Dickens's *Hard Times* includes one of the most memorable introductions in literature. It is offered by Thomas Gradgrind, the teacher at the M'Choakumchild School:

> Thomas Gradgrind, sir. A man of realities. A man of fact and calculations. A man who proceeds upon the principle that two and two are four, and nothing over. . . . With a rule and a pair of scales, and the multiplication table always in his pocket, sir, ready to weigh and measure any parcel of human nature, and tell you exactly what it comes to. It is a mere question of figures, a case of simple arithmetic.

It is apparent from this single excerpt that Dickens's portrayal of Gradgrind has much to do with the fallacies of the Benthamite political economy of his era. The literary philosopher Martha Nussbaum suggests that Dickens's critique of that philosophy is still current, however, and indeed that "Gradgrind economics has an even greater hold over the political and intellectual life of [our] society than it did over the society known to Dickens's characters, or to the narrating voice in his novel."[1] This is because, Nussbaum contends, many of the "rational choice" models of behavior that have gained acceptance, even a sort of hegemony, in critical scholarship "derive, ultimately, from the utilitarianism known to Mr. Gradgrind." Gradgrind's utilitarianism is especially pervasive in corporate law, and Dickens's critique of it can be used to bring a powerful attack against existing corporate law doctrine.

* * *

Dickens uses the character of Thomas Gradgrind to critique the ethic of utilitarianism. Gradgrind not only advocates utilitarianism's theory of mathematical rationalism but also acts it out in his everyday life. Over the course of the novel, however, Gradgrind learns that he cannot sustain his fierce rationalism, admitting at the novel's close, "I mistrust myself now." Nussbaum ascribes this aspect of the character to "his failure to be the sort of person his utilitar-

[†] From *Brooklyn Law Review* 63 (1998): 799–801, 805–08, 811–16, 842–44, 858–59. Reprinted by permission of the authors.
1. Martha C. Nussbaum, *Poetic Justice: The Literary Imagination and Public Life* 8 (1995) [hereinafter Nussbaum, *Poetic Justice*].

ian theory represents." It may be more than that, though. It may be also that Gradgrind has undergone a sort of education at the hands of the author, one as to the proper basis for judgment. By the novel's end he not only mistrusts his own ability to be the sort of person, and to act in the sort of way, that his ethical theory requires; he also begins to mistrust the theory itself.

This Article urges that Gradgrind and Gradgrind's education serve as useful metaphor for understanding one of corporate law's persistent paradoxes: the vitality of the business judgment rule ("BJR") in the face of the director's fiduciary duty to maximize shareholder profits. This Article offers a new explanation for this paradox, drawing on Gradgrind's education as both an analogy and a point of departure.

*　*　*

A key question then, is what makes Gradgrind a compelling character for the reader, "a gripping and ultimately a deeply moving character," when Bitzer and Bounderby are not? The answer is that Gradgrind undergoes an education: the events of the novel work to undermine Gradgrind's confidence in the rationalist method he had adopted in order to understand life. He watches as his son succumbs to gambling and drink and as his daughter is lost in an agonizing, empty marriage, in spite of their rationalist schooling. Gradgrind is also forced to reevaluate his notions of the Coketown "Hands," whom he had previously considered fungible commodities of finite and predictable appetites and capacities. As he meets individual Hands and attempts to make them conform to his larger algorithm, he is forced to concede that "he never could, make out how it yielded this unaccountable product." Gradgrind also is challenged by the presence of Sissy Jupe, a young girl who leaves a circus troupe and comes to live in the Gradgrind household. Gradgrind is forced to admit to himself that:

> he had become possessed by an idea that there was something in this girl which could hardly be set forth in tabular form. Her capacity of definition might easily be stated at a very low figure, her mathematical knowledge at nothing; yet he was not sure that if it had been required, for example, to tick her off into columns in a parliamentary return, he would have known how to divide her.

*　*　*

Gradgrind's starting point—the point from which he is educated—is, of course, utilitarianism, and it is utilitarianism that is the target of much of Dickens's satire and scorn. As one critic has put it, "*Hard*

Times is about an attitude of mind which we define . . . as utilitarianism, [and] the substance of the book is a testing of this 'philosophy.'"
To appreciate the manner in which *Hard Times* "tests" utilitarianism,
a review of that philosophy's core tenets might be helpful.

Philosopher John Rawls has written that "[t]he main idea [of
classical utilitarianism] is that society is rightly ordered, and therefore just, when its major institutions are arranged so as to achieve
the greatest net balance of satisfaction summed over all the individuals belonging to it."[2] Woven into this articulation of utilitarianism are two central, philosophical components: first, the idea
that Rawls calls satisfaction (but what might also be termed happiness or pleasure) is the chief object of value; and second, that
its maximization therefore represents the optimal arrangement of
society.

The first component of utilitarianism, then, is its use of "happiness" as the unit of value. This is a practical, even descriptive, component to the extent that the utilitarian philosopher is attempting
to characterize what people *do* value, rather than what they *should*
value. This is the so-called "greatest happiness principle," which
characterizes the "ultimate end" as "an existence exempt as far as
possible from pain, and as rich as possible in enjoyments, both in
point of quantity and quality." Its corollary is that "actions are right
in proportion as they tend to promote happiness, wrong as they
tend to produce the reverse of happiness."[3]

If this is so, if actions are right insofar as they promote happiness, then the necessary conclusion is that "[t]he multiplication of
happiness is, according to the utilitarian ethics, the object of virtue."[4] Thus, the second component of utilitarianism, maximization,
would appear to flow from the first. Maximization poses problems,
however. As Rawls has noted,[5] the utilitarian utopia is indifferent
to whether the optimal amount of happiness is distributed evenly
(or even roughly so) or whether one fortunate citizen is in possession of the sum total. Dickens, though, was not indifferent.

*   *   *

In sum, then, Dickens uses *Hard Times* to show that, far from
being an exercise in rationality, utilitarian decisionmaking is pro-

2. John Rawls, *A Theory of Justice* 22 (1971).
3. See John Stuart Mill, *Utilitarianism* 12 (Prometheus Books 1987) (1863) ("[M]en's sentiments, both of favor and of aversion, are greatly influenced by what they suppose to be the effects of things upon their happiness."), 22, 16.
4. Mill, 30.
5. Rawls, *supra* note 32, p. 26. In Rawls's words, [t]he striking feature of the utilitarian view of justice is that it does not matter, except indirectly, how this sum of satisfactions is distributed among individuals any more than it matters, except indirectly, how one man distributes his satisfactions over time. The correct distribution in either case is that which yields the maximum fulfillment.

foundly irrational. Its ruthless algebra is ultimately deficient, both in insisting that value is commensurable and in seeking solely to maximize its aggregate. Confronted with the "unaccountable product" of the myriad variations of human desire and sense of the good, utilitarianism fudges the numbers and tells itself that everything is not so complicated after all. But by the novel's end, Gradgrind has learned better. It is the premise of this Article that his education has implications above and beyond a critique of Victorian utilitarianism.

Before we apply Dickens's critique more specifically to corporate law, it is worth noting that *Hard Times*'s criticism of utilitarianism can be situated within the Aristotelian tradition. In her essay "The Discernment of Perception: An Aristotelian Conception of Private and Public Rationality,"[6] Martha Nussbaum launches an Aristotelian critique of scientific rationality as a method of decision-making, a critique that in many ways mirrors and extrapolates upon Dickens's critique of utilitarianism. Like *Hard Times*'s attack on utilitarianism, Nussbaum's critique focuses upon two crucial premises: "commensurability," the idea that all things may be valued on a single scale, whether dollars, utils or otherwise; and "metricity," the idea that a single algorithm can then provide an adequate basis for sound decisionmaking.

* * *

Dickens and Aristotle thus agree that utilitarianism is, in an important sense, irrational. As we learn from *Hard Times*, individuals who actually try to take the lessons of utilitarianism to heart seem childish, obtuse, or insane. As we argue in the next Part, this is how corporate law requires management to act.

Perhaps the closest living relative of the utilitarianism that Dickens critiques in *Hard Times* is the corporate law of the United States. Corporate law at the end of the twentieth century is characterized by those principles that served as targets for Dickens in the middle of the nineteenth century. According to the majority rule, members of corporate management are to be constrained in their decisionmaking to a single, over-arching goal: the maximization of shareholder wealth. It is [Milton] Friedman, a Nobel-Prize winning economist, who has famously explained the director's fiduciary duty to increase shareholder profits: "In a free-enterprise, private-property system a corporate executive is an employee of the owners of the business. He has direct responsibility to his employers. That responsibility

6. Martha Nussbaum, "The Discernment of Perception: An Aristotelian Conception of Private and Public Rationality," in *Loves Knowledge: Essays on Philosophy and Literature* 54 (1990).

is to conduct the business in accordance with their desires, which generally will be to make as much money as possible . . . ."[7]

The seminal decision in developing and explicating the fiduciary duty to maximize shareholder profits was handed down in 1919 by the Michigan Supreme Court in *Dodge v. Ford Motor Co.* That case involved a suit on the part of minority shareholders against Henry Ford challenging Ford's new policy against declaring special dividends. In particular, the plaintiffs pointed to the fact that, even prior to the new policy, the company's profits had risen much faster than the dividends. In the press, Ford had been defiant, proclaiming his decision to reinvest in the company "[in order] to spread the benefits of this industrial system to the greatest possible number, to help them build up their lives and their homes." The Michigan Supreme Court frowned upon Ford's philanthropic impulses, declaring:

> *A business corporation is organized and carried on primarily for the profit of the stockholders.* The powers of the directors are to be employed for that end. The discretion of directors is to be exercised in the choice of means to attain that end, and does not extend to a change in the end itself, to the reduction of profits, or to the non-distribution of profits among stockholders in order to devote them to other purposes.

* * *

Accordingly. Ford was ordered to pay the dividends.

Corporate law is thus one of those realms where the kind of utilitarianism that Dickens critiques still holds sway. Wealth maximization is the normative goal. But it is not just wealth maximization in general or societal terms that is the touchstone of corporate law: it is the wealth maximization of shareholders only. All choices must be analyzed as to that one value. All other "goods" are to be taken into account only if they are commensurable with that one measure. Choices are well made when they serve that goal and poorly made when they do not. Dickens's critique—that utilitarianism is irrational insofar as it requires a dependence on commensurability and maximization—must be taken seriously when applied to corporate law. If utilitarianism is irrational when applied in the

7. Milton Friedman, "The Social Responsibility of Business Is to Increase Its Profits," N.Y. *Times Magazine*, Sept. 13, 1970, pp. 32–33, 122, 124, 126. Over a century earlier, Herman Melville provided a dramatization of this principle in *Moby-Dick*. When that novel's narrator, Ishmael, joins the Pequod's crew for its infamous voyage, he is assigned a "lay," i.e., a share of the voyage's profits. In figuring Ishmael's lay, one of the ship's "directors" (Captain Bildad) proposes an apparently modest share, but the other (Captain Peleg) objects. Bildad reminds Peleg that "thou must consider the duty thou owest to the owners of this ship—widows and orphans, many of them—and that if we too abundantly reward the labors of this young man, we may be taking the bread from those widows and those orphans." Herman Melville, *Moby-Dick or, The Whale*, pp. 90–91 (Signet Classic ed., 1980) (1851).

real world, then existing corporate law doctrine requires corporate managers to make decisions in an impoverished way. Law is commanding irrationality.

One of the great puzzles of corporate law is the co-existence of the strict duly to maximize shareholder profits with the business judgment rule, a rule of judicial deference to the decisions of corporate management. This Part explores and offers a new explanation for the apparent paradox between the two legal norms.

The business judgment rule includes at least two legal principles. As a presumption, the rule provides that the acts of independent directors will be presumed to be taken in good faith and with appropriate care. As a substantive rule of law, the business judgment rule provides that the directors will incur no liability for an injury or loss to the corporation arising from corporate action when they, in authorizing such action, proceeded in good faith and with appropriate care.

*   *   *

The underlying duty in corporate law—to maximize shareholder returns—forces corporate managers to act irrationally. The development of the business judgment rule has served to mitigate this irrationality and has allowed managers to act in a manner that more closely aligns with Aristotelian rationality. But corporate law is still imperfect, even with the BJR and stakeholder statutes, because it remains closely tied to an irrational underlying duty.

A corporate law that encourages irrationality is not the only choice. Corporate law could be based on a set of legal duties that would allow—indeed expect—directors to act rationally. An expansive elaboration upon such duties and a defense of them lie beyond the scope of this Article. But we can offer a glimpse of what corporate law doctrine might look like if it were based on Aristotelian norms of rationality and decisionmaking.

A few words about the importance of this effort are in order, as existing corporate law doctrine has been under increasing attack recently. The topics of corporate social responsibility, corporate democracy, and communitarianism in corporate law have enjoyed a resurgence of interest in the academy and even among the public at large. Yet the proponents of this new trend have been criticized for failing to provide a theoretical alternative to existing corporate law doctrine. The criticism has been that the "communitarians" only have critiqued and have not been successful in providing a genuine alternative upon which corporate law could be based. Fleshing out an Aristotelian version of corporate law could go far in responding to this criticism and in providing a theoretical basis for communitarian corporate law. *   *   *

* * *

As Dickens and Aristotle tell us, to have one's decisions depend on the calculus of utilitarianism is irrational. Yet within corporate law, the fiduciary duties of managers and directors require them to make decisions based on the very principles—commensurability and maximization—that Dickens and Aristotle criticized so powerfully. This Article has argued that the business judgment rule has sprung up as a corrective to the irrationality of the underlying duty of maximizing shareholder returns. It is as if the law could admit to the words of Louisa Gradgrind: "With a hunger and thirst upon me, father, which have never been for a moment appeased; with an ardent impulse towards some region where rules, and figures, and definitions were not quite absolute; I have grown up, battling every inch of my way." The adoption of the business judgment rule has been an important part of this battle. This Article has also suggested, however, that corporate law could be brought still closer to the norms of good decisionmaking suggested by Aristotle and Dickens.

We must make one important concession. While we believe that corporate law indeed asks corporate managers to make decisions in an impoverished, irrational way, we admit that rationality is not necessarily the sole test for public policy. Sometimes it is better to have a rule, even if it is a very simple, childish rule, than to offer discretion, especially if the people who have responsibility for acting do not have the "practical wisdom" necessary for making good decisions without set rules.[8] The proper test for deciding the contours of corporate fiduciary duty doctrine should mirror the test for most other public policies: which set of legal rules gets us closer to the kind of society we want. Corporate law does not exist in a vacuum of academic thought any more than in the thin air of corporate boardrooms. To decide whether we, as a society, want to retain existing corporate doctrine or move to something more rational, we must decide whether society as a whole is better off when corporate directors have the legal duty to maximize profits or when they have the legal duty to take into account the needs and desires of others affected by the decision. This is in part an empirical question, in part a political question, and in part a moral question. And it is not only for lawyers, corporate executives, or shareholders to answer.

8. Nussbaum, "Discernment of Perception," *supra* note 6, p. 73.

Charles Dickens: A Chronology

1812	February 7: Birth, in Portsmouth, the first son and second of eight children of John and Elizabeth Barrow Dickens.
1812–24	His father, a clerk in the Navy pay office, is sometimes stationed in London but usually in the twin towns of Chatham and Rochester on the south coast of Kent. Charles becomes an avid reader, especially of eighteenth-century novels.
1824	John Dickens is imprisoned in the Marshalsea, a debtor's prison. Charles, no longer attending school, becomes an ill-paid manual laborer in a London blacking warehouse, where he works for a few months.
1824–27	Resumes schooling after his father's release from prison. Leaves school at age fifteen and is awarded prize for Latin.
1827–30	Employed as clerk in law offices.
1830–34	Becomes an expert shorthand-reporter of debates in Parliament, an institution that he likens to a pantomime "strong in clowns." Rounds out his education by reading in the library of the British Museum. Falls in love with Maria Beadnell, a banker's daughter, whose parents regard him as unsuitable. The relationship is broken off after four years.
1833–36	Becomes a newspaper reporter for the *Morning Chronicle* and travels extensively outside of London. Begins publishing short articles and stories that are collected into a volume, *Sketches by Boz* (1836).
1836–37	Marries Catherine Hogarth; first child born (first of ten); publishes his first novel, *The Pickwick Papers*, in twenty monthly installments. Its triumphant success enables him to give up newspaper reporting.
1837–41	Publishes in *Bentley's Miscellany* installments of *Oliver Twist*. Loses his much-beloved sister-in-law, Mary Hogarth, who dies at age seventeen. Writes three more novels: *Nicholas Nickleby*, *The Old Curiosity Shop*, and *Barnaby Rudge*.

1842   Tours America for five months. Loses his original high
             hopes for democracy. Disillusionment with United
             States evident in his *American Notes* and his novel *Martin
             Chuzzlewit*.

1843   *A Christmas Carol*.

1844–49   Pays long visits to Italy, Switzerland, and France with
             his large family. Helps found *Daily News*. Publishes
             only one novel, *Dombey and Son*, but also four more
             Christmas books.

1850   Founds his popular weekly magazine, *Household Words*,
             featuring installments of novels, and also articles deal-
             ing with social issues. Publishes a novel, *David Copper-
             field*, told in first person.

1851–57   Publishes the first three of his so-called Dark Period
             Novels: *Bleak House* (1853), *Hard Times* (1854), and
             Little Dorrit (1857). Takes increasing pleasure in direct-
             ing and acting in amateur play productions.

1858–61   Buys Gad's Hill Place, a beautiful house near Roches-
             ter. Separates from his wife and establishes a relationship
             with a young actress. His sister-in-law, Georgina Hogarth,
             stays with him and the children. Begins paid perfor-
             mances of readings from his own works. Publishes, in
             weekly form, *A Tale of Two Cities* (1859) and *Great Expec-
             tations* (1861).

1861–68   Continues public reading tours in England and, for five
             months in 1867–68, in the northeastern states of Amer-
             ica. The American readings are stunningly successful
             and profitable. In 1865 appears his last completed novel,
             Our Mutual Friend.

1869–70   Continues his public readings, despite failing health,
             until March 1870. In April begins publishing *The Mys-
             tery of Edwin Drood*, of which he finishes six of twelve
             projected parts. After working on that novel he is over-
             whelmed by a stroke and dies the following day, on June
             9, at Gad's Hill. He is later buried in Poets' Corner in
             Westminster Abbey.

Selected Bibliography

I

The Dickens section of *The New Cambridge Bibliography of English Literature* (1969), compiled by Philip Collins, offers a comprehensive list of writings about Dickens. This list may be supplemented by *The Cumulated Dickens Checklist 1970–1979*, by Alan M. Cohn and K. K. Collins (1982). For later studies see "The Dickens Checklist" in *Dickens Quarterly* (formerly *Dickens Studies Newsletter*), the Dickens section of the annual *PMLA* and *Victorian Studies* bibliographies, and the annual review in *Dickens Studies Annual*. For judicious assessments of such studies, see Ada Nisbet's survey in *Victorian Fiction: A Guide to Research*, ed. Lionel Stevenson (1964, pp. 44–153) and also Philip Collins in *Victorian Fiction: A Second Guide to Research*, ed. George H. Ford (1978, pp. 34–113). For a comprehensive bibliography, see Duane Devries, *General Studies of Charles Dickens and His Writings and Collected Editions of His Works, An Annotated Bibliography*, Volume One: *Bibliographies, Catalogues, Collections, and Bibliographical and Textual Studies of Dickens's Works* (2 vols., 2010). For a wide-ranging general bibliography that also focuses on *Hard Times*, see "A Bibliography for Charles Dickens' *Hard Times* (1854)," compiled by Teresa Mangum and Joanne Janssen (2008). The website of the Dickens Project at the University of California, Santa Cruz (http://dickens.ucsc.edu /resources/bibliographies/index.html), contains up-to-date bibliographies compiled between 1999 and 2014 for sixteen of Dickens' novels.

II

Two classic full-length biographies are John Foster's *The Life of Charles Dickens* (1872–74, with annotations by J. W. T. Ley, 1928), and Edgar Johnson's *Charles Dickens* (1952). Later biographies include Angus Wilson's *The World of Charles Dickens* (with illustrations, 1970), Fred Kaplan's *Dickens* (1988), Peter Ackroyd's *Dickens* (1990), Michael Slater's *Charles Dickens* (2009), Robert Douglas-Fairhurst's *Becoming Dickens: The Invention of a Novelist* (2011), Michael Allen's *Charles Dickens and the Blacking Factory* (2011), Robert Garnett's *Charles Dickens in Love* (2012), Robert Gottlieb's *Great Expectations: The Sons and Daughters of Charles Dickens* (2012), and Claire Tomalin's *Charles Dickens: A Life* (2012). On special aspects of his life and career, see Robert Patten, *Charles Dickens and His Publishers* (1978); Michael Slater, *Dickens and Women* (1983); Michael Allen, *Charles Dickens's Childhood* (1988); and Claire Tomalin, *The Invisible Woman: The Story of Nelly Ternan and Charles Dickens* (1990). Also informative are *The Speeches of Charles Dickens*, ed. K. J. Fielding (1960); *Uncollected Writings from 'Household Words,'* ed. Harry Stone (2 vols., 1968); *Dickens' Working Notes for His Novels*, ed. Harry Stone (2 vols., 1987); *Charles Dickens: The Public Readings*, ed. Philip Collins (1975); and *Charles Dickens' Book of Memoranda*, ed. Fred Kaplan (1981). *The Letters of Charles Dickens*, ed. Madeline House, Graham Storey, and Kathleen Tillotson (12 vols., 1965–2002) is the authoritative edition of complete letters. The *Oxford Companion to Charles Dickens: Anniversary Edition*, ed. Paul Schlicke (2011) is useful. So too are Norrie Epstein, *The Friendly Dickens* (1998) and *The Cambridge Companion to Charles Dickens*, ed. John O. Jordan (2001).

III

From the large store of general critical studies of Dickens's novels, the following chronological listing represents only a selective sampling.

    George Gissing, *Charles Dickens: A Critical Study* (1898); Louis Cazamian, *The Social Novel in England, 1830–1850* (trans. from the French of 1903, 1973); G. K. Chesterton, *Charles Dickens* (1906) and *Appreciations and Criticisms of the Work of Charles Dickens* (1911); Edmund Wilson, "The Two Scrooges," *The Wound and the Bow* (1941); George H. Ford, *Dickens and His Readers* (1955, 1965); John Butt and Kathleen Tillotson, *Dickens at Work* (1957); J. Hillis Miller, *Charles Dickens: The World of His Novels* (1965); K. J. Fielding, *Charles Dickens: A Critical Introduction* (1958); Monroe Engels, *The Maturity of Dickens* (1959); A. O. J. Cockshut, *The Imagination of Dickens* (1961); George H. Ford and Lauriat Lane Jr., eds., *The Dickens Critics* (collection of critical essays, 1961); Philip Collins, *Dickens and Education* (1963); Mark Spilka, *Dickens and Kafka* (1963); Robert Garis, *The Dickens Theatre* (1965); Sylvère Monod, *Dickens the Novelist* (1968); Barbara Hardy, *The Moral Art of Dickens* (1970); F. R. Leavis, *Dickens the Novelist* (1970); Alexander Welsh, *The City of Dickens* (1971); Robert Barnard, *Imagery and Theme in the Novels of Dickens* (1974); Garrett Stewart, *Dickens and the Trials of Imagination* (1974); Juliet McMaster, *Dickens the Designer* (1983); Paul Schlicke, *Dickens and Popular Entertainment* (1985); Janet L. Larson, *Dickens and the Broken Scripture* (1985); Harry Stone, *Dickens' Working Notes for His Novels* (1987); Alexander Welsh, *From Copyright to Copperfield: The Identity of Dickens* (1987); Andrew Sanders, *Dickens and the Spirit of the Age* (1990); Anny Sadrin, *Parentage and Inheritance in the Novels of Charles Dickens* (1994); Malcolm Andrews, *Dickens and the Grown-Up Child* (1994); Harry Stone, *The Night Side of Dickens: Cannibalism, Passion, Necessity* (1994); William J. Palmer, *Dickens and New Historicism* (1988); John Bowen, *Other Dickens, Pickwick to Chuzzlewit* (2000); Juliet John, *Dickens's Villains: Melodrama, Character, Popular Culture* (2001); Efraim Sicher, *Rereading the City, Rereading Dickens: Representation, the Novel, and Urban Realism* (2003); Grace Moore, *Dickens and Empire: Discourses of Class, Race and Colonialism in the Works of Charles Dickens* (2004); Malcolm Andrews, *Charles Dickens and His Performing Selves: Dickens and the Public Readings* (2006); Rosemarie Bodenheimer, *Knowing Dickens* (2007); Sally Ledger, *Dickens and the Popular Radical Imagination* (2007); Juliet John, *Dickens and Mass Culture* (2010); John R. Reed, *Dickens's Hyperrealism* (2010); Kelly Hager, *Dickens and the Rise of Divorce: The Failed-Marriage Plot and the Novel Tradition* (2010); John Gordon, *Sensation and Sublimation in Charles Dickens* (2011); Linda M. Lewis, *Dickens, His Parables, and His Reader* (2011); Sarah Winter, *The Pleasures of Memory: Learning to Read with Charles Dickens* (2011); Jonathan H. Grossman, *Charles Dickens's Networks: Public Transport and the Novel* (2012); and Robert L. Patten, *Charles Dickens and "Boz": The Birth of the Industrial-Age Author* (2012).

IV

For studies of various aspects of the Victorian age, the following books are useful: Asa Briggs, *The Age of Improvement* (1959, 1979); Jerome Buckley, *The Victorian Temper* (1951, 1964); Philip Collins, *Dickens and Crime* (1962) and *Dickens and Education* (1963); R. J. Cruikshank, *Charles Dickens and Early Victorian England* (1949); H. J. Dyos and Michael Wolff, *The Victorian City* (2 vols., 1973); Friedrich Engels, *The Condition of the Working Class in England in 1844* (1845, trans. 1958); Judith Flanders, *The Victorian City: Everyday Life in Dickens' London* (2014); Catherine Gallagher, *The Body Economic: Life, Death, and Sensation in Political Economy and the Victorian Novel* (2006); Theodore

Hoppen, *The Mid-Victorian Generation, 1846–1886* (2000); Humphry House, *The Dickens World* (1941); Audrey Jaffe, *The Affective Life of the Average Man: The Victorian Novel and the Stock-Market Graph* (2010); F. D. Klingender, *Art and the Industrial Revolution* (rev. by Arthur Elton, 1968); Steven Marcus, *Engels, Manchester, and the Working Class* (1974); Sally Mitchell, *Daily Life in Victorian England* (2008); Mary Poovey, *Uneven Developments: The Ideological Work of Gender in Mid-Victorian England* (1988); John R. Reed, *Victorian Will* (1989); Herbert Sussman, *Victorians and the Machine* (1968); E. P. Thompson, *The Making of the English Working Class* (1963); H. A. Turner, *Trade Union Growth, Structure and Policy* (1962); Sidney and Beatrice Webb, *The History of Trade Unionism* (1911); and G. M. Young, *Early Victorian England* (1936, 1960).

V

For a review of studies of *Hard Times* itself, see Sylvia Manning's excellent *Hard Times: An Annotated Bibliography* (1984). For individual critical or historical studies, see Harold Bloom, ed., *Hard Times* (essays by Raymond Williams and others, 1987); Patrick Brantlinger, Dickens and the Factories," *Nineteenth-Century Fiction* 22 (1971): 270–85; Geoffrey Carnall, "Dickens, Mrs. Gaskell, and the Preston Strike," *Victorian Studies* 8 (1964): 31–48; Philip Collins, "Queen Mab's Chariot among the Steam Engines: Dickens and 'Fancy,' *English Studies* 42 (1961): 78–90; Daniel P. Deneau, "The Brother-Sister Relationship in *Hard Times*," *The Dickensian* 60 (1964): 173–77; Terry Eagleton, introduction to *Hard Times* (1987); Richard Fabrizio, "Wonderful No-Meaning: Language and the Psychopathology of the Family in Dickens' *Hard Times*," *Dickens Studies Annual* 16 (1987): 61–94; K. J. Fielding, "The Battle for Preston," *The Dickensian* 54 (1954): 159–62, "Mill and Gradgrind," *Nineteenth-Century Fiction* 11 (1956): 148–51, and with Ann Smith, "*Hard Times* and the Factory Controversy: Dickens vs Harriet Martineau," *Dickens Centennial Essays*, ed. Ada Nisbet and Blake Nevius (1971); George Ford, "Dickens' *Hard Times* on Television: Problems of Adaptation," *Papers on Language and Literature* 23 (1987): 319–31; Catherine Gallagher, *The Industrial Reformation of English Fiction: Discourse and Narrative Form* (1985); Robert Giddings, ed., *The Changing World of Dickens* (essays by Roger Fowler and others, 1983); Robin Gilmour, *The Victorians and Social Protest* (1973); Paul Edward Gray, ed., *Hard Times: A Collection of Critical Essays* (1969); Janet Larsen, "Identity's Fictions—Naming and Renaming in *Hard Times*," *Dickens Studies Newsletter* 10 (March 1979): 14–19; David Lodge, *Working with Structuralism* (1981); Robert Lougy, "Dickens's *Hard Times*: The Romance as Radical Literature," *Dickens Studies Annual* 9 (1980): 237–54; Jerome Meckier, *Hidden Rivalries of Victorian Fiction* (1987); Paul Schlicke, *Dickens and Popular Entertainment* (1985); Bernard Shaw, introduction to *Hard Times* (1912); Frank Edmund Smith, "Perverted Balance: Expressive Form in *Hard Times*," *Dickens Studies Annual* 6 (1977): 102–18; David Sonstroem, "Fettered Fancy in *Hard Times*," PMLA 84.3 (May 1969): 520–29; Deborah A. Thomas, *"Hard Times": A Fable of Fragmentation and Wholeness* (1977); Margaret Simpson, *The Companion to "Hard Times"* (1997); Nicholas Coles, "The Politics of *Hard Times*: Dickens the Novelist versus Dickens the Reformer," *Dickens Studies Annual* 15 (1986): 145–79; Patricia E. Johnson, "*Hard Times* and the Structure of Industrialism: The Novel as Factory," *Studies in the Novel* 21.2 (1989): 128–37; Jean Ferguson Carr, "Writing as a Woman: Dickens, *Hard Times* and Feminine Discourse," *Dickens Studies Annual* 18 (1989): 161–78; Paul Schacht, "Dickens and the Uses of Nature," *Victorian Studies* 34.1 (1990): 77–102; Cynthia Northcutt Malone, "The Fixed Eye and the Rolling Eye: Surveillance and Discipline in *Hard Times*," *Studies in the Novel* 21.1 (1989): 14–26; Martha C. Nussbaum, "The Literary Imagination in Public Life," *New Literary History* 22.4 (1991): 877–910; Eric P. Levy, "Dickens' Pathology of Time in *Hard Times*," *Philological Quarterly* 74.2 (1995): 189–207; Alexander Welsh, *Dickens Redressed: The Art of Bleak House and Hard Times* (2000);

David M. Levy, "*Hard Times* and the Moral Equivalence of Markets and Slavery," *How the Dismal Science Got Its Name: Classical Economics and the Ur-Text of Racial Politics* (2002); Julie M. Dugger, "Editorial Interventions: *Hard Times*'s Industrial Imperative," *Dickens Studies Annual* 32 (2002): 151–77; Christine Lupton, "Walking on Flowers: The Kantian Aesthetics of *Hard Times*," *ELH* 70 (2003): 151–69; Christopher Barnes, "*Hard Times*: Fancy as Practice," *Dickens Studies Annual* 34 (2004): 233–53; Elizabeth Starr, "Manufacturing Novels: Charles Dickens on the Hearth in Coketown," *Texas Studies in Literature and Language* 51 (2009): 317–40; David Paroissien, "Ideology, Pedagogy, and Demonology: The Case Against Industrialized Education in Dickens's Fiction," *Dickens Studies Annual* 34 (2004): 259–82; Paulette Kidder, "Martha Nussbaum on Dickens's *Hard Times*," *Philosophy and Literature* 33 (2009): 417–26; Carolyn Valenga Berman, "Awful Unknown Quantities: Addressing the Reader in *Hard Times*," *Victorian Literature and Culture* 37 (2009): 561–82; Nils Clausson, "Dickens's *General Mixta*: What Kind of a Novel Is *Hard Times*?," *Texas Studies in Language and Literature* 52 (2010): 157–80; Tamara Ketabgian, "'Melancholy Mad Elephants': Affect and the Animal Machine in *Hard Times*," *The Lives of Machines: The Industrial Imaginary in Victorian Literature and Culture* (2011); Efraim Sicher, "Dickens and the Pleasure of the Text: The Risks of *Hard Times*," *Partial Answers: Journal of Literature and the History of Ideas* 9 (2011): 311–30; Theodore Dalrymple, "Hard Times Again," *The American Conservative* 11.1 (January 2012): 12–14; Nele Pollatschek, "Discard the Word Fancy altogether!' Charles Dickens's Defense of Ambiguity in *Hard Times*," *Dickens Quarterly* 30 (2013): 278–87; Priti Joshi, "An Old Dog Enters the Fray; or, Reading *Hard Times* as an Industrial Novel," *Dickens Studies Annual* 44 (2013): 221–41; and Darcy Lewis, "Melancholia and Machinery: The Dystopian Landscape and Mindscape in *Hard Times*," *Dickens Quarterly* 31 (2014): 17–31.